The Life of

Huysmans by G. Barlangue

Robert Baldick

The Life of J.-K. Huysmans

With a foreword and additional notes by
Brendan King

Dedalus

Published in the UK by Dedalus Ltd,
Langford Lodge, St Judith's Lane, Sawtry, Cambs, PE28 5XE
email: info@dedalusbooks.com
www.dedalusbooks.com

ISBN 1 903517 43 5
ISBN 978 1 903517 43 7

Dedalus is distributed in the United States by SCB Distributors,
15608 South New Century Drive, Gardena, California 90248
email: info@scbdistributors.com   web site: www.scbdistributors.com

Dedalus is distributed in Australia & New Zealand by Peribo Pty Ltd,
58 Beaumont Road, Mount Kuring-gai N.S.W. 2080
email: peribo@bigpond.com

Dedalus is distributed in Canada by Disticor Direct-Book Division,
695 Westney Road South, Suite 14 Ajax, Ontario, L16 6M9
web site: www.marginalbook.com

First published in 1955
First Dedalus edition in 2006

The Life of J.-K. Huysmans © *Jacqueline Baldick 1955*
Foreword and additional notes © *Brendan King 2006*

Printed in Finland by WS Bookwell
Typeset by RefineCatch Limited, Bungay, Suffolk

THE EDITOR

Brendan King is a freelance writer, reviewer and translator, with a special interest in late nineteenth-century French fiction.

He has just completed a Ph.D on the life and work of J.-K. Huysmans and he has translated for Dedalus Huysmans' *Là-Bas* (2001), *Parisian Sketches* (2004) and *Marthe* (2006).

He lives and works in Paris and on the Isle of Wight

LIST OF ILLUSTRATIONS

CONTENTS

FOREWORD

To those already familiar with the work of the French novelist J.-K. Huysmans (1848–1907) Robert Baldick requires little in the way of introduction. Following the publication of his acclaimed biography in 1955, Baldick's name has become as well-known in Huysmansian circles as that of Lucien Descaves, Huysmans' literary executor and the editor of the 23-volume edition of his complete works, Pierre Lambert, the bibliophile and scholar who amassed the largest collection of Huysmans-related material in private hands, and Pierre Cogny, the critic whose editorial hand guided so many previously unpublished letters and manuscripts into print. Despite the biography's relatively small distribution – it was published in only one English hardback edition in 1955, and in two French paperback editions in 1958 and 1975 – *The Life of J.-K. Huysmans* has become the standard work of reference on its subject in both England and France, and its continuing value to Huysmans scholars is testified to by the fact that it is still regularly cited in academic journals and works of literary criticism.

Robert Baldick was born in Huddersfield in 1927, to an English father and a French mother. He studied Modern Languages at Oxford, where he received first class honours and went on to pursue his post-graduate research under the flamboyant figure of Dr. Enid Starkie, who had already made her name with celebrated studies of Rimbaud and Baudelaire. It was Starkie who advised him to turn his attention to Huysmans and in his doctoral thesis, which he completed in 1952 at the age of 27, he thanked his tutor for her advice and encouragement, which he said had been of inestimable value to him.

In the course of writing his thesis, *The Novels of J.-K. Huysmans: A study of the author's craft and the development of his*

11

thought, Baldick spent an invaluable period researching in Paris, where he met another key figure who was to have an even greater influence on his subsequent life and work, Pierre Lambert, a soft-spoken, delicate man who collected rare books with the same passion he devoted to his extensive butterfly collection. As Richard Griffiths later wrote in an obituary notice for the *The Times*, Baldick became 'a kind of adopted son to Lambert and his wife, with whom he remained on the closest of terms for the rest of his life'. Lambert had been a collector of Huysmansiana for many years and he generously opened up his extensive archive of letters, cuttings and manuscripts, the majority of which were unpublished at the time, to the young scholar, who quoted exhaustively from them in his thesis and subsequent biography. Lambert later bequeathed this collection to the French state on his death in 1969, and it now forms the basis of the Fonds Lambert at the Bibliothèque de l'Arsenal in Paris, the largest holding of primary and secondary source material on Huysmans in the world.

After completing his studies, Baldick became a joint lecturer at Pembroke and University Colleges, and began work on adapting his doctoral thesis into a full-length biography. When it was published in 1955, Enid Starkie summed up the work of her former student with the words: 'He has produced the authorative biography which supercedes all previous ones, and which is the soundest, fullest and most scholarly in any language'. Despite such praise, and despite the enthusiastic reception the book received among dedicated Huysmans scholars in England and France, the biography never achieved the sales its critical acclaim warranted. Although Huysmans had always had his adherents, usually partisans of one particular 'phase' of his writings, whether Naturalist, Decadent or Catholic, he had never been a popular or fashionable literary figure. In France he tended to be overshadowed by the giants of nineteenth-century French literature, by Zola and Flaubert, and by Hugo, Balzac and Baudelaire, while in England he fared even worse: translations of his work were not easy to get hold of, for the most part available only in limited editions printed by small, idiosyncratic presses, or in baudlerised versions that left much to be desired in terms of accuracy and style. Even Baldick's own translations of Huysmans' *Marthe* and *Downstream* in the early 1950s made little impact, having appeared under the notoriously erratic imprint of the Fortune Press. It was only with the publication of Baldick's groundbreaking translation of *Against Nature* for Penguin Classics in 1959 that Huysmans started to be taken seriously in England, both in academic circles and among a wider reading public.

In 1958 Baldick was made a Fellow of Pembroke College, and he quickly gained a reputation as a stimulating and enthusiastic tutor. Over the next decade he divided his time between teaching, writing, and translating: he published a series of vibrant studies of nineteenth-century literary life, most notably *Pages from the Goncourt Journal* (1960), *The First Bohemian: the Life of Henry Murger* (1961), and *The Life and Times of Frederic Lemaître* (1962), and a string of impressive translations including Flaubert's *Sentimental Education*, Sartre's *Nausea* and Restif de la Bretonne's *Monsieur Nicolas*. He was appointed editor of the Oxford Library of French Classics in 1962, and was joint editor of Penguin Classics from 1964 until his death in 1972.

Despite the impressive scope of his work in other fields – his book *The Siege of Paris* (1965) is one of the best accounts of that turbulent period in French history – *The Life of J.-K. Huysmans* is arguably Baldick's most substantial and influential work. It has had a huge impact on the posthumous reputation of its subject, having been instrumental in changing the perception of Huysmans as a writer, and re-establishing his position as a significant cultural figure in the literature of the late nineteenth-century. Of course Baldick's biographical method is not the only way to present the life of the acerbic, contradictory and often controversial writer that Huysmans was, and there are those who might question his recourse to Huysmans' fiction to supply gaps in the autobiographical record. Nevertheless, fifty years after its publication, no one on either side of the Channel has yet produced a work that matches the *Life* in terms of scope, accuracy, scholarly judgement and readability. It is to be hoped that this revised edition of *The Life of J.-K. Huysmans* will introduce a whole new generation of students to the great contribution Robert Baldick made to the study of French literature in general and Huysmans in particular.

Note on the text

In reprinting a book which was written so long ago but which has become a classic in its own right, I was mindful of the difficulties of treading a path between faithful adherence to the original text and the need to produce a work that took new research into account and was therefore relevant to present-day scholars. For the most part, the text of this revised edition remains that of the original, though a handful of literal errors that somehow escaped Baldick's rigorously critical eye have been silently corrected, and some of the textual revisions Baldick made for the French edition of 1958 have been incorporated. Instances in the text where Baldick's conclusions or statements have been invalidated or challenged by new findings are dealt with in the notes at the back of the book.

Acknowledgements

I would like to thank Eric Lane at Dedalus for agreeing to take on this project.

PREFACE

MANY years ago, when I first became interested in Huysmans, I discovered to my surprise that no reliable, fully documented biography of the novelist had then been published; and what was true then is still true at the time of writing. The reason for this is very simple. In his will Huysmans directed that his correspondence and private papers should remain unpublished; and although his executor, Lucien Descaves, was well aware that this ban could not be enforced indefinitely, he did his utmost to prevent the piecemeal and prejudicial publication of his friend's letters for as long as possible. For nearly forty-three years, in fact, he threatened erring authors, journalists, and *marchands d'autographes* with sanctions ranging from legal action and professional opprobrium to personal vilification; and it was only on his death, in September 1949, that the publication of Huysmans' correspondence and the writing of a fully documented Life became practical possibilities. There have, of course, been one or two attempts to recount Huysmans' life without the aid of his letters and diaries, but on the whole it has been agreed that Lucien Descaves spoke well when, at the General Assembly of the Société J.-K. Huysmans on 6 June 1934, he declared: 'I am convinced that the story of the author of *En Route* can be written only when the greater part of his correspondence, which was copious, has been collected and published . . .'

It is my belief that the time has now come for the Life envisaged by Lucien Descaves to be published. The first of the two conditions which he mentioned in 1934 has been fulfilled, for most of Huysmans' letters and papers are now safely preserved in public and private collections. As for the second condition, although only a small part of the correspondence has so far been made public, I have been given access to most of the known collections of unpublished Huysmansiana, and have consulted nearly all the novelist's extant letters and diaries, as well as all the published works and articles on and around Huysmans listed by his bibliographers. I have also been given valuable information and advice by people who knew Huysmans personally, and I now wish to record my gratitude to them and to the many others who have helped me to write this biography.

To my friend and colleague Dr. Enid Starkie, who first suggested that I should undertake this work, and whose advice and encouragement have been of inestimable value, I owe a great debt of gratitude.

I gladly express my thanks to the Provost and Fellows of the Queen's College, Oxford, for a generous grant in aid of my research; to the Académie Goncourt for permission to consult the Huysmans-Goncourt correspondence; and to the Librarians and staffs of the Bodleian Library, the Taylor Library, the Bibliothèque Nationale, and the Bibliothèque Sainte-Geneviève for the courtesy extended to me. My thanks are also due to M. Robert Ricatte, who communicated to me certain unpublished extracts from the *Journal* of Edmond de Goncourt, and to the Right Reverend Abbess of Sainte-Scolastique de Dourgne, the Provincial of the Dominican Order in Great Britain, Mme Paul Valéry, and MM. Alfred Dupont, Emmanuel Fabius, Pierre Jammes, Henri Jouvin, and Louis Massignon, whose collections of Huysmans documents I have consulted or quoted. To the following I am indebted for information, assistance, and advice: Me Maurice Garçon of the Académie française, the late Dom Basset, Mme Andrée Bemelmans, Dr. Pierre Cogny, Dr. Joseph Daoust, M. Félix Fabre, Me Jean Jacquinot, Dr. Cornélie Kruize, M. Gabriel-Ursin Langé, M. Henry Lefai, M. Roger Lhombreaud, Mlle Alice Mamelsdorf, Mr. Alan Raitt, M. René Rancœur, Professor Jean Seznec, M. André Thérive, Dr. Helen Trudgian, and M. Pierre Waldner.

I am deeply grateful to Mme Myriam Harry, Mlle Antonine Meunier, M. René Dumesnil, Professor Louis Massignon, and the late Jérôme Tharaud, who have recalled for me their personal memories of Joris-Karl Huysmans.

My greatest debt of gratitude, a debt I cannot hope adequately to repay, is to my friend M. Pierre Lambert, who has most generously placed at my disposal his immense collection of Huysmansiana and his unrivalled knowledge of Huysmans' life and work. To him, as also to my parents and to my wife, this work is gratefully and affectionately dedicated.

R. B.
OXFORD
January 1955

PART ONE

1. THE BOY

THE ironical fate which sometimes governs our entrances and exits ordained that the first recorded mention of the subject of this biography – a writer whose life was nothing if not unhappy – should be made in a farcical document calculated to provide amusement.[1] This document was drawn up one evening by a young clerk called Jules Badin, at a dinner-party given by his sister Malvina in her little Paris flat, and it concerned the child she was expecting in three months' time. The gist of it was that if Malvina gave birth to a girl, Jules undertook to buy his friend Mme Constance Marchand a *baba glacé* at the famous Lesage *pâtisserie* in the Rue Montorgueil; but that if the child were a boy, Mme Marchand would provide the *baba*, while Jules would treat friends and relations to a round of drinks 'in celebration of the ardently desired birth of a nephew'. After this solemn covenant had been signed and witnessed, Jules entered in the date: 24 November 1847.

He won his wager. A boy, known to posterity as Joris-Karl Huysmans, was born at seven in the morning of 5 February 1848, at No. 11 Rue Suger. It is not known what part of the house his parents were then occupying, but it is thought to have been the third-floor flat overlooking the street: this is the only flat at No. 11 which boasts shutters on the court side, and tradition has it that it was Malvina Huysmans who arranged for these to be fitted. The house itself was often called the Maison Turgot, for it had at one time been the property of Michel-Jacques Turgot, Marquis de Sousmont and brother of Louis XVI's famous minister. In the century which has elapsed since Huysmans' birth, it has seen two revolutions – the first in that same month of February 1848 – and one heroic insurrection, yet it has altered only very slightly. The street having been renumbered, it is now No. 9; and its distinguishing feature – a pair of green outer doors studded with enormous nails – has disappeared. But in spite of the hubbub in the nearby Boulevards Saint-Germain and Saint-Michel, the Rue Suger is still the pleasant and tranquil backwater it was over a hundred years ago.

The child's father, Victor-Godfried-Jan Huysmans, was born in the Dutch town of Breda in 1815, and settled in Paris when a young man. Entering into partnership with a printer called Janson, he was soon earning a fair living as a lithographer and miniaturist. In June 1845 he proposed to a young French schoolmistress, Élisabeth-Malvina Badin, and they were married five months later. Of Godfried's character we know very little, but he appears to have been a meticulous man: there is still in existence a notebook into which he entered an account of every farthing spent on his honeymoon. As for his talents, they were not remarkable, and it is possible that he became an artist as much in deference to family tradition as from any sense of vocation. For it was undeniably a powerful tradition, and a long-established one. Towards the end of the sixteenth century a Michael Huysmans had a studio in Antwerp; his great-grandson Jacob won the approval of Charles II and painted portraits of Izaak Walton and the Duchess of Richmond; while Jacob's brother Cornelius produced studies of peasant life which are still to be seen in the Louvre. More recently, Godfried Huysmans' elder brother Constant had succeeded their father as Director of the important Breda Academy of Art.[2] Godfried's son was to be a great art-critic and a painter in words.

The boy's mother, Malvina Badin, was born at Vaugirard, near Paris, in 1826. When she married she was a slim, pretty brunette, and an accomplished musician. The only other member of her family with any pretensions to artistic talent was her grandfather, Antoine-François Gérard, a Prix de Rome sculptor who has left his mark on the Arc de Triomphe of the Carrousel and the pedestal of the Vendôme Column.[3] Her other male relations were all civil servants. Her father, Louis Badin, was an official at the Ministry of the Interior; so

22

was her brother Jules. Malvina's son was to be a discontented but conscientious pen-pusher.

On 6 February the child was baptized at the parish church of Saint-Séverin and given the names Charles-Marie-Georges. Godfried Huysmans took out French naturalization papers two months after the birth of his son, but the boy was to pride himself on his Dutch ancestry and to adopt what he thought to be the Dutch form of two of his names: Joris (or Jorris)-Karl. In an autobiographical sketch[4] he calls himself 'an inexplicable amalgam of a Parisian aesthete and a Dutch painter'; and his unusual *nom de plume* was at once a tribute to his forebears and an atonement for Godfried's desertion of his native land.

He retained few memories of the apartment-house in the Rue Suger, for his parents left it when he was very young and moved to No. 38 Rue Saint-Sulpice. Here a daily routine was established, which was scrupulously followed for several years. In the morning Georges stayed at home with his mother; in the afternoon, like hundreds of other children, he was taken to play in the Luxembourg Gardens. The little girls he met there were poor company, for they flaunted embroidered drawers and turned up tiny noses at children who were not immaculately dressed – and Georges' clothes rarely won their approval. But with the boys he enjoyed many a rough-and-tumble on the sandy paths, ravaged the tidy flower-beds, and feasted on waffles and sticks of sugar-candy. In the evening he was generally allowed to watch his father as Godfried toiled at minute illustrations for prayer-books and missals; but if he cried, his mother would banish him to the kitchen, where the housemaid sat spelling out a Book of Dreams by candlelight.[5]

Summer brought a little variety to the monotonous pattern of his childhood, for then Godfried and Malvina would take him to stay with his Uncle Constant at Tilburg, or with his grandparents at Ginnikin, near Brussels. He saw very little of his grandfather, who was blind and bed-ridden, but his grandmother made a great fuss of him and taught him a few simple Dutch prayers.[6] From time to time he accompanied

Huysmans' birthplace, showing his mother at the window of her room.

Huysmans in 1856.

Malvina to outlying convents in which various aunts and cousins were immured, and these visits made a deep impression on the child's mind. He never forgot how his diminutive Aunt Maria used to tease him when he was taken to the Turnhout beguinage, or how the serious demeanour of other kinswomen so intimidated him that he hid in the folds of his mother's skirts and trembled as each nun implanted a cold kiss upon his forehead.[7] Indeed, memories of these afternoons spent in waxed convent parlours and dank presbytery orchards were often to be evoked in after-years, when Huysmans himself was drawn to the idea of monastic life.

In the meantime Godfried was finding it difficult to obtain commissions for his work, and his health was deteriorating. Malvina soon grew irritable under the strain of caring for an invalid husband and a young son, with the result that the couple frequently quarrelled. After a few severe scoldings Georges learned to play quietly by himself, out of earshot, and occasionally his behaviour earned him a little insipid praise. Thus when, in May 1856, his father drew a pencil-portrait of the sickly eight-year-old boy,[8] Malvina added the verse:

> Georges s'est bien conduit à table,
> Il a mangé fort décemment,
> S'est amusé sans être diable,
> Enfin, s'est montré charmant.[9]

A month later came catastrophe – for on 24 June 1856 Godfried Huysmans died. There can be no doubt that his son was deeply affected. He never mentioned his parents in his correspondence or in his works, but all his life he treasured three oil-paintings by his father: a self-portrait, a portrait of Malvina, and a copy of Francisco de Zurbaran's *The Monk*. And in his last illness he had the Zurbaran hung in his bedroom, where *The Monk* watched him die, as it had watched his father.[10]

Malvina's grief was less poignant; besides, she was preoccupied with the problem of supporting herself and her son.

Soon after Godfried's death she obtained employment in a large department-store, and she took Georges to live with her parents at No. 11 Rue de Sèvres. In the nineteenth century this was not the busy, commercialized thoroughfare it is today, but a long quiet street in a quarter steeped in religious tradition and calm. In nearly all the adjoining streets one could hear at times the singing of plainchant, and the Rue de Sèvres itself was bordered almost exclusively by convents and bric-à-brac shops. No. 11 had been a Premonstratensian monastery until 1790, when the monks were expelled and when the adjacent Carrefour de la Croix-Rouge became known for a time as the Carrefour du Bonnet-Rouge; after the Revolution the priory chapel had been demolished and the monks' cells converted into a number of large flats.[11] In *De Tout*, Huysmans recalls the immense, high-ceilinged rooms on the first floor where he spent an icy childhood, the corridors 'wide enough to accommodate a cavalry charge', and the staircases 'up which a regiment could have marched with perfect ease'. Here, in fact, he renewed the experience of monastic quiet – and monastic discomfort – which he had first obtained during his visits to Dutch and Belgian convents.

The move to the Rue de Sèvres, and the excitement of exploring a new home, blunted the edge of the boy's sorrow, and soon he stopped brooding over his father's death. However, what happiness he may have enjoyed that summer in the company of Malvina, his grandparents, and his Uncle Jules, did not last long. As winter drew on, he noticed that his mother often went out in the evenings, and that at other times a young man would call at the flat to pay his respects. Then, early in 1857, he was told that the young man was coming to live with them – as his stepfather and Malvina's husband.

About this person we know only that he was thirty-four years of age, Protestant by religion, and Og by name. Since Godfried Huysmans had not been a particularly fervent Catholic, it is improbable that his son was unduly offended by M. Og's religious conviction, and the man's name may have fascinated him by its very ugliness. But the boy had felt great affection for his father, and Malvina's speedy remarriage seemed to him a betrayal, M. Og a usurper. This situation has not, of course, escaped the attention of the psychoanalysts, and in recent years there have been several attempts to explain Huysmans' entire life and works in terms of a mother-fixation, one eminent authority even asserting that the novelist's choice of a bureaucratic career and his occasional holidays in the Château de Lourps were symptomatic of a persistent nostalgia for the womb.[12] Although we may safely discount most of these Freudian fantasies, there can be no doubt that the boy Georges was outraged when his mother married again, and embittered when she later neglected him in favour of Juliette and Blanche, her two daughters by this second marriage. The revenge which he took on Malvina and her husband was unspectacular but none the less significant: he virtually banished them from the pages of his autobiographical novels. Thus M. Og is not represented in Huysmans' works at all, unless perhaps it be in the satirical portrait of M. Désableau in *En Ménage*. As for the mothers portrayed in Huysmans' novels, they are permitted to put in only brief appearances; and with one exception – the silent, dropsical monster in *Les Sœurs Vatard* – they are summarily disposed of in the first chapter. For only in later life, through his devotion to the Mother of Christ, did Huysmans come to know that sense of security and tenderness which was so conspicuously lacking in his childhood and youth.

Whatever psychological effect Malvina's remarriage had upon her son, it undoubtedly brought her certain material benefits, in the form of M. Og's savings. In May 1858 these were invested in a book-bindery owned by one Auguste Guilleminot, and for many years the Ogs derived a small but steady income from this business. The workshop itself could scarcely have been more conveniently placed, for it was installed on the ground floor of No. 11 Rue de Sèvres, in what had once been the monks' refectory.[13] Georges was allowed inside only when it was empty, and he often lay awake at night, listening to the thudding of the presses and the raucous singing of the women, and wondering what sort of people these were who worked for his stepfather and old M.

Guilleminot. Twenty years later he was to describe them, and the bindery, in *Les Sœurs Vatard*.

Although he continued to be starved of affection at home, he came to prefer life there to the wretched existence he led at school. He had begun his studies in the autumn of 1856 at the Institution Hortus, a *pensionnat* established at No. 94 (now No. 102) Rue du Bac, and was finding it an unpleasant experience. The very appearance of the school, with its two bare playgrounds separated by a wooden railing, its drooping acacias whose flowers the pupils used to eat, and its huge clock solemnly mounted on the latrines, was depressing enough; but the food and the discipline inflicted on its inmates were even more distasteful.[14] The boys' diet consisted of 'fatty mutton and watery beans on Monday, veal and chalky cheese on Tuesday, carrots in brown sauce and nauseating sorrel on Thursday, and for the rest of the week unseasoned macaroni, lumpy pea-soup, and potatoes fried in black fat'. Discipline was the special responsibility of the shifty-eyed, scrofulous ushers, all of whom were habitual drunkards, bullied their young charges without mercy, and lived only for the time they could spend in the nearest bar. The boys, for their part, lived only for Sunday morning, when they were released from this soul-destroying captivity and could pass a few hours at home. Even there, however, the dread thought of returning in the evening haunted them all day; and Huysmans has told how after the housemaid, impatient to join some admirer of the moment, had hurried him back to school, he would cry himself to sleep in the bleak, icy dormitory. 'To think', he wrote, many years later, 'that there are some people who claim that their schooldays were the happiest in their lives! That anyone can say such a thing passes my comprehension. However unhappy I might be, I would rather die than live that barrack-life over again, suffering the tyranny of fists bigger than mine and the petty spite of the ushers!'

He was no happier at the Lycée Saint-Louis, which he entered with a bursary in 1862, for here too the ushers regarded the pale, delicate boy as a pre-ordained victim for bullying. In his memories of the years he spent at this school, four figures stood out with nightmare precision. The first was an usher called Bourdat, 'with a threadbare suit that was known in every low bar in Paris, a mangy old hat, a slimy moustache, a pimply skin, and eyes that positively oozed lechery. He used to kiss the younger boys, rifle our pocket-money, confiscate our cigarettes to smoke himself, sell the books he borrowed from us, get as drunk as a lord, and then force us to pay him 2 francs each if we didn't want a gating. He was a remarkable specimen.' There was also a foul-mouthed old woman who screamed abuse at the boys whenever they passed her stall near Saint-Sulpice; and 'Pichi', a Rue de Grenelle shopkeeper whose nickname roused him to apoplectic fury. Last and most horrifying of all, there was the man who sold soup from a canteen outside the school gates, 'a cunning, lying brute with a prodigious belly, the head of a calf and the arms of a Hercules'. He was forever showing the boys a book containing lurid pictures of men who were supposedly ravaged by syphilis. 'You see this drawing, lad?' he would say. 'Well, you'll look like that one day, if you don't take care.' And with a parting cuff on the ears, he would fix the terrifying pictures deep in their minds.

Although the school records reveal that Georges worked well and showed more than average intelligence, the masters gave no encouragement to the 'bursary boy', but instead wreaked their spite on him. At the Institution Hortus he had found some consolation in the company of his schoolmates, but the rich young bourgeois of the Lycée Saint-Louis shunned him on account of his patched and faded clothes. The agony of his isolation is faithfully reflected in André Jayant's bitter commentary on his schooldays, in *En Ménage*:

My adolescence was one of poverty and humiliation. With a widowed mother, reduced boarding fees and a bursary at school, I didn't dare complain when the meat was bad, or when I found cockroaches floating in my wine. I knew that when the servant took the plates up to the master and whispered the names of the boys he was going to serve, my plate would inevitably come back to me heaped with dirty scraps of food, lumps of fat and bones. I knew too that at the end of any particularly inedible meal, I should almost certainly be called on to say grace! On the other hand, the masters treated me generously as regards punishments: when the others were given 100 lines, I always had to write 500. If I was first in the form I got no compliments, but I was certain of black looks if I was third, and harsh words if I was eleventh. My boots were patched and nailed, my Sunday suit worn and shiny, my waistcoats cut down from an uncle's cast-offs; and on holidays the richer boys left me at the school gates because, unlike them, I didn't sport a blue tie and a stand-up collar. Nor for that matter did I slaver on a Manilla cigar, as they did: I never rose higher than a penny cheroot. When I look back upon my youth, in fact, all that I can see is a lamentable, unbroken succession of insults and misfortunes . . .

For four years he patiently endured these trials; then, one day in 1865, he refused to return to the hated *lycée*, or to risk similar hardship and humiliation at any other school. His mother scolded and entreated, but Georges stood his ground with all the determination a seventeen-year-old can muster, and it was finally decided that he should receive private tuition from one of the masters at the Lycée Saint-Louis, a M. Delzons. On 7 March 1866[15] he obtained his Baccalaureate.

2. THE STUDENT

AT a family dinner held to celebrate Huysmans' success in the Baccalaureate examination, the question of his future career was discussed, and it was proposed that he should study law at the University.[1] The thought of paying his stepson's expenses doubtless perturbed M. Og, but his wife and her relations were ready with an acceptable solution to the problem: they urged that Georges should follow the Badin tradition and apply for a post in one of the Ministries, pursuing his law studies in his spare time.

This proposal met with general approval and was rapidly implemented. Huysmans wrote to the Minister of the Interior, asking for admission to the Civil Service, promising to perform his duties zealously and efficiently, and mentioning that an uncle, a grandfather, and a great-grandfather of his had all been *fonctionnaires*. The Minister, impressed by this bureaucratic pedigree, granted his application, and on 1 April 1866 Huysmans began work as an *employé de sixième classe*, at an annual salary of 1,500 francs.[2] Under the supervision of a M. Durangel, he busied himself throughout the summer with the welfare of children, beggars, and lunatics. In the autumn, having become sufficiently conversant with office routine, he enrolled in the Faculties of Law and Letters of the University of Paris, and entered upon a strange double-life as civil servant and student.

Huysmans was always extremely reticent about his student days, and the only trustworthy sources of information about this period of his life are his early autobiographical works, and records of his conversations with Henry Céard and Maurice Talmeyr. One fact, however, instantly emerges: the young Huysmans spent very little time over his law-books. 'The Code', he wrote some years later,[3] 'appeared to have been carelessly drawn up simply to allow certain people to quibble endlessly over each and every word; and it still seems to me that a simple sentence cannot reasonably admit of so many different interpretations.' But if his studies bored him, he found delightful compensation in the life and laughter of the new Boul' Mich'. Every evening he could be seen in some café in the Latin Quarter, talking excitedly over a bock with fellow students and their girls; and these discussions would continue into the small hours in his friends' rooms. In fact, Huysmans was a typical young Parisian student in all but one significant respect: feeling nothing but repugnance for politics, he played no part in the revolutionary societies which abounded on the Left Bank during the last years of the Second Empire. On the other hand, his friends found him a ready listener when they talked of contemporary poets and novelists; and he soon transferred his affections from La Fontaine – whose *Contes* he had read in secret at school – to George Sand and Heinrich Heine.[4] Even more enthralling than the works of these writers was Henri Murger's *Scènes de la vie de Bohème*, a book which the Latin Quarter had adopted as its Bible and which fired the imagination of generations of young students. Baron Haussmann's grandiose plans had drastically altered the face of Paris, and her spirit was constantly changing; but to Huysmans and his friends the Left Bank was still the carefree, romantic Bohemia of Murger's book – and every girl a potential Mimi.

Huysmans' own intimate relations with the opposite sex had begun at the age of sixteen, while he was still at school. One evening, armed with a bottle of eau-de-Cologne, he had ventured down an alley off the Boulevard Bonne-Nouvelle and timidly accosted a middle-aged prostitute. This woman had promptly relieved the boy of his money and his precious eau-de-Cologne, but taking pity on his tender years, she had made some pretence of passion while initiating him in the sexual rites.[5] Even so, the experience had disillusioned him, and many months passed before he was tempted to pursue his researches farther and pay his first visit to a brothel. This too proved disappointing, for here the women treated their customers with ill-concealed indifference, and the tawdry glamour of the place – the gilt and plush furnishings, and the sickening scent of amber and patchouli – filled Huysmans with disgust. He could scarcely foresee that one day he would rank among the *habitués* of this and other brothels – among the unhappy men 'who came here to forget persistent anxieties, lasting grudges, inexhaustible sorrows; who, so to speak, after cutting their lips sipping heady wines from muslin glasses, now chose to drink trashy beer from coarse public-house tankards . . .'[6]

In the meantime, Huysmans was not satisfied with his achievements or his Bohemian reputation; the final distinctive cachet was lacking. It was not lacking for long. In 1867 he took a soubrette as his mistress.

The story of this conquest is also the story of the young man's début as a writer, and of the death of a little theatre. With some other students, Huysmans went one night to Bobino, *alias* the Théâtre du Luxembourg, a ramshackle playhouse in the Rue Madame which in the fifty years of its existence had staged everything from tightrope-walking to tragedy. It had at this time descended to a revue called *Cocher, à Bobino!* which was having a rough passage when Huysmans first saw it. As he later explained, in his novel *Marthe*, 'Bobino was unlike the theatres of Montparnasse, Grenelle and the other old suburbs in that its clientèle was not made up of working-men intent on hearing a piece through to the end; it was patronized rather by students and artists – the noisiest and wildest of God's creatures. They didn't come to this hideous, purple-papered shack to listen in spellbound silence to heavy melodramas or light revues: they came to shout and laugh and interrupt – in short, to have a good time.' Certainly they enjoyed themselves at the expense of the unfortunate company of *Cocher, à Bobino!* – but their catcalls turned to enthusiastic applause on the appearance of one singer, a lovely red-haired girl. 'Her figure', writes Huysmans,[7] 'was tightly encased in a pearl-embroidered costume of exquisite pink – that pale, almost faded pink of Levantine silk – and with her magnificent scarlet mane, her full, moist red lips, she was utterly

33

enchanting, irresistibly seductive!' As soon as he saw her come on to the tiny gas-lit stage, young Georges Huysmans fell in love.

During the days that followed, he tried again and again to attract the attention of this popular artiste, leaving flowers, letters, and poems for her at the Bobino stage-door. Perhaps he even sent her the strange sonnet which he later published in *Marthe*:

> Un fifre qui piaule et sifle d'un ton sec,
> Un basson qui nasille, un vieux qui s'époumonne
> A cracher ses chicots dans le cou d'un trombone,
> Un violon qui tinte ainsi qu'un vieux rebec,
>
> Un flageolet poussif dont on suce le bec,
> Un piston grincheux, la grosse caisse qui tonne,
> Tel est, avec un chef pansu comme une tonne,
> Scrofuleux, laid enfin à tenir en échec
>
> La femme la plus apte aux amoureuses lices,
> L'orchestre du théâtre. – Et c'est là cependant
> Que toi, mon seul amour, toi, mes seuls délices,
> Tu brames tous les soirs d'infâmes ritournelles
> Et que, la bouche en cœur, l'œil clos, le bras pendant,
> Tu souris aux voyous, ô la Reine des belles![8]

If all his declarations of love were couched in this style, then it is small wonder that they all failed to elicit a reply. Nothing daunted, however, Huysmans looked for some other means of approaching and courting the girl, and he finally hit upon a less conventional plan: by posing as a journalist in search of copy, he would try to gain entrance to the Bobino green-room. As it happens, he had some small justification for describing himself as a journalist, for he had written an article on contemporary landscape-painters which appeared on 25 November 1867 in *La Revue Mensuelle*. This was a very modest periodical which had begun publication in January 1866 and was fated to die an early death; its offices were in a fifth-floor attic in the Rue de la Sourdière, a street close to the church of Saint-Roch, and its editor was a kindly old gentleman called Le Hir, of whom Huysmans later remembered only that he wore a skull-cap and carpet-slippers. Though not a memorable or important figure in the world of journalism, M. Le Hir merits our respect as a discerning judge of new talent, since in his brief introduction to Huysmans' first article he described him as 'a young critic who appears to us to lack neither verve nor perception'. He was doubtless surprised that his budding art-critic should offer to write a notice of Bobino's latest and last revue – an entertainment called *La Vogue parisienne*, with words and music by Oswald and Lemonnier – but he agreed to this suggestion. And that night a little comedy was enacted behind the scenes at Bobino, which was later described by Huysmans in this passage from *Marthe*:

> The company were in a vile temper, as they expected to be given another rowdy reception by the audience; and the director, who because of the shortage of funds also acted as stage-manager, was pacing feverishly up and down the stage, waiting for the curtain to go up. Suddenly someone slapped him on the back, and he turned to find himself confronted by a young man who shook him by the hand and coolly asked:
>
> 'How are you keeping?'
>
> 'But . . . but quite well. And you?'
>
> 'Oh, very nicely, thank you. But now let's get things straight. You don't know me from Adam, and I don't know you either. Well, I'm a journalist and I intend so write a marvellous article on your theatre.'
>
> 'I'm very pleased to hear it – delighted, in fact. But what paper do you write for?'
>
> '*The Monthly Review.*'
>
> 'Don't know it. When does it come out?'
>
> 'Generally every month.'
>
> 'I see . . . Won't you take a seat?'
>
> 'Thank you very much, but not just now.'

And he disappeared into the green-room, where the actors and actresses were chattering away to each other . . .

Within a week Huysmans was a familiar figure backstage, having won the director's confidence, the company's friendship, and the little soubrette's affection. Somewhat to the surprise of the Bobino players, who soon discovered the real object of his visits, the 'marvellous article' which he had promised them was actually written and published. It appeared in the last issue of *La Revue Mensuelle*, on Christmas Day 1867, and contrived to mention almost everyone in the company; but it was scarcely calculated to retrieve the dwindling fortunes of either periodical or theatre. It read as follows:

The Théâtre du Luxembourg is now presenting its last revue: *La Vogue parisienne*. This piece is not perfect, but the verve and zest of the actors are winning applause for it. The part of Routine is taken by Villot and that of Vogue by Mlle Katybulle; both players acquit themselves very well. Mlles Henriette, Melcy and d'Hauteloup contribute in no small measure to the revue's success, but the best performance is that given by M. Ours; it is to be regretted that his part is so small. Mention must also be made of Mme Bartholy, M. Saincenis, Abel and Ducros. To sum up, this is an amusing revue and we wish it every success.

(Georges H . . .)

We do not know, and indeed we may never know, which of the actresses mentioned in this notice was Huysmans' first love. We know, however, that for his initial venture into journalism he received payment – of a sort. One evening, finding that he had scarcely enough money for a meal, Huysmans appealed to Le Hir for help. Unluckily for him, the old gentleman was in the same straits and had nothing to offer but some sample bottles of liqueur provided by an advertiser. These Husysmans stuffed into his overcoat and hawked round the wineshops in the Rue Saint-Honoré, but the shopkeepers took him for a thief and refused to buy. So in the end he went home, drank the liqueurs – and was literally intoxicated by his first author's fee.[10]

La Revue Mensuelle having ceased publication in December 1867, Huysmans went no more to the dark, narrow Rue de la Sourdière. Strangely enough, Anna Meunier, who was later to be Huysmans' mistress for many years, was for a time employed in a clothing factory in this very street; and it is just possible that he met her one day when he was leaving Le Hir's office. In an article published over thirty years ago, M. Francis Baumal stated his belief that Huysmans and Anna lived together before the Franco-Prussian War, in a garret in the Rue du Dragon; but he produced no evidence to substantiate this assertion.[11] Huysmans had certainly left the Rue de Sèvres flat by 1867, but his only serious liaison in the pre-war years would seem to have been with the Bobino singer, and it is unlikely that when they parted he had either the money or the inclination to take another mistress.

By dint of a few weeks' concentrated work, Huysmans had passed his first law examination in August 1867.[12] Any pleasure M. Jules Og might have felt at this success was short-lived, for he died on 8 September. Perhaps this was as well: his stepson was to give little thought in the future to his studies. As he later confessed in *Sac au dos*, he spent the money for his second-year fees on a girl 'who would assure me from time to time that she loved me'.

This girl, the soubrette from Bobino, found him an exacting lover. The crude satisfactions of the brothel were beginning to bore him, and he longed now for 'sensual pleasures seasoned with perverse looks and strange garments'. He would have liked, he writes, 'to embrace a woman dressed as a rich circus artiste, under a wintry, yellow-grey, snow-laden sky, in a room hung with Japanese silks, while some half-starved beggar emptied the belly of his barrel-organ of the sad waltzes it contained'.[13] He expected his mistress to put on blue eye-shadow and rouge, black silk corsets and flounced skirts. A woman, he thought, who came from a world of magic and make-believe, the world of the stage and the sawdust-ring, should surely answer some of these requirements.

It goes without saying that the girl who came home with him one night from Bobino understood none of his extravagant fancies. And the next morning, she looked as pathetically ugly in bed as the other women he had known; she dressed in the same way too, sitting on the edge of the bed and buttoning her boots with a hairpin; she made the same inane, infuriating remarks. Yet there were compensations. If she was not the faery, other-worldly creature he had desired, she still brought him a little unsolicited tenderness – she 'would assure me from time to time that she loved me . . .'

They lived together. For a while, Huysmans tasted the joys of a modest but happy home life; when he came back from the Ministry in the evening, he found the oil lamp burning steadily, the table laid for dinner, and a pretty woman sitting in the arm-chair by the fire. This was not, it is true, the dream he had cherished of passionate love in an exotic setting, but it was the realization of another dream – one of domestic comfort and quiet, born in part of his ardent admiration for Dutch interiors.

It did not last for long. First, the closing down of Bobino and the dismissal of the company brought about a serious reduction in the young couple's joint income. And then, a short time afterwards, Huysmans discovered that his mistress was some months pregnant by another man.

In the train of this major catastrophe came a host of the trivial irritations which were to plague Huysmans all his life and provide material for so many of his works: the chair that was always out of place, the skirts draped over his coat, the persistent smell of food, the washday puddles and steam, and the ironing-board that for ever straddled his desk. To make matters worse, the girl found the novelty of keeping house soon wore off, and instead of preparing dinner herself, she took to buying ready-cooked meals from the local shops. After dinner, she would pull off her clothes, throw them into an untidy heap, and tumble wearily into bed – leaving her lover to clear the table and grumbling at him if he stayed up reading his books. He noticed now that she had grown slovenly in her personal habits, careless of her appearance, and indifferent to his love-making. 'The actress and the mistress', he complained,[14] 'had disappeared. Only the maid-of-all-work remained . . .'

The baby, a little girl, was born towards the end of the winter. From the account given in *Marthe* and in Huysmans' conversations with Céard,[15] it appears that the child's arrival was premature, having been brought on by an accidental fall. Late one night, the girl felt the first pains of labour and begged her lover to go and fetch the local midwife. As soon as this good woman arrived, she commented on the fact that there was no fire in the room, and the girl, fearing that she would ask to be paid in advance if she suspected how poor they were, asked Huysmans to look for the key to the coal-cellar, which she said was either in her dress-pocket or on the mantelpiece. By this time he was so bewildered that he actually began looking for the non-existent key, when suddenly his mistress fell back on the bed and gave birth to the child. After washing the baby and wrapping it in swaddling-clothes, the kindly midwife left without demanding payment from the young couple, whose penniless condition had not, of course, escaped her notice.

The night that followed was one of indescribable misery. Huysmans sat huddled in an arm-chair with the baby in his arms, while the wind rattled the windows and scattered the ashes of the long-dead fire around the room. His mistress lay groaning on the bed; he himself was so cold that he could only fumble helplessly with the baby's swaddling-clothes when these came undone; and finally, overcome by a sudden attack of nausea, he was violently sick.

As may readily be imagined, the infant was not particularly welcome to its mother, and in its foster-father it implanted a lifelong detestation of the very young. To those who exalted the joys of parenthood he would henceforth counter with the bitter observation that 'once a child's born, it means perpetual sleepless nights and endless worry. One day the brat bawls because it's cutting a tooth, another day because it isn't; and the whole room stinks of sour milk and piddle . . .'[16] Even the day's work at the Ministry he now considered a pleasure compared to evenings with a tired woman in a cold, cheerless room – and nights made hideous by the wailing of another man's child. If he still possessed a copy of Henri Murger's *Vie de Bohème*, he must surely have burnt it now. For this may have been Bohemia, but it was not very romantic and it was certainly not carefree.

How long this wretched state of affairs lasted we cannot tell; nor do we know the fate of either mother or child. Perhaps the woman died; perhaps, like the heroine of *Marthe*, she went into one of 'the slaughterhouses of love, where desire is slain at a single stroke'. In any event, the unhappy liaison eventually came to an end, and the young man's finances and spirits slowly recovered. In this, his first love-affair, he had lost a good deal of money and a few illusions, and he accordingly considered himself a man of the world. He was wondering where to look for new experiences, when the choice was made for him.

'By his clumsy diplomacy,' he writes in *Sac au dos*, 'the late Emperor made a soldier of me. The war with Prussia broke out. Truth to tell, I didn't understand the motives for this wholesale butchery, and I felt neither the desire to kill others nor the desire to have others kill me.' Moreover, as he later explained in a later autobiographical sketch, he was conscious that there existed strong temperamental affinities between himself and the hated foe, and that he instinctively preferred the 'big, phlegmatic, taciturn Germans' to the exuberant Latins 'with their skulls covered with curly astrakhan, and their cheeks lined with ebony hedgerows'.[17] However, there was no time in that summer of 1870 to ponder racial preferences: the die was cast. Already, in March that year, Huysmans the civil servant and student had been officially registered as No. 1377 in the Garde Nationale Mobile of the Seine.[18] And on 30 July, only a few days after the outbreak of war, he was ordered to present himself at seven in the evening at the Rue de Lourcine barracks, there to join the 6th Battalion on its way to the front.

3. THE SOLDIER

THE 6th Battalion of the Garde Mobile went off to war in high spirits, exultant at the thought of doing battle with the Prussians, confident that they would soon he celebrating victory in Berlin.[1] They went dressed in dark blue jackets, blue linen breeches, and monstrous *képis* adorned with tinplate tricolours; they went unarmed and very drunk. Under a sky streaked with summer lightning, the contingent from the Rue de Lourcine barracks reeled across Paris, accompanied by a throng of parents and friends, shrieking the *Marseillaise*, cursing their heavy packs, and drinking steadily all the way. When they arrived at the Gare d'Aubervilliers, they took leave of their weeping relations and were herded into cattle-trucks. And at eight o'clock, to the accompaniment of sobs, final exhortations, and patriotic songs, the troop-train moved out of the station.

The journey that followed was long and wearisome, the trucks being continually shunted into sidings as munition-trains rattled past on their way east. Whenever this happened, Huysmans clambered down on to the embankment to stretch his legs and enjoy a snack of bread and wine in comparative comfort. Inside the trucks, the stench and the heat were well-nigh unbearable; some of the men chanted drunken ditties throughout the night, some dozed fitfully, some wept, and the rest sat in dejected silence. The morning sun revealed to them the bleak, chalky plains of Champagne, and at three o'clock in the afternoon they finally arrived at their destination, Châlons.

Nothing was ready for them. The units that had just left the town had taken everything with them except their lice-infested tents; and in these the 6th Battalion settled down, without straw, blankets, or food. The next few days were spent in enforced idleness, relieved only by brief spells of arms–drill. As for food, the troops were left to fend for themselves, and had to subsist on an occasional saveloy and bowl of coffee, bought dear from the profiteering local inhabitants. 'All this', writes Huysmans in *Sac au dos*, 'was not calculated to endear to us the calling which had been inflicted upon us.'

In these circumstances it was singularly tactless of Marshal Canrobert to remark, at a parade on 4 August, that the battalion was well fed and equipped: there ensued one of the most remarkable displays of insubordination in French military history. Remembering that the Marshal had once expressed his eagerness to crush a threatened insurrection in Paris, if necessary by shooting down a hundred thousand men, the Parisian *gardes mobiles* now screamed at him: '*Ran, plan, plan! cent mille hommes par terre, à Paris, à Paris!*' They touched upon a sore spot. White with anger, Canrobert rode his horse into the midst of the jeering troops, bellowing: 'Hats off before a Marshal of France!' But in the face of continuous barracking, he at last turned tail and rode off with his officers, promising to take dreadful vengeance on *messieurs les Parisiens*.

A week later the battalion was at the front – but without Huysmans. Down with dysentery, he had been ordered into a field hospital near Châlons, under the command of a swearing M.O. who prescribed liquorice infusions for the syphilitic and the wounded alike. Here Huysmans stayed for nine or ten days. His companions were for the most part villainous cut-throats from the shadiest quarters of Paris; but he was lucky enough to win the friendship of his two neighbours – a young artist called Anselme,[2] and a bugler who in private life was a cobbler by day and a pimp by night. Discipline in the wards was not strict, and during the hot August nights the men would squat around Huysmans' bed, to feast by candlelight on smuggled food and wine. They were gradually accustoming themselves to the tedium of hospital life when startling news reached them of the Prussian advance, for at five o'clock one morning the M.O. woke them to announce that the enemy was marching on Châlons. Twenty-four hours later the entire hospital was evacuated. Suspected malingerers were bundled off to their units; the other patients, hoisted in pairs on to lop-sided mule-litters, arrived at Châlons in a cloud of dust, more dead than alive. And there they found the inevitable line of cattle trucks, waiting to take them to an unknown destination.

Late that night their train stopped at Reims, and the sick, rising as one man, bore down upon the station buffet, over-powering the unfortunate proprietor and stripping the shelves of everything from sausages to toothpicks. No one heeded the whistle of the departing train, which soon shunted back into the station to pick up the truants. The rest of the night was spent in an orgy of eating and drinking, with the nimbler invalids scrambling along the footboard and dropping in on the parties with the richest booty. Huysmans dozed off towards dawn, but he was woken by the cry of 'Paris!' and caught sight of the familiar skyline silhouetted against a ribbon of pale, golden light. As the train steamed slowly into the Gare du Nord, the troops leaped on to the platform and tried their Reims tactics on the station exits. Some succeeded in escaping; the rest, including Huysmans and Anselme, were herded back into the stifling heat of the trucks. An hour later they resumed their journey westward.

At Arras, where the troops arrived at four o'clock and spent a couple of days, Huysmans was allotted a bed in the old men's ward of the local hospital. Here he had an unnerving experience on the second night: woken by the sound of a sinister chuckle, he found he had to defend himself against an aged homicidal maniac, while the other inmates of the ward sat speechless in their beds, waving their cotton nightcaps and gibbering with fright. Much to his relief, the troop-train left Arras the next morning and went on to Rouen, where the men were granted an hour's leave. This was Huysmans' first visit to the old city, and he and Anselme were so enthralled by the medieval houses and the church of Saint-Ouen that they became oblivious of time; when they finally returned to the station, they discovered that the train had long since left without them. It was midnight before the two friends reached their journey's end – the little cathedral city of Évreux, standing on the slopes of the Iton valley.

After spending the night in a hayrick, they went into the town for breakfast and then reported to the hospital. Only Anselme was admitted; Huysmans was directed to the austere-looking *lycée*, a former Capuchin monastery built early in the eighteenth century. In this claustral setting – which doubtless reminded him of his childhood home in the Rue de Sèvres – he spent several days of excruciating boredom. The other patients were incapable of conversing in words of more than one syllable, permission to visit Anselme at the hospital was refused, and the only reading matter in the place consisted of pseudo-mystical verses scrawled by the monks on the walls of their cells. For want of anything better to do, and prompted by that documentary fervour which was to inform the whole of his later life, Huysmans laboriously deciphered and transcribed this pitiful doggerel, with the intention of subsequently incorporating it into an account of his war-time experiences. He could have added descriptions of the actual fighting if the M.O. at the *lycée* had had his way, for that gentleman had made it a principle to send three of his patients back to their units every day, whether they were cured or not. Huysmans nearly fell a victim to this practice, but a friendly medical student arranged for his transfer to the hospital, where he was reunited on 21 August with an astonished and overjoyed Anselme.

While he was unlacing his pack, he was introduced to the nun in charge of the Saint-Vincent ward, Sister Angèle. This smiling, sweet-natured young woman in her white-winged coif made a deep impression on Huysmans, and the monastic sympathies revealed in several of his works undoubtedly owed much to her. In later years he would recall how outrageously she spoilt him during his stay at Évreux, how she commiserated with him in his boredom, and how she often appeared at his bedside in the early morning, bearing a bowl of steaming hot chocolate and explaining that the soup that day was far too thin for her liking. 'Knowing her, one could not but love her,' he writes in *Sac au dos*; 'and yet the sight of her made me

44

rather sad, for under the sober mask she wore, one could distinguish a bright and carefree disposition. Sometimes, indeed, her eyes lit up and her languid smile became deliciously roguish; but then, as if reproaching herself with this moment of forgetfulness, she would frown and walk slowly away with downcast gaze, while I would follow her with my eyes until she disappeared . . .'

In spite of Sister Angèle's attentions and his friend's intelligent conversation, Huysmans found life in the hospital unutterably dreary, and one day he and Anselme conspired to escape for a few hours. Clambering over the wall of a secluded courtyard, and skirting the main buildings of the hospital, they soon found themselves in Évreux, where they intended to hunt out a good restaurant. Before they had gone very far, however, they were ambushed by a pair of prostitutes, in whose company they later consumed a gargantuan lunch and passed a merry afternoon. At five o'clock they were back in the Saint-Vincent ward, innocently waiting for Sister Angèle to bring round the evening meal.

The next morning the two truants found that the door leading to the courtyard was locked, so they decided to bluff their way out through the main gate and told the concierge that they had to go to the Commissariat. This time they indulged in no amorous adventures but made straight for the Cathedral, where they studied the sculptured porch and were themselves closely inspected by an irate-looking old gentleman. Boldly returning his stare, they left the Cathedral and adjourned to a nearby café for a *demi-tasse*. There Huysmans made a surprising discovery. Looking through a copy of the local newspaper, he came across the name of an old friend of his family – a Me Louis Chefdeville who, he remembered, was an Évreux solicitor. He at once resolved to pay him a call, and left Anselme to buy a black tie and gloves and make himself presentable.

He was graciously received by Mme Chefdeville in her house in the Rue Chartraine; and when her husband came home, Huysmans asked if the solicitor could possibly prevail upon the military authorities to grant him a few weeks' sick-leave. Promising to do all he could to help, Chefdeville escorted the young man to the headquarters of the divisional M.O., who was obviously surprised to see one of his patients outside hospital walls but agreed to put his case before the General. Huysmans was assured that, all being well, he would probably be able to return to Paris within a few days. After thanking the kindly solicitor, he rejoined Anselme and the two friends made their way back to the hospital.

They were accorded a chilly reception. It appeared that the old gentleman who had stared at them so curiously outside the Cathedral was none other than the General himself, and that he had made angry inquiries at the hospital. Sister Angèle, instructed to find out which of her patients were missing, had nobly withheld her favourite's name; but the concierge had not been troubled by any such scruples. The result was that Anselme, whom the authorities considered the more culpable of the two miscreants, was ordered to report back to his unit, while a guard was set upon the Saint-Vincent ward to prevent any further escapes. Huysmans himself took to his bed for several days, suffering from a particularly severe attack of dysentery and obsessed by the fear that Chefdeville had forgotten him. But the solicitor soon furnished proof of his loyalty: on 6 September he wrote to tell his protégé that the General had relented sufficiently to grant the young soldier's application for leave.[3]

In the meantime news had reached Évreux that on 2 September the Emperor had surrendered with his army at Sedan, and that two days later a Republic had been proclaimed by the people of Paris. The Prussians were reported to be marching on the capital, and Huysmans was naturally impatient to get home before the roads and railways into the city were blocked. However, he was still confined to the hospital until the 8th, when at last his leave permit arrived from Divisional Headquarters. He went for the last time to the Rue Chartraine to thank the Chefdevilles again for their kindness, and then, before catching the train to Paris, he sought out Sister Angèle in the hospital gardens. Blushing a little, she wished him Godspeed and added: 'Be good now –

and above all don't get into bad company on your way home!'
Huysmans promised.

The promise was soon broken. On the train he lost his heart to a fair-haired girl called Suzanne, and would have taken her home with him that night, had not her brother met her at the station and whisked her away in a cab. Huysmans was left to make his way across Paris to the Rue de Sèvres, where his mother had supper ready for him, and then to his own lodgings.

Here he found everything just as he had left it.

I lit all the candles [he tells us in *Sac au dos*], and the room sang a *Te Deum* in colour, a Hosanna in flame! The brasses threw out rays of red and yellow fire, the Chinese pictures writhed and grimaced against a background of crude vermilion, the scarlet flowers blossomed out on the grey curtains, and a terra-cotta nymph on the chimney-piece proffered her rosy body. Then the books in their multicoloured jackets joined in the celebrations, the grotesques on the Moustiers and Rouen plates cut capers and shook their crimson horns, pink and gold butterflies fluttered across the blue enamel of the Japanese dishes, the old table creaked with joy, and my arm-chair stretched out its arms like one of Greuze's loving fathers. And while Zurbaran's monk, clutching a death's-head in his mystical ecstasy, seemed to be imploring forgiveness for my sins, a Boucher nymph lifted up her skirts and looked at me appealingly with bold, lecherous eyes . . .

To this rapturous and colourful welcome, Huysmans came home from the war.

4. THE DÉBUTANT

THOUGH Huysmans was naturally glad to be home again, he soon realized that he could not have chosen a worse place in which to spend his sick-leave. In mid-September two Prussian armies entered the outskirts of Paris, and by the 19th the city had been completely cut off from the outside world. Within a few weeks, food stocks in the besieged capital had fallen so low that the diet of the poorer sections of the population was reduced to a few grammes of coarse bread and horseflesh a day. To make matters worse, the winter proved exceptionally severe; all street lighting was turned off, with the result that there was an alarming increase in crime; while after Christmas the Prussians began a steady bombardment of the city, pouring hundreds of shells every day into the thickly populated districts on the Left Bank. As the winter drew on, an eerie silence descended on Paris, broken only by the sound of exploding shells and the slow, shuffling tread of the women and children queuing outside the food-shops in the early morning. For Huysmans the spectacle of a great capital being slowly demoralized by hunger and bombardment held a horrifying fascination, and it seems that he kept a careful account of the many strange incidents and rumours which came to his notice. In later years he was to use this material for a novel of the siege of Paris; but unfortunately this work was never completed, and he destroyed the manuscript shortly before he died.

As soon as his sick-leave expired he had reported for duty, and on 10 November he was attached to the staff of the Ministry of War as an invoicing clerk.[1] This post was not as safe as might be supposed, for Huysmans later told Céard that in January 1871 he was often under fire while at work in the Fort d'Issy. Sometimes he would sit smoking under the trees, trying to make out the enemy's positions at Meudon, and timing the shells as they burst around him. Once, when a shell exploded only a few yards away, he followed the grim fashion of the day and kept the fragments to be used as paperweights.

In February, after the capitulation of Paris, the National Assembly and the staffs of Government departments moved to Versailles, and it was there that Huysmans – once more a civilian clerk at the Ministry of the Interior – passed the next few months. He therefore saw nothing of the terrible drama of revolution and civil war that was enacted in Paris during April and May – nothing, that is, except the crimson glow which spread across the sky as the hard-pressed Communards fired churches and public buildings in the capital. It was only on 2 June, when he went into Paris on official business,[2] that he understood what the city had suffered during the 'Bloody Week'. The Palais de Justice had been destroyed; the Tuileries and the Hôtel de Ville were charred and blackened ruins; streets and boulevards on both banks of the Seine bore the scars of battle; and the mortuaries were still full of the bodies of the 20,000 men and women shot down by the Government troops or executed by the firing-squads. Huysmans returned to Versailles after a few days, sickened by the stories of carnage he had been told, and ashamed to think that the Prussians encamped in the north-eastern districts of Paris had witnessed with amusement the most violent civil strife in the city's history.

Later that summer, although still employed in the Versailles offices of the Ministry, he took his belongings back to Paris. There, first at No. 114 Rue de Vaugirard, and later at No. 73 Rue du Cherche-Midi, he would entertain his friends in the evenings and at weekends. His most constant companion at this time was a young man bearing the proud name of Ludovic de Vente de Francmesnil, who had been his classmate at the Institution Hortus and had studied law with him under a Polish tutor called Chodsko.[3] The two friends had the same interests, the same tastes in art and literature, even the same occupation – for Ludo (as he was known to his intimates) was a clerk at the Ministry of War. Together they used to explore the Left Bank on Sunday afternoons, deploring what they called the 'Americanization' of the old *quartiers*, and rejoicing at the discovery of some peaceful courtyard or sordid cul-de-sac. Sometimes they went into Saint-Séverin or Saint-Sulpice to listen to the choirs, but they were more often to be seen at the Louvre, where Huysmans spent countless hours studying the Dutch masters in the recently acquired Lacaze collection. Other evenings were devoted to discussion of the literary work which Huysmans had in hand, ranging from the first draft of his war memoirs – *Le Chant du départ* – to a Romantic verse-drama with the pretentious title of *La Comédie Humaine*.[4]

In 1873 Huysmans produced for his friend's inspection the manuscript of a finished work. This was neither memoir nor drama, but a collection of prose-poems in the manner of Baudelaire and Aloysius Bertrand, which Huysmans had entitled *Le Drageoir à épices*. The spices, Ludo discovered, were strangely assorted. There was a landscape of the humble Bièvre district in Paris which reminded him of their Sunday walks, a piece in praise of Villon which recalled their literary evenings, and lively sketches of Adrian Brauwer and Cornelius Bega which were obviously inspired by Huysmans' visits to the Louvre. There were descriptions of a *bal populaire* at Grenelle, and of a *fête* in a Picardy village; of a pink-and-crimson boudoir filled with azaleas, and of a Paris market heaped high with vegetables. There was an impassioned address to a prostitute, and a significant little piece called 'L'Extase', which told of a young idealist's horror at finding that his beloved was a slave to the baser natural functions. And lastly, after a delicate portrait of a Japanese geisha-girl, there was a splendid portrait of a bloater, 'robed in the palette of setting suns, the patina of ancient bronzes, the golden-brown tones of Cordovan leather, the saffron and sandalwood tints of autumn foliage . . .'

Ludo was completely captivated by this exotic work, and he assured the author that it was not only worthy of publication but certain of success. Unfortunately the publishers to whom Huysmans submitted his manuscript had other views.

One after the other, they politely rejected it, until in desperation the young man sought the advice of his mother, who as part-owner of the Rue de Sèvres bindery had business relations with several publishers. It is difficult to believe that Mme Og actually read *Le Drageoir*, for she gave her son a letter of introduction to a publisher who in his leisure hours wrote children's books and innocuous almanacs: P.-J. Hetzel. A few days later Huysmans received a letter from Hetzel which was calculated to chill the blood of the most optimistic young author.[5] After stating that he had read Huysmans' manuscript the publisher continued:

> What I have to say about it is easier to say than to write. If you can come to see me one morning at eleven, and if you are not afraid of the truth – or at least of sincerity which may be at once pleasant and very unpleasant – we shall have a serious talk together. I have the greatest respect for your mother, and if I could help her son to go right instead of left, I should regard it as my duty to do so. In any case it would be impossible for me to speak to you except with absolute frankness. I must warn you therefore that what I have to say is not entirely complimentary.

When he called on Hetzel in his office in the Rue Jacob, Huysmans found that he had little or nothing to say that was complimentary. Recalling his 'serious talk' with Hetzel many years later, he told Edmond de Goncourt that the publisher had indignantly informed him 'that he had no talent whatever, that he never would have any talent, that he wrote in an execrable style, that he was starting a revolutionary Commune de Paris in the French language, and that he was mad to believe in the existence of superior epithets, to think that one word was better than another . . .'[6] The young author went back to his lodgings with the dismal conviction that his literary career was over, but his friends all urged him to pay no attention to Hetzel's opinions. Acting on their advice, he arranged with the House of Dentu to have the book published at his own expense; and on 10 October 1874, *Le Drageoir à épices* made its appearance on the bookstalls – a slim grey volume which bore in scarlet letters the strange-sounding name of Jorris-Karl Huysmans.

It aroused little interest at first. The public, according to Huysmans, bought only four copies in as many weeks, and the Press ignored the book. Indeed, *Le Drageoir* and its author might have passed into oblivion but for the kindness of two influential men of letters, Arsène Houssaye and Octave Lacroix.[7] Houssaye published extracts from the book in the November issue of *L'Artiste*, and Lacroix wrote to a number of important critics, warmly recommending his young protégé. The result was that in December *L'Illustration* and *L'Événement* printed enthusiastic reviews by Jules Claretie and Charles Monselet; while on 18 January Théodore de Banville described Huysmans' work in *Le National* as 'a skilfully cut jewel from the hand of a master goldsmith'. Within the next few weeks, the newly-founded periodical *Le Musée des Deux-Mondes* opened its columns to Huysmans, seasoned writers like Léon Cladel offered him their friendship, and his little book ran into a second edition – published this time by the Librairie Générale under the definitive title of *Le Drageoir aux épices*. The only note of criticism was sounded in a letter from Constant Huysmans, who suggested that in future works his nephew would do better to treat pleasant, homely subjects.[8] This suggestion was coldly received.

In the meantime, Huysmans had made many new friends who, like Ludo, used to come to his lodgings every Wednesday evening. Two of these friends were Ludo's colleagues at the Ministry of War: Henry Céard, a former medical student, and Jean-Jules-Athanase Bobin, nicknamed 'the Professor' on account of his pedantic manner and immense erudition. The others included Gabriel Thyébaut,[9] a legal pundit and practical joker, Maurice du Seigneur, architect son of the Romantic sculptor Jehan du Seigneur, and Albert Pinard, who was later to write the famous novel *Madame X*. In a fug of cigarette smoke they would sit drinking endless cups of tea, composing obscene parodies of Victor Hugo's poems, listening to the learned Bobin as he demolished Molière's reputation or defended Bossuet's, and discussing the merits and demerits of nineteenth-century novelists.[10] Of these, Hugo was at this time generally considered the greatest, but Huysmans and his friends held that Balzac's novels were infinitely superior to *Notre-Dame de Paris* and *Les Misérables*. Stendhal they condemned out of hand for what Huysmans called 'the truly infamous aridity and poverty of his style',[11] while Daudet was contemptuously bracketed with such sentimental popular writers as Cherbuliez and Feuillet. Gustave Flaubert, on the other hand, won the ardent admiration of them all, and Céard and Thyébaut even went so far as to commit the whole of *L'Éducation sentimentale* to memory. But much as Huysmans revered the master of Croisset, he gave pride of place in his literary affections to Edmond and Jules de Goncourt, on account of the bizarre style, the neurotic sensibility, the haunting melancholy of their works. On Wednesday evenings, when he read some favourite passage of prose to his guests, it was generally taken from *Germinie Lacerteux*, the Goncourts' realistic study of a depraved servant-girl, or from *Manette Salomon*, their novel of artist life in Paris under the Second Empire. And some years later, he told Edmond: 'The urge to write came to me from reading your books. Your novels were the first to attract me, and they appealed to me more profoundly than any others . . .'[12]

Huysmans' own work was now appearing regularly in *Le Musée des Deux-Mondes* and in Catulle Mendès' review, *La République des Lettres*. It consisted for the most part of *transpositions d'art*, brilliant evocations of such pictorial masterpieces as Greuze's *Broken Pitcher*, Rubens' *Kermis*, and Franz Hals' *Boon Companion*. Readers of the two reviews enjoyed his contributions, but his friends complained that he was wasting his time on trifles, and begged him to attempt something more ambitious. They could not know that for many months he had been at work on a literary project that was nothing if not ambitious – the writing of a monumental novel about the siege of Paris.

In this novel, which he had entitled *La Faim*, Huysmans

intended to describe every aspect of life in the invested capital; to tell of the wild rumours that swept the city, of the spy-mania that took hold of the people, of the fantastic relief schemes that were proposed to the Commandant, and of the crimes and follies committed by starving men and women. The central figure in the book would be a nineteen-year-old girl from the provinces, employed during the siege by a firm that supplied greatcoats to the Garde Nationale; she was to be shown in a pitiful plight – bullied by the manager, debauched by her workmates, underfed and overworked.[13] Huysmans' manuscript notes for *La Faim*, which are still extant, reveal that this unhappy heroine was no figment of his imagination. A year or two after the war he had had a brief love-affair with a young midinette called Anna Meunier, a native of Metz, who had described to him in detail her harrowing war-time experiences. It was her story that Huysmans now proposed to tell in *La Faim*.

He got no further than the first chapter. Perhaps, as Céard has suggested, he realized that the public was beginning to be bored with the countless stories and memoirs of the siege which covered every bookstall in Paris; perhaps, too, he saw that the vast novel he had planned was as yet beyond his powers. He began work instead on a book of more modest dimensions – a volume of sardonic short stories called *Joyeu-setés navrantes* – but fared no better. Then, at one of the Wednesday reunions in the winter of 1875, something happened which determined the course of his future career as a writer. The conversation had turned to the eternal themes of love and war, and Huysmans suddenly launched out into an ironical account of his tragi-comic liaison with the Bobino soubrette, and of his uninspiring adventures in the Garde Nationale. His audience listened in fascinated silence, and, when he had finished, Céard asked why he did not publish these reminiscences of student and army life in the form of one or two novels. Huysmans' reply was that he doubted whether such works would interest the public, but his friends countered with references to *L'Éducation sentimentale* and eventually persuaded him to make the attempt.

As a result of this conversation, *Le Chant du départ* – the first draft of Huysmans' war memoirs – was taken out of the drawer where it had lain for three years, re-entitled *Sac au dos*, and rewritten as a short personal novel. Next, Huysmans started to write the story of his first love-affair. Fearing, however, that one love-affair would not make a novel, he decided to relate it to other episodes – real or imagined – in the soubrette's life. Thus she would be shown working in an artificial pearl factory, serving as a prostitute in a licensed brothel, and living with a drunken actor-manager called Ginginet; she would end up in the gutter, and Ginginet on the table of a hospital autopsy-room. Of the settings to be described in his novel, Huysmans was familiar with the brothel, the theatre, and the student's rooms, but for the factory and the hospital he had to enlist the aid of his friends. Ludo arranged for him to visit a workshop where artificial pearls were processed; and Céard, after taking him to Lariboisière to witness an autopsy, was invited to 'come and eat a cutlet with me, and see if my hospital is all right'.[14] The heroine's name was also provided by one of Huysmans' friends. He had originally intended to call her Marie – as perhaps she was called in real life – but finally chose the name of Marthe Landousé, which Ludo remembered having seen on a signboard or in a newspaper. The novel itself – a slight work not much longer than *Sac au dos* – was nearing completion, when the even tenor of Huysmans' life was suddenly disturbed. On 4 May 1876 his mother died, leaving in his charge her two young daughters and the Rue de Sèvres bindery.

Some months before, Huysmans had moved from the Rue du Cherche-Midi to the fifth-floor flat at No. 11 Rue de Sèvres – possibly in anticipation of such an emergency. Even so, he feared that the daily journey to and from Versailles would leave him with little time for his new responsibilities, and he therefore asked the head of his department if he might be transferred from the Versailles delegation to the Ministry's offices in the Rue de Varenne, within easy reach of his home. The Ministry granted his application, but were unable to accommodate him at the Rue de Varenne; instead, he was given a post at the Sûreté Générale in the Rue des Saussaies, over on the Right Bank, where he was to be employed for the next twenty-two years.[15] The problem of his half-sisters was less troublesome, and Huysmans seems to have made adequate provision for them until Blanche married and Juliette came of age. As for the bindery, he learned to keep the accounts of the business, but he left much of the day-to-day work to his partner, Mme Guilleminot. And if we consult *Les Sœurs Vatard*, we find the bindery girls agreeing that 'the boss is a good sort, but he doesn't know a thing about this job . . .'

As soon as he could, Huysmans resumed work on his novel, profiting from the long leave which the Ministry had granted him; and by July he had completed the final draft of the manuscript. He was convinced that this work, provocatively entitled *Marthe, histoire d'une fille*, was the first French novel to represent the life of a prostitute in a licensed brothel, and he therefore received a shock when the newspapers announced that Edmond de Goncourt was writing a similar book, with the equally provocative title of *La Fille Elisa*.[16] Since this novel was due to be published in November, Huysmans had no time to lose. He knew, of course, that the publication in France of a book like *Marthe* involved both author and publisher in considerable risk; he knew that Jean Richepin had recently been sentenced to a month's imprisonment and a heavy fine on account of his *Chanson des gueux*; he knew, too, that in Richepin's case the magistrates had singled out for special condemnation a poem called *Fils de fille* . . . There was only one thing for a French author to do in these circumstances, and Huysmans did it. On 11 August 1876 he left Paris to look for a publisher in Brussels.

From the letters and articles which he sent his friends at home, it appears that Huysmans found life in the Belgian capital inexpensive but incredibly dull.[17] During the day, it is true, he was happy enough strolling along the banks of the little River Senne, visiting the church of Sainte-Gudule, and admiring the old masters in the Musée Royale or the modern paintings at the Waux-Hall. But in the evenings, when the boulevards were deserted and the theatres offered no worthwhile entertainment, he felt bored and irritable. Sometimes he would linger for hours in the Maison des Brasseurs, sampling the local brews, but generally he returned to the bleak room at No. 94 Rue du Midi which he rented from a Widow Débonnaire, and there sat reading and writing by the light of a solitary candle.

In one respect at least, Huysmans was not disappointed in Brussels: he soon found a publisher for his novel. It seems that on his arrival in the capital he at once sought out Camille Lemonnier, who like Huysmans was a contributor to *Le Musée des Deux-Mondes*, and who had also reprinted some of Huysmans' work in his own review, *L'Art Universel*. Lemonnier gave his colleague a warm welcome, and listened sympathetically while he explained the purpose of his visit to Brussels. He finally advised Huysmans to have his novel printed by Félix Callewaert and published by Jean Gay, pointing out that Gay specialized in reprints of eighteenth-century erotica and thus had considerable experience of smuggling literary contraband into France. The necessary arrangements were soon made, and three weeks later the young author was busy with the proofs of his book. A letter he wrote to Eugène Montrosier,[18] the proprietor of *Le Musée des Deux-Mondes*, suggests that by the end of August he had completely recovered his spirits, for in it he looked forward exultantly to the publication of 'a wonderful book, with tinted paper, elzevir type, titles in red, framed pages, floral ornaments and tail-pieces – and all for half the Paris price!' He also boasted to Montrosier that he had been lucky enough to find a 'dear old woman' who was letting a room to him, with service and coffee every morning, for only 20 francs a month. 'This must be the Golden Age!' he declared. 'I'm actually saving money! I've never spent so little in my life!'

In the meantime, Lemonnier had introduced Huysmans to some of his colleagues on *L'Art Universel* (or *L'Actualité*, as it was now called), notably the etcher Félicien Rops and the poet Théodore Hannon. Huysmans took an immediate liking to Hannon, whose licentious verses he had already admired in various literary reviews, and the two soon became firm friends. Every day the high-spirited, impish poet – whom Huysmans nicknamed 'the Suffete' after his lordly namesake in *Salammbô* – took him on a tour of the capital's churches and museums; at night they visited less reputable haunts. And after spending several evenings with Hannon in the brothels of the Rue Saint-Laurent, Huysmans had to admit that Brussels was not the staid city he had thought, but 'the Promised Land of beer and whores, the Canaan of drink and debauchery'.[19]

He could no longer claim to be saving money; on the contrary, he was now spending much more than he had expected. To make matters worse, Callewaert suddenly put up his charges for printing Huysmans' novel, and the unhappy author complained in a letter to Céard that 'this damned *Marthe* is costing me dear!'[20] He was therefore glad to accept an invitation from his Uncle Constant to spend a fortnight at Tilburg. Before leaving for Holland, he sent an appeal to Bobin for information about Musset's *Gamiani, ou deux nuits d'excès*, explaining that some publisher – probably Gay – had commissioned him to write a preface for this erotic work. Bobin's notes reached him a few days later at Tilburg, and it was there that he wrote the preface – in the company of his bluff, unsuspecting uncle. Unfortunately the text of what he wrote is not available to us, for not a single copy of the 1876 *Gamiani* has yet come to light.[21]

The printing of *Marthe* had been completed on 12 September, while Huysmans was in Holland. He returned to Brussels towards the end of the month, arriving in time to see his book put on sale. In a letter to Céard[22] he wrote:

I saw the first copy being sold yesterday. It was the President of the Brussels Catholic Circle who bought it at Lemonnyer's. We both had a good laugh over this comical send-off. It's true, of course, that *clérical* is synonymous with *cochon*, and no doubt this good man, attracted by the title, imagines he's going to be regaled with a lot of smutty stories . . .

The President must have been sorely disappointed, for despite its alluring sub-title there is nothing pornographic about *Marthe*, and the book contains only one brief description of a brothel. The greater part of the novel is devoted to an account of an unhappy liaison between Marthe and a young journalist called Léo.[23] Here Huysmans, remembering his first ill-fated love-affair, has skilfully and ruthlessly unpicked the fabric of romantic illusion woven by such writers as Henri Murger: unlike Mimi, Marthe is no handmaid of the Muses, but an unintelligent slattern who stifles her lover's poetic talent. This misogynistic theme, the episodic structure of the book, the weak-willed characters and the vibrant, garish style are all reminiscent of the Goncourt brothers' *Manette Salomon*; and in later life Huysmans himself described *Marthe* as 'an old ovary of my youth, fertilized by a stray spermatozoon from de Goncourt'.[24] But if in some respects it is manifestly derivative, *Marthe* has a rare quality of its own, not to be found in later and more famous *histoires de filles* – a certain febrile charm which compares favourably with the portentous solemnity of *La Fille Élisa* and the monotonous crudity of Zola's *Nana*.

Whatever the novel's literary merits, Huysmans could scarcely expect the authorities in France to look upon it with a kindly eye. Yet he had decided against smuggling *Marthe* across the frontier – on account of the risk and expense involved – and now hoped to take some 400 copies with him through the French Customs. Jean Gay had done his best to give the book an innocuous appearance: he had heroically refrained from commissioning illustrations such as the famous frontispiece designed by Forain for a later edition of *Marthe* – an etching which showed the heroine naked except for stockings and umbrella – and on the title-page he had printed the dubious but high-sounding proposition that 'whores like Marthe inspire in men a yearning for decent women'. But these precautions were of no avail. The customs officers at the frontier impounded all but a few copies of *Marthe*, to prevent what they called 'an outrage on public morals'; and when Huysmans offered to make certain cuts in the text, they replied that this would serve no useful purpose, since the subject of the book was itself sufficient to justify confiscation.[25]

Huysmans returned to Paris under a cloud of official disapproval. In the first place, news of the publication and seizure of his novel provoked an ominous flutter in the Ministerial dovecotes. Secondly, his superiors in the Rue des Saussaies pointed out that his leave of absence had expired in August, and reproached him with a betrayal of trust. His career as an unpopular novelist had begun auspiciously.

5. THE DISCIPLE

HUYSMANS' first thought on arriving home in October 1876 was to send one of his few remaining copies of *Marthe* to his literary idol, Edmond de Goncourt. In a covering letter, he told of the fate which had overtaken his novel, and respectfully begged the veteran writer to 'spare a glance for my poor *fille*, so foully done to death'. Goncourt's reply was typical of the man – kindly but reserved. While praising Huysmans' originality and descriptive skill, he criticized him for 'not always resisting the temptation to use a mannered expression, a brilliant, showy or curiously archaic word'.[1] Coming from the premier exponent of the notorious *écriture artiste*, this reproach must have surprised Huysmans, as it surprises us today; but it can doubtless be explained by Goncourt's annoyance that he, the great innovator and leader of literary fashion, should have been forestalled by a young and unknown writer. His *Journal* reveals, too, that Huysmans' letter had given him a bad night. Alarmed to hear of the measures taken against *Marthe*, he had dreamt that the authorities had arrested him for writing *La Fille Élisa* – without even waiting for the book to be published – and had cast him into prison.

It was scarcely to be expected that Gustave Flaubert would appreciate a novel whose style even a Goncourt considered extravagant; and so for the moment Huysmans wisely refrained from sending a copy to the master of Croisset. There remained only one other contemporary novelist whose judgement Huysmans respected, and whose sympathy for a work like *Marthe* was assured: Émile Zola.

It seems that Huysmans' acquaintance with Zola's writings was little more than a year old, for Céard states that in 1875 he used his profits from *Le Drageoir* to buy the early volumes of the Rougon-Macquart series. These he had read and re-read and discussed with his friends, marvelling at the conservatory scene in *La Curée*, the descriptions of the markets in *Le Ventre de Paris*, the account of Albine's death in *La Faute de l'Abbé Mouret*. He was convinced that the Rougon-Macquart novels were the work of a great writer, an author who brought to the realism of Flaubert and the Goncourts new vigour, audacity, and breadth of vision. Céard and Francmesnil shared this belief, but Bobin had his doubts. Whenever the subject was discussed at Huysmans' flat, the 'Professor' would expatiate on the folly of treating human beings as if they were simply chemical compounds, pouring scorn on Zola's scientific pretensions, and questioning the validity of a fictional work entitled *Histoire naturelle et sociale d'une famille sous le Second Empire*. Nothing that he said, however, could check his friends' enthusiasm, which was excited anew in April 1876, when *Le Bien Public* began serial publication of the sensational *L'Assommoir*.[2] One Sunday in April, Céard plucked up his courage and called at Zola's house in the Rue Saint-Georges. He afterwards reported to Huysmans that the great man had accepted his stammered homage with simple modesty, and had said that he would be glad to see any of Céard's friends who cared to come out to Les Batignolles. So, later in the year, Huysmans in his turn went to see Zola, taking with him copies of *Le Drageoir aux épices* and *Marthe*.[3]

Zola, he discovered, was a short-sighted, paunchy little man with a pronounced lisp; but his uninspiring person was matched with a genial personality. He made his young visitor welcome, and after reading *Marthe* wrote to assure him that he was 'without doubt one of our novelists of tomorrow'.[4] Huysmans was pressed to repeat his visit, and soon he and Céard were on very friendly terms with the Zolas. In the Rue Saint-Georges house he renewed acquaintance with Paul Alexis, Zola's devoted but untalented Boswell, whom he had first met at a masked ball; and Alexis introduced him to two other young writers, the little-known Léon Hennique and the unknown Guy de Maupassant. 'Henceforth', wrote Alexis some years later,[5] 'we were five. Our little group was indestructibly established. One fine Thursday evening we betook ourselves, all five of us in column of route, to Zola's house. And there every Thursday has seen us return.'

There can be no doubt that the five friends enjoyed these weekly gatherings. In the comfortable bourgeois drawing-room crowded with *chinoiseries* and dominated by Manet's portrait of their host, Mme Zola would regale them with cups of tea from a gigantic samovar, while her husband talked end-lessly of his literary theories, of the opposition his books were meeting, of his plans for the future. Often they stayed until long after midnight, and then Huysmans and Céard would walk home together through the deserted streets, recalling everything that had been said during the evening. Zola, for his part, enjoyed sunning himself in the warmth of their admir-ation. For many years his ego had craved the satisfaction to be derived from a literary 'school', and he already regarded his young friends as disciples committed for life to the Naturalist cult. In this he was mistaken. With the exception of Alexis they would all eventually rebel against his tutelage, and Huysmans was to deal Naturalism a blow from which it has never fully recovered.

At this time, however, the five were cheerfully engaged in defending Zola against the storm of criticism and abuse which *L'Assommoir* had stirred up. Outlawed by scandalized subscribers from the pages of *Le Bien Public*, this novel had taken refuge in Catulle Mendès' review, *La République des Lettres*, where it was serialized from July 1876 to January 1877. Every instalment was the subject of outraged comment by Press and public; and when Charpentier brought out the novel in book form, Zola and his work were attacked from many different quarters. August critics and scurrilous pamph-leteers denounced him; parodies of his story were staged at several theatres; and Galipaux amused his audiences with reci-tations of *En r'venant de l'Assommoir*. But above the general clamour, two young voices were heard speaking in Zola's defence. In the Salle des Conferences on the Boulevard des Capucines, Léon Hennique gave an enthusiastic lecture on *'L'Assommoir' et Zola*, which had the effect of infuriating the critics and putting the young poet beyond the Parnassian pale.

And in Brussels, *L'Actualité* published four important articles by Huysmans, under the title *Émile Zola et 'L'Assommoir'*.[6]

Early in March, Huysmans had told Zola that a Belgian review had asked him for '(1) a study and portrait of you, (2) my opinions on Naturalism, (3) a rapid outline of the Rougon-Macquart cycle, (4) a review of *L'Assommoir*'; and he had begged the elder novelist's permission 'to tell the truth about you, once for all, to the Brabantines, who are even more convinced than the French that you are an extraordinary creature living on the fringe of society'. It is unlikely that Zola had any fault to find with the introductory article, which was submitted to him for approval, as it presented an engaging picture of 'a Zola in carpet-slippers, the unknown Zola'.[7] The other articles followed the pattern outlined in Huysmans' letter, and were chiefly remarkable for a vigorous defence of the modern novelist's right to treat any and every aspect of life. Here Huysmans denied that Zola and his friends were interested only in squalor and vice, and declared:

> Green pustules and pink flesh are all one to us; we depict both because both exist, because the criminal deserves to be studied as much as the most perfect of men, and because our towns are swarming with prostitutes who have the same *droit de cité* there as prudes. Society has two faces; we show those two faces, we use every colour on the palette, the black as well as the blue . . . Whatever some may say, we do not prefer vice to virtue, corruption to modesty; we applaud both the coarse, spicy novel and the tender, sugary novel – provided each is well founded, well written, and true to life.

'You are raising a flag', wrote Zola when Huysmans sent him the promised brochure.[8] He was not the only one to recognize that *Émile Zola et 'L'Assommoir'* was one of the first important manifestos of the Naturalist movement, and the slim booklet caused something of a stir when Charpentier issued it in Paris. But few of those who read it noticed that Huysmans paid no attention to Zola's pseudo-scientific theories, and that the Naturalism which he advocated was nothing more than 'a patient study of reality, an overall picture obtained by the observation of details . . .'

In the meantime, Huysmans and his friends had taken to dining once a week at a little restaurant in Montmartre, on the corner of the Rue Coustou and the Rue Puget; it was kept by a certain Mother Machini, and it bore the hallowed name of *L'Assommoir*. 'In this appalling chop-house', Huysmans recorded later,[9] 'we hacked away at unconscionably raw meat and gulped down atrociously sour wine. It was unpleasant and it was perilous, but I doubt whether any of us have ever known happier mealtimes.' After dinner, they would adjourn to Maupassant's rooms in the Rue Moncey, where they listened to their host declaiming his poems or reading extracts from *La Comtesse de Rhune*. When Maupassant moved to an apartment-house in the Rue Clauzel, other guests joined these parties: his fellow tenants were all young prostitutes of convivial disposition, and they would often interrupt some serious literary discussion for a drink and a chat.

Mother Machini's food grew worse from week to week, and after one never-to-be-forgotten meal of putrescent kidneys, the five friends transferred their affections to *Chez Joseph*, a noisy *crémerie* in the Rue Condorcet. Zola dined with them here one evening, but obviously did not relish the experience. He was therefore invited to a better meal at Trapp's, a restaurant at the junction of the Passage du Havre and the Rue Saint-Lazare, together with two other guests of honour – Edmond de Goncourt and Maupassant's illustrious mentor, Gustave Flaubert.

This dinner, which was held on 16 April 1877, was a great success. Goncourt, who secretly envied Zola the renown he and his brother Jules had never achieved, was rather aloof at first, but Flaubert soon infected everyone with his boisterous good humour. As for the meal itself; *La République des Lettres* had announced that it would consist of such dishes as *Potage purée Bovary, Truite saumonée à la fille Élisa* and *Parfait 'naturaliste'*. Needless to say, this menu was a pure fabrication, but it gave Paul Alexis the idea of attracting attention to his friends by satirizing them anonymously in *Les Cloches de Paris*. Press and public swallowed the bait. Before long, lampoons on the new 'school' were being sung in the cabarets, caustic reference was made in the newspapers to 'Zola's tail', and cartoons appeared which depicted a snub-nosed Zola riding a sow and leading a procession of grimy piglets. Five young men, four of whom had written nothing of note, found that a modest dinner at Trapp's had brought them fame.

Another gathering to which Huysmans was invited at this time was accorded less publicity. On 19 May he was one of the select company present in Georges Becker's studio in the Rue de Fleurus, when Maupassant and his friend Robert Pinchon gave a performance of their farce *A la Feuille de Rose, Maison turque*. This play, which for obvious reasons has never been published, concerned a newly married couple who put up at a brothel under the impression that it was a respectable hotel. Its Rabelaisian humour delighted the audience, and Flaubert was helpless with laughter; but it is recorded that the actress Suzanne Lagier, one of the two masked women admitted to the studio, walked out with a great show of indignation.[10]

During Flaubert's periodic stays in Paris, Huysmans and Maupassant often went together on Sunday afternoons to his flat in the Faubourg Saint-Honoré. Flaubert himself would open the door to them and show them into the study, where a veil of red silk covered the desk, hiding the master's quills and manuscript from profane eyes. The Russian novelist Turgenev, a giant like his host, was usually there when they arrived; later Zola and the faithful Alexis would put in an appearance, followed by Edmond de Goncourt and little Alphonse Daudet. Flaubert, wearing his chestnut-coloured dressing-gown and smoking a clay pipe, would discourse for hours to this appreciative audience on the sublimity of art and the imbecility of man, pausing only to note down the choice absurdities which his friends brought him for the famous *sottisier*. Sometimes, at the end of one of these reunions, Huysmans was honoured with an invitation to Goncourt's Oriental treasure-house at Auteuil, where the old man lived with his housekeeper Pélagie; sometimes Zola took him home to the Rue Saint-Georges for dinner. But if the disciple spent a great deal of time with his three masters, he did not feel it was time wasted, nor did he neglect his own work.

Articles by Huysmans, including prose-poems and critical studies of modern artists, were now being published regularly in two Belgian reviews – Camille Lemonnier's *L'Actualité* and Théodore Hannon's *L'Artiste* – as well as in various French periodicals. What is more, he had begun work early in 1877 on a new novel, *Les Sœurs Vatard*, which was intended to be 'a very searching study in realism'.[11] This novel told the story of two girls employed as book-stitchers in an establishment which bore a striking resemblance to the Maison Huysmans et Veuve Guilleminot; and about this time the girls in the Rue de Sèvres bindery were surprised to find the *patron* taking an unaccustomed interest in their work. With ample opportunities to make a close study of working-class life, Huysmans had soon filled several notebooks with details of his employees' conversation, besides descriptions of the slum dwellings which he visited with officials of the Sûreté Générale.[12] But the fabrication of a story proved so difficult that at one point he gave up hope of finishing the novel. Zola, who was in the habit of writing four pages – no more and no less – every morning, was profoundly shocked to hear of this. 'Huysmans simply must keep on working,' he told Henry Céard;[13] 'and you must tell him so. He is our hope; he has no right to abandon his novel just when the group has need of new books.' Céard must have passed on this message, for Huysmans wrote to Zola at the end of July,[14] promising to turn over a new leaf; and pleading in extenuation of his offence that 'the two cannon-balls chained to my legs – the Ministry and the bindery – have weighed more heavily than usual these last few months, and in the evenings I've been too stupefied by figures and accounts to produce a single word or idea.' He continued:

There's my confession – will you give me absolution? All the same, in spite of my laziness, I've already written the typographical equivalent of *Marthe*, plus ten pages. But there's no action in it, no action at all! – and it's constructed as haphazardly as a foreign novel. It's making slow progress, its style is rather garish and slipshod, and there are no extraordinary or poignant happenings. I've spiced this dull dish with a few daring passages – but these are just what the censor and the public will find hardest to swallow! Every time I think about it, I break out in a cold sweat.

To this Zola replied: 'Press on boldly with your book, without wondering whether it contains sufficient action, or whether it will be a success, or whether it will take you to Sainte-Pélagie prison . . .'[15] Thus exhorted, Huysmans set to work again, taking advantage of an unexpected opportunity to discard his two 'cannon-balls' for a short time. Early in August he learnt that he was about to be called to the colours for three weeks' reserve training, and hurriedly arranged for Théodore Hannon to send him a letter and a telegram announcing the illness and imminent death of a near relation.[16] The trick worked, and Huysmans spent the next few weeks at Hannon's home in the Rue de la Vanne, in the Brussels suburb of Ixelles. Here he was able to write a chapter of *Les Sœurs Vatard* and to put the finishing touches to *Sac au dos*, which began serial publication in *L'Artiste* on 19 August.[17] It aroused little comment, and Camille Lemonnier was the only critic to give it a favourable review. Huysmans himself expressed dissatisfaction with *Sac au dos* only a few months after it had appeared in print; and he told Lemonnier[18] that he hoped one day to produce a revised version of the story – the version which was eventually published in *Les Soirées de Médan*.

During the autumn and winter months, Huysmans devoted nearly all his leisure time to *Les Sœurs Vatard*; and on a foggy December day he and Céard, playing truant from their respective Ministries, prepared the final draft over a bottle of Schiedam. The 'daring passages' which he had mentioned to Zola were modified in the process – or, as he put it in a letter to Hannon,[19] 'some ashes were thrown on to the libidinous fire which burned in the book'. Next, Huysmans set about finding a publisher. Georges Charpentier, whose yellow-backed editions of works by Flaubert, Zola, and the Goncourts were already famous, was the first to be approached; but not until July 1878 did he come to a decision about Huysmans' novel. It was favourable. 'Thanks to the support you so kindly gave them,' Huysmans told Edmond de Goncourt, 'my little bindery girls will appear in the bookshop windows towards mid-autumn, wearing beautiful yellow dresses . . .'

With the manuscript of *Les Sœurs Vatard* off his hands, he attempted to pick up the threads of an earlier work, *La Faim.* 'I am making a start on my first novel,' he wrote to Lemonnier; 'and my opening scene is so troublesome, so vast, that I rack my brains trying to obtain the desired effect. Some day, perhaps, it will come.'[20] However, while inspiration continued to elude him, he was plagued by business troubles, extra work at the Ministry, and severe attacks of neuralgia. It was therefore with a feeling of relief that he left Paris on 8 August, to spend a short holiday in Belgium with Céard. He explained to Zola that they intended to pass their time 'going into ecstasies in front of Rubens' pictures, drinking copious draughts of *faro* and *lambic*, and exploring the twisting, teeming streets of Antwerp' – but a letter they sent Théodore Hannon from Antwerp hinted at less innocent distractions.[21] And before returning home, they paid a brief visit to Brussels, where the incorrigible 'Suffete' initiated Céard in the mysteries of the Rue Saint-Laurent.

It seems, however, that Huysmans' object in visiting Brussels was literary no less than erotic, for he brought with him the manuscript of a preface he had written for Hannon's *Rimes de joie.* He also had some serious criticism to make of Hannon's style, so that what with alterations to the poems and the inevitable search for a publisher, the *Rimes de joie* were not brought out until 1881.[22] In the preface, which was post-dated August 1879, Hannon was praised for taking his inspiration, not from Victor Hugo or the Parnassian poets, but from an artist whom Huysmans considered the greatest poet of modern times.

I refer [he wrote] to the poet of genius who, like our great Flaubert, can open up infinite perspectives with a single epithet; to the abstractor of the quintessential qualities of our corrupt nature; to the singer of those troubled hours when a worn-out passion seeks to satisfy the strange longings of the flesh by impious means. I refer to the poet who has rendered all the immense vacuity of simple affections, the implacable domination of spleen, the confusion of jaded senses, the delicious pain of long thirsty kisses; to the painter who has introduced us to the melancholy charms of rainy days and dilapidated joys. I refer to the prodigious artist who has gathered together the *Fleurs du mal*: Charles Baudelaire!

This passage, while of considerable interest and importance for the light it sheds on Huysmans' future literary development, was not strictly apposite to Hannon's poetry – as both Huysmans and Hannon later recognized. The friendship of novelist and poet came to an end in 1883, and when the *Rimes de joie* were reprinted four years later, Huysmans' preface was omitted.[23] By that time Hannon was squandering his talents on cheap theatrical revues; and it seems probable that the librettist of *Tout le monde descend* and *Bruxelles-Attractions* did not care to be reminded that he had once been compared with the poet of *Les Fleurs du mal*.

In September 1878, when the proofs of *Les Sœurs Vatard* began to arrive from the printers, Huysmans consigned *La Faim* to a drawer which served as a limbo for unfinished manuscripts. He dealt rapidly with the proofs of his novel, but the printing took longer than he had expected. The book was finally brought out on 26 February 1879, dedicated to Émile Zola by 'his fervent admirer and devoted friend'.

To read this novel is to understand why a critic once dubbed the Naturalists 'a generation of authors of *morceaux choisis*'; for it consists almost entirely of descriptive passages, of Parisian landscapes, street scenes, and interiors. All the author's skill has been used to convey to the reader the sights, sounds, and smells of the Montrouge district – to evoke the atmosphere of a music-hall in the Rue de la Gaieté, a railway siding behind the Rue Vandamme, a workshop, a fairground, and a *bal de barrière*. For one scene Huysmans claimed a peculiar distinction, declaring in an autobiographical sketch that it was the first prose-picture of a railway in modern literature.[24] Perhaps it was, but it also merits our admiration as a typical product of Huysmans' Impressionist technique: it is the literary counterpart of Monet's picture *La Gare Saint-Lazare*, just as a river scene in *Marthe* is the counterpart of Whistler's celebrated Nocturnes. No French writer – not excepting the Goncourt brothers – has ever shown greater awareness of the niceties of colour, or of the delicate interplay of light and shade, than Huysmans in his early novels.

The story of *Les Sœurs Vatard*, such as it is, concerns the unhappy love-affairs of two young working-girls, Céline and Désirée. Céline Vatard is the mistress of an artist of independent means, Cyprien Tibaille, who comes to detest her stupid talk and vulgar habits as much as she resents his superior attitude; after months of bickering, she leaves him for a man whose beatings she accepts as proof of profound affection. Her mild-mannered younger sister, Désirée, is more suitably matched with a lethargic simpleton called Auguste, but fares no better: their love dies of sheer inertia. The two couples are admirably portrayed, and Huysmans' study of their gradual estrangement could scarcely be bettered. One feels, however, that while he regarded three of his principal characters with distaste, he was prejudiced in favour of the fourth – Cyprien Tibaille. And Cyprien, endowed with the novelist's own morbid temperament, extravagant ideas, and peculiar foibles, seems strangely out of place in this humdrum story of the Parisian working class. He is the first of Huysmans' exceptional characters – a des Esseintes in embryo.

To the author's surprise and delight, the book sold reasonably well. Céard saw copies 'on display from the Boulevard de Beaumarchais to the Opéra, and selling like hot cakes in a bookshop in the Rue de Rennes'; and within two days of publication, a second edition was printed.[25] On 4 March Zola gave sales a further fillip with a laudatory review in *Le Voltaire*.

Asserting that a simple 'human document' like *Les Sœurs Vatard* was superior to any sensational romance, he earnestly recommended the novel to his readers; but he also expressed the hope that Huysmans would be 'dragged through the gutters of literary criticism, denounced to the police by his colleagues, and hounded by a pack of envious, impotent fools – for then he will know his strength'. This hope was soon fulfilled. A score of journalists, led by Louis Ulbach in *La Revue Politique et Littéraire*, accused Huysmans of a grave libel on the French working class. Aurélien Scholl, the urbane literary critic of *L'Événement*, reported that after reading Huysmans' novel he had felt the need to 'pour a little menthe over a lump of sugar and inhale deeply'. And in *Le Figaro*, Albert Wolff complained that *Les Sœurs Vatard* revealed 'no sign of imagination, no whisper of poetry, no hint of illusion, nothing but life in the raw – bleak, hateful, and infinitely sad . . .'

Zola's praise and Wolff's censure came as no surprise to Huysmans, for it was a simple matter to gauge the two men's reactions to a book such as *Les Sœurs Vatard*. On the other hand, it was not so easy to tell what Flaubert and Goncourt would think of the novel, and the anxious author lost no time in sending suitably inscribed copies to Croisset and Auteuil.

Flaubert delivered judgement on 7 March, in a letter[26] that began with an ominous quotation from Racine – '*Et maintenant, Seigneur, expliquons-nous tous deux.*' In his opinion, *Les Sœurs Vatard* was 'a powerful and outstanding work', the characterization 'masterly', the descriptions 'excellent', and the denouement 'verging on the sublime'. But the overall plan of the novel failed to win his approval – for the unexpected reason that it seemed to have been modelled on that of *L'Éducation sentimentale*. Indeed, Flaubert criticized both Huysmans' novel and his own for their lack of perspective, and insisted that 'every work of art should come to a point or summit, like a pyramid, or else the light should strike one spot on a sphere'. Nor was this the only criticism he had to make. He also protested against Huysmans' use of slang in impersonal narrative; and he raised the strongest objections to

Cyprien Tibaille's theory that 'wallflowers withering in a pot were more interesting than roses blossoming in the open air'. This *boutade* was merely an expression of Huysmans' personal tastes intended to shock readers with conventional ideas of beauty; but to the enemy of all the 'isms' it sounded like a fundamental tenet of the Naturalist heresy. 'Neither wall-flowers nor roses', he thundered, 'are interesting in themselves: what is interesting is the manner in which they are depicted. The Ganges is not more poetic than the Bièvre, but neither is the Bièvre more poetic than the Ganges . . . It pains me to see a writer of your originality spoiling his work with such child-ish absurdities. Have a little pride, *nom de Dieu*, and beware of formulas.'

A fortnight later, Edmond de Goncourt wrote Huysmans a similar letter from Auteuil.[27] Like Flaubert, he warned the young novelist not to confine his attention to the seamy side of life – though it is to be feared that his advice, unlike Flaubert's, was not entirely disinterested. He was now pathetically envious of the fame Zola had achieved by writing working-class novels on the pattern of *Germinie Lacerteux*; and the chance of weaning a disciple from his successful rival was too good to miss. 'If an old man might offer you a little advice', he wrote, 'I would suggest that *Germinie Lacerteux, L'Assommoir* and *Les Sœurs Vatard* have exhausted what I call *la canaille littéraire*, and I would urge you to choose another and a higher social stratum for the setting of your next book.' At the same time, in the preface to his novel *Les Frères Zemganno*, he declared that the triumph of Realism would not be assured until other writers followed his example and applied the documentary method to the study of 'cultured beings and exquisite things'.

Huysmans, who in *Émile Zola et 'L'Assommoir'* had claimed that the Naturalist novel embraced every class in society, could not deny the justice of these comments, and he told Goncourt: 'We young writers will certainly take to heart the advice you have given us concerning *la canaille littéraire*.'[28] There was an element of personal pride in this resolve: he had no wish to see every novel he wrote dubbed 'a little *Assommoir*' by some contemptuous critic. Zola, of course, imagined that *Les Sœurs Vatard* was merely the first of many similar studies of working-class life which his disciple was to produce under his aegis. In point of fact, however, it was the last.

6. THE JOURNALIST

THE next two years were for Huysmans a period of intense journalistic activity. His *Salons* established his reputation as a brilliant and unorthodox art-critic; he obtained his first experience of writing feature-articles for a national daily newspaper; and for a brief spell he actually occupied the editorial chair of a literary review.

His first big opportunity occurred in May 1879. In that month the controlling interest in *Le Voltaire*, the newspaper which had recently taken the place of *Le Bien Public*, passed into the hands of a certain Jules Laffitte. Eager to make a success of his new undertaking, Laffitte secured from Zola the serial rights of his novel *Nana*, and in return promised to place *Le Voltaire* at the disposal of Zola and his friends.[1] Zola took him at his word. He sent Laffitte a fiery article entitled 'Lettre à la jeunesse: Morale et patriotisme', to be printed on the front page; and he told him that if he required a competent critic to report on the official Salon of that year, he could not do better than engage Huysmans. After reading the entertaining and inoffensive essays in art-criticism which Huysmans had written in 1876 for *La République des Lettres*, Laffitte decided to give him this assignment. It was agreed that he should write a series of twelve articles covering every aspect of the exhibition, and the first of these was published on 17 May.

It took the readers of *Le Voltaire* completely by surprise. They expected their art-critic to approach the Salon in a spirit of reverence and humility, and to show proper respect for names burdened with official honours or consecrated by public opinion. Instead, they were bluntly informed that of the 3,000 paintings on view, fewer than a hundred were worthy of consideration – and those the work of artists they did not know, such as Guillemet and Raffaëlli. The sticky-fingered babes and bereaved mothers which, year after year, moved the public to laughter and tears, were mercilessly ridiculed. So were the imposing compositions of the traditional artists – 'their Virgins dressed in pink and blue like Christmas crackers, their grey-bearded God-the-Fathers, their Brutuses made to order, their Venuses made to measure, and their Oriental pictures painted at Les Batignolles on a dull winter's day'. Indeed, it seemed that there was nothing sacred to this egregious critic, for he claimed to prefer the crudest posters advertising a cabaret or a circus to what he called the 'fiddle-faddle and jiggery-pokery' of the École des Beaux-Arts.

That same day, many subscribers wrote cancelling their orders for *Le Voltaire* and expressing doubts as to Huysmans' sanity, while dozens of indignant letters soon reached Laffitte from the maligned artists themselves. These worthies, whom Zola had trounced in 1866 when he was championing Manet and Daubigny, recognized in Huysmans an even more formidable adversary; for whereas Zola could scarcely tell black from white and had to be coached by his friends, this newcomer to the lists wrote with knowledge as well as conviction. What is more, he drew the most odious comparisons between their work and that of the universally despised Impressionists and Independents, whom he described as 'distilling the essence of their time, just as the Dutch realists expressed the savour of their own'. It was obvious to the veterans of the École des Beaux-Arts that they would lose both their reputation and their livelihood if the public ever adopted Huysmans' views, and they accordingly clamoured for his dismissal.

Laffitte, for his part, was dismayed by the storm of protest which Huysmans' first article had aroused, and fearful of the effect it would have on his newspaper's circulation. He would certainly have given the young art-critic his notice if Zola had not written him a strongly worded letter, complaining that the 'Lettre à la jeunesse' had been altered and relegated to the centre pages, and insisting that Laffitte should honour the promises he had made to Zola and his disciples. Writing to Zola on the 19th,[2] Henry Céard said that this letter had saved both Huysmans and himself from dismissal, but prophesied that the uneasy partnership between Laffitte and his new contributors would not last much longer.

You can't imagine [he wrote] what terror – and that's not too strong a word for it – our articles have struck into the hearts of the entire staff. They squeal about sacrilege, throw up their hands in horror, and talk about our friend's *Salon* in accents of despair which are simply killing. It has left journalists and readers gasping, and caused a tremendous scandal – which Guillemet applauds in a letter he's written. But the best moment of all came when they asked Huysmans about his second article, and he told them it was even stronger than the first. Laffitte and Étiévant looked at him in consternation, as if they were faced with a raving lunatic . . . We are having tremendous fun, but we mustn't have any illusions about the future: whether we like it or not, we shall have to clear out. We are going to arrange things so that we can march out in triumph when the time comes, with all the honours of war . . .

In the meantime, Huysmans went ahead with his articles, carrying fire and the sword into the traditionalist camp. And at the end of the series, as at the beginning, the 1879 exhibition was condemned as 'the shameless negation of all that we understand by modern art, the insolent triumph of the conventional and the commonplace'.

The sensational *Salon de 1879* was the only contribution Huysmans made to *Le Voltaire* before he 'marched out in triumph', although on one memorable occasion he was offered another assignment. Taking him into his office one day, Laffitte showed him an immense pile of foreign newspapers, explained that they contained appreciations of Zola's work by English, Russian, German, Italian, Swedish, Rumanian, and Dutch critics, and asked him to use them for an article entitled 'Zola à l'étranger'. When Huysmans objected that the only language he understood was his own, the editor blandly replied: 'In that case, I shall call a cab, you will take this bundle of papers home, and there, since you don't understand foreign languages, you will pick out the most striking passages, you will mark them in blue pencil, and I shall have them translated for you . . .' Needless to say, this proposition was not accepted.[3]

Huysmans now began work on a new novel called *En Ménage*, and made considerable progress with it in September while on holiday at Cayeux-sur-Mer, a little Channel coast resort.[4] But it was his first novel, the luckless *Marthe*, which engaged his attention when he got back to Paris. Since the authorities had recently relaxed their censorship of new works, and stories of prostitution were now in vogue, Huysmans had decided to bring out a French edition of his own *histoire de fille*. It was published on 12 October by Léon Derveaux, a bookseller in the Rue d'Angoulême, with a preface in which the author stated his unpretentious literary creed: 'I set down what I see, what I feel, what I have lived, writing it as well as I am able – *et voilà tout!*' Unfortunately, the book went unnoticed for some time, as Laffitte had begun to plaster Paris with huge bill-boards advertising *Nana*, and Derveaux thought it wiser to postpone the more modest publicity campaign he had arranged for *Marthe*.[5] The press reviews, when at last they appeared, were generally unfavourable, often offensive. And several critics, with unconscious irony and no respect for chronology, suggested that Huysmans had written the novel to exploit the success of Zola's monumental contribution to brothel-lore . . .

The other members of what Flaubert nicknamed 'the Zola circus' had been far from idle during the past two years, although their work was still not widely known. Céard and Hennique had published two uninspiring but well-documented novels, *Mal-éclos* and *La Dévouée*; Alexis had written countless articles publicizing the group, and was now toiling at *La Fin de Lucie Pellegrin*; while even Maupassant, whose life seemed to be dedicated to river sports and sexual pursuits, had found time to write a play, *Histoire du vieux temps*.

The five friends no longer dined together every week, but

on Sundays they often met at Médan, a riverside hamlet some twenty miles from Paris, where Zola had bought a villa in the summer of 1878. He had described this house to Flaubert[6] as 'a modest rustic asylum which has the merit of being far from any railway station and of not having a single bourgeois in the vicinity'; but within a few months it had assumed the nightmarish proportions and aspect of every nineteenth-century bourgeois' ideal home. Massive towers were appended to the original structure, to accommodate the vast quantities of bric-à-brac and the spurious 'antiques' which Zola bought from disreputable dealers in Paris. The windows were fitted with stained glass. Stables were built, populated with horses and cows, and furnished with a gallery from which Zola could observe the habits of his animal kingdom. And in his study the master installed an immense writing-table in carved oak, a great chair to match, an aspidistra, and a fireplace inscribed with the device *Nulla dies sine linea*. Yet although everything in this monstrous dwelling-place bore witness to Zola's vanity and vulgarity, his friends found that the welcome he gave them was as sincere and unaffected as before.

In their reminiscences[7] Céard and Mme Émile Zola have left us an intimate record of the Sunday house-parties at Médan. The guests used to arrive in the morning – Maupassant rowing down the Seine from Sartrouville and the others walking from Triel, the nearest railway station. Zola joined them as soon as he had completed his statutory four pages, and then they smoked and lazed in the sun, or stalked rabbits through the wilderness of a garden. After a picnic lunch on an island in the river, Maupassant would take his friends and hosts for an excursion in the rowing-boat *Nana*, with Alexis singing songs from his native Provence and Huysmans drawing on his inexhaustible fund of sardonic anecdotes. And in the evening, if it was a parish feast-day, the young men went down to the village green, where, to the strains of an ancient barrel-organ, they danced the polka with the girls of Triel and Médan.

It would be tempting to suppose that the famous *Soirées de Médan* originated, as the title implies, in this rustic setting –

if it were not known that the book was really the outcome of a conversation at Zola's Paris home[8] in the winter of 1879. At this time anti-Prussian feeling, inflamed by Paul Déroulède's chauvinistic songs, was running high in France; and one day Hennique suggested to his friends that they should publish a collection of war stories, under Zola's aegis, which would serve to put the events of 1870 and 1871 in their true perspective. Welcoming the opportunity to do his disciples a good turn, Zola straightway offered them a long story entitled *L'Attaque du moulin*, and Huysmans assured him that they would all 'dress their babies up as quickly as possible and bring them along'. Two of 'their babies' – Céard's *La Saignée* and Huysmans' *Sac au dos* – had already made public appearances in Russia and Belgium; Hennique had recently finished *L'Affaire du Grand 7*, and Alexis was working on *Après la bataille*; only Maupassant's story had yet to be written. At last, one evening in January 1880, the five young authors met in Maupassant's rooms in the Rue Clauzel to read out their contributions. Maupassant read his story last of all. When he had finished, his friends stood up and with one accord saluted it as a masterpiece. It was called *Boule de suif*.

There remained the problem of choosing a title for the collection. Someone proposed *L'Invasion comique*, but this and other suggestions were rejected on patriotic grounds. Finally it was decided to call the book *Les Soirées de Médan*, because, as Céard put it, 'this sentimental appellation paid homage to the dear house where Madame Zola treated us like a mother and delighted in making great spoilt children of us'.[9] Maupassant, however, encouraged the public to take the title literally, and in a mischievous letter published in *Le Gaulois* on 17 April, he depicted Zola and his friends telling each other tales by moonlight in a Boccaccio setting. The book was brought out by Charpentier the same day, with a defiant preface challenging the critics to do their worst. 'I trust my colleagues will not be taken in by any of these schoolboy tricks', wrote the redoubtable Albert Wolff.[10] '*Les Soirées de Médan* is not worth a single line of criticism. Except for Zola's story, it is the last word in mediocrity . . .'

Fortunately the public thought otherwise, and within a fortnight the collection ran through eight editions. The critics, for their part, gave it ample publicity; goaded to fury by the accusations of bad faith and ignorance made in the preface, they ignored Wolff's warning and devoted long articles to abuse of the book and its authors. The brunt of their attacks was borne by Huysmans, whose *Sac au dos* was condemned as unpatriotic, scatological, and obscene. It differed in several respects from the 1876 version published in *L'Artiste*: such gentle passages as the lyrical description of Sister Angèle were omitted, and the story now ended with an expression of the hero's thankfulness that he could at last satisfy the demands of nature in comfort and quiet. To the modern reader it may appear unremarkable, not to say dull, but that is very probably because his personal experience – reinforced by the war stories of the last few decades – has taught him that war is generally a drab and dirty business. This was not, however, a view with which the reader of 1880 was familiar. To him it seemed scandalous that an author should strip war of its glamorous associations, that he should represent it with such uncompromising realism, and that he should finally reduce it to the simple terms of dirt and dysentery.

The only important critic with a good word to say for Huysmans was Jean Richepin, of *Gil Blas*.[11] He observed that the most striking stories in the collection – *Boule de suif* and *Sac au dos* – were the work of two talented artists who had no real affinities with Naturalism; and he remarked especially on the difference between Zola's flat, colourless prose and Huysmans' captivating style, composed of 'rare nouns, curious adjectives, unexpected combinations of words, archaisms, neologisms, mutilated syntax, splashes of colour, flashes of wit, assonance and discord – everything under the sun, in fact!' He went on to draw pen-portraits of the six authors, hitting off Huysmans' likeness in these few lines:

He has a bushy head of hair, the golden beard of a Primitive, the parchment skin of a neurotic. A prominent Adam's apple too, the colour of powdered brick, which bobs up and down his throat every time he swallows. He ambles along, a gaunt hollow-chested figure, ferreting things out with his nose, spearing them with his eyes, pouncing on them like a tom-cat at play . . .

At Croisset, Flaubert was following the fortunes of *Les Soirées de Médan* with the keenest interest, and he was hugely amused by Richepin's satirical sketches of 'the Zola circus'.[12] But when, a fortnight later, news came to Paris of Flaubert's death, none mourned him more sincerely than Zola and his disciples. They and Edmond de Goncourt and Alphonse Daudet were among the faithful few who accompanied him to his last resting-place on 11 May, walking behind the bier along the dusty roads from the parish church of Canteleu to the monumental cemetery overlooking Rouen. After the funeral ceremony, there occurred an incident which would undoubtedly have appealed to Flaubert's sense of irony. Huysmans and several of his friends had adjourned to Mennechet's, a quay-side restaurant, and were about to order lunch when superstitious Théodore de Banville protested that they were thirteen at table. To reassure the old poet, someone went out on to the quay and invited a soldier who was passing by to join the company of mourners. The soldier accepted, overawed at the prospect of meeting and lunching with François Coppée. But he had never heard of Flaubert.[13]

Huysmans' first task on returning home from Rouen was to write a report on the Salon of 1880 for *La Réforme*, a periodical which the Médan group now patronized in preference to *Le Voltaire*.[14] In this report he renewed his attacks upon the pontiffs of traditional art, and re-affirmed the superiority of the Impressionists and Independents. There were, however, a few paintings in the official exhibition which won his approval, including Gustave Moreau's exotic *Helen* and *Galatea*. These 'fantastic visions of an opium-eater' exerted a curious fascination upon him, and he was later to devote a whole chapter of his novel *A Rebours* to consideration of Moreau's hieratic art; but at the moment he was more interested in the pictorial studies of contemporary life on view in the Rue des Pyramides, where the Impressionists were holding their fifth annual exhibition. The paintings shown here by Caillebotte and Pissarro, Degas and Forain, Mary Cassatt and Berthe Morisot, inspired him to write his *Exposition des Indépendants en 1880* – perhaps the finest of his critiques and a brilliant treatise on Impressionist art. But it seems that not a single editor had the courage or the enterprise to publish the study, for there is no evidence that it appeared in print before 1883, when Huysmans included it in *L'Art moderne.*

His critics were soon given another opportunity to air their dislike of his writings, for on 22 May his *Croquis parisiens* was brought out by Henri Vaton. It was printed by Félix Callewaert of Brussels, illustrated by Forain and Raffaëlli, and composed for the most part of articles which had previously appeared in *Le Drageoir aux épices* or various minor periodicals. The first of the new articles was 'Les Folies-Bergère en 1879', and it was dedicated to Ludovic de Francmesnil, Léon Hennique, and Paul Daniel – the three friends who used to accompany Huysmans to the music-hall to see the dancing-girls and those famous English acrobats, the Hanlon-Lees. As well as describing some of the artistes, this piece evoked the atmosphere of the great auditorium, with its gilt-framed mirrors and scarlet curtains, its plaster nudes holding gas-lit torches, and its pervasive stench of sweat, cigar-smoke, and opoponax. Next came sketches of some typical figures of the Paris scene – a washerwoman, the conductor of a horse-drawn omnibus, an ageing prostitute, and a roast-chestnut seller – followed by descriptions of those desolate quarters of the city whose pathetic, somewhat squalid charm Huysmans could never resist. There was also a 'Poème en prose des viandes cuites au four', which dwelt on the plight of the middle-aged bachelor, torn between fear of marriage and disgust for the 'spurious beefsteaks and illusory chops' served in the restaurants. This last piece, dedicated to a civil-servant friend called Alexis Orsat, was perhaps the most significant in the book, for it later served as the basis for Huysmans' epic of an unhappy *fonctionnaire*, the novel *A Vau-l'Eau.*

A few of the press reviews of *Croquis parisiens* paid tribute to the author's descriptive skill, remarking that his sketches of Paris life were so vivid as to make the Forain and Raffaëlli etchings appear superfluous. The majority, however, waxed indignant over a Baudelairian prose-poem called 'Le Gousset', in which Huysmans had striven to differentiate the diverse odours of feminine arm-pits; and even friendly François Coppée thought it necessary to express regret 'that M. Huysmans' rather unhealthy imagination should have led him to write such pages as these – pages which ensure the relegation of his book to the *phi* section of every public library'.[15] Thanking Zola for a favourable review, Huysmans wrote: 'You have done me a great service in defending "Le Gousset", which has aroused a lot of fierce criticism. People are beginning to regard me as an erotomaniac . . .'[16]

Meanwhile Arthur Meyer, the wealthy newspaper magnate, had invited Huysmans and Maupassant to become contributors to *Le Gaulois*. The two friends each undertook to write a series of weekly articles throughout the summer, for which they were to be paid 500 francs a month. These were attractive terms, yet it seems that Huysmans began to rue the arrangement almost as soon as it had been made. Thus, towards the end of May, he wrote to Zola:[17]

I'm not really counting on this business, as Meyer seems such a perfect fool. He wants me to teach the public something new about the Parisian scene, and at the same time to give them a thrill with a few dramatic incidents! He'd like something spicy, but he wouldn't mind a little milk-and-water too.

The main thing, he says, is that it shouldn't read like something out of *La Revue des Deux Mondes*. This he's told me a hundred times, so presumably the blighter thinks I write like Perret! All the same, it's going to be rather difficult to bring off the peculiar amalgam he's asked for. I suppose I'll just have to stir all those ingredients into a mayonnaise, add a few highly-flavoured words, and hope for the best. Anyway, I'm going to try

84

my hand at these articles. They are to be published under the title *Mystères de Paris* (!!!) – which I beg you to believe I didn't choose myself. As for Maupassant, he's doing a series called *Les Dimanches d'un canotier*, which seems to be right up his street . . .

Maupassant certainly experienced no difficulty in turning out regular instalments of *Les Dimanches d'un bourgeois de Paris* (as his series was finally named). They were scarcely worthy of the author of *Boule de suif*, and Maupassant later refused to admit them to the canon of his works; but it appears that Arthur Meyer enjoyed their rather ponderous humour. Huysmans' relations with *La Gaulois* were not so satisfactory. It irked him to produce a scheduled amount of copy at a scheduled time, and it infuriated him to find sub-editors toning down passages in his *Mystères de Paris* that might offend nice-minded readers. 'How lucky I am', he remarked to a friend,[18] 'to have a job in the Civil Service! Because one of these days, Meyer is going to sack me for sure.'

Ironically enough, it was not Meyer but Huysmans' superiors in the Civil Service who brought his association with *Le Gaulois* to an end. 'After the articles it published about the Jesuits,' he told Zola in July,[19] 'they gave me clearly to understand that I should have to choose between remaining at the Ministry and working for that wretched paper.' The choice was soon made. With nothing more to his credit than four *croquis parisiens* – of a workshop, a tavern, a dance-hall, and a séance – Huysmans tendered his resignation to the editor.[20]

Far from discouraging him, this unfortunate episode acted as a spur to his journalistic ambitions. For many years he had dreamt of founding a paper of his own, in which he and his friends might publish whatever they wished, without having to pander to editorial whims or public prejudices; and early in 1880 he had submitted a project for a Naturalist weekly to Zola and the Médan group. Now, after delivering the manuscript of *En Ménage* to Charpentier, he spent a fortnight at Cayeux-sur-Mer working out the details of this plan.

In the first and only issue of *La Chronique Illustrée*, published by Eugene Montrosier in December 1875, Huysmans had declared that the ideal Parisian review would 'present a complete and accurate picture of the capital's fugitive, frivolous fashions, its passing fancies and fleeting aversions; so that if one day a writer wanted to do for the nineteenth century what the Goncourt brothers have done for the eighteenth – to wit, reveal the pattern of an epoch in its most minute details – he could consult this review with profit'.[21] Five years later, he evidently intended his own review to accomplish all this and more, for he gave it the grandiose title of *La Comédie Humaine* – a title which, it will be remembered, he had also bestowed upon an unpublished Romantic drama in verse. The list of contributors that he drew up was no less imposing: it bore the names not only of Zola and the five members of the Médan group, but also of Edmond de Goncourt, Eugène Montrosier, Camille Lemonnier, and the young novelists Robert Caze and Harry Alis. For the first issue, Zola promised an introductory letter and an instalment of his story *Un Communard*; Goncourt offered some impressions of Paris; Maupassant, Alexis, and Céard submitted articles on the Jesuits, Jules Ferry, and the bicentenary of the Comédie-Française; while Huysmans himself prepared a *croquis parisien* of Pantin and a study of Alexander Herzen, the Russian revolutionary.[22] Everything seemed to augur well for the success of *La Comédie Humaine*, and the letters Huysmans wrote his friends bubbled over with enthusiasm and confidence – but not for long.

It had been decided that Derveaux, who a year before had brought out the French edition of *Marthe*, should be entrusted with the publication of *La Comédie Humaine*, and on 18 October he and Huysmans signed a contract to that effect. The fortunes of the review then went into a steady decline. Originally scheduled for 1 November, the appearance of the first number had to be postponed for a week. On the 4th Huysmans complained to Zola that Derveaux was creating difficulties, and that 'the old sheeny has prepared some odious posters and charlatanical puffs!' And on the 15th he wrote to tell Zola that 'all our plans for the paper have fallen through'.

It appears that two days before, Derveaux had asked Huysmans to let him have Zola's introductory letter at once, at the same time promising that he would not show it to anyone. Huysmans' suspicions had been aroused, and he had replied that if Derveaux would come to his flat that week-end and explain why he wanted the letter, he would consider giving it to him. Derveaux, however, had not accepted this invitation, but had written to say that by refusing to give him Zola's letter Huysmans had deprived him of his last trump. He added that he had now no funds at his disposal and was therefore unable to launch the review. 'It's quite obvious', Huysmans told Zola, 'that he wanted to use your letter in an attempt to borrow the necessary capital. Which is not exactly consistent with the oaths he swore in Saturday's letter . . .'[23]

The full extent of the disaster was at first kept hidden from the review's contributors, who were merely informed that financial difficulties made it necessary to postpone publication of the first number. But on the 18th Huysmans wrote to Théodore Hannon, whom he had appointed Belgian correspondent, acquainting him with the facts of the matter and concluding: 'We are in a truly glorious mess – with our expenses already paid, the posters printed, the office furnished, etc., etc. You can imagine what a stew I'm in.' The only ray of hope came from the bookseller Marpon, who proposed to resurrect the review on an outlay of 30,000 francs; but Huysmans was convinced that this sum was totally inadequate. He also rejected Zola's suggestion that they should use Marpon's money to start a four-page 'rag' printing nothing but copy furnished by the authors of Les Soirées de Médan, on the grounds that this would result in absolute monotony. When Zola persisted in his idea, he resigned his post as editor, and on 14 December he wrote to Hannon:[24]

This has been a terrible disappointment for me. I can see more trouble ahead, and fear we are going to sink to the level of a Latin Quarter weekly. What is more, the differences of opinion which have already arisen are certain to become more serious . . . We are now divided into two camps over this issue – Zola, Céard, Alexis, Hennique on one side, in favour of the rag; Maupassant and myself on the other, against it. As things are at present, instead of founding a stylish shop, a real 'Louvre', the only sort which could possibly be a success, we are setting up a paltry haberdashery, a tuppenny-ha'penny street-stall.

And that, my dear fellow, is the end of the story of *La Comédie Humaine*. We are going into battle without munitions, and we shall probably come out of it without glory. Keep all this to yourself, for such matters are no concern of the public. We shall carry on, since needs must, but our hearts are not in it.

In the end, however, nothing came of Zola's plans. 'He tried to establish the review on new foundations,' Huysmans told Edmond de Goncourt,[25] 'but like mine they collapsed.' As for the ill-fated *Comédie Humaine*, it was the subject of two actions for breach of contract brought before the Tribunal de Commerce de la Seine. Huysmans and Hennique, as editor and sub-editor of the review, had instructed one Me Henri Allart to lodge a claim for a month's salary and heavy damages from Derveaux, while Derveaux had retaliated with a counter-claim for damages amounting to 5,000 francs. On 30 December the tribunal referred the two cases to an arbitrator, M. Masson, who summoned the litigants to his chambers in the Boulevard Magenta, at 4 p.m. on 4 January 1881. The anxiety which the impending legal battle caused Huysmans is reflected in a fragment of a novel which he began but never completed, and which was found among his papers after his death.[26] In this fragment he described the feelings of one Jean Chayrol as he sat in a café on the Boulevard Magenta, counting the minutes until four o'clock and the fateful appointment with the arbitrator; and he continued:

The only positive information he had been given was that the Tribunal de Commerce almost invariably accepted the recommendations contained in the

Huysmans in 1881.

arbitrator's report. It was therefore on this M. Plêtre, the official arbitrator attached to the Tribunal, that his case, his fortune, and his life depended. Although he was convinced of the justice of his cause, he could not help dreading the judgement of this perfect stranger. Moreover, his opponent was a man of such great eloquence and bad faith that he felt sure he would be ignominiously defeated in the coming discussion. And then, he thought, the enemy's advócate might very well be a wily, pettifogging rogue who would confuse him with his crafty questions and completely silence the young man whom, for financial reasons, he had been obliged to choose from among the new-comers to the bar . . .

As it happened, Huysmans' fears were groundless, for M. Masson's report went against Derveaux and recommended an award of a month's salary, damages, and costs to Huysmans and Hennique. This award was made by the Tribunal on 13 April 1881, when Huysmans' damages were fixed at 1,500 francs and Hennique's at 500 francs.[27] Although there is no evidence that Derveaux discharged these obligations, it seems probable that at least Huysmans recovered the money he had lost in the affair. But never again did he devote himself to any journalistic project with the same enthusiasm; and never again did he refer to *La Comédie Humaine* in conversation or correspondence. The failure of this particular enterprise had hurt him more deeply than he cared to admit.

7. THE PESSIMIST

'A page of human life, banal yet poignant', was how Zola described Huysmans' novel *En Ménage* when it was published in February 1881;[1] and his judgement still holds good. Nothing could be more commonplace than this tale of an unhappy young writer; but the recital of his misfortunes in boyhood and manhood, in bachelorhood and marriage, in literature and in love, is somehow deeply affecting. It is the story of André Jayant, a novelist of moderate means, who marries solely in order to escape the tyranny of such fearful trivialities as frayed cuffs, dirty linen, and unappetizing meals. Marriage brings him the material comfort he desires; but when he discovers that his wife, Berthe, is not only wilful and petty-minded but unfaithful to boot, he leaves her and tries to pick up the threads of his life as a bachelor. Once more he has to suffer the stupidity and negligence of a housekeeper, and he also falls victim again to those urgent cravings for female love and companionship which Huysmans calls 'petticoat crises'. For solace he turns first to a well-bred prostitute called Blanche, and then to a midinette called Jeanne who had been his mistress five years before. Neither liaison, however, proves entirely satisfactory, for Blanche resents his jealous inquiries about her other clients, while Jeanne has to leave him to take up employment in London. And in the end, wearied by these unsettling affairs, and incapable of tackling life's problems unaided, André goes back to his wife.

Like Huysmans' earlier novels, *En Ménage* abounds in descriptive passages, from the first shadowy glimpse of a Paris street at midnight to the last brilliant picture of the crowds in the Cité Berryer market; but it differs from *Marthe* and *Les Sœurs Vatard* in that its most impressive feature is character-ization rather than description. This shift from pictorial to

psychological interest is illustrated by the number of perceptive character studies – notably those of Berthe Jayant, her
uncle M. Désableau, and the maidservant Mélanie – which are
to be found in the novel. It becomes even more obvious when
one considers the two friends André Jayant and Cyprien
Tibaille; for here Huysmans performs a remarkable *tour de force*
of characterization, projecting his own personality into both
men and then subjecting it to a searching and fearless scrutiny.
He was very proud of the results he achieved; and in an autobiographical sketch, donning the disguise of an imaginary
critic, he wrote of the 'petticoat crisis': 'Note how accurately
this crisis is represented, and remember that Huysmans was
the first to discover this minute district of the soul.'[2] But such
discoveries as this were really of secondary importance compared with the new method of characterization which
Huysmans had adopted. In *En Ménage*, for the first time, he
tries to recount his own experience of the inner life, with
all its complexities and its strange inconsistencies, using a
technique very similar to the 'inner monologue' beloved of
twentieth-century novelists. *En Ménage*, in fact, is no typical
Naturalist work, no sociological study in the Zola tradition,
but a personal novel that looks back to Benjamin Constant
and forward to Proust.

It is also an intensely pessimistic novel, or, as Huysmans
once put it, 'the song of Nihilism, a song punctuated by bursts
of sinister gaiety and expressions of ferocious wit'.[3] Viewing
his fellow men with a jaundiced eye, the author produces in
every chapter fresh evidence of the folly of human love, the
absurdity of human institutions, the monotony and futility of
human life. Both his pessimism and his use of irony are reminiscent of Flaubert, as are also some of the characters and situations in the novel. Berthe Jayant, who finds married life
deplorably unromantic and adultery as platitudinous as marriage, is an Emma Bovary in little; while Désableau, like the
immortal Homais, believes whole-heartedly in the twin
deities of the nineteenth century, Science and Progress. Again,
André Jayant's recurrent disillusionment in affairs of the heart
recalls Frédéric Moreau's ill-starred pursuit of happiness in

L'Éducation sentimentale; and both novels end with a melancholy summing-up by the hero and a childhood friend. Huysmans himself eventually acknowledged that, whatever the original merits of his novel, in certain respects it invited comparison with Flaubert's work – and inevitably suffered by that comparison. 'You would like me to write another *En Ménage*', he told an admirer in 1891.[4] 'But what would be the good of that? For isn't *L'Éducation sentimentale* a hundred times better than that book of mine?'

For the biographer, the chief interest of *En Ménage* lies in the glimpses it affords of Huysmans' character, his appearance, his home, and his private life. Thus we can obtain insight into the novelist's temperament from a study of André Jayant, who 'could never make up his mind about even the simplest things, but would hesitate, discovering difficulties everywhere, solving them sometimes with the desperate courage of a coward, and then regretting his decision two minutes later'. If, on the other hand, we are looking for a full-length portrait of the author, we shall find it in this description of Cyprien Tibaille:

> He was tall and thin, fair-haired and pale-faced, with a blond beard, long slender fingers, hands that were never still, piercing grey eyes, and a few white bristles showing in his shaggy head of hair. He had a habit of knocking his ankles together when walking, with the result that he soon wore out the ends of his trousers; these, incidentally, were always too short and too wide for his spindly tibias. With his back slightly bowed and his left shoulder a little higher than his right, he looked poor and sickly. As for his manner out of doors, it was singular to say the very least. He would advance in fits and starts, marking time for a while and then swooping forward like a great grasshopper, tearing along at full speed with his umbrella tucked schoolmaster-fashion under one arm, and rubbing his hands for no apparent reason . . .

When André Jayant leaves his wife and moves into lodgings, he turns his rooms into a miniature treasure-house of books and pictures, Japanese porcelain, and old brasses, giving pride of place to two contemporary water-colours: the one a study of ballet-dancers resting in the wings of a theatre, the other a formal drawing-room scene. Huysmans' friends were quick to recognize here a description of the novelist's own flat in the Rue de Sèvres. There too, they remembered, 'rows of books in Charpentier's yellow uniforms or the red tunics of Hachette's foreign legion paraded along the shelves'; there too, pictures by Degas and Forain occupied a place of honour. But the walls of Huysmans' study, draped in Turkey-red cotton after the fashion of the day, boasted many other pictures not mentioned in *En Ménage*, including a still-life by Cezanne and a snow-scene by Raffaëlli, as well as drawings by Constantin Guys and Félicien Rops.[5] And in one corner of the room, surveying visitors with a quizzical air, there hung a pastel portrait of Huysmans himself, drawn by his friend Forain in 1878.

It was in these intimate surroundings that Huysmans and André Jayant entertained their friends and their mistresses – or rather their mistress, for Anna Meunier and Jeanne were one and the same person. Critics have hitherto been unable to establish the identity of the two women, but the recent discovery of a copy of *En Ménage*[6] dedicated to 'Jeanne – Anna Meunier' leaves no room for doubt: it was Anna who served as the model for Huysmans' portrait of the young midinette, with 'her slim, supple figure and elegant appearance, her adorable arms and dainty hands and feet, her tiny upturned nose and sparkling eyes under a cloud of fair hair, her pert and provocative *laideur*'. There is reason to believe that Huysmans first met Anna in 1872, when she was employed at Hentenaar's, a dressmaking establishment in the Rue du Quatre-Septembre, and that he was introduced to her by one of her work-mates, a girl who later married the etcher Louis Bescherer and who is portrayed in *En Ménage* under the name of Virginie Lateau. Like André Jayant and Jeanne, they quarrelled and parted after a few months, and five years passed before they were reunited. By this time Anna had founded her own dressmaking business at No. 21 Rue du Cardinal-Lemoine, and two daughters had been born to her – Blanche-

Antonine and Antonine. She and Huysmans never set up house together, but she often spent week-ends at his Rue de Sèvres flat, leaving her children in the care of Virginie Bescherer, and sometimes she accompanied him on his holidays. It is with unusual tenderness that Huysmans recounts in *En Ménage* the beginnings of this placid relationship, which, only a few years later, was to end in stark and horrible tragedy.

Though it was undoubtedly Huysmans' best work to date, *En Ménage* was given a hostile reception by the critics. They could scarcely dismiss it as another sordid tale of low life, for Huysmans had taken Goncourt's advice and abandoned *la canaille littéraire*, but they could and did criticize its pessimistic philosophy and vestigial plot. It also shared in the ridicule that was heaped upon Céard's *Une Belle Journée*, a recently published novel of 346 pages in which nothing whatever happened; and Aurélien Scholl, who for some reason passed for a wit in journalistic circles, won fresh laurels by nicknaming the two authors 'Chouya and Boulou'.[7] On the other hand, warm praise for Huysmans' book came from an unexpected quarter: the artistic confraternity at Pontoise. Writing to thank Zola for introducing him to Huysmans, Paul Cézanne pronounced *En Ménage* a delightful work; and a fortnight later he reported that Camille Pissarro, to whom he had lent his copy of the novel, was 'lapping it up'.[8]

Two months after the publication of *En Ménage*, Huysmans received an invitation to a literary gathering at the Rue Viète studio of the painter de Nittis. There, on Wednesday, 6 April, he listened to Edmond de Goncourt reading the first chapters of his new novel, *La Faustin*, to an audience that also included the Daudets, the Heredias, the Zolas, the Charpentiers, Céard, and Alexis.[9] In a letter to Zola written a few days later, Huysmans referred slightingly to Goncourt and his book, but in fact he had been considerably impressed by the reading. What is more, his loyalty to the master of Médan was at this time undergoing a severe strain. For the past four years Zola had been in the habit of employing his young friends to gather the material for his novels which he was unable or unwilling to collect himself; and although Huysmans for one had proved his worth with several major works of his own, Zola persisted in treating him as a prentice writer. Thus, in the space of one month, he was called upon to provide the master novelist with detailed information about his own family history, the work of diocesan architects and their relations with the clergy, the rates of pay of copyists employed by students at the École Centrale, the interior and exterior appearance of houses in the Rue Saint-Roch, and the designs of rare postage stamps.[10] He became increasingly contemptuous of Zola's arm-chair methods of documentation, and increasingly irritated by the demands which this unrewarding and unrewarded research made upon his time. But three years were yet to pass before he asserted his independence.

Throughout the spring of 1881 Huysmans suffered severely from attacks of neuralgia, and in June he told Zola that he intended to spend the next three months in the 'pseudo-countryside' of Fontenay-aux-Roses, coming into Paris every morning to attend to his work at the Ministry. Before making this move, he arranged for the publisher Édouard Rouveyre to bring out a slight but attractive work he had recently written in collaboration with Léon Hennique. This was *Pierrot sceptique*, a macabre pantomime in thirteen scenes which had been inspired by a performance given by the Hanlon-Lees at the Folies-Bergère.[11] The author's friends were surprised to read that six other pantomimes were in preparation, for they knew that Huysmans did not share Hennique's interest in dramatic art and often described the theatre-going public as an unintelligent rabble. Events proved them right. Of the six pantomimes advertised, only one – *Le Songe d'une nuit d'hiver* – actually appeared, and that was signed by Hennique alone.

It is not known for certain where in Fontenay-aux-Roses Huysmans settled when he left Paris in mid-July, but it may well have been at No. 10 Rue du Plessis-Piquet (now Rue Boris Vildé). Four years later his friend Léon Bloy moved to this address from Asnières, probably on his recommendation;[12] and there are indications in *A Rebours* that the fabulous des Esseintes also made his home in this neighbourhood.

No. 10 is still to be seen; it is a very ordinary house. But it is built on to a house so bizarre in appearance that it might be more suitably termed a folly. This strange building cannot have failed to intrigue Huysmans, who saw it every day for three months on his way to and from Fontenay station; and the memory of it was doubtless still green in his mind when he came to describe the 'refined Thebaid' of des Esseintes.

During his stay at Fontenay he resumed work on *La Faim*, but that refractory first novel was soon abandoned in favour of a story called *A Vau-l'Eau*. This is the tale of a wretched little *fonctionnaire*, Jean Folantin, whose life is a succession of misfortunes and disappointments. He loses both his parents at an early age; at school he is crippled in an accident; and in the Civil Service, which he joins as a junior clerk, promotion constantly eludes him. His amorous experiences are no less unsatisfactory: after a brief liaison with a working girl who leaves him 'a keepsake from which he found it hard to recover', he enters into sordid relationships with various prostitutes and finally abandons all interest in the opposite sex. The consolation of good food is denied him, for he finds that everywhere – in high-class restaurants as well as humble chop-houses – 'the wine is full of lead-oxide and diluted with pump-water, the eggs are never cooked to one's liking, the steaks are never juicy, and the vegetables look like garbage from the local jail'. People and things continually conspire to torment him. His life is made miserable by insolent waiters and dishonest shopkeepers, importunate acquaintances and incapable housekeepers, cigarettes that go out and fires that fail to kindle; and in the end, as a crowning humiliation, he is accosted by a purposeful young woman and bullied into her bed. As he makes his way home, he recalls Schopenhauer's dictum that 'man's life swings like a pendulum between suffering and boredom'; and he decides that, since happiness is clearly a pathetic illusion, there is nothing to do but ship one's oars and drift downstream . . .

It appears that Huysmans originally intended to make a full-scale novel of *A Vau-l'Eau*; but after working on it for a few weeks, he realized that Folantin's life-story was not very different from that of André Jayant. 'As a result', he told Zola later,[13] 'I decided that this story would have to be much shorter than I had planned. Even so, the subject necessarily involved a repetition of situations I had already explored in *En Ménage*, and I was obliged to deal once more with the housekeeper problem and the drawbacks of the solitary life – but I think I was right to measure my lines parsimoniously and to be as brief as possible.'

What it lost thereby in length, *A Vau-l'Eau* gained in power and intensity. It became a masterly essay in everyday pessimism – or, as Huysmans called it in his autobiographial sketch, 'the Missal of minor misfortunes' – and its hero one of the great types in French literature. Huysmans' Folantin has been succeeded by Duhamel's Salavin and Sartre's Roquentin, unhappy heroes of the twentieth century who resemble him in more than name: they too are 'little men' whose wretchedness and perplexity attain epic proportions.

In December the finished manuscript was sent off to Henry Kistemaeckers, a young publisher in Brussels. This Kistemaeckers was a curious, rather disreputable character. In 1874, while working as a purser for an English shipping company, he had suddenly taken it into his head to set up in business as a publisher. His first ventures in this direction – some radical works by exiled Communards – had been singularly unsuccessful, so he had turned his attention to the more profitable business of supplying the French public with all those erotic works, ancient and modern, which Marshal MacMahon and Casimir Périer tried so hard to keep from their fellow citizens. By publishing sensational novels by young Naturalists such as Louis Desprez and Lucien Descaves, he gained not only considerable profits but also a thoroughly undeserved reputation as a courageous and unselfish patron of letters. Thus in 1884 Edmond de Goncourt bestowed on him the accolade of his approval, allowing him to bring out a new edition of *En 18 . .*, the Goncourt brothers' first novel. Gradually, however, his best authors left him to his pornographic devices; and after playing a cat-and-mouse game with him for many years, the Belgian authorities finally decided to put an end to his activities. In 1902 he was condemned for a series of obscene advertisements which he had published in *Le Flirt*, and he fled the country. Ironically enough, it was in France that he ended his days, for the country which had done so much to keep out his publications generously gave him refuge, and all Belgian requests for his extradition were politely but firmly rejected.[14]

Kistemaeckers' relations with Huysmans had begun when the novelist had authorized him to buy 350 unsold copies of *Marthe* from Jean Gay and to dispose of them cheaply. He had subsequently undertaken to bring out *Monsieur Folantin* (as it was then called) in his 'Édition du Bibliophile' series; and he had gone to great pains to give this work wide advance publicity. At the last moment, however, when the book was almost ready for press, Huysmans decided upon a change of title.[15]

Zola [he wrote] thinks that the title of *M. Folantin* is deplorable, that it conveys nothing to the reader, and that in view of the story's philosophical basis it is quite unsuitable – for the hero is not M. Folantin but any and every lonely bachelor. And I can't deny that in this respect he is right: my story does in fact derive from an abstract idea. Both Zola and Céard are therefore of the opinion that I should call the book *A Vau-l'Eau*, for want of a better title which we've all hunted for and failed to find. So *A Vau-l'Eau* it shall be. It's a mediocre title, and I fear that with all your advertisements announcing *Folantin*, the change may cause you some embarrassment. But on the whole I think they are right, *M. Folantin* signifies nothing, weakens the philosophical impact of the story, and would not sell the book any better than *A Vau-l'Eau*.

Kistemaeckers accepted this decision with remarkably good grace, and the book was published under the new title on 26 January 1882. Two things about it now annoyed the author: a printer's error which he had corrected in vain on the first and second proofs, and a lamentable portrait of himself, done from a photograph by one Amédée Lynen.[16] On the other hand, the press reviews that he read afforded him a certain sardonic pleasure. 'At the moment,' he told Hannon on 15 February,[17] 'I'm enjoying myself immensely in my Rue de Sèvres belvedere, because the newspapers are busy firing faecal bombshells at *A Vau-l'Eau*. It gives them something to do, and it amuses me. How that book infuriates them!'

The chief complaint made about Huysmans' novel was that its subject was too trivial to inspire interest. Yet it would be wrong to see in *A Vau-l'Eau* simply an account of a little clerk's material woes and digestive disorders; the book has a deeper significance. Like Flaubert's indefatigable seekers after truth, Bouvard and Pécuchet, Folantin is searching in his very humble way for spiritual satisfaction; and his quest for a palatable meal symbolizes this pursuit of happiness. Similarly his attempts to turn his rooms into a snug haven of refuge, his hankerings for the seclusion of the cloister, and his sudden intuition that 'religion alone could heal the wound that plagues me', all indicate a profound fear of life and an ardent desire for spiritual security. And lastly, of course, his story is of interest for the light it throws upon Huysmans' own life – for though M. Folantin may owe something to Restif de la Bretonne's *Monsieur Nicolas* and to M. Patissot, the comical hero of Maupassant's *Dimanches d'un bourgeois de Paris*, there can be no doubt that *A Vau-l'Eau* is largely autobiographical.

Huysmans, it is true, was no lame, middle-aged nonentity, but the material circumstances and daily routine of his life and Jean Folantin's were very similar. Like Folantin, he could not afford what was at that time the modest luxury of a full-time maidservant or housekeeper, and had to attend to most domestic matters himself; his friends, for instance, often found him laying the fire or carefully checking items of laundry in a notebook. He used to leave home every day at about ten in the morning and make his way to *La Petite Chaise*, an old-fashioned restaurant in the Rue de Grenelle where he lunched with Alexis Orsat. On the stroke of eleven, he arrived at the offices of the Sûreté Générale in the Rue des Saussaies. Here he spent the next six hours, copying out official letters, adding up columns of figures, and – like so many other young authors employed in various French ministries – working on his own books and articles. From the room which he shared with another clerk, he could look out upon a little garden with ivy-clad walls and 'the marble statue of a woman whose cheerful, vacuous expression was a positive inspiration to him'.[18]

The Civil Service offered him no other amenities: his office was fusty with the smell of files and inkpots, his room-mate chattered endlessly about political events and the state of his health, and his salary in 1881 was the meagre stipend of 3,000 francs earned by Folantin in *A Vau-l'Eau*. On the other hand, he confided to Gustave Coquiot that in entering the Civil Service he had chosen the lesser of two evils, for it was by no means as soul-destroying and stultifying as the legal profession.[19]

After five o'clock, the hour of his release from bureaucratic bondage, Huysmans would cross over to the Left Bank and stroll along the quay between the Rue du Bac and the Rue Dauphine, rummaging in the dusty book-boxes on the parapet, admiring the morocco-bound volumes smugly ensconced in their glass cases, and peering into the antique shops on the other side of the road. This walk never failed to delight him, but soon – all too soon – he had to make up his mind where to have dinner.

In this respect he was as hard to please as Folantin, and the restaurants that won his approval were few and far between. There was, of course, *La Petite Chaise*, which he once described as 'the only eating-house in all Paris where one was not immediately and ineluctably poisoned'.[20] There was also the Restaurant Lachenal, on the corner of the Rue Bonaparte and the Place Saint-Sulpice, from which he could watch people coming out of the church, and the seminarists filing past in a long black-and-white procession. These were both peaceful, well-conducted houses, and the meals they produced were not unsatisfactory; but everywhere else, according to Huysmans, the service was insufferable or the food uneatable. He considered himself something of an authority on these matters – and with good reason, for in the past fifteen years he had patronized every type of restaurant in Paris and ferreted out most of the horrifying secrets of the catering trade; he knew, for example, how certain drinks were adulterated, what chemicals went into the making of various soups, and what sauces were used to disguise the flavour of decaying meat. Indeed, he was so knowledgeable that his presence at table could embarrass the most stout-hearted hostess; and one good lady was reported as saying: 'I love having Monsieur Huysmans to dinner – but if I so much as give him a thought while the maid is serving, my sauces turn!'[21] It must be admitted, however, that often the fault lay not with the food itself but with Huysmans' ailing stomach, which remained impervious to all the stimulants in Folantin's well-stocked bedroom pharmacy – to 'every variety of citrate, phosphate, protocarbonate, lactate, sulphate of protoxide, iodide and iron-proto-iodide, Pearson's liquors, Devergie's waters, Dioscorides' salts, pills of arseniate of soda and golden arseniate, and tonic wines made from gentian and quinine, coca and colombo'. There was undoubtedly an element of exaggeration in Huysmans' never-ending culinary complaints, but his stomach troubles were real enough. His correspondence reveals that, like the hero of *A Vau-l'Eau*, he was a life-long martyr to dyspepsia.

Like Folantin again, he was a confirmed bachelor, holding the idea of marriage in abhorrence. To him married life meant poverty and frustration; it meant 'being obliged to lie still in bed, to suffer the contact of a woman in and out of season, and to satisfy her when one simply wanted to sleep'; it meant bearing with 'a brat that bawled one day because it was cutting a tooth, and another day because it wasn't'. But considerations of comfort alone were not enough to account for the extreme bitterness of Huysmans' views on women; there were other, more fundamental reasons. In the first place, the thought of his mother's second marriage and her subsequent coldness towards him still rankled in his mind, as did also the memory of his disastrous liaison with the Bobino soubrette. In the second place, it is just possible that, like the little clerk in

102

his novel, he had contracted a venereal disease in early manhood. And finally, as he admitted in certain letters to Théodore Hannon, he suffered from periods of sexual impotence.[22] It was this factor, above all others, which really conditioned his attitude to the opposite sex. Anna Meunier brought him unfailing tenderness and understanding, but he came to dread intimate contact with other women, just as Folantin shrinks from the boisterous embrace of the prostitute in *A Vau-l'Eau*. Huysmans' misogyny, in fact, was no superficial affectation; it was rooted – deeply rooted – in fear.

His pessimistic view of life, which found such perfect expression in the title and text of *A Vau-l'Eau*, derived partly from his unhappy experiences at table or in alcove, partly from the impact which an imperfect world made upon his neurotic sensibility. He used to say that he was as sensitive as a man who had been flayed alive, and it is certain that in his eyes the petty irritations of life assumed the character of physical torments, a thoughtless action became a piece of criminal stupidity, and a minor setback was magnified into a major catastrophe. An acquaintance of his has told how, when some chance remark was made in his presence, Huysmans, 'without looking up, and without taking the trouble to speak distinctly, picked up the phrase, transformed it, more likely transfixed it, in a perfectly turned sentence, a phrase of impromptu elaboration. Perhaps it was only a stupid book that someone had mentioned, or a stupid woman; as he spoke, the book loomed up before one, became monstrous in its dullness, a masterpiece and miracle of imbecility; the unimportant little woman grew into a slow horror before your eyes . . .'[23] There was something masochistic about the way in which Huysmans would thus dwell upon the unpleasant aspect of things, deliberately exposing himself to ugliness and stupidity and pain. But he knew that to suffer was also essential to his art and to his beliefs; to his art because, as his friend Paul Valéry explained,[24] 'everything that revolted his senses excited his genius', and to his beliefs because pain and misfortune lent support to his and Folantin's contention that 'one can expect nothing but the worst'.

He found confirmation of this melancholy opinion in the most trivial occurrences. For example, taking a friend into a café and ordering two different apéritifs, he would guarantee that the waiter would get the orders mixed; not once was he proved wrong, according to Gustave Kahn,[25] and this peculiar constant became known among his intimates as 'the Huysmans law'. Rather more weighty authority for his pessimistic beliefs was provided by Schopenhauer's *Aphorisms*, which caused a sensation in intellectual circles when they were first translated into French in 1880. Huysmans discovered that they reflected many of his own most cherished ideas – that life was futile and unpleasant, that woman was fundamentally ignoble, that suffering was a sign of superiority, and so on – and it is not surprising that he gave unhesitating adherence to Schopenhauer's philosophy. He even attempted to convert Zola to his point of view, as the following letter reveals.[26]

Consider [he wrote] that it is the theory of resignation, precisely the same as that of *The Imitation of Christ*, except that here the future panacea is replaced by a spirit of patience, by a determination to accept all afflictions without complaining, and by a calm expectation of death, which, as in religion, is not feared but welcomed as a deliverance. I know, of course, that you don't hold with pessimism, and that Bourdeau, in his preface to Schopenhauer's *Pensées*, declares that that prodigious man was afraid of death. But the theory is greater than the man, who merely failed to practise what he preached. And since no intelligent person can possibly believe in the Catholic faith, his ideas remain the most consoling, the most logical, and the most convincing there can be. After all, if you aren't a pessimist, you can only be a Christian or an anarchist; you must be one of the three.

Though this last argument failed to impress Zola, Huysmans remained convinced of its validity; and when he abjured his pessimistic beliefs some years later, it was to enter the fold of the Catholic Church. In 1882, however, the author of *A Vau-l'Eau* still considered Christian dogma to be absurd, the clergy intolerant, and religion 'a consolation for none but the feeble-minded'.

8. THE ART-CRITIC

PERHAPS the only thing which could arouse Huysmans' enthusiasm at this time and make him oblivious of the misery of life was the cause of modern art. For several years he had been closely associated with the Impressionists or Independents, and indeed had identified himself with their cause to a degree unusual and probably unique in the history of art-criticism. He had singled out the artists of exceptional promise, explained their aims and methods to the public, and defended them against the bitter attacks of the traditionalist critics; he had criticized them and praised them, deplored their faults and lauded their virtues, regretted their failures and rejoiced at their successes. Now, in 1882, although the Impressionists had broken up into small groups and no longer presented a united front to academic attacks, he thought he could see in much of their work the fulfilment of earlier promise, and he decided that this was an opportune moment to gather together his *Salons* of the past few years into a single book. This work, which because of Huysmans' ardent yet not uncritical championship of the Impressionists constitutes a valuable record of an important phase in the history of modern art, was published by Charpentier in 1883. It was entitled, not unreasonably, *L'Art moderne*.

Of the pieces printed in *L'Art moderne*, some had already appeared in *Le Voltaire, La Réforme*, and *La Revue Littéraire et Artistique*, while the rest seem to have been unpublished; they comprised articles or notes on the four official Salons held from 1879 to 1882, and the unofficial 'Expositions des Indépendants' held in 1880, 1881, and 1882. This was not, of course, the sum of Huysmans' art-criticism to date: he had contributed articles on various exhibitions or individual paintings to *Le Musée des Deux-Mondes, La République des*

Lettres, and *L'Actualité*, and it will be remembered that his first published work, an article which appeared in *La Revue Mensuelle* in November 1867, was a study of contemporary landscape-painters. But on the whole these early essays in art-criticism had been innocuous and undistinguished, as if the young writer had not yet acquired either convictions or the courage of them. It was only in 1879 that he launched the first of his violent attacks upon academic art and its exponents. The violence of his onslaught upon the 'ancients' and of his enthusiasm for the 'moderns', which may seem shocking to present-day readers accustomed to the pale innuendoes of twentieth-century critics, was natural to a man who believed that the true critic should be passionately partisan in his judgements, if he was to avoid the dilettante's 'promiscuity in admiration'. Thus, some years later,[1] he explained:

> The truth is that one cannot understand art and truly love it if one is an eclectic, a dilettante. One cannot sincerely go into ecstasies over Delacroix if one admires M. Bastien Lepage; one does not like M. Gustave Moreau if one accepts M. Bonnat, nor M. Degas if one tolerates M. Gervex. Fortunately the profitable estate of the dilettante has its drawbacks: in these excesses of pusillanimity, these debauches of prudence, language inevitably grows feeble and fluid, reverts to the dreary, murky style of the Instituts, liquefies into the damp diction of M. Renan. For one cannot have talent unless one loves passionately and hates passionately; enthusiasm and contempt are indispensable to anyone wishing to create a work of art; talent belongs to those who are sincere and fanatical, not to those who are indifferent and afraid.

There was certainly nothing feeble, fluid, or murky about the style of Huysmans' *Salon* of 1879, as the unfortunate exhibitors discovered to their cost. But except as an exciting and instructive exercise in invective, this series of articles scarcely repays reading today, for Huysmans' ridicule did so much to turn the tide of popular and critical opinion that most of the artists whom he attacked have by now been completely forgotten. There were only a few exhibitors whom he considered worthy of praise: Guillaumin for a bleak seascape; Raffaëlli for his melancholy suburban landscapes; and Manet for two canvases illustrating the accurate observation, the 'open-air' technique, the skilful use of colour, and the contempt for convention, which had made this painter one of the pioneers of modern art. Otherwise the critic's incidental praise of the Impressionists and Independents – he explained that he used the two terms interchangeably for the sake of convenience – made it clear that he would rather be reporting the annual Impressionist exhibition than wasting his time on the 'Champs-Élysées stock exchange in oils'.

This opportunity came the following year, when Huysmans wrote an account of the fifth Impressionist exhibition or 'Exposition des Indépendants'. Here, after pouring scorn upon the painters schooled in the École des Beaux-Arts, who used the same lighting effects for interiors and landscapes and 'whether the scene they were depicting was laid in winter or summer, at midday or five o'clock, under a clear or a cloudy sky', he went on:

> It is to the little group of Impressionists that credit is due for having swept away all these prejudices and thrown overboard all these conventions. The new school has proclaimed this scientific truth: that every colour fades a little in broad daylight, that the silhouette and colour of, say, a house or a tree, painted indoors, are completely different from the silhouette and colour of the same house or tree, painted in the open air. This truth, which could not possibly occur to people accustomed to the more or less restricted light of a studio, was of course discovered by the landscape artists who, leaving their curtained rooms, went out into the open to paint Nature with simplicity and sincerity.

At the same time he expressed his admiration for the Impressionists' favourite technique, which at that time puzzled the public and angered the critics – 'the use of tones which are not to be found on the palette, but which are obtained on the canvas by the juxtaposition of other colours'. Taking as his example the Degas portrait of Duranty,[2] he wrote:

> Here there are patches of bright pink on the forehead, green in the beard, blue on the velvet coat-collar; the fingers are done in yellow edged with bishop's-purple. From close to, it is an appalling jumble of colours that war with one another and seem to overlap; but if one steps back a little, harmony is established, and all this blends into an exquisite flesh-tint – a palpitating, living flesh-tint such as no other French artist seems able to produce.

Important though these technical discoveries and innovations were, Huysmans considered that greater significance should be attached to the essentially modern subject-matter and style of the Impressionists' work. He himself had often urged artists to abandon the neo-classical and historical subjects still in vogue, and to depict instead those familiar aspects of contemporary life which Goncourt and the Naturalists represented in their novels. In *En Ménage*, for example, he had suggested that the Gare du Nord was just as worthy of admiration and attention as the Parthenon, while the Venus de Milo – 'a pin-headed prude with the torso of a fairground wrestler' – had been unfavourably compared with 'the young street-walker, dressmaker, milliner, or errand-girl of today, with her pale face, her roguish, pearly eyes, her pert little nose, her jaunty breasts and swinging hips'. It is small wonder that he was captivated once more by Raffaëlli's paintings of factory chimneys vomiting black smoke into leaden skies – paintings which he acclaimed as expressing 'the poignant note of spleen in landscape, the plaintive delights of our suburbs'. Small wonder, either, that he was attracted to the work of his friend Forain, whom he considered the supreme painter of the prostitute – 'for no one has observed her more closely, no one has rendered more exactly her impudent smile, her provocative eyes, and her lecherous air; no one has understood better the absurd caprices of her fashions, the enormous thrusting breasts, the arms as thin as matchsticks, the whittled-down waist, and the bust straining under its armour-plating . . .' And still less surprising is the admiration he conceived for Degas, who 'although reputed to have painted only ballet-dancers', had in fact depicted 'washerwomen in their shops, dancers at rehearsal, café-singers, theatres, race-horses, models, American cotton-merchants, women getting out of their baths, and scenes in boudoirs and boxes'. With Degas, he maintained, 'a painter of modern life was born, a painter who derived from no one and resembled no one, who brought with him entirely new techniques and an entirely new artistic savour'.

The later articles included in *L'Art moderne* are written from the same standpoint and with the same anger or enthusiasm. Courbet, Millet, and Puvis de Chavannes are damned or derided; Degas, Renoir, Monet, Pissarro, Caillebotte, Sisley, Forain, Raffaëlli, Mary Cassatt, and Berthe Morisot are praised. Laurels are bestowed, too, on Walter Crane, Kate Greenaway, and Randolph Caldecott, in an unexpected digression on illustrated children's albums, while in the *Exposition des Indépendants en 1881* Gauguin is lauded for having 'fully succeeded' in what Huysmans considered to be the first attempt in modern times to paint truthfully a truly contemporary nude. And finally, in his notes on the 1882 Impressionist exhibition, the critic salutes the achievement of the Impressionist landscape-painters. 'MM. Pissarro and Monet', he declares, 'have at last emerged victorious from the terrible struggle. One can now state that the difficult problems of light in painting have finally been solved in their canvases . . .'

There are two names mentioned in *L'Art moderne* which must strike the reader as out of place in such a work, since they belonged to artists who had little or nothing in common with Degas and the Impressionists: Gustave Moreau and Odilon Redon. Neither of these two artists used Impressionist methods or took his subjects from contemporary life, for while Moreau conjured up 'the faery visions and bloody

110

apotheoses of other ages', Redon produced drawings suggestive of anatomical and entomological nightmares. Huysmans'
praise of these exotic or macabre dream-like pictures fore-
shadowed his own future development; and in this respect it is
particularly interesting to note that he described Redon as
one of Baudelaire's spiritual offspring and added: 'With him
we delight in loosing our earthly bonds and floating away
into the world of dreams, a hundred thousand leagues away
from all schools of painting, ancient or modern.' Soon
Huysmans, too, was to look to Baudelaire for inspiration, to
seek to escape from his 'earthly bonds', and to turn from the
study of contemporary life to an exploration of the world of
dreams.

Huysmans was personally acquainted with many of the artists he praised in *L'Art moderne*, and some of them were close
friends. However, we have regrettably few documentary
accounts of these relationships. There is an anecdote Degas
recounted to the novelist one evening,[3] an occasional reference to the times he and Forain had 'gone on the spree
together in Paris',[4] and a letter from Raffaëlli inviting him to
share a 'frugal dinner' with him at Asnières, where the painter
lived 'with my wife, my little daughter, two hens, a cock, and
two pigeons'.[5] But to obtain some idea of the affection which
the ferocious critic could feel for one of his protégés, we must
turn either to the letters he wrote to Redon and his wife,[6] or
to this account by Redon[7] of their friendship:

How did I meet Huysmans? It happened like this. I had
held a little exhibition of my charcoal sketches at
the offices of either *Le Gaulois* or *Le Figaro*. He had
written to ask if he could buy one particular sketch.
Unfortunately I hadn't any more copies, or that was the
only one left, so I replied regretfully that it wasn't possible. At that time he had already published his *Croquis
parisiens, Marthe* and *Les Sœurs Vatard*, and these works
had earned him the reputation of being one of the best
pupils of Zola's Naturalist school. One day – we were
then living in the Rue de Rennes – the doorbell rang.

111

I opened the door, and saw a tall, thin silhouette: 'Huysmans'. I asked him in, and he was extremely charming. For me he was always charming . . . My house, our house, was, I believe, one of the few which he entered with pleasure, his 'refuge' . . . He used to say of my wife: 'It's a woman like her, if only I could find one, that I should marry. She's the ideal companion for an artist.' One dish she cooked especially for him sent him into raptures of delight. He always felt at home with us, in our rather old-fashioned surroundings. We were poor then, but not uncomfortable. There were some old pieces of furniture in the studio, including an old arm-chair of which he grew very fond. When we moved house and Huysmans found that we had left that old arm-chair behind, he stayed away for several days to 'punish' us . . . The dear man had a kind heart. Though he claimed to detest children, he sat up with my wife and myself all through one night until the morning, with the child we lost. And he used to say, as if to excuse himself: 'It's because your children aren't like those of other people . . .'

It would be a mistake to imagine – as one might on reading this testimony by Redon – that Huysmans praised certain artists only because they were his friends: as a general rule it was because he had praised their work that artists entered into correspondence with him, met him, and occasionally were admitted to his friendship. Moreover, even when he was personally attracted to an artist and felt deep admiration for his character, he would not laud his paintings unless he was genuinely convinced of their merit. This can be seen most clearly from his treatment of Cézanne in *L'Art moderne*, where a sympathetic reference is made to the artist's contribution to Impressionist landscape-painting, but nothing more. When Pissarro later reproached Huysmans for saying so little of Cézanne, the critic explained[8] that this was partly due to the fact that Cézanne had not shown any work since 1877, but added:

Look – Cézanne's personality appeals to me tremendously, for Zola has told me of his struggles, disappointments, and defeats when he tries to create a new work. Yes, he has temperament, and he's an artist, but on the whole, with the exception of some excellent still-lifes, the rest is, to my mind, unlikely to survive. It's interesting, curious, thought-provoking; but it's the product of a special ocular condition of which, I gather, he himself is aware . . .

It is a little disconcerting to find a critic as perceptive as Huysmans writing about Cézanne with so little understanding. But it must be remembered that his opinions of Cézanne's work had largely been formed – or rather, malformed – by his conversations with Zola; and that he was later to make ample amends in *Certains*, with a passage in praise of Cézanne which shows that he had rid himself of the prejudiced notions inculcated at Médan.

L'Art moderne should have been brought out by Charpentier in the autumn of 1882, for Huysmans had delivered the manuscript to him by June of that year. However, there were long delays, as the publisher objected to Huysmans' criticism of some of his own illustrators,[9] and it was not until April 1883 that the book went to press. 'There are some curious things in it,' the author told Théodore Hannon;[10] 'and I think it will raise a good many howls of protest – for I have told the truth, once for all, about our painters.' This was a bold claim to make, but it was not unjustified. As Roger Marx has since observed,[11] 'one would have to go back to Thoré to find so infallible a diagnosis, and back to Baudelaire to find that double gift of divination and expression which gives Huysmans' aesthetic writings their definitive quality, and which ensures for their author abiding fame – not as one judge among many, but as a unique personality: the modern art-critic'.

Huysmans' great achievement as an art-critic was, of course, his staunch championship of the Impressionists. Before him, Duranty and Théodore Duret had recognized the importance of the new movement, but they had lacked the perspicacity and the ability to do much more. It was left to Huysmans to pick out the foremost exponents of modern art and do battle for them against public apathy and critical incomprehension. The remarkable skill with which he separated the wheat from the chaff – the artists whose work would endure from those whose very names would soon be forgotten – is still a source of astonishment. To take but one of many examples, he wrote of Degas:

When will this painter be accorded the high place which is due to him in the world of art? When will it be acknowledged that this artist is the greatest we possess today in France? I am no prophet, but if I am to judge by the ineptitude of the enlightened classes, who despised Delacroix for so long, and who still have not the least suspicion that Baudelaire is the poetic genius of the nineteenth century, dwarfing every other poet including Hugo, or that the masterpiece of the modern novel is Gustave Flaubert's *L'Éducation sentimentale*, then I can well believe that the truth of what I write – and am today the only one to write – about M. Degas will not be recognized for many, many years.

Though his faith in the future of one painter outside the Impressionist movement – Gustave Moreau – is now thought to have been misplaced, posterity has ratified nearly all his critical judgements on the Impressionists themselves. He did more than any other man to establish their reputations, and it is no disparagement of them to say, as did Félix Fénéon,[12] that he was 'the inventor of Impressionism'.

It is, of course, impossible to calculate exactly what effect Huysmans' criticism had on the development of modern art, but at least two of the artists whose work he discussed later testified – in word or deed – to the influence which his writings had exerted on their individual careers. Thus Odilon Redon acknowledged[13] that Huysmans' praise of his work 'spread my reputation widely among the artists who read his books'. And Gauguin, on reading Huysmans' criticism of the paintings he submitted to the 1882 Exposition des Indépendants – 'M. Gauguin is not making any progress, alas! . . . Nothing worthy of note this year . . . dull, scurvy colours' – was confirmed in his decision to abandon his career in the broking world, and set out in search of colours which could not possibly be described as dull or scurvy . . .[14]

However, when *L'Art moderne* was first published, in May 1883, it met with a very mixed reception. The art-critics of the old guard greeted it, as the author had expected, with 'howls of protest', while even Zola, in a letter which revealed how little he really sympathized with the Impressionists,[15] quarrelled with Huysmans' high opinion of Degas, whom he dismissed as 'nothing more than a constipated artist'. On the other hand, Gustave Geffroy, who was soon to make his mark as an art-critic, gave the book an enthusiastic review in *La Justice*; young Paul Bourget praised it in *Le Parlement*; and Mallarmé, thanking Huysmans for a copy of the work,[16] assured him that he was 'the only *causeur d'art* who can induce one to read *Salons* of yesteryear from beginning to end, and to find them more interesting than those of today . . . What a fine passion for truth you display, with a penetrating eye and a persuasive voice to serve it!' And finally Claude Monet was to write, a few years later,[17] that 'never has anyone written so well, so nobly, of modern artists'.

By the time *L'Art moderne* appeared, Huysmans had almost finished another book. In February 1882 he had told Théodore Hannon that he was working on a story called *Le Gros Caillou*,[18] and had already produced a very lively description of 'a dance-hall full of soldiers, tobacco-girls, and whores'. But the writing of the rest of *Le Gros Caillou* did not go as well as he had expected, and he eventually turned to a more congenial subject. He explained to Zola, in November 1882: 'I felt the need for a complete change, and so I embarked on a wild and gloomy fantasy, something crazy but at the same time realistic.' This 'wild and gloomy fantasy' was to bring Huysmans world-wide fame, lead to his break with Médan, and start a powerful reaction against Naturalism.

It was *A Rebours*.

PART TWO

1. THE DECADENT

WHEN he wrote *A Rebours*, Huysmans neither intended nor expected it to launch a new literary movement, becoming, in Arthur Symons' memorable phrase, 'the breviary of the Decadence'. On the contrary, he tells us in an autobiographical sketch that he believed he was 'writing for a dozen persons, fashioning a sort of hermetic book which would be closed to fools'.[1] He wrote this book because he was intensely dissatisfied with his earlier works, and tired of following in the footsteps of Flaubert and the Goncourts; because he wanted to give free rein to his imagination and his style, ignoring the dictates of literary convention; because, as he confessed to Henry Céard,[2] 'he was afraid of getting his pen trapped in the inkpot, and of having to stir up the same old ink for the rest of his life'. The other young writers of the Médan group were conscious of much the same anxiety and uncertainty as to the future, though perhaps in a lesser degree. Their dilemma was summarized by Huysmans in the important preface to *A Rebours* which he wrote in 1903:

> Naturalism was just then in its heyday; but this movement, which rendered literature the notable service of depicting true-to-life characters in true-to-life surroundings, was condemned to go on marking time, repeating itself *ad nauseam*. In theory at least, it refused to admit of anything exceptional; it therefore confined itself to representing the course of everyday life and, under the pretext of painting lifelike portraits, sought to create characters that were as like to the average run of humanity as possible. This ideal had already been realized in a masterpiece which, much more than *L'Assommoir*, served as a model for every Naturalist writer:

L'Éducation sentimentale, by Gustave Flaubert. To us, the young authors of *Les Soirées de Médan*, this novel was a veritable Bible – but a Bible from which we could derive little profit; for it was finished in every detail, and even Flaubert himself could not write another book like it. As a result, we were all reduced to exploring the more or less beaten tracks around it, and to prowling about in its shadow.

The Virtues, in Huysmans' opinion, were a closed book to the Naturalists, who in any case dismissed them as being both unusual and uninteresting; while of the Vices, the only one that they were qualified to depict was carnal lust. 'Invent what you please,' he remarks, 'the theme of the average novel could be summed up in these few words: why M. So-and-so did or did not commit adultery with Mme What's-her-name. If a writer wanted to give himself airs and stand out as an author of distinction, he presented an intrigue between a Count and a Marchioness; if, on the other hand, he wanted to pose as a popular novelist, a writer who knew what was what, then he described the mating of some low ruffian with a common tart. Only the background varied.' It was, of course, the background which rescued Zola's novels from mediocrity; and his readers, impressed by such monumental décors as the market in *Le Ventre de Paris*, the department-store in *Au Bonheur des Dames*, and the mine in *Germinal*, often failed to notice that Zola's characters were merely puppets, governed only by instinct and the author's whim. But Zola's young colleagues, no longer blinded by the Master's dazzling descriptive talent, opened their eyes at last to the psychological poverty of his novels, and to the monotonous sameness of their own. 'We began to wonder', writes Huysmans, 'whether Naturalism was not advancing up a blind alley, and whether we might not soon be running our heads into a wall.' He himself felt that the only possible solution to the problem lay in an attempt 'to shake off preconceived ideas, to extend the scope of the novel, to introduce into it art, science, history: in a word, to use this form of literature only as a frame in which to insert more serious work'. These encyclopaedic ambitions, and Huysmans' oft-expressed desire to 'be original at all costs', were to find fulfilment in *A Rebours*.

The book was originally conceived as an extension of *A Vau-l'Eau*, but in another milieu. 'I pictured to myself,' writes Huysmans, 'a M. Folantin, more cultured, more refined, more wealthy than the first, and who has discovered in artificiality a specific for the disgust inspired by the worries of life and the American manners of his time. I imagined him winging his way to the land of dreams, seeking refuge in extravagant illusions, living alone and apart, far from the present-day world, in an atmosphere suggestive of more cordial epochs and less odious surroundings.' Folantin's poverty and humble upbringing had limited the number and degree of his escapist experiments; but the more fortunate hero of *Seul* (as *A Rebours* was first called), Duc Jean Floressas des Esseintes, would be rich enough to indulge his every caprice. Whereas Folantin, in literature as in art, 'could only take to works that were rooted in real life', des Esseintes would seek solace in the unreal, the artificial, and the exotic. Whereas Folantin had been powerless to relieve the monotony of his diet, des Esseintes would occasionally take his nourishment *à rebours*, by means of enemas. And whereas Folantin's sexual experience had been confined to traffic with common prostitutes, des Esseintes was to enjoy 'unnatural loves and perverse pleasures'. Yet in the end, both heroes were to suffer the same fate, the same utter disillusionment. Both reality and artifice were to be tried – and found wanting.

As is well known, des Esseintes himself was not entirely the product of Huysmans' imagination, nor simply a refined reincarnation of M. Folantin. What is less well known is the fact that Huysmans used not one but many models for the fabulous hero of *A Rebours*. Thus there was the eccentric Ludwig II of Bavaria, whose happiest hours were spent alone in painted indoor forests where mechanical lizards crawled through artificial grass.[3] There was Edmond de Goncourt, who had recently catalogued every exotic detail of his Auteuil home in *La Maison d'un artiste*. There was Jules Barbey d'Aurevilly, the disciple and biographer of Beau Brummel; and Charles Baudelaire, who as a young dandy had furnished his apartments at the Hôtel Lauzun in something like the style adopted by des Esseintes for his 'refined Thebaid' at Fontenay-aux-Roses.[4] There was also Francis Poictevin, a wealthy and eccentric young writer whom Huysmans had lately befriended. And lastly, of course, there was Robert, Comte de Montesquiou-Fezensac.

This elegant and somewhat ridiculous person hoped to achieve immortality as a poet; but even before his death in 1921 it became painfully clear that he was fated to be remembered only as the prototype of Huysmans' des Esseintes and Proust's Charlus. It must be admitted that for this he had no one but himself to blame. In matters of dress, for example, he was studiously eccentric, and his eccentricities were paraded across every salon in Paris. It was widely known that he suited his clothes not only to the occasion, the season, and the weather, but also to the tastes and temperament of his host; and it was rumoured that sometimes, in lieu of a cravat, he would wear a bunch of Parma violets tucked into a low-necked shirt. If his clothes were unconventional, the furnishings of his home in the Rue Franklin were fantastic in the extreme – but these were rarely displayed, and then only to carefully chosen friends. In 1883, to his eternal regret, Montesquiou admitted Stéphane Mallarmé to this select company. It was late at night when the poet was shown over the house, and the only illumination came from a few scattered candelabra; yet in the flickering light Mallarmé observed that the door-bell was in fact a sacring-bell, that one room was furnished as a monastery cell and another as the cabin of a yacht, and that a third contained a Louis Quinze pulpit, three or four cathedral stalls, and a strip of altar railing. He was shown, too, a sled picturesquely placed on a snow-white bearskin, a library of rare books in suitably coloured bindings, and the remains of an unfortunate tortoise whose shell had been coated with gold paint. According to Montesquiou, writing his memoirs many years later,[5] the sight of these marvels left Mallarmé speechless with amazement. 'He went away', records Montesquiou, 'in a state of silent exaltation, which, though not unusual with him, rarely attained such a temperature. I do not doubt, therefore, that it was in the most admiring, sympathetic, and sincere good faith that he retailed to Huysmans what he had seen during the few moments he spent in Ali-Baba's Cave.' Whatever the poet's true opinion of 'Ali-Baba's Cave', it cannot be denied that Huysmans made good use of the information he provided. All the bizarre features of Montesquiou's home are, in fact, reproduced in *A Rebours*, with suitable embellishments – as in the famous episode where the young des Esseintes preaches to his assembled tradesmen from the pulpit, 'adjuring his shoe-makers and tailors to conform strictly to his encyclicals on matters of cut, and threatening them with pecuniary excommunication if they did not follow the instructions contained in his monitories and bulls . . .'

The knowledge that Montesquiou was used as a model for des Esseintes has led some critics to suppose that *A Rebours* was intended as a caricature of the aesthetes or 'Decadents' of the eighties, just as *The Green Carnation* was written as a satire on Oscar Wilde. There are two fundamental reasons why this view cannot be accepted. The first is that the 'Decadent' move-ment did not really gain impetus until after the publication of *A Rebours*; and the second is that the true prototype of des Esseintes, as Léon Bloy later remarked, was Huysmans himself. This is not, of course, to suggest that Huysmans was an effete scion of a noble family, or that he indulged in his hero's eccentric pastimes; but it is clear that des Esseintes became the repository of Huysmans' secret tastes and untold dreams, and that in their sickly sensibility, their yearning for solitude, their abhorrence of human mediocrity, and their thirst for new and complex sensations, author and character were one. Even des Esseintes' sexual vagaries may have reflected a brief phase in Huysmans' own experience, for the novelist certainly had some acquaintance with the 'unnatural loves and perverse pleasures' of which he wrote. This was first revealed in 1904, when Dr. Marc-André Raffalovich published Huysmans' reply to a questionnaire he had circulated among various

French and English writers.[6] Thanking Raffalovich for his letter, and for a copy of his treatise *Uranisme et unisexualité*, Huysmans wrote:

> Your letter and your book bring back to mind some horrifying evenings I once spent in the sodomite world, to which I was introduced by a talented young man whose perversities are common knowledge. I spent only a few days with these people before it was discovered that I was not a true homosexual – and then I was lucky to get away with my life . . . In particular, I remember seeing one of our matinée-idols coming into a tavern in the Rue des Vertus that was much frequented by rad-dled old 'boys' of sixty . . . Never in my life have I seen anything so sinister. It was obvious that he hated and despised himself for coming – and yet there he was, with his coat-collar turned up, looking ghastly pale and path-etically unhappy. When you have seen something like that, you really feel like thanking God that you aren't made the same way . . .

Had all this been known to Huysmans' bourgeois con-temporaries, they would have felt little or no surprise, ready as they were to believe the worst of anyone who could write so perverse, so 'Baudelairian' a book as *A Rebours*. For it is, of course, of Baudelaire that the reader is irresistibly reminded when reading Huysmans' novel. In the first place, there can be no doubt that the title and theme of *A Rebours* owe much to Baudelaire's paradoxical praise of artifice, and that his revolt against conventional ideas of the beauty of Nature inspired des Esseintes' comment that 'Nature has had her day; the disgusting monotony of her landscapes and skyscapes has finally proved too much for refined and sensitive tempera-ments'. What is more, the spirit of Baudelaire's *Correspond-ances* pervades Huysmans' book, the idea of transposing sense-impressions being developed to its furthest limits in the famous episode of the 'mouth-organ' – an arrangement of liqueur-casks so contrived that des Esseintes can perform upon his palate sapid symphonies, 'silent melodies, mute funeral marches, *crème-de-menthe* solos, rum-and-vespetro duets'. And quite apart from these and other aesthetic analogies,[7] a study of *A Rebours* affords evidence of a very real spiritual kinship between the two authors, and shows how well Huysmans understood the terrible sickness of the soul which lies at the root of *Les Fleurs du mal*.

While many critics have recognized the Baudelairian inspiration of *A Rebours*, very few have remarked upon the considerable debt which the author also owed to Edmond de Goncourt.[8] Since the appearance of *Les Frères Zemganno* in 1879, Huysmans had given careful consideration to Goncourt's advice to portray 'cultured beings and exquisite things'; he had often listened respectfully to an exposition of Goncourt's aesthetic beliefs, which were closely related to those of Baudelaire; and he had been deeply impressed by Goncourt's most recent novel, *La Faustin*. On 19 January 1882, shortly after the publication of this book, he had written assuring the author that 'I cannot think of a work which has set my nerves tingling in such a painful yet exquisite way.' In particular, he had praised Goncourt's study – 'so curious, so novel, so essentially modern' – of La Faustin's strange character; and in the following passage from his letter one can already detect a hint of the even stranger des Esseintes:

> For sheer nervous sensitivity, the carnal side of *La Faustin* is equalled only by certain of Schubert's adorable and disturbing melodies. This is no coarse, bestial mating, but the union of bodies refined by cerebral excitation; it is something new to our literature and very true to life – something characteristic, it seems to me, of the eighteenth century, that corrupt, aristocratic, and exceptionally refined epoch. This subtle and elegant depravity, this studied erethism which was known to the Latins of the Decadence, and which Petronius described in his curiously elaborate style – this exists too in our own time, and I knew it without being able to put it into

125

words, none of our modern novelists having yet brought it to light. And so your account of the night Lord Annandale spends with La Faustin sent a shiver of delight through me, for this analysis of the sensual and cerebral pleasures of refined and neurotic creatures opened up to me new, if not unsuspected, horizons.

It was not long after writing this significant appreciation of Goncourt's novel that Huysmans began work on *A Rebours*. He originally intended this work to be no longer than *A Vau-l'Eau*, but he soon found himself compiling something more in the nature of an encyclopaedia than a novelette; and in one of his last letters to Théodore Hannon before the poet broke off their friendship,[9] he described the book as containing 'the quintessence of everything under the sun: literature, art, flori-culture, perfumery, furnishing, jewellery, etc.' Like Flaubert with his *Bouvard et Pécuchet*, he consulted countless specialist works on all these subjects, and then composed an abstract of his notes for each chapter; his hero's survey of late Latin litera-ture, skilfully adapted from Ebert's *Allgemeine Geschichte der Literatur des Mittelalters*, is perhaps the most notable instance of this technique.[10] Much of his material was derived from rather more obscure sources – the idea of the famous 'mouth-organ', for example, coming from an anonymous eighteenth-century volume with the unpromising title of *Chimie du goût et de l'odorat, ou principes pour composer facilement et à peu de frais les liqueurs à boire et les eaux de senteurs*.[11] The subject of *A Rebours* obviously called for researches of this kind rather than the 'field-work' to which Huysmans was accustomed; but sometimes an opportunity occurred to collect material for some incidental *croquis parisiens*. Thus in a letter[12] to Émile Hennequin – a young friend who gave him some assistance in his encyclopaedic studies – he wrote:

Alas! you are quite right, my dear Hennequin, in sup-posing that I've been leading a fast life these last few days. I think I spoke to you not long since of an old friend of mine who teaches biology, philosophy, etc., at the Academy of Porto Alegre. Well, ten days ago this mahogany-coloured gentleman hurled himself into my arms with a roar of delight, and ever since, my life has been a wild cavalcade through beer-houses and brothels. It really is time for this buccaneer to head back to Brazil, because I can't stand much more of the revolting meat and *homard à l'américaine* with which the monster has been stuffing me . . .

In spite of Huysmans' plaints, the evenings he spent with the gentleman from Porto Alegre were not entirely wasted, for it was probably on one of their joint expeditions that he discovered the bodega on the corner of the Rue Castiglione, and the tavern known as Austin's Bar in the Rue d'Amsterdam, which are patronized by des Esseintes in the course of his abortive London journey.[13] We can imagine the fascinated interest with which our author watched some 'big-boned, long-toothed, apple-cheeked Englishwomen' attacking their rump-steaks in Austin's Bar, before settling down himself to a magnificently English meal of ox-tail soup, smoked haddock, roast beef washed down with two pints of ale, Stilton cheese, rhubarb tart, and a tankard of porter. For a brief hour or two the intestinal agonies of M. Folantin were completely forgotten.

One of the most important features of *A Rebours* was to be a commentary on contemporary French literature, as Huysmans explained in his first letter to Stéphane Mallarmé,[14] on 27 October 1882:

Mon cher confrère [he wrote], I am at present working on a strange story, the subject of which is briefly as follows: The last representative of an illustrious race, appalled by the invasion of American manners and the growth of an aristocracy of wealth, takes refuge in absolute solitude. He is well-read, cultured and refined. In his comfortable retreat he substitutes the pleasures of artifice for the banalities of Nature; he delights in reading the authors of the Latin Decadence – I use the word 'Decadence' for the sake of convenience – and also the works of the Early Church, such as the deliciously primitive poems of Orientius, Veranius of Le Gévaudan, Baudonivia, etc., etc. In French literature, he dotes on Baudelaire, his translations of Poe, and the second half of *La Faustin*. You can see what it's going to be like. You can see, too, how I can pay out those cretins who have never understood anything of the penetrating style which some of us try to achieve. For when it comes to modern poetry, my hero naturally worships Tristan Corbière, Hannon, Verlaine; and I propose to give a few quotations from these delicate artists, these delightful and disturbing poets. This will be easy enough, as I possess copies of their works; but in your case I am having some difficulty, which is why I am writing to you now.

He went on to ask for the text of certain poems by Mallarmé which he had been unable to trace, notably *L'Après-midi d'un faune* and *Hérodiade* – the latter 'because my hero possesses the admirable Gustave Moreau water-colour . . . and I want to quote from your *Hérodiade* while attempting to describe Moreau's magical pictures'. Mallarmé gladly lent Huysmans copies of the works he required, and by the spring of 1883 Huysmans had completed the two chapters devoted to a study of contemporary writers. Though he could not know it, these chapters were to have a profound influence on literary tastes and trends in both France and England, an influence which even now shows no signs of diminishing. For they at once revealed and consecrated a new literature – the literature of Baudelaire, Mallarmé, and Verlaine.[15] Huysmans' comments on Mallarmé may now be considered misleading, his praise of Verlaine too extravagant; but his appreciation of Baudelaire's genius still commands our respect:

According to des Esseintes, writers had hitherto confined themselves to exploring the surface of the soul, or such underground passages as were easily accessible and well-lit . . . Baudelaire had gone further; he had descended to the bottom of the inexhaustible mine, had picked his way along abandoned or unexplored galleries, and had finally reached those districts of the soul where the monstrous vegetations of the sick mind flourish. There, near the breeding-ground of intellectual aberrations and diseases of the mind – the mystical tetanus, the burning fever of lust, the typhoids and yellow fevers of crime – he had found, hatching in the dismal forcing-house of *ennui*, the frightening middle-age of thoughts and emotions. He had laid bare the morbid psychology of the mind that has reached the October of its sensations, and had listed the symptoms of souls visited by sorrow, singled out by spleen; he had shown how blight affects the emotions at a time when the enthusiasms and beliefs of youth have drained away, and nothing remains but the barren memory of hardships, tyrannies, and slights, suffered at the behest of a despotic and freakish fate . . . In a period when Literature attributed man's unhappiness almost exclusively to the misfortunes of unrequited love or the jealousies engendered by adulterous love, he had ignored these childish ailments and sounded instead those deeper, deadlier, longer-lasting wounds that are inflicted by satiety, disillusion, and contempt upon souls tortured by the present, disgusted with the past, terrified and despairing of the future.

In May 1883,[16] writing to thank his new friend for a copy of *L'Art moderne*, Mallarmé asked after 'the noble gentleman, whom I often picture to myself in the midst of his books and flowers'. The 'noble gentleman' was almost ready to make his appearance on the French literary scene, for Huysmans was now engaged on the last chapter of his novel. This is the famous chapter in which des Esseintes, ordered back to Paris by his doctors, gives vent to his feelings in a long and wrathful indictment of modern society, pouring forth his maledictions upon every class and every institution in France.[17] In this hour of anguish one would expect him to take refuge in Schopenhauer's philosophy, which he earlier described as 'the great comforter of lofty souls'; but instead he decides that 'the arguments of pessimism were powerless to console him, and the only possible cure for his misery was the impossible belief in a future life'. Jean Folantin, too, had observed that 'religion alone could heal the wound that plagued him'; but while the little clerk had gone no further, des Esseintes abjures his pessimistic beliefs, and finally appeals to God for comfort and enlightenment:

> 'It is all over', he said. 'Like a flowing tide, the waves of human mediocrity are rising to the heavens and will engulf this refuge, for I am opening the flood-gates myself; against my will. Ah! but my courage fails me, and my heart is sick within me! – Lord, take pity on the Christian who doubts, on the sceptic who would fain believe, on the galley-slave of life who puts out to sea alone, in the darkness of night, beneath a firmament no longer illumined by the beacon-fires of the ancient hope!'

Wise after the event, we can recognize in this despairing plea one of the first signs of Huysmans' return to the faith he had abandoned in his youth. Yet at the time he wrote *A Rebours*, there seemed little likelihood that Huysmans would ever take the road to Rome, for he knew no practising Catholics, he never had occasion to meet a priest, and he had not set foot inside a church for many years. Even when his conversion was an accomplished fact, he was still unable to explain how he had come to write that spontaneous and impassioned prayer of des Esseintes.

Huysmans spent the summer of 1883 copying and recopying the manuscript of his novel, which he was to deliver to Charpentier in early October. A little-known writer called Francis Enne, who visited him in his Rue de Sèvres flat one hot August afternoon, records that he was far from anticipating success for *A Rebours*.[18] Indeed, after they had drunk several pints of iced beer together, and demolished several famous literary reputations, Huysmans told his visitor: 'It will be the biggest fiasco of the year – but I don't care a damn! It will be something nobody has ever done before, and I shall have said what I want to say . . .'

In fact, when it was published in May 1884, his novel proved to be anything but a fiasco. As Huysmans stated in the preface he wrote twenty years later, *A Rebours* 'fell like a meteorite into the literary fairground, provoking anger and stupefaction, especially among the Press'. He was naturally delighted to find that the book was causing such a sensation, and he told Zola:[19]

> From the letters I'm getting, and from what people tell me, I gather that there's a tremendous rumpus going on! I seem to have trodden heavily on everybody's toes. The Catholics are exasperated; the others accuse me of being a clerical in disguise – when in fact I'm nothing, *saperlotte!* – the Romantics are furious about the attacks on Hugo, Gautier and Leconte de Lisle, while the Naturalists are offended by my hero's loathing for modern life.

The vogue which *A Rebours* was enjoying, however, was no mere *succès de scandale*. For every outraged literary critic who condemned the novel there were a hundred admiring readers who, like Paul Valéry five years later,[20] made it their 'Bible and bedside book'. And Huysmans, who had imagined that he was 'writing for a dozen persons', found that he had given expression to the aspirations of all those who scorned accepted aesthetic standards, who delighted in the perverse and the artificial, and who sought to extend the boundaries of emotional and spiritual experience: the writers and artists, in fact, of that movement in France and England which came to be known as the Decadence. Just how closely the paradoxical ideas and exotic style of *A Rebours* approximated to the ideals of this new movement was shown in April 1886, when the first issue of *Le Décadent* carried an editorial that might well have been written by des Esseintes himself. Moreover, the following years were to witness the appearance of many works which were manifestly inspired by Huysmans' novel – among them Remy de Gourmont's *Sixtine*, George Moore's *A Mere Accident* and *Mike Fletcher*, Oscar Wilde's *The Picture of Dorian Gray, Salome*, and *The Sphinx*. Nor did the authors of these works attempt to hide their admiration for *A Rebours*. Remy de Gourmont, interviewed by Jules Huret in 1891,[21] insisted that 'we should never forget what a great debt we owe to that memorable breviary'. George Moore called it 'that prodigious book, that beautiful mosaic', and declared that 'a page of Huysmans is as a dose of opium, a glass of something exquisite and spirituous'.[22] And in *The Picture of Dorian Gray*,[23] Wilde paid an eloquent tribute to the potency of Huysmans' novel, telling how, as his hero turned its pages, 'it seemed to him that in exquisite raiment, and to the delicate sound of flutes, the sins of the world were passing in dumb show before him. Things that he had dimly dreamed of were suddenly made real to him. Things of which he had never dreamed were gradually revealed . . .'

Huysmans' friends in Paris were no less enthusiastic. The artist Whistler wrote to him the day after *A Rebours* was published, praising his 'marvellous book'; Paul Bourget congratulated him on his penetrating study of 'the neurosis of an intellect'; and Maupassant told him that 'it bewitched me, it set me laughing and dreaming, it captivated me with its style, with its strange truthfulness, with its deliciously droll philosophy'.[24] In an entry in his *Journal*, Edmond de Goncourt wrote on 16 May that 'they may say what they like against the book, it brings a touch of fever to the brain – and only writers of merit can produce books which do that'. A week later, a letter reached Huysmans from Paul Verlaine,[25] who was then living at Coulommes with his mother, praising *A Rebours*, and adding characteristically: 'Of course, the first thing I looked at was the paragraph about myself, for which I send you my warmest thanks.' And Stéphane Mallarmé, though doubtless a little amused by Huysmans' interpretation of the Symbolist aesthetic, also sent the novelist an enthusiastic letter[26] of appreciation:

Here it is [he wrote], the one book that had to be written – and how well you have written it! – at precisely this moment in our literary history! Considering it now as it lies on the table before me, its treasures of learning gathered together beneath my gaze, I really cannot imagine it other than it is; yet you know how, in the hour of reverie after reading a book – even a work one admires – the mind almost always conjures up a *different* book. But no! here everything is as it should be, nothing is missing: scents, music, liqueurs, old books and books that almost belong to the future – not forgetting, of course, the flowers! – all these together form a complete picture of the paradise which sensation alone can offer a man in search of modern or primitive pleasures . . . As for what you said about me, I know it was not said to please, so I will not thank you for it; but I must tell you how truly and profoundly happy I am that my name should appear in this beautiful book, this inner room of your mind, feeling so much at home there, and wearing such magnificent robes woven in the most exquisite spirit of sympathy!

In comparison, Zola's reaction to *A Rebours* was chilly in the extreme. He wrote a long letter to Huysmans from Médan on 20 May,[27] in which he indulged in piecemeal criticism of the novel, while carefully ignoring its deeper implications; and when in the end he ventured a prophecy, it was only that 'this book will at least count as a curiosity among your other works . . .'

This letter placed Huysmans in something of a quandary. He could see that the master of Médan had been puzzled and annoyed by *A Rebours*, and although he no longer respected Zola's literary creed, he still valued his friendship. He therefore sought to reassure the older writer in a letter which combined genuine modesty with deliberate untruth. First of all, he admitted that the form of his novel was far from satisfactory, and that the absence of dialogue produced a monotonous effect; but he pleaded that 'given the subject,

I couldn't arrange the book in any other way, even though this was bound to result in a certain incoherency'. He went on to deny that des Esseintes' tastes in contemporary literature bore any resemblance to his own, concluding with a hint that the entire novel was nothing more than a literary leg-pull.

> I threw my opinions overboard [he wrote], and put forward views which are diametrically opposed to those I hold, and which nobody could possibly attribute to me, since I wrote the very opposite in *L'Art moderne*. Thus I stated that des Esseintes preferred *La Tentation* to *L'Éducation, La Faustin* to *Germinie, La Faute de l'Abbé Mouret* to *L'Assommoir* – that's clear enough! – and this complete reversal of my real preferences enabled me to express some extremely unhealthy ideas and also to sing Mallarmé's praises (which I considered rather a good joke!) . . . The sceptics are beginning to suspect that the whole thing is just a colossal hoax, and they are probably pretty close to the truth. The long and the short of it is that I had a book on the brain, I've written it out of my system – and now it's finished with![28]

But Zola was not so easily deceived, and he forced the matter to an issue when Huysmans visited Médan in early July. In the 1903 preface to *A Rebours*, Huysmans tells how, 'one afternoon while we were taking a stroll together in the country, he suddenly stopped, and with a frown reproached me with this book, saying that I had delivered a terrible blow to Naturalism, that I was leading the school astray, that I was burning my boats with such a novel, since no type of literature was possible in this genre, exhausted by a single volume; and amicably – for he was a good fellow – he urged me to return to the beaten track, and set to work on a novel of manners'. In reply, Huysmans had to admit that he no longer had any sympathy with Zola's theories, and that 'the novel as he conceived it seemed to me hackneyed, moribund, and – whether he liked it or not – totally lacking in interest'. With this conversation in a country lane near Médan, the ties that bound Huysmans to Zola were completely severed: the author of *A Rebours* might remain Zola's friend, but he could not now be numbered among his disciples.

Strangely enough, only two of Huysmans' contemporaries appear to have foreseen this development; and these two were also the first critics to appreciate the profound spiritual significance of *A Rebours*. One was the fiery Catholic pamphleteer, Léon Bloy. The other was his friend and mentor, the ageing 'Connétable des Lettres', Jules Barbey d'Aurevilly.

Bloy's review of the book appeared in *Le Chat Noir* on 14 June, under the title of 'Les Représailles du Sphinx'. It described Huysmans as 'formerly a Naturalist, but now an Idealist capable of the most exalted mysticism, and as far removed from the crapulous Zola as if all the interplanetary spaces had suddenly accumulated between them'.[29] According to Bloy, Huysmans' supreme achievement was to have demonstrated that man's pleasures were finite, his needs infinite – and also that everyone had to decide for himself 'whether to guzzle like the beasts of the field or to look upon the face of God'.

I know of no contemporary work [he wrote] which puts this alternative in a more definitive or a more terrifying form than *A Rebours*. There is not a single page in this book where the reader can enjoy a breathing-space and relax in some semblance of security; the author allows him no respite. In this kaleidoscopic review of all that can possibly interest the modern mind, there is nothing that is not flouted, stigmatized, vilified, and anathematized by this misanthrope who refuses to regard the ignoble creatures of our time as the fulfilment of human destiny, and who clamours distractedly for a God. With the exception of Pascal, no one has ever uttered such penetrating lamentations . . .[30]

The following month, *Le Constitutionnel* and *Le Pays* published an article on Huysmans' novel by Barbey d'Aurevilly which ranks among the most outstanding reviews written in the last century.[31] Like Bloy before him, Barbey noted that 'behind the hero's boredom and his futile efforts to conquer it, there is a spiritual affliction which does even more to exalt the book than the author's considerable talent'. He went on to draw a suggestive parallel between *A Rebours* and *Les Fleurs du mal*; and finally, with astonishing prescience, he looked forward to Huysmans' eventual conversion.

Baudelaire [he wrote], the satanic Baudelaire, who died a Christian, must surely be one of M. Huysmans' favourite authors, for one can feel his presence, like a glowing fire, behind the finest pages M. Huysmans has written. Well, one day, I defied Baudelaire to begin *Les Fleurs du mal* over again, or to go any further in his blasphemies. I might well offer the same challenge to the author of *A Rebours*. 'After *Les Fleurs du mal*,' I told Baudelaire, 'it only remains for you to choose between the muzzle of a pistol and the foot of the Cross.' Baudelaire chose the foot of the Cross. But will the author of *A Rebours* make the same choice?

Twenty years later, Huysmans was to answer in all simplicity: 'The choice is made.'

2. THE COUNTRYMAN

FOR Huysmans the spring of 1884 was doubly fateful: it witnessed not only the end of his active association with Émile Zola, but also the beginning of his famous and ill-omened friendship with Léon Bloy. We do not know exactly when François Coppée brought the two men together, but it was probably about the time *A Rebours* was published, since Bloy's press copy of the novel[1] bore the rather formal dedication: '*A Monsieur Léon Bloy, A Rebours, cette haine du siècle*'. Though they seemed a strangely assorted pair – the cold, cynical northerner and the dynamic little southerner – their acquaintance soon ripened into friendship; and after reading 'Les Représailles du Sphinx', Huysmans cast aside his habitual reserve.

> I need hardly tell you [he wrote[2]] how pleased and proud I was to read such magnificent praise – you can imagine how I felt. For a man who has been accustomed to having only insane and insulting remarks flung at him all his life, it's an indescribable, an almost physically unbearable, joy to find someone appreciating and explaining his poor writings . . . Thank you again for the delightful consolation you have brought me, my dear friend, and on this icy white paper allow me to send you a warm handshake.

In the same letter, however, he administered a gentle rebuke which could be cited as proof – if proof were needed – of his essential kindness and loyalty. Although Bloy knew nothing of the work of Mallarmé and Verlaine, he had blandly condemned the two poets as 'crazy simpletons' in his review of *A Rebours*. Huysmans chided him for this 'virulent attack' and begged him to consider that 'they are two down-trodden artists, that the public doesn't know them, that they've never had any success, and that they'll probably die without even finding a publisher – while so many worthless rhymesters prosper and grow fat'. And he urged Bloy to 'spare the poor artists whom everyone scorns, even if you too dislike their work'.

Bloy had good reason to take this appeal to heart. A few weeks earlier he had been dismissed from the staff of *Le Figaro*, after hundreds of readers had protested against his scathing articles; and now, at the age of 38, the author of *Propos d'un entrepreneur de démolitions* found himself without a job and without a public. In any case, none but his friends – Jules Barbey d'Aurevilly, a clerk called Georges Landry, a Swiss librarian called Louis Montchal, and Huysmans himself – honestly admired his work, which alternated between the scatological and the sublime; though they made up in enthusiasm what they lacked in numbers. Thus when Huysmans received a copy of *Le Révélateur du Globe*, Bloy's study of Christopher Columbus, he wrote[3] to the author:

This book is full of a strange beauty, born of unassuaged sorrow and unquenchable, righteous anger at the endless infamy of mankind. I love you for these explosions of holy wrath, for this hatred which you vent upon the vomitory ignominy of this age; and from the professional point of view, I particularly admire your high art for the oratorical innovations you produce, the marvellously decisive adverbs, the precise and vigorous epithets. Read aloud, your prose has superb sonorous and rhythmic qualities not to be found in any other writer's work – and yet some half-witted polygraphs think it clever to call you a little Veuillot! A colossal gulf separates your art from his, but what hope is there of ever getting the public to understand that? For them you are simply a little Veuillot, and I'm a little Zola. The labels have been stuck on, and we shall carry them all our lives – for we are no longer young enough to believe in literary justice, present or future . . .

During the summer of 1884 the two men became firm friends and almost inseparable companions. Indeed, they spent so much time together that Barbey d'Aurevilly would occasionally complain that Bloy was forsaking the Rue Rousselet for the Rue de Sèvres. In July, however, they were parted, for Huysmans then decided to take his annual holiday in the country – alone. 'I leave tomorrow for an authentic village', he told Mallarmé on 11 July;[4] 'and I shall probably stay there for three weeks, unless I find it just too boring. This I may well do, as I'm not much of a countryman and have always preferred art and artifice to the wide open spaces . . .'

The 'authentic village' was Jutigny, a hamlet four miles from Provins, in the department of Seine-et-Marne. Huysmans had been introduced to the district in 1882 by Louis Bescherer, whose wife Virginie was a native of Jutigny.[5] On that occasion he had visited the then dilapidated Château de Lourps, which stands on a nearby hillside overlooking the valley of the Voulzie, and which Huysmans chose to be des Esseintes' birthplace in *A Rebours*. The owner of the château was a florist called Simonot who had formerly been steward of the Lourps estate; and it was at Simonot's house in Jutigny that Huysmans stayed in July 1884. As he had expected, country life proved rather tedious at times, but he admitted in a letter to Zola[6] that it was acting as a soothing poultice for his tortured nerves.

On the 12th [he wrote] I landed here at Jutigny, a canton of Donnemarie, where I found a country cottage prepared for me that looks like a theatrical décor – complete with big fireplace, tall dressers and raftered ceiling. I'm now settled in and am savouring the pleasure of doing absolutely nothing – nothing, that is, except chatting with the local rustics, who are really interesting . . . I went with one of them to buy a calf at the market at Bray-sur-Seine – an extraordinary operation that lasts an hour and is accompanied with potations of white wine. Insults are exchanged all the time, and finally they decide on the calf that was picked out right at the beginning! What a crafty and yet what a stupid lot they are!

To while away the time, Huysmans took notes on the people of Jutigny, starting with the yokels he met at market or in the village inn on Sundays, and finishing with Jules and Honorine Legueux – the aged peasant couple who leased the Lourps farm from Simonot and who were later portrayed as Antoine and Norine in *En Rade*. Sometimes, too, he climbed the hill to the deserted Château de Lourps, which he found 'suffering from all the infirmities of a horrible old age, with its catarrhal gutter-pipes, its blotchy plaster, its rheumy windows, its fistular stonework, and its leprous bricks . . .'[7] Even allowing for our author's penchant for grisly descriptions of this kind, it is clear that the building was in a ruinous condition – yet Huysmans apparently thought it had possibilities as a rural 'Thebaid'. And before he left for Paris on 6 August, he arranged to rent a few rooms in the château the following summer.

Shortly after returning home, Huysmans told Zola that he was once more at work on his war novel, *La Faim*; but it seems that he soon realized the impracticability of disinterring this youthful project, for he gave up the attempt. Nor had he much cause to be satisfied with his next published work, *Un Dilemme*, which appeared in the September and October issues of *La Revue Indépendante*. This story had been written in the spring of 1884, as a kind of matter-of-fact antidote to the extravagant fantasy of *A Rebours*, and Huysmans himself dismissed it[8] as merely 'a simple little tale intended to show once again the unalterable turpitude of the bourgeoisie'. It tells how, after the death of his only son, a business-man and his rascally lawyer conspire to cheat the boy's mistress of her rightful inheritance. It reads rather like a *conte* by Maupassant.

While Huysmans was beginning to wonder whether he would ever write another novel, Léon Bloy was struggling manfully with his first – *Le Désespéré* – which had been commissioned by his publisher, the young and enterprising Pierre-Victor Stock. There was, of course, nothing of the

ordinary novelist about Bloy, and *Le Désespéré* was certainly
no ordinary novel: written largely on the model of *A Rebours*,
it partook of autobiography, theological dissertation, and
scurrilous pamphlet. Its hero, Caïn Marchenoir, was a barely
disguised self-portrait, and its heroine was drawn from Bloy's
former mistress, Anne-Marie Roulé, a prostitute turned
visionary who had implanted in her lover's mind the belief
that he was a new Elijah. After living with him for five years,
this strange woman had been committed to the mental
hospital of Sainte-Anne in June 1882. Bloy always held her
memory sacred, but her place had soon been taken by a
girl called Berthe Dumont, a gentle creature he had found
begging barefoot in the Paris streets. Poor though he was,
Bloy had taken her under his protection, and in October 1884
he moved with Berthe and her mother into rooms at Asnières,
where Huysmans and Anna Meunier used to visit them at
week-ends.

Sometimes Bloy would take an early-morning train into
Paris and spend the whole day with Huysmans, in his office at
the Ministry and in his Rue de Sèvres flat. At this time his
admiration for Huysmans knew no bounds. 'Huysmans is an
unhappy man because he is a great man', he told Louis
Montchal; and in another letter to Geneva he declared that 'if
you knew Huysmans you would realize that his greatness as a
writer is nothing compared with his greatness as a man'.[9] One
can therefore imagine his feelings when he heard that the
doyen of French critics, Francisque Sarcey, intended to pillory
his friend in a public lecture on *A Rebours*. This lecture was
given in the Salle des Capucines towards the end of October
and was attended by Huysmans and Bloy, the one listening
with a sardonic smile on his lips, the other bursting with
suppressed indignation. 'I can assure you', Bloy wrote to
Montchal,[10] 'that it was only because Huysmans didn't want
to be noticed in the hall and begged me to keep quiet that I
refrained from telling that old hypocrite just what I thought
of him. As it was, I confined myself to bawling out a few
woefully inadequate interjections . . .'

For the past few weeks Bloy had been living on a loan of

500 francs from Louis Montchal – one of several hundred loans which his friends made him and which he rarely, if ever, repaid. But now some other source of income had to be found, to support Bloy and his two protégées while he was writing his novel. After several unsuccessful attempts to raise money in an orthodox fashion, he despairingly resolved to strike out on his own and publish a weekly review written entirely by himself. When Huysmans was told of this project he immediately offered his collaboration, and on 8 December Bloy wrote[11] optimistically to Louis Montchal that the pamphlet, which had been entitled *Le Pal* (The Stake), 'should be a success – because of the violent tone we should adopt, and also because of the unexpected association of our two names'. Between them, however, they found they had barely enough money for the printing of a periodical, let alone the necessary publicity; and Huysmans, doubtless remembering the fiasco of *La Comédie Humaine*, abandoned his share in the scheme and tried to persuade Bloy to do the same. Finding that this was impossible, he loyally gave his friend what help he could, lending him money for the first issue and drawing up a contract with a printing house;[12] but even so, only four issues of *Le Pal* were published. As Huysmans had feared, the publicity it received was hopelessly inadequate – but this was not simply due to a shortage of funds. On 10 March the newspaper *La France* named thirty-eight prominent writers whom Bloy had 'dragged through the slime', and called for an embargo on all articles dealing with *Le Pal* or its author; the resultant 'conspiracy of silence' accomplished the ruin of Bloy's first editorial enterprise.

His funds were now completely exhausted, and he felt great anxiety for his womenfolk, whom he had left without money or food in Huysmans' former lodgings at Fontenay-aux-Roses. Since his friends were at present unable to help him, he turned in despair to an old enemy, Edmond de Goncourt; and citing Huysmans as a common friend, he boldly asked the veteran novelist for 50 francs. Not unnaturally, Goncourt suspected blackmail, and indignantly rejected Bloy's request; he also accused Huysmans of complicity, and the author of *A*

Rebours was obliged to write denying that he had authorized Bloy to use his name. As for Bloy himself, he was once again saved by a loan from Geneva – but only to be overwhelmed a little later by a new catastrophe. On 11 May, after suffering excruciating pain for eight hours, Berthe Dumont died of tetanus, and Bloy found to his horror that he could not afford to give his mistress a decent burial. This time he applied for help, not to an enemy, but to an old and wealthy friend – the novelist Paul Bourget. But Bourget, like Goncourt, shut his heart and his purse to Bloy's pleas, and in the end it was Huysmans and Georges Landry who bore the expense of the funeral.[13]

In the following months Huysmans did everything in his power to help and comfort his friend, who wrote to Montchal[14] praising 'my good Huysmans, on whom I have leaned continually in these trying days, and who has cared for me like the most patient and devoted of nurses'. Yet, wretched though his situation was, Bloy told Montchal that Huysmans was even unhappier.[15] 'I am less to be pitied than Huysmans,' he wrote, 'for I have not yet abandoned all hope . . .'

Soon, however, the two friends were to enjoy a brief respite together. In August 1885 Huysmans travelled to Lourps to spend a few weeks there with Anna Meunier, one of her daughters, and her sister Joséphine. Writing to his friend Alexis Orsat on the 19th,[16] he lauded the picturesque charms of the château, which he described as 'a romantic ruin, quiet and remote, overgrown with moss and ivy; a huge building with vaults and dovecotes, swarming with pigeons and swallows, buffeted by every wind that blows, yet preserving an air of majesty in its distress'. This, however, was only one side of the picture, and he went on to paint the other, in what he called 'a naturalistic study of the dilapidated domain of the old Marquesses of Saint-Phale'. Only five or six rooms in the château were habitable, the rest being at the mercy of wind, weather, and birds; the local butcher refused to climb the hill to Lourps with their meat, even for extra money; they had to leave a basket at the bottom of the long drive where the baker deposited their bread as he went by; and any water they needed had to be laboriously drawn from a deep well in the courtyard.

> I can see you shuddering [he wrote] over this far from Rabelaisian *résumé* – but on the whole, what with plenty of meat and eggs every day, we are not doing too badly. On the other hand, Anna is feeling dead-tired just now. She isn't sleeping well, and at night she's terrified by the long dark corridors, the echo of our footsteps, and the shindy made by the birds. I only hope she will get over it and pay no attention to the local rustics, who believe the château has been haunted ever since the last of the Saint-Phales died.
>
> At the moment, Joséphine is having a nap, I'm nodding off, and Tonine, worn out by her little games, is snoozing with her fists tightly clenched.
>
> Well, that's nearly all our news. Recently we've taken to dining in Jutigny and drinking rather more than usual. During the day, I explore the delightful woodland paths, I sit reading on the lawn, I live in perfect peace. In the evening, when we are by ourselves, bezique helps to pass the time, and of course there's always the bed . . .

From this peaceful retreat Huysmans' thoughts went to Bloy, who was now working twelve hours a day illuminating *souvenirs de première communion* for the Maison Lebel-Bouasse. 'I want him to come out here,' he told Georges Landry;[17] 'for only the sovereign bromide of country life could soothe him and set him to rights after the appalling shocks he has sustained.' And to Bloy himself he sent money for the journey, with this characteristic invitation:

> Ah, Bloy! I am filled to overflowing with wrath, ready to join with you in vomiting bellyfuls of bile upon the despicable world we live in – so if you came here we could have some good days together! In spite of the pecuniary sump into which a diabolical fate has plunged us, like sippets in a soft-boiled egg, you would find

here a momentary haven of refuge, a temporary berth, a shelter from the raging tempest of human folly.

Bloy's arrival was delayed for a few days, and it was not until 2 or 3 September that he irrupted into Jutigny, clutching a pillow and blankets, and scowling ferociously at the bemused inhabitants. But at Lourps he was able to relax, enjoying peace of mind and body for the first time for many months. Mlle Antonine Meunier, as a gracious and charming old lady, could still recall the scene at Lourps in those far-off September days. While her mother and her aunt were resting indoors she used to play with her ball on the lawn, close to where 'Papa Georges' and the gentleman with the bushy moustache sat perched on little canvas stools, talking and gesticulating excitedly. She remembered too that she could not understand what they were saying – which is perhaps as well, for they were probably 'vomiting bellyfuls of bile upon the despicable world'. On the 7th, however, Bloy had to go back to Paris, and the others left Lourps with him. 'Our unhappy des Esseintes', he wrote,[18] 'is also returning to a life of misery – the misery of a man of genius harnessed to the administrative dung-cart. What a monstrous fate!'

In Paris Huysmans and Bloy rejoined a third unhappy friend: 47-year-old Jean-Marie-Mathias-Philippe-Auguste, Comte de Villiers de l'Isle-Adam. The brilliant author of *Claire Lenoir, Axël* and the *Contes cruels*, whom Baudelaire and Wagner had proclaimed a genius at the age of twenty, had recently been reduced to the status of a human punch-ball: for the pitiful wage of 60 francs a month, he was employed as a sparring-partner in a Paris gymnasium. Huysmans had first met him in the offices of *La République des Lettres* in 1876, and like the hero of *A Rebours*, he had always had the greatest admiration for Villiers' work. But it was only now, during the last few years of Villiers' life, that the two men became close friends.

Villiers had good news for Huysmans and Bloy when he saw them on their return. He told them that a new daily newspaper called *La Journée* was soon to be launched in Paris, and that by a fortunate coincidence he happened to be on good terms with the editor. As a result, at an interview on 2 October the three writers were each invited to contribute a weekly article or story to *La Journée*, and were promised a high rate of pay. They were naturally jubilant over this unexpected change in their fortunes, but a succession of rejection slips soon chilled their enthusiasm. When it finally went out of circulation, in March 1886, *La Journée* had published only five stories by Villiers, one article by Bloy – and nothing by Huysmans.[19]

Huysmans fared rather better with two other commissions he received about this time. The first was from *La Revue Illustrée* for some articles on the poorer suburbs of Paris – the sort of assignment which Huysmans could still enjoy, though he grumbled to Zola about 'the great booby of an artist' he had to take with him on his Sunday excursions.[20] The other commission was for a brief autobiography,[21] to be included in Léon Vanier's series *Les Hommes d'Aujourd'hui*. Huysmans wrote this with his tongue in his cheek, for it eventually appeared under the pseudonym 'A. Meunier' and contained some amusing parodies of his critics. Thus we find 'A. Meunier' delivering himself of the opinion that:

> One of the great faults of M. Huysmans' books is, I consider, the unique type who plays first fiddle in each of his works. Cyprien Tibaille and André, Folantin and des Esseintes, are in fact one and the same person, situated in different milieux. And it is perfectly obvious that this person is none other than M. Huysmans himself. Here we are a long way from the perfect art of Flaubert, who effaced himself behind his work and created characters of such astonishing diversity: M. Huysmans is clearly quite incapable of a like effort. His sardonic, puckered face can be seen lurking behind every page, and I feel sure that the constant intrusion of the author's personality, however interesting that personality may be, detracts from the quality of his work and ultimately wearies the reader . . .

On the other hand, he thought fit to prophesy that 'if there is any justice in this world, then it will eventually favour M. Huysmans'. The cover of this pseudo-biography bore a lively cartoon by Coll-Toc, showing Huysmans thrusting his 'sardonic, puckered face' through a list of his works.

The year ended on a note of despair, with Bloy informing François Coppée on 31 December[22] that Huysmans was 'lying on the road from Jerusalem to Jericho, stripped of his garments and three-quarters dead . . . with not a Samaritan in sight!' It seems that the Rue de Sèvres bindery had been losing money so heavily that Huysmans was now threatened with bankruptcy and, *ipso facto*, with dismissal from the Civil Service. But he was too proud to beg from his friends, and it was without his knowledge that Bloy wrote to Coppée, imploring the poet to help 'a victim of the highest literary probity . . . one of the rarest writers of this *fin de siècle*'.

Coppée's help saved the situation, but 1886 saw little improvement in Huysmans' finances. The only major work which he published during the year was a new and enlarged edition of *Croquis parisiens*, and the profits from this source were negligible. Then, later in the year, his hopes were raised by the death of his uncle Constant Huysmans, but a promised legacy of 25,000 francs failed to materialize. Bloy told Montchal[23] that 'after wealthy relatives had worked on him for a long time, the old man arranged that Huysmans should inherit the money only after the death of *six* other people, who are to have a life-interest in it while the real heir won't be able to touch a single centime!' The relatives in question had apparently turned Constant against his nephew by representing him as a depraved and dissolute wastrel. They could not have known that he had once edited Musset's *Gamiani* under Constant's very nose, but they had found other convincing 'proofs' of his immorality – including an article in which Félicien Champsaur hinted that the author of *Les Sœurs Vatard* was on intimate terms with the girls in his workshop. And as a result of their machinations, Huysmans had been virtually disinherited by the one member of his father's family whose trust and affection he had never doubted.

Strangely enough, Félicien Champsaur also had some connexion with the death of one of Huysmans' friends, Robert Caze, in March 1886. A journalist by profession and a novelist by inclination, Caze was often to be seen at literary gatherings, notably at Edmond de Goncourt's famous *grenier* at Auteuil. He also had his own *grenier* at No. 13 Rue Condorcet, where he entertained many of the leading Impressionist painters and such writers as Huysmans, Hennique, and Félix Fénéon. In February 1886 a quarrel with Félicien Champsaur led to a duel in the Meudon woods between Caze and a journalist called Charles Vignier, and in this encounter Caze was mortally wounded. He died six weeks later, on 28 March, leaving a widow and two young children without any resources except the profits from his last novel, *Grand'mère*, published a few days before his death.[24] Huysmans' last, harrowing visit to Robert Caze is described in this extract from Edmond de Goncourt's *Journal*:

> *Tuesday, 23 March* 1886 . . . I sit down in the little study, where Huysmans, Vidal, and an Impressionist painter are waiting. Through the open door I can hear the *glouglous* of all sorts of drinks the wounded man keeps tossing down, one after the other, in his unquenchable thirst; I can hear the incessant coughing of his consumptive wife; I can hear the scolding voice of the maid, as she tells one of the children: 'You're taking advantage of your father's illness to do no work.'
>
> The surgeon is expected, but he doesn't come. After waiting for half-an-hour, Huysmans and I get up and go, talking about the dying man and his preoccupation with his novel . . . Huysmans saw him today for a moment, and the only thing he had to say was:
>
> 'Have you read my book?'

Huysmans also told Goncourt that he had received a letter from a Dutch novelist who, though he did not know Caze, offered to send the wounded man a cheque for any sum he cared to name. This generous Dutchman was Arij Prins, a young writer of independent means who had recently left his native town of Schiedam to settle in Hamburg. He had the greatest admiration for Huysmans' work, which he had introduced to the Dutch public in a number of important articles in *De Amsterdammer* and *De Nieuwe Gids;* and in the summer of 1886 he made the first of several visits to Paris to see the French novelist. The two men took an immediate liking to each other, and they corresponded regularly until Huysmans' death.[25]

In the late summer Huysmans again spent a few weeks in the Château de Lourps. There he began writing a short story entitled *En Rade*, based on his previous stay in the château with Anna Meunier. It was a cheerless tale of discomfort and disappointment, in which popular misconceptions of country life were attacked and Romantic illusions rudely shattered. Thus Huysmans recounted at length the material cares which beset his hero and heroine, Jacques and Louise Marles; the peasants he portrayed were not the gentle creatures of George Sand, nor yet the loquacious nymphomaniacs of Émile Zola, but cunning, silent brutes; the golden corn of tradition was described as 'a dirty orange colour', and the harvesters beloved of poet and painter were shown to be 'hairy, bare-chested men, stinking of sweat, and sawing away in strict time at rusty-coloured undergrowth'. Into his grim narrative Huysmans introduced descriptions of three dreams – perhaps simply for the sake of the contrast between bleak reality and colourful fantasy, but more probably in order to achieve a new and comprehensive realism by depicting both a man's conscious and his subconscious life. At this time the world of dreams perplexed and fascinated Huysmans, and in his novel *Là-Bas* he was later to condemn the Naturalists for 'rejecting the supersensible, denying the importance of dreams, and failing to understand that Art only becomes interesting when the senses cease to help us'. But whatever his reasons for writing the three dream-sequences, the effect was to turn what had been a short story into a novel;[26] and Huysmans was still writing *En Rade* when *La Revue Indépendante* started serializing it in November 1886.

The editor of *La Revue Indépendante* was now no longer Félix Fénéon but 24-year-old Édouard Dujardin, who was eventually to establish its reputation as the classical review of the Symbolist movement. Naturalists such as Henry Céard who had written for the old *Revue Indépendante* were now discarded, but the author of *A Rebours* remained a welcome contributor. He sometimes found it difficult, however, to appreciate the tastes and theories of his colleagues – their veneration for Richard Wagner, for example. Dujardin, who had founded *La Revue Wagnérienne* the previous year, has related how on Good Friday 1885 he took Huysmans and Mallarmé to a Wagner concert conducted by the famous Lamoureux, and asked Huysmans to write an article on the music he heard. For Mallarmé this concert was a revelation, and he sat through the performance in silent ecstasy. Huysmans, on the other hand, was observed to be 'noting with amusement a hundred picturesque details, such as the facial expressions assumed by the audience, the paunch of the bass-tuba – and the paunch of Lamoureux himself'. As for 'L'Ouverture de Tannhæuser', the article he wrote after the concert, Dujardin discovered that it was nothing more than a brilliant adaptation of the programme notes.[27]

When Huysmans, Villiers, and Bloy dined together – as they did every Sunday at Huysmans' flat – Villiers would sometimes chaff his host about his heretical indifference to Wagner's music. But usually these meetings of what Bloy called 'the Council of Paupers' were melancholy occasions. Thus in May 1886 Bloy wrote to Louis Montchal: 'Huysmans, Villiers, and I had dinner together again last Sunday – and this dinner of desperate men was really quite a romance! You won't, I hope, think me vain if I say that we three formed a unique group, of great interest for the future of French literature. Well, we were an absolutely defeated group, outlawed by the Press and reduced to dire poverty – and we spent three hours establishing these dismal facts!' And again, in October, Bloy told Adèle Montchal: 'I very much fear that those three unfortunates, Villiers, Huysmans, and Bloy, have tumbled into

No. 10 Rue Boris Vildé, Fontenay.

The Chateau de Lourps.

The Maison Notre-Dame.

No. 31 Rue Saint-Placide.

a paupers' grave, where not even a cross will mark their presence . . .'[28]

Bloy was still hard at work on *Le Désespéré*, and in the course of these dinners he would often ask Huysmans and Villiers for details of the journalistic and literary circles with which they were familiar. After Villiers had told his famous story of the editor who rejected a story of his because 'it bore the hallmark of genius', Huysmans would follow up with anecdotes about the eminent critics and best-selling authors of the day, never dreaming that everything he said would later be held against him. For in 1890, when their friendship was at an end, Bloy reproached Huysmans for having supplied the very information he had asked for, and alleged that Huysmans had 'used me as a devoted catspaw to avenge his own griev-ances and to attack enemies he didn't dare to attack himself'.[29] When one remembers the virulent *Propos d'un entrepreneur de démolitions*, written before Huysmans and Bloy had even met, it becomes obvious that this profession of injured innocence was nothing but a sham – yet it convinced many of Bloy's disciples, and eventually it even convinced Bloy himself. However, his devoted biographer, M. Joseph Bollery, has admitted that there was probably no basis for Bloy's accus-ation.[30] *Amende honorable*.

The printing of *Le Désespéré* began in October 1886, and by mid-November the complete first edition of a thousand copies was almost ready for publication. At the last moment, however, the Press got wind of what was afoot, and threatened to extend the deadly 'conspiracy of silence' to Stock and his firm if he dared to publish Bloy's book. Never a brave man, Stock did not dare. Though Huysmans and Bloy went to his office near the Théâtre-Français, argued with him and pleaded with him, he steadfastly refused to bring out *Le Désespéré* or even to sell the printed paper to another pub-lisher. It seemed likely that Bloy's most important book to date, the product of two years' unceasing work, would never see the light of day.

His few remaining friends – notably Huysmans, Montchal, and the Catholic historian Charles Buet – rallied round magnificently in this crisis. Huysmans wrote to the Belgian author Jules Destrée, asking him to approach the publishers he knew in Brussels and Charleroi on Bloy's behalf;[31] and when eventually a publisher was found in Paris, he went over the manuscript of *Le Désespéré* with Bloy, carefully striking out any passages which might give grounds for a libel action. The actual printing of the book took rather longer than had been expected, for it was done by an old revolutionary on a press which was better adapted to tracts than to full-length novels, but at last *Le Désespéré* made its appearance on the bookstalls, on 15 January 1887. It was much discussed in literary circles, but the general public showed no eagerness to buy a book which all the leading critics – even, surprisingly enough, Barbey d'Aurevilly – studiously ignored. Once again, in fact, the 'conspiracy of silence' proved hideously effective.

Huysmans' novel *En Rade*, which appeared in book form on 26 April, also failed to find favour with the public. It was published by Stock – with whom Huysmans had rashly signed a ten-year contract some time before the Bloy fiasco – and perhaps the young man's publicity methods were not as skilful as Charpentier's. But the principal reason why *En Rade* was not a success was that neither the critics nor the public liked the mingling of dreams and reality in the novel; they felt that exotic visions of Esther and dream-journeys to the moon were out of keeping with descriptions of cattle mating – descriptions of such brutal realism that one critic declared they 'would make even a cowman blush'. Zola voiced the general opinion when he told Huysmans[32] that 'I should have preferred to see the peasants on one side, the dreams on another . . . It seems to me that the contrast you wanted hasn't come about, or at least that it has come about with a confusion which isn't art.' In his reply, Huysmans admitted the justice of this criticism.

As for your opinion [he wrote] on the two legs of this pair of trousers, one down-to-earth and the other up-in-the-air, it is – alas! – mine too. Your comments are absolutely correct. I started with a preconceived idea, a plan to divide the book into reality by day and dream by night. Given that idea, I'd have done infinitely better to have applied it in all its rigour – writing alternately one chapter of reality and one of dreams. It would not have been entirely satisfactory and there would still have been some unevenness, but at least it would have been better than these three devilish big chapters, which look rather as though they'd been scattered haphazardly through the book.

Many critics dismissed the novel as an obvious case of regression, because, apart from the dream-sequences, they could see no connexion between *A Rebours* and *En Rade*, between the exotic story of des Esseintes and the sordid story of Jacques Marles. Yet both tales follow the same pattern of hope, disillusionment, and despair. Both heroes attempt to escape from the misery of life, the hateful company of their fellow men, and both are eventually forced to abandon the attempt. That Huysmans shared to the full the anguish expressed by des Esseintes and Jacques Marles is shown by this extract from one of the *Croquis parisiens* of 1886, significantly entitled 'Obsession':

Inevitably I begin counting the days. One more week, and then I shall have to pack my bags, go into the town, and find a cab. I shall have to endure the ear-splitting noise of a railway-carriage crammed with creatures whose faces can inspire nothing but repugnance. There will be the arrival in Paris and then, after a restless night, the return to a life made hideous by the tortuous torments of the mind, by the forever frustrated hopes of the senses, by the lively antipathies which must be overcome if one wants enough food to eat, enough money to pay the rent. Ah! to think that there will always be a Before and an After, and never a Now which endures!

The same note of disillusionment was sounded in an entry Huysmans made in his diary on 10 May 1887.[33] That evening he was disturbed by noises in the courtyard of No. 11, and looking down from his narrow balcony, he saw a wagon being loaded with luggage and furniture from one of the flats. He guessed that the tenants, like so many Parisians, were migrating for the summer months to some little village in the country, not far from the capital. How foolish, he thought, was the idea that happiness could be found by escaping from Paris to 'a poor but peaceful Médan – the dream everyone has at the approach of summer!' And yet, this was the dream he too had cherished for several years, the idea which had led him to seek refuge in the lonely Château de Lourps. He had learnt his lesson. He knew now that though his surname might signify 'countryman',[34] the countryside could offer him nothing more than temporary physical and mental relaxation. He knew that henceforth he would have to look elsewhere for 'a Now which endures' – abiding spiritual content.

3. THE FRIEND

AMONG those who knew him only slightly or by hearsay, Huysmans was reputed to be irascible, ill mannered, and virtually inaccessible. His friends and colleagues, on the other hand, always described him as considerate, warm-hearted, and extremely hospitable. The truth probably lies somewhere between these two estimates of his character. Huysmans certainly did not suffer fools gladly – if, indeed, he suffered them at all; and strangers or casual acquaintances who tried to intrude on his privacy were assured of a chilly reception. But his forbidding manner, as those near to him soon discovered, was assumed as a disguise and protective covering for a gentle nature and a delicate sensibility. He was, in fact, never happier than when surrounded by his friends at dinner on a Sunday evening, delighting in their company and revelling in their conversation. As for his guests, they did not go to the Rue de Sèvres as they would to Médan, Auteuil, or the Rue de Rome – to worship at a literary shrine: they went to Huysmans' home because they knew him for a good host and a good friend.

In the Rue de Sèvres circle, the aristocracy of blood was represented by Villiers de l'Isle-Adam, and the aristocracy of wealth by Francis Poictevin – an eccentric millionaire who took such care over his writings that he is said to have burst into the bedroom of a honeymooning friend to ask his opinion on a stylistic point. But the two most faithful members of the circle, whom Lucien Descaves called 'the firedogs of Huysmans' hearth', were men of humble birth, modest means, and no talent whatsoever: Georges Landry and Henri Girard.[1]

Landry was the elder of the two, being the same age as Huysmans. Remarking on his heavy build and rugged features, one writer has said that 'he looked like a wooden saint in a reredos carved by a medieval craftsman, and he had the soul of a saint to match'. But if he was pious, humble, and meek – so meek, indeed, that Bloy said 'he melted in the hand like a piece of chocolate' – he was also extremely sensual, and he spent most of his life vacillating between concupiscence and contrition. Bloy, who had known him in his youth, introduced him to Barbey d'Aurevilly after the Franco-Prussian War, and soon he was vying with Louise Read, Barbey's secretary and companion, in his devotion to the Connétable des Lettres. He took a room adjoining Barbey's famous *tournebride* at No. 25 Rue Rousselet; he ran the great man's errands, tied his parcels, copied out his manuscripts. All this was a labour of love, but it was richly rewarded, for through Barbey the humble little clerk met many of the greatest writers of the age, and won the friendship of Huysmans and Villiers de l'Isle-Adam. For nearly twenty years he was employed as a book-keeper in a haberdashery in the Rue du Sentier, but in 1891 Huysmans obtained for him the post of chief clerk in the publishing house of Savine. After Huysmans' death he received a small pension from Léon Leclaire, another of the novelist's friends, and this enabled him to spend his last years in modest comfort, reading and re-reading the hundreds of autographed books he had gathered together in his Rue des Bergers flat. He died in a nursing home at Saint-Cloud in July 1924.

Henri Girard was an amiable young man who earned a precarious living for thirty years by playing walking-on parts in small touring companies. He was introduced to Huysmans in 1886 by a clerk at the Ministry of the Interior, and although the novelist affected to despise the theatrical profession, he took a great liking to the young actor. Perhaps this is because Girard was such a very bad actor – for it is recorded that when he was given the part of a valet in a play at the Gymnase, he could not even catch the overcoat which another character had to throw him on entering. He was often away from Paris for long periods, but as soon as he returned from a tour in the provinces or abroad, he would hunt out Georges Landry, and the two friends would then descend on Huysmans – or 'J.-K.' as they affectionately called him. Huysmans later dedicated *Le*

Quartier Saint-Séverin to the young man, and in his will he left Girard the famous portrait of himself by Forain which now hangs in the Versailles Museum. When he eventually left the stage, friends found Girard various jobs including a post as keeper of the non-existent archives of the Théâtre des Variétés – until in 1923 he used his life-savings to buy a little bookshop in the Rue Saint-Sulpice. Before this shop was opened, however, he died suddenly on 30 August 1923, at the age of fifty-eight.

Another frequent visitor to the Rue de Sèvres was Lucien Descaves, who in September 1882, while he was still a young bank clerk in the Crédit Lyonnais, had brought Huysmans a copy of his first novel, *Le Calvaire d'Héloïse Pajadou*, published by Henry Kistemaeckers.[2] The next four years he had spent in military service at Le Havre, where he collected the material for his famous tales of army life, *Les Misères du sabre* and *Sous-offs*. During his leaves in Paris he often enjoyed Huysmans' hospitality, and the older writer continued to give him valuable encouragement and advice when he had completed his term of service and was trying to establish himself in the world of letters. Yet although the two men were soon firm friends, they could not be described as intimates. Descaves always shrank from using the familiar 'J.-K.' form of address which came so easily to Landry and Girard, and it is possible that his attitude to Huysmans was too respectful and reserved to allow of any close relationship between them. In the end, however, Huysmans showed that he fully appreciated the sterling worth of his friend's character, for it was Lucien Descaves whom he chose to act as his executor.

Descaves was not, of course, the only young writer whom Huysmans befriended during the eighties. There was also Maurice de Fleury, then a medical student at the Sainte-Périne nursing home; Gustave Guiches, a former employee of the Gas Company who saw his first novel published when he was twenty; and Gabriel Mourey, who was later to win considerable repute as an art-critic and as a translator of Swinburne and Poe.[3] But Huysmans' greatest affection and solicitude was always reserved for older and unhappier artists who had fallen on evil days. As Gustave Guiches writes in his memoirs,[4] 'Huysmans' nose, which sniffed contemptuously at Nature, spurned womankind, derided enthusiasm, insulted the sun, sullied the blue sky, and disheartened the very flowers – this nose of his would suddenly quiver with pity and emotion at the recital of an artist's misfortunes, thus revealing a good fellow who was capable of sharing to the full a friend's distress, of comforting him with all his heart, and of assisting him with all his money . . .'

The most deserving object of Huysmans' compassion at this time was, without a doubt, Villiers de l'Isle-Adam. Poverty and sickness had prematurely aged this great artist, and only rarely now did the fire come back into his pale blue eyes, to recall the youth of genius who had captivated Baudelaire and Wagner. With his toothless mouth, his hair and beard shot with grey, and his skin the colour of old ivory, he looked some twenty years older than he really was. Yet however poor or ill he might be, he took a pathetic pride in his appearance: his cheeks were always clean-shaven, his silk scarf was kept spotlessly white, and his top hat still sported two pearls – his 'bath-taps' as Forain irreverently called them – out of the nine which had once formed his insignia. The same pathetic pride showed itself in his references to his mistress and his son. Everyone knew that the mother of little Victor or 'Totor' was Marie Dantine, the ugly middle-aged servant who cooked Villiers' meals, mended his clothes – and sometimes shared his bed; but Villiers always maintained that Totor was the fruit of a passionate encounter with a beautiful princess at a reception given by the Princess Ratazzi. Since it would obviously be impossible to offer money to anyone so proud without causing offence, Huysmans had to resort to charitable subterfuge whenever he saw that Villiers was in need of help. And once Bloy confided to Guiches that, although Huysmans would never admit it, the anonymous gifts which occasionally arrived at Villiers' bare rooms in the Rue Blanche were dispatched from No. 11 Rue de Sèvres.

Another friend whom Huysmans frequently helped was Paul Verlaine. The two men first met in the summer of 1884, and afterwards Huysmans told Émile Hennequin that he had found the poet 'a fascinating personality – a combination of a brutal, wheedling pederast and a confirmed drunkard'.[5] If, in the years that followed, he often gave a scolding to the pederast and the drunkard, he would also give a helping hand to the poet – buying him a meal from time to time, persuading his publishers to let him have an advance, or even arranging for him to leave Paris for a retreat at La Grande Chartreuse.[6] Verlaine took Huysmans' criticism in good part, coming as it did from a friend, and he was sincerely grateful for the novelist's help. Thus in a letter to Léon Vanier,[7] after quoting an example of Huysmans' kindness, he added: 'I can always count on more practical sympathy – a billion times more – from one of my peers than from the best of our journalists.' And to Huysmans himself he sent the following sonnet in token of his affection and gratitude.

J.-K. HUYSMANS

Si sa douceur n'est pas excessive,
Elle existe, mais il faut la voir,
Et c'est une laveuse au lavoir
Tapant ferme et dru sur la lessive.
Il la veut blanche et qui sent bon,
Et je crois qu'à force il l'aura telle.
Mais point ne s'agit de bagatelle
Et la tâche n'est pas d'un capon.
Et combien méritoire son cas
De soigner ton linge et sa détresse,
Humanité, crasses et cacas!
Sans jamais d'insolite paresse,
Ô douceur du plus fort des J.-K.,
Tape ferme et dru, bonne bougresse![8]

Huysmans' preoccupation with the troubles of Villiers and Verlaine does him honour, for at this time he was far from well, and Anna Meunier's health was causing him grave anxiety. She had been suffering for some years from a strange malady which one doctor diagnosed as neurosis, another as metritis, and yet another as chlorosis. At first it had taken the form of headaches and nervous prostration, but more recently Anna had also been subject to severe lightning pains in both legs. The doctors whom she consulted, whether qualified or quack, had to admit they were unable to cure her; and in *En Rade*, where Louise Marles is afflicted with the same mysterious disease, Huysmans records that 'all the cauteries, all the blood-lettings, all the probes, all the distressing examinations and abominable operations the poor woman had been forced to endure, had proved of no avail'. One scene from the last chapter of *En Rade* deserves particular mention here, for time has invested it with tragic significance. Jacques Marles and his wife are watching the death-agony of a stray cat stricken with a form of paralysis, when suddenly Louise recognizes the symptoms of her own disease in the animal's convulsive movements, and cries out to Jacques that she knows she will die the same horrible death. It is more than likely that Anna had recently made a similar prophecy when she and Huysmans had watched his cat 'Barre-de-Rouille' dying from gradual paralysis brought on by a fall. We are not told in *En Rade* what eventually happened to Louise Marles, but we know the ultimate fate of Anna Meunier. When she died, a few years later, it was from general paralysis of the insane.

Though modern medical science recognizes only one explanation of this condition, the accompanying neurosis in Anna's case may have had other, subsidiary causes. Thus Gustave Guiches was led to suppose that Anna had once witnessed a railway accident, and that she had never recovered from the shock sustained on that occasion.[9] We shall probably never know what truth there was in this supposition, though it can be revealed that Anna's life was indeed affected by a railway accident: her father, an employee at the Gare du Nord, had been crushed to death between two wagons in the goods yard. But whatever the causes of her illness, its effect was to change the lively, carefree midinette of *En Ménage* into the languid, plangent invalid of *En Rade*. It was a desperately sick woman whom Gustave Guiches met on his first visit to the

Rue de Sèvres, and whom he described in this passage[10] from his memoirs:

> From the dining-room an imploring voice calls: 'Georges! They still haven't arrived, and the joint will be overdone – as usual!'
>
> It is a sweet, plaintive voice, and it is followed by the appearance of a young woman at the study door. She cannot be more than thirty-five years of age. At first sight, it is impossible to tell her social rank: she is not a woman of the working class, but on the other hand she is not exactly a bourgeoise. She is dressed simply, yet with a certain coquetry, and she might easily attain real elegance if it were not for the obvious weariness which oppresses her. A hidden sickness has long been sapping her vitality, until now she is powerless to resist it. She is tall, with pretty features under a mass of fair hair. But her eyes are of so pale a blue, her lips so colourless, her complexion so pallid, that her white face in its golden setting has the languid beauty of a lily stricken unto death.
>
> Huysmans introduces me. She gives me her hand, with a murmured 'Bonjour, monsieur.' But just as I am putting her hand to my lips, she pulls it away so quickly that Huysmans has to explain, with an awkward smile: 'It's her nerves . . . she isn't used to it . . .'
>
> After dinner, I watch her slowly getting up, wearily moving to and fro, listlessly sitting down again: a white-and-gold silhouette, like the gentle ghost of a great joy that has passed away. I watch her suffering, and I can see that out of the corner of his eye, Huysmans is watching her suffering too . . .

Anna's condition grew steadily worse, and by the autumn of 1887 Huysmans was convinced that she had not long to live. He confided his fears to Léon Bloy, who on 27 October wrote to a friend of the Montchals,[11] Mme Henriette L'Huillier:

If only you knew how miserable those around me are! Huysmans, that devoted but unhappy friend of mine, came here to spend Sunday evening with me, and after eating we talked together, by ourselves, for several hours. The unhappy man had just left poor Anna, who appears to be at death's door. You can imagine what a cheerful conversation we had – especially as I was in agony myself.

I have seen something, Henriette, which I had never seen before, and which very few people would think possible.

I have seen the author of *A Rebours* crying. Ah! but he must have been utterly sick at heart, for he is not at all like me and tears do not come easily to him! Life is really too wretched. In his case, the terrible concern which he feels over Anna's condition is aggravated by almost insuperable money troubles, and it is really infuriating to think that this should be the lot of the half-dozen writers who today bring honour to French letters, while unspeakable mountebanks have only to lift their little fingers to obtain the paltry sum of money which would make all the difference to us . . .

Three days later, Louise Read wrote on Huysmans' behalf to Dr. Seligmann, friend and physician of the Connétable des Lettres, begging him to examine the sick woman.[12] She explained that Anna was not receiving proper medical attention because the greater part of the money Huysmans gave her went on food for her mother, her sister, and her two little daughters. 'Huysmans is not the father of these children,' she added, 'but he loves the woman deeply, and has loved her for many years. It is because he loves her that he has asked me to write to you, for he doesn't know where to turn! He has these five mouths to feed, and all on the pittance he gets from the Ministry and the sale of his books. . .' Dr. Seligmann responded nobly to this appeal, and under his care Anna made a partial recovery.[13] But being an honest man as well as a capable doctor, he could hold out no hope of a permanent cure.

Though anxiety was now the keynote of Huysmans' life, he was still able to enjoy some brief interludes of happiness with his friends. One such interlude occurred on 14 July 1887. He had spent the day with Descaves, Bloy, and Louis Montchal – the latter being on a short visit to Paris – and towards evening Descaves suggested that they should all go out to Montrouge, to take pot-luck at his father's house. On the way they called for Villiers, whom they found working in bed, and who accepted Descaves' invitation on condition that Totor might come with him – a condition to which Descaves readily agreed. The evening that followed was unforgettable. Huysmans tells how 'after dinner Villiers sat down at the piano, and, completely lost to the world, sang in his cracked and quavering voice pieces from Wagner interspersed with barrack-room ballads, linking them together with shouts of laughter, crazy jokes, and weird verses'. But the most popular item in this impromptu programme was Villiers' rendering of Baudelaire's poem *La Mort des amants*, sung first to the music of Maurice Rollinat and then to his own. When the party finally broke up, it was too late for Totor to be taken home, so Descaves offered to put father and son up for the night. The others trudged happily back to Paris, convinced that this had been the most joyous and exhilarating *quatorze juillet* of their lives.[14]

Huysmans' host on this occasion was to incur his disapproval a few weeks later, for Descaves was one of the signatories to the *Manifeste des Cinq*, the spectacular denunciation of Zola's *La Terre* that was published in *Le Figaro* on 18 August. In this notorious manifesto he joined with Guiches, Paul Bonnetain, J.-H. Rosny, and Paul Margueritte in attacking 'the indecency and filthy terminology of *Les Rougon-Macquart*' – which the Five attributed to 'a malady of the author's lower organs' – and in repudiating Zola's works 'in the name of our sane and virile ambitions, in the name of our cult, our profound love, our supreme respect for Art'. The five young men actually had little right to call themselves one-time disciples of Zola, and the master of Médan protested that he knew them but slightly, some of them only by name. They had even less justification for sanctimoniously posing as champions of 'decent' literature, for Margueritte had depicted Lesbian love in his novel *Tous quatre*, while Bonnetain had produced a naturalistic study of masturbation entitled *Charlot s'amuse*. As for their wounding allusions to Zola's physical deficiencies, these were quite unpardonable and only brought discredit on the five authors.

Although Huysmans now had as little respect for Zola's writings as Goncourt and Daudet – who were said to have inspired the attack on their more successful colleague – he deplored what he called 'this pompous and remarkably stupid manifesto'. He was relieved to hear that his young friends Descaves and Guiches had played only a minor part in the affair; and in a letter assuring Zola of his sympathy, he suggested that they were not as blameworthy as the others.

> I have not been to Goncourt's house [he wrote] since his return from Champrosay, and that is the only place where one can hear all the gossip and tittle-tattle. But I gather from Orsat, who has it on good authority, that the ill-bred person who concocted the manifesto is Rosny (that was obvious, anyway) and that Bonnetain conceived and launched the affair. The others, it seems, were merely compliant.[15]

Zola replied on the 21st: 'Thank you, my dear Huysmans, for your kind letter. I had already recognized Rosny in the tortuous pedantry of the sentences, and only Bonnetain could have started it. It's all very childish and dirty.'[16] In the course of time the authors of the *Manifeste des Cinq* were themselves to come round to this opinion, and all except Bonnetain eventually made public apology to the man they had so grossly maligned.

Literary circles in Paris saw very little of Huysmans at this time, but he was unable to resist one invitation – a rhymed summons composed by Mallarmé for Édouard Dujardin, bidding him to the 'housewarming' of the new *Revue Indépendante* offices in the Rue de la Chaussée d'Antin on

26 November.[17] Others who responded to this invitation were Mallarmé himself; Jacques-Émile Blanche, George Moore, Teodor de Wyzewa, Jean Ajalbert, Maurice Barrès, Paul Adam, and Théodore Duret. There was also Villiers, enjoying another personal triumph as he regaled his colleagues with an account of his tragi-comic experiences as a candidate for the throne of Greece – or as a candidate for the hand of a prim English Miss. Jean Ajalbert, who was present at this and subsequent dinners given by Dujardin, has left us an intimate record of the scene in his memoirs.[18] Through his eyes, we can see Dujardin proudly displaying his exquisitely tinted waistcoat to a friend; Villiers brushing away a troublesome lock of hair with a familiar, impatient gesture of the hand; Mallarmé tenderly drawing up Méry Laurent's furs over her shoulders; and Huysmans' sardonic smile fading from his lips as he listened in spell-bound admiration to the author of the *Contes cruels*.

The only other literary gathering which Huysmans attended in November was at Goncourt's house on Sunday the 27th. Although he had lately replaced the Marquis de Chennevières as one of Goncourt's future 'academicians', and knew that after Goncourt's death the 'academy' was due to benefit from the sale of the Auteuil art treasures, he only rarely put in an appearance at the famous *grenier*. He explained to Gustave Guiches, whom he was taking on his first visit to Auteuil,[19] that Sunday afternoons at Goncourt's house were generally tedious to the point of boredom.

'It wouldn't be so bad', he said, 'if one could hurry through one's devotions and then dash away. But it just isn't possible, and you have to stay there to the bitter end.'

Surprised, I asked why.

'Why?' he exclaimed in mock horror. 'Why, because every *greniériste* knows that if he were so imprudent, so insane as to leave before everyone else, the door would scarcely have closed behind him when the others would fling themselves upon his work, and that in no time at all it would be dismembered, disembowelled, and devoured, so that not a shred of it, not a crumb of it remained! So, to avoid being eaten up, you sit tight and stay on. And Goncourt, who is only interested in effects and never goes back to causes, is pleased to proclaim that his house is too small to hold so many friends!'

Guiches found that Huysmans' cynical comments on the *grenier* were not as unjust as they seemed. He was, of course, impressed by the books, *bibelots*, eighteenth-century drawings, and Japanese prints which lined the staircase of the Auteuil house and covered the walls of the two rooms on the second floor where Goncourt received his visitors. He was fascinated too by Goncourt himself: an erect, white-haired figure sitting in state at one end of the *grenier*, a white handkerchief knotted about his neck, his delicate hands nervously twisting an old felt hat into tortured shapes. But he also sensed the boredom of Goncourt's guests, and he noticed that on the stroke of seven the *grenier* suddenly emptied, like a classroom at the end of the day.

Another writer, testifying to Huysmans' dislike of the *grenier*,[20] has described his reactions when accosted by some importunate guest – 'lighting a cigarette, as if to drive away an insect, edging away gradually, and looking like a martyr who would dearly love to turn executioner'. He preferred more intimate gatherings such as the Christmas dinner given that year by Gustave de Malherbe to a small circle of friends.[21] Malherbe was a kindly and intelligent man who used his position in the publishing house of Quantin to help many unknown or indigent writers. On this occasion Huysmans, Villiers, Bloy, Guiches, and Maurice de Fleury enjoyed the hospitality of his flat in the Rue Darcet, where they consumed a turkey sent from Geneva by Louis Montchal. Inspired by this rich and unaccustomed Christmas fare, they conceived the idea of founding a literary review of which Malherbe was to be the director, Huysmans the editor, and Montchal the sub-editor. With passionate enthusiasm the six friends discussed the smallest details of this project late into the night, and Bloy wrote to Montchal the next day to acquaint him with the idea. Needless to say, however, this pipe-dream was soon dispelled by the chill winds of reality, and nothing more was heard of it.

During the winter Huysmans contrived to do good turns to both Villiers and Bloy. The paper-merchant Soirat, who had brought out *Le Désespéré* the year before, had recently gone bankrupt, and Bloy was eager to sell the 250 copies of the book remaining in his possession to some other publisher. After several unsuccessful attempts, he appealed to Huysmans, who in December persuaded Léon Vanier to buy the books for 100 francs.[22] Then, in February 1888, after seeing Villiers off on a trip to Brussels, Huysmans wrote to tell Jules Destrée[23] that he was convinced his friend had no definite plans and little money, and begged him to arrange some readings and lectures for Villiers, 'to keep an eye on him, and to see that he doesn't get into trouble'. As a result of Huysmans' intervention, Villiers' visit to Belgium was extremely successful. It brought little profit, however, to poor Marie Dantine – for on his return to Paris, Villiers was waylaid by unscrupulous acquaintances who encouraged him to spend the entire proceeds of his lecture-tour in their company.

Huysmans himself was still in exceedingly poor spirits. *Un Dilemme*, issued in book form by the firm of Tresse et Stock, had been virtually ignored by the critics and was not selling well. The Rue de Sèvres bindery was doing so badly that Mme Guilleminot judged it opportune to retire, ceding her share in the business to a certain Léon Leroux.[24] Anna Meunier's health showed no real improvement; Bloy, as usual, was in the depths of misery; while a macabre note was sounded by Huysmans' charwoman – or rather, his charlady, for she was the widow of a M. Enguerrand de Marigny, a descendant of Philip the Fair's ill-fated minister. Like his ancestor, this man had died by the rope, and Mme Enguerrand de Marigny would sometimes re-enact his suicide in gruesome detail, in a misguided attempt to amuse her employer.[25] It is small wonder that at this period of his life Huysmans' correspondence breathed a spirit of despair. The letter he sent Maurice de

Fleury, for example, congratulating him on his forthcoming marriage, was scarcely calculated to cheer the heart of a young bridegroom.[26]

> Favourable examination results [he wrote], and the prospect of a few joyous days ahead, that's wonderful, my dear Fleury. And I really envy you, for I can't see that the future holds any chance of happiness for me. The discovery of a dry and disinfected spot in the ignominious sewer in which we are paddling is truly an occasion for shouts of joy and loud hosannas. Remember that, so that you may enjoy all the more the delicious drops which the Celestial Pharmacist is about to distil into your potion. Forget Sainte-Périne and all your other troubles, and drink the exquisite liquor slowly and thankfully!
>
> Nothing new here. Snow and wind, then a thaw covering the streets – and my tired old boots – with caramel cream. My Choubersky stove narrowly saved from death when I get home late at night, but keeping me up for hours while I nurse it through its convalescence. Rosy visions, but a life of mauve and muddy hues . . .

Spring, however, brought a promise of better things, for in March Huysmans was invited to become a contributor to a new cosmopolitan periodical, *The Universal Review*. This was the brain-child of one Harry Quilter, a prosperous barrister who dabbled in journalism and art-criticism, with uniformly disastrous results. Obsessed by the idea of founding what he called *une grosse revue internationale*, he sought the collaboration of the most eminent French writers of the day, aided and abetted in this by his friend George Moore.[27] Zola refused his support, possibly because he mistrusted anything even remotely connected with George Moore; but Daudet agreed to serial publication of his novel *L'Immortel*, and Huysmans promised a short story for the first number of the review. The initial instalment of Daudet's serial duly appeared in this issue, on 15 May: Huysmans' story did not. Since the beginning of

April he had been under treatment for conjunctivitis, and consequently his story was not ready in time for publication.

This contretemps was not without its compensations, since it resulted in a meeting between Huysmans and Miss Edith Huybers, a young Englishwoman who acted as the *Universal Review*'s representative in France. It would appear that Miss Huybers spent several years in Paris, where she lodged at No. 13 Rue du Montparnasse, and that she was acquainted with many leading French writers and artists; but as far as is known she is not mentioned in any memoirs of the period. From the letters she sent Huysmans, however, it is possible to form an impression of a woman possessed of considerable charm, intelligence, and tact. It is obvious that she was also extremely loyal to her employer, even though Quilter rarely appreciated or understood the writers she recommended to him. Thus, writing to Huysmans on 9 May, she defended Quilter's action in rejecting a story by Villiers, on the grounds that 'it was more in the nature of a political satire and could not have the same appeal in England as in France'. But she added that 'Mr. Quilter only knows the work of M. Villiers by hearsay, not having had an opportunity to appreciate it personally (all this *strictly between ourselves*, please). On the other hand, he knows your books very well, Monsieur, and admires *A Rebours* as much as anyone. So he is able to judge whether English readers of his review will be capable of understanding you . . .'

In spite of Miss Huybers' assurances, however, Huysmans was to undergo the same humiliation at Quilter's hands as Villiers. He finished writing his story, *La Retraite de Monsieur Bougran*, in the first week of May, and sent it off to London. It was returned to him a fortnight later, accompanied by the following letter from Quilter's Savile Row office, dated 17 May:

I don't think that this nouvelle is at all such a one as you would wish to be represented by in such an important Review as ours. It is so short and uninteresting except to those who are acquainted with the bureaucratic life of Paris, that it would have little significance or attraction in England. What I want from you is a bit of your best work – *intriguant* [*sic*], something which will make a decided stir when I insert it in the Review. As you say you would have no difficulty in placing this special nouvelle with another journal, I beg to return it to you herewith, and to say that as soon as you can conveniently send me another, about half as long again, and with some strong *female* interest, I shall be greatly obliged to you . . .

Needless to say, Huysmans was in no mood to pander to the sexual appetite of the English reading public, and he did not reply to Quilter's letter. As for the rejected story, it was never published, and all trace of the original manuscript has now been lost.[28] However, M. Pierre Lambert, who read it many years ago when it made a brief appearance in the sale-room, has kindly given the present author an account of this unknown work. It told of a *fonctionnaire* whose life loses all meaning and purpose when he retires from the Civil Service. He therefore furnishes one room of his flat with the trappings of his office at the Ministry, hires a retired messenger, and spends his days writing official letters to himself. After a time, of course, he tires of this unrewarding activity; and since some form of clerical work is essential to his well-being, he finally sets up as an ordinary copy-clerk.

Even from this bare summary, it is easy to see why Huysmans decided against publishing this story in France, although he had told Quilter he 'would have no difficulty in placing this special nouvelle with another journal'. He evidently realized that French readers would see his tale for what it was: a mere *réchauffé* of *A Vau-l'Eau* and *A Rebours*, with an ending reminiscent of *Bouvard et Pécuchet*. Innocuous and amusing, if not exactly original, it had seemed to him eminently suitable for an English periodical. But then, how was he to know that English editors expected every work of fiction from across the Channel to contain 'some strong *female* interest'?

Miss Huybers, for her part, was still eager to secure

Huysmans' collaboration, but she knew better than to press him for another story. On 2 June she accordingly wrote to ask if he would consider writing an article for Quilter on Odilon Redon, to be illustrated by the artist. Huysmans' reply was kindly, but not encouraging. He thanked her for her friendly efforts 'to force hazardous drawings and perilous prose upon a recalcitrant review', agreed to consider her proposal, but explained that it was difficult to arrange at the moment as Redon was on holiday. There was another reason why he was reluctant to commit himself. 'I've just been looking', he wrote, 'at the copy of the Review which you were good enough to leave with me. The illustrations are so far removed from anything by Redon that I feel quite alarmed. Are you sure that you have given the matter sufficient thought?'

The illustrations he mentioned were of pictures hung in that year's Royal Academy exhibition, and they accompanied an article in which Quilter praised the exhibitors for refusing to be led astray by 'the flashy dexterities of the French school'. Considering that the other contributions were on the same pedestrian level, it is scarcely surprising that Huysmans' article on Redon, with its promise of 'hazardous drawings and perilous prose', remained unwritten; or that the still more perilous prose of Léon Bloy, whom Huysmans introduced to Miss Huybers, never affronted the readers of *The Universal Review*. In the end, the only member of the 'Council of Paupers' whose work appeared in the review was Villiers, for Quilter relented sufficiently to publish his story *L'Amour sublime* in April 1889.

By this time Miss Huybers had apparently left Paris, and it was only after eight or nine years had passed that Huysmans heard from her again. She was then married to a Mr. Reverdy, and was living in Winchester, Massachusetts.[29] With a nice sense of irony, she wrote to ask Huysmans if he could possibly place a short story she had written with some French periodical, explaining that 'to have published something in French would be most useful to me in my work here'. We may be sure that Huysmans did his best to help her,[30] for she had greater claims on his affection than she can have supposed: it seems, indeed, that he had fallen in love with her at their first meeting. But he had not told her of his love – or if he had hinted at it, she had not understood. And in June 1898, ten years after they had parted, we find him writing in his diary[31] a wistful postscript to this ephemeral love-affair: '*La petite Anglaise pas compris . . .*'

Not all his memories of that summer of 1888 were so melancholy. There was the episode of Verlaine's suit, for example, which in later years he often recalled with amusement.[32] The poet had then only recently come out of the Hôpital Broussais, and was lodged in a dark, squalid, ill-furnished room at No. 14 Rue Royer-Collard. Hearing that he was unwell and practically penniless, Huysmans and Bloy made arrangements for him to spend a holiday with a childhood friend, the Abbé Dewez, in the little Belgian village of Corbion. Money for the journey to Corbion was subscribed by Verlaine's friends, and notably by the publisher Albert Savine; but at the last moment the Abbé Dewez had doubts about the wisdom of introducing a notorious wastrel into his parish, and he withdrew his offer of hospitality. Verlaine's reaction to this was characteristic: he showed no indignation at the priest's conduct, but evinced considerable interest in the money his friends had collected for the journey. Assuring Huysmans that he could be trusted to put this viaticum to a worthy use, he wrote: 'If you can, send me the money as soon as you receive this letter, so that I can buy some clothes with it and die decently – for to die I am resolved, on my honour as a man and as your friend, P. Verlaine.' But Huysmans was not deceived. He knew very well that Verlaine would never bring himself to spend good money on clothes while the bars of Paris were still stocked with absinthe; and the poet was accordingly informed that he would shortly be fitted out at the Belle Jardinière – under the strict supervision of his friends.

On the appointed day, Huysmans, Bloy, and Guiches made their way to the Rue Royer-Collard, where they found Verlaine in a surly, uncooperative mood. The fancy had taken him to have a suit in corduroy velvet, and he made it clear to his friends that he would accept nothing else. In vain did

Huysmans argue that a velvet suit would be too expensive, or that it would soon be ruined by the absinthe with which Verlaine bespattered all his clothes: the poet was adamant. 'I should like to look like a carpenter,' he announced, 'because carpenters are the most magnificent exemplars of human beauty! I want a jacket in ribbed velvet, and baggy trousers with that little pocket for the yellow yardstick – and if I can't have what I want, I swear I shan't wear any clothes at all, but go stark naked like St. John the Baptist!' And with that he nodded his great, Silenus-like head, and angrily pounded the floor with his stick.

In the end, despite his protests, he was frog-marched to the Belle Jardinière and there equipped, not with the corduroy *complet* he so admired, but with a suit in some more humble and hard-wearing material. He bore his benefactors no malice, however, and when he needed sympathy or support it was still to Huysmans that he came. Often, in the late afternoon, he would settle at a café close to the Ministry of the Interior, and send his friend an urgent summons on a dirty scrap of paper. If Huysmans did not immediately leave his office, the messenger would return a few minutes later with a reproachful: 'Monsieur Verlaine is still waiting for Monsieur – and he is crying.' It was impossible to resist such an appeal. With a sigh, Huysmans would tidy away his papers and hurry out to the café, where an ugly, sinister figure sat hunched over a table, sobbing like a child, and waiting to be comforted.

4. THE MENTOR

PARIS in the summer of 1888 was a sunny, joyous place, already busy with preparations for the next year's Exposition Universelle. But nothing of that sunshine and joy and excitement penetrated to the Rue de Sèvres. There Huysmans sat in solitary gloom, fretting over the account-books of his workshop, the ill health of his mistress, and the persistent misfortunes of his friends. He felt desperately unhappy, he told Jules Destrée on 18 June,[1] and his friends were in no better case:

> Bloy is working, but can scarcely be described as happy. Villiers spends his time in the *brasseries*, surrounded by beer-mugs and holding forth to a set of fools. Poor Verlaine is very sick in both body and spirit, and d'Aurevilly is slowly petering out as a result of his recent illness. In fact, when I look around me at those I love, I can see nothing but sorrow and ruination . . .

A month later, to complete his unhappiness, he learnt that his young friend Émile Hennequin had been drowned while bathing with Odilon Redon at Sannois. The news provoked the sad reflection that he had written to Hennequin only a few days before his death,[2] praising his *Études de critique scientifique*, and assuring him that a great future lay before him.

At long last the time came for Huysmans' annual leave from the Ministry. It was clearly unsafe to return this year to Lourps, where irate villagers lay in wait for the author of *En Rade*, so he decided to accept a long-standing invitation from Arij Prins to visit him at Hamburg.[3] He also intended to take the opportunity to see the art collections of Cologne and Berlin. 'I'm off to Germany at the end of the month,' he told Verlaine,[4] 'to enjoy the sight of a few Primitives – and to escape from the company of our abominable compatriots!'

He left Paris on the night of 31 July, and for the first time in his life he travelled in a sleeping-car. He did not relish the experience.[5] The presence of two heavily scented women in the small compartment made breathing difficult, while the movement of the train and the narrowness of the bunks made sleep well-nigh impossible. Poor traveller that he was, Huysmans began to wish that he had never left his comfortable flat to embark on this nightmarish journey, but he comforted himself with the thought that next day he would see the Cathedral and the world-famous Primitives of Cologne. Unfortunately, both the great church and the altar-pieces within were something of a disappointment.[6] The façade offended his eye with its harsh lines and bleak contours, while Stephan Lochner's *Dombild* and other paintings in the Cathedral and the Museum struck him as gross and uninspiring. Nor was this impression simply the result of a sleepless night, for another inspection of these paintings at the end of August, on his way home, only confirmed him in his unfavourable opinion of the Cologne school.

From Cologne, he travelled north, and found that the Hanseatic ports offered ample compensation for the discomforts of the sleeping-car and the disappointments of the picture-gallery. The old city of Lübeck, where he spent a day visiting medieval churches and taverns, delighted him; and with his penchant for unusual experiences, he particularly enjoyed dining in a restaurant installed in the Town Hall cellars.[7] But it was Hamburg which fascinated him most of all – 'that city with the lilac-coloured sea and the blotting-paper sky; that city which, every evening, turns from a busy trading centre into a fairground, where the money earned by day is scattered and spent by night in opulent *readdeks*'.[8] Thus on 13 August he wrote[9] to Maurice de Fleury:

> After a visit to Lübeck, a city which has kept its personality as well as its old houses, and which has a thirteenth-

century Dance of Death in one of its churches, I'm back in Hamburg, feeling dog-tired and dead beat.

This is a city of mists and melancholy. The firmament is invariably grey; the atmosphere is invariably humid; and in spite of prodigious activity, everything here is quiet.

I feel in my element here, with all these twisting medieval streets and these good Germans whose inexhaustible complaisance I find enchanting – not a single gesture or exclamation! And the seamy side of this huge port at night! But you are a married man and therefore a virtuous one, Herr Doktor, and I can no longer write Latin well enough to describe for you certain of the city's streets at nightfall.

In the meantime I've been taking notes, and yet more notes. In other words I'm working hard, and I hope I'll soon have the makings of a book of impressions of Hamburg and North Germany . . .

With other friends Huysmans was less reticent about the 'seamy side' of life at Hamburg. One correspondent was told of a female acrobat who performed her tricks naked before him; she reminded him, he said, of the strange, twisted figures of the German Primitives.[10] To Goncourt he described the hierarchy of *maisons publiques* in Hamburg,[11] ranging from 'the brothels for seamen, infinitely superior to the Maisons Tellier of the Latin Quarter' to 'the brothels for bankers, where the girls are young Hungarians of 15 or 16, and the bedrooms are filled with orchids'. And in a conversation he had with Gustave Coquiot some years later,[12] he recalled the fervent patriotism of the Hamburg prostitutes, maintaining that 'before performing the sensual rites, they insist on saluting the portrait of their Emperor which hangs above every bed', and that as a mark of affection one woman had presented him with a photograph of von Moltke inscribed: 'To my dear little flower . . .'

On 18 August Huysmans and Prins left Hamburg and set off on a brief tour of Germany. Their first stop was at Berlin, a city which impressed Huysmans as the ugliest he had ever seen. Its River Spree he considered 'a trickle of dirty water', its Brandenburger Tor 'a cheap imitation of the Propylaea at Athens', its Unter den Linden 'even more mediocre than our Champs-Élysées', and its people as hideous as their surroundings.[13] However, he decided that much should be forgiven a city which possessed an art collection as fine as that in the Berlin Museum, for it was here that he saw the triptych by Roger Van der Weyden which he afterwards held to be the purest of all prayers in paint, the most splendid representation of the Nativity. He saw nothing to compare with it in the Thuringian towns to which he and Prins now travelled – Weimar, Erfurt, and Gotha – although he noted a bizarre and captivating *Mass of St. Gregory* in the Grand Duke's collection at Gotha.[14] But at Cassel, which was their next stopping-place, he found a picture of such terrifying realism and mystical beauty that he cried out in horror and admiration as he entered the little museum gallery in which it was hung. This great painting – a *Crucifixion* by Matthaeus Grünewald – had a profound influence on Huysmans' aesthetic and psychological development, and his impression of it as he first saw it at Cassel deserves to be quoted here at length.[15]

> Never before had realism attempted such a subject; never before had a painter explored the divine charnel-house so thoroughly, or dipped his brush so brutally in running sores and bleeding wounds. It was outrageous and it was horrifying. Grünewald was the most daring of realists, without a doubt; but as one gazed upon this Redeemer of the doss-house, this God of the morgue, there was wrought a change. Gleams of light filtered from the ulcerous head; a superhuman radiance illumined the gangrened flesh and the tortured features. This carrion spread-eagled on the cross was the tabernacle of a God; and here, his head adorned with no aureole or nimbus but a tangled crown of thorns beaded with drops of blood, Jesus appeared in his celestial supra-essence, between the Virgin, grief-stricken and blinded

with tears, and St. John, whose burning eyes could find no more tears to shed.

These faces, at first sight so commonplace, shone with the ecstasy of souls transfigured by suffering. This was no common criminal, nor this a poor beggar-woman, nor this a country yokel: these were supra-terrestrial beings in the presence of a God.

Grünewald was the most daring of idealists. Never had painter so magnificently scaled the mystical heights, or so courageously leapt from the topmost peak of the spirit up into the very sphere of the heavens. He had gone to both extremes; and from the depths of squalor he had extracted the finest cordial of charity and the most bitter tears of woe. In this picture was revealed the masterpiece and supreme achievement of an art which had been bidden to represent both the invisible and the tangible, to manifest the piteous uncleanness of the body, and to sublimate the infinite distress of the soul.

For many months after his visit to Cassel, Huysmans remained under the spell of this painting; and towards the end of the year he wrote in a letter to Jules Destrée[16] that 'the Primitives are art in its highest form, and supernatural realism is the only formula, the only true formula, which can exist for me'. The importance he attached to Grünewald's achievement can also be judged by the prominence he gave to the Cassel *Crucifixion* in his writings. The idea of producing a book about Hamburg and North Germany, which he had mentioned to Maurice de Fleury, was abandoned;[17] and his impressions of Cologne, Hamburg, Lübeck, Berlin, and Gotha were not published until, many years later, they were introduced into *La Cathédrale* and *De Tout*. But his description of the Grünewald *Crucifixion* was given a place of honour in the first chapter of *Là-Bas*, where it was used to illustrate Huysmans' conception of 'supernatural realism' or 'mystical naturalism'.

On his return to Paris, Huysmans found Léon Bloy as loud as ever in his complaints of poverty, and as unwilling as ever to

179

do anything to remedy his situation – anything, that is, except beg 'loans' from his friends. 'I recognize a friend', he used to say,[18] 'by the fact that he gives me money'; and at first there had been no lack of good people to provide him with the only proof of friendship which he understood. They discovered, however, that they were expected to give further proof of their affection for Léon Bloy at regular intervals, however straitened their own financial circumstances might be. If they were behindhand with their contributions, they suffered the onslaught of his righteous wrath in some vituperative article or pamphlet; but even if they poured their hard-earned francs into the Bloy exchequer, they rarely received a word of thanks in return. This was because Bloy held that his mission on earth was divinely ordained, and that in subsidizing him his friends were simply acquitting themselves of their duty to God; he even declared ingratitude to be one of the highest Christian virtues, and proudly styled himself 'the Ungrateful Mendicant'. These sophistries, of course, were scarcely calculated to endear him to his friends, especially if those friends were themselves poverty-stricken. And Villiers de l'Isle-Adam, the true prince of paupers, voiced the general opinion when, pronouncing solemn judgement upon Bloy,[19] he said: 'He has brought poverty into dishonour.'

The author of the *Contes cruels* knew from bitter experience how unscrupulous Bloy could be in money matters. On the rare occasions when Villiers succeeded in obtaining some payment for his stories, he would usually find Bloy standing outside the publisher's offices, waiting to exact what he considered his rightful share of his friend's earnings. It was Bloy too who, in the hope of bigger profits, led Villiers into one of the most cruelly disappointing adventures of his life. In the autumn of 1887, hearing that the Marquess of Salisbury was staying at Dieppe, he urged Villiers to go and ask the British Prime Minister, as one nobleman to another, for a loan. Outlining his plan in a letter to Montchal,[20] he wrote:

The noble lord won't see anything of me, but I shall be standing in the wings, whispering to Villiers the manly words of advice which only I can give him and which he accepts only from me. It is essential that this English autocrat should find him a good position, and that meanwhile he should give him a small capital sum which we could bring back to Paris . . . I'm absolutely convinced that this plan of mine will succeed. I have a genius for laying sieges, and this one looks like child's play. But our friend is a difficult engine of war to man-oeuvre. The day before yesterday I practically had to carry him to his publisher's pay-office. Anyway, my will is usually stronger than his, and I hope to win him over again.

It seems, however, that the 'engine of war' refused to be manoeuvred into position, and the siege of Salisbury was regretfully postponed. During the following months Bloy must have made strenuous efforts to persuade his friend that there was nothing dishonourable in his scheme, for in September 1888 Villiers finally travelled to Dieppe to see the Marquess. On his return he told his friends that something was sure to come of his visit, since the English peer had listened to him for five hours without once interrupting him.[21] But it soon became apparent that this lengthy monologue had had no effect whatever – and he was forced to conclude that this was because Robert Cecil, third Marquess of Salisbury, was as deaf as the proverbial post.

The hurt which this fiasco caused to Villiers' pride may have been fatal to his friendship with Bloy, for in October we find the latter informing Montchal[22] that 'Villiers and I have fallen out'. Bloy's friendship with Huysmans was also in growing danger at this time. The first signs of dissension had appeared in August, when Huysmans had written to Gustave Guiches[23] from Hamburg:

I've just received a letter from Léon Bloy. He complains as usual of a miserable life – a life which, after all, is of his own making. He's certainly very unhappy, and although he's doing scarcely any work of any sort, he deserves our sympathy. The trouble is that I can't see any solution to his problem. I've written to several people recently, asking them to help him, but all have refused. They charge him with incurable laziness, and it's clear that he has exhausted everybody's patience. But don't tell him this, as it would only upset him and would serve no useful purpose . . .

Gradually Huysmans himself began to lose patience with the 'Ungrateful Mendicant', and to think that those who criticized Bloy's 'incurable laziness' might not be far from the truth. He knew that Villiers' health did not permit him to undertake any form of regular employment, but he saw no reason why Bloy should not try to earn his daily bread, instead of living on gifts and loans – 'subsidies to which the *fonctionnaire* gave a less charitable name, and to which he referred with ever-increasing contempt'.[24] Gustave Guiches, seeing how strained relations between the two men had become, looked forward to the inevitable quarrel with a certain *Schadenfreude*. 'I can see a conflict coming', he wrote,[25] 'between these two proud wills; and when this storm breaks, I know that if Bloy is the thunder, Huysmans will be the lightning.'

Even now, however, Huysmans was looking for means of helping Bloy, and in November he succeeded in finding a new opening for him in journalism. It so happened that Camille Lemonnier had been summoned to Paris to answer a charge of offending public morals with a story published in *Gil Blas;* and the editor, René d'Hubert, then asked him to recommend some other writers who might also be relied upon to give fresh impetus to the newspaper's affairs. On Lemonnier's advice, Huysmans was asked to become a contributor, but he only accepted on the condition that Bloy shared this good fortune. D'Hubert accordingly invited his two new recruits to dinner at the Café Américain on the 27th, in order to discuss with them the terms of their contracts. At this meeting Huysmans promised a series of descriptive articles, beginning with a piece called 'Le

Sleeping-car', while Bloy offered to celebrate every Sabbath with a scathing attack on some contemporary writer or public figure. Ten of Bloy's articles, all on a dead level of vituperation, appeared in *Gil Blas*, from December 1888 until February 1889; but by that time both public and paper had tired of his Sunday harangues, and he was dismissed. Even so, he had better luck than his friend. When René d'Hubert read Huysmans' first offering, and found that it described the *wagon-lit* in terms of the torture-chamber, he was filled with fear for the complimentary travel-vouchers which *Gil Blas* received from the railway companies. Huysmans refused to alter the offending passages in 'Le Sleeping-car', and it was therefore rejected.[26] His second contribution also met with a discouraging reception, as he revealed in a letter to Jules Destrée.[27]

You ask me [he wrote] about *Gil Blas*. It's a sink of iniquity. They only engaged Bloy in the expectation of some scandal, and me in the hope of some smut. Instead, I let them have a quasi-pious piece. It would take too long to tell you how stupidly they behaved, and how this article had to wait two months before it was published. But one thing is certain – I've no desire to deluge them with my prose.

The 'quasi-pious piece' which he mentioned in this letter was published in *Gil Blas* on 18 January 1889, under the title of 'L'Accordant'. It described a visit to the belfry of an unspecified church in Paris, and a conversation with the bell-ringer. It is of interest because it later reappeared, with considerable modifications, in Huysmans' novel *Là-Bas*, where the bell-ringer was given the name of Carhaix, and the church stood revealed as Saint-Sulpice.[28]

Huysmans saw very little of Bloy in the New Year. He saw even less of the other member of the 'Council of Paupers', for in February he and Villiers were both confined to their rooms – Huysmans with rheumatism,[29] and Villiers (though he did not know it) with the cancer which was to kill him within a few months. Probably the last evening the two men spent together before illness overtook them was at a small dinner-party arranged by Mallarmé. Evidence of this modest reunion subsists in a letter from Huysmans to Mallarmé[30] in which the novelist wrote:

> This dinner you mention – yes, we really must have it. When and where you like. Just for the three of us. No more cormorants such as we met with in the not very fraternal ambuscades of the *Lion d'Or*. But we ought to plan it all beforehand with Villiers so that he doesn't have to worry about certain details which might other-wise cause him serious embarrassment.

On the envelope containing his reply, Mallarmé penned one of his famous rhymed addresses:

> Rue (as-tu peur) de Sèvres onze
> Subtil séjour où rappliqua
> Satan tout haut traité de gonze
> Par Huysmans qu'il nomme J.-K.

The next letter which Mallarmé sent Huysmans was written in a more serious vein. Villiers' condition had sud-denly grown so serious that Mallarmé had made arrange-ments for him to move from the Rue Fontaine to a villa at Fontenay-sous-Bois, overcoming his scruples with references to a non-existent advance on the royalties from Villiers' unpublished masterpiece, *Axël*. He then wrote to some of Villiers' closest friends – Méry Laurent, Huysmans, Coppée, Léon Dierx, and Francis Poictevin – asking whether they could pledge themselves to send him 5 francs each, every month, so as to relieve Villiers of financial anxiety. Huys-mans was the first to respond to this generous appeal, with a not less generous offer. He wrote to Mallarmé on 15 March 1889:[31]

> Agreed. But I can let you have ten francs a month with-

out feeling the pinch. Please arrange matters, my dear Mallarmé, in such a way that our poor friend isn't caused any offence or embarrassment. I myself am beginning to feel a little better – but all the same, what a filthy hole is this carnal hostelry in which someone has seen fit to coop us up . . .

Saved by his friends from utter destitution, Villiers was to cling to life a little longer, thus outliving by a few months his friend the eighty-year-old Connétable des Lettres. For Jules-Amédée Barbey d'Aurevilly breathed his last on the morning of Tuesday, 23 April, in his *tournebride* in the Rue Rousselet. He died from old age, from an internal haemorrhage – and also, it was said, from the shock caused by a mysterious telegram he had received from Mme de Bouglon, his 'White Angel' and the sworn enemy of Louise Read. When Huysmans went to pay his last respects to the Connétable, on the Thursday evening, he found Louise Read and Georges Landry mounting guard over the bier, and wondering whether the woman whom they held responsible for their master's death would arrive in Paris before the funeral.[32] A solitary candle was burning in Barbey's room. The dandy's scarlet cloak was spread out upon the bed, while on the coffin a few wild violets had been arranged in the shape of a cross. Huysmans and Landry talked together in low tones while a succession of priests came and went – among them Father Sylvestre, the Franciscan chaplain to the nearby alms-house of the Brothers of Saint-Jean-de-Dieu, whom Huysmans was to meet again in even more tragic circumstances. The novelist was told that there had been an unwelcome visitor to the house earlier in the day – a member of Barbey's entourage who was devoted to the scheming Mme de Bouglon. This was the self-styled Sâr Joséphin Péladan, a notorious charlatan who claimed to be descended from the Chaldean Mages – conveniently forgetting his humble Parisian début as a bank-clerk in the Crédit Français – and who used to perambulate the boulevards in a silver waistcoat and flowing black burnous, his hands folded upon his breast. He had appeared at the door of Barbey's *tournebride* flaunting a doublet of violet corduroy, and had been unceremoniously hustled downstairs by Léon Bloy. And when Huysmans saw him the next day, standing among the mourners at the Montparnasse Cemetery, he noticed that the 'Sâr' looked paler and was more soberly clad than usual.

Barbey's death received little attention from either Press or public, for their interest was occupied by events of greater moment than the passing of an eccentric octogenarian. Only a few days before, General Boulanger had fled ignominiously to Brussels; and only a few days later, the Exposition Universelle of 1889, held to celebrate the centenary of the Revolution, was to open its doors to the public. Huysmans, for his part, regarded both the General and the Exposition with contemptuous amusement. His connexion with the Boulanger affair has been described in the following passage[33] from Gustave Guiches' memoirs:

At a time when almost the whole of France was going wild about Boulanger, when the mob was acclaiming the *brav' général, Père la Victoire* and his *pioupious d'Auvergne*, and when enthusiastic orators were declaring that he would avenge our defeats and restore our national pride, Huysmans waved a thin file of papers before my eyes and said:

'You see these papers? They are copies of the love-letters that silly old fool has been writing to the woman he loves – a woman who is probably being paid to keep him out of mischief! And while all these crowds are enthusing over the blond beard of their *brav' général*, the gangling schoolboy is busy writing: "My dearest, if only you knew how I detest them for preventing me from spending all my time with you. Because nothing exists for me but you, my love!!" And so on for page after page! Comical, isn't it . . .'

As for the Exposition, Huysmans visited it several times in the company of thousands of gaping Parisians, provincials, and foreigners. Unlike them, however, he directed a critical and derisive gaze upon the garish buildings in the Champ de Mars, with their brass genies and gilt goddesses, their cast-iron columns and mosaic pillars, their turquoise-and-gold cupolas and sky-blue arcades. Another object of his scorn was the much-discussed tower of M. Eiffel, which he was later to describe in *Certains* as 'that infundibuliform lattice-work, that bottle wickered in painted straw, that solitary suppository riddled with holes'. And in a letter to Mallarmé[34] he wrote that he was 'extracting from the belly of the Tour Eiffel a few symbols which I hope will please you when my work on that gravy-coloured ironmongery appears . . .'

One of Huysmans' friends was meditating a work on the very same subject – for Villiers, who in April had moved from Fontenay to a villa at Nogent-sur-Marne, told Mallarmé in June that he had drafted the plan of a story called *Le Revenant de la Tour Eiffel*. But Villiers, though he may have visited the famous tower, was never to complete his ghost-story. Early in July his friends were informed that his doctor, Dr. Albert Robin, had diagnosed his illness as cancer of the stomach, and that he had only a few weeks to live. On the 5th Huysmans wrote[35] to Mallarmé:

I enclose with this letter the wretched prebend for our poor Villiers. Guiches has seen Robin – and now we know from what incurable and diabolical disease he is suffering. Decidedly the Almighty has special prebends of suffering and dispensations of horror for artists. For which, it seems, one ought to praise him . . .

Villiers remained ignorant of the sentence of death which had been passed upon him, since Dr. Robin told him only that he was suffering from a temporary dilatation of the stomach. Even so, he felt too ill to work, and he came to the conclusion that the Nogent villa, instead of promoting his recovery, was having the opposite effect. In a letter to Robert du Pontavice de Heussey,[36] Villiers' cousin and first biographer, Huysmans

187

later told of a fateful visit he paid his friend at Nogent, early in July.

> One day [he wrote] when he was ailing more than usual, the sick man complained to me about the house he was in. It was, as a matter of fact, as cold as a vault, absolutely sunless, and almost rotten with damp. As he said he would like to leave it, and added that he needed skilled nurses to lift him and move him in his bed, I mentioned the Brothers of Saint-Jean-de-Dieu in the Rue Oudinot in Paris. Two days later I had a letter from him saying that he was settled in their house, thanks to the mediation of Coppée, who had obtained exceptionally favourable terms for him from the Director. I found him there delighted with the change, convinced that he would soon recover, and full of plans for the future. He said he was resolved to give up going to the boulevard *brasseries*, and meant to work quietly in some peaceful corner, far from the hubbub of journalism . . .

The sick man had moved into this house – No. 19 Rue Oudinot – on Friday, 12 July. Did he, one wonders, realize then that the convent gardens he could see from his bed were the selfsame gardens the dying Connétable des Lettres had looked upon, three months before, from his *tournebride* in the Rue Rousselet? And did he guess that the bare room he had been given would shortly witness, not only his death, but also an event worthy of inclusion among his own *Contes cruels* – the marriage of the Comte de Villiers de l'Isle-Adam, descendant of a Grand Master of the Knights of Malta, to humble Marie Dantine, his servant and mistress?

A great deal has been written about this marriage *in extremis*, most of it in ignorance or bad faith. The majority view – though not, it should be said, the view taken by any of Villiers' biographers – appears to be that Huysmans isolated Villiers from his friends and then forced him to marry Marie Dantine, simply in order to humiliate a proud artist whose genius he envied. This melodramatic idea stemmed, of course, from the fertile imagination of Léon Bloy, who himself came in time to believe it was the truth. It is as well to remember, however, that in a letter to Mme Henriette L'Huillier written three weeks after Villiers' death,[37] Bloy confessed that 'we had stopped seeing each other some months ago, and he refused to see me before he died'; and that although he complained that Huysmans 'has not been a friend to me in this affair', he admitted that to Villiers the novelist had shown 'admirable devotion'. Only later, after he had finally broken with Huysmans, did he conceive the theory expounded in *La Femme pauvre*,[38] where he told how 'Folantin', in his envious hatred of 'Bohémond de l'Isle-de-France', 'took a hideous revenge, in which I think he must have displayed the cunning and the perseverance of the devil himself. For the result was worth it. Just think of it! To bring the black swan that was Bohémond, the last scion of a proud race, an almost royal line, to give his magnificent Name – if only in the twilight of life – to a scullery drab! To force him to end his days like an old rake who in his dotage falls into the clutches of his cook! What a revenge!'

This plausible theory, so plausibly advanced by Bloy, has gradually gained currency, although friends of Huysmans who knew his admiration for Villiers and the essential kindness of his nature have never ceased to protest against it. However, certain letters and documents have recently come to light, which go a long way to disproving Bloy's allegations. As will be seen, they show that it was always Villiers' intention to marry Marie Dantine before he died, and also that Mallarmé's part in the affair was as great as, if not greater than, that played by Huysmans. No one would think of accusing Mallarmé of having sought to humiliate Villiers on his deathbed: similarly, there seems to be no reason why anyone should have thought of levelling that accusation at Huysmans – had not Léon Bloy been looking for a stick with which to beat his former friend.

Throughout the month of July Villiers' condition grew steadily worse. In his letter to Pontavice de Heussey, Huysmans recorded that 'the stomach no longer functioned properly, his strength failed, his emaciation became frightful.

A sort of straw-coloured shadow crept over his features, and in the wasted face only the eyes lived on, seeming to pierce the very soul of any visitor with their terrifying gaze. Despite the efforts of Mme Méry Laurent, a friend who nursed and petted him, bringing him nourishing food and authentic wines, Villiers was unable to eat, and death came ever nearer.' By the end of the month his friends had decided that consideration of his son's position could no longer be delayed. Villiers, it seems, had for a long time been concerned about Totor's future status, and had said that he meant to legitimize the child before he died. He knew, of course, that 'legitimization' of a child necessarily involved the marriage of the parents, whereas 'recognition' involved nothing more than a formal admission of paternity; but he wished his son and heir to enjoy the status of *enfant légitimé* rather than the inferior status of *enfant reconnu*. However, he was not eager to confer his name and title upon poor Marie Dantine before the approach of death rendered this inevitable; and his friends were therefore faced with the problem of persuading him to marry without telling him that he was a doomed man.

It was Mallarmé who took the first steps in this delicate matter.[39] Early in August he came to Paris from Valvins to arrange for the legal transfer of Marie Dantine's modest belongings to his name, in payment of a non-existent debt: this was to protect her against the demands of creditors after Villiers' death. At the same time he broached the question of marriage with Villiers, but was told that a 'dilatation of the stomach' was not sufficiently alarming to justify such extreme measures. Mallarmé was also unsuccessful in collecting the necessary papers for the marriage, notably the medical certificate which he thought was necessary to secure dispensation from publication of the banns: the doctor of the house, Dr. Mène, refused to sign such a certificate unless Villiers himself asked for it – and Mallarmé still wished to spare his friend the knowledge that he was a dying man. However, the chaplain, Father Sylvestre, agreed to persuade Villiers to ask for a certificate that he was 'in danger of death', ostensibly as a mere precaution. And in a letter which he wrote from Valvins on 8 August, Mallarmé gave Huysmans explicit instructions as to the steps he should take once Dr. Mène had signed the certificate.[40]

On Friday the 9th, Huysmans saw Villiers for an hour and tried, unsuccessfully, to induce him to agree to an early marriage. He later told Pontavice de Heussey:

> I was sick with anxiety, but suddenly it occurred to me to apply to the Chaplain of the Brothers of Saint-Jean-de-Dieu, a Franciscan from the Holy Land, the Rev. Father Sylvestre. He was a gentle and compassionate monk, who had already helped Barbey d'Aurevilly to die. I reminded him of the lamentable story, which he knew already, for Villiers had confessed to him and had received communion from him. He simply answered: 'Just wait for me here. I will go up and have a word with him.' Five minutes later he came out of the sick-room. Villiers had consented to an immediate marriage.

Huysmans gave this news in a letter to Mallarmé the next day.[41] He added: 'Marie told me something very illuminating. Villiers' only concern with regard to the various documents we need is to have Totor's birth certificate altered. It describes the mother's profession as charwoman, and he would like to substitute *property-owner* . . .' The novelist had already traced most of the relevant papers, thanks to a clerk called Raoul Denieau at the local *mairie*; but he told Mallarmé that, even if Father Sylvestre managed to obtain the vital medical certificate, it would still be impossible to have the banns dispensed with altogether. Mallarmé's immediate reaction to this disquieting news was to appeal for help to his friend Paul Beurdeley, Mayor of the Eighth Arrondissement.[42] He explained in his letter to Beurdeley that Villiers was dying, and added: 'He has a child, and if he legitimized it by a marriage *in extremis*, I and a few friends could do something for both mother and son. This is Villiers' own idea, but he wishes to give effect to it only at the very last moment – for if he recovered, he would suffer from the lowly condition of the good-hearted and devoted creature who is looking after him.' Though important in that it gives the lie to Léon Bloy's accusations against Huysmans, this letter served no useful purpose at the time, since unknown to Mallarmé the banns of marriage were being read for the first time that same day. Huysmans told the poet in a brief note[43] that 'yesterday Marie, horrified by Villiers' growing weakness, took it upon herself to have the banns published today, Sunday. The marriage can therefore take place on Thursday. I don't quite know how Villiers will take the news . . .'

The news, it seems, was broken to him on Sunday evening by Father Sylvestre, who probably told him quite frankly that he was near to death and should resign himself to the fact. As a result, the Franciscan was able to inform Mallarmé on Monday that he had at last persuaded Villiers to ask for the medical certificate, which was still necessary if further publications of the banns were to be avoided.[44] He added that as Villiers was much weaker and had agreed to 'regularize the situation', he thought that the marriage should be celebrated as soon as possible. He appears to have expressed the same opinion to Huysmans, whom he saw in the afternoon, for on Monday evening the novelist wrote[45] to Méry Laurent:

The banns were published for the first and only time yesterday, Sunday. Allowing for the delay laid down by the Code, the marriage can take place on Thursday. But I am terribly anxious. I have just seen the Franciscan, who thinks Villiers is in a very bad way – worse than I thought he was myself – and that man knows what he is talking about. Tomorrow, I hope to get the public attorney to dispense with the second publication, but even so, shall we be in time? I doubt it, because that never-ending diarrhoea is weakening him . . .

On Tuesday the 13th, Huysmans dispatched two telegrams to Mallarmé at Valvins.[46] The first, at nine o'clock, announced that Villiers' condition had improved slightly. But the second, at eight in the evening, read: 'Marriage tomorrow Wednesday – come immediately.'

When he arrived at the house the next morning, Mallarmé found Villiers looking desperately ill and unhappy, and his depression deepened as the day wore on.[47] Unforeseen legal difficulties arose, due to the fact that Marie Dantine was a native of Luxembourg, but at four o'clock the Deputy Mayor of the Seventh Arrondissement arrived and the civil ceremony began. There were four witnesses: Huysmans, Mallarmé, Léon Dierx, and Gustave de Malherbe. Marie's elder son, Albert, does not appear to have been present, but Totor was there, full of boyish high spirits quite unsuited to the occasion. His presence acted as a reminder of the real reason for the marriage, and after the Deputy Mayor had read the relevant articles of the Code, Villiers asked him to confirm that Totor would henceforth be recognized as legitimate. At a later stage in the civil ceremony, there occurred a horrifying incident which Huysmans described in this passage from his letter to Pontavice de Heussey:

When the time came to sign the registers, the woman stated that she could not write. There was a terrible silence. Villiers lay in agony, his eyes closed. Ah! he was spared nothing: his cup overflowed with bitterness and humiliation. And while we were all looking at one another, almost broken-hearted, the woman added: 'I can make a cross as I did for my first wedding.' And we took her hand and helped her to make the mark . . .

Afterwards, a pathetic attempt was made to infuse a little gaiety into the proceedings when Marie produced some biscuits and a bottle of Veuve Cliquot. The champagne, like the bride's wedding-ring, was a present from Méry Laurent, but poor Marie had been obliged to buy glasses specially for the occasion. Toasts were drunk to the bride and bridegroom, and then Father Sylvestre came in to conduct the religious ceremony. When it was over the kindly priest told Villiers and Marie: 'Although women are not allowed to spend the night here, I have arranged that now you are married you shall no longer be separated.' But Villiers was almost fainting with fatigue and would not be comforted. The last words his friends heard him say as they left the sickroom were: 'And now let me die . . .'

Huysmans went to see Villiers every day that week, and on Sunday the 18th he wrote[48] to Méry Laurent:

Our poor friend is in a bad way. He is fighting hard to get better, but is getting weaker every day. His face, which was already so hollow-cheeked, looks thinner than ever and is really frightening. He can now scarcely sit up in his bed, talks very little, and just murmurs: 'My God, is it possible?' In an attempt to keep his strength up, I have got him to take a yolk of egg through a straw every day, but he's growing sick of it – just as he grew sick of the meat extracts, the peptones, the beef-tea and everything else – and that dreadful diarrhoea continues! . . . He is tortured too by the idea that he's dying in an alms-house. I do my best to calm him, promising him that as soon as he's convalescent I shall find him lodgings. But . . . but . . . I fear what I say no longer carries much weight with him – since I did so much to hurry on the marriage, he obviously thinks I regard him as a doomed man.

That this was, in fact, how Huysmans regarded him is clear from the rest of the novelist's letter to Méry Laurent. He answered in detail Méry's anxious inquiries about the funeral expenses: the Ministry of Public Instruction, the Société des Auteurs Dramatiques and *Le Figaro* would each, he thought, contribute from 100 to 250 francs. And he added: 'Villiers is to receive extreme unction this evening, which means, alas! that there seems little hope of his dragging out his life to the end of this coming week . . .'

That evening Huysmans saw his friend again after he had received the last sacraments.[49] He later recorded that 'Villiers lay half-conscious, his wan face grown hollow and his throat rattling. I saw that the end was near, but overwhelmed with emotion as I was, I had to hurry away, for it was late and the house was closing for the night . . . A ring at the bell the next morning made me jump out of bed. "Villiers is dead", I said to myself, and so it proved to be; his wife sank sobbing onto a chair in my room.' Marie told him that Villiers had died peacefully at eleven o'clock. His last words to her had been a moving, childlike appeal: 'Hold me close, that I may go gently.'

Villiers' funeral took place on Wednesday, 21 August, exactly a week after his marriage.[50] Huysmans and Mallarmé led the procession of mourners from the church of Saint-François-Xavier to the Batignolles Cemetery, where, in drizzling rain, their friend was buried. Between the two men, sheltered by an umbrella and holding a rose in one hand, walked little Totor, for whom his father had suffered such bitter humiliation, and in whom Villiers had placed such high hopes. He was to die twelve years later, long before any of those hopes could be fulfilled.

5. THE OCCULTIST

THE day before he died, Villiers had named Huysmans and Mallarmé as his executors. For some weeks, therefore, Huysmans' correspondence was chiefly concerned with his friend's affairs. In one letter,[1] to a woman who had known and admired the author of the *Contes cruels*, he wrote:

> Poor Villiers has now been laid to rest in the Batignolles Cemetery. We had arranged a modest but quite heraldic ceremony for him, but it was spoilt by a certain Marras, a friend of Mendès, who felt the need to obtain a little self-advertisement by pronouncing a futile speech at the graveside.
>
> Just now, as Villiers' executor – a capacity I share with Mallarmé, who is out of town – I'm beset by publishers who want to bring out Villiers' books without delay: a real flock of vultures fastening upon a corpse. And Villiers' papers are in the most incredible disorder. I don't know how I'm going to bring out *Axël*, which he has left in a pile of half-altered proofs . . .

A little later, he wrote to the same correspondent:

> It was very good of you to offer to go and see the Marquess of Salisbury about Villiers' child. Unfortunately, it's too late, for I see from a dispatch which arrived this morning that the big white chief of tea and ham left Calais for London at four o'clock yesterday afternoon. So there's nothing to be done for the time being – otherwise Mallarmé (whom I saw yesterday) and I would have gladly accepted your kind offer.

The woman to whom these letters were addressed was one of the strangest of Huysmans' acquaintances; but if she deserves consideration, it is not simply on account of her manifold eccentricities, but because she was to play an important part in the novelist's life.[2] Her name was Caroline-Louise-Victoire (or, more simply, Berthe) Courrière, and she was born at Lille in June 1852. At the age of twenty she came to Paris, where she met and conquered George Sand's son-in-law, the sculptor Clésinger. She was a buxom young woman, and Clésinger often used her as his model for sculptures in the grand manner, such as the figures of the Republic which he executed for the Sénat and for the Exposition Universelle of 1878. He also introduced her to high society, whereupon she assumed the noble particule, pretended that 'Courrière' was her married name, and posed as Clesinger's niece. When the sculptor died in 1883, Berthe suffered a temporary eclipse, but three years later, she found a new publicist in young Remy de Gourmont, whom she promptly identified as a long-lost cousin. Just as her 'uncle' had sought to immortalize her in his statues of the Republic, so now her 'cousin' depicted her in a flattering light in his novels *Sixtine* and *Le Fantôme*, and also *Portraits du prochain siècle*, where she appeared[3] as 'a cabbalist and occultist, learned in the history of Asiatic religions and philosophies, fascinated by the veil of Isis, initiated by dangerous personal experiences into the most redoubtable mysteries of the Black Art . . . a soul to which Mystery has spoken – and has not spoken in vain'.

The late Pierre Dufay has described Berthe Courrière less kindly as 'a madwoman whose lucid intervals were not entirely free from the disordered notions which haunted her'. Her mind was certainly unbalanced. Twice in her lifetime – at Bruges in 1890 and in Brussels in 1906 – she was certified as insane and committed to a mental asylum; and once she published a violent attack on Charcot, entitled 'Néron, prince de la science', which betrayed the hatred felt by many mental patients for mental specialists. It has been said too that she harboured an unwholesome passion for the priesthood, and would often admit to the most horrifying practices in the hope of tempting or shocking some inexperienced confessor; while Rachilde claimed to have seen her take consecrated hosts from her shopping-bag and dispense them to stray dogs. Her ideas on interior decoration were apparently governed by the same sacrilegious impulse, for Henry de Groux wrote[4] of her flat:

> Mme de Courrière's home is quite the oddest thing one could possibly imagine in the style of her half-pagan and supposedly half-Catholic world. Wherever one looks, one sees the paraphernalia of worship put to the most unexpected uses – chasubles, altar-cloths, monstrances, corporals, dalmatics, candelabra with multi-coloured tapers flickering mysteriously in shadowy corners, and a superb eagle-lectern bearing upon its outstretched wings works by Félicien Rops or the Marquis de Sade. And in the suffocating atmosphere, the effluvia of benzoin, ambergris, and attar of roses mingle with those of incense . . .

It seems that Huysmans was introduced to Berthe Courrière by her protégé, publicist, and lover, Remy de Gourmont.[5] The younger man, then an assistant librarian in the Bibliothèque Nationale, had called at the Ministry of the Interior one day in 1889, bearing the manuscript of a story entitled *Stratagèmes* which he wished to dedicate to Huysmans.[6] The novelist had taken a liking to both the story and its author, and Gourmont soon became a frequent visitor to the Ministry and to No. 11 Rue de Sèvres. Huysmans in turn was invited to the flat in the Rue de Varenne which Gourmont shared with Berthe Courrière; and there he sat through many a long evening, listening to his hostess as she discoursed on the occult arts or recalled the 'dangerous personal experiences' which she had undergone. His friendship with Gourmont and his mistress lasted almost three years; then they drifted apart. Huysmans continued to read Gourmont's articles in the *Mercure de France*, and occasionally he was told of some new folly Berthe had committed; but he never visited the house in the Rue des Saints-Pères to which the ageing 'cousins' moved, and where they died within a few months of each other during the First World War.

Berthe Courrière was not the only woman to give Huysmans instruction in the occult arts: there was also Henriette Maillat, a person of considerable beauty and some learning, with whom he had a brief, unsatisfactory love-affair.[7] He was by no means the first of her lovers, for while Berthe pursued men of God, Henriette made a practice of seducing men of letters. By the time she met Huysmans, in 1888, her conquests included the Sâr Joséphin Péladan – who portrayed her in his first novel, *Le Vice suprême*, as the Princess d'Este – and Léon Bloy. From Bloy she turned her attention to Huysmans, asking him for an assignation in an intriguing letter which she signed: 'Mme Dorval, poste restante, Rue Bonaparte.' Huysmans' reply – 'Remember, Madame, that nothing happens as one would wish it' – was discouraging; but his curiosity had evidently been aroused. After a suitable interval it was satisfied: 'Mme Dorval' revealed her true identity, and invited Huysmans to the fifth-floor flat in the Rue des Beaux-Arts where she lived with her brother.[8] At their first two meetings, however, she was coquettish and unapproachable, refusing even to let him kiss her; and she met his pleas with the astonishing claim that, being versed in the mysteries of incubus and succubus, she could have commerce with him or with any other man, living or dead, whenever she pleased. But at last, after Huysmans had been driven to the point of calling her 'hell incarnate', she relented and wrote to him:

> Very well, then. Come this evening to the Rue des Beaux-Arts, at a quarter to eight. My brother will stay only a little while with us, as he has some work to do. And I promise you that I shall have a heart – since you call *that* having a heart . . .

With Henriette Maillat Huysmans would apparently have liked to maintain a placid, sensual relationship such as he and Anna Meunier had enjoyed, spending an evening with her every week. But the arrangement he suggested smacked too strongly of bureaucratic routine for her liking, and she decided that it would be better to bring their liaison to an end. 'Thank you', she wrote in a farewell letter, 'for the fond affection, carefully regulated by the calendar, which you offer me; but that is not my measure – my heart takes a larger size of glove'. Even now, however, all was not over between them, for Henriette had a habit of applying to her former lovers whenever she found herself in financial straits. Twice in 1889 Huysmans gave her money in response to urgent appeals for help, although on the second occasion he made pointed reference to the fact that he had yet to pay his own and Anna Meunier's rent.[9] And in the spring of 1891, as will be seen, he discovered that Henriette Maillat dabbled in blackmail as well as black magic.

Although Berthe and Henriette undoubtedly did much to stimulate Huysmans' interest in the occult, that interest was already active long before he met the two women. The first obvious signs of it appeared in *En Rade*, where Huysmans speculated upon the existence of incubi and succubi, and also referred knowingly to the Cabbala. Soon his friends noticed that the supernatural, which he had hitherto regarded with indifference, was beginning to loom larger in his conversation. Thus Édouard Dujardin, recalling the *Revue Indépendante* dinners of 1887,[10] wrote forty years later:

I was struck by the importance which Huysmans attached, not yet to things religious, but to what I shall call things of mystery – in other words, anything transcending the tangible and the rational. He used to tell us weird stories of secret cults, of werewolves and witchcraft and satanism; and he would usually conclude by saying, after a long pause: 'It's all very strange . . . very strange . . .'

Huysmans himself once tried to explain to a friend the fascination which the supernatural had come to hold for him,[11] saying that he hoped to find in the occult sciences 'some compensation for the horror of daily life, the squalor of existence, the excremental filthiness of the loathsome age we live in'. But his occult investigations, like des Esseintes' aesthetic experiments and Jacques Marles' scholarly researches, were much more than the diversions of a bored dilettante; they represented an earnest attempt to obtain that spiritual satisfaction which life, love, and literature had all failed to afford him. The clearest expression of his motives is perhaps to be found in the following record of a conversation he had with Gustave Guiches in 1887.[12]

'Ah, women!' he said. 'When I think of what mine is suffering! That dreadful disease is gaining ground all the time, and nothing seems able to check its progress, least of all the doctors. And the end of it all is madness! There are times when I feel greater despair than the *Désespéré* himself – who can at least relieve his feelings by howling abuse at all the powers of heaven and earth. Ah, now if only I had the faith . . .'

'But you have got faith – in your work.'

'My work! But I'm no luckier with that than with anything else. Look at *En Rade*, for instance. I was really in love with that book, and I thoroughly enjoyed displaying the vileness of people and the emptiness of things. But now it's all over, and I want nothing more to do with that naturalistic filth! So what remains? . . . Perhaps there's still occultism. I don't mean spiritualism, of course – the cheap swindlers with their shady tricks, the mediums with their buffoonery, and the doddering old ladies with their table-turning antics. No, I mean genuine occultism – not above but beneath or beside or beyond reality! Failing the faith of the Primitive or the first communicant, which I should dearly love to possess, there's a mystery there which appeals to me. I might even say that it haunts me . . .'

In his efforts to find a solution to this mystery, Huysmans came in contact with several of the leaders of the occultist movement in Paris. Thus when Villiers took him to Edmond Bailly's bookshop in the Rue de la Chaussée d'Antin, where the review *La Haute Science* was published, he met Édouard Dubus,[13] a young poet addicted to magic and morphine; the Marquis Stanislas de Guaita, another morphinomaniac, who had recently revived the ancient Rosicrucian Order; the novelist Paul Adam, a member of the Supreme Council of the Rosy Cross; and Gérard Encausse, a humble medical officer who published popular works on occultism under the proud style of 'Papus, Mysteriarch, Unknown Superior'. At the Exposition Universelle of 1889, in a reconstruction of an alchemist's laboratory, he met Dr. Michel de Lézinier, a scholarly scientist to whom he later applied for information about the hermetic arts and their modern practitioners.[14] Another friend he made in occultist circles that summer was Jules Bois, a young man who gained his sympathy with an admirable necrologic article on Villiers, and who told Huysmans that he was preparing a work entitled *Le Satanisme et la magie*.[15] Finally, at Berthe Courrière's flat, despite his declared contempt for spiritualism, Huysmans took part in a very ordinary séance, and was profoundly impressed by what he saw – possibly because the 'table-turning antics' were performed not by 'doddering old ladies' but by young Édouard Dubus. Describing this séance in his memoirs,[16] Remy de Gourmont wrote:

After Édouard Dubus had arrived, we bent our efforts towards persuading a pedestal-table to turn. It showed itself extremely accommodating, for some of the illustrious dead were summoned and gave edifying replies about the condition of the departed as they wandered through the eternal spaces. I found it all very amusing, but everyone else was in deadly earnest – Huysmans in particular was never satisfied, and after pondering a while would ask for more. Finally the table eluded us and began to jig round the room by itself, with Dubus gently guiding it with one finger between the chairs. I must say that if there was any deception at that moment, I could not see how it was practised.

Other opportunities for meeting prominent occultists occurred when Huysmans became associated with a cause which owed much to supernatural revelation, and which had attracted a considerable following of prophets, spiritualists, and miracle-workers. This was the cause of Naundorff's son, a gentleman styling himself Prince Louis-Charles de Bourbon, who as 'Charles XI' pretended to the throne his father had claimed as 'Louis XVII'. Early in 1886, in the prospectus of a review called Le Légitimiste,[17] there appeared the names of Wuitsmans [sic], Williers de l'Ile Adam [sic], and Léon Bloy; but Huysmans for one displayed no further interest in the Naundorffist cause for over a year. Then, in the autumn of 1887, he informed several of his friends that he was hard at work on a novel about 'the fringe of the clerical world and the followers of good King Charles XI . . . a set of cranks I've been watching for some years'.[18] He told Jules Destrée[19] in November:

> You can't imagine the reading I've had to do in hagiography, alchemy, the medical theories of Matteï, and the history of the Empire, as well as piles of brochures and newspapers on the survival of Louis XVII. Though I'm still dazed and bewildered by it all, I must try now to condense this mass of material – and the very thought of it makes me sweat. But if I could bring it off, the result would be a very curious book describing a hitherto unexplored milieu, a book full of weird fancies and cruel realities, a book which would inevitably fall flatter than the flattest pancake with the great reading public . . .

On 12 November he wrote a similar letter to the editor of La Revue Indépendante.[20] Dujardin had asked if he would be willing to sit for a group-portrait of the review's contributors, to be painted by Jacques-Émile Blanche, and Huysmans replied that he was 'out of circulation for the time being, partly on account of the peculiar books I'm reading, but above all because I'm expecting invitations to some diplomatic gatherings – invitations which I've solicited and which I couldn't possibly refuse'. It is known that Huysmans was in correspondence with the Marquis de Meckenheim, one of Naundorff's most devoted followers, but there is no evidence that he was ever invited to any 'diplomatic gatherings' held in support of the Pretender. Probably the only functions he attended at which he could count on meeting a few Naundorffists were the parties given by Charles Buet, the Catholic historian and novelist, at his home in the Avenue de Breteuil. These parties were later described by Huysmans in *Là-Bas*, where he told how, in a house 'on the fringe of the clerical world', the historian used to gather together 'the oddest collection of guests imaginable – bigots from the sacristy and poets from the slum, journalists and actresses, partisans of the Naundorffist cause and professors of equivocal sciences'. Buet himself, whom Jules Renard summed up as 'Catholicism at its greasiest and dirtiest', was portrayed in almost as unflattering a light in *Là-Bas*, as the sanctimonious and rather sinister Chantelouve. He bore Huysmans no malice, however, and the two men maintained cordial relations up to the time of Buet's death in 1897.[21]

Over three years were to elapse before the novel which Huysmans had mentioned to his friends in 1887 actually appeared in print; and during this period the character of the work underwent a considerable change. The work he originally had in view seems to have been a complex political novel, a tale of intriguing eccentrics, of plot and counterplot. For some reason which he never stated, Huysmans eventually abandoned this plan, even though this meant discarding the 'mass of material' which he had accumulated on the Naundorffist cause. Perhaps, as Céard later suggested,[22] he feared that readers who remembered Daudet's novel *Les Rois en exil*, first published in 1879, would think his own work unoriginal. But doubtless a more important consideration was the fact that in 1888 he adopted a new artistic formula which was obviously ill suited to the political novel he had planned. As he explained in the opening chapter of *Là-Bas*, he had for some years been searching for this formula – one which would resolve the contradiction between his respect for the documentary method employed by the Naturalists, and his dislike for their gross materialism, their inability to understand that 'Art only becomes interesting when the senses cease to help us.' *En Rade*, with its somewhat crude opposition of dream and reality, had pointed the way; but it was only in the summer of 1888, standing before the Grünewald *Crucifixion* in the Museum at Cassel, that he found the solution to his problem – in a dichotomy of matter and spirit, a 'supernatural realism', a 'spiritual naturalism'. Explaining how he would apply this medieval formula to the modern novel, he wrote in *Là-Bas*:

It was necessary to keep the accurate documentation, the precision of detail, the rich and vigorous style of the Realists; but it was also necessary to sink well-shafts into the soul, instead of trying to explain its every mystery by some malady of the senses. The novel, if that were possible, ought to be divided into two parts – that of the soul and that of the body – which would be welded together, or rather intermingled, as they are in life; and it should tell of their mutual reactions, their conflicts, their points of agreement. In a word, the novelist must follow the highway so strongly marked out by Zola; but he should also trace a parallel road in the air, a second highway reaching out to the regions beyond and hereafter; he should, in fact, fashion a spiritual naturalism that would be far finer, more powerful, and more complete!

The petty intrigues of a Naundorff were clearly not ideal material for a novelist newly converted to 'spiritual naturalism', and eager to 'represent both the invisible and the tangible, to manifest the piteous uncleanness of the body, and to sublimate the infinite distress of the soul'. But the history of the Middle Ages was, he knew, rich in subjects admirably fitted for such treatment; and so he turned his attention from the reign of the pseudo Charles XI to that of the authentic Charles VII. It was, of course, understandable that the declared enemy of contemporary mediocrity and materialism should regard with nostalgic admiration an age of high villainy and high virtue, when it seemed that rich and poor alike dedicated themselves wholeheartedly to God or to Satan. And it was natural too that he should choose to study in particular a man who was perhaps the greatest sinner and the greatest penitent of that age – Marshal Gilles de Rais, the so-called 'Bluebeard' of Tiffauges. For this 'fifteenth-century des Esseintes', as Huysmans termed him, was the very antithesis of the nineteenth-century 'little man' beloved of the Naturalists: he had touched the uttermost boundaries of human experience, plumbed the depths of satanic vice, and scaled the heights of Christian fervour – all in the short life-span of thirty-six years. Huysmans was tempted by the difficulties which the study of such a character presented, notably the problem of explaining 'how this man, who was a good soldier and a good Christian, suddenly turned into a monster of sacrilege and sadism, cruelty and cowardice'. Possibly he was also encouraged by the example of Paul Adam, who in Être, a recently published novel of fifteenth-century life, had portrayed a diabolical character very similar to Gilles de Rais – a woman called Mahaud who vies in wickedness with the Seigneur of Tiffauges, who like him defies her judges when brought to trial, and who like him is finally overcome with sudden, sincere, and unexpected remorse.[23] Adam's Mahaud is an impressive, unforgettable figure; and Huysmans doubtless resolved to demonstrate in like manner the true greatness of Gilles de Rais, to rehabilitate the man whom unthinking generations had confused with the Bluebeard of fairy-tale and legend.

His plans for a novel 'about King Charles and the fringe of the clerical world' were accordingly shelved, and he began work instead on a biographical study of Gilles de Rais. For some months he consulted all the available documentary sources, drawing chiefly upon the Abbé Bossard's monumental work on the subject.[24] Then, in September 1889, he decided that a visit to Tiffauges itself was indispensable. With Francis Poictevin he spent a few days at a modest hostelry in the village, which lies in the shadow of the castle keep, close to the borders of La Vendée and Brittany. In the evenings the two friends used to stroll along the banks of the

Sèvre, watching the shadows spread across the vast ruins of the Marshal's stronghold; while an old woman dressed in black with a medieval coif waited for them at the inn, candle in hand, ready to bolt the door as soon as they returned. During the day, according to an entry in Edmond de Goncourt's *Journal*,[25] 'Huysmans amused himself by troubling Poictevin's feeble wits with his Mephistophelism, looking in the latrines of a ruined castle for the remains of children slaughtered by Gilles de Rais, and for want of better booty, carrying off a priest's *caecum* which they found in a monastery graveyard . . .' The novelist certainly enjoyed his brief holiday in the west, and in a letter he wrote to Odilon Redon towards the end of the month[26] he enthusiastically recalled the melancholy charm of the Breton moors, the splendour of the caves at Morgat, and the sinister attraction of the oubliettes in the castle at Tiffauges. Unfortunately, the sudden transition from the medieval atmosphere of Tiffauges to the hubbub of Paris in Exposition Year spoilt much of his pleasure. Giving vent to his irritation in the same letter to Redon, he wrote:

Enjoy the good country air while you may. Here it is foul and pestilential. And the streets are swarming with provincials trailing bewildered wives and squalling brats behind them – all with their noses in the air, gaping at the rooftops and spelling out the names of the streets. The need for a little wholesale slaughter becomes evident.

Anyway, what the blazes do they want here, all these people? There were hundreds of them at the Louvre yesterday, exuding a damp canine odour and polluting the pictures with their filthy breath. One of them, a bald and obese monstrosity, was explaining what the paintings were about to his frumpish wife; and she was standing there with her hands folded on her belly, rolling her mucilaginous eyes, and murmuring: 'Ah, but them pictures is old, very old!'

Oh, for a bloody massacre!

Sentiments scarcely less violent were expressed in a letter which Huysmans wrote to Paul Verlaine at about this time.[27] Though commiserating with the poet on his enforced return to the Hôpital Broussais, he added:

> In one way, however, you can count yourself lucky to be shut up just now: you are at least spared the sight of a city completely taken over by South American gigolos and English tourists. It's enough to make one vomit. And the frightful, podgy, squealing balls of fat produced by foreign spermatozoa are simply beyond belief!
>
> There is undeniably something to be said for the tortures ordained by the Holy Office!

Huysmans employed the same tones of horrified disgust, and sounded the same note of exasperated misanthropy, in *Certains*, a collection of articles on art and architecture brought out by Stock in November 1889. In this book he no longer celebrated the tawdry splendour of the Paris streets, but spoke with loathing of 'the boulevards lined with trees which the Highways Department has squeezed into orthopaedic corsets and fitted with cast-iron trusses; the roadways shaken by enormous omnibuses and wagons plastered with ignoble advertisements; the pavements swarming with a hideous crowd in search of money, with women degraded by childbirth and worn out by odious trafficking, and with men reading infamous newspapers or thinking about fraud and fornication, while they in turn are spied on from the windows of shops and offices by the licensed pirates of business and banking'. Similarly, he no longer exalted the new iron-age architecture which he had glorified in *En Ménage*, but fulminated against the Tour Eiffel and the shoddy Exposition buildings in the Champ de Mars. And the artists whom he now thought fit to praise were not those who discovered beauty in aspects of modern life, but those who fled in horror from nineteenth-century reality to other times and other worlds. Thus in the introductory chapter of *Certains* he wrote:

The theory of environment, as applied to art by M. Taine, operates even in the case of great artists – but in reverse, for then the effect of environment is to fill the artist with hatred and revulsion. Instead of modelling and fashioning the spirit in its own image, it creates a lonely Edgar Poe in an immense Boston City, while in a depraved and worthless France it creates a Baudelaire, a Flaubert, an Edmond and Jules de Goncourt, a Villiers de l'Isle-Adam, a Gustave Moreau, a Redon and a Rops – exceptional beings who retrace their steps down the centuries and, out of disgust for the shameful promiscuities which they are forced to suffer, throw themselves into the abyss of the ages, into the tumultuous spaces of dream and nightmare.

Huysmans' growing interest in the occult, and more particularly in satanism, was made manifest in his studies of these 'exceptional beings'. Of Gustave Moreau's art he wrote that it inspired thoughts of 'sacramental formulas of obscure prayers, insidious appeals to rape and sacrilege, to torture and murder'. One of Odilon Redon's bizarre creations was described as linking him with 'the fantastic Bestiaries of the Middle Ages, the clairvoyant devotees of the Monster'. Whistler's female studies were termed 'phantomatic', his Nocturnes likened to 'fluidic dreams', and the painter himself called 'a psychic artist capable of disengaging the suprasensible from the real'. And finally, in an essay on *Les Sataniques* of Félicien Rops, Huysmans praised the Belgian artist for celebrating 'the supernatural aspects of perversity', and made the significant statement that all art 'must gravitate, like humanity which has given birth to it and the earth which carries it, to one of these two poles: purity and wantonness, the heaven and hell of art . . . and to be truly great, a work of art must be either satanic or mystic, for between these extremes there is only a temperate zone, an artistic purgatory, filled with more or less contemptible works of purely human interest'.

This masterly study of *Les Sataniques* is important also for the light it throws upon the development of Huysmans' attitude to the opposite sex. As a natural consequence of the frustration which Anna Meunier's illness caused him, he had become increasingly misogynistic in recent years, and this tendency was reflected in his writings. Thus in both *A Rebours* and *En Rade*, woman was represented as unclean and diseased; while in an article on Degas reprinted in *Certains*, Huysmans congratulated the artist on his courage in showing the idolized creature 'tubbing herself in the humiliating postures demanded by her toilet', in depicting her 'frog-like and simian attitudes', and in laying bare 'the humid horror of a body which no washing can purify'. From the medieval contempt for the flesh expressed in these works, it was but a short step to the medieval concept of woman as an *instrumentum diaboli* – and Huysmans found it easy to accept this idea. In all his early novels he had shown how woman inflicted untold physical and spiritual suffering on man, stifling his artistic talent or implanting disease in his body and doubt in his mind; he was, therefore, a willing convert to the belief held by Baudelaire and Barbey d'Aurevilly before him – that woman was 'bewitched by the Devil, and then transferred the maleficent spell to any man who touched her'.[28] Following his usual practice of illustrating his theories with references to pictorial art, he first expounded this concept of woman in his essay on Félicien Rops, where he asserted that even if one repudiated the theory of demonic possession, the fact remained that woman had always fomented evil, that she was 'the great vessel of crime and iniquity, the store-house of shame and misery, the mistress of ceremonies who introduced into our souls the ambassadors of all the vices'. And he made no secret of his personal conviction that woman was essentially 'the naked and venomous Beast, the mercenary of the Powers of Darkness, the absolute slave of the Devil'.

Huysmans was to reaffirm this belief in a story of modern satanism which he had decided to link with his biography of Gilles de Rais. If it was a novel by Paul Adam which had encouraged him to undertake his study of the Marshal, it was probably a little-known work called *Un Caractère*, a tale of spiritualism by his friend Léon Hennique, which prompted him to adopt this binary form for *Là-Bas*. In his novel, which was published in 1889, Hennique had presented scenes from two eras, alternating episodes from the life of Agénor, nineteenth-century Marquis de Cluses, and dreams of the age Agénor most admired – the seventeenth century. Huysmans was quick to see the advantages offered by this plan, especially as it would enable him to make use of some of the material he had gathered for his Naundorffist novel; and he accordingly decided to make a study of satanism both contemporary and medieval, interweaving the two narratives, revealing similar motives and effects, and achieving what he called 'a parallel demonstration that the same spiritual phases occur in the same sequence – that they have not changed in character but have merely been cloaked by hypocrisy'.[29]

In order to satisfy himself that the cult of satanism was indeed practised in his own day, Huysmans was eager to meet some of its devotees and, if possible, to witness their secret rites. Whether, in fact, he was ever present at a Black Mass is uncertain; but there is good reason to believe that, in this respect at least, Durtal's confession in *En Route* corresponds to the general confession made by Huysmans himself after his conversion. Admittedly, Remy de Gourmont stated that the Black Mass in *Là-Bas* was purely imaginary,[30] and added: 'It was I who hunted for details of this fantastic ceremony. I found none, for the simple reason that none exists.' But Gourmont, on account of his connexion with Berthe Cour-rière and his hostility to Huysmans, must be regarded as an unreliable witness. The evidence of the Abbé Mugnier,[31] who in 1930 assured a young research student that Huysmans had never witnessed the celebration of a Black Mass, is also suspect – though not, of course, for the same reasons. On the other hand, it is unlikely that on this point Huysmans' old friend Léon Hennique had any axe to grind; and in that same year of 1930,[32] Hennique stated in an interview with Frédéric Lefèvre: 'Huysmans had been present at a Black Mass, and afterwards he had told me how frightful and diabolical the spectacle had seemed to him.' Even more striking is the tes-timony of Baron Firmin Van den Bosch, an unimpeachable

211

witness, who claimed that Huysmans had furnished him with a detailed account of his researches into contemporary satanism.[33] In this account Huysmans was alleged to have stated that through the mediation of certain occultists he had once been given the chance to attend a Black Mass, and that during the office he had noticed a priest dressed in a cassock and some sort of hood standing apart from the congregation, not far from the altar, and watching the ceremony most attentively. Not long afterwards he had seen a photograph of the same priest, this time wearing an unusual chasuble, in the window of a bookshop specializing in works on satanism and occultism; and he had eventually succeeded in identifying the man as the Abbé Van Haecke, Chaplain of the Holy Blood at Bruges. According to Baron Van den Bosch, Huysmans' statement had continued:

> I discovered many curious facts concerning this man. He has paid three visits to Paris, where he moved in satanist and occultist circles. On his second visit he put up at the Hôtel Saint-Jean-de-Latran, in the Rue des Saints-Pères, an establishment of doubtful repute which is known chiefly for its clientèle of renegade priests. It is certain that he has at one time been a satanist, and that he has even had a cross tattooed on the soles of his feet, so that he may have the pleasure of continually walking upon the symbol of the Saviour.
>
> Later I went to see Van Haecke at Bruges. He seemed very suspicious of me. I made it clear to him that I didn't understand what could have induced him to compromise his reputation by associating with satanists and by attending the Black Mass at which I had seen him. He replied: 'Haven't I the right to be inquisitive? And how do you know that I wasn't there as a spy?'

At first sight, this explanation of the priest's conduct seems quite feasible, for the Abbé Louis Van Haecke was known to his intimates as an exceptionally inquisitive person. Out of curiosity, he once attended a religious ceremony of some eastern sect, and afterwards went to great pains to obtain an oriental chasuble – doubtless that in which he was photographed; while he also confided to a friend that he had spent the whole of one night locked in a temple of the Greek Orthodox Church, simply in order to explore the sacristy and ransack the tabernacle.[34] Huysmans can scarcely have had visual proof that the priest had crosses tattooed on the soles of his feet, and this detail may have been taken by some informer from the history of the notorious Cantianille affair. As for the photograph in the bookshop window, it seems that Van Haecke was very vain of his good looks and his ecclesiastical vestments, and that he was in the habit of presenting Parisian shopkeepers with portraits of himself in various poses and costumes; thus, according to Huysmans' preface to *Le Satanisme et la magie*, another study of the Belgian priest was to be seen in a photographer's shop-window at the Carrefour de la Croix-Rouge.[35] Lastly, if we are to believe M. Herman Bossier, who knew the man in his old age and questioned many of his friends, Van Haecke was always held in love and respect by the good people of Bruges; and they would certainly have laughed to scorn any accusations of devil-worship levelled at the silver-haired priest who led the Procession of the Holy Blood through the city streets each Good Friday, and who died in October 1912, in his eighty-fourth year, mourned by all his parishioners.[36]

It should not be supposed, however, that the sight of Van Haecke at a Black Mass, or the discovery of his photograph in an occultist bookshop, was sufficient to convince Huysmans of the priest's guilt: more evidence was required before the novelist would represent him in *Là-Bas* as the diabolical Canon Docre, the modern counterpart of Gilles de Rais. This evidence was provided by Édouard Dubus and Berthe Courrière, who on various occasions both enjoyed Van Haecke's hospitality at Bruges. It was probably Berthe to whom Huysmans referred in his preface to *Le Satanisme et la magie*, when he wrote that 'one of Docre's victims has described to me how, in the evening, this priest would sometimes fall into a panic, trembling with fright and screaming:

"I'm afraid! I'm afraid!" – and how he could only recover his self-possession by lighting all the lamps in the house, vociferating diabolical imprecations, and committing nameless acts of sacrilege with the Eucharist.' And it was doubtless from Dubus that Huysmans obtained the substance of this indictment of Van Haecke, which he published in the same preface:[37]

This man has organized a demoniacal clan of young people in Belgium. To attract them, he spins them tales of experiments designed to uncover 'the hidden forces of Nature' – for that is the excuse made by all who are caught in the act of devil-worship. Then he strengthens his hold on them with the aid of lovely women, whom he hypnotizes, and lavish meals; and, little by little, he corrupts their morals and excites their senses by means of aphrodisiacs which they absorb in the form of brandy-nuts, at dessert. Finally, when the neophyte is completely in his power, bound and defiled by reciprocal services, he forces him into the darkest devilries and into the company of his horrible flock.

Attempts have, of course, been made to discredit this evidence, on the grounds that both Édouard Dubus and Berthe Courrière were mentally unstable, not to say insane; and it must be admitted that during one of her visits to Bruges, Berthe conducted herself in a most peculiar manner. On the night of 8 September 1890, in fact, the Bruges police found her hiding in the bushes on the Rempart des Maréchaux, clad only in her undergarments, and promptly arranged for her to be interned in the mental asylum of Saint-Julien. When Remy de Gourmont obtained her release from this institution, a month later, she told him that the police had refused to accept her explanation of her strange behaviour – to wit, that she had just escaped from the house of Van Haecke, who had been trying to implicate her in his satanic practices. Considering the reputation which Van Haecke enjoyed in his native city, it is not surprising that the Bruges police should have dismissed Berthe's story as the ravings of a lunatic; and one would indeed be inclined to agree with them – but for one significant fact. When M. Herman Bossier was conducting his thorough and impartial investigation into the Van Haecke affair, he discovered that the dossier on Berthe Courrière opened by the police at the time of her arrest, and that which was opened by the asylum authorities when she was admitted to the Institut Saint-Julien, had both mysteriously disappeared.[38]

Whatever truth there may have been in the charges laid against Van Haecke, there can be no doubt that Huysmans sincerely believed him to be a satanist. If he had suspected, even for a moment, that he had wronged the Belgian priest, he would certainly have felt obliged to retract his allegations of devil-worship, in private if not in public; but his correspondence reveals that he persisted in these allegations long after his conversion. Thus, in an article on Bruges published in the *Écho de Paris* on 1 February 1899, he wrote: 'You will find witches' thimble growing in a certain little square, and there, in a shuttered house which is painted yellow like the homes of criminals in the Middle Ages, the Black Mass is celebrated at sacrilegious gatherings of young people.'[39] In the summer of the same year, he showed Michel de Lézinier[40] a recent photograph of 'that blackguard Docre', and told the Abbess of Sainte-Cécile de Solesmes that an enemy of his had been to Bruges 'to ask for help from a frightful demoniacal priest whom I portrayed in *Là-Bas*, under the name of Canon Docre. It seems, however, that the spells cast by the wretched woman and that sorcerer are somewhat lacking in vigour, because the results she has obtained are nil . . .'[41] To another correspondent, an Abbé Moeller, who had asked for details of the real Canon Docre,[42] he wrote:

As for Docre, that's a very delicate question, as it's difficult for me to avoid saying too much or too little. The documents which I possessed have been given to the proper authorities for examination, and have been accepted as valid. But I can say no more, for I'm no longer concerned with the affair. I think that the truth, the whole truth, will only be known if and when they release from the seal of the confessional a Belgian priest *who knows everything*. But will Rome do this? In the meantime, there's nothing to be done. The people who have been to see you *know very well what they are about*, believe me. In any case, they know whom to ask, if their investigations are incomplete. There are women mixed up in this affair, and that's one reason why I'm holding aloof from it all, seeing that otherwise I could expect nothing but trouble. Besides, I've done all I could to help the authorities. Why, then, have they spared Docre? Why, after such a fierce blaze, has everything petered out? I don't know . . .

The inquiry to which Huysmans referred in this letter had been opened by the Bishop of Bruges, Mgr Waffelaert, after rumours identifying Van Haecke with the Canon Docre of *Là-Bas* had reached the episcopal ears. Huysmans was invited to submit evidence, and he sent a twelve-page memorandum on the affair to Baron Firmin Van den Bosch, who forwarded it to the Bishopric of Bruges. In conversation with M. Herman Bossier, the Baron later recalled that this memorandum contained references to Van Haecke's presence at a Black Mass, to the photograph in the bookshop window, to the priest's relations with Berthe Courrière and Édouard Dubus, and to two incriminating letters which Dubus had sent Huysmans from Bruges in 1889.[43] Common courtesy demanded some acknowledgement of the trouble Huysmans had taken to help Mgr Waffelaert in his inquiries; but no such acknowledgement was made, and the results of the investigation were kept a closely guarded secret. What is more, when the indefatigable M. Bossier attempted to carry his researches into the Bishopric of Bruges, he found that Huysmans' memorandum and the Van Haecke dossier, like the Berthe Courrière dossiers in the Ministry of Justice and the Institut Saint-Julien, had unaccountably vanished. One can only assume that the authorities had decided to suppress all evidence of Van Haecke's Jekyll-and-Hyde existence, in the hope that the world would eventually forget that a Chaplain of the Holy Blood had served as the model for one of the most diabolical characters in modern literature. Or, as Huysmans put it,[44] in a bitter postscript to the whole affair, 'they preferred *silentium . . .*'

6. THE MAGICIAN

IN the Abbé Louis Van Haecke, Huysmans thought at first that he had discovered the greatest satanist of his time, the Gilles de Rais of the nineteenth century. Towards the end of 1889, however, he heard of a defrocked priest whose diabolical practices were reported to surpass anything attempted by the Chaplain of Bruges. A study of this priest's private papers, recently discovered in a remote French village by M. Pierre Lambert, and of a 'confession' which he wrote in the prisons of the Holy Office, leaves no doubt that these reports of his depravity were well founded. Yet this man, who has been colourfully but not unfairly described[1] as 'a pontiff of infamy, a base idol of the mystical Sodom, a magician of the worst type, a wretched criminal, an evil sorcerer, and the founder of an infamous sect' – this man was to exert a powerful and largely beneficial influence on Huysmans' life and thought. For this reason, and despite the fact that it makes unpleasant reading, some account of his life must be given here.

His name was Joseph-Antoine Boullan, and he was born on 18 February 1824 in the little village of Saint-Porquier, in the Department of Tarn-et-Garonne. Ambitious to become a priest, he studied first at the local seminary and later at Rome, where he obtained his doctorate with distinction. He then joined the Missionaries of the Precious Blood and took part in several missions to Italy, before settling down in 1853 in the Maison des Trois Épis, one of the Society's houses, not far from Turckheim in Alsace. Within two years he had become superior of this establishment; but in 1856, for some unknown reason, he left Alsace and came to Paris as an independent priest. Here his attention was soon divided between his first periodical, *Les Annales du Sacerdoce*, and a young woman called Adèle Chevalier, a former member of the community of

Saint-Thomas-de-Villeneuve at Soissons. In 1856, two years after a 'miraculous' cure which she attributed to the intercession of Our Lady of La Salette, this nun had been summoned by supernatural voices to the mountain shrine; and the monks of La Salette had been so impressed by her account of her mystical experiences that they had asked the Bishop of Grenoble for permission to entrust her spiritual direction to the Abbé Boullan, who was known to them as an eminent theologian. As it happened, the good monks could not have made a more unfortunate choice.

At first, the association of the Abbé Boullan and Sister Adèle Chevalier promised well. They busied themselves with the publication of *Les Annales du Sacerdoce*; they lived ostensibly holy lives; and in 1859 they founded at Bellevue, near Paris, a religious community with the imposing title of the Society for the Reparation of Souls. In fact, however, this community was nothing more than a cloak for an amorous liaison between the two founders, and for sacrilegious practices of a particularly revolting nature, culminating in ritual murder. Thus whenever a nun fell sick or complained of being tormented by the Devil, Boullan would apply remedies compounded of consecrated hosts and faecal matter; and on 8 December 1860, at the end of his Mass, he sacrificed upon the altar a child which Adèle Chevalier had borne him at the moment of Consecration. This abominable crime was never discovered by the authorities; but complaints were made to the police and the Bishop of Versailles about certain fraudulent devices and strange medicinal remedies employed by the Society for the Reparation of Souls, with the result that in 1861 Boullan and his mistress were put on trial for fraud and indecency. They were found guilty on the first count and sentenced to three years' imprisonment, which Boullan served at Rouen from December 1861 till September 1864. A few years later, in the spring and summer of 1869, the Abbé again found himself behind prison walls – this time at Rome, in the cells of the Holy Office. It was here, on 26 May 1869, that he began writing the 'confession' of his crimes known as the *cahier rose*: a horrifying document which Huysmans found among the priest's papers after his death, and which Professor Louis Massignon delivered into the safe-keeping of the Vatican Library in 1930. Rehabilitated by the Holy Office, Boullan returned to Paris in the winter of 1869; and on 1 January 1870 he brought out the first issue of a new periodical, *Les Annales de la Sainteté au XIXe Siècle*. It was not long before the attention of the Cardinal Archbishop of Paris was drawn to certain heretical views propounded in this review, and to reports that the Abbé Boullan was once more indulging in indecent practices, under cover of his considerable reputation as an exorcist. For as his first biographer revealed in 1912,[2] whenever Boullan's good offices were invoked by Mother Abbesses whose nuns had complained of diabolical visitations, he did not confine himself to exorcizing the unfortunate women, but also 'taught them how, by means of auto-hypnosis and auto-suggestion, they could dream that they were having intercourse with the saints or with Jesus Christ, and showed them what postures and occult methods they should adopt to enable supernatural entities – and more particularly his own astral body – to visit and possess them . . .'

When the Archbishop of Paris finally summoned Boullan to his Palace, in 1875, it was ostensibly to inquire into the case of an epileptic whom the priest professed to have cured with the help of Christ's seamless coat, the famous relic kept at Argenteuil; but in fact, he wished to question Boullan about the less orthodox remedies which he used against evil spirits. At the end of the interview between priest and prelate, Cardinal Guibert roundly condemned the 'infamous doctrines' promulgated in *Les Annales de la Sainteté*, placed Boullan under a solemn interdict, and ordered him out of the Palace.[3] He straightway appealed to Rome to remove the interdict, but the Vatican upheld Cardinal Guibert's judgement. And on 1 July 1875, after bringing out the last issue of his review, Joseph-Antoine Boullan left the Church.

He lost no time in forming new ties to replace the old, for in that same month of July 1875 he entered into correspondence with Pierre-Eugène-Michel Vintras, the ageing miracle-worker of Tilly-sur-Seulle, who taught that he was a reincarnation of the prophet Elijah, sent to prepare the world for the Third Reign, the Era of the Paraclete, the coming of the Christ of Glory. The two thaumaturgists met for the first time in Brussels on 13 August, and again in Paris on 26 October; and at their second meeting Vintras presented Boullan with some of his 'miraculous' hosts, marked in blood with mysterious symbols. As Vintras had been bestowing these hosts upon his followers for the past thirty years, this could scarcely be interpreted as anything more than a friendly gesture; yet when the prophet of Tilly died, on 7 December 1875, Boullan announced that he had been chosen to succeed him. He spent the following months fitting himself for his position as high priest of the Vintrasian sect and leader of the heretical Society of Mercy. In February 1876 he arrived in Lyons, to study the Society's archives and to familiarize himself with its mystico-erotic jargon, which he discovered was not unlike that employed by the ill-fated Society for the Reparation of Souls. Because Vintras had dubbed himself the New Elijah, Boullan now proclaimed that he was a reincarnation of John the Baptist; and since Vintras had proudly displayed a mark in the shape of a dove in the centre of his forehead, his successor had a cabbalistic pentagram tattooed at the corner of his left eye. However, despite these precautions and his excellent qualifications, many members of the Society of Mercy were suspicious of so recent a convert; and by the end of the year only three of the nineteen pontiffs consecrated by Vintras had accepted Boullan as their leader. Undaunted, he set up his headquarters in Lyons, first at the house of one François-Ours Soiderquelk, *alias* 'Adhalnaël, Vintrasian Pontiff of Cordial and Holy Unification', and later, in 1884, at No. 7 Rue de la Martinière, the home of the newly instituted 'Pontiff of the Divine Melchizedean Chrism', an architect known to the unenlightened as Pascal Misme.

The names of some of those who forgathered at Misme's house have come down to us either through Boullan's archives or through Huysmans' correspondence. They included a clairvoyante called Mme Laure, a certain Laverlochère and his wife, two young dressmakers called Claudine and Joséphine Gay, and the faithful Soiderquelk; there was also Boullan's middle-aged housekeeper, Julie Thibault, otherwise known as 'Achildaël' or 'the Apostolic Woman', who was later to assume an important role in Huysmans' life and works. Among Boullan's disciples these were the elect. Others might be permitted to watch Boullan or Julie Thibault celebrating such strange rites as the 'Sacrifice of Glory of Melchizedek' or the 'Provictimal Sacrifice of Mary'; but only a faithful few were privileged to participate in the most important ceremonies in the Boullan liturgy – his 'Unions of Life'. He taught these chosen disciples that 'since the Fall of our first parents was the result of an act of culpable love, it was through acts of love accomplished in a religious spirit that the Redemption of Humanity could and should be achieved'; and he therefore advocated intercourse with celestial entities if an adept wished to redeem himself, or with 'inferior beings' if, out of charity, he wished to help them up the 'ladder of life'.[4] As Stanislas de Guaita pointed out in *Le Temple de Satan*, this doctrine led 'firstly, to unlimited promiscuity and indecency; secondly, to adultery, incest, and bestiality; thirdly, to incubism and onanism . . . all exalted to meritorious and sacramental acts of worship'. One can, therefore, understand Boullan's anxiety that profane eyes should on no account witness the celebration of these intimate rites.

In 1886, however, Boullan threw caution to the winds and admitted three comparative strangers to his confidence. The first was Canon Roca, a priest with Socialistic leanings and occult interests who edited a review called *L'Anticlérical*; he was initiated by Julie Thibault in the mysteries of the 'ladder of life', and soon afterwards left Lyons in disgust, determined never to return. Stanislas de Guaita, who spent a fortnight in Lyons in November 1886, also professed disgust for Boullan's doctrines, although according to the ex-Abbé[5] he had gone down on his knees before Julie Thibault and assured her that he was 'only a little child at school'. But Guaita's hypocritical pretence was as nothing compared with the gross deception practised on Boullan by a third initiate, the occultist Oswald

Wirth. For over a year this unscrupulous young man simulated the most ardent enthusiasm for Boullan's ideas; then, in December 1886, having obtained a written statement of the master's 'secret doctrine', he wrote him a brutal letter explaining how he had been tricked. Early in 1887 Guaita and Wirth came together, compared notes on their experiences at Lyons, and set up an 'initiatory tribunal' to judge Boullan. As was only to be expected, the ex-Abbé was found guilty; and on 24 May 1887, in a letter dictated by Guaita and signed by Wirth, his self-appointed judges informed him that he was a condemned man. Wirth afterwards maintained that he and Guaita had never intended to do more than expose Boullan's practices to the public, which they did in 1891 in *Le Temple de Satan*; but Boullan was convinced that he had been condemned to death, and that attempts would be made to carry out the sentence by magical means. The house in the Rue de la Martinière was accordingly placed on a war footing, and Boullan made ready to ward off the spells and incantations which he had taught Guaita and Wirth, and which he believed would now be turned against him.

The battle had been raging for more than two years when Huysmans first heard of Joseph-Antoine Boullan. The sinister rumours circulating in Paris about the ex-Abbé suggested that here was a source of 'documents' on occultism which he could not afford to neglect, but for some time he was not sure how to set about tapping it. Finally Gustave Guiches, who had heard that the editor of *L'Anticlérical* was a member of the Lyons sect, wrote to ask whether Roca could put his friend Huysmans in touch with Boullan.[6] The Canon replied:

In answer to your letter of the 27th instant, I hasten to inform you that I have broken off all relations with M. Boullan of Lyons, and that I shall take good care never to renew them ... The man is not known to have any friends, and I very much doubt if there is a single one whom M. Huysmans might ask for an introduction. But I can refer him to a decent young fellow in Paris who knows all Boullan's infamous secrets and can enlighten you completely on both the man and his abominable occultism. Write to the initiate Oswald Wirth, mentioning my name . . . and perhaps also to the young Baron Stanislas de Guaita, who should be in Paris just now and who knew Boullan in the same circumstances as I did, though more briefly. He too is well up in the subject . . .

Roca was apparently under the impression that Huysmans was a pictorial artist, for after warning him of the dangers of dabbling in the black arts, he asked him if he would agree to draw 'a head of Christ in glory for the cover of our review, to take the place of the dolorous Christ who is no longer in fashion or in season [sic]'. Vexed more by the priest's philistine views than by his ignorance of modern literature, Huysmans ignored both Roca's warnings and his astonishing request. However, he wrote to Guaita and Wirth, as Roca had advised him to do, explaining that he was collecting material for a book on contemporary satanism, and asking for information about Boullan.[7] Guaita's reply was unhelpful, but Oswald Wirth expressed his readiness to give the novelist 'all the information I possess concerning the person you mention, being only too happy if I can thus help you to put our contemporaries on guard against the most dangerous of all human aberrations'. The two men met at Wirth's flat in the evening of 7 February 1890. Huysmans was not impressed by what the young occultist had to tell him, as can be seen from these notes[8] which he made on their conversation:

O. Wirth – a shuffler and stammerer – denies that the Abbé Boullan is a satanist. He's a Naundorffist, hopes for the coming of the great King and wants to be Pope. He dreams of a Religion of 'Pure and Free Love'. Alleged to be a swindler and a rogue. His occult powers? – Wirth denies these and claims to have exposed Boullan's depravity to Roca and the other occultists. What he's seen, in the country: animals howling like furies, which the Abbé calmed at will. Wirth met him through a family at Châlons. This is how he described him to me:

'He's a little man, all chest and no legs – shifty eyes, tousled beard, nothing of the priest about him save the "soapy" gestures.' This man Misme with whom Boullan lives – and whom he dominates completely – is an architect who was trained at the Châlons works.

If Wirth hoped to dissuade his visitor from making contact with the Lyons sect, he was already too late. Only a few days earlier, Huysmans had discovered that Berthe Courrière, whose connexions with the occultist world were nothing if not extensive, knew Boullan as well as Van Haecke. In answer to his inquiries, she had told him something of Boullan's history, supplied him with Boullan's address, and assured him that the ex-Abbé, whom she described as 'a charming man', would welcome the opportunity of helping him in his work.[9] And on 5 February, two days before his interview with Oswald Wirth, Huysmans had written a long letter introducing himself to the Lyons thaumaturgist.[10] In this letter he explained to Boullan that he was preparing a study of modern satanism, and that in order to document himself for this book he had applied to various occultists in Paris, but that these persons had expounded 'some idiotic theories wrapped up in the most appalling verbiage' and had shown themselves to be 'perfect ignoramuses and incontestable imbeciles'. He went on:

Several times I heard your name pronounced in tones of horror – and this in itself predisposed me in your favour. Then I heard rumours that you were the only initiate in the ancient mysteries who had obtained practical as well as theoretical results, and I was told that if anyone could produce undeniable phenomena, it was you and you alone. This I should like to believe, because it would mean that I had found a rare personality in these drab times – and I could give you some excellent publicity if you needed it. I could set you up as the Superman, the Satanist, the only one in existence, far removed from the infantile spiritualism of the occultists. Allow me then,

Monsieur, to put these questions to you – quite bluntly, for I prefer a straightforward approach. Are you a satanist? And can you give me any information about succubi – Del Rio, Bodin, Sinistrari and Görres being quite inadequate on this subject? You will note that I ask for no initiation, no secret lore – only for reliable documents, for results you have obtained in your experiments . . .

Boullan replied promptly but guardedly the next day,[11] politely refusing Huysmans' offer of publicity, denying that he was a satanist, and posing as 'an Adept who has declared war on all demoniacal cults'. He also claimed, not without justification, to be an authority on incubi and succubi; but he refused to give any detailed information until Huysmans stated the purpose of his inquiries. At the head of his letter he had scrawled his enigmatic motto *Quis ut Deus?* and he had signed it: 'Dr. Johannès' – the 'Adept's name' under which Huysmans was to portray him in *Là-Bas*.

In his next letter,[12] written on the day he met Oswald Wirth, Huysmans changed his tactics and protested that he intended, not to glorify satanism, but simply to prove its continued existence and power.

It happens [he wrote] that I'm weary of the ideas of my good friend Zola, whose absolute positivism fills me with disgust. I'm just as weary of the systems of Charcot, who has tried to convince me that demonianism was just an old wives' tale, and that by applying pressure to the ovaries he could check or develop at will the satanic impulses of the women under his care at La Salpêtrière. And I'm wearier still, if that be possible, of the occultists and spiritualists, whose phenomena, though often genuine, are far too often identical.

What I want to do is to teach a lesson to all these people – to create a work of art of a supernatural realism, a spiritual naturalism. I want to show Zola, Charcot, the spiritualists, and the rest that nothing of the mysteries which surround us has been explained. If I can obtain proof of the existence of succubi, I want to publish that proof, to show that all the materialist theories of Maudsley and his kind are false, and that the Devil exists, that the Devil reigns supreme, that the power he enjoyed in the Middle Ages has not been taken from him, for today he is the absolute master of the world, the Omniarch . . .

Replying to this letter,[13] Boullan expressed unqualified approval of Huysmans' opinions, and promised the novelist his co-operation in the great task he had undertaken. In confirmation of Huysmans' belief that satanism still flourished, he asserted that devil-worship was now practised with even greater fervour than in the Middle Ages, all over Europe – in Rome and Paris, at Lyons and Châlons, and also at Bruges. 'I can put at your disposal', he wrote, 'documents which will enable you to prove that satanism is active in our time, and in what form and in what circumstances. Your work will thus endure as a monumental history of satanism in the nineteenth century.'

He was as good as his word and soon the Rue de Sèvres flat was engulfed in a flood of documents from Lyons, giving not only the desired information on succubi, but also voluminous details of the art of casting spells, the Sacrifice of Glory of Melchizedek, the Black Mass, and other practices of satanists and exorcists. Nor was Boullan content to give Huysmans only documentary help: in May 1890, and again in July, he performed what he called 'magical operations' to protect the writer from evil spells cast by Guaita and his fellow Rosicrucians, the second of these 'operations' lasting two whole days.[14] However, there is no reason to suppose that, at this stage at least, the occultists of Paris resorted to any force other than that of argument in their efforts to separate Huysmans from Boullan. Two attempts to do this are known to have been made by Oswald Wirth. On 13 February 1890 he sent Huysmans a letter referring him to those passages in *Les Congrégations religieuses dévoilées*, a book by Charles

Sauvestre, which dealt with the criminal activities of the Society for the Reparation of Souls.[15] And a few weeks later, on a visit to Huysmans' office at the Ministry of the Interior, Wirth and Édouard Dubus tried to open his eyes to Boullan's depravity by describing the 'secret doctrine' and obscene practices of the Lyons sect.[16] But Huysmans was unmoved, and refused to treat their revelations seriously. 'He listened to us with a smile on his lips,' reported Wirth, 'and then remarked that if the old man had found a mystical dodge for obtaining a little carnal satisfaction, that surely wasn't so stupid of him . . .'

In June 1890[17] Huysmans wrote to tell Boullan that, thanks to his copious documentation, the novel had made good progress and was now two-thirds finished. This was doubtless very gratifying to Boullan, but in fact 'Dr. Johannès' was by no means Huysmans' sole source of information on nineteenth-century satanism. As we have seen, the novelist had been documented by Berthe Courrière and Édouard Dubus on the subject of the reputedly diabolical Abbé Van Haecke. He also consulted a considerable number of occultist works, such as Bibliophile Jacob's *Curiosités des sciences occultes*, and even abstracted records of contemporary magicians from the files of the Ministry of the Interior.[18] If we are to credit the statement he made to Baron Firmin Van den Bosch, the 'field-work' which he did in preparation of his book included attendance at a Black Mass, although the ceremony described in *Là-Bas* was based on papers from the Vintrasian archives and on the famous account of a Mass celebrated over the body of Mme de Montespan – probably because these sensational documents were more satisfying than any Black Mass which Huysmans could have witnessed.[19] Finally, when his documentation was complete, Huysmans filled out the fabric of his story with the information Boullan had provided on incubi and succubi, passages copied almost verbatim from Henriette Maillat's letters, conversations he had had with Michel de Lézinier and other friends, and notes he had made on subjects ranging from alchemy to astrology, from theosophy to therapy. Only the success of his bold experiment in form – that 'parallel demonstration' which Paul Valéry described[20] as a landmark in the development of the modern novel – saved his book from becoming, in Léon Bloy's spiteful words,[21] 'an extraordinary hotchpotch, a mix-up, a hugger-mugger, a farrago, a cataclysm of documents'.

Dealing with such a mass of material in a comparatively short space of time, Huysmans was, of course, bound to make some mistakes. Thus, trusting blindly to his authorities, he innocently confused the poet Longfellow with a Scots occultist and satanist of the same name; and according to a letter Charles Buet sent him after the publication of *Là-Bas*,[22] his account of the famous Cantianille affair was 'altogether inaccurate'. Similarly, a misprint in the list of his bell-ringer's campanological works reveals that, anxious as ever to give an impression of wide reading, Huysmans had merely copied out a defective bibliography.[23] But his most serious mistake – a mistake which exposed him to caustic criticism from Papus and other authorities on occultism – was to overlook the fact that the source from which he drew most of his material was polluted. As Joanny Bricaud has pointed out,[24] Boullan deceived Huysmans in much the same way as he himself had been deceived by Wirth, 'by reversing the roles, and attributing to Canon Docre or the occultists of the cabbalistic Rosy Cross his own demoniacal practices . . .'

Boullan certainly had good reason to be pleased with the portrait Huysmans painted of him in *Là-Bas*, where he appeared in the guise of a master magician and exorcist, 'a highly intelligent and very learned priest . . . a much sought-after theologian and a recognized master of canon law'. But while Huysmans did everything to publicize the real Dr. Johannès short of giving Boullan's name and address, he was at pains to disguise the true identity of Canon Docre. The statement that Docre was living near Nîmes, the home of Canon Roca, combined with the similarity of the two names, was designed as a red herring to deflect readers from the trail leading to Bruges. So was Docre's *curriculum vitae*, which mentioned that he had served as chaplain to a queen living in exile; for although Huysmans claimed to have proof that the sometime chaplain to Isabella II of Spain had been a satanist, only the physical characteristics of this priest were used in portraying Docre.[25] Another composite portrait in Huysmans' gallery of diabolists was that of Mme Chantelouve, for here the novelist took as his models no fewer than four women: Mme Charles Buet, Berthe Courrière, Henriette Maillat, and a certain Jeanne Jacquemin,[26] who was the mistress of the Marseilles painter Auguste Lauzet. Chantelouve himself was, of course, modelled on Charles Buet;[27] and the mysterious Gevingey, the friend of Dr. Johannès, was in reality an astrologer called Eugène Ledos, of whom Huysmans used to say that 'he looked as though he had been born with a three-legged stool fastened to his rump'.[28] As for Carhaix, the kindly Quasimodo of *Là-Bas*, his prototype was a man called Contesse, who had been bell-ringer at Saint-Sulpice since 1878; but Carhaix's panegyric of the art of bell-ringing was largely taken from Lamiral's *Art de la sonnerie*, and the *pot-au-feu* with which he regaled his guests was really cooked by Berthe Courrière for the friends who dined at her Rue de Varenne flat.[29] Huysmans had met Contesse in the winter of 1888, when he was preparing the article 'L'Accordant' for *Gil Blas*, and he had paid several visits to the bell-ringer's home in the north tower of Saint-Sulpice. Recalling these visits many years later,[30] in a conversation with Michel de Lézinier, he said:

The poor man imagined that I went to see him in order to pay court to his daughter, a strapping wench of some twenty summers who wasn't exactly retiring in her ways. One day he accused me of trifling with her affections, then flew into a passion and threw me out, shouting: 'Be off with you! Be off with you!' I can still see him waving his hands in my face – the hands of an old man, with the veins standing out on them like the wire fillets in cloisonné enamels. And all this time, the girl was shaking a salad basket containing some chicory leaves of a green so dark that it was almost black. I know

– they were just the colour of Remy de Gourmont's three hairs . . .

Huysmans himself appeared in *Là-Bas* in the guise of two characters – des Hermies and Durtal – not, as in *En Ménage*, in order to reveal complementary aspects of his own personality, but simply to motivate the discussion on Naturalism in the first chapter of the novel. His duty as foil done, des Hermies was soon to die a convenient death, but Durtal established himself as the protagonist of all Huysmans' later novels: more than any other character which the novelist created in his own image, he was the essential Huysmans, the retiring author, the confirmed bachelor, the sinner in search of his soul. As can be seen by consulting the manuscript of *Là-Bas*,[31] Huysmans originally intended to call the hero of his novel Runan – a name taken, like most of the names he gave his characters, from a railway time-table. The decision to substitute the name of Durtal was made, curiously enough, at a restaurant in the Place Saint-André-des-Arts – only a few yards from the street where Huysmans himself was born, and not far from the church where he was christened – in the course of a lunch-time conversation with Michel de Lézinier.[32] The doctor had been telling Huysmans that his family name was that of a village which lay between Angers and La Flèche, close to the town of Durtal.

'Durtal!' exclaimed Huysmans, who seemed to have something in mind. 'But that doesn't sound like a French name. In the languages of the North, it would mean "Valley of Aridity" or "Valley of the Door". Dürer, you know, had a door on his coat of arms. And that hefty fellow Lilienthal, who's just killed himself trying out some sort of balloon, cheerfully bore the ridiculous name of "Valley of the Lilies". But to get back to the town – have you ever been there?'

'Yes, some years ago. I'd travelled from Angers to Lézinier out of curiosity, to see if I could still find any trace of my family there. It's a mean little hole, with a few houses grouped round the station – the last stop before Durtal. As it wasn't far, I went to catch the train at Durtal itself, which is an unpleasant haunt of coopers and vine-growers.'

'Durtal!' said Huysmans once more. He asked the waiter for a railway time-table, hunted through it, and scribbled a few words in pencil in a notebook . . .

Some of the last details required for *Là-Bas* were supplied in September 1890 by Gustave Boucher, a bookseller on the Quai Voltaire whom Henri Girard had introduced to Huysmans, when he sent the novelist a brochure on the prophecies of the *Liber Mirabilis* and a cutting from an old folio dealing with the Mass of Melchizedek.[33] By a curious coincidence, during the same month of September, Huysmans received a visit from a woman who performed these rites daily, and who, only a few years later, was to make her home in his bachelor establishment in the Rue de Sèvres, as his housekeeper and friend. This woman was Julie Thibault.[34] His first impression was of a little peasant woman in a cheap black dress and a ruched bonnet, with an umbrella and a prayer-book tightly clutched in her hands, a tin crucifix dangling on her chest, and a pair of pince-nez perched on the very tip of her nose. But he quickly dismissed the idea that she was a mere country bumpkin when he saw her face in profile – the austere profile of a Caesar's death-mask – and when, after quoting from memory from the works of an obscure sixteenth-century mystic, she recounted to him some of her own pious exploits. It seemed that she had spent many years visiting shrines to the Virgin all over the Continent, trudging the highways of Europe for over 25,000 miles, taking with her only her umbrella and a bundle of clothes, and living only on milk, bread, and honey. With his penchant for exceptional characters, Huysmans was naturally fascinated by this astonishing woman, who spoke of conversations she had with the Virgin and the saints as of some very ordinary occurrence. She, for her part, took an immediate liking to the author, and henceforth referred to him affectionately as 'our friend' – while he invariably called her 'Maman' Thibault.

A month later Huysmans wrote *finis* to his book, and left Paris for a brief visit to Lyons to thank Boullan personally for his help.[35] On his return he told Edmond de Goncourt[36] that *Là-Bas* was finished and would appear in the spring of 1891; but he added that he was afraid no newspaper or review would publish it in serial form, 'on account of the terrible details furnished by the Lyons priest I have just been to see'. However, events soon proved him wrong. He was approached by Henry Bauër on behalf of one of the least sensational of the Paris newspapers, with the result that on 15 February 1891 the first instalment of *Là-Bas* appeared in print, in the columns of the *Écho de Paris*.[37]

It made an immediate impression upon the public. The more conservative subscribers to the *Écho de Paris* threatened to cancel their orders for the newspaper if Huysmans' serial were not withdrawn; but the editor, Valentin Simond, stood firm, and was rewarded with an immense influx of new and appreciative readers. Even Edmond de Goncourt, normally chary of praise, gave *Là-Bas* his unqualified approval after reading only three instalments. 'It is really very good, this novel by Huysmans in the *Écho de Paris*', he wrote in his *Journal*.[38] 'It is the sort of prose one rarely finds on the serial page of a newspaper, and which is a pleasure to read when one wakes in the morning. Yes indeed, this is rich writing, with some bold thinking behind it.' But the majority of Huysmans' readers were, of course, attracted more by the sensational subject-matter of the story than by its stylistic qualities. And when, on its publication in book form in April, the Bibliothèque des Chemins de Fer banned the novel from all railway bookstalls, its success was assured.

Reviews of the book were on the whole favourable, although Charles Maurras reacted sharply and characteristic-ally[39] to Huysmans' attack on 'the accursed Latin race', and the Rosicrucians of Paris rushed into print to defend their discredited reputations. Thus Péladan, who was referred to in *Là-Bas* as 'that cheapjack magician, that mountebank from the

Midi', retaliated by asserting[40] that Huysmans' book revealed 'an absolute and definitive ignorance of the laws of satanism', while Papus hinted that the novelist's principal source of information was *Larousse*.[41] Huysmans ignored these attacks, but felt obliged to reply to an anonymous article in *L'Éclair*[42] which, treating *Là-Bas* as the *livre à clé* it undoubtedly was, sought to identify Canon Docre with the ex-Abbé B . . . of Lyons. He immediately wrote an open letter to Valentin Simond,[43] protesting that the ex-Abbé B . . ., far from being a satanist, was 'a remarkably erudite mystic and one of the most brilliant thaumaturgists of our time', and stating that Canon Docre had been modelled on a royal chaplain, long dead, and on a priest who still officiated in Belgium, 'in a town not far from Ghent'. The only other serious attempt to identify one of the characters in *Là-Bas* – a very accurate attempt this time, made by a singularly well-informed reader – was dealt with by Huysmans in strict privacy. It occurred in March 1891, when he received a letter from one Eugène Cross, informing him that if, as was suspected, the letters of Hyacinthe Chantelouve had been copied from the letters of Henriette Maillat, he would be well advised to get in touch with Cross at once. The writer of this letter had evidently forgotten that Huysmans was an official of the Sûreté Générale, but he was quickly reminded of that fact. And as soon as the would-be black-mailer and his accomplice learned that a detective was making inquiries about them on Huysmans' behalf, they relapsed into a discreet silence.[44]

As it happened, Huysmans' somewhat ungentlemanly pub-lication of extracts from Henriette Maillat's letters was one of the factors leading to the final break between himself and Léon Bloy. It cannot, however, be said to have affected their friendship in any way, for that friendship was already dead. As Bloy explained in a letter to Louis Montchal,[45] in January 1890: 'I have fallen out with Huysmans, completely and irremediably. We may still see each other occasionally and speak courteously to each other, but our friendship is des-troyed for ever. The remarkable thing is that the break cannot be explained by any serious circumstance: we have simply stopped seeing each other, just as one drops a burden one has grown tired of carrying.' However, while Huysmans quickly reconciled himself to this situation, Bloy tried twice to heal the breach between them. Huysmans' refusal to encourage these misguided efforts has often been represented by Bloy's biographers as evidence, at best, of callous indifference to the claims of friendship, and at worst, of base treachery. In fact, it showed nothing more than a realistic appraisal of the true state of affairs, and recognition that satisfactory relations between the two men were no longer possible.

Bloy's first attempt at reconciliation was made in May 1890, when he informed Huysmans by letter that he was about to marry Johanne Molbech, the daughter of the Danish poet Christian Molbech, and invited him to the wedding.[46] Considering that Huysmans believed marriage to be fatal to art, that he disapproved strongly of anyone who married without the means to support a wife and children, and that in this case he is reported[47] to have said he could not understand why Bloy should want to marry 'a woman with a Gorgon's head', it is more than likely that he meant to ignore Bloy's invitation. On the 19th, however, the two men met by chance for the first time for many months, and Huysmans agreed to come to the wedding.[48] Not satisfied, Bloy wrote to him again on the 21st, asking him to be a witness to the marriage cere- mony, and demanding an immediate reply.[49] Huysmans was not unnaturally vexed by such persistent importunity, and unwilling to place himself once more at the beck and call of the 'Ungrateful Mendicant'. He refused, in a note which has apparently not survived, but which Bloy described[50] as 'of insulting brevity'.

Huysmans heard nothing more of Bloy until February 1891, by which time the pamphleteer and his wife had settled at Bagsvaerd in Denmark. Bloy had arranged for Georges Landry to keep him supplied with copies of the *Écho de Paris*, and after reading the first two instalments of *Là-Bas*, he felt moved to congratulate Huysmans on his conception of 'spir- itual naturalism'. 'You are becoming an out-and-out Catholic', he wrote.[51] 'You can no longer control the movements of your soul, which is evidently dragging you along the frightful roads which separate literature from the contemplative life. I find that a unique and, upon my word, a sublime spectacle.' Huysmans did not reply – partly because he had no wish to renew his association with Bloy, and partly, no doubt, because he knew that Bloy's enthusiasm would cool when he discovered that *Là-Bas* was a study of satanism and not a religious work written by 'an out-and-out Catholic'. That he was right was shown by Bloy's bitter comment on the novel, made in an article[52] four months later: 'I mistook the adverb. Huysmans had written *Là-Bas* and I persisted in reading *Là-Haut*.' But this disappointment was not the only reason for the savage attacks which Bloy made on Huysmans' novel. Recognizing Henriette Maillat's tactics in the description of Mme Chantelouve's approaches to Durtal, and his sometime mistress's style in Mme Chantelouve's letters, he assumed that Huysmans had made use of his confidences and had also obtained some of the woman's letters from Joséphin Péladan; the idea that Huysmans could have aroused in Henriette Maillat a passion such as he, Léon Bloy, was capable of inspiring, never occurred to him.[53] He also believed – for he knew nothing of Joseph Boullan or his doctrines – that the theory of the Third Reign propounded in *Là-Bas* was based on his confidences regarding the prophecies of Anne-Marie Roulé. 'Huysmans' book', he told a friend,[54] 'is made up of the rags and tatters of ideas with which I've been supplying him for the past six years. And not content with stealing my ideas, he has travestied and prostituted them in the most odious way . . .'

If any hope of reconciliation still remained, it vanished at the beginning of April. The journalist Jules Huret was at this time conducting his famous inquiry into the state of French literature, on behalf of the enterprising *Écho de Paris*, and on 6 April he published in that newspaper an account of his interview with Huysmans. Like all the other writers interviewed by Huret, the novelist took the opportunity of publicly attacking his literary *bêtes noires* – such as Moréas, who 'writes *coulomb* simply to avoid writing *pigeon*', or Bourget 'with his novels for Jewesses, his tea-table psychology' – and publicly praising his friends – Verlaine and Mallarmé, Jean Lorrain and Lucien Descaves, Paul Margueritte and Remy de Gourmont. Léon Bloy, who could not be considered as either friend or foe, was not mentioned – an omission which the outraged pamphleteer interpreted as a deliberately hostile act. 'Now it is *war* between us', he told Georges Landry.[55] 'And you know what war with me can mean.' In this case it meant that Bloy was to pursue Huysmans to the grave – and even beyond the grave – with a series of defamatory articles and brochures. Huysmans never retaliated; and on several occasions, when he heard that Bloy was suffering hardship, he sent money to the enemy who for six years had been his friend.[56] Although he must have been grieved by Bloy's venomous attacks, only once is he known to have commented on the pamphleteer's conduct. Replying to a friend who had questioned him about Bloy,[57] he wrote in June 1900: 'The man is so well known in Paris, and held in such contempt, that his attacks have no effect. He's an unhappy wretch whose pride is truly diabolical and whose capacity for hatred is immeasurable . . .'

Apart from the enmity of Léon Bloy, the publication of *Là-Bas* created other problems for Huysmans – some of them apparently of a supernatural nature. In one of his first letters to Huysmans[58] Boullan had asked the novelist if he was armed to defend himself in occult warfare with the Rosicrucians, explaining that 'if you write the book you have outlined to me, you will certainly incur the full fury of their hatred'. Finding that Huysmans was totally unprepared for such an eventuality, 'Dr. Johannès' gave him some instruction in the art of combating evil spells during his visit to Lyons, and later sent him the weapons he would need in his battle with the occultists. One of these weapons was shown to Jules Huret when he called at the Rue de Sèvres flat to interview the novelist.[59] Huret told the readers of the *Écho de Paris* how Huysmans had suddenly turned to him and asked:

'Would you like to smell some exorcistic paste?'
'Yes', I said. 'You have some here?'

He got up, opened a box, and took out a square tablet of brownish paste. Then he collected a little red-hot ash from the fireplace on a shovel, and laid the tablet on top of it. The paste sizzled, a thick cloud of smoke rose into the air, and a strong smell filled the tiny room – a smell in which there mingled with the perfume of incense the pungent, oppressive smell of camphor.

'It's a mixture of myrrh, incense, camphor, and cloves – the plant of St. John the Baptist', he told me. 'What's more, it has been blessed in all sorts of ways. It was sent to me from Lyons, by someone who told me: "As this novel of yours is going to stir up a host of evil spirits about you, I am sending you this to get rid of them." '

There was a long silence. I began to understand des Esseintes and Gilles de Retz, and in the red rays of the setting sun which came slanting in through the fiery window-panes, I almost expected to see twisted forms fleeing from the torments of exorcism . . .

No 'twisted forms' appeared to Huysmans in the evenings, but he became conscious of certain eerie sensations which he attributed to the malignant influence of the occultists. News of this reached Edmond de Goncourt by way of Jean Lorrain, and he recorded[60] that the author of *Là-Bas* was 'troubled by the feel of something cold moving across his face, and rather alarmed at the thought that he might he surrounded by an invisible force'. For several years Huysmans continued to experience these strange 'attacks', which invariably occurred when he was about to retire for the night, and consisted of what he termed 'fluidic fisticuffs' aimed at his head. He thought at first that these might simply be symptoms of some nervous disease, but then, as he told a friend,[61] he discovered that 'my cat, which is scarcely likely to be suffering from hallucinations, feels the same kind of shock as I do – and at the same time'. Moreover, his doctors were unable to account for the peculiar sensations of which he complained, and he himself could think of nothing comparable to these 'fluidic fisticuffs' until one day he called on Dr. Maurice de Fleury and asked him to direct the blast of a static electricity machine into his face.[62] 'After feeling this,' reports Fleury, 'he declared that everything was clear to him now, explaining that he frequently felt a fluidic blast of the same sort, which he undoubtedly owed to the hatred of Stanislas de Guaita.' A statement which, one feels, must have left the good doctor shaking his head sadly over his friend's apparent mental degeneration.

In the meantime, Huysmans religiously followed the instructions and advice which were sent to him from Lyons. Once, after Boullan had warned him not to go to his office on any account, he dutifully played truant for a day, and on his return found that a heavy gilt-framed mirror behind his desk had fallen where he should have been sitting.[63] At other times Boullan advised him to make use of the exorcistic paste which he had shown to Jules Huret, or the scapular and blood-stained host which Jean Lorrain had been privileged to see. According to Joanny Bricaud,[64] Huysmans would shut himself up with these occult weapons at the first sign of an attack. A tablet of paste would be burnt in the fireplace, a defensive circle drawn on the floor. And then, 'brandishing the miraculous host in his right hand, and with his left hand pressing the blessed scapular of the Elijan Carmel to his body, he would recite conjurations which dissolved the astral fluids, and paralysed the power of the sorcerers'.

After a few months Huysmans' neighbours at No. 11 Rue de Sèvres became increasingly familiar with the sound of incantations and the smell of incense and myrrh, for the novelist was now afraid to go to bed without performing the elaborate precautionary ritual. Even so, he did not regret his incursion into the realms of the occult. It had taught him to fear and respect things supernatural; and on the more material plane, it had brought him his first important success with the reading public. But the price which he paid for it, in health and peace of mind, was heavy.

7. THE CONVERT

In July 1890 the publishing house of Genonceaux had brought out a minor work by Huysmans which, although it boasted fewer than fifty pages, was probably closer to the author's heart than the bulky volume which he later consecrated to the study of nineteenth-century satanism. This work described the pitiful condition to which modern industry had reduced the second river of Paris – the river which Rabelais took as the subject of one of his most famous anecdotes, but which in recent years has vanished from sight into the vast underground sewerage system of the capital. It formed part of the series *Les Vieux Quartiers de Paris*, and it was entitled *La Bièvre*.

Huysmans had been attracted to the Bièvre and its environs ever since his youth.[1] He had read Balzac's description of the Bièvre in *La Femme de trente ans*, and admired Hugo's picture of the valley in *Les Misérables*; and he was deeply impressed by the Goncourt brothers' evocation, in *Manette Salomon*, of 'that poor oppressed little river, that foul-smelling stream, that thin, unhealthy trickle of water'. Following their example, he devoted one chapter of his first book, *Le Drageoir à épices*, to the Bièvre district, remarking that the river banks, lined with grim tanneries and soot-stained poplars, possessed for him a melancholy charm which 'seemed to evoke distant memories, or the plaintive strains of Schubert's music'. As a young man, too, he often explored this poverty-stricken *quartier* on Sundays, in the company of Ludovic de Francmesnil and Alexis Orsat, Henry Céard and François Coppée. Recalling these Sunday excursions,[2] Céard wrote after Huysmans' death:

> We used to wander along in the fetid summer twilight, admiring the reflection of the setting sun in the brown

waters dotted with green weeds. Ah! the Rue Croule-barbe and the Passage Moret – how well he has described them! And when we came to the end of the long lane skirting the Gobelins factory, we would make for a restaurant on the Avenue d'Italie, the *Restaurant de l'Homme décoré*. This was not the restaurant's real name, but an allusion to Coppée, who was then the only one among us who wore a red ribbon in his buttonhole. One evening he failed to join us for dinner. The manager of the establishment, which, incidentally, used to serve us with excellent wine, expressed his regret at the absence of *l'Homme décoré*, and the name stuck. After dinner, in a night full of the sounds of children at play and of washing flapping against the windows of sordid laundries, we would continue our exploration of districts that are now neither accessible nor recognizable – for the Highways Department of the City of Paris has diverted the Bièvre from its course, dried it up and disinfected it, while the Orléans Railway Company has filled in its leprous swamps in order to lay the foundations of its locomotive depots. Nothing now remains but Huysmans' pages illustrated by Raffaëlli's etchings . . .

In February 1877 the first fruit of these walks appeared in *La République des Lettres*, in an article on the Bièvre which Huysmans subsequently reproduced in Théodore Hannon's review, *L'Artiste*, and in *Croquis parisiens*. This, however, was merely a preliminary version of *La Bièvre*: the definitive work was not written until 1886, when it appeared in the Amsterdam review *De Nieuwe Gids*,[3] before being published in book form by Genonceaux in 1890. In this final version, Huysmans neglected the purely picturesque aspect of the Bièvre riverscape in order to reveal its spiritual significance – as a symbol of human suffering, 'the most perfect symbol of feminine poverty exploited by a big city'. For like the Goncourts before him, who had called the Bièvre 'that little slut of a river', and M. André Thérive after him, who gave it the charming name of 'the brown nymph', Huysmans saw the river as a girl – a fresh and innocent country maid who, as soon as she approached the city, was stripped of her rural finery, imprisoned between drab grey walls, and then brow-beaten, overworked, and corrupted by her employers. To François Coppée, poet of the humble folk and poor quarters of Paris, this picture of the river was sure to appeal; and when Genonceaux brought out *La Bièvre* in 1890, he wrote[4] to Huysmans:

I knew her when she was still something of a rustic, my dear Huysmans, this Bièvre to whom you have devoted such intensely artistic pages. How right you are to compare her to a girl of the fields debauched by the big city! To think that perhaps, at her source, she sets the water-cress a-quivering – and that she dies in squalor, like a beggar-woman of the Faubourg Saint-Marcel! You have put this into the most marvellous words, and all Parisians who truly love their Paris will be grateful to you for your work.

Time proved Coppée right, for with his little book Huysmans accomplished something neither Balzac nor Hugo nor even the Goncourts had succeeded in doing: he made the Bièvre valley a place of pilgrimage. Often, on Sunday afternoons, young men were seen roaming the streets and alleys between the Poterne des Peupliers and the Rue Geoffroy-Saint-Hilaire, map and camera in hand, trying to trace the erratic course of the Bièvre, and exulting whenever they caught a glimpse of the river over a factory wall or through courtyard railings. From the first, the local populace were naturally suspicious of these inquisitive strangers, who gazed in ecstasy upon the slimy waters of the Bièvre and breathed its foul odours with every appearance of delight; and when they were seen taking photographs and scribbling in notebooks, the suspicion that they were spies or surveyors crystallized into certainty. According to Dr. Michel de Lézinier, who knew the district well and accompanied Huysmans on some of his later visits to the Bièvre, the would-be explorers were often set upon in the dark river-side alleys, or contracted tetanus from glass disks that were catapulted into their faces.[5] 'That', he declared in his memoirs, 'is how *La Bièvre* made victims of its innocent readers. They still remember those cases at the Hôpital Broca. But when I told Huysmans about them, he could not believe his ears; and to convince him that I was telling the truth, I had to take him one day to the receiving hall at the hospital . . .'

This grim object-lesson seems to have had little effect on Huysmans: henceforth he always took a friend or 'protector' with him on his visits to the poorer quarters of Paris, but his taste for this kind of excursion was unimpaired. The winter of 1890, indeed, found him exploring the insalubrious district around Saint-Séverin and the Place Maubert, gathering material for a second work in the series *Les Vieux Quartiers de Paris*. At first the results of his investigations were disappointing. He thought he had discovered a den of thieves at the Crémerie Alexandre, an establishment incongruously lodged beneath the medieval bas-relief of St. Julian in the Rue Galande; but the 'thieves' did not allow him to get any farther than the staircase leading to the first-floor room. 'As soon as you poked your head out of the staircase well,' he reported,[6] 'everybody in the room stopped talking, and some of the men came nearer, ready to kick your teeth in if you climbed another step.' Similarly, at Père Lunette and the Bal du Château-Rouge, two other low haunts in the Rue Galande, he found that while one could meet some picturesque loafers in the public rooms, there was no sign of the criminals who were believed to frequent these places. He was beginning to despair of ever entering a genuine 'thieves' kitchen' when a friend told him of a likely spot – a tavern-cum-dance-hall on the road to Vanves. In an entertaining account[7] of the visit he and Huysmans paid to this place, one evening after dinner, Gustave Guiches relates how, as they sat in an evil-smelling arbour in the garden, listening to an accordion playing the polka *Le Beau Nicolas*, they suddenly saw a few dark shapes entering by a little side-door. Within seconds there was uproar inside the dance-hall, with candlesticks brandished, windows broken, and screams of '*A mort! A mort! A l'assassin!*'

We made our escape [writes Guiches] under cover of the darkness and confusion. Out in the street we stood and waited for a tram.

'Those are men', said Huysmans. 'Real men, such as we should all be but for our namby-pamby education and our niminy-piminy civilisation! Wild beasts!'

But then a little breeze brought us the sound of the accordion once more, playing:

Viens avec moi pour fêter le printemps,
Nous cueillerons des lilas et des roses.

Huysmans smiled, a smile of bitter disappointment, and exclaimed in accents of the most poignant disgust and disillusionment:

'Ah, *zut!* They're only sentimental idiots after all . . .'

Huysmans soon forgot this disappointment when he was introduced to some of the more sinister *habitués* of the Bal du Château-Rouge by Gustave Boucher – himself a rather shady character who combined the occupation of bookseller with the more lucrative profession of police-spy.[8] Also known as the Cabaret de la Guillotine, the Bal du Château-Rouge occupied one of the oldest houses in the district – No. 57 Rue Galande – a house which has since been demolished to make room for the Rue Dante. The huge bedroom on the first floor, where according to legend Henri IV had often lain with Gabrielle d'Estrées, was used in Huysmans' time as a common dormitory for the riff-raff of the *quartier*. Downstairs, the two bar-rooms were presided over by the proprietor, a giant called Pierre Trolliet, whose fame rested on the fact that he had betrayed the murderer Gamahut to the police, and whose authority was supported by an armoury of loaded sticks, black-jacks, and revolvers which he kept behind the bar. Three of Trolliet's regular customers attracted Huysmans' attention when he visited the Bal du Château-Rouge – either in the company of Boucher or Henri Girard, or under the protection of one de Bray, a curious individual who claimed to have been Barbey d'Aurevilly's secretary. The first was Louise Hellouin, known as Tache-de-Vin on account of the birth-mark which covered part of her face, and respected in the Paris underworld as the sometime mistress of Midi, Gamahut's accomplice in the murder of Widow Ballerich. The second was an old woman of seventy called Pauline or Pau-Pau, whose speech and manners suggested that she had once moved in higher social circles; rumour had it that she was the mother of a barrister who had committed suicide because of her hopeless addiction to drink. The third, and most attractive, was a young thief called Antoinette or Mémèche, whom Boucher described as 'a little tousle-haired tomboy who made a great show of affection for Huysmans', and whom Huysmans remembered, several years later, as 'a dumpy, moon-faced kid of seventeen, with a turned-up nose, the prettiest mouth imaginable, and the ingenuous eyes of a virgin'.

Huysmans derived considerable enjoyment from his weekly visits to the Château-Rouge, for these brought him in contact with men and women very different from the colourless nonentities he met in everyday life, and gave him a taste of the full-blooded life of François Villon and Gilles de Rais, which he had described with such nostalgic regret in *Le Drageoir* and, more recently, in *Là-Bas*. Thus, after performing the New Year's Day duties prescribed by the laws of etiquette, he wrote[9] to Gustave Boucher:

> The dread day is over at last. It has left me with my pockets empty and my heart filled with ineffable disgust. After seeing the honest citizens who belong to my family, I can only say that I hanker after the company of the down-and-outs of the Place Maub' and consider Tache-de-Vin and Mémèche to be exquisite princesses with pure and unspotted souls . . .

A few days later, however, events at the Château-Rouge taught him that these 'exquisite princesses' were neither suitable nor safe acquaintances for an official of the Sûreté

Générale. It so happened that Mémèche had been arrested by the police in a raid on the Central Market, and her friends of the Place Maubert suggested that Huysmans should use his influence with the authorities to secure her release. He not unnaturally showed no enthusiasm for this proposal, and was warned by Henri Girard that in consequence the *habitués* of the Château-Rouge had made plans to set upon him on his next visit to the Rue Galande. According to Girard, Mémèche had taken up the cudgels for her friend as soon as she was released from Saint-Lazare, and de Bray had joined her in denouncing the conspirators. Describing what had then occurred,[10] Huysmans wrote to Boucher on 16 January:

> Girard has doubtless told you about the terrible happenings at the Château-Rouge – how my protector de Bray was practically clubbed to death, while the waiter had his throat slit. And how yesterday, at the Hôtel-Dieu, Trolliet laid into the murderers with a loaded stick, and killed one of them. A real massacre! And it isn't over yet. Mémèche, who came out of Saint-Lazare a few days ago, tore into the den like a fury, and screamed that the first to lay a hand upon me would have to reckon with her as well. And for a start, she gave a good thrashing to Tache-de-Vin, who was the cause of the whole rumpus. You can believe me when I say that I'm lying doggo and ignoring the invitations Mémèche has sent me to go and see her again. I'm lucky not to have been killed one evening when all this trouble was brewing, and that's enough for me . . . But what a pity, all the same! We find a delightful haunt, different from all the others – and now it's finished. The truth is that Mémèche had told everybody that I slept with her. I was known to them all as Antoinette's lover, and that was why they put up with us for so long. Her little trip to Saint-Lazare spoilt everything. But she has a nerve, that girl, to say that I sleep with her . . .

Mᵉ Maurice Garçon, who some years ago made a careful

study of the records for January 1891 at the Paris police head-quarters,[11] could find no trace of the 'massacre' at the Hôtel-Dieu, and discovered that the 'terrible happenings' at the Château-Rouge amounted to nothing more than a brawl in which the waiter was slightly wounded. Both Huysmans and Boucher, however, were convinced that the former had nar-rowly escaped death at the hands of a band of assassins, and they gave the Château-Rouge a wide berth from then on. Not until 1898, when he began revising his study of the dis-trict for the Stock edition of *La Bièvre et Saint-Séverin*, was Huysmans prompted to make inquiries about the fate of his former boon-companions. Pau-Pau, he learnt, had died of drink and old age. Tache-de-Vin had become involved in another murder and was serving a long prison sentence. And Mémèche, the 'little tousle-haired tomboy' whom he still remembered with affection,[12] had fallen to her death from a fourth-floor window, in a fit of delirium tremens.

Huysmans' colleagues at the Ministry of the Interior would doubtless have been surprised and shocked to learn that he was in the habit of consorting with prostitutes and petty crim-inals in one of the lowest haunts of Paris; but they would have been doubly surprised and shocked had they known that, in this same winter of 1890, he was often to be seen sitting, and even kneeling, in churches and chapels on the Left Bank. Alone, or with Georges Landry or Gustave Boucher, he had taken to visiting Saint-Séverin or Saint-Sulpice on Sunday evenings, to listen to the choirs; and on one unforgettable occasion he and Boucher heard Vespers in the little Franciscan chapel in the Rue de l'Èbre which is now the parish church of La Glacière. They discovered this chapel shortly before Christmas, while exploring the Bièvre district together; and Huysmans at once fell in love with the sanctuary which, in *En Route*, he described as 'being to Notre-Dame de Paris what its neighbour, the Bièvre, is to the Seine'. Going in, the two men found the chapel filled with white-robed nuns, girls from the convent school, and poor women of the neighbourhood. After Vespers the beadle came up to them and, explaining that it was customary for any men who were present to walk behind the Blessed Sacrament, asked if they would lead the procession which was about to form up. As they were the only men in the congregation they could not refuse, and with feelings compounded of embarrassment and shame they took the lighted tapers that were handed to them and made their way to the altar. When the procession had been round the chapel several times Boucher and Huysmans were asked to kneel at the altar-rail, where they remained, still holding their lighted tapers, until Benediction was over. Unaccustomed as he was to such religious exercises, Huysmans suffered agonies of cramp and discomfort; but he was deeply moved by the ethereal voices and simple piety of the nuns, and resolved to return early in the New Year. And in the same letter in which he told Boucher how he longed for the company of Mémêche and Tache-de-Vin,[13] he wrote: 'I shall be going with Landry next Sunday to La Glacière – where I shall try not to wear out my knees!'

Another religious ceremony which impressed Huysmans about this time, and which, like his first visit to the Rue de l'Èbre, he later described in *En Route*, was a clothing at the Carmelite convent in the Avenue de Saxe, where he and Remy de Gourmont were taken one morning by Berthe Courrière.[14] 'On that occasion,' wrote Gourmont, 'we listened to a very tiresome sermon preached by Cardinal Richard, but although Huysmans spattered that mediocre prelate with sarcastic comments, he was moved by what he saw.' Gourmont imagined, however, that for Huysmans, as for himself, such ceremonies had only an aesthetic appeal, and that in the splendours of the Liturgy the novelist saw nothing more than a romantic décor. 'I was far from supposing', he wrote later,[15] 'that behind the curtains of purple and gold Huysmans was looking for dogmatic realities: our discussions were so very unedifying, so very free from any hint of religiosity . . .'

Gourmont was not alone in imagining that Huysmans' interest in the Church was slight and superficial, for Léon Bloy, in his review of *Là-Bas*,[16] stated categorically that 'Huysmans' soul has not the remotest connexion with the illusion of Christianity which this gibberish may produce.' Yet in January 1891 the author of *Là-Bas* was already so concerned about the state of his soul that he told Georges Landry he had been thinking seriously of confessing his sins to a priest.[17]

> But what phenic acids [he asked], what copper solutions could cleanse the great sewage tank into which my carnal iniquities are still pouring? It would need casks of carbolic, barrels of disinfectant – and then what Milleriot could handle a pump powerful enough to draw the residual waters from the old sewers? The breed of divine pumpmen who rejoiced in such labours is extinct. And so there seems no reason, brother, why things should not go on as before. Though it's true that when they are as bad as this! . . .

Beneath the light badinage of this letter, as also beneath the 'gibberish' of *Là-Bas*, there was a deep-seated, ill-concealed spiritual anguish, or, as Huysmans later described it,[18] 'a desperate desire to believe'. Attempting to account for his return to the Church, after the event,[19] the Naturalist was careful to note the probable influence of heredity – 'the atavism of an old, devout family scattered among a dozen religious houses' – but attributed his conversion chiefly to two causes: his love for art and his growing hatred of existence. The pleasures of life, all of which he had tasted in fact or in fancy, had not only failed to content him, but had awakened in him feelings of shame and self-disgust; so that, like Durtal in *Là-Bas*, he had begun to look for 'a means of throwing off his earthly bonds, of escaping from the sewer of sensuality, of winning through to regions where the soul loses itself in infinite altitudes of bliss'. By the time he came to write *Là-Bas*, he was convinced that only through Christian art and mysticism could he satisfy this desire for spiritual exaltation, and that only through faith in Christ could he satisfy the yearning for spiritual tranquillity which possessed his questing and weary soul. At the end of the novel, therefore, we find Durtal, like des Esseintes before him, praying for the gift of faith – that faith which is movingly described as 'the breakwater of life, the only mole behind which the dismasted ship of humanity can run aground in peace'.

The principal obstacle to Huysmans' conversion had always been his inability to accept the validity of Christian dogma. As he wrote in *Là-Bas*, 'it demands such a repudiation of common sense, such a determination to be surprised at nothing, that he shied away from Christianity, while still keeping an inquiring eye on it'. However, as a result of his researches into occultism and satanism, he was eventually able to overcome these intellectual scruples, resembling in this respect James Tissot and August Strindberg – Tissot who was converted to Catholicism after attending a spiritualist séance, and Strindberg who once remarked on the similarity between Huysmans' spiritual development and his own, as recounted in *Inferno*.[20] Huysmans was not one to refuse credit where it was due, and in a revealing letter to Baron Firmin Van den Bosch,[21] he later declared that 'it was through a glimpse of the supernatural of evil that I first obtained insight into the supernatural of good. The one derived from the other. With his hooked paw, the Devil drew me towards God.'

Strangely enough, when at last Huysmans' spiritual aspirations were fulfilled, and the grace to believe was granted him, he was taken by surprise. He had half expected some tremendous revelation, some blinding illumination, such as St. Paul experienced on the road to Damascus, in the classic instance of conversion. Instead, as he revealed in *En Route*, he woke up one fine morning and – without knowing how or why – he believed. Havelock Ellis, in a penetrating study of our author,[22] has described this as 'the sudden emergence into consciousness of a very gradual process'. The Abbé Mugnier has likewise testified[23] that Huysmans' conversion was 'a very slow advance towards a logical and necessary end'. But it was left to Huysmans himself to find the most striking definition of his spiritual progress. Characteristically spurning the vague, high-flown phrase for the honest, earthy, and expressive image, he stated in *En Route* that 'it was something analogous to the digestive processes of the human stomach, functioning without one's being aware of it . . .'

Huysmans' novels had always borne the impress of his opinions and experiences, and it was therefore inevitable that his new-found belief in God should be reflected in his future works – all the more so because he was now more confident of his literary powers, more determined than ever to strike out something new and original. He was encouraged in this resolve by tributes from young French and English writers, for it was about this time that Paul Valéry came to Paris from Montpellier, and Arthur Symons and Havelock Ellis from London, to pay homage to Huysmans as a master in his own right.[24] It is true, of course, that there were others who still disputed his originality – that Edmond de Goncourt, for instance, seeing perhaps something of La Faustin in Mme Chantelouve, believed that in *Là-Bas* he had sired another Huysmans novel, and that he even went so far as to claim that the erotic hallucinations of Gilles de Rais in Tiffauges Forest were 'a plagiarism from *Germinie Lacerteux*, who was hallucinated in the same way in her own kitchen'.[25] But Huysmans had nothing more to learn from Goncourt, and in November 1891 he wrote to an anonymous critic: 'I believe as you do in exact and true-to-life documentation, and I have no intention of renouncing that belief, but I am travelling towards regions uncharted by Zola or even by the Goncourts, towards little-known, intriguing, and troubled realms of the spirit.' In this same letter[26] he insisted that his desertion of his old masters was not due simply to his belief that Naturalism was dead and the 'bourgeoisie of subjects' exhausted, but also to his spiritual development.

Formerly [he wrote] I admired Schopenhauer: now I find him disappointing. I can still appreciate the accuracy of his assertions, but the emptiness of his conclusions repels me. In the unintelligible abomination which is life, there simply cannot be nothing at all. During the past year, I have seen something of monastic life, and I know that among the religious are souls possessed of undoubted truths – but then, alas, they are so very extraordinary, so very exceptional in character!

251

But, you will say to me, this is surely Catholicism! Yes – or rather the art of Catholicism, mysticism. There are some extraordinary things in mysticism – as there are, of course, in satanism – exciting happenings, terrifying spiritual adventures, battles of which the profane have not the slightest inkling . . . an immense, unexplored field of strange and complex spiritual activity. And these things are more interesting – to me at least – than all the psychological studies of *femmes du monde* and fishwives that have been turned out in recent years . . .

To all but his closest friends, Huysmans refused as yet to reveal the profound change of heart which he had undergone. His churchgoing, his reading of the mystics, even his oft-expressed intention of going to confession, were all explained – often with a Mephistophelian smile – as necessary documentation for his next novel.[27] Most of his acquaintances were completely deceived by this explanation – some, like Jules Renard,[28] so completely that, long after Huysmans' conversion was an accepted fact, they persisted in regarding him as an arch-hypocrite, 'a literary Léo Taxil'. But it is significant that for many months Huysmans obviously had no clear conception of the novel he was supposed to be busily preparing, and referred to it vaguely[29] as 'a white book' or 'an antidote to *Là-Bas*'. And it is interesting, too, to note the suggestion of proselytism in such letters as this to Jean Lorrain,[30] written in March 1891, more than a year before Huysmans' own return to the Church was made absolute:

This evening [he wrote], in the café, I've been looking through the back numbers of the *Courrier Français*. Lorrain! Lorrain! You are blaspheming with such deliberate intent that when the angels in leather jerkins and two-pointed hats take you 'up there' to appear before the Definitive Assizes, you will undoubtedly be given the maximum sentence. Your guardian angel in his wig and gown will plead your case in vain. The red-robed, ermine-clad archangels will have no pity for you. The comparative youthfulness of your soul will not be accepted as a defence. Take care! Take care!

One mustn't play about with such things too much, for who knows? who knows?

For my part, I intend to have nothing more to do with satanism, and I mean to write a mystical work after my *Saint-Séverin*, which is just a diversion, an interlude. I shall have a bath, a rub-down, and a purge – and then, with a clean and wholesome body, I shall go to confession. After which, I hope to be in a state of such purity that I can lose myself in a mystical *à rebours* of *Là-Bas*. But first I shall have to get my nerves back into shape, for otherwise I might lose my senses for good!

There were other reasons for delay. Huysmans wanted his return to the Church to mark the beginning of a new phase in his life. 'I cannot conceive of Catholicism', he wrote in *En Route*, 'as a lukewarm, faltering faith, continually warmed up by a water-bath of bogus zeal. I want no compromises and truces, no alternations between sacraments and sprees, pious and immoral shifts; no, I want all or nothing, a complete change or no change at all.' Unfortunately, he had grown so accustomed to a life of sexual indulgence that he knew it would be no easy matter to reform. Cheated by Anna Meunier's illness and Henriette Maillat's passionate pretensions of any hope of a satisfying liaison with a mistress of his choice, he had taken once more to buying his pleasures on the open market; and by this time he was as much a prisoner of the Paris brothels as the inmates themselves. One woman in particular, a prostitute called Fernande, held a powerful fascination for him. She was an adept in her profession, and thoughts of the perversities she practised haunted him even in church, so that he would often leave Saint-Séverin or Saint-Sulpice only to go to her at *La Botte de Paille*, the Rue Mazarine brothel where she lived.[31] All his good resolutions proved of no avail, and seemed indeed to heighten the attraction of Fernande's physical charms. And after hours of mental strife, like Durtal in *En Route*, 'he would end up, defeated, in the woman's room, which he left feeling sick at heart and almost sobbing with shame and disgust . . .'

It became increasingly obvious to Huysmans that, if he really wished to lead a chaste life, he would have to seek the help and advice of an experienced spiritual director. But here again a difficult problem presented itself. Our author had an extremely low opinion of the secular clergy, whom he regarded as the skimmed milk of the seminaries – the cream having been taken off, he believed, by the monastic and missionary orders. He was afraid, therefore, that he would be unable to find in Paris a priest capable of understanding his spiritual and moral problems, of encouraging him in his sincere desire for reform, of sympathizing with his vague mystical aspirations, and of nursing him back to spiritual health with tact and intelligence.[32] But when Berthe Courrière, with a charitable zeal which is difficult to explain, tried to put him in touch with a Carmelite of her acquaintance, one Léonce de Saint-Paul, the friar objected – on account of the 'pride and perversity' which he discovered in *Là-Bas*.[33] Though deeply discouraged by this rebuff, Huysmans asked his friend to continue her search for a spiritual director, if necessary among the secular clergy. At her second attempt, she was fortunate enough to find a priest who was not only more amenable than her Carmelite friar, but who seemed to fulfil all Huysmans' requirements. His name was Arthur Mugnier.

The Abbé Mugnier was born in 1853 in the village of Lubersac, some thirty miles south of Limoges, and educated in the seminaries of Nogent-le-Rotrou, Issy-les-Moulineaux, and Saint-Sulpice. After teaching at the seminary of Notre-Dame-des-Champs for three years and occupying the curacy of Saint-Nicolas-des-Champs for nine, he was appointed curate of the church of Saint-Thomas-d'Aquin in 1888. By the time he met Huysmans, three years later, he had already won a considerable reputation as an *abbé de cour* who combined wit with wisdom and was as well read in profane as in religious literature. It must be admitted, however, that he had never read any of Huysmans' works and that his tastes ran rather to Chateaubriand and George Sand; indeed, there is a story that one day in 1876, while unwrapping a pair of shoes sent him by his mother, the young priest was overwhelmed to see a newspaper report of Lélia's death, and promptly went down on his knees to pray for the soul of *la bonne dame de Nohant*.[34] But curiously enough, it was the Abbé Mugnier's passion for George Sand – a passion which Huysmans, for his part, had outgrown over twenty years before – which helped to bring the two men together. In an account which he gave later of the circumstances which led to their first meeting,[35] the Abbé explained that towards the end of 1890 he had been introduced to Berthe Courrière at a charity bazaar in the Rue de Grenelle, and that on discovering he was an admirer of George Sand she had said she would very much like to come and see him to talk about Sand and Clésinger. He continued:

This visit was followed by many others. Mme Courrière used to come almost at a run into the imposing sacristy of Saint-Thomas-d'Aquin where at that time I was curate, and whose windows overlooked some gardens which have since disappeared. As soon as she was seated, and showing scant regard for the fact that this was not the place to read such things, she would take out of her handbag a number of newspapers and reviews – among them the *Mercure de France*, on whose cover she would indicate with an infallible finger the names of the literary giants of the future, and also the latest issues of the *Écho de Paris*, which had nearly completed its serialization of *Là-Bas*.

'I know the author of this novel, M. Huysmans, very well', she told me one day. 'He is a very talented writer. For some time now, he has been prowling round the churches and looking for a priest in whom to confide. I mentioned your name to him, and he would be glad to see you if you have no objections.'

I had not read a single line of his; I knew that he belonged to the Médan group, and that was all. But I was not averse to a meeting such as Mme Courrière proposed; and though the idea of doing a little good was sufficient in itself to encourage me, I was also tempted by the opportunity of showing that the Church, which recognizes all forms of government, can live on good terms with all schools of literature.

A meeting was arranged for the evening of Thursday, 28 May 1891.[36] On that day Berthe Courrière came tripping as usual into the sacristy of Saint-Thomas-d'Aquin, accompanied this time by 'a thin man with close-cropped hair and a short moustache, who showed signs of the embarrassment which one normally feels in an unfamiliar place'. Berthe left after making the necessary introductions, and Huysmans sat down by the fireplace, opposite the Abbé. He was silent for a few moments, fixing the priest with his cold blue eyes; but what he saw seemed to reassure him, for without any encouragement he launched into an explanation of the purpose of his visit. He had written, he said, a satanic book, full of Black Masses. He now wanted to write another which would be *white*, but he knew that first it would be necessary to whiten himself. And so he had come to the Abbé Mugnier for the help which only a priest of the Church could give him.

'Have you', he asked, 'any chlorine for my soul?'

8. THE PENITENT

THE impression which the Abbé Mugnier obtained from his first conversation with Huysmans was not of that 'pride and perversity' which Father Léonce de Saint-Paul had expected to find in the author of *Là-Bas*, but rather of a very real humility and sincerity.[1] This humility was most apparent whenever Huysmans referred to his spiritual condition. For instance, talking of Zola, he said: 'I spoke to him one day about death, and I saw him go pale. But what has one to fear when one is a materialist? As for myself, I'm no materialist, but my soul is sick and I don't feel proud of myself . . .' The advice which the priest gave him on this occasion was simply to pray as much as he could, at home and in church, and to avoid occasions of sin. Like the Abbé Gévresin in *En Route*, the Abbé Mugnier probably had to explain to a somewhat dissatisfied penitent that since God had dispensed with all human mediation in bringing him back to a Christian way of life, he could be counted on to complete his work of mercy as he had begun it: 'Have patience and he will explain himself; put your trust in him and he will help you; say to him, like the psalmist: *Doce me facere voluntatem tuam, quia Deus meus tu . . .*'

During the following months Huysmans returned several times to Saint-Thomas-d'Aquin, or called at the presbytery in the Rue du Bac, to report to the Abbé on the progress of his spiritual cure. Fortunately the good Abbé could not know that at the same time his protégé was receiving advice and protection of a sort from a defrocked priest – to wit, the ex-Abbé Boullan. The protection which 'Dr. Johannès' gave Huysmans consisted in more magical defensive measures, such as the Sacrifices of Glory which he offered up on 13 June to thwart another 'lethal operation' by the Rosicrucians; while

257

the advice he gave was that, if Huysmans was not satisfied with a projected visit to La Grande Chartreuse that summer, he should accompany Misme and Boullan on a pilgrimage to La Salette and also spend a few weeks in Lyons.[2] Huysmans accordingly travelled a month later to Lyons, whence he reported to Berthe Courrière[3] on 17 July that 'life here is very pleasant, what with occasional walks, a climb to Notre-Dame de Fourvière, family dinners, and camomile tea guaranteed to rid one of all carnal desires. White with purity and sulphurous with magic, that's the present state of your friend.' In the same letter he inquired after the health of Stanislas de Guaita; and then, doubtless feeling that some explanation of this surprising solicitude was called for, he added:

As a result of certain circumstances which I shall explain later, he ought now to be in bed, and the arm he usually injects with morphine should be looking like a balloon. This is what is supposed to have happened:

Here at Lyons, at the home of our good friend Boullan, a battle royal is in progress at the moment, and assisted by a quite amazing clairvoyante as well as by Mme Thibault, he's flinging himself about all over the place. I'm told that de Guaita poisoned the little clairvoyante, who promptly counter-attacked by virtue of the law of return. So that it would be interesting to know whether, in fact, de Guaita had been laid low. The two women here see him in bed!

Ouff! – There's no denying that I'm having a quite extraordinary time with all this going on – including the brandishing of hosts to ward off evil spirits. Lord, what a restless rest-cure this has turned out to be!

However, though the atmosphere of the house in the Rue de la Martinière was not exactly soothing to Huysmans' nerves, he assured his correspondent that 'all the same, magic is always more interesting than the tittle-tattle of society folk or the chit-chat of the grocer at the corner-shop'. Even so, he must have felt some relief when, after a few days, Boullan decided to start on the pilgrimage to La Salette. Describing this pilgrimage in letters to Boucher, Landry, and Berthe Courrière, Huysmans stressed his aversion to the mountain scenery of the Dauphiné; and in *La Cathédrale* he described the church and the bronze statues at La Salette as examples of 'the frightful appetite for ugliness which at present dishonours the Church'. But in conversation with his intimates, and in the first chapter of *La Cathédrale*, he admitted that La Salette had made a profound and lasting impression upon him; and though he never returned to the mountain shrine, he later devoted an entire work to its history – a work which was unfortunately never published and which Huysmans burnt a few days before his death, in order to avoid stirring up certain old theological controversies.[4] He was most moved, it seems, by the ecstatic faith and piety of a small band of peasant women from Savoy whom he watched climbing laboriously up to the plateau, praying in the church, and then beginning their long and dangerous journey down the mountain. 'These humble creatures,' he wrote in *La Cathédrale*, 'with their uncouth feelings and rudimentary ideas, barely literate and scarcely able to express themselves, wept with love before the Inaccessible, which they forced by their very humility and simplicity to reveal itself unto them.' They were led, it should be added, by none other than the redoubtable and ubiquitous Maman Thibault.

After La Salette, La Grande Chartreuse proved something of a disappointment, as Huysmans revealed in this letter to Berthe Courrière,[5] written on his return to Lyons, on or about the 26th:

> The mountain scenery I found either distressing or boring. La Salette is situated at such a height that there isn't a single tree growing there. Imagine immense masses of pumice-stone, a couple of blades of grass, and, further up still, the eternal snows. Below, tremendous chasms – all unspeakably sinister, and yet the monotony of those rocks barring the horizon and shutting out the sky, the lifeless appearance of that forever motionless stone,

wearied and disgusted me. How I prefer the sea, which is at least a living and limitless thing!

As for La Chartreuse, it's hostelry of the very lowest order and, except for the night office, beneath contempt. The Abbé Mugnier was right. Even the scenery is overrated and is really only a comic-opera décor. The precipices are little more than gentle slopes and the famous desert is just a reproduction of the Vaux-de-Cernay on a rather bigger scale. In fact, the only tolerable part of the monastery is the cell, and I finished by spending most of my time in mine . . .

For years past, of course, Huysmans had toyed longingly with the idea of escaping from the world to some secluded retreat, and this idea had recurred in all his major works. In *A Rebours* he had glorified the conception of a 'refined Thebaid'; in *En Rade* he had told of his attempts to obtain some respite from modern life in a rural refuge; while in *Là-Bas* he had dreamt of living 'the healing life of solitude' in the north tower of Saint-Sulpice, and had written of 'the fabulous joy of dwelling here, oblivious of the passage of time, and while the tidal wave of human folly broke at the foot of the tower, of turning the pages of very ancient books in the warm glow of a shaded lamp'. Now, in the quiet of his cell at La Grande Chartreuse, he was at last able to sanctify and spiritualize his yearning for solitude and his loathing for human society. But however seriously he might consider the problems of religious experience, he was not yet prepared to talk seriously about them, and the only comment on his spiritual condition in his letter to Berthe Courrière was this:

As for my soul, my poor soul, *tonton tontaine*, it is doing nicely, thank you. I've been treating myself to a foretaste of the contemplative life, in a cell with whitewashed walls and only a prayer-stool as furniture. That has calmed me down tremendously and now I'm like a little angel, all white. Which is quite a change!

La Salette and La Grande Chartreuse, he added, 'can't hold a candle to Lyons and Boullan!' Certainly neither shrine nor monastery ever witnessed such strange or picturesque ceremonies as those which took place in the Rue de la Martinière on Huysmans' return to Lyons. Warned of impending danger by his astrological computations, by Mme Laure's visions, and by Maman Thibault's interpretation of the flight of the sparrow-hawks which brushed against the windows, Boullan several times celebrated the Sacrifice of Glory of Melchizedek, attired in the vestments of the Vintrasian Carmel – a red robe, with a red-and-white girdle, and a white mantle cut in the shape of a cross, which was upside down to signify that the reign of the dolorous Christ was ended. On at least one occasion Huysmans was told that he was in imminent danger of attack and induced to take part in the ceremony. He sat in front of the altar while Mme Laure stationed herself beside him, ready to enter into a somnambulistic sleep if necessary. Standing barefooted at the altar, Boullan recited the prayers of the Sacrifice and then, at the Consecration, placed his left hand on Huysmans' head, lifted up a host in his right, and called upon the heavenly powers to strike down the spell-workers.[6] Reports of the ceremony differ as to whether he named Stanislas de Guaita or Joséphin Péladan in his invocations, and it may be that he named both: neither he nor Huysmans seems to have been aware that the Rosicrucian camp was by now divided, and that the Marquis and the Sâr were unlikely to combine forces in any occult offensive. Péladan was apparently the object of Boullan's exorcistic prayers in the ceremony described in this passage from Huysmans' long letter to Berthe Courrière:

In this amazing house I've actually seen Mass said by a woman! Glory be to the regenerated sex and to the celestified organs (to use the style favoured by these people)! I'm having my fortune told by the little somnambulist I told you about, and just now she's reading the future in some glasses of water. After that I'm going to consult another woman who practises the Mozarabic

Rite and casts horoscopes with chick-peas and broad beans. And lastly I've an appointment with a former Benedictine Abbess and hope to get some curious documents from her. As you can see, I'm not wasting my time.

The battles have begun again since I last wrote to you – Wagrams in space. For a time I thought I was in a lunatic asylum. Boullan jumps about like a tiger-cat, clutching one of his hosts. He invokes the aid of St. Michael and the eternal justiciaries of eternal justice; then, standing at his altar, he cries out: 'Strike down Péladan, strike down Péladan, strike down Péladan!' And Maman Thibault, her hands folded on her belly, announces: 'It is done.'

To Berthe Courrière, who like Huysmans had heard reports of Boullan's mystico-erotic aberrations, this description of the Sacrifice of Glory seemed very tame; and on 27 July, showing scant regard for the purity of her friend's newly-whitened soul, she wrote[7] to him:

Since you have some celestified female organs at hand, why don't you tell the Abbé Boullan that you wish to contract a *spiritual marriage* with one of the persons possessing these organs? I know that you are inclined to have scruples about these things, but when one is investigating such strange affairs one shouldn't allow anything to stand in one's way. It would be *such* a shame if you came back without having ferreted out the truth about this part of the secret doctrine. Come now, show a little daring and find out just how Boullan sets about forming these unions of his . . .

In this case it is clear that Huysmans, to his credit, remained firmly attached to his scruples and made no attempt to enter into one of Boullan's *unions de vie*. Perhaps his refusal to countenance Berthe Courrière's suggestions was also due to a fear that closer investigation would confirm all that Guaita and

Wirth had told him about 'Dr. Johannès'. After Boullan's death he did in fact obtain documentary proof that the initiates of the Carmel had practised incubism and succubism, but he remained convinced that they were not fundamentally evil in character but merely unbalanced, and he continued to defend them against the Rosicrucians' charges of sexual immorality on a material plane. Thus, in a letter to Adolphe Berthet, or 'Esquirol', a young disciple who was preparing a book on the heresies of Lyons, he wrote[8] on 1 May 1900:

As for the unions, I very much doubt whether they were material. After Boullan's death I took possession of a paper which I have in my archives and which listed the unions proposed for certain days. Well, among the males reserved for the women in the list were Raymond Lully and a host of other dead men. It was all a matter of succubism such as is practised in the monasteries (about which I have some voluminous documents which I likewise obtained after Boullan's death). I really can't see Mother Thibault fornicating with Father Misme, in whose house Boullan was living at that time. They were a lot of old crocks for whom such pastimes would have been both unwise and unattractive. On this point Guaita's book is full of errors – and makes no mention, of course, of the shabby conduct of which he and Wirth were guilty. The Gays were decent folk, and I find it hard to believe that those two girls, whom I know well and who live with their parents, were ever the abandoned creatures they were made out to be. The trouble, I think, was that the mystical phraseology used by that circle created the wrong impression. Boullan was a satanist, that's certain, and Guaita was another. Only each claimed to be with God. And both were lying. As for the people who congregated about Boullan, they were *minus habens*. Father Misme, if he hadn't gone astray and become a heretic, would have been a saint, for no man ever had a finer soul or a more charitable nature. And Mother Thibault too, though she was cursed with cranky ideas and an insane pride, was a decent sort and a staunch friend . . .

It can be seen that Huysmans never entirely lost the respect which Boullan and his friends inspired in him during the early stages of their association. He might scoff at their weird ceremonies, he might later shudder over the horrifying *cahier rose*, but he never forgot the kindness that was shown to him at Lyons, the brilliance of Boullan's conversation, or the astonishing proficiency in the occult arts which the Lyons sect displayed. One incident illustrating this proficiency – the episode of the mirror at the Ministry of the Interior – has already been cited; another occurred towards the end of Huysmans' stay at Lyons in July 1891. While Mme Laure was in one of her somnambulistic trances, he asked her what was happening at that moment in his Rue de Sèvres flat. She answered that a sick man was lying in his bed – and was laughed at for her pains, for the novelist knew that he had given his keys to the concierge, who could be trusted to admit no one to the flat. But on his return to Paris he was told by an apologetic concierge that the floor-polisher he employed had been taken ill while working in Huysmans' flat, had crawled into the bed, and had been inadvertently locked in for the night.[9] After this convincing demonstration of clairvoyance, Huysmans tended to accept almost without question the truth of any communication he received from Lyons – an attitude which was perhaps understandable, but which was later to involve him in unpleasant and even dangerous notoriety.

According to Gustave Guiches,[10] Huysmans' return to Paris was followed by a violent scene with Léon Bloy. The two men met accidentally in the street, and within a few minutes Bloy was loudly proclaiming that 'he was the benefactor of all who had received the magnificent almsgift of his friendship, and that since Huysmans had irremediably offended him by his ingratitude and insolence, he intended to break for evermore with all those who made common cause with the novelist'. Recounting this scene to Guiches, Huysmans warned him that soon he would doubtless receive a 'terrible epistle' from Bloy, instructing him to choose between the two former friends. Others who were presented with a similar ultimatum were Lucien Descaves, Maurice de Fleury, and Georges Landry. They all chose to follow Huysmans, and in consequence were all excommunicated by Léon Bloy – figuratively and, if we are to believe a typical passage from *Le Mendiant ingrat*[11] relating to Landry, literally as well. 'Georges L . . .', thundered Bloy, 'had been entrusted with a mission, the accomplishment of which was essential to the salvation of his soul. *He had been entrusted with the mission of being a faithful friend to Léon Bloy.* Having deserted this post, it was only to be expected that he should abandon himself shamelessly to atheists and satanists. May God have pity on him . . .'

Bloy may perhaps be forgiven for having held Huysmans to be an 'atheist and satanist', for the novelist had given no public indication of his conversion, and his private life revealed little or nothing of the change of heart he had undergone. From Lyons, it is true, he wrote to Berthe Courrière[12] in July 1891: 'If you see the Abbé Mugnier, tell him that I haven't forgotten him and am being very good.' But in August we find him confiding in Gustave Boucher[13] that 'after a spell of exemplary behaviour while on holiday, I was afflicted on my return to Paris with another pruritus of lewdness and have spent many hours lingering over Fernande's musky cassolettes'. Nor was his behaviour in the autumn all that the Abbé Mugnier might have wished. In September he complained in a letter to Boucher[14] that he was now obliged to patronize other brothels than *La Botte de Paille*, since 'I have lost Fernande, whose . . . delighted me – she is being kept by another man. *Zut alors!*' And a month later he reported[15] to Berthe Courrière: 'Time is hanging heavy on my hands. Some diverting practices, now religious, now obscene, cheer me up a little, but not for long. And then . . . and then . . .'

Gradually, however, the practice of religion took first place. In the evenings Huysmans would sometimes go to Saint-Sulpice or Saint-Séverin with Boucher, who at this time was apparently torn between similar religious and erotic cross-currents; and on a Sunday morning in November[16] the two friends obtained their first experience of the Benedictine Liturgy, when they attended a clothing in the chapel of the Benedictine convent in the Rue Monsieur – a ceremony presided over by the Abbot of La Grande Trappe and later described by Huysmans in one of the most moving chapters of *En Route*. By the New Year the convert was already showing signs, not merely of repentance for the sins of his past life, but also of that proselytizing disposition which was to have so marked an effect on the character of his later works. Aware that his incursions into spiritualism and satanism had been in some degree responsible for his return to the Church, he felt that it might be possible to lead others back to the Faith by the same devious route, through what he characteristically called 'the latrines of the supernatural'. Boucher was selected as a suitable subject for a first experiment in this strange method of conversion, and on 16 January he received a card from Huysmans[17] inviting him to inspect whatever 'disconcerting abominations' might appear at a séance in the Rue de Sèvres the following evening.

When he arrived at Huysmans' flat, Boucher found that his host had also invited Orsat, Bobin, Landry, and a friend from the Préfecture de la Seine, Paul Daniel. The visiting medium or magnetizer was a certain François, a militant occultist and one of the founders of the famous Martinist Lodge in the Rue de Trévise. He opened the séance with a little elementary table-turning and went on to summon up the ghost of General Boulanger – to the great distaste of the pious Landry, who did his best to hinder proceedings by muttering exorcistic prayers in a corner of the room. Eventually Boucher thought he perceived a shadowy apparition in the form of a human silhouette and cried out in terror, whereupon Huysmans brought the lamp back into the darkened room, declaring that 'the health of our good friend Boucher is more precious to us than the presence of that scoundrel Boulanger'. Perhaps he was also satisfied that his experiment had been successful, and thought it unnecessary to prolong the séance. If so, he must have been disappointed the next morning, when

Boucher came to see him with a plausible explanation of the 'apparition'. However, his friend added: 'I know with what excellent intentions you organized yesterday's gathering . . . You wanted to introduce us into the spiritual world by way of its inferior circles, in the hope that like you we should soon aspire to the light above . . . Well, for my part, I don't wish to disappoint you, but nor do I wish to give the Devil credit for my conversion: I should prefer to attribute it entirely to your friendship and your fraternal prayers, which I feel sure have obtained for me the grace to believe.'

Huysmans could now justifiably claim that he had helped to bring an unbeliever into the Church, but meanwhile his own spiritual problems continued to cause him difficulty and distress. In his perplexity he turned for advice, now to the Abbé Mugnier, now to the ex-Abbé Boullan; and this two-sided spiritual direction is reflected in the advice which the Abbé Gévresin gives Durtal in *En Route*. Thus, while it would be pleasant to suppose that the Abbé Mugnier, like the Abbé Gévresin, explained to Huysmans how Carmelites and Poor Clares in far-off convents could take upon themselves the greater part of his trials and temptations, it must be admitted that the curate of Saint-Thomas-d'Aquin was no mystic, and that in all probability Huysmans learnt about this doctrine of mystical substitution or mystical reversibility − a doctrine which was to become the very mainstay of his faith − from Joseph Boullan and Léon Bloy, both of whom preached it throughout their lives.[18] Indeed, the Abbé Mugnier later confessed, in a brochure on Huysmans' conversion,[19] that in the year following his first meeting with the novelist he did nothing but recommend to him 'a few precepts of moral hygiene', while waiting patiently for what Bossuet called 'the moment of God'. At last it came. Early in June 1892 Huysmans told the good Abbé that, after two years of mental strife, he now felt that he should 'knock at God's door'. He was still a little fearful of approaching the sacraments lest he should later fall back into his old and sinful ways, but he asked the priest to tell him of some religious house, if possible outside Paris, where he could make a retreat and perhaps even take the decisive step.

The ex-Abbé Boullan.

The Abbé Mugnier.

Notre-Dame d'Igny in 1903.

The Abbé Mugnier's thoughts went at once to a little Trappist monastery which he had discovered on one of his holidays and where he had since made several retreats. Its name was Notre-Dame d'Igny, and it was situated in the country between the Aisne and the Marne, a few miles from Fismes. Founded by St. Bernard in 1127, it lent support to the adage *Benedictus colles, valles Bernardus amabat*, for it lay hidden in a narrow valley where the silence was broken only by the trickle of a stream, the tolling of the abbey bell, and the flight of migrating herons in the autumn.[20] When describing the monastery to Huysmans, the Abbé Mugnier did not lay stress on the beauty of this austere landscape, knowing that the novelist was no nature-lover; he spoke rather of the tranquillity of the setting and the sympathetic character of the monks. Huysmans hesitated for a while, partly out of shame at the thought of confessing his sordid misdeeds to a man who had dedicated his whole life to God; partly – and characteristically – because he dreaded the physical suffering Trappist austerity, and particularly the Trappist diet, might cause him. On 19 June, however, he told the Abbé Mugnier that he was prepared to go to La Trappe in July, when he would have a month's leave from the Ministry.[21] 'You who have always had the Faith,' he wrote, 'if only you knew what it costs to recover it! But I'm so weary, so utterly disgusted with my life, that it's surely impossible for Him not to have pity on me!'

At Huysmans' request, the priest wrote a letter of introduction for him to the Guestmaster at Notre-Dame d'Igny, Father Léon. In this letter he forbore from mentioning that his friend was a novelist and a civil servant; but on the other hand, remembering how des Esseintes had fulminated against the commercialism of the monastic orders, he thought it wiser to warn Huysmans that the monks of Igny manufactured chocolate. Huysmans' comment on this news[22] was reassuring:

The chocolate doesn't worry me [he wrote], provided that they have some potent bleaching-waters and some extraordinary benzines with which to clean me up! All the same, if anyone had told me, when I was writing *En*

269

Ménage, that one day I should go to La Trappe, I should have felt outraged. Now, it seems a little painful, but very simple. How stupid I've been all these years – how incredibly stupid!

Early in July Father Léon wrote[23] agreeing to receive Huysmans for a week's retreat, beginning on Tuesday the 12th. On the eve of his departure from Paris, Huysmans packed his portmanteau with spiritual and material provisions for his stay at Igny – selections from the works of Ruysbroeck, the recorded visions of Catherine Emmerich, chocolate and tobacco, matches and napkins, pencils and paper, packets of antipyrine and a phial of laudanum – and then went out to have a farewell dinner with Lucien Descaves at the Restaurant Mignon on the Boulevard Saint-Germain.[24] Descaves, whose sympathies at this time were more Communard than Catholic, was naturally a little sceptical as to the probable success of his friend's expedition to La Trappe. Nor was he alone in this respect, for even the Abbé Mugnier had his private doubts. 'I knew very well', he wrote,[25] 'what an irresolute character I had to deal with. Would he, I wondered, get as far as the Gare du Nord? And supposing that he did, might not the story of des Esseintes, whose journey to London went no further than the Rue d'Amsterdam, be repeated here?'

This time, however, the journey was made in earnest; and it was not until Huysmans had been deposited at the abbey door, and had watched the gig which had brought him from Fismes disappearing behind the trees, that he was overcome by panic – a panic such as any small boy might feel on his first day at a new school. Describing this difficult moment in *En Route*, he wrote:

Durtal remained standing before the door, his portmanteau at his feet, feeling utterly desolate; his heart was beating violently; all his assurance, all his enthusiasm vanished, and he stammered: 'What will happen to me in there?'

And in a swift rush of panic, a vision of the terrible

life of the Trappes passed before him: the body ill-nourished, exhausted from want of sleep, prostrated for hours on the stone flags; the soul trembling, squeezed dry, drilled and disciplined, probed and ransacked even to its innermost recesses; and, brooding over it as it lay on this inhospitable shore, like a wreck thrown up by the sea of life, the stillness of the prison cell, the awful silence of the tomb!

'My God, my God, have pity on me!' he prayed, wiping his brow.

Unconsciously he looked around, as if he expected someone to come to his aid; the roads were deserted and the woods empty; not a sound could be heard either in the country or in the monastery. He told himself that he would have to make up his mind to ring the bell – and at last, his heart sinking within him, he pulled the iron chain.

A few minutes later Huysmans was in the presence of Father Léon, a smiling young monk wearing the white robe and black scapular of his order, who after bidding the novelist welcome showed him to his room. This contained a bed, a cupboard, two tables, three chairs, and a prayer-stool – luxurious furnishings by Trappist standards, yet simple enough to satisfy Huysmans' tastes. After asking him to mention anything he might need which had not been provided, Father Léon left him to admire the view from his window – a view of the abbey orchard with a wide vista of fields and wooded slopes beyond – and to consult a copy of the rule of the house. This last made depressing reading. Huysmans learnt that although retreatants were not obliged to rise with the monks at two in the morning, they were expected to begin their long daily round of offices and meditations at four. Even more disquieting was a note which read: 'Retreatants are requested to make their confessions at an early date, in order to have their minds more free for meditation.' Thus reminded of the real reason for his visit to La Trappe, Huysmans was once more filled with apprehension. His fears abated to some extent when Father Léon returned and presented him to the other occupant of the guesthouse, a M. Charles Rivière who is portrayed in *En Route* under the name of M. Bruno. He was a retired wool-dealer from Reims who on his mother's death had settled at Igny as an oblate – that is to say, a person who shares in the life of a religious community without taking the full and final vows of the order. The kindness and sympathetic understanding which he showed Huysmans during the following days earned him the novelist's lasting friendship, and the two men were to meet and correspond regularly until Huysmans' death.[26]

Their first meal together was a pleasant surprise to the retreatant, who had expected a diet of bread and water, since it consisted of fried eggs, rice and beans, honey and wine. As with the hour of rising, however, he discovered that the monks themselves followed a stricter rule: for at least six months of the year they were allowed only one meal a day, and that of coarse vegetables washed down with vinegary wine. Noticing that his companion was not subjected to this grim diet, and that he had a room of his own in the guesthouse instead of a plank-bed and a blanket in a chilly dormitory, Huysmans questioned him closely about the duties and privileges of oblatehood. It is unlikely that he already had some vague intuition that one day he, too, would become an oblate, of the Benedictine Order; but there can be no doubt that the thought of the devout, austere, but not too uncomfortable life which Charles Rivière led at Igny influenced him in later years.

After supper Huysmans went out into the grounds to smoke a cigarette, and then hurried to the chapel for Compline. He considered the eighteenth-century sanctuary 'alarmingly ugly', but the monks' impassioned rendering of the *Salve Regina*, followed by a silence in which the Angelus rang out pure and clear, moved him to tears. Still dreading the thought of his confession, which Father Léon had told him would be heard the next morning, but comforted and uplifted by the office he had just attended, he went to his room and prepared for sleep.

The night which followed – a night which he had hoped would be one of sweet repose and religious calm – proved, in fact, to be the most disturbed and horrifying he had ever experienced. Again and again he woke from some dreadful nightmare, trembling with fear and convinced that he had been visited by just such a succubus as he had described in his study of satanism. As he later explained in *En Route*, these were no ordinary sexual nightmares:

It was not at all that involuntary and commonplace act, that vision which is blotted out just at the moment when the sleeper clasps an amorous form in a passionate embrace. It happened as in nature, differing only in degree: it was long and complete, accompanied by every prelude, every detail, every sensation, and the orgasm occurred with a singularly painful acuteness, an incredible spasm. Apart from the fact that certain caresses which could only follow each other in reality were united in the same moment in this dream, there was one curious circumstance which underlined the difference between this condition and the unconscious uncleanness of ordinary nightmares: the sensation, clear and precise, of a being, a fluidic form, which disappeared with the sound of a percussion cap exploding or a whip cracking close by, at the very moment of waking. And this being was felt so near and so distinctly that the sheet, disarranged by its flight, was still in motion, and one was left staring in terror at the empty place . . .

Unnerved by this phenomenon, which recurred at brief intervals throughout the night, Huysmans finally decided to leave his bed and go out into the fresh air. He spent a few minutes in the open smoking a cigarette, and then made for the chapel. As he opened the door and stepped inside, he tripped over a body. Looking down, he beheld, in the dim lamplight, a scene suggestive of a battlefield swept by grape-shot. Human forms were scattered over the floor in agonized postures – some lying flat on their faces, some kneeling with arms uplifted, some clawing at their heads or breasts, and all silent. One figure in particular arrested the novelist's attention: an eighty-year-old monk kneeling before a side-altar in an ecstasy of adoration, his coarse and weatherbeaten features utterly transformed and illuminated by an inner spiritual radiance. Even in the paintings of his beloved Primitives Huysmans had never before seen such transcendent fervour, and he sank to his knees, humbling begging God to forgive him for soiling this holy place with his presence.

This first night at La Trappe taught him to pray with genuine warmth and true humility, but it left him in a state of spiritual and physical exhaustion. The result was that when, later in the morning, he found himself in the presence of the Prior, the saturnine Father Bernard, he was quite unable to make a coherent confession, admitting only that he had not practised his religion since childhood, and then bursting into tears. Seeing his plight, the monk asked him to return the following day, at an earlier hour, when he would feel more composed and they would have more time at their disposal.

The next morning, after Mass, Huysmans went into the grounds to collect his thoughts, and sat for a few minutes beside one of the abbey's two great ponds. This pond was in the shape of a cross, and at its head there stood an immense crucifix of wood bearing an eighteenth-century figure of Christ, of natural size, carved in white marble. Huysmans' feelings as he gazed at the reflection of the cross in the dark waters are recounted in this moving and symbolic passage from *En Route*:

> Seen from behind, the crucifix sank into the water, trembling in the ripples stirred up by the breeze, and appeared to be plunging dizzily into the inky depths. And of the marble Christ, whose body was hidden by the wood, only the two white arms which hung below the tree could be seen, twisting in the black waters. Sitting on the grass, Durtal looked at the blurred image of the recumbent cross, and thinking of his soul, which, like the pond, was tanned and soiled by a bed of dead

leaves, a dunghill of sins, he pitied the Saviour whom he was about to invite to bathe himself there. For this would be quite unlike the martyrdom of Golgotha, which was at least suffered on a hilltop, head high, by daylight, and in the open air! This would be martyrdom by an increase of outrages, the abominable plunging of the crucified body, head down and by night, into a muddy morass!

'Ah, but it is time', he told himself, 'to spare him this ordeal, by filtering and purifying my soul.' And the swan, till then motionless in an arm of the pond, swept forward over the lamentable image, and whitened the moving mourning-cloth of the waters with its peaceful reflection.

Just as the swan's white plumage relieved the blackness of the waters, so peace came a few hours later to Huysmans' soul, when the Prior, after hearing his confession, stretched out his white-sleeved arms like two great wings and pronounced the blessed words: *Ego te absolvo*. The penitent shuddered from head to foot, feeling, as he wrote in *En Route*, that 'Christ was present in person, was there beside him in that room; and although he could find no words to thank him, he wept out of sheer happiness, bowed down under the great sign of the cross in which the monk enveloped him . . .'

Unfortunately the rest of the day was less happy, being spoilt for Huysmans by doubts as to whether his penance consisted of ten Aves every day or ten Rosaries; by a marathon recitation of 500 Aves through which he plodded in case the second hypothesis should be correct; and finally by remorse at having prayed so badly and performed his first penance so grudgingly. Even after this matter had been settled by the Prior, who assured him that he had prescribed only one dec-ade of the Rosary and described his scruples as a stratagem of the Devil, the novelist was still troubled by the question of communion. As luck would have it, none of the Trappist priests was available the next day to give him communion, since the Abbot himself was ill, the Prior was celebrating a

Mass at which it was not possible to communicate individually, and the two other consecrated monks were away from the abbey. Worse still, a visiting priest, to whom Huysmans had taken an intense dislike on account of his crass good humour and vapid wit, had kindly offered to celebrate a special Mass before he left Igny on the Friday morning, to enable the novelist to take communion the day after his confession. Try as he might, Huysmans could not overcome a certain repugnance at the thought of receiving the Eucharist from the hands of such a jovial, coarse-grained member of the secular clergy, or a certain chagrin at having come specially to La Trappe only to be communicated by a priest of passage. He even went so far as to pray that, if his communion were pleasing to God, a monk might take the priest's place as a sign of divine approval. His prayer was granted. To his great joy and relief, it was not the visiting curate whom he saw entering the chapel next morning, but a younger, more majestic figure, wearing the white Trappist robe under his vestments, and on one finger the episcopal amethyst. The monk's features were pale and drawn, for, as Huysmans later discovered, he had risen from his sickbed in response to a mysterious intimation that he should celebrate his Mass that day. And so it happened that Huysmans was communicated for the first time since his childhood by Dom Augustin Marre, Bishop of Constance, Abbot of Notre-Dame d'Igny, and future General of the Cistercians.

Curiously enough, this first communion did not produce in Huysmans the state of spiritual exaltation which he had expected and which he had experienced after confession, but rather, as he wrote in *En Route*, 'a condition of absolute torpor, of spiritual anaesthesia'. And in a letter he wrote to the Abbé Mugnier the same day[27] he described his mood as one 'of infinite sadness, with an impression of complete unworthiness, of a patched-up soul which has given of its best but can stand only with the aid of crutches'.

On the whole, though [he added], I'm perfectly happy here, terribly spoilt and on good terms with everyone.

I'm taking notes on the Abbé Péchenard's book which you recommended to me, praying, meditating, smoking, daydreaming beside the pond, strolling up and down the avenues, and generally having a silence and open-air cure. Unfortunately it has been raining a lot, but the cell is not without its charms.

I shall probably be leaving here next Tuesday, pushing on to Reims to see the Cathedral again, spending a day or two in Paris, and then going to Lyons for a few weeks. To think that I've missed the National Holiday – what luck! And how sweet life at La Trappe is, when you come to think of it! What more can I say to you, except that it's to you that I owe all this? You have done so much to help me see it through. I really don't know how to thank you for everything . . .

Sweet though Huysmans found life at Notre-Dame d'Igny, the rest of his stay in the abbey was not entirely untroubled. Kneeling beside his bed one day, he was suddenly visited by memories of Fernande – the perverse Florence of *En Route* – with 'her street-arab smile and her adolescent haunches, her mania for nibbling his ears, for drinking toilet waters in little glasses, and for eating dates with slices of bread and caviare'. He was now able to resist the appeal of such memories, but he was also beset by other, newer temptations which caused him far greater anguish of mind and spirit. Thus he occasionally fell a prey to blasphemous impulses, as when he had to bite his lips till they bled to prevent himself from shouting abuse at a statue of the Virgin. And though he felt neither the courage nor the inclination to follow in the steps of a St. John of the Cross, he too suffered the mystical 'night of darkness' which is part of the purgative life, when after nine hours of doubts and scruples he suddenly imagined that God's grace had been entirely withdrawn from him in the hour of his greatest need.

During his last few days at La Trappe, however, Huysmans enjoyed moments of great happiness and perfect peace. He was taken on a tour of the abbey buildings by Father Léon and shown the treasures of the library by Father Bernard. He met the saintly swineherd of Igny, Brother Isaac – the Brother Siméon of *En Route* – whom he recognized as the old monk he had so admired in the chapel on his first night at La Trappe. He went for many walks down the avenue of limes and beside the two great ponds, and earned a minor title to fame when he glimpsed an otter which had made its home in the abbey grounds – a legendary beast which had never been seen before. And finally, to set the seal on his contentment, he tasted that ecstasy of joy after his second communion which he had failed to experience after his first. He has described in *En Route* how, 'gently, almost insensibly, the Sacrament took effect; Christ opened, little by little, the shuttered lodging of his soul, and light and air came streaming in'. At the same time his vision of Nature was transformed:

> He experienced that sensation of expansion, of almost childish joy, which comes to the sick man on his first outing, and to the convalescent who, after languishing in a single room, finally sets foot outside: everything grew young again. These paths, these woods through which he had so often wandered and whose every twist and turn he was beginning to know, appeared to him in a new light. A restrained gladness, a quiet contentment emanated from this landscape which, instead of spreading outwards as before, seemed to him to be drawing near, to be gathering round the crucifix, to be turning attentively towards the liquid cross. The trees were trembling and rustling in a whisper of prayer, and bowing before the Christ, who no longer twisted his tortured arms in the mirror of the pond, but constrained the waters before him in a wide embrace, blessing them. They themselves were different: their inky fluid was filled with monastic visions in white robes which the reflected clouds left there in passing; and as the swan swam forward, making great circles around itself, it spattered and splashed them with sunlight . . .

Such transcendent happiness as this inevitably made the

moment of departure, when it came, extremely painful and difficult. Leaving Notre-Dame d'Igny, Huysmans was afflicted with the despair des Esseintes had felt on leaving Fontenay, but with greater reason – for whereas des Esseintes could regret only the solitude of his 'refined Thebaid', his creator had discovered an ideal community, whose life he knew he was temperamentally and constitutionally unfitted to share for more than a few days. He knew, too, that those few days had spoilt him for the outside world. Having been confessed by the Prior of Igny, he felt he would never be satisfied with the platitudinous homilies of a secular priest; and without the spiritual guidance of the Trappists, he envisaged 'the anxiety of a conscience skilled in self-torment, the permanent reproach of an acquired lukewarmness, the apprehension of doubts regarding the Faith, the fear of the furious clamour of senses aroused by some chance encounter'. Again, after seeing the monks of Igny at worship and hearing them sing, he doubted whether he would be able to endure 'the crass stupidity of the churchgoing fraternity' or 'the theatrical warblings of the Paris choirs'; and he was certain that the conversation and books of his fellow writers would never hold the same interest for him as the 'divine ebriety' of a Trappist swineherd. As he wrote in *En Route*, he appeared to be condemned to a life of frustration, since he was 'still too much the man of letters to make a monk, and yet already too much the monk to remain among men of letters'. His problem was, in fact, to find some middle course between an impracticable and an insufferable way of life. It was a problem which was to occupy his attention during most of his remaining years.

PART THREE

1. THE NEOPHYTE

FROM the moment of leaving Notre-Dame d'Igny, Huysmans found it difficult to readjust himself, either physically or spiritually, to the world which he had abandoned for nine fateful days. The physical process of rehabilitation was especially unpleasant in its earliest stages, for the meal which he hungrily devoured as soon as he got to Reims made him violently sick.[1] As for the spiritual aftermath of his stay at Igny, he wrote in August[2] to Gustave Boucher:

> My soul feels absolutely shattered. The effect produced by La Trappe and the reaction it has had on me are bizarre and tenacious. I'm suffering from an unspeakable moral fatigue, an unconquerable boredom with everything, almost a nostalgia for the cloister. I tell myself that it's fortunate (or unfortunate) that I should have hit upon an order whose life is so hard that you can't share it for long without falling ill, for if I'd immured myself in a more intellectual and more comfortable house I should probably have returned there by now – for good.

Luckily Huysmans did not have to plunge back into the literary and bureaucratic life of Paris as soon as he arrived home, for his summer leave had not yet expired. Instead, after less than three days in Paris, he left on the 25th for a fortnight in Lyons.[3] There he rose early every day – a habit contracted at La Trappe – and spent the morning strolling along the banks of the Rhône or visiting the city's churches and convents, before going to the Rue de la Martinière to lunch with Joseph Boullan. One afternoon he went out to Mont Cendre, a few miles from Lyons, to meet and converse with a Capuchin friar who lived there in a peaceful hermitage; but generally he passed his afternoons at Pascal Misme's house, studying letters Boullan had received from the superiors of various convents, with the intention of using them in his next novel. 'There are some stupefying demoniacal struggles described in these letters,' he told Georges Landry, 'and a truly beautiful mysticism of a high order. I shall bring a lot of these documents back to Paris after we have sorted them out.'

The life led by Boullan and his disciples had changed very little in the year since Huysmans' last visit. The only remotely orthodox ceremony which the novelist attended with members of the Carmel was the wedding of the somnambulist Laure, whom he had the privilege of giving in marriage to a painter and decorator, in the sight of all the occultists and mediums of Lyons. In the Rue de la Martinière, Boullan was continually engaging in long-distance warfare with sacrilegious priests, and Maman Thibault having visions of militant archangels, while Huysmans lay on a divan sardonically watching their activities through a haze of cigarette smoke. And he complained to Landry that his study of Boullan's letters was going slowly because 'from time to time we interrupt our work to win a battle . . . in space'.

In spite of these wearisome eccentricities, however, Huysmans still held Boullan in high regard. He told Boucher that the defrocked priest was 'a prodigious mystic who smilingly explains to me the phases through which I shall have to pass'; while to Landry he wrote:

> This Boullan is disconcerting. As a theologian, as a mystic, and as an experienced confessor, he was incomparable. Why the devil had this man, who would otherwise have become an ecclesiastical high-up a long time ago, to get mixed up with the crazy notions of a Vintras!

The extent of Huysmans' admiration and liking for the man was shown later in the summer, when Boullan was charged at Trévoux with practising medicine illegally, convicted on the evidence of the newly-married Laure, and sentenced to a fine of 2,000 francs. According to his biographer, Joanny Bricaud, it was Huysmans who paid this heavy fine.[4]

While Huysmans was still in Lyons, news of his conversion was broken to the public by the Paris Press. Various newspapers published reports that he had made a retreat in some unspecified monastery, and on 30 July *Le Figaro* stated:

Rumour – a rather persistent rumour – has it that one of our writers, whose last novel created a sensation, but whose work, on account of its extreme subtlety, is known to only a limited public, has immured himself in a Trappist monastery, determined never to leave the shelter of its walls. The truth is that M. Huysmans, for it is he who is concerned, is at this moment in Lyons, where he is resting in a religious house until the end of his leave.

The novelist was infuriated to discover that his closely guarded secret was out, and he told Boucher that he suspected Stock of having spread the news as a publicity device. Fearing that his superiors would look with disfavour upon a civil servant whose conversion attracted so much attention, he wrote at once to the editor of *Le Figaro*, denying that he had retired to a Trappist monastery or was staying in a religious house, and as an additional precaution sent his Lyons address to a colleague at the Ministry.[5] In fact, his attempts at this time to suppress the news of his conversion were superfluous, for few people believed that he was sincere in his religious aspirations. 'The author of *Là-Bas* has no desire to be converted,' stated the *Écho de Paris* on 31 July, 'for his path lies very far from the road to Damascus.' And when, in mid-August, Huysmans went back to his office, no one thought fit to mention the reports which had appeared in the Press.

One of his first visitors on his return to Paris was the Abbé Mugnier, who entered the following record[6] of their conversation into his diary:

17 August 1892. Last night, on the balcony of his flat, Huysmans told me his impressions of La Trappe. He was entranced by the lay-brothers. Temptations and scruples assailed him. The diabolical influences were such that he thought of committing suicide. In the chapel, he felt strange 'effluvia' arising and enveloping him. Absolution produced the effect of a wind uplifting him. Communion made less of an impression on him. He detests the idea of taking communion for his own benefit instead of doing it simply for God. In Huysmans' opinion there are no sudden conversions or blinding revelations. When he woke up in the Hôtel Jeanne d'Arc at Reims, on his way back, he experienced a feeling of profound disenchantment. 'I suppose I ought to settle down to a life of humdrum piety,' Huysmans said to me, 'but that's impossible.' This novelist, through reading the mystics, has refashioned his soul in their image. Zola, hearing that his sometime disciple had left for La Trappe, said: 'He's off his head.' Zola himself is going to Lourdes to collect material there for a book.

One might have expected that after mentioning Zola's plans Huysmans would make some reference to the work he himself had in hand, but none appears to have been made. We know that the novel he was writing was very different from the book he brought out in 1895 under the title of *En Route*, but as yet we have only a few indications as to its character.[7] On completing *Là-Bas*, Huysmans had asserted that he intended to embark on a mystical work, although he was obviously undecided as to what variety of mystical experience he should treat. At first he had been tempted to make a study of the secular clergy, and in April 1891 he had stated[8] in an interview with Jules Huret:

Ah, but there's always the priest! Nobody has ever made a proper study of *him* – but I fear nobody ever will. You would have to have been a priest yourself, to have lived that life of the seminary which pulverizes your brain, completely changes your personality, and so affects you that should you ever deny the Faith, grow a beard, and efface your tonsure, some phrase, some gesture, some inflexion of the voice would still reveal that you had been a seminarist. Yes, in a priest's life there is something special which evades all outside investigation, and which we are forbidden, as it were, to imbibe. I've known some priests in my time – that is to say, some former priests – and lately I've seen quite a few while preparing *Là-Bas*. They are unanalysable.

This refractory subject had to be abandoned, but Huysmans refused to be discouraged from his high purpose. 'I mean to try and concoct an antidote to *Là-Bas*,' he told Émile Edwards[9] the next month; 'the absolutely white book of pure and divine mysticism. In it I may possibly reach new heights, but it's very difficult and I'm afraid it will probably break my back – anyway I shall have a try . . .' However, the purity of this 'absolutely white book' is open to question, for it is known that Huysmans intended to call it *La Bataille charnelle*,[10] and also that Boullan was inciting him[11] to present in it 'the spectacle of people abandoned to every sort of satanic obscenity, yet at the same time enjoying the illumination of divine life'. And even after his stay at Notre-Dame d'Igny, we have seen that Huysmans examined Boullan's case-histories of 'possessed' nuns with a view to incorporating them into his novel. But this project was also abandoned, as Huysmans came to see that there was greater interest and unity in the story of his own conversion and the mute heroism of Trappist monks than in any study of sexual perversion and demonic possession in the convents of France.

Was there, one might ask, any reason for his decision to write an account of his conversion other than interest in the psychological processes involved? Léon Bloy had a ready answer to this question,[12] and declared: 'Converted at little or no cost to himself, without experiencing any revelation or expending any effort, he set to work producing convert-literature, the sort that pays . . .' In the light of our present knowledge of Huysmans' character, this malicious comment can be discounted: if the novelist was inspired by the example of other converts to relate this vital phase of his existence, it was by the quality of their writings rather than the extent of their earnings. Although certain passages of *En Route* and also Huysmans' aesthetic approach to Christianity are reminiscent of Chateaubriand, Huysmans was neither impressed by the great Romantic's style nor convinced of his sincerity; asked by the Abbé Mugnier if he liked Chateaubriand,[13] he replied briefly: 'Not much.' He felt no such repugnance for the works of his friend Francis Poictevin, and had doubtless read the story of Poictevin's conversion, *Petitau*, which his own novel was to resemble in many respects, particularly in its subtle evocation of church interiors. Like Poictevin, too, he wished to discountenance legendary conversions of the Pauline type, and would present the truth as he saw it, banal though it might seem, applying the naturalistic methods he had always employed to the study of his soul. His 'documents' would this time be of a spiritual order, but his scrupulous regard for truth, his disdain for precedent, were unaltered. Writing to Jules Huret shortly before *En Route* was published,[14] he gave this brief outline of the book as he had planned it:

> The plot of the novel is as simple as it could be. I've taken the principal character of *Là-Bas*, Durtal, had him converted, and sent him to a Trappist monastery. In studying his conversion, I've tried to trace the progress of a soul surprised by the gift of grace, and developing in an ecclesiastical atmosphere, to the accompaniment of mystical literature, liturgy, and plainchant, against a background of all that admirable art which the Church has created.

A secondary purpose is revealed in these last lines: the glorification of monastic life, of ecclesiastical art. As Huysmans explained to another correspondent,[15] his novel was not only 'the true confession of a soul' but also 'an attempt to celebrate the splendour of the Liturgy, the glorious art of the Church'.

The neophyte turned proselyte also hoped that *En Route* would lead to other conversions, and wrote to a friend[16] that the book 'is addressed less to safe, practising Catholics than to the intellectual élite of Paris. It's a question of attracting these people and making them think about a religion which they don't know or don't practise, on account of the devotional fiddle-faddle with which it's been overloaded to please the pious.' As will be seen, Huysmans' subsequent novels were to have this same dual character: they were to be both frankly autobiographical and unashamedly didactic.

Once the purpose and plan of *En Route* had been established, Huysmans began amassing notes on those aspects of the Liturgy and art of the Church which he proposed to discuss. His work went well, and to a reporter who found him at his office, annotating a work on plainchant,[17] he confessed that 'his pleasure consisted *entirely* in this documentation and detailed research; that it was sheer bliss to him, like wallowing in a bath; and that he only ceased to enjoy himself when he had to begin writing the book'. However, not all his information was derived from the printed page: for the theological part of his novel he consulted his confessor, the Abbé Gabriel-Eugène Ferret, a curate at Saint-Sulpice. This priest had become his spiritual director soon after his return from Igny and Lyons. He had been reluctant to choose the Abbé Mugnier as his confessor, possibly because he found him too worldly and too literary after the monks of Igny; and he had therefore decided to follow the advice which M. Bruno gives Durtal in *En Route:*

If you want to find a truly zealous priest, go to Saint-Sulpice. There you will meet some good-hearted, honest, and intelligent ecclesiastics. In Paris, where the parish clergy are such a motley crew, they are the pick of the bunch – which is easily understood when you consider that they form a separate community, live in cells, don't dine out, and, since the Sulpician rule forbids them to aspire to high positions or honours, run no risk of being spoilt by ambition.

There still remained the problem of selecting one priest from the many who served the parish of Saint-Sulpice. Remembering that St. Teresa had said one should allow God to make a choice of this kind, Huysmans plunged blindly into a confessional one evening, resolved to accept as his spiritual director whatever priest he might find there, but making a mental reservation regarding a forty-year-old curate of somewhat uncouth appearance whom he had often observed with dislike ambling around the church.[18] To his disgust, he found that he had chanced upon this very priest, and had to make his confession – or 'delouse his soul', to use his characteristic phrase for this operation – in the hearing of a man whom he took to be an ignorant peasant. Disgust turned to surprise when he left the confessional, for the curate leapt upon him and embraced him, exclaiming: 'I have you now, and I shan't let you go!' He then introduced himself to the astonished Huysmans as the Abbé Gabriel Ferret, and explained that for months he had been intrigued by the novelist's nocturnal visits to the church; that, as Georges Landry's spiritual director, he had learnt of his conversion and had looked forward to meeting him; and that he regarded this encounter in the confessional as an act of Divine Providence. Huysmans, already captivated by the priest's extraordinary enthusiasm, was later to consider their meeting in the same light, for from being an object of suspicion and dislike, the Abbé Ferret eventually became, in the novelist's words,[19] 'everything – father, brother, and friend'.

With his confessor elucidating any theological problems that confronted him, Huysmans worked at his book through most of the autumn and winter of 1892. He enjoyed a brief respite, however, when Joseph Boullan came to Paris on some mysterious errand, putting up at the Hôtel des Missions Catholiques under an assumed name. Huysmans did his best to repay the hospitality he had received in Lyons, and Gustave Boucher later remembered being taken out to dinner with Boullan at one of the few eating-places favoured by M. Folantin – the peaceful Restaurant Lachenal, on the corner of the Rue Bonaparte and the Rue du Vieux Colombier.[20] This and other pleasant memories of Boullan's visit were to linger for many years, for neither Huysmans nor Boucher saw him again. The last letter he sent the novelist,[21] on 3 January 1893, was full of foreboding, as the following extracts reveal:

Quis ut Deus!   Lyons, 2 January 1893
    My very dear friend J.-K. Huysmans,
    We received with much pleasure the letter which brought us your good wishes for this New Year. It opens with ominous presentiments, this fateful year, and its figures 8–9–3 together form a terrible warning . . .
    3 January. I ended my letter there last night to wait for dear Mme Thibault to finish hers; but during the night a terrible incident occurred. At three in the morning I awoke with a feeling of suffocation and called out twice: 'Madame Thibault, I'm choking!' She heard, and came to my room, where she found me lying unconscious. From three till three-thirty I was between life and death. At Saint-Maximin, Mme Thibault had dreamt of Guaita, and the next morning a bird of death had called to her – prophesying this attack. M. Misme, too, had dreamt of it. At four I was able to go to sleep again: the danger had passed . . .

Boullan died the next day. In a letter to Huysmans describing his last hours,[22] Julie Thibault wrote:

    In the evening he sat down to table and dined well; he was in a jovial mood and went as usual to pay his little daily call on Mlles Gay. When he got back he asked me if I should be ready soon for prayers. We came to pray; a few minutes later he felt ill and cried out: 'What's that?' With these words he crumpled up, and M. Misme and I were only just in time to catch him and help him into his arm-chair . . . He died after an agony lasting two minutes . . .
    I was afraid things would end unhappily like this,

what with all those battles he fought for himself and for others. I'm surprised only that he lasted as long as he did. I believe that he had accomplished his task on earth. Already, more than six years ago, I had received forewarning of his death, and a few days ago, just as I was getting into the train at Saint-Maximin, a bird came and called to me several times. It was then six o'clock and not yet light. I said aloud, in the hearing of one or two people: 'Ah, merciful Heaven, that bird is warning me of somebody's death!' And I felt it was to be our poor Father. I rejected this inspiration, little knowing that it was to be fulfilled five days after my return to Lyons . . .

Even before he received this letter, Huysmans had formed and expressed his own opinion as to the cause of Boullan's death. Thus, in answer to a telegram from Lyons giving him the news, he wrote[23] to his 'poor dear friend' that '1893 must be a terrible year if it can begin with the triumph of Black Magic!' He also communicated his suspicions – and the text of Boullan's last letter – to his friend Jules Bois, who was himself a disciple of the late Dr. Johannès. Unfortunately for Huysmans, Bois was a naturally incautious person, and the temptation to avenge his former master in print, while at the same time turning an honest journalistic penny, proved irresistible. He accordingly published a violent article in the *Gil Blas* of 9 January, in which he wrote:

I consider it my duty to relate these facts: the strange presentiments of Joseph Boullan, the prophetic visions of Mme Thibault and M. Misme, and these seemingly indisputable attacks by the Rosicrucians Wirth, Péladan, and Guaita on this man who has died. I am informed that M. le Marquis de Guaita lives a lonely and secluded life; that he handles poisons with great skill and marvellous sureness; that he can volatilize them and direct them into space; that he even has a familiar spirit – M. Paul Adam, M. Dubus, and M. Gary de Lacroze have seen it –

locked up in a cupboard at his home, which comes out in visible form at his command . . . What I now ask, without accusing anyone at all, is that some explanation be given of the causes of Boullan's death. For the liver and the heart – the organs through which death struck at Boullan – are the very points where the astral forces normally penetrate.

This attack on the Rosicrucians was pressed home the next day with another article by Bois in *Gil Blas* and a report by one Blanchon in *Le Figaro* of an interview Huysmans had given him on the subject of Boullan's death. In this interview Huysmans was alleged to have said:

It is indisputable that Guaita and Péladan practise Black Magic every day. Poor Boullan was engaged in perpetual conflict with the evil spirits which for two years they continually sent him from Paris. Nothing is more vague and indefinite than these questions of magic, but it is quite possible that my poor friend Boullan has succumbed to a supremely powerful spell.[24]

Guaita still affected to ignore these allegations, but the publication in *Gil Blas* of yet another defamatory article by Bois finally stung him to action.[25] On the 13th he sent his seconds, Maurice Barrès and Victor-Émile Michelet, to the Ministry of the Interior to demand satisfaction from Huysmans, whom he accused of being 'the propagator and source of the vile and ridiculous gossip about me which has been circulating in the Press for some days'. Asked to name his seconds, Huysmans chose Gustave Guiches and his old friend Alexis Orsat. He instructed them to try to reach an amicable agreement with Guaita,[26] but added that 'if such an arrangement is impossible, we shall just have to fight. We'll exchange a few sword-thrusts or bullets which will be sure of achieving one result at least – that of making people laugh.' However, the seconds of both parties were eager to avoid the scandal which would surround a duel of such a sensational character, and all four did their best to placate Guaita. The consequence was that a statement was published on 15 January in which Huysmans discreetly disassociated himself from the views expressed by Bois, and declared that he had never had any intention of impugning Guaita's honour as a gentleman. A second statement in the same conciliatory vein put an end, for the time being, to Guaita's quarrel with Bois – but this flared up again in April when the unrepentant journalist made another attack on Guaita in *L'Événement*.[27] This time the Marquis would accept no apology for the affront, and a pistol-duel was fought at the Tour de Villebon. Guaita's only recorded comment on the encounter, which was indecisive, was that Bois had conducted himself courageously on the duelling-ground.[28] A more colourful account of this affair, as also of a subsequent sword-duel between Bois and Papus, was later given by Bois in *Le Monde invisible*, and by one of his seconds, a journalist nephew of Victor Hugo called Paul Foucher, in *Le Sud-Ouest Toulouse*.[29] They told of a bullet which was magically prevented from leaving a pistol-barrel, of a horse which collapsed on the way to the duelling-ground, upsetting its carriage, and of another horse which halted for twenty minutes in the roadway, trembling as if it had seen the Devil in person. Though these details were probably the products of a fertile journalistic imagination, there can be no doubt that Bois was convinced that Guaita possessed occult powers. Certainly he and Huysmans persisted in their belief that Joseph Boullan had been done to death by magic, as the following letter from Huysmans to Julie Thibault, written in August 1893,[30] bears witness:

No news of the occultists – except for the unhappy Dubus, who is in the grip of persecution mania and spends his time defending himself against phantoms which are trying to kill him. What do you think of that for a terrible punishment?

That kind of madness is incurable. From what Bois tells me, I gather that before he was shut up at Charenton he was boasting it was he who had struck down the

Father at Lyons. If he wasn't lying he's paid the penalty soon enough.

As for Guaita, we know nothing except that since he's been deprived of his best auxiliary he's gone to ground. His punishment seems slow to come, but doubtless we shall see it in time.

It came five years later, when Guaita died of an overdose of drugs, at the early age of 27. He had outlived his supposed accomplice by three years, for Dubus died in 1895. Released from the asylum at Charenton, the young poet called on Huysmans in April that year, apparently in the hope that he would receive some comfort and spiritual guidance from the author of *En Route*. He spoke of voices which pursued him wherever he went, and admitted that he had formerly practised black magic and cast mortal spells.[31] In June, a few days after a second conversation with Huysmans, he was found dead in the urinal of a restaurant in the Place Maubert. It was whispered in occultist circles that a spell had been put upon him, either by the Rosicrucians or by Boullan's disciples. But in fact, his death owed as little to supernatural causes as did Guaita's: it was due to morphia, not magic.

Meanwhile, in Lyons, the faithful of the Carmel continued to practise the Vintrasian cult despite the death of their 'Father'. Huysmans was, of course, unable to attend Boullan's funeral, but he bought a fifteen-year grant of a grave in a Lyons cemetery for the man whom the tombstone described as '*J.-A. Boullan (Docteur Johannès), noble victime*'. The grant was not renewed, for in 1908 Julie Thibault, Pascal Misme, and Huysmans himself were dead, and Lyons – a city notorious for its heretics – had already half-forgotten Joseph–Antoine Boullan.

A few weeks after Boullan's death, Huysmans was involved in another distressing affair which affected him even more closely. The mental condition of his former mistress, Anna Meunier, had steadily worsened during the last few years, and she had recently been obliged to leave the Rue du Cardinal-Lemoine for No. 15 Rue Monge, after an attack in which she knocked over an oil-lamp and almost set fire to the apartment-house. Her daughters having left her, it soon became obvious that she was a potential source of danger both to herself and to her neighbours, and it was decided to have her interned in the mental home of Sainte-Anne. Huysmans himself tried to take her there, on 12 April 1893, before calling in the police, and later gave Guiches an account[32] of Anna's preparations for the journey:

Calmly, with only a slight flickering of the eyelids that betrayed the inner torments he was suffering, he described every detail: the childish femininity of her toilet, for she wanted to make herself beautiful, not knowing where she was about to be taken; and her delirious speech as she became excited and insisted on knowing more, while he struggled to conceal his agony of mind in order to reassure and amuse her with a little light banter . . .

At Sainte-Anne, Dr. Magnan noted the symptoms of Anna's illness – infantile satisfactions, wandering speech, and erratic pupils – and diagnosed it as general paralysis of the insane. After a few days she was transferred to the asylum at Villejuif for two or three weeks and then brought back to Sainte-Anne, probably at Huysmans' request. Just as she had come to his Rue de Sèvres flat every Sunday, so now he visited her on the same day each week, while his maid, a Mme Giraud whom he described in his letters to the asylum authorities as 'the sick woman's oldest friend', went to see her on Thursdays.[33] His regular visits to Sainte-Anne did him honour, for they must have been an unspeakable ordeal to a man of his sensitivity. In later life he talked about Anna to Mme Myriam Harry, who writes[34] in her memoirs:

He spoke to me of his harrowing visits to that poor remnant of humanity, who recognized him only intermittently, looking at him then with glimmers of such appalling distress that he would come away feeling physically and spiritually crushed, and, going into Saint-Séverin, would throw himself, quivering with emotion, at the Virgin's feet. And then there were the nights, when her anguished eyes appeared again before him, reproaching him with not having forseen her illness; with having aggravated it by taking her to stay at the haunted château – the Château de Lourps – by his eccentricities, his taste for occultism and satanism, his endless soliloquies; and with having pushed her, a carefree, light-hearted little midinette, towards the domain of terror and despair . . .

Insufficient knowledge of these circumstances has led several writers into error when dealing with the history of Anna's incarceration. Thus Gustave Guiches, whose sense of chronology was notoriously deficient, declared[35] that it was after her entry into Sainte-Anne that Huysmans sought comfort in religion; while Léon Deffoux created a touching Huysmans legend when he stated that immediately after Anna's death in the asylum Huysmans paid that first visit to the chapel in the nearby Rue de l'Èbre which is recounted in *En Route*.[36] 'This was for him', he wrote, 'the first step towards conversion, the first stage on the road to Notre-Dame d'Igny.' We now know, of course, that Huysmans was converted some time before Anna's incarceration and long before her death – which occurred in 1895, only a few days before the publication of *En Route*. On the other hand it is true that her illness had done much to turn his thoughts to religion, and that the plight of this wretched inmate of Sainte-Anne whom he had once loved so dearly caused him to ponder more often and more earnestly a problem which had always interested him and was to preoccupy him until his death: the problem of human suffering.

Huysmans would appear to have been born to suffering, both physical and spiritual. A martyr to innumerable ills, of which neurasthenia was perhaps the one which affected him most deeply, he was abnormally sensitive not only to physical pain but also to the petty miseries of life; he found his personal relationships unsatisfying and the company of his fellow men frequently intolerable; and his mind was perpetually torn by fears, doubts, and scruples. Early in life he recognized that suffering was essential to his art, and in a letter to a friend[37] he explained that 'health is egoism ... it produces chubby-cheeked, heavy-footed literature, a Zola and a Maupassant, art that is meaty and vulgar'. However, for many years he refused to admit that suffering could be necessary or beneficial except as a stimulus to artistic creation. Thus while des Esseintes declared that sickliness was an invaluable asset to the modern artist or writer if he wished to treat a subject 'unintelligible to precise or vulgar persons, and comprehensible only to minds shaken, sharpened, and rendered almost clairvoyant by neurosis', he was full of praise for the Schopenhauer who inveighed against 'that useless, incomprehensible, unjust and inept abomination, physical suffering', and agreed with the philosopher that 'if a God has made this world, I should hate to be that God, for the world's misery would rend my heart'. Yet twenty years later, when Huysmans wrote his famous preface to a new edition of *A Rebours*, it was these last passages that he singled out for condemnation. 'I would not acknowledge', he wrote, 'that suffering could be inflicted by a God, and I fondly imagined that pessimism could be the great comforter of lofty souls. What stupidity!'

His conversion to the belief that suffering was necessary, sublime, and God-given was due partly to his desire to discover some meaning and justification for his own frequent illnesses and Anna Meunier's mental and physical degradation; partly to his reading of Baudelaire, who glorified what he called *l'indispensable douleur*; partly to his association with those two apostles of pain, Léon Bloy and Joseph Boullan. Bloy wrote[38] of himself that 'as a child he had lusted after suffering and coveted a paradise of tortures', and in his works and correspondence[39] he never ceased to advocate 'the education given by great suffering' and to insist that 'time spent in suffering is time well spent'. During the five years of their close friendship he may well have expounded to Huysmans the doctrine of mystical substitution which he preached in *Le Désespéré* and which Huysmans later made his own; he must surely have tried to persuade him that suffering was not the work of a baleful fate, but the gift of a God – that 'it is he who gives us suffering, because none but he can give us anything, and suffering is so holy that it idealizes or magnifies the most miserable of creatures'.[40] As for Boullan, he constantly taught and practised the doctrine of substitution, explaining in *Les Annales de la Sainteté*[41] that many Christians engaged in the work of expiation suffered from mysterious diseases, which were not to be confused with diabolical maladies and which no doctor should attempt to cure. He may even have suggested to Huysmans, when the two men met in 1890, that Anna Meunier's strange illness was of divine origin; certainly this aspect of his doctrine impressed the novelist, who often referred to it in his later works and derived great comfort from it in the last months of his life.

The teaching of Bloy and Boullan was reinforced by the example of the contemplative orders. Already, as early as 1881, in a brief consideration of the monastic virtues, Huysmans had written in *A Vau-l'Eau* that 'those who can accept the adversities and afflictions of this life as a passing trial are happy indeed'. Closer acquaintance with monastic life had evoked his admiration for those orders whose members dedicated their lives to suffering, and after a visit to a Carmelite convent he was moved to praise the nuns in this passage from *En Route*:

> The life of these women! To sleep on a prickly horsehair mattress without either pillow or sheets; to fast for seven months out of twelve except on Sundays and feast-days; to eat, standing, nothing but vegetables and other meagre fare; to have no fire in the winter; to sing psalms for hours while standing on a freezing stone floor; to mortify the body and to be humble enough, if one has been brought up in luxury and comfort, to agree joyfully to wash the dishes and to perform the vilest tasks; to pray from early morning till midnight, to pray until one faints from exhaustion, to pray thus unto death! How they

must pity us, and how anxious they must be to expiate the imbecility of this world which dismisses them as hysterical lunatics, for it is incapable of understanding the agonizing joys of such souls as these!

Long before his conversion, Huysmans had noted[42] that 'many common, red-faced women acquire a certain delicate charm after a prolonged illness'; and similarly, in *En Route*, he remarked that although the female voice was generally impure and sensuous it was refined by the austerities of monastic life – a typical expression of his belief that woman, odious and unclean by nature, cannot be purified or redeemed except through suffering, and cannot otherwise attain spiritual or physical beauty. But it was chiefly their heroic adherence to the doctrine of mystical substitution which inspired his admiration for the contemplative orders as a whole, male and female. This was the doctrine which the Abbé Gévresin expounded to Durtal in *En Route*, when he described those religious who took upon themselves the sufferings and temptations of the world as 'the lightning-conductors of society . . . they draw on to their own heads the demoniacal fluid, absorb temptations to vice and protect those who live as we do, in sin; they appease, in fact, the wrath of the Most-High that he may not place the earth under an interdict'. It was the doctrine which, more than anything else, led Huysmans to acknowledge the necessity for suffering, and to write in *En Route*:

In the shipwreck of human reason which occurs as soon as it tries to explain the terrifying enigma of the why and wherefore of life, a single idea remains afloat in the midst of sinking intellectual debris: the idea of an expiation felt rather than understood, the idea that the sole end assigned to life is suffering. According to this idea, everyone has a sum of physical and spiritual suffering to pay, and whoever does not settle his account here on earth, discharges it after death; happiness is only lent, and must be repaid, while even a semblance of happiness is like duty paid in advance on a future succession of sorrows. Who knows, in that case, whether anaesthetics which suppress corporal pain do not bring into debt those who use them? Who knows whether chloroform is not a means of revolt and whether humanity's unwillingness to suffer is not a treacherous rebellion against the will of Heaven? If this be so, the arrears of torment, the debits of distress, the score of pain avoided must accumulate interest at an appalling rate up above . . .

As yet, however, Huysmans was not prepared to follow the painful example of Blessed Lydwine of Schiedam, who was 'greedy of wounds and gluttonous of sores', nor even to accept the logical implications of what has been called the Dolorist philosophy.[43] It is true that he now recognized that suffering was not only inevitable and universal but also necessary, that it was 'the sole end assigned to life', and that 'without suffering, human nature would be too ignoble, for it alone can uplift and purify the soul'. But he knew that he himself was guilty of that unwillingness to suffer, that 'treacherous rebellion against the will of Heaven', of which he had written. Thus in *En Route*, remembering how he had shrunk from the prospect of enduring a week's discomfort in a Trappist monastery, he admitted that 'I'm not Lydwine or Catherine Emmerich who, when you struck them, Lord, cried out: "Again!" You scarcely touch me and I complain – but what would you? You know better than I how physical suffering oppresses and dismays me.' And again, in a letter to Charles Rivière,[44] after mentioning that he had recently read the *Stabat Mater* while confined to his room with rheumatism and acute stomach disorders, he added:

There is one verse in which one begs the Blessed Virgin to allow one to share in the corporal sufferings of her Son. I'm very much afraid that my petition has been only too well received, and I must confess that I have no courage for that sort of thing . . .

He little knew what terrible physical agonies lay in store for him in later life – nor with what unsuspected courage he would then shoulder his burden of suffering, gladly joining the religious he so admired in their work of reparation.

2. THE PROSELYTE

THROUGHOUT the troubled year which followed his first visit to Notre-Dame d'Igny, Huysmans had been haunted by what he termed 'claustral nostalgia . . . the dream of retiring far from the world, of living peacefully in seclusion, close to God'.[1] Though he knew that there was no possibility of his ever being able to endure Cistercian austerity for more than a few days, and though the memory of his meals at Igny and subsequent experience at Reims still made him wince, he none the less decided to make another retreat at La Trappe in the summer of 1893. 'I shall be leaving next week', he told Landry[2] in late July, 'to stay with my good washermen, who are going to scrub my soul clean again.' This operation cannot have lasted as long as it had the previous year, for Huysmans arrived at Igny on 5 August and was back in Paris by the 10th; but it was conducted in far more pleasant conditions. The novelist told Gustave Boucher on the 11th that he had been allowed to rise later and to talk to some of the monks, and he concluded that on his first visit he had been put through a rigorous test. Unfortunately he had suffered the same 'demoniacal attacks' as in August 1892, and these continued when he returned home.[3]

> Here in Paris [he wrote to Boucher], since I got back, it has been worse than ever, and all yesterday and last night I suffered martyrdom. I had to go to communion this morning at Saint-Sulpice to put an end to it, and now I can write to you in peace. But . . . but . . . I'm still terrified by these hard ways along which I'm being led. Religion is really no joke when so much is asked of you, and I'm devilishly envious of those simple, pious souls

who make their humdrum way through life without going through all these crises . . .

A few weeks later, unexpected honour was paid to Huysmans when, on 3 September, he was made a Chevalier de la Légion d'honneur. This mark of distinction took him by surprise, for some years earlier he had refused the offer of another official decoration, in a scene which Gustave Guiches described[4] in this passage from his memoirs:

One day the Minister of the Interior summoned Huysmans to his room and said to him: 'It is not the chief clerk whom I wished to see, but the writer . . . the great artist . . . the author of that magnificent book which has become deservedly famous . . . that . . . let me see . . . that . . . er . . . the title . . . that curious title . . . *A l'Envers!'*

'*A Rebours.*'

'*A Rebours!* That's it! What a wonderful book! Des Esseintes! The perfumes . . . a masterpiece! . . . Well now, since I have the honour to have a great writer on my staff, I haven't hesitated to indicate to my colleague, the Minister of Public Instruction, that it was his duty to award that writer a highly merited distinction. And I now have the pleasure of informing you that he has agreed to confer upon you – in the next Honours List – the Academic Palms!'

Huysmans had to invent a tall story of considerable proportions in order to avoid this humiliation, and in the end the Palms went to one of his cousins . . .

This time, however, it was not the writer the Government sought to honour, but the *fonctionnaire* with twenty-seven years of faithful service to his credit – or, as Huysmans himself put it, 'twenty-seven years as a bottle in the administrative cellar'.[5] He did not complain; indeed, he told the Minister, Charles Dupuy: 'The civil servant is delighted to see his services appreciated. The novelist would have been less pleased to appear in the same section of the Honours List as M. Georges Ohnet . . .'[6]

Though his friends were indignant that the Government should still refuse to recognize his literary achievements, we may be sure that Huysmans was not displeased by the tribute paid to his work for the Ministry. But after twenty-seven years he was naturally beginning to weary of bureaucratic life, and his dreams were all of some claustral retreat – preferably 'an easy-going monastery served by an indulgent order that loves liturgies and adores art'.[7] In 1894 these dreams seemed close to realization, for in the spring of that year Gustave Boucher introduced him to a Benedictine monk with similar tastes and, what was more, the power to satisfy them: Dom Jean-Martial Besse. Boucher and the Abbé Mugnier had met Dom Besse while in retreat at the Benedictine Abbey of Saint-Martin de Ligugé, near Poitiers, and they had spoken to him of Huysmans' conversion and his monastic leanings. Seeing that monk and novelist had much in common, Boucher decided to bring them together on Dom Besse's next visit to Paris, and he then arranged a rendezvous at the same Restaurant Lachenal where the ex-Abbé Boullan had been entertained little more than a year before.[8]

Dom Besse was a strapping, corpulent monk in his early thirties, endowed with a forceful personality which made a tremendous and immediate impact upon the retiring Huysmans. The novelist later described him in *L'Oblat*, under the name of Dom Felletin, as 'big and robust, with the blood under the surface of the skin dotting his cheeks with crimson pinpricks like the peel of an apricot, a protuberant nose which twitched whenever his face broke into a smile, light-blue eyes, and thick lips'. But Dom Besse, unlike his literary counterpart, did not yet exude 'an atmosphere of tranquil piety': his piety was eloquent and energetic, forever evolving grandiose schemes for the greater glory of God and the Order of St. Benedict. Shortly before he met Huysmans, he had been charged with the restoration of the ancient and ruined Abbey of Saint-Wandrille, and he saw in this task, not simply a problem of organization and administration, but an opportunity to erect a treasure-house of all the arts, a wondrous basilica whose fame, spreading to every part of the world, would outshine that of Vézelay and Cluny. He had no difficulty whatever in infecting Huysmans with his enthusiasm, and he left the novelist dreaming of escape to a Thebaid more religious, but not less refined, than that of des Esseintes, where he would be able to work among other writers, painters, sculptors, and musicians, in an atmosphere of plainchant and ecclesiastical art.

At the beginning of July Huysmans and Boucher arrived at Saint-Wandrille to see what progress had been made in realizing this ideal.[9] In truth, little had been done. The task of restoring an edifice ruined by successive generations of French and English vandals, and of making the few buildings that had been left standing safe and habitable, would have daunted the most experienced of monks: it was far beyond the capabilities of Dom Besse's band of untrained novices, many of them callow young men with romantic ideas of monastic life who had been drawn to Saint-Wandrille by the Superior's eloquent discourses. Yet Huysmans was as blind as Dom Besse himself to the difficulties and dangers inherent in this tremendous enterprise. Talking with Dom François Chamard, the irascible but kind-hearted old monk who until recently had been Prior of Saint-Maur de Glanfeuil, or with Brother Ernest Micheau, a tormented little exegetist who oscillated between presbytery and cloister for many years before pronouncing his final vows in 1900; listening to the choir, whose singing seemed to avoid both the extreme virility of the Cistercians and the extreme languor of convent choirs, and particularly to the 'lovely, pure, filiform voice' of the young Guestmaster, Dom Georges Guerry; or admiring the splendid setting provided for the abbey by the little River Fontenelle, the avenues of great ash-trees, and the woods stretching up to the crest of the hill – all this was happiness such as Huysmans had rarely tasted before, and he was in no mood to find fault with Dom Besse's extravagant plans for Saint-Wandrille.

He stayed at the abbey for a week. Much of his time he spent in his cell or on the banks of the Fontenelle, reading various mystical works he had borrowed from Dom Besse, including a treatise on prayer by Mme Cécile Bruyère, Abbess of Sainte-Cécile de Solesmes, which Huysmans was to mention in *En Route* as 'containing several bold propositions which Rome read with displeasure', and whose author was later to become one of his most devoted friends in the monastic world. After meals in the refectory, he and Boucher would walk up and down the cloisters with the Superior, discussing the past and prophesying the future of Saint-Wandrille, and followed by a little troop of novices – or Dom Besse's chicks, as Lucien Descaves called them[10] – who 'clucked liturgical chants behind him and pecked at old texts in the shelter of his black wings'. With several of these novices, who were for the most part artists with similar ideals to his own, Huysmans was soon on the friendliest terms, and the young men afterwards visited him in Paris whenever they were passing through the capital.

At last, on Sunday, 8 July, Huysmans left Saint-Wandrille for Paris, more than ever convinced, as he wrote in the abbey guest-book,[11] that 'happiness consists in being shut up in a closed place where a chapel is always open'. Indeed, for some days he could think and talk of nothing but Saint-Wandrille; the sound of plainchant sang in his ears wherever he went; and he walked the streets of Paris 'like a drunken man who is not quite sure where he is'.[12] His enthusiasm and gratitude even led him to be unjust to the Cistercians of Igny, for when he wrote to Dom Besse on the 11th, he thanked him 'for having helped me to understand the intimate affection and gentle indulgence of the Benedictine family – something of which La Trappe had given me no idea . . .'

As was always the way with Huysmans, this enthusiasm for Saint-Wandrille cooled somewhat after a little while, especially when one of the novices called on him in Paris to warn him that all was not well with the new community. La Trappe now regained first place in his affections, and he decided to make another retreat there in October, after a projected visit to Saint-Wandrille with the Abbé Ferret. Forgetting his ungracious remark to Dom Besse about the Cistercian way of life, he told Boucher[13] that his retreat at Igny would be made 'in a more serious frame of mind', and added maliciously that 'after being with those other monks the silence of La Trappe will doubtless be doubly welcome'. It even seems possible that he was considering becoming an oblate at Igny rather than at Saint-Wandrille, if we are to judge by a letter he sent Julie Thibault on 18 September.[14] After telling her that Dom Augustin Marre had promised to release his monks from their vow of silence the next time he visited Igny, he continued:

As you can see, all these saints are marvellously disposed towards me, and this naturally increases my longing to become an oblate. Anyway, I'm hoping that after my book has come out something will happen. I don't quite know what – an unexpected arrangement, help of some sort from God, something at least which would relieve me of the prospect of enduring this abominable lay-man's life for another four years, and enable me to settle at long last in a monastery.

I know perfectly well, both from earlier evidence and from what I'm told by the monks who come to see me here in Paris, that monastic life is not a bed of roses – but nothing could be worse than the nerve-racking, stupefy-ing life I've been leading these past six weeks. As long as I can remember that, I shall never regret leaving the world. Ah, no! Between laying telegrammatic eggs all day and singing the delicious melodies of plainchant from morning till night, my choice is soon made! Pray God to help me, my very dear friend, for the cloister is truly the only haven I desire.

There is no evidence that Huysmans went to Igny in the autumn of 1894,[15] and it is probable that after the three ecstatically happy days he spent at Saint-Wandrille he felt no inclination to enter La Trappe 'in a more serious frame of mind'. During their stay at Saint-Wandrille, which began in the evening of 29 September, Huysmans and the Abbé Ferret were taken on two excursions into the surrounding country-side, first to see the little medieval town of Caudebec and later to visit the ruins of Jumièges.[16] Here, walking in the great triple avenue of trees and looking at the branches meeting overhead, the novelist was struck by the resemblance to the nave and side-aisles of a cathedral, and concluded that Chateaubriand had been right to suppose that a similar natural formation had inspired man to invent the Gothic arch. Three years later he gave a detailed description of this scene in *La Cathédrale*, prompting Dom Besse to ask whether he had returned to Jumièges after his first visit in 1894. Huysmans' reply was significant, in that it helps us to appreciate the acuteness of his vision and the photographic quality of his memory.[17] 'No,' he answered. 'Once I've observed something, it stays in my mind for ten years or more. And whenever I need to do so, I can picture it as clearly as on the first day I saw it.'

After three short days, which he described to a correspondent as the happiest of his life,[18] Huysmans returned to Paris with the Abbé Ferret, hoping that he would soon be able to leave the capital for ever and make his home at Saint-Wandrille. But this hope was never to be fulfilled. The old Abbot of Ligugé, Dom Joseph Bourigaud, had for some months been watching with growing concern while Dom Besse squandered the Saint-Wandrille funds on foolish and extravagant projects. At last, losing patience with the improvident monk, he struck. Dom Chamard was appointed Superior in place of Dom Besse, but only to be succeeded by the illustrious Dom Pothier, while Dom Besse himself was ordered into exile to the Spanish monastery of Silos.[19]

News of this catastrophe was brought to Huysmans in mid-December by a young friend of Dom Besse, the Abbé Hirigoyen, who naturally said nothing of the true causes of the former Superior's disgrace. The novelist was left with the impression that a group of reactionary dullards in the mother-house of Ligugé, alarmed by Dom Besse's literary and artistic sympathies, had removed him from office from motives of spite. Such at least was the version of the affair which he gave his friends, as for example in this letter[20] to the painter Auguste Lauzet:

> While you've been swallowing bitter dittanies, I've been gently laid on my back by my good friend Robin, who found me ailing and left me positively ill. He decided I was suffering from a deficiency of gastric juice, due to rheumatism. This seems plausible enough – but the treatment he prescribed has given me such appalling headaches that I've consigned all his strychnines and banyans to the dustbin and gone on living . . . without gastric juice! . . . For the beginning of a new year this isn't very pleasant – but what has affected me most is the unhappy tale of my Abbey of Saint-Wandrille. I had dreamt such wonderful dreams with Father Besse, an extraordinary monk who is obviously intended by God to regenerate his order. Well, all the old fogies of the reactionary party, the whole Benedictine mediocracy in fact, conspired against us, and my poor monk has been exiled to a Spanish monastery. I saw him on to his train and I can assure you that if he suffered all this in the true monastic spirit of obedience, I couldn't disguise my indignation at this triumph of monastic imbecility. Isn't it dreadful to think that nothing can kill human stupidity and spite, not even the cloister! Meanwhile my refuge has disappeared and the sky grows darker . . .

All the letters Huysmans wrote at this time spoke of his despair at the news from Saint-Wandrille. 'I feel completely crushed', he told Gustave Boucher.[21] 'My dreams of a peaceful haven have gone up in smoke, and the future looks gloomier than ever.' And to Brother Micheau, who had recently left Saint-Wandrille to become parish priest of Mondion,[22] he wrote: 'Ah, Lord! What dreams I dreamt of taking refuge in a monastery when I retire in three years, and now everything is finished!' He never entirely recovered from this harsh blow Fate had dealt him, for although he eventually forgave the 'old fogies' of Ligugé and even made his home in the shadow of their monastery, he never mentioned Saint-Wandrille in any of his works, nor did he ever pay another visit to the valley of the Fontenelle.

A few weeks later, more sad tidings reached Huysmans: Anna Meunier had died in Sainte-Anne on Tuesday, 12 February 1895. In his memoirs[23] Lucien Descaves recalls meeting Huysmans one day in the Place du Théâtre-Français and being told that Anna had been buried the day before; when he reproached his friend for having withheld the news of Anna's funeral, Huysmans replied that 'only the family was represented'. By 'the family' he presumably meant Anna's two daughters and her sister Joséphine. The latter died a few years ago and was buried beside her sister in the Montparnasse Cemetery. Blanche-Antonine Meunier, Anna's elder daughter, was married on 26 November 1895 to a Dr. Gaston Comar,[24] with Huysmans attending the ceremony as her 'tutor *ad hoc*'. Her sister, Mlle Antonine Meunier, had a brilliant career in the *corps de ballet* at the Opéra, which Huysmans and Coppée helped her to enter; she lived in Paris and until her death cherished affectionate memories of the man whom she used to call 'Papa Georges'.[25]

Huysmans scarcely had time to recover from his grief at Anna's death before he found himself attacked from all sides for his novel *En Route*, which was brought out by Stock on 23 February. He himself was somewhat dissatisfied with the work, and before it was published he wrote[26] to Auguste Lauzet:

This book has nearly killed me and now it disgusts me, for I haven't been able to achieve the result I had hoped for. It's pale and flabby. But then, how can one render sensations which can't be unravelled, sensations which defy analysis and description? How terrible it is to feel inadequate to a task one has set oneself! I've experienced things vividly, but now – working like a madman on my proofs – I realize that I haven't expressed them well enough. But no language could possibly live up to a subject like this – least of all French . . .

As it happened, few criticisms were made of the style of *En Route*, except by prudish Catholic critics who objected to such expressions as 'delousing the soul'. There was also Léon Bloy, of course, who sneeringly dismissed the book[27] as 'a compilation identical to the earlier compilations of this author, but infinitely more boring'. But the eminent *jury* which recently named *En Route* one of the twelve major French novels of the nineteenth century evidently preferred the opinion of Paul Valéry,[28] who after reading the work wrote to Huysmans:

> You have hurled the contemporary novel where it belongs – into the cauldron of the lowest fairground hell – and you have created something which recalls the masterpieces cast in the great literary foundries of old; something rugged and primeval, with a mighty current running strongly through it; something which one would have thought could never be produced in this era of bits and pieces, of bubbles and pinpricks . . .

Contemporary critics who viewed the book from a moral standpoint were generally less perceptive and less complimentary in their comments. Thus the Jesuit Father Jean Noury declared[29] in *Études*: 'A book such as this cannot be put into the hands of girls or young men or decent women . . . Even if Durtal were converted in earnest and for good, it is not to him that I should entrust the moral and religious education of any neophyte.' There were many others who, though even less qualified to judge than Father Noury, also questioned the sincerity of Huysmans' conversion. Léon Bloy told a correspondent[30] that 'his conversion is founded on bric-à-brac and is the most suspect that I know', while René Doumic, in the March issue of *La Revue des Deux Mondes*, remarked of rumours that Huysmans intended to become a monk: 'Nothing of the kind! On the contrary, all his devotional practices have been turned to the greater glory of literature, for M. Huysmans has merely been collecting documents. Is there any need to point out that Christianity doesn't enter into it?' Worse still, some of the novelist's friends were among the doubters. Lucien Descaves wrote[31] that he saw in *En Route* 'less an act of faith than an explosion of art', and Henry Céard declared[32] that 'for Huysmans religion is a bizarre and beautiful flower which attracts him only because he has never seen its like in the hot-houses of the world'. Gustave Coquiot went even farther, and told Huysmans to his face that he did not believe him to be a true convert.[33] To which the novelist, marvelling inwardly that any friend of his could be so stupid, replied simply: 'Well, you're wrong, that's all.'

Those who were prepared to declare their belief in Huysmans' sincerity and orthodoxy were few indeed. Prominent among them were the Abbé Félix Klein, who assured readers of *Le Monde*[34] that Durtal's conversion was genuine, and Mgr d'Hulst, who, generously forgetting that Huysmans had called him a 'bellicose old duffer' in *En Route*, stated publicly[35] that 'there are spiritual experiences which it is impossible to invent'. Other members of the secular clergy, however, were less disposed to forgive an author who compared them unfavourably with their monastic brethren, and many would have been delighted to learn that *En Route* had been placed on the 'Index Prohibitorum'. Indeed, it soon became clear that if the book was to avoid this fate, some eloquent and authoritative defence of the author would have to be made by an ecclesiastical figure of distinction. Such a defence was made on 19 March, when the Abbé Mugnier gave a public lecture in the Salle Sainte-Geneviève on Huysmans' religious evolution. In this lecture, which was well attended and widely reported, he denied that he was the Abbé Gévresin but stated that he could vouch for the sincerity of Huysmans' conversion, which he classed with such famous conversions as those of St. Augustine, Chateaubriand, and Lacordaire. After hearing from the Abbé Ferret that the audience in the Salle Sainte-Geneviève had been completely won over by the speaker's eloquence, Huysmans wrote[36] to the Abbé Mugnier:

> I want to send you my thanks and my congratulations straight away. Thank you, then, for having defended me

against the accusation of pride which I see repeated *ad nauseam* in the Press. When I wrote the book I certainly had no intention of decking out my soul and singing its praises. Moreover, it seems to me that I rarely triumph except at La Trappe and that I don't confess very much. Still, it's like that fellow who imagines that I went to La Trappe to enjoy myself. He has only to do as I did and he'll see just how enjoyable it is to kneel at the feet of a silent monk, and how much one thinks about literature at that moment! Lord, how stupid all those people are!

However stupid or severe the criticisms which had been made of *En Route*, Huysmans hoped that at least the book would help to bring about a few conversions. 'In intellectual circles in Paris,' he told Brother Micheau,[37] 'there is a kind of mystical current which has gone astray and which *En Route* might be able to canalize.' But sometimes he doubted his ability to achieve this object, especially when he remembered that his last attempt to proselytize in print – in his preface to Remy de Gourmont's *Le Latin mystique*, published in 1892 – had resulted only in a broken friendship.[38] Since Gourmont's interests were strictly literary, he had failed to appreciate Huysmans' statement that any author wishing to write a mystical work would have to return to the Church and 'repudiate the vain existence which we all lead in the world of letters'. He had also complained to his friends that Huysmans was no latinist, causing Bloy to ask: 'Why then this preface which makes the beneficiary blush? They must have killed somebody together.'[39] However, the beneficiary did not blush for long, for when two new editions of *Le Latin mystique* were published in 1895, Huysmans' preface was omitted from both.

Fortunately, *En Route* met with a more widespread and encouraging response. The book rapidly went through edition after edition, while nearly every periodical in the country reviewed it, in some cases several times. 'One thing is clear,' Huysmans told Dom Besse,[40] 'and that is that the subjects of mysticism and monasticism don't leave people indifferent but make them howl.' And he added with amused satisfaction that 'when you come to think of it, it's funny to be able to make an unbelieving public swallow doses of mysticism and liturgy, and to shout at them that there's nothing enviable or decent in the filthy times we live in except the cloister'. The very violence of his attack started many readers on the road to conversion – as Huysmans pointed out to those who criticized the tone of certain passages in *En Route* and the crudity of his vocabulary. Thus to the parish priest of Mondion[41] he wrote:

I agree that some pages could have been suppressed – but if you consider the non-Catholic public at which I was aiming, I risked compromising everything by not being frank and outspoken. For after all, what is a Catholic? – a man who is either healthy or cured. The others, sick men. To cure them, would you give them all the same medicine? Surely not. You would admit, would you not, that the very ill, such as I was myself – and they are many – cannot be cured with soothing drugs: they have to be given an emetic and forced to bring up their past lives. Well, for them my book has been something of the kind – a spiritual vomitory! It is powerful medicine – and perhaps unpleasant to take – but if it cures only one sick man (*and this it has done*) what doctor of the soul could condemn it? The book *has* effected conversions of which I have certain knowledge, and others are ready. This phenomenon astonishes many of the priests who witness it, but they testify to its reality. As for the patients, they must have been seriously ill to have taken that horse-medicine! And isn't the knowledge that they are cured the finest reward God could give me for my efforts?

Soon, however, Huysmans discovered that the role of proselyte was no easy one, for every post brought letters from abroad and from all parts of France, asking for his advice on spiritual matters. Remembering his past misdemeanours, the novelist could not help smiling wryly at the trusting tone of these letters and the virtuous nature of his replies, as when he told[42] the Abbé Mugnier:

> There's a young woman of 23, living somewhere in the provinces, whom I don't know personally, and who wants me to give her a push to help her into the nearest convent. Shades of the Vatard sisters – and Marthe! You must admit, though, that life is full of surprises. In the old days, after a book of mine had appeared, I used to get letters from Chantelouve – and the effect on my poor soul was far from beneficial. At present, things happen on a mystical plane, and I find myself writing love-letters on behalf of God!

Of all the correspondents who treated him as their spiritual director, none aroused his interest more than a certain Dutch reader called Alberdingk Thijm. Telling Dom Besse[43] what he knew of this 'admirable soul', he described Thijm as a rich man who, after reading *En Route*, had given all he possessed to charity and settled in a slum district of Amsterdam, where he intended to devote his life to the service of the poor. 'The idea of giving advice to a man like that', wrote Huysmans, 'would be comical if it were not truly humiliating. God evidently shows such people a mirage, making them apply for help to good-for-nothing souls, under the impression that these are worthy of respect. Certainly this holy man's mistake has taught me a lesson that I shan't forget . . .'

It was only later in the year that Huysmans learned that this 'holy man' was, in fact, a woman.[44] The daughter of a famous Dutch author and scholar, Catharina Alberdingk Thijm was born in the same year as Huysmans and was to survive him by only a few months. She had established a considerable reputation in Holland as a writer of plays, short stories, and historical novels when, in 1895, she abandoned her literary career to found an institution for homeless women and children in Amsterdam. It was doubtless because of Huysmans' notorious antipathy to his fellow writers and to women in general that in her correspondence with the novelist she deliberately concealed her profession and her sex. As it happened, this was an unnecessary subterfuge, for when one of Huysmans' friends revealed to him the true identity of his Dutch correspondent, in October 1895, his only comment[45] was: 'Thank you for your information on Alberdingk Thijm. This Magdalen is truly admirable and I should be sorry not to be in correspondence with her. She writes very well, too, and in a singularly virile style, this good repentant.' Respecting her epistolary disguise, he continued to address her as *Cher Monsieur* or *Cher ami*, and their relationship pursued an uneventful course for several months. At the end of 1896, however, Huysmans wrote[46] to the friend who had uncovered Catharina's secret: 'I must tell you the story of a strange incident concerning that heroic soul Catharina Alberdingk Thijm, myself and . . . Our Lady, which has just occurred at Chartres . . .'

To understand why this story should have had Chartres as its setting, it is necessary to have some knowledge of Huysmans' literary plans on the completion of *En Route*. Just as in 1884, there were several critics in 1895 who declared their belief that his career as a novelist had come to an end, that he could not advance any farther and would not retrace his steps. Yet the very title of his latest work should have informed these critics that Huysmans' autobiography was not complete, and that he would probably continue the story of Durtal's spiritual and material existence in another novel. In 1896 he announced publicly that this was, in fact, his intention.[47] He explained that in *En Route* he had already revealed 'the influence of sacred music on a tormented, irresolute soul, on a soul which longs for calm and quiet, and which seeks to overcome a debilitated body, blood heated to fever-pitch, and nerves exasperated by sensual excess'. Now, showing the same unfailing interest in cause and effect, he intended in *La Cathédrale* to study Durtal's soul as it underwent the permeating influence of medieval architecture and art. He recognized that art had played an important part in his conversion and believed that it would now take him farther in his search for spiritual contentment. 'Be that as it may,' he said, 'the influence of my cathedral on Durtal will be such as to lead my hero into a Trappist monastery, which he will enter definitively, but without pronouncing definitive vows. That will be the subject of *L'Oblat*.' In mystical parlance, *En Route* had corresponded to the purgative life, *La Cathédrale* was to represent the contemplative life, and *L'Oblat* the unitive life.

Another reason why Huysmans chose to depict a cathedral in his next novel was that this afforded him an opportunity to play the pedagogue, to give his readers further instruction in the glories of medieval art. While writing *En Route*, he had told a reporter[48] that 'in his new book he would like to do for plainchant what he had done for campanology in *Là-Bas*'. And now he stated to another reporter[49] that 'what I have done for sacred music in *En Route*, I want to do for the religious architecture, painting, and sculpture of the Middle Ages, in *La Cathédrale*'. Nor was this all, as he explained in this letter[50] to Auguste Lauzet:

> I must also deal with all branches of medieval symbolism: the symbolism of ecclesiastical forms, of painters' colours, of stained glass, etc . . . There is work there for two or three years. But if I could succeed in doing all this, I should have expressed the very soul of the Church in its totality – mysticism, symbolism, liturgy, and literary, pictorial, sculptural, musical, and architectonic art. As you can imagine, it's a formidable task, but I'm patiently grinding away at it and amassing material from every quarter. As my main example I'm taking the Cathedral of Chartres, the most beautiful and the most easily decipherable of them all, and grouping the others around it – just as in my study of the symbolism of colours I'm gathering certain Primitives around the Fra Angelico, the most clearly readable of all such paintings . . .

It would, indeed, be a mistake to see in Huysmans' choice of setting simply a desire to instruct the public in aesthetics and an attempt to elucidate the development of Durtal's character. The pedagogue and the psychologist in Huysmans were inseparable from the proselyte, and the latter, having discovered in Notre-Dame de Chartres a symbolic and comprehensive commentary on religion and life, was resolved to communicate it to the unenlightened. Chartres appeared to Huysmans as Nature had appeared to Baudelaire – as 'a forest of symbols' – but the 'living pillars' of this petrified forest spoke to him in a language that admitted of little confusion. As he wrote in *La Cathédrale*, they revealed to him 'the Scriptures, the philosophy of religion, the history of the human race in its broad outlines; for, thanks to the science of symbology, a macrocosm has been created from a heap of stones, and everything is contained in this building, even our material and moral life, our virtues and our vices'. The commentaries of Hugues de Saint-Victor, Yves de Chartres, and Isidore de Séville gave him considerable pleasure, and though he was aware that their interpretation of certain symbols was somewhat fanciful, he hoped that his readers would come to share his enthusiasm for the 'analogical marvels and purely mystical concepts' of Christian symbology. He hoped, too, to convince them that God's teaching was everywhere manifest to those who had been schooled in the science of interpretation. 'Everything in this world is symbolic', he explained to a friend;[51] 'everything must serve in some way as a spiritual looking-glass; everything has its function and its meaning; and everything is a lesson or a warning for us all . . .'

Strangely enough, Huysmans never actually resided in Chartres, even though in his novel Durtal rents spacious rooms in a house facing the Cathedral. Indeed, he rarely stayed there more than a day, usually arriving early in the morning with the Abbé Mugnier or Georges Landry, taking communion in the crypt, and returning to Paris in the evening.[52] True to the technique of the Impressionist painters, he spent much of his time at Chartres studying the interior and exterior aspects of the Cathedral at all hours, in all seasons, and in all weathers: in dazzling sunshine and grey mist or drizzle; at dawn, as the basilica slowly took shape in the gathering light; at dusk, as it wrapped itself in the advancing shadows. Often, however, he went to Chartres with no thought but to pray – as at Christmas 1896, when the strange incident occurred of which mention has already been made.[53]

With Georges Landry, Huysmans heard Midnight Mass in the crypt, where it was so cold that after taking communion the two friends went up to the nave. They had scarcely arrived there before a priest left the choir and pushed his way through the crowd towards them. 'You are Monsieur Huysmans?' he asked the novelist, and on receiving an affirmative reply said: 'I have a letter here for you.' The missive which he handed to Huysmans had been posted in Amsterdam the day before and bore the following address:

> *Monsieur J.-K. Huysmans, littérateur, Cathédrale,*
> *Crypte de la Vierge, à Chartres, France.*

Huysmans gave some indication of the contents of this letter when he wrote[54] to the Abbé Ferret the next day:

> I must tell you about a kindness done by the Blessed Virgin, who this Christmas turned postwoman – and a very skilled postwoman, I can assure you – to give an answer to a soul in torment. It was terribly cold at Chartres, with snow falling and coffee-coloured sherbets to paddle through in the streets – but I didn't care. As always, I was perfectly happy there, enjoying happiness such as I can find nowhere else. I prayed hard and hope that I didn't annoy Her with too many requests. But there is so much to ask for, both for oneself and for others. What I've discovered is that She loves Alberdingk Thijm, who has been going through a testing period with doubts about the Faith. I think she has had a reply to her questions . . .

It appears that in her letter Catharina announced that she had lost the Faith, but said that if a certain condition were fulfilled she would believe again. The condition was that the letter with its curious address should reach Huysmans in the Cathedral of Chartres on Christmas morning. Fortunately, it had been shown to several curates, one of whom remembered a certain Abbé de Sainte-Beuve pointing Huysmans out to him, and searched the Cathedral for the novelist. After reading Catharina's letter, Huysmans waited until the post office opened its doors and then dispatched a telegram to Amsterdam. It consisted of two comforting words:

LETTER RECEIVED.

3. THE RETREATANT

WITHIN a few months of the publication of *En Route*, another work bearing Huysmans' name made its appearance on the bookstalls – or rather in the shop-windows of the Rue Saint-Sulpice. This work was entitled *Petit Catéchisme liturgique;* it was written by an Abbé Henri Dutilliet who had died in 1891; it had been revised by the Abbé Vigourel, choirmaster and master of ceremonies at the Saint-Sulpice seminary; and it was adorned with a preface by J.-K. Huysmans. The explanation of this surprising state of affairs which the novelist turned liturgist had given in advance to Dom Besse[1] was that he had found the catechism on the quays a few years before and had recently shown it to some of the clergy at Saint-Sulpice, suggesting that the book could render immense service by explaining to the public, at little cost, everything it heard and saw in church. The publisher had been approached and had agreed to bring out a new edition of the work if Saint-Sulpice would revise the text and Huysmans would write a preface. 'Strange though it may seem', the latter remarked, 'for me to preface a liturgical catechism, I feel that it's my duty, for I believe that it's worth doing and that everyone should do what he can to make known the liturgical splendours of the Church.'

This early enthusiasm for the project gradually cooled. Writing to Dom Besse in June,[2] Huysmans admitted that he was beginning to find the role of expert liturgist somewhat embarrassing, and added: 'It's all rather ridiculous, because I'm really incompetent to deal with such matters.' And his final comment on the catechism, contained in yet another letter to Dom Besse,[3] was that of a man who has performed a disagreeable duty in difficult circumstances. 'With Saint-Sulpice putting its name to the book,' he wrote, 'I couldn't ride my hobby-horse where and how I liked – for I shan't be telling you anything new when I say that the Sulpician mind is appallingly timorous. But in any case, it really doesn't matter, because when I feel like talking liturgy again I can do it in my own books, where I'm completely free and not imprisoned in an ecclesiastical strait-jacket . . .'

Huysmans' work on this preface and *La Cathédrale* was frequently interrupted in the spring and summer of 1895 by unexpected visitors, some of whom were sufficiently remarkable to merit a mention in his letters to various correspondents. The most striking of them all was undoubtedly Édouard Dubus,[4] then in the grip of diabolical obsessions and the final stages of morphia poisoning, who on taking leave of Huysmans for the last time, whispered pathetically: '*They* have forbidden me to come and see you, and now I shall have to pay for this visit with dreadful tribulations . . .' Then there was a naval officer just arrived from India, who called on Huysmans to discuss his own experience of diabolical possession, pausing every few minutes to utter some frightful blasphemy.[5] And lastly, as a refreshingly calm contrast to these tormented visitors, there came to the Rue de Sèvres a young English artist who wished to add a portrait of Huysmans to his studies of eminent French personalities. The late Sir William Rothenstein has left us two records of this visit: one, an admirable drawing of the novelist, now in the possession of the Société J.-K. Huysmans, and the other this brief but vivid pen-portrait[6] in his memoirs:

During this visit in 1895 I made a drawing of Huysmans, whom I had met before, at one of Edmond de Goncourt's parties at the Grenier. Huysmans, a small, shrunken, nervous man, with a parchment skin – looking rather like a *fonctionnaire*, I thought, with his bourgeois collar and tie, and provincial clothes – was then at work on *La Cathédrale*. He had become absorbed by Catholicism – so absorbed, indeed, that he was soon to retire from the world. He smoked cigarettes one after the other, rolling them incessantly between his quick, slender fingers, yellow with nicotine. He asked about George Moore, who was writing about nuns, he had heard, but wondered – for he said that when he last met Moore, Moore didn't know a Poor Clare from a Sister of Charity . . .

The mention of nuns was significant, for Huysmans was still obsessed by the idea of monastic life. 'Paris is terrible', he told Catharina A. Thijm.[7] 'To have a little peace here, you have to shut yourself up, apart from other people, and even then you are distracted and enervated by your environment. So I want to get away from it all.' And to the Abbé Henry Moeller, a Belgian magazine editor with whom Charles Buet had put him in touch, he wrote[8] that 'in the three years since my first visit to La Trappe, not a day has passed without my dreaming of the cloister'. Now, once again, it seemed possible that his dreams were about to be fulfilled, thanks to a certain Antoinette Donavie, a seventy-year-old nun whose name in religion was Mother Célestine de la Croix, and who thirty years before had founded a convent at Fiancey, near Valence. Her first letters to Huysmans, written in May 1895, had convinced him that she was 'a modern St. Teresa',[9] and he described her to Dom Besse[10] as a 'brilliant organizer' who, besides her own convent, had founded a home for old men and, more recently, a Kneipp hydrotherapeutic institution.

What an astonishing woman she is! [he wrote] After reading my book she wrote me an enthusiastic letter about it, saying the most amazing things. For example: 'You see, my child, like all intellectuals you have been living on your mind, on your brain, on your pride, and your heart is dried up. It's truly pitiful. Why, you have never even loved women!' Incidentally, the good Mother knows the Abbé Ferret. At the moment she is thinking of founding an order for artists, to help restore and revive ecclesiastical art; and she is urging me to go and see her about this! I shall probably go next month with Ferret and Boucher . . .

He made no mention in this letter of the disquiet which Mother Célestine's hydrotherapeutic venture was causing him. Towards the end of May she had sent him a photograph of herself taken with a group of doctors and a German masseuse. This glimpse of 'Kneipp Abbey', as Huysmans called it in one of his letters to Boucher,[11] bore no relation to the novelist's dreams of a semi-monastic, semi-artistic foundation; yet he refused to be disheartened. Ignoring Boucher's warnings, and forgetting the lessons learnt in the Saint-Wandrille fiasco, he persuaded himself that Mother Célestine would be willing to abandon her interest in hydrotherapy in favour of art and literature. 'How wonderful it would be', he wrote hopefully to the Abbé Moeller,[12] 'to live in an abbey where, as you can imagine, there would be only plainchant and things of beauty, and where I could work in peace on a Life of the good Lydwine! And how splendid to attempt this revival of religious art in a really propitious environment . . .'

In less exalted moments Huysmans admitted to his friends that the Fiancey project presented many problems. 'What appals me', he told Catharina A. Thijm,[13] 'is the prospect of our dealings with the Bishop, the difficulty of obtaining the sanction of the Holy See, and the suspicion which we are certain to arouse among the clergy.' Nor did he relish the idea of settling in the torrid south; and after spending a stifling June day in bed with neuralgia, he wrote feelingly[14] to the Abbé Mugnier:

The ideal would be a melancholy clime from which the sun had been banished – or where it had become a mere trickle of gold-dust as in Rembrandt's pictures. And in that clime, a very old monastery where one would be able to write the lives of saints with no distractions save the perfume of incense and age-old psalms. Unfortunately, if this dream is realized, it will be in a region where the sky is of a blatant blue and entirely lacking in distinction . . . Oh, those blue skies! How crudely coloured the heavens seem in the south, and how adorable by contrast is the northern firmament!

Another problem was that of peopling the 'refined Thebaid' of Fiancey with artist-monks. Apart from Huysmans himself, who was clearly destined to be Superior of the new foundation, there were so far only four candidates: Gustave Boucher, the Abbé Ferret, and two former novices from Saint-Wandrille, Gonzalez and Schilling, who had left the Benedictine Order in disgust when Dom Besse was exiled to Spain. Both Boucher and the Abbé Ferret had family ties which made it difficult for them to enter a monastery, and even Huysmans had recently taken on a new personal responsibility. 'I have had to give a home', he told his Dutch correspondent,[15] 'to an old woman, a strange visionary who has lost all her friends at Lyons; and I can't abandon the poor creature just now.' This 'strange visionary' was, of course, Julie Thibault, whom Huysmans had with some reluctance invited to share his home after Pascal Misme's death in March. Towards the end of April she had taken possession of a small spare room in Huysmans' flat, where she had installed on a chest of drawers a little altar in white marble, adorned with a pattern of intertwining hearts.[16] Standing before this altar every morning and evening, dressed in green-and-white vestments and with her cat as congregation, she celebrated the Provictimal Sacrifice of Mary instituted by Eugène Vintras, and took communion in red wine – the species of white wine being reserved for priests.[17] Friends who called on Huysmans while she was in the novelist's service retained affectionate memories of Maman Thibault, who while performing her household duties would recite prayers from a black missal stuffed with devotional images.[18] Had they looked more closely at this missal, however, they would have seen that it was also stuffed with consecrated hosts, which Huysmans was in the habit of removing surreptitiously, one by one, and taking to a priest to be consumed. For the time was past when the novelist would tell Jules Bois[19] that his surest protection against occult attacks was 'the unassailable sanctity of Mme Thibault'; that illusion had been destroyed in the summer of 1894, when he had taken the opportunity afforded by a brief visit to Lyons to read Boullan's private papers and the infamous *cahier rose*. Yet he patiently put up with his housekeeper's eccentric and even sacrilegious practices – partly because he considered that he owed her and Boullan a debt of gratitude; partly because she worked devotedly for him and refused to accept any wages; and partly, no doubt, because he found it convenient to live at close quarters with the model for Mme Bavoil, that endearingly comic character of *La Cathédrale* and *L'Oblat*. He knew, however, that the Abbé Ferret would never tolerate the presence of 'the old sorceress', as he called her,[20] within a hundred miles of Fiancey; and he could only hope that she would soon find a post as housekeeper to someone as indulgent as himself.

On Monday, 1 July, Huysmans left Paris with Boucher and the Abbé Ferret,[21] hoping for the best but half afraid that the Fiancey project would prove to be just 'a mirage of the Midi'. On the way south, they visited Paray-le-Monial, a town in the Abbé Ferret's native district, where they lodged with a friendly bookseller called Diard. During their stay here, the priest introduced his friends to an orphan protégé of his, Arnaud by name, an irresponsible but likeable young man in whose career, as we shall see, Huysmans was to take considerable interest. They also talked with Arnaud's sister, a nun in one of the Paray convents, and later visited a convent of Poor Clares where another of the Abbé Ferret's protégés, thinking that he was alone, launched out into a flood of complaints about the austerity and misery of monastic life.[22] But if this incident dampened their ardour, their next stopping-place, Cluny, provided the three friends with a happier augury – the sight of 'three Benedictines installed in a minute monastery which they were building with debris from the old abbey'.[23]

After a brief visit to the church at Brou, which Huysmans was to describe in *La Cathédrale* as 'a masterpiece of architectural coquetry', they came at last to Fiancey. Describing their reception at the abbey in a letter to Dom Besse,[24] Huysmans wrote:

Imagine the most delightful of monasteries, with spring water, avenues of poplars, and a splendid view over the

Alpine chain. And in it a sprightly little old lady of the eighteenth century, very indulgent and very broad-minded. We were received with open arms and treated like kings. There's a little saint there, too, who might almost be a daughter of Brother Siméon – a cowherd of extraordinary simplicity and uncommon power in prayer. In short, we spent some deliciously pious hours in the abbey. But I didn't settle anything with the good Mother, who, unlike the mystics, seems to me to have no practical common sense whatever.

Arriving hot and weary at Fiancey, Huysmans had apparently been shown to a cool cell by Mother Célestine, who made him lie on the bed while she sat beside him, holding his hands and talking in the darkness of her plans for the abbey.[25] The horrified novelist learnt that she intended his friends to train under Kneipp as masseurs, while he was to extol the virtues of hydrotherapy in pamphlets and prospectuses. 'I felt something crumbling away in my heart', he told the Abbé Moeller;[26] and in a letter to Catharina A. Thijm[27] he pronounced the Abbess of Fiancey to be 'an excellent woman, but slightly cracked and suffering from delusions of grandeur; quite sensible, in fact, in her mystical ideas, but not at all reasonable with regard to practical matters'. Subsequent events confirmed this verdict, for the Kneipp Institution soon foundered for lack of funds, and when Mother Célestine died, in January 1907, she was the sole occupant of her abbey.

In spite of his disappointment at the abortion of this second monastic venture, Huysmans' stay at Fiancey was extremely happy. He took communion every morning with Boucher and the Abbé Ferret; he kept all the canonical hours in the little chapel; and he met an old friend, Louis Le Cardonnel, whom he had not seen since the poet had left the world of letters to train for the priesthood in Rome. On Sunday the 7th Le Cardonnel came over from Valence, where he was spending his summer holidays at his parents' home, to lunch with Huysmans and his friends. He brought with him his younger brother Georges, who over thirty years later[28] remembered the novelist as 'still young-looking, dressed entirely in grey, with a lithe figure that was somewhat feline in appearance. His close-cropped hair and his beard were already going grey. Sometimes he would poke his head forward or cock it a little to the left; and when he looked up out of his grey-green eyes, he wrinkled his brow and smiled gently at people and things with a curious mixture of kindness and irony.' At one point in the conversation over lunch, Mother Célestine put into words what Le Cardonnel had been thinking, observing that to her Huysmans looked like a big grey cat. And when he smilingly admitted to being 'an old rooftop prowler', she exclaimed in delight: 'That's it! Monsieur Huysmans, you got into the Church by way of the roof! I must say I rather approve of that method of approach . . .'

Huysmans and Boucher returned to Paris without the Abbé Ferret, stopping on the way north to spend two days at Dijon. There they received communion at Notre-Dame, in the chapel of the Black Virgin, before inspecting the treasures of Dijon's museum and churches which Huysmans was later to describe in detail in *L'Oblat*. The farther the novelist travelled from Fiancey, the more keenly did he regret the impossibility of ever settling there; and on the 13th he wrote[29] to the Abbé Ferret:

What a shame not to be able to occupy a monastery like that! It seems to me that it wouldn't have spoilt us too much – but alas, that's only a dream! The truth is that the monasteries are very sick in spirit. When I got back I found a letter waiting for me from Father Parisot, which his Abbot had clearly not read: a sorrowful and rather bitter letter about his order, which he says keeps none of the promises it makes to postulants. I don't know what to say in my reply. In any case, it seems that there is absolute chaos at Ligugé. We obviously can't allow little Arnaud to go there, for I'm convinced that even a retreat in that place would be bad for him. How can God be expected to protect an order like that? One thing is certain, and that is that it isn't meant for us. Ligugé and

Fiancey, what a sorry pair! – But what I want to say to you now, my dear friend, is how attached I am to you and how grateful I feel to the Blessed Virgin for having brought us together. In what a princely fashion She arranges matters! Ah, if only She would consummate her kindness by giving us a little monastery . . .

Two months later, Huysmans' hopes of finding 'a little monastery' were raised again when the Abbé Mugnier proposed a retreat at the Abbey of Saint-Maur de Glanfeuil, in Anjou. 'I'm dreaming of your Glanfeuil,' Huysmans told him,[30] 'and I think that at the beginning of October I shall probably make up my mind to go there . . .' But in October a severe attack of influenza prevented him from visiting either Glanfeuil or Saint-Pierre de Solesmes, whose Abbot, Dom Delatte, had sent a pressing invitation to the author of *En Route*.[31] All that he could manage – for he was still very weak – was a rapid tour, later in the month, of the cathedrals of Tours, Bourges, and Amiens.[32] This tour convinced him that Chartres was superior to all other French cathedrals, spiritually as well as architecturally, having retained an atmosphere of sanctity which the others had wholly or partly lost. 'It is quite certain', he told Dom Besse,[33] 'that Chartres is full of mystery and piety, while the same can no longer be said of Amiens. But to put this into words will be like doing a difficult balancing feat. Still, with much prayer I think it can be done . . .'

During the winter Huysmans travelled frequently to Chartres, and at Christmas, as was his custom, he attended Midnight Mass in the crypt. It is small wonder that he often sought refuge in this peaceful sanctuary, for in Paris he had recently been brought in contact with another distressing case of insanity. His old friend Francis Poictevin had lost his reason early in November, and Huysmans and Georges Rodenbach had made themselves responsible for his care and supervision.[34] Poictevin's mistress, Alice Devaux, was in scarcely better case, and towards the end of December expressed a wish to be confessed before she, too, went mad or died. In a letter asking the Abbé Ferret to come and hear her confession,[35] Huysmans gave the impression that he was living in a world peopled with mad friends, mad visitors, and even madder correspondents.

> Yesterday [he wrote], she made me go through a bad day, because listening to her ravings evoked far from pleasant memories of Igny. This morning, I saw Father Parisot, who is an odd person and difficult to assess, and received an absolutely crazy letter from the Abbess of Fiancey, in which she asks me to perform the most compromising and ridiculous services for her. This time I'm going to break completely with her and not reply at all. She it is who ought to be living with Poictevin, for the one is just as insane as the other. Mother Célestine is, in fact, most decidedly a monomaniac . . .

The New Year was to bring some measure of peace and a large measure of respectability to the Poictevin household, for on 25 March, having temporarily recovered his wits, 'Coco' married Alice Devaux in his Champs-Élysées home, with Huysmans and Landry acting as witnesses.[36] But if Poictevin was now apparently out of danger, Huysmans lost two other friends in 1896: Paul Verlaine and Edmond de Goncourt. As was to be expected, he paid loyal tribute, in word and deed, to the memory of both these writers. He wrote eloquent prefaces to Cazals' book *Paul Verlaine, ses portraits*, published in 1896, and to an edition of Verlaine's religious poetry, published in 1904; he was a moving spirit in the campaign to erect a monument to the poet in the Luxembourg Gardens; and he quietly persuaded Father Pacheu of the Society of Jesus to change the title of his book *De Dante à Huysmans* to *De Dante à Verlaine*.[37] Unlike Verlaine, Edmond de Goncourt left explicit instructions as to what measures should be taken to maintain his posthumous reputation; and Huysmans loyally carried out these instructions, even though he detested the publicity which was thrust upon him as a member, and later as the first President, of the Académie Goncourt.

In April 1896 two important friendships were formed in Huysmans' circle. The first was between Lucien Descaves, the rough, outspoken ex-sergeant with no affection for the Church, and the Abbé Mugnier, the courtly curate of Sainte-Clotilde and the darling of the Faubourg Saint-Germain, whom Huysmans brought together in his flat on Low Sunday.[38] Contrary to all expectations, the writer and the priest conceived a great liking and respect for each other, and their friendship lasted until March 1944, when the 'apostle of pardon and of letters' died, in his ninetieth year. The second friendship, just as unexpected in its way, was between Huysmans and a nondescript married couple, Léon and Marguerite Leclaire by name, who like the novelist were spiritual charges of the Abbé Ferret. Leclaire was born in 1862, and at the age of twenty became joint-manager with his brother Henri of the Leclaire quarries at Montmartre. A little later, however, he married, retired from the family business, and took charge of his bride's embroidery shop in the Rue Villedo. Dr. Michel de Lézinier, a great traveller, has left us a description of the Leclaires[39] which reads rather like a whimsical passport entry: 'The husband was of medium height, with a military bearing and an officer-type moustache; the wife was tall and slim, with the most beautiful teeth I have ever seen.' Others who met them were more impressed by their moral and intellectual qualities – or deficiencies. Gustave Boucher considered Mme Leclaire to be an inveterate trouble-maker,[40] while Descaves wrote[41] that 'their company lacked charm, the woman being invariably ill, and the man devoting himself to photography in an attempt to cast off old industrial ties'. Yet the fact remains that this was the couple in whose company Huysmans later resolved to spend the rest of his life, and with whom he conducted what is perhaps his largest extant correspondence.[42] In this connexion it is interesting to note that Huysmans and Léon Bloy, both exceptional personalities, both chose an obscure middleclass couple to be their confidants – for the Leclaires were to Huysmans what the Montchals were to Bloy. And it was to Léon Leclaire that Huysmans entrusted his most intimate secrets, remarking[43] on one occasion: 'To whom should I tell all this, if not to you? For everyone else I must keep my lips sealed . . .'

Huysmans' first letter to the Leclaires was in response to a gift of flowers, and it consisted largely of a fanciful essay on floral symbology which he later developed in *La Cathédrale*.[44] Other motifs of that novel were mentioned in an interesting letter which Huysmans addressed to Dom Besse at about the same time.[45]

I'm still immersed [he wrote] in that enormous book of mine. It's wearing me out, but it seems to me there is so much to say about those two spiritual conditions called the Romanesque and the Gothic that I somehow keep going. Towards the end of last year I visited several Romanesque churches, and these sombre, penitent buildings appear to me to allegorize the reign of pious fear, the Old Testament, just as Gothic architecture, so bright and gracile, seems to symbolize the Gospels. The ideal would therefore be to unite the two books, binding them together in a single volume – the transitional style – or better still, Chartres, with its Romanesque crypt and its Gothic nave – the Old Testament supporting the New, as depicted in one of the stained-glass windows. And then I keep thinking of planning a little garden of symbolical flowers, of virginal and floral litanies. A garden liturgy! It would be something interesting to attempt – with especial reference to the flowers carved on capitals, the sacred botany of Reims, for instance, where the various species have all been catalogued. And lastly, I think that in Fra Angelico's masterpiece in the Louvre I've discovered the key to the symbolism of colours – the range of pious hues, with diabolical or merely profane hues excluded – which would explain why that monk used so few colours in his paintings. I've already written a long essay on this subject, and on the symbology of Sister Mechtilde and Catherine Emmerich, as well as that of the old medieval symbolists . . .

Still chafing at the bureaucratic bit, Huysmans half thought of accepting an invitation from Dom Georges Guerry to visit Saint-Wandrille in June, when two novices whom he had befriended were making their profession; but he was unable to obtain leave from the Ministry.[46] At the same time Dom Delatte, who on Huysmans' and the Abbé Ferret's recommendation had recently accepted young Arnaud as a novice at Solesmes, was pressing the novelist to make a retreat at the great Abbey of Saint-Pierre; while Dom Romain Banquet, Abbot of En-Calcat, the Benedictine monastery at Dourgne, called on Huysmans in Paris and tried to 'carry him off' to the south.[47] However, when the Ministry granted his application for leave, in July, it was to Notre-Dame d'Igny that he went – for the last time.

Writing to the Abbé Mugnier about the middle of the month,[48] he described the abbey as 'a changed monastery, a place of luxury and comfort', for he was now allowed meat, coffee, and an extra egg for each meal, and in the mornings he could rise at the 'sybaritic' hour of 4.30. He told his friend that he was spending the time between offices lazily smoking on the banks of the great pond, admiring the turquoise dragon-flies streaking the surface of the water, and watching for the elusive otter – which he claimed to have seen again.

So you see [he wrote] that you have reason to rejoice, my dear country-lover, for I've been captivated by Nature, enraptured by the water. And then the pleasure of having my good friend Rivière as Guestmaster may have something to do with it, for he's a real saint, and not at all Cistercian – at least in his attitude to other people. My Brother Siméon is still alive, but so old . . . so old that he can no longer take care of his children. He's allowed to go and see them, though, and it's infinitely moving to see the good Brother visiting his little flock. As for myself, physically I'm keeping moderately well, and spiritually I'm enjoying almost idyllic happiness in this sweet domain of the Virgin . . . The cloister! The cloister!

On his return to Paris, Huysmans wrote[49] to the Abbé
Ferret that 'this retreat at La Trappe has wound up the clockwork of my soul again and reawakened all my unsatisfied
longings for monastic life'. And in another letter[50] the Abbé
Mugnier was told:

The fact is that there are people who need to go hunting
every year, and who are thrilled by the smell of game.
For my part, I need to live among monks, where I can
smell the smell of old cloister walls. After the first five
minutes, I feel so much at home in that atmosphere! I
was born to be a cloister cat and not to remain forever
prowling the rooftops of a city, eating my spiritual fleas.
But then, life is so stupidly organized . . .

Inspired though he was by his retreat at La Trappe, it was
not at Igny that Huysmans now thought of ending his days,
nor at Saint-Wandrille, nor at En-Calcat, nor yet at Ligugé: it
was at Saint-Pierre de Solesmes. Little Arnaud, full of ingenuous pride at being a member of the great Benedictine community, wrote urging Huysmans to come and see him, and
ended his letter with a boyish quip which the novelist could
not resist quoting in *La Cathédrale:* 'If only you knew how
provincial the Benedictines of Paris seem, once you've heard
the nuns at Solesmes!'[51] As it happened, Huysmans had
already resolved to visit Solesmes, if only 'to finish with my
obsession with the place';[52] and at the end of September he set
off for the Abbey of Saint-Pierre, full of hope.

He stayed at the abbey until 13 October, and was considerably impressed by all that he saw there and at the Abbey
of Sainte-Cécile de Solesmes. In letters to his friends[53]
Huysmans described Dom Delatte as 'a very simple and very
good man', and the Abbess of Sainte-Cécile as 'a person of
almost superhuman intelligence and, what is more, a saint'.
Mme Bruyère's treatise *De l'Oraison*, which in *En Route* he
had condemned on Dom Besse's authority, was now read
again and approved; and he promised the Abbess to make
amende honorable in his next novel.[54] As for her nuns, whose

singing Brother Arnaud had vaunted to him, he was lost in admiration for them. 'They spend ten years', he told the Abbé Moeller,[55] 'in continuous study of Latin and exegesis, and they paint miniatures and do embroidery like the artists of old.' Of their singing he wrote[56] some years later:

> To know the art of plainchant, it's there one must go. I remember one night in particular, which stands out among a lifetime's memories as sublime. It was the eve of the Feast of the Dedication. I was at Solesmes. The good Mother said to me: 'Come to Matins tonight; the serving-nun will be warned to expect you.' I went, and in the darkened church I found beside the altar a little table, with a lamp lit and the offices all ready. The enclosure screen lifted, and there appeared before me the whole choir, with the Abbess at the back. I listened then to the most wonderful singing from voices such as one can rarely hear today, and the beauty of the Liturgy struck me so forcibly that, kneeling in my little corner, I wept . . .

Similarly, writing to the Abbé Ferret on 10 October,[57] Huysmans told his confessor that at Mass in Sainte-Cécile that morning the *Kyrie* had moved him to tears, and that the choirmaster, Dom Mocquereau, had sung the Preface as he had never heard it sung before. But knowing that the priest was eager for news of the Abbot and Brother Arnaud, he went on:

> The Abbot, with whom I've spent several hours, is a very simple and very good man – which doesn't preclude him from being also a skilled manipulator of souls, like the Abbess. He has said some truly beautiful and profound things to me, and unwound my soul like a cocoon after hearing me in confession. He's certainly a remarkable man.
> The day before yesterday there was a great gathering here for the pilgrimage to Notre-Dame-du-Chêne,

including the Bishop of Angers and the Abbot of Saint-
Maur . . . I need scarcely say that I didn't join the crowd.
They let me have the little one, and the two of us went
for a walk on the hills. He seems happier than ever and
preaches the Benedictine life to me with real fervour,
saying that he can't understand my hesitation. How
fortunate he is to be so young and so adaptable! . . .

The novelist found it more difficult to come to a decision.
Brother Arnaud might be happy at Solesmes, but the Abbey
of Saint-Pierre was far bigger than the modest cloister of
Huysmans' dreams, and he found Dom Delatte − nicknamed
'Colonel' Delatte by his monks − a shade too authoritarian for
his liking. 'I really don't know where I stand,' he wrote to the
Abbé Ferret, 'and that's why I mean to visit Chartres on my
way home. There's less and less light in the crypts of my soul,
and when I peer into them I see only a dark void. Let's hope
that Our Lady will shed a little light on all this . . .'

As always, Chartres delighted him and eased his anxiety. He
spent some hours praying in Notre-Dame, and he probably
revisited two peaceful spots he had recently discovered in the
city:[58] 'a delicious convent of Carmelites' and 'a dream of a
pious shanty, standing in a bleak garden from which the
Cathedral appears to have only one spire'. We cannot tell
whether any light penetrated the dark crypts of his soul during this visit, but a letter he wrote to the Abbé Moeller on his
return to Paris suggests that he had become reconciled to a
major decision which had been somewhat brutally forced
upon him at Solesmes.[59]

It appears that after several long conversations with the
novelist, Dom Delatte had taken him into his cell, fixed his
eyes upon him, and asked: 'When are you coming to us?' 'I
was rather shaken,' Huysmans told the Abbé Moeller, 'for I'm
not a very brave soul. Finally, not knowing what to say in
reply, I simply took his hand and kissed his ring as a mark
of submission. He embraced me, and it was settled.' And
Huysmans concluded: 'It is therefore probable that towards
the end of next year, I shall enter the cloister − for good . . .'

4. THE SYMBOLOGIST

THE year 1897, which seemed to hold such promise for Huysmans, was in fact overshadowed by disappointment and death: the disappointment of his dreams of monastic life, and the death of his friend and confessor, the Abbé Ferret.

The first signs of the cancer from which the priest was to die appeared during the winter, and in February he left Paris to take what he intended to be a short holiday at Hyères, the Mediterranean resort. For some time Huysmans believed that the Abbé Ferret was suffering from nothing more serious than overwork, and the letters he wrote his friend were concerned more with monastic affairs than with questions of health. The Abbé had sent him details of another of his innumerable protegées, a Mlle Mathilde Prache who wished to enter a Benedictine convent; and the novelist, discovering that the would-be novice was extremely poor, offered to send her what money she might need in order to take this step, on condition that his name was not mentioned.[1] At the same time he gave his confessor news of two Benedictine monks who in recent years had been creating scandal and schism in every monastery they inhabited: Dom Martin Coutel de La Tremblaye and Dom Joseph Sauton. In April 1892 they had addressed a *Mémoire sur Solesmes* to the Holy Office, accusing Dom Delatte of heresy and immoral conduct with Mme Cécile Bruyère. After careful investigation the Holy Office refuted these accusations, and the two monks were sent in disgrace to Ligugé.[2] When that monastery established a *pied-à-terre* in the Rue Vaneau in Paris, for monks passing through the capital, it was entrusted for some reason to Dom de La Tremblaye; he abandoned his charge in January 1897, taking with him, according to some reports, the entire priory library, and seeking romance in the arms of an attractive widow.[3] As for Dom Sauton, he was appointed Prior of Ligugé by Dom Bourigaud, whom he then denounced to the Holy Office as senile and incompetent. This time Rome simply forwarded the accusing letter to Dom Bourigaud, and after biding his time for six months the Abbot deposed his incorrigible Prior, appointing Dom Chamard in his place. News of these intrigues naturally did nothing to improve Huysmans' already unfavourable opinion of Ligugé, and as the spell of Solesmes wore off he also began to wonder whether he was really destined to enter the strictly regimented community of 'Colonel' Delatte. 'The Benedictine Congregation', he told the Abbé Ferret,[4] 'seems anything but ideal at the moment. On the one hand there's a general hurly-burly, and on the other a barracks . . .'

La Cathédrale was still monopolizing Huysmans' leisure hours, for the novelist was obsessed by the fear that 'unless I go thoroughly into every branch of symbology, people will say that it isn't a serious, scholarly work'.[5] He was fortunate to be helped in his researches by two monks at Solesmes, Dom Bouré and Dom Thomasson de Gournay, who collected data for the book from the abbey library; and also by a young friend called Austin de Croze, who made notes for him on the medieval bestiaries kept in the Bibliothèque Nationale. Even so, all this information had still to be assimilated into the novel, and Huysmans found this no easy task. He complained[6] to the Abbé Ferret:

I've got myself into a pretty fix with this study of symbolism. When I began I had no idea of the proportions it would take, the mass of documents I should need, and, from the stylistic point of view, the worry that all this would cause me. It's a repository of erudition, a *consommé* of ecclesiastical art, but it looks as though it had been written with albumin; there's no doubt that it's difficult to make anything out of these lists and quotations, squeezed together as in a hydraulic press and then squashed into chapters. Still, it completes *En Route*. And if, after all this trouble, I get no reward on earth, I hope that Our Lady, who is the real subject of the book, will ask for it to be given me hereafter.

He was greatly heartened about this time by the discovery of some lithographs by a young religious artist, Charles-Marie Dulac, whom he was to praise highly in *La Cathédrale*. 'Of all our pious painters,' he told his confessor,[7] 'young Dulac is the only one with any talent. I'm very pleased about this, because having to slate Tissot I'm delighted to be able to praise somebody and show that Catholic art, though it has fallen so low, is not yet completely dead . . .' Perhaps, too, he was already thinking of Dulac as a founder-member of that ideal community of religious artists and writers which still occupied his thoughts and dreams.

A little later Huysmans had another inspiring experience when Mlle Mathilde Prache called at his home on her way to the novitiate at Wisques. 'Her visit had an excellent effect on me,' he wrote to the Abbé Ferret,[8] 'for truly she has a sweet-scented soul and is so obviously happy to go!' And some years later, recalling this meeting in a letter to the artist Forain,[9] he wrote:

Only once in my life have I seen radiant beauty, divine beauty, the only true beauty. It was in the face of a very plain woman who came to see me one evening. I saw her for ten minutes and I shall never see her again, since the following day she entered a closed convent of the strict observance. Through a priest I had been privileged to enter for a moment into the life of this astonishing creature. In the short time she spent with me she spoke to me of the joys of sacrifice and the delights of suffering – and this plain woman's face was transfigured. Her eyes took on an extraordinary, indefinable expression – but how can one possibly render anything like that? True beauty doesn't lie in form or feature, for these are transformed by a sudden surge of the spirit: religion ennobles everything . . .

The same could scarcely be said, however, of a ceremony which Huysmans attended in April 1897: the funeral of Charles Buet, the Catholic author whom he had portrayed as Chantelouve in *Là-Bas*. In recent years Huysmans had given financial help to Buet and his sons, one of whom had entered the army and another the Premonstratensian Order. Writing to the Abbé Moeller,[10] who had known Buet, Huysmans described his death and funeral, and added:

> There was one frightful detail which added a note of atrocious irony to the scene. Poor Buet's hearse was practically bare, and there was only one big wreath to be seen, bearing this inscription: *Le Grand Guignol*!!! It had been brought by the buskers of a little theatre of that name where they were rehearsing one of Buet's plays. Imagine the coffin of a Catholic writer with that dangling behind it, and followed by two sons, one dressed as a soldier and the other as a monk! The whole affair made one feel utterly wretched. Still, the poor man was unhappy enough in this life for God to welcome him with open arms in the next . . .

In that same month of April news reached Huysmans that the Abbé Ferret, who had recently been moved to his home at Palinges, in the Department of Saône-et-Loire, was seriously ill. He promptly made arrangements to go to Palinges on Holy Thursday, and urged the Leclaires to accompany him, remarking[11] that 'considering how weak he is, I begin to wonder whether we shall see him again in Paris'. The Leclaires, however, were unable to get away, and it was with Georges Landry that Huysmans left Paris on the 15th to spend two or three days at Palinges. He found the priest's doctors unable to make a definite diagnosis, and with his customary contempt for the medical profession he concluded that they had been exaggerating the gravity of the sick man's condition. The first letter to reach him after his return to Paris was encouraging, and he wrote to Landry[12] that 'the improvement has continued since we left'. It did not continue for long. On 8 May we find Huysmans writing[13] to Mme Cécile Bruyère:

> Alarmed by a letter from my poor friend, I went to see him during Holy Week. I thought he looked better than I had been told he was, though terribly weak, and I returned to Paris full of hope. Since then the little news we have had of him has been worse and worse. And in his last letter the Curé of Palinges informed me that he had just received extreme unction. All this is quite heartbreaking, and here we are leading a miserable life, waiting anxiously for letters and feeling sick whenever a telegram arrives. Still, I haven't lost hope yet – if medical science, as usual, proves ineffectual, there is always Our Lady who, if she wishes, can cure that poor body. But in these dark days it's hard to know what to think, and when one considers the appalling catastrophe which has taken place here in Paris, one wonders whether the substitution in suffering of the best for the worst isn't what God requires at the moment . . .

The catastrophe to which he referred was the fire at the Charity Bazaar in which many leaders of charitable organizations lost their lives. This event reinforced Huysmans' belief in the doctrine of substitution, and he regarded the victims of the disaster as having been chosen to redeem their country in the eyes of God. On 11 May, a week after the fire, Edmond Le Roy of *Le Journal* wrote to Huysmans, asking him what he thought of an article by Édouard Drumont in which this theory had been advanced. The rough draft of the novelist's reply has survived.[14] In it he wrote:

> I had read the courageous and admirable article by Drumont which you have been good enough to send me and which develops the thesis that 'innocent blood can expiate crimes without number'. My opinion? But you know it already, since you refer in your letter to *En Route* – in short, this is a case of mystical substi-

tution, the substitution of the innocent for the guilty in the punishment meted out. All the saints practised it, and it is the *raison d'être* of certain of the contemplative orders, such as the Trappists, the Poor Clares, and the Carmelites, who expiate the sins of others every day in their monasteries. Perhaps these orders are not sufficiently numerous to perform this onerous task, since such appalling catastrophes occur, furnishing visible proof of the necessity for substitution in suffering. This is the only moral that I would draw from this sad story.

As we have seen, the possibility had occurred to Huysmans that the Abbé Ferret had also been chosen by God to be an expiatory victim, but he preferred to believe that the priest could still be saved. He therefore wrote to his friends and acquaintances in monasteries all over France, appealing to them to pray for his confessor's recovery. The measure of his affection for the Abbé Ferret and of his distress at the priest's plight can be gauged from this letter[15] he addressed to Léon Leclaire:

This morning, just as I was going out, a letter arrived from the curate at Palinges. This sentence sums it up: 'Our dear friend is growing weaker and, as M. le Curé told you, is suffering from a tumour on the stomach.' No change, in fact, and so I'm throwing more troops into the battle. The novena at La Trappe continues till tomorrow, and the Abbess of Solesmes, for her part, has asked for prayers from all her nuns. At Solesmes, the Abbot has his choir reciting the prayer *pro infirmo* every day. And according to a letter I received today, both the monasteries at En-Calcat are supporting the attack. We must go on stirring up the cloisters, for they form our best line of defence. I still have the Cistercians of Aiguebelle in reserve. Will you bring in the Carmelites, since Heaven obliges us to adopt strategic methods? We simply must try to win this battle and not despair until the very last moment . . .

In June the news from Palinges was better, and it seemed possible that the Abbé Ferret would recover. 'What a good doctor Our Lady is,' Huysmans exulted,[16] 'compared with the ignoramuses who are attending him!' The novelist was delighted, too, to learn from Dom Besse that the exile of Silos had been pardoned and would soon be able to return to Ligugé.[17] Yet he himself was far from happy. He had recently completed *La Cathédrale* and was profoundly dissatisfied with the result, complaining[18] to Mme Bruyère:

> Now that my book is finished it pains me to see that I've accomplished nothing of what I had set out to do. It's terrible, I assure you. I try to cheer myself up by telling myself that I've done my best, that I've spared myself neither time nor trouble, that whatever happens the book may help people to a greater love for Our Lady and her house at Chartres – but I know only too well that this hybrid work, which is neither fish, flesh, nor fowl, is unlikely to please anybody, myself least of all. Still, God will decide . . .

Towards the end of June Charles Rivière arrived in Paris on a brief visit, and on the 26th he lunched with Huysmans.[19] He brought the sad news that the saintly swineherd of Igny was at the point of death, 'smiling and opening his arms to the invisible'. In the afternoon the two men went on a pilgrimage through the broiling streets of Paris, stopping at every church they saw to say a prayer for Brother Isaac and the Abbé Ferret. The latter had just suffered a relapse, and a fortnight later, on 8 July, Huysmans travelled to Palinges to spend a few days at his friend's bedside. He found the priest terribly changed, and the sick man's straw-coloured features reminded him at once of Villiers de l'Isle-Adam in his last illness.[20] The Abbé Ferret's doctors, too, had at last come to a definite opinion and diagnosed cancer of the stomach. Though Huysmans still refused to admit defeat and begged his friends to redouble their prayers, he must have known in his heart that his confessor could not live much longer.

While he was in the south Huysmans took the opportunity to visit the Dominican chapel at Oullins, to inspect the frescoes painted there by Paul Borel, a modern artist to whom the novelist was to give equal honours with Dulac in *La Cathédrale*. He also stopped at Lyons on his way home from Palinges, and went up to Notre-Dame de Fourvière to pray for his sick friend. 'There,' he assured the Abbé Ferret,[21] 'I was the happiest man alive. It seemed to me that my prayers were heard and that our Mother would decide to cure you . . .' By mid-September, he added, he hoped to be able to escape from his bureaucratic gaol once more and join the priest at Palinges. In fact, however, this journey was never made.

One of the last persons Huysmans had seen in Paris before boarding the train for Palinges was Paul Valéry, and in the course of their conversation the novelist had settled a curious misunderstanding which had arisen between Stéphane Mallarmé and himself. Mallarmé had been afraid that Huysmans' feelings towards him had changed, and that the author of *Là-Bas* even suspected him of practising the occult arts. 'The last time he came to see me,' he had told Valéry, 'he observed that the lamp was burning with an alarming noise and that the chairs were creaking in a some-what ominous fashion, and I felt that he was worried by this assemblage of symptoms around me.' After his meeting with Huysmans Valéry was able to assure the poet that his fears were unfounded, and in the following winter he had the pleasure of bringing his two elders together again in the famous English tavern in the Rue d'Amsterdam and seeing them engaged in friendly discussion of the proofs of a new selection of Villiers' stories.[22]

Though Huysmans' friendship for Mallarmé remained unaffected, it is safe to assume that he had, in fact, regarded the noisy lamp and the creaking chairs as evidence of the presence of some evil spirit. In 1895 he had still been afflicted with diabolical obsessions, as can be seen from a study of the pref-ace he wrote in that year for a book by Jules Bois entitled *Le Satanisme et la magie*. Again, according to Gustave Boucher,[23] he showed such terror at the thought of diabolical attacks while on a visit to Solesmes that the monks feared for his reason and Dom Delatte scolded him in his sharp and soldierly way. This may have been during the stay he made at Solesmes in July 1897. He had returned from Palinges on the 16th, and on the 24th he set off once more for Solesmes, where he wished to do some additional research for *La Cathédrale*. From a letter he wrote to the Abbé Ferret before his departure,[24] it appears that if he expected to be attacked it was by Dom Delatte rather than by the Devil.

> I shall write to you from Solesmes [he wrote] as soon as I'm settled. I've had a letter from the Abbot in which he alludes more and more to my definitive entry into his monastery. Ouch! – Personally, I shall do what Our Lady wishes. I think I know what my own feelings on the matter are, but as yet I've no idea what She wants. So I can't come to a decision, however much they may press me. And I know they are going to throw little Arnaud at me!

In the promised letter, written on the 28th, Huysmans confided to his friend that he felt unwell and unhappy: unwell because of the food at Solesmes and unhappy about the general atmosphere. He had been made very welcome by the monks, whom he described as 'charming, and from the point of view of piety and behaviour quite irreproachable'. Yet he found that he was suffering from that same boredom and uneasiness that he had experienced on his first visit to Solesmes: he could not feel at home in the great abbey as he had done at Notre-Dame d'Igny. Moreover, he was annoyed when none of the monks would hear his confession but advised him, apparently on the Abbot's instructions, to await the return of 'Colonel' Delatte. 'I must leave you now,' he wrote to Leclaire on the 28th, 'to go and have my soul deloused by the Abbot, who came back last night. I've been unable to make my confession to anyone else. Hmm!' And to the Abbé Ferret he wrote: 'My opinion, my dear friend, is that it's not at Solesmes that I shall end my days . . . In spite of all young Arnaud's persuasive eloquence, it's curious how little inclination I feel to remain here.'

On Saturday the 31st Huysmans left Solesmes for Chartres, where he joined his friends the Leclaires. They stayed the night at the Hôtel du Duc de Chartres, heard Mass in the Cathedral on the Sunday morning, and returned to Paris together in the afternoon.[25] A week later Huysmans was overwhelmed with work at the Ministry, for an Italian anarchist had assassinated the Spanish Prime Minister at Agreda, and the Sûreté Générale had to arrange for extra supervision of all suspected anarchists in France. The frenzied activity in the Rue des Saussaies offices made the novelist's memories of Solesmes more pleasant by contrast, and he began to think that perhaps he had judged the Abbey of Saint-Pierre too harshly. On 22 August he wrote[26] to the Abbé Ferret:

> I'm writing to you in a moment of comparative peace from the evil den to which I'm confined. I'm so bored here that I wonder whether Heaven is not inflicting all this trouble on me to make me more appreciative of Solesmes. What's certain is that it's a joy to follow the canonical hours, and that the Liturgy is far superior to the twaddle that the telephone spits and splutters into my ear . . .

It now seemed unlikely that Huysmans would be released from the Ministry before the end of September, but he assured the Abbé Ferret on the 4th that he would come to Palinges as soon as he obtained leave. This was the last letter he wrote to his confessor, for news arrived within the next few days that the priest was in great pain and sinking fast. On Monday, 13 September, he died. A grief-stricken Huysmans wrote the next day[27] to Mme Bruyère:

> This morning I received a letter from the Curé of Palinges informing me that poor Ferret was dead. For some days the news had been so alarming that, losing all hope, we, his friends in Paris, begged Our Lady to put an end

to so much suffering by taking him with her. This was the only prayer She granted; blessed be her name. But if the Abbé Ferret, who was a saintly priest, is now happy, that isn't true of those who loved him in this life, and the thought of the gap he leaves behind him makes us despair. He was everything – father, brother, and friend . . .

For some weeks Huysmans' correspondence was full of heartbroken references to the departed priest. Gradually, however, the despair tinged with bitterness which was apparent in the letters he wrote when he learnt of the Abbé Ferret's death gave place to a more reflective and resigned mood. Thus, towards the end of October, we find him writing to the Abbé Mugnier[28] that 'when I think of what that poor soul, condemned to the icy Gehenna of Saint-Sulpice, suffered, resolutely and silently, I tell myself that certain hesitations are very cowardly and that I shouldn't be so fearful of necessary and purificatory suffering in the future . . .'

On the title-page of *La Cathédrale*, the manuscript of which was delivered to the printers on 20 September,[29] Huysmans penned a farewell tribute to the friend who had watched over every stage of the book's evolution: *Patri, Amico, Defuncto Gabrieli Ferret, Presbyt. S.S. Mœste, Filius, Amicus, J.-K. H.* Whether the Abbé Ferret would have admired the finished work, if he had lived to read it from cover to cover, is perhaps doubtful, for Huysmans was not exaggerating when he described it[30] as 'a real old curiosity shop, something like one of those medieval electuaries composed of every conceivable ingredient and a few more besides'. In an attempt to present the reader with all the information on medieval symbology which he and his friends had painstakingly collected, Huysmans had reduced many a page of his book to little more than a dry list of names and facts, and he was obliged to admit to Dom Pothier[31] that the result made 'arid, penitential reading – monastic in that respect, at least'. But if this is fair criticism of the chapters on symbolism, it cannot be applied to the descriptive passages, such as the justly famous description of the interior of the Cathedral at dawn. Nor is it true of that part of the novel which comprises a further instalment of Huysmans' autobiography.

The book is not, of course, autobiographical in every sense, nor even to the extent of *En Route*. In it Durtal settles at Chartres, partly because he regards the cathedral city as a comfortable half-way house between the world and the cloister, and partly because the Abbé Gévresin has been appointed vicar-general to the Bishop of Chartres, Mgr Le Tilloy des Mofflaines. Now it is known that Huysmans never stayed at Chartres for any length of time and that the Abbé Mugnier, who is generally taken to have been the model for the Abbé Gévresin, never held any ecclesiastical office at Chartres. Until recently it was supposed that for the purposes of his novel Huysmans simply transferred his *alter ego* and that of the Abbé Mugnier to Chartres, but in 1950 Dr. Pierre Cogny suggested[32] that the vicar-general at Chartres does not represent the Abbé Mugnier at all, but is a portrait of Joseph Boullan. He pointed out that the priest's housekeeper, Mme Bavoil, is obviously modelled on Julie Thibault, and that Durtal accompanies these two characters on a pilgrimage to La Salette – the shrine which Huysmans had visited with Boullan and his priestess-disciple in 1891. While the present author thinks it is important to remember that there are also elements of Boullan's character and beliefs in the Abbé Gévresin of *En Route*, he would support this thesis, and might perhaps mention another indication of the identity of Boullan and Gévresin which Dr. Cogny has apparently overlooked: in *La Cathédrale* the priest is called 'the Father', a term reserved for Boullan by the Lyons community and not usually applied to members of the secular clergy in France. If this theory stands, it is permissible to regard the novel as an attempt by Huysmans to pay his debt of gratitude to those who had guided his steps along the road to conversion: thus in the first place he lovingly erects his cathedral, word by word, to be a monument to the glory of the Mother of God, and in the second he envelopes his two humbler and heretical mentors, Joseph Boullan and Julie Thibault, in a flattering odour of sanctity.

Though the details of Durtal's material existence given in

La Cathédrale do not always correspond with what we know of Huysmans' life, the spiritual side of the book is strictly autobiographical. Every prayer, every plaint, every passage of introspection in the novel has its counterpart in Huysmans' diaries and correspondence. Like Huysmans, Durtal falls an easy prey to scruples, constantly reproaching himself with a lack of humility, with spiritual aridity – 'that desiccated condition as a result of which, every time he went into a church or knelt in prayer at home, frost entered into his prayers and ice formed on his soul' – and with that splenetic boredom to which Baudelaire and Huysmans were both martyrs. Again, like Huysmans in his correspondence with Catharina A. Thijm, Durtal admits that for all these spiritual torments he is himself largely to blame – that 'it is my perpetual constraint, my lack of confidence in God, and also the paucity of my love which have reduced me to this state; these ills have in time engendered the disease from which I am suffering, a profound spiritual anaemia, aggravated by the fears of the sick man who, not knowing the nature of his complaint, exaggerates it'. Neither character nor author is yet capable of putting his entire trust in God, or of accepting the necessity for such spiritual afflictions; and it is the grace to do this that Durtal finally implores, in an appeal as moving in its shame and sincerity as des Esseintes' plea for faith:

> Alas! we are no longer like those humble workmen of the Middle Ages who praised God as they laboured, and submitted to the master's authority without argument. We, by our lack of faith, have exhausted the dittany of prayers and the soothing balm of orisons; and henceforth everything seems difficult and unjust to us, and we kick against the pricks, we demand pledges and promises, we are slow to begin our appointed task, and we are so despicable in our distrust that we should like to be paid in advance! Ah! Lord, grant us the grace to pray and not to have even the idea of asking you for earnest-money; grant us the grace to obey and to be silent!

Whereas *La Cathédrale* was dedicated to the Abbé Ferret, Huysmans' next work, *Sainte Lydwine de Schiedam*, was to be dedicated to Léon Leclaire and his wife – not, as might be imagined, out of mere politeness, but in a spirit of sincere affection. The strangely assorted trio drew closer together after the Abbé Ferret's death, in deference to his last wishes – for he had summoned the Leclaires to his death-bed to tell them that Huysmans was to be 'their brother'.[33] And it was in their company that Huysmans left Paris towards the end of September on a journey through Belgium and Holland.

The object of this journey was to study the background for a Life of Blessed Lydwine – or, as Huysmans always called her, St. Lydwine – of Schiedam. Since the time of his conversion, the mystic in Huysmans had been inspired by the heroic example of this fifteenth-century exponent of the doctrine of substitution, while the Naturalist had been fascinated by the number and nature of the unspeakable diseases from which she had suffered. His Hamburg friend, Arij Prins, had collected for him a considerable number of documents on Lydwine's life, and now, with *La Cathédrale* off his hands, he wanted to visit Schiedam himself, to walk where the beata had walked, and to absorb the atmosphere of the little town where she had lived and died. During the journey he recorded his impressions of Belgium and Holland in a notebook which is now in the possession of Professor Louis Massignon.[34] Turning the pages of this little book and reading the faded handwriting, we may recognize the man of many parts – art-critic, gourmet, tourist – whom we saw travelling through Germany in the eighties and through Belgium in the seventies. But we note also that, while discarding none of his old roles, Huysmans has since assumed a new one: he is now a devout pilgrim.

The first stopping-place of the little party was Brussels, where Huysmans spent most of his time in the Museum and the chapel of the Carmelite friars. Everything else in the capital displeased him. To his disgruntled gaze every shop appeared to be a tobacconist's or a confectioner's and every Belgian seemed to be eating, drinking, or smoking: the church of Sainte-Gudule, he remarked, had obviously been 'fashioned in the image of the Belgian soul – gross and heavy'. The night-life of Brussels, which he had so enjoyed with Théodore Hannon twenty years before, now merely revolted him; and his notebook contains a disgusted comment on 'the awfulness of the evenings, of this Boulevard Anspach, with its mad riot of electric light, its prostitutes, and the coarseness of these gorged and bloated crowds'.

After 'ignoble Brussels' it was a relief to come to Bruges, where the churches were open and there was an atmosphere of piety – even though that piety took the form of tinkling church bells, theatrical organ-music, and raucous singing. While in Bruges Huysmans went with his friends to look at the house with the yellow shutters where the Abbé Van Haecke lived, and noted down the address: No. 36 Rue du Marécage. However, they were unable to catch a glimpse of Van Haecke himself; either there or in the nearby church of Saint-Jacques, where he normally celebrated his Mass. But if the thrill of seeing the supposedly satanic priest was denied them, a curious adventure befell them in Saint-Jacques, which Huysmans recorded in this passage from his notebook:

> Everyone smiles when we mention Van Haecke. A bookseller with her hair in bandeaux said: 'He's a scream!' And the sacristan at Saint-Jacques told us: 'He says a Mass now and then.' People say he's droll, eccentric, and extremely amusing in the pulpit. We had gone to the church to find out when he said his Mass there – for he sometimes says it there and sometimes in one of the religious houses. Suddenly I heard the beginning of a Mass. I got up to go and see – and Mme Leclaire, who was some distance from me but could hear what I heard, beckoned me with a glance, and we made our way towards the place from which the sound of the two voices was coming. And there was nothing there – no Mass was ever said at that time in that church . . .

After passing hurriedly through Ghent, a place which

Huysmans immediately qualified as gloomy, sinister, and impious, the three pilgrims came to Antwerp. The Museum here claimed Huysmans' attention for many hours, and especially its 'priceless jewel' – the *Sacraments* of Roger Van der Weyden. In the evenings he divided his time between the churches and the docks, describing in his notebook the seven naves of the Cathedral and a transatlantic liner which he had visited; a Way of the Cross by pupils of Leys and the loading of cargo-boats; the 'stevedore saints and fishwife Magdalens' of Rubens, and a woman on the emigrant ship *Armenia* whom he saw calmly ridding herself of vermin in full view of the quays. These various aspects of life in Antwerp fascinated him, but the people impressed him as unfavourably as anywhere else in Belgium. The verdict he passed on the Belgians after leaving their country was that they were 'coarse and sly', whereas the Dutch were 'coarse but good-natured'. He added a petulant and rather pathetic rider to this verdict, condemning 'the boorishness of these people, always trying to elbow you out of your place in the latrines'. And pursuing this sanitary train of thought still further, he concluded that the symbol of Belgium was to be seen in 'the superb cesspool-drainage wagons at Antwerp, with their brasses gleaming like gold – for they, too, are clean outside . . .'

At the end of September Huysmans and the Leclaires arrived at Schiedam, where they put up at a boarding-house kept by a Mme Engering at No. 140 Hoogstraat. On the morning after their arrival Huysmans called at the church of the Visitation of Our Lady and introduced himself and his friends to the parish priest, the Abbé Poelhekke, who with his prominent blue eyes and long pipe reminded the novelist of his Uncle Constant. Encouraged by the hospitable welcome which this kindly priest gave him, he spent the next few days gathering information about Lydwine from anyone else who could tell him or show him anything connected with the beata; a Jansenist pastor, a Jesuit historian, a Catholic plumber, and a Protestant businessman were among those who helped him. Wherever he went he was impressed by the piety of the townspeople, and in his notebook he remarked that 'at Mass the men take communion, return to their places with their hands folded, and remain deep in prayer; the churches are nearly always open and constantly crowded'. He was also captivated by the charm of the town, with 'its canals, its drawbridges, its broadbuilt boats, and its superb windmills, nearly all dating back to the eighteenth century, built in mellowed brick with wooden collarettes and little ash-green windows'. In a letter he wrote to Julie Thibault on 4 October[35] Huysmans complained that it was 'heartbreaking to have to leave this good town', but the next day he and the Leclaires were obliged to set off on their return journey. Afterwards he recorded this final comment on his stay at Schiedam:

We've had wonderful weather, except for one rainy Sunday at Schiedam, which at least let us see the town drowned in mist and water, with its windmills waving ghostlike arms in a drizzly haze. What I remember with most pleasure – in spite of the surveillance and shadowing of which I was the object at Schiedam (pronounced Skrridam) – is the kindness of the people there; the endearing shyness, the breadth of outlook, the saintly simplicity of the parish priest; the delightful charm of the landlady, prattling away all the time, and so pleased and proud to have me there; and little Lydwine, one of her six children, so very sweet with her sea-green eyes and fair hair. She went to so much trouble to make me comfortable, and the bill at the end was so reasonable – those Engerings are really splendid people!

From Schiedam Huysmans and his companions travelled to The Hague – 'a pretentious city playing at being a little Paris' – and Haarlem, before arriving at Amsterdam. Here he admired the contents and organization of the Museum, was disappointed by the port and the zoological gardens, and was appalled by the squalor of the Jewish quarter around the Lazarusstraat. By accident or design he eventually found himself in the street where one of his correspondents lived, but it seems that he did not call on her, merely scribbling in his

354

notebook: 'Rosengracht, 196. The street where Alberdingk Thijm lives: the Avenue des Ternes with a few trams in it, and a windmill and a canal at one end.' At last, at seven-thirty in the morning of the 8th or 9th, Huysmans and the Leclaires left Amsterdam, and at six in the evening they arrived back in Paris. As a holiday, their journey to Schiedam had been extremely enjoyable; as a pilgrimage, it had been inspiring. And in a satisfied postscript to his record of their travels Huysmans wrote: 'To sum up, the best of the journey was a bit of Bruges, a lot of Antwerp – and everything at Schiedam.'

Back in Paris, Huysmans was confronted with the first of many problems concerning *La Cathédrale:* an offer made by the *Écho de Paris* to publish the work in serial form as it had published *Là-Bas*. He later told the Abbé Poelhekke[36] that he had rejected this offer, 'not wishing to put Our Lady in bad company', but that the editor of the *Écho de Paris*, nothing daunted, had then asked for some extracts from the book, promising to publicize it if he agreed, and threatening to attack it if he refused. Knowing the power such newspapers wielded, he had been obliged to 'go through the Caudine Forks', with the result that the *Écho de Paris* published fourteen lengthy extracts from *La Cathédrale,* beginning on 27 October. But Huysmans had not gone back on his original decision to keep the Virgin out of the popular press, for the fourteen chosen passages were all of purely artistic interest.

In the meantime, as the proofs of his novel began to arrive from the printers, Huysmans was plunged into 'a whirlpool of moral and typographical torments'.[37] The moral torments to which he referred were doubtless the result of his continued uncertainty about the future. He told Boucher[38] that his anti-clerical superiors at the Ministry, hearing that *La Cathédrale* was to appear early in the New Year, had advised him to retire from the Civil Service: 'They gave me to understand that they'd had enough of my opinions and that besides they had a protégé to put in my place. So next year I vamoose.' However, he still did not know what to do with himself once he had left the Ministry, and in an unhappy letter to Brother Ernest Micheau[39] he complained that he was 'just eating my heart out, tired of living in Paris, away from God, and longing to be near him – and then drawing back, seeing obstacles everywhere, worrying about the poor state of my health'. He tried to comfort himself with the thought that after his book had come out and his pension had been settled he might see things more clearly; but he knew that if he decided in favour of the cloister he would only be confronted with the necessity to make another difficult decision – which monastery to enter.

This last problem was growing ever more difficult as one possibility after another was rejected. Solesmes had now fallen from favour, for in October Huysmans had assured Leclaire that he had no intention of 'putting myself under the thumb of my imperious Abbot'.[40] He added that there was a possibility of his joining the Premonstratensians, 'in whose Rue de Sèvres house I've lived since I was a boy, and who have asked me to go and see them. They are in Normandy, and I mean to go there when I'm free.' But he was beginning to grow weary of this search for a claustral home, and doubtful of his chances of ever finding a monastery approximating to his ideal. And he qualified his remarks about the Premonstratensians with the disillusioned comment: 'I really think that literature is fundamentally incompatible with monastic life as it is lived today – and that Schiedam is worth much more.'

Huysmans' unhappiness at this time was matched by that of his friends. To the Leclaires, who suffered a bereavement in December, he wrote on the 30th:[41]

What a wretched end to the year! You are in tears, the little one sees his vocation being frustrated and is in despair, while Alice has written me a letter so full of misery that I don't know what to say in my reply to cheer her up. And on New Year's Day there will be an empty place at the dinner-table here, where poor Ferret used to sit. Let us pray, let us pray! For there are storm-clouds lowering on the horizon and the skies are dark . . .

When he spoke of darkening skies, Huysmans little suspected what storm-clouds of wrath were gathering in the clerical firmament, ready to burst upon him when his novel was published at the beginning of February. There were many priests who had neither forgotten nor forgiven the gibes at the secular clergy which he had made in *En Route*, and they were determined to take this opportunity to revenge themselves. The more perceptive of the novelist's friends, seeing on the one hand the danger of an attack by influential clerics and on the other the possibility that political events might distract the public's attention, did their best to publicize the book and to win sympathy for its author. Thus on 22 January, in the Rue du Luxembourg, the Abbé Mugnier delivered a lecture on Huysmans and his forthcoming novel to an appreciative audience almost entirely composed of ladies of the Faubourg Saint-Germain. Thanking him in advance for this service, Huysmans expressed the hope that 'you may save the unfortunate book from being overlooked in the midst of all this clamour about Dreyfus'.[42] This certainly seemed an unpropitious moment to publish a novel whose rebarbative character Huysmans was the first to acknowledge, but he was not in the least dismayed. On 27 January he wrote to Leclaire:[43]

> Wherever I go I meet people who tell me that I must be mad to think of bringing the book out at a time like this. What they say is perfectly true! But I can count on the support of someone whom I naturally don't mention to them: the Black Virgin of Chartres. Everyone declares that the Press simply won't review the novel. From the purely human point of view this is possible, but there are signs that, however improbable it may seem, the contrary may prove to be true . . .

That, in fact, the Press gave extensive publicity to La *Cathédrale* was due in no small measure to an article entitled 'Huysmans intime', inspired by the indefatigable Abbé Mugnier, written by the journalist Julien de Narfon, and published by *Le Figaro* on 29 January. In this article Narfon stated that Huysmans would enter the novitiate at Solesmes soon after the appearance of his novel – an assertion which aroused the public's interest and the novelist's wrath. 'It's really too bad!' he complained to Leclaire.[44] ' "Huysmans intime" indeed – by a M. de Narfon I've never set eyes on, who's never even been to see me! These people treat my soul like a public urinal . . .' And a fortnight later, although he was reaping the benefits of the publicity Narfon had given him, he made no mention of the offending article in this triumphant letter[45] to Gustave Boucher:

> *La Cathédrale* is selling in the most amazing way. With the Dreyfus affair killing any and every book that dared to appear, there was every likelihood that it would be sunk. Yet it was put on sale on the 1st and it's now in its 18th thousand, without benefit of reviews or anything. Stock guarantees a sale of more than 20,000 by the end of the month – a figure *En Route* took four years to reach! It's incredible! But no, I think there's an explanation: our poor dear Abbé Ferret must have pleaded eloquently with the Madonna of Chartres for the novel to have this astonishing sale, for never has a book been so difficult for the public to read nor appeared at such a deplorable moment.

However, if *La Cathédrale* enjoyed greater success than any of Huysmans' earlier novels, it also suffered more violent criticism, from both clerical and anticlerical writers. At first Huysmans affected surprise that his fiercest critics should be members of the clergy, writing[46] to Boucher: 'They are furious with me now that I've dropped Florence. Could it be that these pious people miss her? For after all, it's strange how the indignation of the bigots is worse over *La Cathédrale* than over *En Route*.' In fact, this 'indignation of the bigots' was caused by Huysmans' harsh strictures on contemporary Catholic literature and art, and on the priestly philistinism and prudery which he saw exemplified at Chartres in a piece of paper pasted over a medieval representation of the Circumcision. One of the priests who reacted violently to Huysmans' charges was a friend of the Abbé Mugnier's, the Abbé Frémont, who after reading *La Cathédrale* commented in his diary[47] that 'this man is to Chateaubriand what a toad is to a nightingale'. He followed up this judgement by joining with several like-minded members of the clergy in denouncing Huysmans to the Congregation of the Index at Rome. The others were Dom Sauton, who detested Huysmans on account of his friendship with Mme Cécile Bruyère, and who by now was highly skilled in this kind of underhand bigotry; a curate at the Sainte-Trinité called the Abbé Périès, who in the spring published a defamatory brochure entitled *La Littérature religieuse de M. Huysmans*; and a priest at Bourges, the Abbé Belleville, who castigated the novelist and his works in a study of *La Conversion de M. Huysmans*.[48] Public denunciation to Rome of Huysmans' latest novel was made in April by Canon J. Ribet, who in *L'Univers* declared that 'however much he may pretend to be a Christian, Durtal exhales a spirit of intense and infectious unbelief'. Commenting on this latest attack,[49] Huysmans wrote to Leclaire on the 6th April:

It was to be expected that we shouldn't get through Holy Week without trouble. *L'Univers* of 4 April contains an abominable article about me by a Canon Ribet, the writer on mysticism, saying that I'm not really converted and denouncing me to the Index. From what I'm told, this appeal to the Index, in a newspaper dear to the Pope's heart, will set the secret tribunal at Rome in motion. So now we can expect anything – the condemnation of *La Cathédrale* and perhaps also of the earlier works. As some Belgian friends of mine say in a horrified letter they've written to me, this is one of the worst attacks I've suffered. Nor can I see any way of warding off the blow. Rome condemns you without appeal, without hearing your defence, without even explaining its decision, and without even notifying you. It's monstrous, but that's how it is . . .

The situation was complicated by the intrigues of a Spanish Countess who had recently been trying, without success, to seduce the unfortunate novelist. This woman, whom Huysmans always called La Sol or Sol, but whose real name was the Countess de Galoez, had entered into relations with Huysmans some months earlier, probably on the pretext of consulting him about some question of satanism; at all events he had presented her with a medal of St. Benedict, which was what he did with anyone who complained to him of diabolical attacks.[50] In his letter to Leclaire of 6 April he wrote about her:

As the last straw, I've received a disconcerting telegram from La Sol, in which she informs me that she's spent three hours with the Papal Nuncio, who knows her family and is himself going to take her religious instruction in hand. And her telegram ends thus: 'God of my Karl! Protect us and help us *to be reunited soon!* Let him be cured and I shall believe in you, his God and soon mine too, I hope.' She's obviously resorting to new tactics here: having lost the first game she's taking the second on to different ground. If it's true that she's seeing a lot of the Nuncio, I can hope for nothing but trouble from that quarter; as for her conversion, I don't wish to cast doubts on the efficacy of the medal of St. Benedict, but, knowing the woman and her truly devilish determination to have me as her lover, I'm more and more suspicious of what she says . . .

Meanwhile Huysmans had retired from the Civil Service, on 16 February, with the honorary rank of head clerk. 'I left the Ministry', he told a friend,[51] 'between two rows of officials brandishing censers; the Minister bombarded me head clerk *in extremis* and sent me a letter expressing his sorrow at losing such a devoted servant!!' In more serious mood he wrote[52] to Lucien Descaves: 'The old civil servant has had his day, and is still rather bewildered at no longer having to plod along the same streets at the same times like an omnibus horse. Freedom

– the freedom to go for a stroll when one likes – is a strange thing . . .'

He found that freedom was also a troublesome thing, for he could now no longer escape the problem of how to employ it. He was still haunted by a longing for monastic life, and still deterred by unhappy memories, the tittle-tattle of friends, and a deep-seated distrust of any form of human association. As he wrote[53] to a theology student at the beginning of June, 'I'm convinced that the cloister is the most beautiful thing on earth, the truly divine way of life. I believe that in it one can be very happy and very unhappy at the same time – happy to be close to Him at last, and unhappy because of the human failings which one retains and which one can't help noticing in others . . .' Soon after writing this letter he once more underwent the familiar process of attraction and repulsion, for Dom Delatte wrote urging him to come to Solesmes on a final trial visit, while Brother Arnaud wrote complaining that he had been banished without a word of explanation from Saint-Pierre de Solesmes to Saint-Maur de Glanfeuil. In a diary which he kept from 15 to 20 June Huysmans left this record of his perplexity:[54]

The storm has burst. This monastic business was quiescent – then with a word the Abbot of Solesmes stirs it up again, gathering together these stray thoughts of mine as if he had sounded a horn – and it seems to me that I'm ready for anything, or at least ready to make an honest effort. And then comes the letter from the little one at Glanfeuil, bewildered by the Abbot's silence and not knowing what to think. The repulsion I felt for Solesmes on my first day there, and which nothing has been able to overcome, gets worse. If I haven't even a single friend there! You feel so clearly that the other people there are almost incapable of affection. And then I've never felt at home there, always sensing hidden intentions, a lack of sincerity. Is this a pointer to Saint-Maur? Everything is in conflict within me. Anyway, to enter a monastery you must at least feel some attraction.

Do I feel any? Vaguely, it seems to me that I must do it. But what uncertainty, what silence when I need a reply!

It was the absence of supernatural guidance of which he complained: on the human plane his friends and acquaintances were only too ready to suggest answers to his problem. Charles Rivière advised him to follow his own example and enter a monastery as an oblate. Everyone else – the Abbot of Igny, the Abbé Mugnier, old friends such as Bobin, and his new confessor, the Abbé Bouyer of Saint-Sulpice – tried to dissuade him from embarking on a way of life for which they all considered him to be ill suited and ill equipped. The most ardent opposition to the idea of his entering a monastery came, of course, from the Countess de Galoez, who declared that Solesmes wanted him only as a living advertisement, and added that if he truly loved God he would long ago have made his vows. Her arguments evoked the memory of a woman with very different views, and he wrote in his diary:[55]

The joy of Sister Prache when she left for the convent! Where is mine? It's true that I don't give myself wholeheartedly, that the little one's departure upsets all my resolutions, that on the one hand I try to see in it a new indication, and that on the other it increases my dislike for that barracks. And then the Abbot's behaviour in this affair worries me; his silence is inexplicable and the little one's letter, with its comments and its assured tone, is incomprehensible. What a mess! – a muddle worse than La Trappe, for then I *knew* that I had to go there, and now I don't know. Ah, if only poor Ferret were alive today! All this is becoming an obsession with me. I'm perpetually miserable, perpetually breaking out into obviously unjust anger against Solesmes. 'You don't know how to discipline yourself', says Mme Leclaire. 'You are like the hero of *En Rade*.' And I can't deny it.

In a pathetic attempt to 'discipline himself' and to put an end to his indecision, he went on to draw up the following balance-sheet of arguments for and against his entry into Solesmes:

BALANCE-SHEET

Against	For
Everyone.	Obscure feeling.
State of health.	Vague attraction before and after.
Instinctive repulsion.	Reaction against the Spanish-woman's arguments.
Distrust of those people.	Bored with journalism.
No holiness.	Problem of how to live settled.
Feel like running away when I'm there.	
Don't feel at home.	
The argument: 'You can do more good with your books by remaining in the world.'	

Trying to make a cool appraisal of the arguments and emotions listed in his balance-sheet, Huysmans found that he was being distracted by an old enemy who for many years had left him in peace: the devil of the flesh. 'In the midst of all this muddle,' he wrote in his diary, 'thoughts of the Spanish-woman haunt me, and I have to fight against my sensual instincts as well as everything else.' A day or so later his defences were subjected to a severe test in a scene with the Countess which he described in this letter[56] to the Abbé Mugnier:

I've just suffered the most astonishing attack I've ever experienced. The Spanish Countess came here and for *an hour and a half* by the clock she remained on her knees beside my desk, kissing my hands and begging me to love her and allow her to love me! She's a pretty minx, and though I resisted her without killing her as in *Antony*, this scene left me feeling shaken and fearfully perturbed . . . The woman is quite incomprehensible. She's a strange compound of a child of twelve, a raving lunatic, and a crafty jade. The worst of it all is that although I've forbidden her to come back, come back she will. The very thought sends cold shivers down my back!

His diary reveals that this incident had affected him far more deeply than the humorous tone of his letter to the Abbé Mugnier would suggest, for in his entry for 20 June he wrote:[57]

Atrocious scene with La Sol: terribly upset by that woman. I tell her: 'You don't want to have the faith so much as to take it from me.' And the truth of the matter is that with that creature on her knees in front of me, kissing my hands, I feel everything collapsing . . . La Sol's voice saying: 'The cloister, no! You shan't do that if I can help it!' She's possessed by the Devil, unwittingly perhaps. A cunning monkey, a flashy wench, and yet also a child who can be sweet and impulsive. What a nuisance she is, and how she'd cling if you gave her the chance! She certainly fired my senses in this scene lasting an hour and a half. And now I'm so miserable, so perplexed, so tired, and above all so bored . . . But let's be fair: I deserved to suffer this attack by La Sol, for with my filthy imagination I dreamt of it and asked for it. And the devilish idea occurs to me that with all my dreams collapsing about me, she offers me love, a return to life, real devotion perhaps. Who knows but I shan't regret spurning this fleeting chance of human happiness, the happiness of all other men? . . . Now a telegram from La Sol saying: 'You treat me like a common tart, you are a cruel man and not worthy of me. Adieu.' She adds that she's in bed, ill as a result of the scene we had together.

It's true that I was cruel, but what about her? Is she sincere? And what does the strange creature want? But I mustn't think about her – that will be so much less to worry about. All the same, she excited me, the minx, with her slim waist, her broad hips, and her firm buttocks. She looks rather like D's wife, with the same moon-face, but not as pretty because of her protruding lips, though more elegant and more petite. Poor woman – insulted and abused when perhaps she really wanted to be kind . . .

Kindness was indeed what Huysmans craved at this time, and not without reason. On the 18th an agency had sent him a batch of press-cuttings reporting that *La Cathédrale* had been officially denounced to the Congregation of the Index, and he had gone out on to the streets feeling miserable and oppressed, and longing to escape to some distant retreat far from the hostile world of religion. Then had come news of the fall of the Ministry, an event which he believed would involve a reduction in the size of his pension. And with a despair which would be comical if it were not so pitiful, he complained in his diary that 'it's a bit steep: Rome, Paris, and Solesmes combining against one man!'

It was at times such as this that he yearned for the company and solace of woman and wished that he had married. The sight of a young married couple at the window of the flat opposite his excited envy and regret in his heart, and he sadly recalled the women to whom he had been attracted since the time of Anna's illness: a person called Eugénie of whom nothing is known, a mysterious 'Zka.' who can be identified as the Czech artist Zdenka Braunerova,[58] the English journalist Edith Huybers, a woman whom he associated with Saint-Lazare and who was probably Mémèche of the Château-Rouge, and finally the Spanish Countess de Galoez. Remembering these abortive love-affairs, recalling his fruitless attempts to find a congenial monastic home, and considering his equivocal position with regard to the world of letters, he began to wonder whether he might not have been happier living a humdrum married life, practising the ordinary devotions of the average churchgoer, and writing commonplace novels in an unexceptional style. In a mood of bitter regret he wrote in his diary on 20 June:

I'm marking time, I'm stagnating, and above all I'm so bored, so very bored. I no longer have any taste for the world, or for the cloister, or indeed for anything. Across the way I can see that working-class couple, a pair of young, healthy people, and I envy them. They are living a normal life, married and light-hearted. But I'm always outside. Marriage? But if the Eugénie affair came to nothing, that wasn't my fault. Lived outside the bounds of conventional literature, derided and attacked as a Naturalist. Zka. turned up at the time of La Trappe, but that wasn't serious, and in any event it would have put a stop to my conversion, which was out of the question. My conversion followed, and afterwards I found myself outside the world of letters, spurned even by the Naturalists, and certainly by the Catholics. I'm condemned to perpetual isolation. In whom can I confide? With women, nothing has gone right. The little Englishwoman didn't understand. Since then, there was the Saint-Lazare tart, but by that time I was converted. It's the same with Sol. No, nothing has gone right, nothing. If I don't enter a monastery I shall have failed in everything: a bachelor life without women, marriage, and the cloister.

It was midsummer; he was only fifty years old, independent and famous. Yet never before had he felt so lonely and unhappy; never before had the past appeared so drear and futile, and the future so bleak.

5. THE OBLATE

In spite of the repulsion which Huysmans felt for Solesmes, he decided to pay one last visit to 'the barracks of the Sarthe' in July 1898, in the hope that either the atmosphere there or his own reactions to it might have changed. He wrote in his diary on 20 June: 'I shall leave for Solesmes on the 6th. I must settle this question. I don't feel optimistic about it, but my present life is impossible.'[1]

This visit to Solesmes was decisive. Although Dom Delatte pressed him to follow the dictates of his reason and become a monk, and even suggested that La Sol had been divinely appointed to harry him into the cloister, Huysmans now felt sure that he was not destined to settle at Solesmes. On 8 July he wrote to Léon Leclaire:[2]

> The longer I spend here, the more convinced I am that this isn't the place where I shall end my days. It's impossible for me to pray in real earnest in the church here, and I remember what little Esquirol said about his seminary: 'I prayed better outside.' Add to this a perpetual state of boredom, of uneasiness, of a lethargy such that I have to make a real effort to write a letter. The result is constant distraction, day-dreaming, and general sottishness – none of which is of any use to God. No, this is not the place for me – and from what I've heard of it, I should be very surprised if Saint-Maur turned out to be the monastery of my dreams . . .

Huysmans remained at Solesmes for the opening of the new refectory and the celebration of the Feast of St. Benedict, and left for Saint-Maur de Glanfeuil on Wednesday the 13th. In his diary he had written that 'perhaps Our Lady, knowing my repugnance for Solesmes, wants to see me installed there instead'. But Saint-Maur, if less intimidating than Solesmes, was no less disappointing, and Huysmans' first impressions of the place, recorded in a letter to Leclaire on the 14th, were of 'monks weighed down by their years, a horrible chapel, and a high-society Abbot'. He found the sub-prior, Dom Logerot, more likeable and very understanding, for after hearing his confession the monk advised him not to enter the cloister but to become an oblate instead, attached to some monastery but living outside its walls.[3] Huysmans was also warned against monastic life in general, and Solesmes in particular, by Brother Arnaud, who spent several hours unburdening himself of his petty grievances against Dom Delatte. By now the novelist was willing to believe anything he was told to the discredit of Solesmes, and in his letter to Leclaire he wrote:

> I've got the truth out of little Arnaud. This visit to Solesmes opened one of my eyes, and he's just opened the other. That monastery is to be shunned at all costs!! Our Lady has answered my questions after all, and now I know that there's nothing to be done there or at Saint-Maur either – that the Benedictine Order will never count me among their number. It's better to know where one stands, and now I feel sure that my life will have to be ordered in some other way. The cloister is all very fine in imagination, but frightful in reality; and it's certainly more difficult to work out one's salvation there than in the world . . .

The Countess de Galoez would have been delighted to hear of this development, for she had not given up hope of seducing Huysmans, and indeed had warned him that if he became a monk she too would enter a convent, there to commit nameless acts of sacrilege.[4] Knowing that she would launch fresh attacks upon his virtue as soon as she learnt of his disappointment, Huysmans resolved not to return to Paris until reports that she was on holiday were confirmed. On 18 July he left Saint-Maur for Blois, where he was met by

Lucien Descaves, and together they walked on to Macé, near Saint-Denis-sur-Loire. There Descaves had rented a cottage for the summer, and it seems that Huysmans intended to follow his example. Two days later, however, he returned to Paris, explaining afterwards in a letter[5] to Dom Thomasson de Gournay: 'I fell among a pack of crafty and rapacious peasants who, imagining that I was determined to rent one of their wretched hovels, asked for fantastically high rents – whereupon I packed my suitcase and left them high and dry.' Though he did not know it, his decision not to spend the rest of the summer at Macé was to have momentous consequences.

Shortly after his return to Paris Huysmans had a visit from Gustave Boucher, who was staying in the capital for a few days. On being told that Huysmans had made no plans for a summer holiday, Boucher invited him to spend a week or two at Ligugé, where he himself was now established as editor of a newspaper, *Le Pays Poitevin*, and curator of a small folk-lore museum which he had founded.[6] Huysmans shook his head regretfully, so that Boucher was extremely surprised when the novelist wrote to him on 30 July, announcing that he would arrive at Poitiers four days later. However, a room was prepared for his guest at the house where he lodged, the Villa Saint-Hilaire, and on Wednesday the 3rd he travelled to Poitiers to meet Huysmans' train.

Boucher has left us a detailed account of this first day of Huysmans' visit.[7] It appears from his notes that Huysmans arrived at Poitiers early in the afternoon and that there was no connexion for Ligugé until six in the evening. To pass the time Boucher took Huysmans on a tour of Poitiers, showing him in particular Notre-Dame-la-Grande and the church of Sainte-Radegonde, before calling on some of his clerical friends. In the space of a few hours the novelist was introduced to Canon Omer Péret, the Bishop's secretary, Canon Clément Gaborit, choirmaster at the Cathedral, Canon Henri Lavault, headmaster of a church school, and the Abbé Robert de la Croix de Castries, a Jesuit archaeologist. He was greatly impressed by the intelligence and kindness of these priests, for most of them knew and admired his works, and all invited him to lunch with them during the following week. Their hospitality proved no less impressive, and on the 8th Huysmans complained in a letter to Leclaire that 'as they are equipped with magnificent cellars, it was all quite overpowering . . .'

Another warm welcome awaited Huysmans at the Abbey of Saint-Martin de Ligugé, where he was reunited with Dom Besse and Dom Chamard. After Solesmes the little monastery of Ligugé seemed delightfully intimate, and the monks – with the exception of Dom Sauton – much friendlier than the troops of Dom Delatte's garrison. Even Dom Bourigaud, whom Huysmans had always held responsible for Dom Besse's disgrace in 1894, now found favour in his eyes, and he told Leclaire[8] that 'while the Abbot is obviously the feeblest from the intellectual point of view of all the monks I've met here, on the other hand he's certainly the holiest'. The novelist lunched at the abbey several times, taking coffee in the Abbot's rooms with Dom Bourigaud and Dom Chamard, and afterwards chatting with his friends in the garden. His afternoons were generally spent strolling round the countryside with Gustave Boucher, and the latter records that it was on one of these walks that Huysmans noticed a plot of land bordered by pines and watered by a spring, which overlooked the abbey. He observed to Boucher that this would be an ideal spot on which to build a house for beguines or lay-sisters, whereupon his friend asked: 'Why not a house for an oblate?' Boucher's query was echoed by Dom Besse, who reminded Huysmans that the third novel in his Catholic trilogy was to be called L'Oblat, and insisted that he was destined to live outside rather than inside monastery walls. Huysmans was tempted by the idea, especially as he realized that at Ligugé he could live in greater comfort on his pension of 2,800 francs than he could in Paris on an income twice as large.[9] Deciding to extend his stay at Ligugé for a few days, he wrote to Leclaire on 13 August:

Getting away involves a struggle with everyone here,

including myself – for the longer I stay here, the more delightful I find this part of the country, where it's hot but where the mornings, evenings, and nights are exquisite. And then, the setting is perfect. Since my last letter I've lunched with nearly all the parish priests of the neighbourhood and, just as at Poitiers, I've been astounded to find myself among pious, well-bred, and learned clerics. What's more, the monastery here is not at all like Solesmes, for there's a family atmosphere and a spirit of freedom here such as I never felt at the other place. I lunch frequently at the abbey and they entertain me simply and well . . .

Surprisingly enough, the author of *En Rade* was even impressed by the local peasantry, and after the Feast of the Assumption, when he saw all the adults taking communion and listened to the children singing plainchant, he assured Leclaire[10] that Ligugé was in truth 'a monastic village'. Meanwhile Dom Bourigaud was urging him to make his home in the village, where there were two vacant building sites, one the plot of land which Huysmans had pointed out to Boucher and the other a somewhat bigger plot not far away. On the 17th Huysmans told Léon Leclaire:

I've thought a lot about all this, and discussed the question at length with the Abbot and Father Besse; and I've come to the conclusion that this is exactly what I want. The Abbot said to me, just like Dom Logerot: 'Don't become a monk but stay outside the abbey as an oblate. In that way you will be able to enjoy all the advantages of monastic life without suffering any of the disadvantages. Besides, you'll never find a better site anywhere – ten minutes from the woods, four from the monastery, four from the station. And as there are only two of them for sale, you would be well advised to make haste.'

Making haste was never Huysmans' *forte*, but that same day

371

something happened to force his hand. Canon Péret had been invited to lunch at Ligugé, and Huysmans and Boucher went to meet him at the station. On the way to the monastery the three men passed the smaller of the two building sites and Boucher told the priest that Huysmans was considering buying it. Turning to the novelist, Canon Péret exclaimed: 'This land shall be yours tomorrow. I know the man who owns it – a retired solicitor called Monsieur Piard. Yes indeed, my dear Monsieur Huysmans. You have promised *L'Oblat* to your public: you must live it and write it here!' Huysmans merely smiled, but the next day he and Boucher received a telegram inviting them to lunch at Poitiers, and at the Canon's table they found M. Piard waiting for them. There followed what Huysmans called[11] 'a Homeric battle with this pious Pharisee', which ended with the novelist agreeing to buy the land for 4,000 francs.[12] Convinced that he had been lured into an ambush and robbed by an astute trickster, Huysmans was in an irascible mood on the journey back to Ligugé, and he complained to Boucher: 'What a fool I've been to let myself be hoaxed like that! And why the blazes did I ever come to this place with its clinging canons and its bothersome businessmen!' However, the beauty of the countryside and the thought that he had at last found a home combined to set his fears at rest. Boucher tells how, that evening, he was sitting with the novelist on the verandah of the Villa Saint-Hilaire when the abbey bell tolled for Compline. Without a word, Huysmans crossed himself and went down on his knees to give thanks to God, and his friend, deeply moved, knelt beside him in silent prayer.

The next day Huysmans wrote to the Leclaires, giving them his news, and within a week they too had arrived at Ligugé. According to Boucher 'their enthusiasm astonished Huysmans', and he suggests that it was largely due to Dom Chamard's flattery of Mme Leclaire. Whatever the cause of it, the result was that on 27 August the Leclaires bought for 9,000 francs the only remaining site in the village, a building plot separated from Huysmans' land by the property of a Mme Gibouin. Early in September Huysmans returned to

Paris with his friends, confident that he would soon possess the home of his dreams – 'the house of a country priest, standing at the end of a garden, with green-painted shutters and a vine running along the wall'.[13] But once again, as will be seen, his plans were to go awry.

The thought that the houses which they planned to build would be separated by a peasant's cottage irritated both Huysmans and the Leclaires, and after little more than a week in Paris the novelist hurried back to Ligugé to see whether Mme Gibouin could be persuaded to sell her house. He found that she could not. The old peasant woman, whom he nicknamed 'La Chouanne' or 'the woman with the yataghan nose', had all the peasant's traditional distrust of strangers from the city, and each of Huysmans' offers met with a stubborn shake of her old head in its starched white bonnet. At last, in desperation, Huysmans bid for a former policeman's house which was put up for auction on 18 September, bought it for just over 5,000 francs, and offered it to Mme Gibouin in exchange for her cottage. To his surprise, instead of accepting this generous offer, 'La Chouanne' temporized, consulted her children and her neighbours, submitted the house to a critical inspection, and finally declared that she would agree to the exchange only if she were given 500 francs to cover the costs of removal. On Huysmans' indignant refusal, she decided to remain where she was, and he was obliged to lease the newly acquired house; in November 1900 he sold it to a M. Dubois for the derisory sum of 3,000 francs.[14] Another attempt to link Huysmans' and the Leclaires' properties, by the purchase of a field which belonged to the commune and which skirted Mme Gibouin's garden, also came to nothing because the novelist considered the price asked to be exorbitant.[15] The net result, in fact, of all the complicated negotiations in which Huysmans was involved during the autumn of 1898 was that he was left with an unwanted house on his hands and the conviction that his 'monastic village' was inhabited by grasping peasants no better than those of Macé.

Foiled in his efforts to join the two sites, and fearful of the mounting expenses of the Ligugé enterprise, Huysmans welcomed a proposal which the Leclaires made to him one day: to split the costs of the house he was having built and share it between them. The idea of a modest house with green shutters was now abandoned in favour of plans for a large three-storied building with a miniature cloister at the front. Perhaps this cloister was merely an expression of the novelist's taste for things monastic; but perhaps, too, it was intended as a token of independence. What is certain is that, with memories of Solesmes in mind, Huysmans had no intention of becoming deeply implicated in the life of the Abbey of Saint-Martin, for on 2 October he wrote[16] to Dom Thomasson de Gournay:

> I should like to explain to you the lines on which, in my own interest, I'm determined to conduct my life at Ligugé. I'm convinced that the only way to have peace is to stay at home ... Otherwise, with the way the monasteries have of looking at things and their unconquerable addiction to tittle-tattle, I should inevitably get into trouble. So since my return to Ligugé ... I've been putting this theory into practice. I've been to confession at the abbey twice, and that's all. I've attended the various offices and afterwards come back to my provisional retreat. To be quite frank with you, my relations with the abbey matter less to me than my relations with the clergy at Poitiers, who are cultured, broad-minded, and well-informed on artistic matters. I go to see them at Poitiers and they come to see me at Ligugé. My main connexions are there.

Work on the house, which was to be called the Maison Notre-Dame, began on 11 October, and on 7 December the foundation-stone was solemnly blessed by Dom Bluté, one of the monks of the Abbey of Saint-Martin.[17] Neither Huysmans nor the Leclaires were present at this ceremony, and indeed they had to rely on Boucher to keep them informed of the progress of the building work. In his notes Boucher tells how, on his own initiative, he persuaded the architect to transfer Huysmans' study from the ground floor to the first floor, which was then arranged as a self-contained flat. The news of these alterations to the architect's plans apparently infuriated the Leclaires, who themselves had hoped to occupy the first floor, where they would have been less accessible to importunate visitors and would have enjoyed a better view of the surrounding countryside. The second floor of the Maison Notre-Dame was to consist of a number of guest-rooms, which Huysmans hoped would be permanently occupied by fellow oblates. Although in several letters written at this time he poured scorn on the rumour that he meant to found a community of religious artists and writers at Ligugé, this was in fact his intention. Already, in April 1898, he had considered founding such a colony in association with the Franciscans of the Rue des Fourneaux, but this project had been abandoned.[18] Now the idea was revived, and a list of prospective members of the community was drawn up. It included the names of two artists: Charles-Marie Dulac, the young painter whose work Huysmans had praised in *La Cathédrale* and who, like the novelist, had recently decided that he had no monastic vocation; and Jean de Caldain, a charming but unscrupulous person whose real name was Jean Marchand and who, after a chequered career as circus trainer and art-student, was trying to live by his drawing when Huysmans met him.[19] It was also hoped that the Ligugé community would include Charles Rivière of Notre-Dame d'Igny, and the Abbé Broussolle, a young art-historian and an admirer of *La Cathédrale*.[20] Huysmans felt increasingly confident that at last the dream which had drawn him to Fiancey three years before was about to be realized; and in October, referring to Leo XIII's recent brief on the reconstitution of the Benedictine Oblatehood, he wrote[21] to Gustave Boucher:

The Pope's sudden appearance on the scene, and the unexpected arrival at my flat of little Dulac, who has left the Franciscans of Assisi after a disappointment similar to that which I suffered at Solesmes, strike me as auspicious omens. Perhaps Our Lady is in a greater hurry than we are, since she brings people to us before anything is ready . . .

This optimism gradually faded, however, as winter brought fear and disappointment in its train. The Countess de Galoez, after trying in vain to win the friendship and support of Mme Leclaire, informed the horrified bourgeoise that she meant to follow Huysmans to Ligugé; and when the novelist heard from Boucher that an elderly gentleman had arrived in the village, announcing that he wished to rent a house there whatever the cost, he at once suspected that this person was an agent acting for La Sol.[22] Even more disturbing was the news from Rome, where Cardinal Vicenzo Vannutelli was reported to be presenting the case against *La Cathédrale* to the Congregation of the Index. Huysmans had but little faith in the efficacy of the help which his friends offered him in this emergency. He refused to believe that a letter[23] from the aged Dom Bourigaud, testifying to his good character would carry much weight at Rome; and he rejected out of hand the advice of the former Princess Bibesco, Prioress of a Carmelite convent at Algiers, who urged him to make public disavowal of all the works he had written before his conversion.[24] Instead, he addressed a submissive letter to the Prefect of the Congregation of the Index, Cardinal Steinhuber, acting on a suggestion made by Dom Delatte.[25] Writing to Leclaire on 15 December,[26] he explained:

He advised me to write to the Cardinal Prefect of the Index, telling him that I was prepared to submit to his authority, and asking him if he would therefore point out to me which were the offending passages. Now in Rome they hate to be explicit about anything, and in any event they never reply to letters, considering that to be unworthy of their Lordships. But it means a good mark for you in the dossier, and this often saves the day. So I sent a letter of this sort, full of salaams and salutations and genuflexions, off to Poitiers, whence they will forward it to the sinister schoolmaster in charge of that calamitous Congregation . . .

While waiting to see whether his letter would have the desired effect on the 'calamitous Congregation', Huysmans continued to make preparations for the move to Ligugé and the establishment of his colony of Catholic artists. Furniture and bedding was sent to Ligugé to fit out a room in the former policeman's house for Dulac, who was to leave Paris as soon as his affairs there had been put in order; ornaments were bought to fill the mantelpieces of the Maison Notre-Dame and books to provide against any deficiencies in the abbey library; and a large painting by Forain entitled *The Brothel*, which for many years Huysmans had kept in his bedroom for fear of scandalizing visitors, was now quietly disposed of as being unsuitable for a semi-monastic residence.[27] Unfortunately, as fast as plans for the Ligugé community were made, they were nullified by the secession, voluntary or not, of most of the prospective members of that community. Thus Charles Rivière and the Abbé Broussolle both abandoned the idea of settling at Ligugé, and Jean de Caldain informed Huysmans that he would not join the community if he could not have Dulac as a companion – for the latter had fallen ill early in December, and it was feared that his delicate health might prevent him from taking part in the Ligugé enterprise.

These fears were only too well founded. On the 20th Huysmans went to see Dulac, and he afterwards reported to Leclaire that the young man had been bleeding from the nose for over five hours and was in 'a lamentable condition'.[28] The next day he conferred with two of Dulac's best friends in Paris: the art-patron Henry Cochin and the sculptor Fernand Massignon, better known under his self-explanatory pseudonym of Pierre Roche. The three men decided that they should arrange for Dulac to be admitted to a religious house such as that of the Brothers of Saint-Jean-de-Dieu, but before they had time to do this the young artist was rushed to the Hôpital Beaujon in a critical condition. On Christmas Eve a note from Roche informed Huysmans that Dulac was '*gravely ill* but as comfortable as possible'; and on Christmas Day the novelist, himself still weak from a long attack of influenza, wrote to the ailing Leclaires:[29]

I've just come back from Beaujon. I found the little one as ill as Roche says – feverish and in a comatose condition, having had a horrible night. But he had received communion in the morning: the problem of a priest which was worrying me has been settled, his own confessor having been informed. This letter from Roche made me terribly miserable last night. At Midnight Mass at the Benedictine convent my soul felt like a cemetery and my mood was scarcely in keeping with that of the liturgies! What an unhappy business this is! Anyhow, we must hope that things will get better once we are out there. Just now I'm in pretty poor condition, with stomach-ache and rheumatic pains in my feet. I dragged myself along to the Rue Monsieur, feeling half-dead, and to cheer me up guess who was saying Mass and gave me communion – Sauton!!!!! Alas! Get better quickly so that we can cheer each other up a little. I'm in a pitch-black mood, with a soul like a chimney – coated with soot from top to bottom . . .

As the year drew to its close his melancholy deepened, and he found himself 'literally and spiritually in a cemetery'.[30] For on the 28th he attended the funeral of his old friend Georges Rodenbach; and on the 29th Dulac died at his mother's home at Charonne, where he had been taken at his own request two days before. 'I have never seen anything', Huysmans told Boucher,[31] 'as beautiful as that child on his death-bed.' And on the 31st he wrote[32] to the Abbé Mugnier:

The beginning of this New Year finds me sad at heart. Tomorrow I bury my poor little Dulac, who was to have been the foundation-stone of our community of oblates. He was a living answer to my prayers, and his death plunges me back into darkness, into the unknown, into I know not what. All this bodes ill for our venture, and to add to the unhappy omens, when I went to see St. Benedict this morning at his convent, I heard funeral chants and found that they were burying the Prioress . . .

The prospect was brighter, however, in the New Year. In the first place, although Huysmans was still afraid that the Countess de Galoez would pursue him to Ligugé, she at last recognized that he would never requite her love; and in what appears to be the only letter[33] from her that the novelist failed to burn – a letter written in reply to one of his less courteous communications – she declared: 'Already I love you just a little bit less . . .' A second and even more welcome piece of news which reached Huysmans early in 1899 was that the Vatican had no intention of placing *La Cathédrale* on the Index. 'The Rome affair', he told a correspondent[34] in February, 'is closed.'

In the spring Huysmans busied himself with preparations for an exhibition of Dulac's work organized by Henry Cochin and Pierre Roche. At their request he wrote a preface to the exhibition catalogue, in which he mourned the young artist 'who was the incontestable hope of the mystical painting of our time'. The exhibition was held in the Vollard Galleries in the Rue Laffitte and attracted considerable notice, thanks to an article on Dulac which Huysmans contributed to the *Écho de Paris* of 12 April and which he later reprinted in *De Tout*.

Meanwhile he continued to make plans for the move to Ligugé, and his letters to the Leclaires at this time were full of details of his latest purchases. He was more than ever determined to pursue a policy of peaceful isolation in the Maison Notre-Dame, as he stated in this letter[35] to Gustave Boucher:

Have had a visit from a noble marquess of those parts. He gave me to understand that he and his family would always be happy to see me. I thanked him, but told him that I was settling at Ligugé in order to avoid seeing anyone at all. This is the beginning of the invasion!

What these good folk seem unable to understand is that if I wanted to see people I'd stay in Paris, where at least the natives are slightly less stupid. Fortunately the Leclaires are in complete agreement with me on this point. As soon as we arrive we are going to bolt the door and get rid of all these gad-flies. I want peace, and whatever it may cost I'm going to have it.

Another decision Huysmans had taken was to dismiss Julie Thibault in the summer, in spite of the fact that her 'voices' assured her that she was destined to accompany him to Ligugé. Having discovered that she was portrayed in *La Cathédrale* as Mme Bavoil, and that Bavoil was a name which appeared on the tombstone of the Huysmans family grave, Maman Thibault had grown proud and presumptuous. Not only had she accepted money from the Countess de Galoez and promised to help her in her attempts to seduce Huysmans; she had also countenanced the publication in *Le Figaro* of an article by one Jane Misme, a relative of Pascal Misme of Lyons, which asserted that the novelist's conversion owed much to her and that she still wielded great power over him.[36] Yet it was not simply on account of these indiscretions, serious though they were, that Huysmans had decided to dismiss his housekeeper. He had come to see that a Vintrasian priestess would be as out-of-place in a house dedicated to the Virgin as would erotic paintings by Forain; and in a letter to Georges Landry,[37] explaining why Maman Thibault was to be pensioned off, he stated emphatically: 'I want no devilry in my new home!'

On a brief visit to Ligugé towards the end of May, Huysmans found the Maison Notre-Dame almost ready for occupation, and he returned to Paris to arrange for the removal of his books and furniture.[38] Reporting on the state of the newly-built house and his thoughts on leaving Paris, he wrote[39] to the young Lyons novelist Adolphe Berthet on 10 June:

In defiance of the agreed plan the architect, suddenly

taking leave of his senses, decided to build Moresque instead of Romanesque arches, and the whole cloister had to be begun again. At the moment I'm feeling terribly bored. Mother Thibault is full of gloom at the idea that we shall soon be parted, and I can't get a word out of her. Even the cat, who's going to have a new owner this week, prowls around looking pitifully distressed among the parcels which are piling up on all sides. And with all my friends reproaching me for going away, I too am beginning to fall into a melancholy mood, which is made worse in every way by the farewell dinners I'm given . . .

Two days later Huysmans wrote to inform Boucher that he and the Leclaires would travel to Poitiers on Saturday the 17th, staying the night at the Hôtel du Palais before going on to Ligugé. His last week in Paris, which promised to be uneventful, was made memorable by two unexpected and very dissimilar visitors to the half-empty flat. The first, as he later told a correspondent,[40] was 'one of the leaders of the Franciscan Order. He came to thank me for the articles I had written about his order and insisted on girding me with St. Francis's cord. So the ceremony was performed then and there, in my own home.' The second and last visitor was the Countess de Galoez, of whom Huysmans wrote[41] to Mme Cécile Bruyère:

On the day of my departure the satanic Spanish-woman succeeded in squeezing between two of the furniture-removers and getting into the flat. I had to go through yet another of her scenes, but in the end I put her out. An interesting detail is that before this she had gone to Bruges to ask for help from a frightful demoniacal priest whom I portrayed in *Là-Bas*, under the name of Canon Docre. It seems, however, that the spells cast by the wretched woman and that sorcerer are somewhat lacking in vigour, because the results she has obtained are nil . . .

Even at Ligugé Huysmans did not feel secure against the attacks of the irrepressible Countess, especially as she had written an alarming letter to Dom Besse, threatening to descend on the Abbey of Saint-Martin. In mid-July the novelist told Landry[42] that 'she has to go back to Spain to join her husband, and the express stops at Poitiers – so we shall be lucky if she doesn't come to Ligugé'. However, there is no evidence that La Sol carried out her threat to visit Huysmans at Ligugé, and it seems indeed that he never met her again after that last scene in the Rue de Sèvres flat. As will be seen, his only contact with her in later years was through a meeting with her daughter, whom he discovered to his astonishment to be a Carmelite nun at Lourdes.

As for La Sol's accomplice, Julie Thibault, she retired with a pension from Huysmans to the little village of Venteuil in Champagne, where she died in 1907, and where in 1951 M. Pierre Lambert discovered the archives of the Lyons sect, the old woman's missals, notebooks, and private papers, and the little marble altar in front of which she celebrated her heretical masses. Huysmans was amused to think of Julie practising her strange cult in this tiny, God-fearing hamlet, and in July 1899 he wrote[43] to Georges Landry:

I've had a letter from Mother Thibault, who has just left for La Sainte-Baume. She goes into dithyrambs about her lodgings at Venteuil and seems to be very happy. She adds that everyone there is full of admiration for her little altar – which is all to the good, provided the parish priest doesn't poke his nose into it!

Huysmans too was happy in his new home, as he revealed in this, his first letter[44] to the Abbé Mugnier from Ligugé:

I live in a perpetual day-dream, with my soul wandering away out of this world, to a continuous accompaniment of church bells . . . All that I know for certain is that once it is finished I shall have an exquisite home. We've worked out a combination of green doors and woodwork with red wallpaper which is a great success, and by emptying all our boxes of prints we hope to be able to fill the enormous gaps on our walls ... The heat is diabolical here just now, but in the evenings it's cool in the little cloister, and I sit there smoking and breathing in the smell of the pines and listening to a concert performed by frogs, magpies, and above all tree-crickets ...

It seems unlikely that Huysmans considered the ground-floor rooms of the Maison Notre-Dame to be 'exquisite', for the Leclaires had furnished them in the very worst bourgeois taste, even going so far as to install a piano-player in the sitting-room. Upstairs, however, everything about the novelist's study and bedroom recalled his flat in the Rue de Sèvres: the antique walnut table supported by carved angels' heads, the bust of St. Sebastian, the huge rusty key used as a paperweight, the brass candlesticks and delft vases, the fifteenth-century monstrance, the pictures by Callot and Raffaëlli, the shelves lined with books. Only the view had changed: instead of a narrow courtyard, the windows looked out on to a large field which sloped gently down towards the spires and belfries of the Abbey of Saint-Martin. Huysmans' nearest neighbours were the Sisters of St. Philomena, who had obtained his permission to pass through his garden on their way to and from the abbey church; and he reported to Landry[45] that from his windows he could often see 'white coifs bobbing in greeting to me, and busy fingers telling beads'. One wonders whether he remembered how des Esseintes had instructed his housekeeper to wear a white coif whenever she had occasion to pass the windows of his 'refined Thebaid', in order to create a religious atmosphere such as the author of *A Rebours* could now enjoy.

During Huysmans' first few weeks in Poitou several of his friends travelled to Ligugé to see him, including Dr. Michel de Lézinier – who took some photographs of the novelist and his new home[46] – Georges Landry, Henri Girard, and Lucien Descaves. Each visitor was shown some new acquisition or told of some new project – Lézinier seeing a recent photo-graph of the Abbé Van Haecke, and the others hearing of an unusual plan for the garden. Thus Huysmans assured Descaves[47] that the next time he came he would find the grounds divided into two plots: a liturgical garden with plants symbolizing the saints, and a medicinal garden 'based on that which the old monk Walhafrid Strabo celebrated in his poem *Hortulus*'. Needless to say, this last project came to nothing. The ground was prepared, seeds were sown, plants were planted. But only the weeds survived.

While staying at the Maison Notre-Dame Descaves was amused by the behaviour of the cook's husband, a certain Jean Fort, who served Huysmans and the Leclaires as butler, handyman, valet, gardener, and hairdresser. This Jack of all trades was in the habit of waiting at table with a cigarette drooping from his lips and of joining in the conversation when so inclined – much to Huysmans' amusement and Mme Leclaire's intense irritation.[48] Soon, however, even Huysmans was obliged to admit that both Fort and his wife were insolent and inefficient, and at the beginning of September the two servants were given a week's notice. They promptly sued the Leclaires for a year's wages, asserting that they had been engaged for that period, and also claimed damages for unjust dismissal. Huysmans was called as a witness, and on 29 September he wrote[49] to Georges Landry:

At Jean Fort's request we've recently appeared before a Justice of the Peace complete with black robes and white bib-and-tucker. Judgement was postponed for a fortnight. I can't say that I feel very optimistic about it, as the magistrate looks like an old Radical and we seem to have fallen into the clutches of a bunch of Freemasons. Still, we shall see. Whatever happens I can't help feeling rather sorry that we've seen the last of that amusing scrounger with his peculiar smile.

Fortunately the magistrate, Radical and Freemason though

384

he may have been, maintained a strict impartiality, and on 11 October Huysmans was able to inform Landry that 'we've won our case against the poor simpleton you met here, and he's been ordered to pay costs. He would have done better to have kept quiet in the first place.'

The Jean Fort case was an unusually disturbing occurrence for Ligugé, and on the whole Huysmans still considered the village to be a charming and peaceful place. His notorious aversion for the vaunted beauties of Nature was rapidly disappearing, and one letter he sent the Abbé Mugnier[50] was almost lyrical in its enthusiasm for the smell of resin from the firs and cedars, the reddish-brown leaves of the chestnut-tree, and the soft blue tint of the autumn sky. Indeed, only twice in the autumn and winter of 1899 could he be persuaded to leave his new home and garden for more than a few hours. The first occasion was in early October, when he accompanied Dom Besse on a brief but enjoyable tour of La Vendée. On his return he wrote to Descaves:[51]

We've seen some extraordinary châteaux inhabited by still more extraordinary people – a strange old aristo-cratic society living on its lands far from any town or city and playing antediluvian card-games. Doesn't it sound just too eighteenth-century! In these châteaux whose owners have reverted to a country life, peculiar women spend their time cultivating green roses, and yet these lunatic princesses are closely in touch with literary trends! It's all quite astonishing – like a rather jolly nightmare. The worst of it is that my stomach's in a stew, because these people dined and wined me far too well . . .

The second time Huysmans left Ligugé was on 15 November, when he travelled to Paris to send out press copies of his latest publication. This was not his Life of Blessed Lydwine, the bulk of which had still to be written, but a selection of innocuous passages from his works, published under the aegis of the Abbé Mugnier and the title of *Pages catholiques*. Many years later[52] the Abbé told how, in his anxiety to avoid offending a public of prudish piety, he had omitted *Marthe, histoire d'une fille* from a list of Huysmans' works in his introduction – but remedied the omission when the novelist reproachfully asked him: 'Since I wrote the book, why not say so?' *Pages catholiques* brought Huysmans many new readers who had hitherto been afraid to read his works, but he himself regarded the book with good-natured contempt and described the selected passages[53] as 'herbal infusions for spiritual colds in the head'.

He spent only two days in Paris and was glad to return to Ligugé, where, as he had written to a correspondent[54] at the beginning of the month, 'we offer God a luxurious cult, with magnificent and truly monastic offices and real plainchant; and today, All Saints' Day, going across in the darkness for Matins, I was met with a blaze of light and colour from the lamps and copes, and waves of incense'. At Christmas, too, the splendours of the Liturgy overwhelmed him with delight, and at Midnight Mass he was 'in a state of indescribable joy'.[55] If he still had any regrets at having left Paris, it was only because he sometimes missed those of his friends who remained in the capital. 'Otherwise,' he told the Abbé Broussolle,[56] 'I'm infinitely happier in this life of walks, work, and offices. I feel rather like an old rag which has been soaked and squeezed for year after year, and which has now been put out to dry on the river-bank . . .'

His postulancy was now nearly over, and he began to prepare for the ceremony of his clothing as an oblate novice. He was under no illusions as to how the public would react to the news that he had taken this step, and on 21 January 1900 he wrote[57] to the Abbé Mugnier:

> The fun will really start the next time I come to Paris. When they see that I'm not wearing a monkish robe they'll say: 'What did I tell you? He's been unfrocked! It didn't take long . . .' And there'll be more fodder in the troughs of my journalist colleagues. All this

goes unnoticed here; the village doesn't even suspect that the Press is talking about me, and the abbey is silent . . .

The village was soon to realize that Huysmans was the object of widespread public interest, for on the 30th the great Jules Huret, one of the country's leading reporters, descended on Ligugé to interview the novelist. He afterwards reported to his readers[58] that Huysmans was leading a happy and holy life, beginning each day with Matins at five and ending it with Compline at eight, but that if his habits had altered, his physical appearance had not. In his account of his interview with Huysmans he wrote:

He has not changed. The pointed, grizzly beard; the neat moustache; the regular line of the long nose and of the wide but gently humorous mouth; the big grey-green eyes and the somewhat diabolical curve of the eyebrows; the hair cut very close to the head. Yes, this is the faun-like face whose image had remained fixed in my memory . . .

Huret's article may have convinced the readers of *Le Figaro* of the reality of Huysmans' conversion, but there were still many eminent clerics who regarded the novelist with suspicion and distaste, and who sometimes gave voice to their suspicions. Huysmans bore these attacks with commendable patience, comforting himself with the reflection that whatever muddle-headed prelates might say against his books, these were known to have brought about many conversions. Thus on 23 February we find him writing[59] to Adolphe Berthet:

Here I've seen a strange creature, a former occultist who has been saved from suicide and converted by *En Route*, and who has just made his confession and washed away the sins of his past life in this monastery. In a way this is an answer to a pastoral letter which the Bishop of Annecy

387

has just published in his *Semaine Religieuse*, saying that I'm not a true convert, that I ought to be unmasked, and that *En Route* is an obstacle to conversions . . .

The good Bishop would clearly not have been surprised to learn that about this time Huysmans was to be seen in the company of a fraudulent Archbishop who later 'ordained' two priests in Paris, was denounced by Cardinal Richard, and was finally excommunicated.[60] Huysmans first saw this curious person in the refectory at the Abbey of Saint-Martin, when he was lunching there one day with a young friend of Dom Chamard's called Aubault de la Haulte-Chambre. In a record of the incident[61] Aubault writes that they suddenly espied 'a clean-shaven, coarse-skinned giant of Herculean stature, who looked like an American athlete, and whose thighs were encased in pale green trousers'. They afterwards discovered that 'this powerful-looking man was Mgr Vilatte, Old-Catholic Archbishop of Babylon, who had come to Ligugé to study the apostolic succession of the Jacobite bishops in order to prove to Rome, into whose communion he wished to enter, the validity of his episcopal consecration'. After tracing the history of René Vilatte's subsequent relations with the Church, Aubault concludes briefly but charitably: 'He is dead now; may his soul rest in peace, for his Havanas were excellent.'

Meanwhile it had been arranged that the ceremony of Huysmans' clothing, which was due to take place with that of Gustave Boucher on 18 March, should be held in the chapel of the novitiate, a fastness which neither Parisian journalists nor Poitevin peasants would be allowed to enter. Writing to the Abbé Mugnier[62] Huysmans asked him to discourage *Le Figaro*'s ecclesiastical correspondent, Julien de Narfon, from travelling to Ligugé, as his journey would be wasted, and added: 'If he wants details of the ceremony I can send you some, with a description: sugar-loaf on the Right Reverend Abbot's head, modest attitude of J.-K. during the *Induat te Dominus novum* etc., and little Father Mayol, a delicious stained-glass-window monk, posing in the midst of the tapers. Why, one could write the article in advance!' It seems, indeed, that the rather formal account which he eventually sent the Abbé Mugnier for publication[63] might well have been written beforehand. It reads as follows:

My dear Abbé,

The ceremony of oblation took place on the 18th after the first Vespers of St. Joseph. It was simple and very private. To prevent the intrusion of sightseers it was held in the chapel of the novitiate, where not even a priest may penetrate. Imagine a little chapel at the end of a corridor, a very small room painted the colour of dried rose-petals. There, on the altar, the Benedictine habit was placed in a silver-gilt bowl, covered with violets and anemones. The well-known historian, Dom François Chamard, Prior of the Abbey, officiated, and it was he who, after the beautiful prayers which precede the ceremony, clothed me in the habit, saying: '*Induat te Dominus novum hominem*, etc.' Then the great relic of St. Benedict, which had been brought there specially for the occasion, was taken from behind a fiery barrier of tapers and given to me to kiss. Finally, after Matins the next morning, Father Bluté, the master of novices, celebrated in the same chapel the Communion Mass, during which I took communion with the novices. There, my dear Abbé, you have a succinct account of this ceremony which no one save the monks was allowed to attend.[64]

Yours very truly,
J.-K. Huysmans.

A few days after his clothing as an oblate novice Huysmans announced to the Abbé Mugnier that he had obtained the Prior's permission to come to Paris for a meeting of the Académie Goncourt. This body had recently attained legal existence after prolonged litigation dating back to 1897.[65] In August of that year the Civil Tribunal had dismissed the objections to Edmond de Goncourt's will raised by his natural heirs, ruling that the formation of a literary corporation bearing his name was 'not in itself impossible, nor inimical to public order and morality', and this decision was upheld by the Court of Appeal on 1 March 1900. Of the eight 'academicians' named in Edmond's will – Alphonse Daudet, Huysmans, Octave Mirbeau, Joseph Rosny, Justin Rosny, Léon Hennique, Paul Margueritte, and Gustave Geffroy – the first had died in December 1897, so that three new members had to be elected to make up the statutory number of ten. Huysmans hoped that Descaves would be one of those elected, and it was chiefly for his friend's sake that he tore himself away from Ligugé to attend this meeting. Writing to the Abbé Mugnier on 1 April,[66] he confessed that he hated leaving the monastery during Holy Week, as he found the offices there more interesting than 'all that literary jiggery-pokery' and there was also a danger that he might miss the paschal dinner on Easter Sunday. 'My only consolation', he added, 'is that at least I shan't see the Exposition. The Mecca of universal mediocrity will have to do without a visit from this particular pilgrim . . .'

Huysmans arrived in Paris in the evening of the 6th and put up at the Hôtel du Vatican in the Place Saint-Sulpice. The following afternoon he joined the other members of the Académie Goncourt at Hennique's flat in the Rue Decamps, where, after a meeting lasting over three hours, Élémir Bourges, Léon Daudet, and Lucien Descaves were elected.[67] As the oldest of the 'academicians', Huysmans himself became *ipso facto* President of the newly-constituted corporation. He made an admirable President according to the elder Rosny, who writes in his memoirs[68] that 'Huysmans behaved towards the members of the Academy like an old gentleman brimming over with consideration and respect. He seemed to have grown more compassionate, and he took a brotherly interest in our work . . .'

Returning to Ligugé in good time for the paschal dinner, Huysmans sent the following account of the great occasion[69] to the Leclaires, who were spending Easter with relatives at Vincennes:

Little of interest has happened since you left, except that we had the paschal dinner, with the lamb brought on to the refectory table. It was horrible – a twisted carcass with its mouth open, showing white teeth and a seemingly endless black tongue. Father Babin and Father Bluté were the sacrificers, and they carved the meat for us. It tasted less like young lamb than like old ram – bootleather, in fact. But old Chamard, who has no teeth left in his head, took three extra helpings!!

The following month Huysmans dated his letters not from the Maison Notre-Dame but from the Hôpital Notre-Dame – a grim touch of humour occasioned by prolonged paroxysms of toothache. The first dentist he consulted in Poitiers operated on him for a locked tooth with such ferocity that for some time he was unable to drink without difficulty and unable to sleep at all. A second dentist, to whom he appealed for help, informed him that his jaw had been injured by the extraction of the malformed tooth, and that he could look forward to a few more weeks of pain. 'I'm patiently waiting', he told a correspondent,[70] 'for the epilogue to this dental drama. At the moment it looks as if the tooth-doctor's predictions were accurate.' In fact, however, it was not weeks but years before the 'epilogue to this dental drama' was enacted; for there is every reason to suppose that the pains which Huysmans now began to suffer in his teeth and jaw were early symptoms of the cancer which was to carry him off seven years later.

He found compensations for his sufferings in the religious celebrations which took place at Ligugé during the summer months. Describing the first of these celebrations, held on 14 June, the Feast of Corpus Christi, he wrote[71] to the Abbé Mugnier:

We've been in a turmoil these last few days, with the Feast of the Blessed Sacrament and its Octave! And just think of it – it was the Maison Notre-Dame which served as the altar of repose! The cloister was specially decorated for the occasion, and all the old statues, delftware and reliquaries came out of the house to receive Our Lord amid a mass of flowers. It all went very well. Father Mayol officiated, and our little cloister rang with the sound of the monks' Gregorian chant. The whole village was there. In the Rue de Sèvres I never dreamt that Our Lord would come to my home except in the Viaticum. Anyway, I hope that he feels we did our best to give him a fitting reception.

Yesterday, Thursday, the ceremony was repeated, this time in the abbey gardens, and on Sunday it will be held in the village itself. We live in a cloud of incense, in a thunder of *Tantum ergos*, in a glow of tapers. The most amusing thing was the decoration of the house. I'd been lent the novices to help me, and like untethered kid-goats they suddenly appeared at all the windows, in the cellars and on the roofs, like a pantomime by the Hanlon-Lees! And then we had a little troop of our neighbours, the Sisters, busily arranging bouquets of flowers. It was terribly hot, with a fierce, blistering sun; and we watered the ground with pious perspiration . . .

At the beginning of July the Leclaires left Ligugé to spend six weeks at Vincennes, and Huysmans was left alone in the Maison Notre-Dame – alone, that is, except for Louise and Laurent, the young couple who had replaced the Forts, their new-born child, a dog called Bibelot, and a cat called La Moute. There were also the novelist's friends, many of whom came from Paris to stay with him for a few days during the summer and autumn of 1900. One of his first visitors was the Abbé Mugnier, whom Huysmans had taken to calling 'the mad Abbé' in affectionate mockery of his irrepressible gaiety. He came to Ligugé for a retreat, but the abbey was so crowded with priests in retreat that Dom Bourigaud recognized the Maison Notre-Dame as an annexe *pro hac vice*, and allowed the Abbé Mugnier to eat and sleep under Huysmans' roof.[72] Passionate nature-lover that he was, he spent as much time as he could in the 'annexe' garden; and on the 19th, a few days after he had left for a holiday at Scheveningen, Huysmans wrote to Leclaire[73] that 'here he was kissing the leaves on the trees and uttering cries of delight, and there he's probably drinking the waves as they roll on to the shore!'

Others who came to see Huysmans at Ligugé that year were Descaves, Girard, Landry, Pierre Roche, Charles Rivière, and the Abbé Broussolle.[74] There was also an unexpected but none the less welcome visitor, who arrived at Ligugé on the afternoon train on 27 October. Huysmans described him to Leclaire[75] as 'the most charming young man you could wish to meet. He was the bearer of a letter from Roche, introducing his son!' The young visitor was, in fact, Louis Massignon, who went on to become a professor at the Collège de France. Professor Massignon told the present author of the profound impression Huysmans made upon him that afternoon and evening – and of the unpleasant impression created by Gustave Boucher, who dined with them at the Maison Notre-Dame and afterwards accompanied the young man to Poitiers. But these were hard times for Boucher. With debts to the monastery totalling 15,000 francs, *Le Pays Poitevin* had been obliged to cease publication; and its proud editor had been reduced to asking Dom Bluté for a job as an apprentice in the abbey printing works.[76]

The only person known to have been a guest of the Leclaires at Ligugé was their niece, Mme Gault, a young woman who spent four or five weeks at the Maison Notre-Dame in September and October 1900. A pretty, pleasure-loving creature, she found life in the little village indescribably boring; and to have her uncle ordering her to bed at eight in the evening, as if she were still a child, must have been an added irritation. To revenge herself she took a malicious delight in doing and saying things calculated to shock her staid uncle and aunt. She shocked them by affecting unconcern at the fact that her husband was far away in Haiti; by making her toilet or reading Lorrain novels all day; and most of all by repeatedly declaring that she was interested only in wealth and pleasure and envied the fate of the great courtesans of the day. As for Huysmans, he was too great a connoisseur of female perversity to be impressed by this adolescent affectation, but in a letter to Landry he confessed to being amused by 'this *de luxe* doll, who seems to have no soul at all'.[77]

Throughout the summer and autumn of 1900 he continued to work on his Life of Blessed Lydwine. This was completed on 6 November,[78] and the following month he began to make a fair copy of the manuscript for the printers. He also wrote a preface to the Abbé Broussolle's monumental treatise on *La Jeunesse du Pérugin et les origines de l'École ombrienne*, which was printed by the monks of Ligugé in December.[79] Earlier in the year he had made arrangements with a book society called the Société des Bibliophiles du Pavillon de Hanovre to publish in October a collection of miscellaneous articles of his under the title of *De Tout;* but the society had suddenly gone bankrupt, leaving Huysmans in an embarrassing position as Stock came to hear that he had secretly been dealing with another publisher.[80] Relations between publisher and author were unaffected, however, and it was Stock who finally brought out *De Tout,* in November 1901.

There was little mention in Huysmans' correspondence at this time of Brother Arnaud, for the young man had proved so troublesome at Glanfeuil that he had been exiled to the Benedictine Abbey of Farnborough, under Dom Cabrol. In the summer of 1901 he left the Benedictine Order to become an oblate of St. Francis de Sales; and after teaching in Athens for many years he returned to France, where he died in the military hospital at Dijon in 1917, aged 46. His place in Huysmans' affection had been largely filled by the priest-poet Louis Le Cardonnel, who had entered the novitiate at Ligugé in February 1900. It is recorded[81] that Le Cardonnel scandalized Dom Mayol de Lupé by reciting poetry – and, what was worse, *French* poetry – in the latrines; but Huysmans for his part was delighted to have a friend at Ligugé with whom he could read and discuss the poems of Verlaine and Mallarmé. Thus, after describing to the Abbé Broussolle[82] a dinner of the local archaeological and historical society which he had attended at the abbey on 22 November, Huysmans added that 'these people with their incessant flow of commonplaces literally wore me out – and if I hadn't succeeded in escaping and gone to freshen up my brains with Le Cardonnel, I don't know what would have become of me'.

A friend of longer standing than Le Cardonnel, and whom Huysmans had never thought to see within the precincts of a monastery, descended on Ligugé on Christmas Eve. Huysmans afterwards wrote[83] to the Abbé Broussolle:

> Christmas Eve was magnificent here, and made more memorable for me by a truly joyous event. Just imagine – I'd seen nothing of the painter Forain for twenty years, although recently I'd heard vague rumours that he'd returned to the Church, when suddenly, on Christmas Eve, I had a telegram from him asking if I could put him up for the night, I wired him to come, and later saw the wicked rascal of old piously taking communion at Midnight Mass. It was certainly an odd experience for two friends who had been sceptics together and gone on the spree together in Paris, to meet again after so many years . . . at midnight, in the church at Ligugé!

In spite of the very real pleasure this incident gave to Huysmans, the end of the year found him in melancholy mood. The cause of his unhappiness was the threat of expulsion which had hung over the religious orders in France since the Prime Minister, Waldeck-Rousseau, had introduced his Bill relating to the Contract of Association. This Bill, which stipulated that every congregation must apply for legal authorization or be dissolved, was to be voted on in 1901, and Huysmans had no doubt that it would be passed. The position of the Abbey of Saint-Martin seemed to him particularly precarious, for friends of his in the Ministry of the Interior told him that the Prefect of Poitiers, a Freemason called Joliet, had sent the Government an unfavourable report on Ligugé.[84] What is more, there was growing hostility to the Benedictines in the village itself – hostility for which Huysmans blamed the mayor, another Freemason, who according to the novelist[85] had 'poisoned the place with hatred and alcohol'. In the summer, at the time of the elections, drunken women had paraded outside the Maison Notre-Dame, singing the *Carmagnole* and shouting: 'Down with the Benedictines! Down with their lackeys!'[86] To make matters worse, the monk who had served the village as parish priest had died, and a secular priest had been appointed in his stead, apparently with the object of annoying the monks and weakening their influence in the parish. Wherever our author looked at the close of the year, he saw only hatred and dissension; and on 31 December 1900 he sent Léon Leclaire[87] 'best wishes for the health required to face this new century, which seems to me to open on to a porch beyond which stretches an endless avenue of abominations'.

With this mournful and, it must be admitted, not unjustified prophecy, Huysmans entered into the twentieth century.

6. THE HAGIOGRAPHER

Two works by Huysmans were published in the first year of the century. In January 1901 *La Bièvre; Les Gobelins; Saint-Séverin* was brought out by the Société de Propagation des Livres d'Art in a limited edition illustrated by Auguste Lepère; and on 11 February Huysmans sent the manuscript of *Sainte Lydwine de Schiedam* to Stock.[1] Of the latter work he wrote to Princess Bibesco[2] that 'it will go its little way, whether its enemies like it or no. I believe it may do some good, console the sick, give people a more virile idea of religion, and reveal the monastic spirit to those who don't know it.' These were incidental aims: the main purpose of the book, as he revealed in an important letter[3] to a sick woman who had applied to him for spiritual comfort, was 'to throw a little light, however uncertain, upon the dark and terrifying mystery of suffering'. In this letter he stated explicitly his belief in the doctrine of mystical substitution, which he explained to his correspondent in these terms:

> It is quite certain that humanity is governed by two laws of which it knows little or nothing: the law of solidarity in evil and the law of reversibility in good; solidarity in Adam, reversibility in Our Lord. In other words, everyone is responsible to a certain extent for the sins of others and must to a certain extent expiate them; and everyone can also attribute the virtues he possesses or acquires to those who possess none or can acquire none. God was the first to submit to these laws when he applied them to himself in the person of his Son, allowing Jesus to pay the ransom of others in order that his virtues, which were of no use to him since he was innocent and perfect, should profit the sinners who

397

could not otherwise attain virtue. He wished Jesus to give the first example of mystical substitution – the substitution of one who owes nothing for one who owes everything – and Jesus in turn wishes certain souls to accept the legacy of his sacrifice and, in the words of St. Paul, to complete what is lacking in his Passion. For in fact, Christ could no longer suffer by himself after his Crucifixion. His mission was fulfilled with the shedding of his blood; and if he wishes to continue suffering here on earth, he can do this only in the members of his mystical body . . .

After stating that this was the explanation and justification of the sufferings borne by the saints and the contemplative orders, Huysmans continued:

Unfortunately there are now fewer saints, and the contemplative orders are dwindling in numbers or becoming less austere, so that Our Lord is obliged to turn to us, who are not saints. Hence our illnesses and afflictions, which undoubtedly ward off catastrophes. Lydwine was one of God's chosen expiatory victims, but it took her a long time to realize this. She suffered physical agonies such as may never be suffered again, simply because she did not wish to suffer. From the day that understanding dawned upon her, God helped her, and she lived in that strange condition in which pain is a source of joy. She came to that understanding through meditating on the Passion, and particularly on that agony in the Garden of Olives which only one person in modern times – Sister Emmerich – has truly comprehended . . . One should take no account of the spiritual aridity or lethargy, or the impossibility of praying properly, which one experiences when suffering. One should simply offer up one's continuation of the Passion to God. That is all that I know, and all that I can write in *Sainte Lydwine*, about suffering. It seems to me to be the truth, and what is more a consoling truth, for one is never nearer to God, and never more accessible to his influence, than when one is in pain.

Huysmans could scarcely have foreseen that the publication of these opinions in *Sainte Lydwine*, while comforting many sick people by convincing them of the value of their sufferings, would also cause acute mental distress to at least one member of the medical profession. On 12 August 1901 a Dr. Gabriel Leven wrote to him from Munich, complaining that no Catholic doctor who shared his beliefs could reasonably continue to practise, since there was a danger that he might thwart the designs of Providence by curing an expiatory victim whose very mission it was to suffer. In his reply[4] Huysmans made the point that no sick person, saint or sinner, could be cured except by the will of God, and that therefore the good doctor had no cause for concern. He also took the opportunity to reaffirm his adherence to the doctrine of mystical substitution, stating that 'if the clergy rarely preach the necessity for suffering and expiation, for fear of scaring away their flocks, that still remains the essence of Catholic belief, the lesson taught us by Calvary, the purest mystical theology'.

It was largely because Lydwine of Schiedam was one of the leading medieval exponents of this doctrine of substitution that Huysmans had chosen to write her Life; he had observed that she was born in 1380, the year that St. Catharine of Sienna died, and he was convinced that with her fellow stigmatists and contemporaries, St. Colette of Corbie and St. Francesca of Rome, she had been appointed by God to succeed St. Catharine in the work of expiation. Another reason why he had selected Blessed Lydwine as the subject of his first essay in hagiography was that she was a native of Holland, a country which, as has been seen, commanded his affection and hereditary loyalties. But perhaps the most compelling motive for his choice had been the realization that an account of Lydwine's appalling sufferings would give him an opportunity to achieve that 'mystical naturalism' or 'supernatural realism' which he had so admired in the Grünewald *Crucifixion* at Cassel. Any reader able to support a recital of physical ills more harrowing than any medical dictionary will agree that Huysmans succeeded in this ambition. For the milk-and-water of the average hagiography he substituted a compound of blood-and-pus; and into the tormented frame of his Lydwine he infused life and sanctity.

As often happened with Huysmans, he had gradually lost confidence in himself while writing *Sainte Lydwine*, and he was profoundly dissatisfied with the finished work. To Princess Bibesco he wrote[5] that he had 'failed to write the book I had dreamt of – a book far superior to this'; while he confided to the Abbé Broussolle[6] that 'if the book hadn't been advertised, and if I didn't need the money so badly, I should certainly shut this monstrosity up in a drawer, because that's undoubtedly where it belongs'. How close he came to doing this was told, many years later, by Georges Aubault de la Haulte-Chambre.[7] From his account it appears that after Huysmans had completed his Life of Lydwine, he bought the relevant volume of the new and carefully revised Palmé edition of the Bollandists' *Acta Sanctorum*. To his horror he found that according to this edition the beata was not born in 1380, as stated by Gerlac and Thomas à Kempis, but '*anno millesimo trecentesimo octogesimo decimo quinto kal. aprilis*' – which he took to mean 'in 1395, at the kalends of April'. The theory on which he had based his Life of Lydwine – that she was born in the year of St. Catharine's death in order that there should be no break in the succession of expiatory victims – came toppling to the ground; and in his despair he told Dom Besse that he would have to abandon the book. Fortunately the monk refused to believe that both Gerlac and Thomas à Kempis could be mistaken, and he therefore asked his young friend Aubault to consult the folios of the first edition of the *Acta Sanctorum* kept in the library of the Faculty of Theology at Poitiers. In his memoirs Aubault writes:

Very conscious of my importance, I rushed to Poitiers and went straight from the station to the library of the Faculty of Theology. There I read in the July volume: '*Nata est die Palmarum, anno millesimo trecentesimo octo-*

gesimo, decimo quinto kal. aprilis' ('She was born on Palm Sunday, in the year 1380, on the fifteenth day of the kalends of April'). Comparing the texts I saw that a comma of capital importance had been omitted from the Palmé edition. I copied out the passage from the *Prima Primaria*, and at the vital spot I inscribed in red ink a monumental comma with a tail like a comet. I then sent the precious rectification post-haste to Huysmans, together with a note giving him my address in case he should have further need of my services. The next day I received a telegram of forty-four words, a veritable letter, in which he told me that I had saved St. Lydwine and invited me to go and see him, declaring that he would always be at home to me. I called on him to pay my respects a few weeks later. He received me like a cousin of the Queen of Sheba, pressed me to stay for lunch, opened in my honour a bottle of the delicious Bourgueil wine, the colour of a fire opal, which an admirer whom he had never met sent him every year, paid me every sort of compliment, and sent me away in a rapture of delight.

On account of the costume which he affected – purple stockings, jabot, and cloak, silver-buckled shoes, jewelled snuffbox and amethyst ring – Georges Aubault de la Haulte-Chambre was nicknamed *Monsieur le Cardinal* by his friends.[8] But after his fruitful research into the life of Blessed Lydwine, he was always known to Huysmans as 'the young noble who found the comma' – much as Huysmans himself was known to the monks of Igny as 'the gentleman who saw the otter'.

Reprieved from banishment to the drawer which Huysmans reserved for unfinished or unsatisfactory works, the manuscript of *Sainte Lydwine* was furnished with an affectionate dedication to the Leclaires, 'my friends and companions at Schiedam and Ligugé', and posted to Paris on 11 February 1901.[9] Stock had grandiose plans for this work, which he outlined to Huysmans on a flying visit to Poitiers the following month.[10] While Darantière of Dijon would print an ordinary edition of *Sainte Lydwine*, a limited *édition de luxe* was to be printed by a Hamburg firm, with type designed by the Imperial Printer, Georg Schiller, and specially cast by the Imperial Press. Stock suggested that as a token of gratitude for these privileges, the first copy in the limited edition should be sent through diplomatic channels to Kaiser Wilhelm II. Huysmans agreed – never dreaming that this book would be returned to Paris (Imperial protocol forbidding the acceptance of gifts from private persons) and would eventually come into the possession of Mme Waldeck-Rousseau.[11]

Two days after Stock's visit, on 21 March, Huysmans made his solemn profession as a Benedictine oblate. Before the ceremony he carefully wrote out his charter of oblation, which is preserved in the Archives of the Abbey of Saint-Martin:

PAX

In nomine Domini Jesu-Christi,
Amen.
Ego, frater Huysmans (Georgius-Joannes) me offero Deo omnipo-
tenti, beatae Mariae Virgini et sancto Patri Benedicto, pro monasterio
Sancti Martini de Logogiaco et promitto conversionem morum
meorum ad mentem regulae sancti Patris Benedicti, juxta statuta
Oblatorum, coram Deo et omnibus sanctis.
In festo almi Patriarchae Benedicti, die XXI Martii
hujus anni 1901.

Explaining why he had taken John as his name in religion, Huysmans had already written[12] in a letter to the Abbé Mugnier: 'They told me that I should have to choose a name with which to sign the charter, so I hunted out some Benedictine saints who weren't very busy and could therefore take a greater interest in this poor creature. I finally discovered a Jean de Gorze, a Benedictine Abbot, perfect in every way, loving plainchant, art, etc . . . So I shall be Brother Jean . . .'

In his charter of oblation Brother Jean had solemnly promised to lead a holy life, and this promise he kept *usque ad mortem*. But his way of looking at life and describing it did not change, as can be seen from a letter written to the Abbé

Mugnier shortly after Easter 1901,[13] in which with typical humour he depicted the paschal lamb behaving in a most refractory manner on Holy Saturday, 'casting suspicious glances at the monks who were visibly calculating how much fat there was on him', and proving even more refractory when they ate him the next day. This letter also contained a characteristic complaint – that 'Holy Week was rather exhausting, as domestic complications and interminable offices quite wore me out – so that afterwards I could summon up only a faint *alleluia* . . .' The domestic complications to which he referred had been caused by the departure of Louise and Laurent, but partly remedied by an 'exquisite sister-oblate who has given me her maid so that I shan't be completely helpless'. His first recorded mention of this 'exquisite sister-oblate', in a letter to Mme Bruyère written in July 1899,[14] had been less complimentary: 'There's a strange person here who has come from Solesmes – a Mme Godefroid [*sic*] who poisons the atmosphere of the poor church of Saint-Martin with a scent of musk.' However, even for a misogynist like Huysmans, it was impossible not to like Mme Godefroy, for she was a sprightly little woman endowed with the enormous appetite and the sweet nature of an unspoilt child. Her habit of appearing every day wearing ribbons of the appropriate liturgical colour amused everyone at Ligugé, but she did not seem to mind teasing remarks about 'walking calendars'. Though Huysmans had disliked her at first, and later referred to her with affectionate disrespect as 'Poulotte', he made ample amends in his novel *L'Oblat*, where Mme Godefroy is immortalized and ennobled as Mlle de Garambois.

Eugénie, Mme Godefroy's maid, was relieved in April by one of Huysmans' former housekeepers, an old woman called Mme Guillemot whom the novelist had summoned from Paris, only to discover that she was now 'a physical and mental wreck'.[15] Fortunately she had only Huysmans to look after, as the Leclaires spent the greater part of this year at Vincennes. In their letters they spoke of their determination to leave Ligugé, where their relations with both village and monastery had deteriorated; and Mme Leclaire suggested that without them Huysmans would perhaps be able to realize his dream of a community of Catholic artists. It is true that there were now three young men living in the village who could be regarded as prospective members of such a community: Antonin Bourbon and Georges Rouault, both former pupils of Gustave Moreau, and the writer Paul Morisse.[16] On the other hand, Louis Le Cardonnel had been afflicted with sickness of both body and mind while at Ligugé, and he left the monastery in May to join the Franciscans of Amiens.[17] And finally, Huysmans himself, disillusioned by close contact with the Benedictines over a period of nearly two years, had decided that even if the monks were not exiled, he could not hope for satisfactory or understanding co-operation from them in any literary or artistic enterprise. Even Dom Besse, the misunderstood hero of Saint-Wandrille, had now lost Huysmans' respect; and on 30 April the novelist wrote to Leclaire:[18]

> In spite of the distress all this causes me, I can't help smiling a little at what your wife says to console me: that I might be able to undertake more easily, by myself, the work we had dreamt of. Alas! I've no desire to undertake anything at all, and I'm convinced that if there were something to be done it would certainly not be with this monastery here at Ligugé. Even supposing that a scheme had some prospect of life, it would be nipped in the bud by the mere fact that Father Besse would assume control of it. He would make it a matter of his personal interest, and that would suffice to encompass its failure. Ah, no! I can assure you that *le bon Dieu* would have to boot me damnably hard in the backside before I took a step in *that* direction . . .

In June Huysmans went to Paris for the publication of *Sainte Lydwine* on the 8th, putting up at the Hôtel Fénelon in the Rue Férou – a hostelry which, in a characteristic letter to Leclaire,[19] he recommended for its cool rooms, its statues of the Virgin in every corridor, and its innumerable privies. During this stay in the capital he lunched and dined with many of his friends, including Descaves, Coppée, the Abbé Mugnier and the Abbé Broussolle, and lastly Jules Bois, the author of *Le Satanisme et la magie*, who had recently followed Huysmans' example and returned to the Church.[20] As for *Sainte Lydwine*, the Press received it kindly, and the reviews of it which Huysmans read were 'nearly all respectful, but insignificant and bewildered'.[21] The only notable exception was an article in *Études*[22] in which the irreconcilable Jesuit Father Noury attacked Huysmans' style as being 'of a crudity and realism which sometimes borders on immorality . . .'

After a brief visit to Dijon, to collect material for his next novel, *L'Oblat*, Huysmans returned to Paris on 16 June and to Ligugé a few days later.[23] He found the monks resigned to the prospect of evacuating their abbey, for Dom Bourigaud was determined not to apply for permission to remain at Ligugé – permission which he felt sure would be refused. Huysmans, on the other hand, was in despair at the thought of their leaving, for however much he might criticize them he was none the less bound to the Abbey of Saint-Martin by ties of affection and loyalty. Accordingly, after making a careful study of the provisions of the fatal law, which was promulgated at the beginning of July, he proposed to Dom Bourigaud the setting up of a spurious archaeological and literary society which would rent the novitiate for its 'reading-rooms' and 'lecture-halls', and whose monkish members would lodge at the Maison Notre-Dame and other houses in the village.[24] However, this over-ingenious scheme was prudently dropped, and new homes were found for the monks at Herck-la-Ville in Belgium and at Cogullada in Spain. Throughout July and August they busied themselves making packing-cases for their furniture and the 25,000 books in their library, while Huysmans wrote to the Abbé Mugnier:[25]

Soon I too shall be packing my books, and next month I must take the express to Paris to find a new home. In September Ligugé will be deserted, and the prospect of spending the winter without any offices is unthinkable. All the schemes I've thought out with the Abbot have come to nothing. This is the big debacle. As I've said before, the Celestial Cabinet-maker now makes only chairs that come unstuck as soon as one touches them. One can no longer sit down in this life . . .

During this unhappy period Huysmans found some amusement in the antics of a Siamese cat which had been presented to him by a Mme Thomassin, a friend of the Abbé Mugnier's who admired his works. He described this pet to Leclaire[26] as 'the most affectionate and garrulous little thing that ever was', and added that 'if she didn't have a mania for nibbling my ears while I'm working at my desk, she'd be perfect'. The unhappy oblate also derived consolation from the company of friends who came down from Paris to spend a few days with him. Girard was at Ligugé at the beginning of August, and on the 27th Huysmans told the Abbé Moeller[27] that Jules Bois was staying at the Maison Notre-Dame: 'He's witnessing the preparations for the debacle, and shaking me out of my melancholy thoughts.' Those melancholy thoughts were not easily dispelled, however, and in a letter to another correspondent[28] Huysmans stated sadly: 'I'm drinking the last bottles of plainchant; before the end of September the liturgical cellar will be empty . . .'

Meanwhile, hearing that Huysmans intended to return to Paris, François Coppée had suggested that he should rent a flat which had fallen vacant in the apartment-house where he lived, at No. 12 Rue Oudinot. Huysmans would probably have done this, but for the fact that Coppée's landlord, discovering that his prospective tenant was a famous man of letters, asked for a fantastically high rent.[29] Instead, the novelist decided to accept an offer of accommodation made through Dom Chamard by the Prioress of the Benedictine convent in the Rue Monsieur.[30] This accommodation consisted of a large flat in the convent annexe, at No. 20 Rue Monsieur. Huysmans visited the annexe twice that autumn – the first time to inspect as much of the flat as the then tenant, a shrewish old lady, would allow; and the second time to arrange with Alexis Orsat's nephew, who was an architect, for the conversion and redecoration of the rooms.[31]

At Ligugé, the last solemn ceremonies – the clothing of three monks – took place on 12 September. After the office, which was celebrated with all due pomp, a splendid meal was served in the refectory. 'An enormous dinner', Huysmans noted in his diary.[32] 'Thick vermicelli soup, fricandeau, mutton with kidney beans, custard and pears. The three new monks have vases of flowers on the table before them. All the same, it's all very sad . . .'

Later in September Lucien Descaves arrived for a short stay at the Maison Notre-Dame, ostensibly to write an account of the monks' departure for the *Écho de Paris*, but in fact to keep his friend company during what he knew would be bitterly unhappy days.[33] On the 27th the last Mass was celebrated in the abbey church. On the 28th most of the remaining monks left Ligugé by an early-morning train. On the 29th Huysmans reported[34] to a friend of Adolphe Berthet's, Comte Henri d'Hennezel: 'Since this morning, when I saw off my Abbot, the last to leave the ship, the Abbey of Ligugé has been completely empty. The bells no longer ring, and the monastery clock has stopped. It is death.' And on the same day he made the following poignant entry in a diary[35] which he had been keeping for some weeks:

Sunday, 29 September 1901. I feel utterly foresaken . . . Truly it's time that I went. One week more. My head aches and I feel sick at heart, as though I were suffocating. I didn't know that this disaster the monastery has suffered would affect me so deeply. Ah! however weak he may be, the Abbot was Jesus Christ being driven away – was Our Father himself. I kissed his hand and was close to tears. Even Houllier, mediocre though he is, seems lovable now that he's there alone, for he represents monk and monastery. Never would I have suspected that I loved them so much, that they had entered so deeply into my life. It's strange how common adversity brings people together . . .

In another entry, dated 6 October,[36] he recorded his debt to Ligugé in these words:

I regret nothing. These two-and-a-half years, though dearly bought, have been good years, even for my soul. I've lost a mass of illusions about the monks and the monasteries. – Or have I? Since their departure the scales have tipped in their favour, and their virtues seem to outweigh their faults. – I've learnt to know the Liturgy; I've gathered together material for *L'Oblat*; I've met people like Poulotte; I've learnt to live a communal life. In short, in spite of everything, it has been an oasis . . .

One monk remained in the monastery to act as caretaker, and with him Huysmans and Boucher chanted the offices until news came from Herck-la-Ville that the liturgical cycle had been resumed in Belgium.[37] After this, there was no reason for Huysmans to stay any longer at the Maison Notre-Dame. In mid-October he paid a brief visit to his new quarters in Paris, and was told that they would be ready for occupation in a few days' time. And on Wednesday the 23rd, after one last pilgrimage to the deserted abbey, and one last look at the tall white house where he had hoped to end his days, Huysmans left the village of Ligugé, never to return.[38]

Writing to Princess Bibesco later in the month,[39] he asked for her prayers, saying that he had 'never been so bewildered or so disturbed as by this return to Paris'. The distress which exile from Ligugé had caused him was aggravated by the difficulty and discomfort which he experienced while installing himself in his new home. His books and other belongings were delayed on the way to Paris; his rooms were dark and cold; and his first days in the convent annexe were spent watching for the removal wagon through rain-lashed windows, or huddled over the kitchen stove between Mme Guillemot and the cat.[40]

On the 30th, a week after his arrival in Paris, he complained in a letter to Leclaire that he was still waiting for the removal men. 'This enforced idleness is intensely annoying', he wrote. 'I go from one room to another like a caged animal, cocking an ear whenever a wagon passes, always hoping that it's mine, spending the time between the offices doing nothing, perishing with cold in body and soul, and making heavy weather of the stodgy food the convent gives us.' And a few days later he was still complaining that he was unable to do any work – but this time because the removal men had unloaded his 3,000 books on the floor of the flat, where they lay in nightmarish disorder, waiting to be sorted and shelved.[41]

There were, of course, compensations which Huysmans soon discovered. It was a rule of the house that the doors of convent and annexe should be locked at nine in the evening, and that no guest or inmate should have a key – a rule which provided the novelist with an admirable excuse for refusing the invitations to dinner which poured in upon him as soon as he returned to Paris. The Prioress showed him great kindness and hospitality, arranging that he should have board, lodging, and service at the convent's expense until he was settled in, and trying to relieve the boredom of his first days in the annexe by showing him the miniatures which her nuns painted under the direction of the illuminator Anatole Foucher.[42] But perhaps the greatest advantage which Huysmans derived from his stay in the Rue Monsieur was the companionship of Dom du Bourg, an old monk who occupied the rooms above his, and who became his friend and confessor. Dom du Bourg was the nephew of Mgr d'Hulst and had been an army officer until 1888, when his wife died and he entered the Benedictine Order; ten years later he was appointed Prior of the Benedictine monastery at Auteuil, but this house was closed in 1901 as a result of the Law on Associations. Huysmans described him affectionately as 'one of God's tough nuts',[43] and was full of admiration for the heroic life of austerity which he led. 'He lives without a fire', he told Leclaire,[44] 'and can scarcely stay on his feet after all his mortifications. He is cruel to himself, this old monk, and gentle to others. The serving-nuns, filled with pity for him, try to make his life a little easier, but in vain. He sleeps on a hard bed, gets up at half-past three in the morning, and doesn't listen when people remonstrate with him . . .' The first Mass at which Huysmans served was one celebrated by Dom du Bourg,[45] and it was generally in his company that the novelist heard the liturgical offices – as he revealed in this impression of Vespers[46] which he sent Léon Leclaire:

> Vespers here are intimate and charming. Father du Bourg and myself, looking like two strays; a couple of serving-nuns; sometimes a vague feminine form huddled in a corner. When it grows dark a lamp is lit, and we gather round it. Then, after the *Pater*, comes the great silence, and everyone is swallowed up again by the darkness. The glow of a few lamps can be seen behind the grille from which the voices are coming. It's all very ghostly. There's only one writer who has succeeded in describing all this, and that's Victor Hugo with his convent scene in *Les Misérables*, the masterpiece of its kind . . .

Despite the restrictions which the early closing of the convent annexe placed on Huysmans' social activities, he renewed many old friendships in this winter of 1901, and formed several new ones. Curiously enough, the two most engaging friends he met or made during this period are both mentioned in a letter he wrote to Leclaire on 15 November. The first[47] was an eccentric old gentleman whose latinizing propensities and political sympathies could be deduced from the inscription on his visiting-cards: 'Auguste Dessus (A. Super), Former Prefect of the Second Empire.' M. Dessus had what he considered the misfortune to live in the same Rue de l'Université apartment-house as Waldeck-Rousseau, and his conversation was full of explosive comments on the iniquities of his fellow tenant, the Government he led, and the Third Republic in general. The comic ferocity of these outbursts endeared the old man to Huysmans, as did his enthusiasm for plainchant – an enthusiasm so extravagant that he once bullied the Cardinal Archbishop of Paris into visiting the dying Abbé Raillard, a neglected Gregorianist, and afterwards showed him to his carriage with the final admonition: 'Your Eminence, *extra Gregorianum, nulla salus!*' Huysmans could always rely on M. Dessus to amuse him when he was in despondent mood, and it was after attending the funeral of Georges Landry's brother that he went to call on the old eccentric on 15 November. 'I went to Saint-Séverin after lunch,' he told Leclaire, 'and dropped in on dear old Dessus, who has just entered into his eighty-eighth year and practically dislocated his shoulder falling downstairs. But he was as excited as ever about events, and as eloquent as ever in his comments. He waits for, he hopes for, he calls for the worst catastrophes . . .' In his memoirs Aubault de la Haulte-Chambre reveals that M. Dessus, whom Huysmans introduced to him as 'the drollest character under the skull-cap of the skies', recovered from his accident and continued to entertain the novelist and his friends for several years to come.

Of the other person of interest mentioned in this letter of 15 November, Huysmans wrote: 'A visit from young Gaëlle, a lovely girl with a sweet little punchinello face. She's terribly upset at the departure of the nuns of Sainte-Cécile for the English island [the Isle of Wight], because but for that she would have gone to see the Abbess this year. All the same, she's just a little tiresome with her invitations (authorized by *maman*) to her Château de la Colombière.'

Several of Huysmans' friends have referred to 'young Gaëlle' in their memoirs, but never by name. Thus Mme Myriam Harry, writing[48] of this 'young girl of the old provincial nobility, brought up in a convent and drawn to the religious life, but prevented by her family from taking the veil', says only that Huysmans always called her 'my little bird'. Similarly, Aubault de la Haulte-Chambre refers to her[49] simply as 'Mlle de X . . . a beautiful and gracious girl of twenty, of excellent family, with a cultured mind and an enthusiasm for all things liturgical and Benedictine, who had chosen Huysmans as her spiritual director.' It can now be revealed that her name was

Henriette (or Gaëlle) du Fresnel, and that her home was the Château de la Colombière in the commune of Mouroux, near Coulommiers (Seine-et-Marne). From a study of her correspondence with Huysmans, part of which is in a private collection and part in the Archives of the Abbey of Sainte-Scolastique de Dourgne (Tarn), the present author has discovered that Henriette du Fresnel first wrote to the novelist in 1899. Other letters followed, in which she sent him Easter or Christmas wishes, described her beloved Château de la Colombière, and discussed the mystical works which her 'spiritual director' recommended her to read. It appears that they did not meet until November 1901, and then only briefly; but later, as will be seen, the 'little bird' was to occupy much more of Huysmans' time and affection. In 1907, taking the name of Scolastica, she entered the Benedictine Abbey of Dourgne, where she died thirty-four years later, on 16 August 1941.

A few days after his first meeting with Henriette du Fresnel, we find Huysmans complaining in a letter to the exiled Abbess of Sainte-Cécile[50] of 'the lack here of ceremonies to which the male religious houses had accustomed me . . . the gloominess of the house, the lack of sunshine, the icy coldness of the rooms'. Nothing seemed to go right in the annexe, from the chimney which caught fire on Huysmans' first night in the Rue Monsieur to the ceiling of the privy which once came falling about his ears; and when, one day, lightning struck the house, the novelist swore that he was being pursued by ecclesiastical larvae, a species of hobgoblin in which he took an almost proprietary interest.[51] Meanwhile, as the winter drew on, the rooms of the annexe became even colder – so cold, in fact, that in December[52] Huysmans could tell Leclaire that 'if only I'd a better stomach for seal-blubber – which, it seems, is extraordinarily calorific – I'd sign this letter: "The Nansen of the Rue Monsieur", and buy some reindeer as soon as I could afford them . . .'

The house was no warmer at Christmas, but at least the 'lack of ceremonies' of which Huysmans had complained to Mme Bruyère was remedied. On Christmas Eve Forain and Landry joined the novelist for Midnight Mass at the convent,[53] and early in the New Year Huysmans wrote[54] to Adolphe Berthet:

That night was magnificent, and ever since there has been a succession of liturgical feasts – clothings, professions, pontifical offices with Dom Pothier, the Abbot of Saint-Wandrille, who is staying here just now, and dinners in the convent. And on New Year's Eve I went down at midnight and was present at the Benediction of the Blessed Sacrament given to the nuns, at Matins, at Lauds, etc. I eat, drink and sleep the Liturgy – and the last verb can be taken literally, because my bedroom is contiguous to the church, and on Christmas Morning I woke at seven to the sound of the *Kyrie eleison*, which with the organ-music was filtering through the wall. At two in the morning, if I'm not asleep, I can hear from my bed distant snatches of Matins. That's something which makes me overlook the drawbacks to living here . . .

During these winter months one book by Huysmans was published and two others were begun. The work which was published was *De Tout*, the collection of articles which Huysmans had given first to the Société des Bibliophiles du Pavillon de Hanovre and then, when that association went bankrupt, to Stock. The book was brought out in November 1901 and, according to its author, was given a rough handling by 'the Dreyfusard Press'. 'The reviews are simply a string of insults', he told Leclaire.[55] 'The note I added at the end raised their hackles, and I'm pleased to see that what I said went home. "Senile" and "monk-ridden" are the kindest terms these good people use to describe me.' The note in question was certainly calculated to raise masonic hackles, if no others, for it suggested that although the Law on Associations had invalidated the articles on the Benedictines and Carmelites, these articles might serve 'to remind readers what the monasteries of these great orders were like before the scum of the

Lodges polluted what was still healthy in the soul, the sickly soul, of this shameful country'.

On 5 December Huysmans began writing *L'Oblat*, the story of his stay at Ligugé and the third novel in his Catholic trilogy.[56] Two months later, however, he laid this work aside in order to devote his time to a second essay in hagiography, an *Esquisse biographique sur Don Bosco*.[57] He first mentioned this undertaking in a letter to Leclaire on 13 February 1902, when he wrote: 'Here I've got the Salesians on my heels. They are begging me to write a brochure for them on Don Bosco and their institution, which they say they would turn out by the million.'[58] It appears that the novelist had discovered that the choirboys whom he saw in the Rue Monsieur chapel on great feast-days were from the Salesian orphanage at Ménilmontant, which he later visited in the company of François Coppée. It was then pointed out to him that the Government was seeking to exile the Salesians on the grounds that, as a charitable institution profiting from tax-exemption and employing child-labour, the Ménilmontant orphanage could engage in unfair competition with commercial firms in the neighbourhood. Coppée urged his friend to do his best to arouse public sympathy for the Salesian Order, and finally Huysmans agreed to write a brief biography of its founder. Unfortunately, the life of nineteenth-century Giovanni Melchior Bosco did not lend itself as well as the life of fourteenth-century Lydwine of Schiedam to treatment in the Grünewald-Huysmans manner; and the eighty-page *Esquisse biographique* which appeared in August 1902 could not be said to possess great literary merit. Still less could it be described as having any artistic merit, for it was illustrated by amateurish drawings with captions in the same glutinous style as Coppée's introductory sonnet. Passing final judgement on the book, the outraged author wrote to Leclaire on 30 August:[59]

As for *Don Bosco*, I'm rather ashamed to send it to you, because those dirty dogs with their infamous illustrations have made an unspeakable hash of it. *What's more, there's a whole page of the text missing.* I pointed this out when I sent back the proofs, but they couldn't bother about a little thing like that and left it as it was – with the result that this work of mine, which for lack of documents was already worse than mediocre, is now absolutely incoherent!!!! I'm keeping it dark and preventing them from sending out review copies. I'm sending you one since you insist, but put it in the privy after reading it.

In the spring of 1902 both Huysmans and his housekeeper went down with influenza. As it was clear that Mme Guillemot was becoming increasingly incapable of performing her duties, she was pensioned off as soon as she recovered, and a younger woman took her place.[60] Huysmans now enjoyed better service, but his health continued to deteriorate. In May, tormented by pains in his teeth and jaw, he consulted first his dentist, a certain Duchesne, and then his doctor, Lucien Descaves' brother-in-law Crépel. 'I'm very rheumaticky', he told Leclaire on the 23rd. 'I've been to Duchesne to have a tooth out, but I've still got pains in my jaw and ear. It must be rheumatism, because when my jaw's all right my back aches. Crespel [sic] has told me to get out of this damp hole I'm in as soon as possible.' He accordingly sought out a new home, and found a suitable fourth-floor flat at No. 60 Rue de Babylone, into which he planned to move in August. But in June it seemed as if convent and annexe would be sold over his head before he had time to leave the Rue Monsieur. On 30 June he wrote to Leclaire:[61]

Just imagine – I've been inside the Benedictines' enclosure! They'd been sued by the State and hadn't paid, so the bailiffs were sent to seize their chattels. When they came the Prioress asked me to help her. It was quite unearthly. She went in front of us ringing a little bell, and all the nuns, fully veiled, scurried away out of sight. The poverty of this convent is unbelievable. A dog wouldn't stay in the squalid holes where the novices sleep. Everything is falling to pieces, and there isn't 500 francs' worth of furniture in the house. The only funny thing about the whole business was the master bailiff, who was dumbfounded by this evidence of poverty, and suddenly asked: 'Madame, where are the mirror-fitted wardrobes?' You should have seen the Prioress's face as she answered: 'But we haven't any mirror-fitted wardrobes.' 'Then where are your pianos?' he said. The man was obviously used to dealing with tarts who owed money, and knew only those two pieces of furniture, which he was in the habit of seizing first . . .

An even stranger adventure, involving an *Arabian Nights* mixture of magic, mystery, and wealth, befell our author in July. This bizarre episode had its origins in a letter he received in May[62] from one L. Delmas of No. 33 Rue Grignan, Marseilles, who wrote:

> An old doctor who lives on the outskirts of Marseilles and once knew your family would like to deliver into your own hands some very important and interesting papers concerning your family, and also to arrange a matter of a legacy. The good doctor, whose name is Rodaglia and who is well known in these parts, feels that he is growing weaker every day, and does not want to die before having a talk with you – not only about the papers I have mentioned above but also about certain bequests to religious charities. He hopes – indeed, he feels sure – that you will come here in answer to his appeal, and come as soon as possible, for it seems that there is no time to lose . . .

Huysmans ignored this letter, but when M. Delmas wrote again on 2 June, assuring him that the matter deserved serious consideration, he acknowledged receipt of the two letters and asked for further details. Instead of a reply from M. Delmas, he then received three long letters, couched in an alternately wheedling and aggressive style, from a Mlle Eulalie Duclos.[63] She was a young woman of thirty-two, a cousin of M. Delmas, a godchild of the mysterious Dr. Rodaglia, and the daughter of a police commissioner called Bernard Duclos, living at No. 9 Impasse du Presbytère at Endoume, Marseilles. In her letters to Huysmans she explained that he was distantly related to Dr. Rodaglia, who wished to see him before dividing his fortune between the novelist and herself. Meanwhile Huysmans set on foot inquiries at Marseilles through a M. Pépin, the uncle of a friend of his called M. Nugues, and through Dom Gauthey, the Benedictine Abbot of Marseilles. Dom Gauthey reported favourably on the Duclos family; and M. Pépin, who claimed to have known Mlle Duclos for many years, wrote that Dr. Rodaglia had originally intended to leave his entire fortune to her, but that she had been unwilling to deprive Huysmans, the doctor's only surviving relative, of his rightful inheritance. On 29 June the novelist, now convinced that this was no hoax, wrote to M. Bernard Duclos, offering to abandon any rights he might have to Dr. Rodaglia's fortune, on the grounds that he was personally unknown to the doctor, whereas Mlle Duclos was the old man's godchild and had earned his gratitude by nursing him in his illness. He added that he could not see how his going to Marseilles would serve any useful purpose, since if the doctor still wished to mention him in his will this could be done in his absence. 'Since I know you to be a man of honour', he went on, 'and have complete confidence in you, couldn't I confer powers of attorney on you and leave it to you to decide whether or not to use them? I repeat that I claim nothing and shall claim nothing. I don't say that because I'm rich, for I'm not; but I've always lived without owing anything to anyone, and I must confess that the mere thought of behaving like a fortune-hunter makes me shudder . . .'

M. Duclos did not reply to this letter, but his daughter and M. Pépin continued to urge Huysmans to make the journey to Marseilles, she reproaching the novelist with cruelty to a dying man, and he deploring what he considered the folly of looking such an attractive gift-horse in the mouth.[64] With each new letter from Marseilles, Huysmans' resolve weakened, and at last, on 11 July, he wrote to announce that he would be travelling south on the 14th. It was his first correspondent, M. Delmas, who replied, offering Huysmans the hospitality of his home and stating, with a melodramatic air which set the tone of the whole adventure, that at half-past ten on the Monday evening he would be standing by the door of the Marseilles station buffet, 'holding a completely unfolded copy of *La Libre Parole*'.

On his arrival in Marseilles, Huysmans discovered to his consternation that Dr. Rodaglia was no ordinary general practitioner, but a magician and miracle-worker who was alleged to have freed Mlle Duclos from an evil spell. He lived in the country at some distance from Marseilles, and Huysmans was informed that inns had had to be built near his house to accommodate the hundreds of sick people who went to him to be cured.[65] With memories of Boullan's abominable cures in mind, Huysmans began to suspect that Dr. Rodaglia was a satanist, and he therefore decided to take all possible precautions. On the morning of the day he was to meet the supposedly dying man, he took communion at Notre-Dame-de-la-Garde and supplied himself with some medals of St. Benedict, which he had always regarded as excellent preservatives against occult attacks. Of the meeting itself we have two different accounts, the first a highly-embroidered narrative from Aubault de la Haulte-Chambre's memoirs, the second a more reliable but not less colourful exposé in a letter from Huysmans to Leclaire.[66] Aubault relates that Huysmans was met at Marseilles by a gentleman in full evening dress, and driven in a superb landau to a palatial country residence, where he was ministered to by a retinue of deferential servants. He continues:

The Master's astonishment knew no bounds when, after he had dined, his guide led him into a magnificent drawing-room, and asked him to be seated in an armchair placed in the centre of the room and facing a double-door. After a few moments this door was flung wide open, revealing a second drawing-room lit *a giorno*. Out of this room came a girl dressed entirely in white, escorted by two ladies in train-dresses of black silk, and followed by the droll figure of an old man who looked like a walking skeleton, but whose eyes shone with an extraordinary brilliance behind his gold-rimmed spectacles. The girl came forward, made a courtly curtsey to Huysmans, who could make neither head nor tail of what was happening, and respectfully presented him with a silver bracelet which she asked him to examine carefully. It was a very handsome bracelet, and Huysmans remarked on its beauty as he handed it back to the girl. She then asked him:

'Doesn't this bracelet remind you of anything, monsieur?'

He replied that it did not, whereupon the two ladies entered into the conversation and said:

'Search your memory, monsieur, and you will remember this bracelet.'

After Huysmans had insisted that this was the first time he had ever seen it, the old gentleman came up to him, fixed his little gimlet-eyes on the author of *A Rebours*, and barked:

'This bracelet belonged to your grandmother.'

What followed was amazing beyond belief. The old doctor solemnly revealed to the Master that he was the true descendant of Louis XVII, that the grandmother who had owned the bracelet was Marie-Antoinette, that he was destined to be restored to the throne of France, but that to do this and to obey the fates he would have to marry the girl in white. He announced that the wedding-present he intended to bestow on Huysmans was a duly signed and authenticated will appointing him residuary legatee of a fortune running into millions of francs, and that all that was required was his consent to the marriage . . .

In a letter to Leclaire which he wrote on 18 July, on his return to Paris, Huysmans gave the following dramatic account of his encounter with Rodaglia, whom he described as 'a villain of the first water, a demoniac worse than all the others I've known':

It was like an explosion of percussion caps. 'What foul depravity!' I said – and he simply replied: 'I've nothing to say', while the poor girl, obsessed by her demoniacal visions, fell screaming to the floor. She had to be carried away. I was rushing at the old swine to throw him out of the window when Delmas grabbed me and said: 'You're mad, he's 80!' Or 20, I thought – because that hell-hound, more skilled in the black arts than Boullan and the rest, can change completely when he wishes.

We came back with the girl unconscious and her mother in floods of tears; and later, after a violent argument I had with the wretched girl about religion, she finally admitted that she was possessed of a devil. What followed was incredible. Apparently that old villain had convinced her five years ago that she was destined to marry me, for reasons too complex for me to explain here. She wept as she told me of this. I refused, of course, telling her that she was a victim of diabolical suggestion. That, I thought, was the end of the matter. But last night her cousins, Delmas and his wife, who though spiritualists are admirable people in their way, saw her after a suicide scene and begged me to put off my departure in order to discuss the marriage question with her. It was mad! A discussion between the two of us would have been worse than anything else. She's inhabited by larvae, *possessed* in the strict Biblical meaning of the word. I haven't the saintliness of the Apostles to fight anything like that. I flatly refused to stay there any longer, and took the night train back to Paris.

A peculiar business, isn't it? I don't care a damn about the legacy – besides, knowing that it came from such a fiend, and that he'd bewitched that poor girl, I wouldn't have taken it. But must you be 53 years old and suffering from a hernia and internal haemorrhoids for young girls to start pursuing and pestering you? I get back and find Gaëlle waiting for me. Ah, no! It's true that she's not in the same class as the other, but still . . . Why the blazes don't they leave me in peace?

To show M. Delmas that he bore him no ill will for having unwittingly lured him into this fantastic adventure, Huysmans wrote to him on the 21st to thank him and his wife for their hospitality, and at the same time sent them a toy for their little daughter. Replying on the 23rd, M. Delmas reported that Mlle Duclos was now calm and resigned, and had told him that 'she no longer heard the spirit-voice which had guided her until then, and that she no longer had any fluidic communication with the notorious Doctor'. On the 25th Huysmans wrote to Leclaire:[67]

I've had a triumphant letter from Marseilles. The poor girl is convinced that I've delivered her from the monster's clutches and agrees that I was right to refuse to marry her. She declares that she is ready to obey me and return to God. Alas! the poor little thing, who incidentally is very well-mannered and attractive, is such a nest of larvae that I doubt whether anything short of a miracle can cure her. She suffers too, like all visionaries, from great pride; I did something to break it, but the pieces soon come together again, and if that old swine of a sorcerer takes an active interest in her once more, I fear he will soon get the upper hand. But still, considering that when I refused to see her again she tried to commit suicide, there has been a definite improvement. Her family are going to take her away for a holiday – perhaps that will cure her of her crazy notions . . .

A letter from Mlle Duclos written three days later seemed to indicate that she was already cured, for in it she referred with shame and regret to 'these bizarre and untoward events', and praised the 'delicacy and nobility' of Huysmans' conduct. At the beginning of August, though busied with preparations for the move to the Rue de Babylone, he sent her a long and kindly letter in reply. After insisting that she should not reproach herself for having induced him to go to Marseilles, since he had very happy memories of the city and of the Delmas family, he went on to warn her of the dangers of dabbling in occultism.

When we left that demoniac [he wrote], you said: 'My life is shattered . . .' But no, you hold it in your hands, intact. You are young, and once you have attained true humility and thus rid yourself of the phantasms and deceitful revelations of spiritualism, you have a whole normal life before you! With God's grace, why shouldn't you be happy one day – as happy, that is, as one can be in this life? For after all, God only acts harshly and plays the surgeon when it is necessary to save a soul; afterwards, why shouldn't he be a good Father to you? He gave you a severe shaking simply to show you the way out of this tangle. It's over now, and as soon as you submit to his will, why shouldn't he welcome with open arms his little prodigal daughter and give her her share of happiness on earth? Don't take an empty pride in all this, but simply see in it the effect of his infinite goodness. The way in which he has treated you shows clearly that he loves you, and you may be sure that he won't abandon you, provided that you show a little willingness to satisfy him.

I can't help but smile a little to see myself giving you this advice which I should do well to apply first to myself, in an attempt to kill that old pride which is the Devil's door to our souls – a door which I sometimes feel swinging open within me. But failing saintliness, I can at least speak to you with a certain amount of experience, as one who has been through satanism – and La Trappe . . .

Unfortunately this excellent advice was totally ignored by Eulalie Duclos, who soon gave herself up once more to her follies and fantasies. We do not know whether this was because she had further communication, fluidic or personal, with Dr. Rodaglia; indeed, the identity of her godfather is still something of a mystery, since all attempts to find traces of his existence in Marseilles and surrounding districts have failed. It seems probable, however, that Eulalie needed little or no encouragement in her eccentric activities, which she was to pursue for another forty years.

Huysmans continued to be the unhappy object of her attentions for some time, and in the autumn of 1903 we find her sending him ten-page letters, flowers, lace-work, miniatures, a framed portrait of herself, and crudely disguised missives signed with the improbable name of Baptistine Gandolfe.[68] In the spring of 1905, having apparently given up hope of melting the novelist's heart, she married one Hilarion Bressier, of whom nothing is known save that he died in November 1931. After his death, Eulalie lived for a while with a Mme Vicenti, who had been several times convicted of drug-trafficking. She studied palmistry, practised a little magic, and amassed a remarkable collection of sea-shells. She wrote long letters to the crowned heads of Europe, and received curt acknowledgements in return. She died in Marseilles on 30 October 1943, perhaps still harbouring resentment against the unkind fate which had willed that she should be neither the bride of J.-K. Huysmans nor the Queen of France.

7. THE PILGRIM

On 7 August 1902 Huysmans moved from the Rue Monsieur to the Rue de Babylone. He was not sorry to leave a place which was associated in his mind with one of the unhappiest periods in his life – a period when, as he later told Mme Myriam Harry,[1] 'I had nothing in the world, neither books nor *bibelots* nor habits nor friends – and one night I came close to committing suicide.' Moreover, he was delighted with his new home. 'The move went like clockwork,' he told Leclaire,[2] 'with the bookcases installed beforehand and a smart decorator doing the place up in a couple of days. The flat is really charming and very cheerful, which makes a pleasant change from the *in-pace* of the Rue Monsieur.' A few days later, however, his housekeeper began to show signs of dangerous insanity. Huysmans gave her notice, but since she had brought her own furniture to the Rue de Babylone, he had to keep her in the flat until she found lodgings elsewhere – a difficult task considering her condition. Writing to Leclaire on the 26th, Huysmans complained: 'This delightful situation has lasted nearly twelve days, and you can imagine how enjoyable it is. I'm paying for my sunny little flat and the easiness of the move. You obviously can't have something for nothing in this life . . .'

The Leclaires, too, were thinking of moving house, and in his letter of the 26th Huysmans wrote: 'The plan your wife mentions of going to Lourdes seems excellent to me, for it would certainly be better to be close to the Blessed Virgin, with plenty of offices, than to stay in that unspeakable hole, Ligugé.' The expected move took place in mid-October, when the Maison Notre-Dame was put up for sale and the Leclaires installed themselves in the Villa Saint-Antoine on the outskirts of Lourdes. Soon all the oblates of Ligugé had left the Poitevin village, and at the same time most of them went out of Huysmans' life. Antonin Bourbon became a farmer in the Department of Ain; Paul Morisse returned to Paris, where Huysmans resolved[3] to 'keep him at a distance, having no desire to renew acquaintance with him'; while Gustave Boucher, who was now held in contempt by all who knew him, renounced his oblatehood and took a wife. 'I've had a letter from the ineffable Boucher,' Huysmans told Leclaire,[4] 'announcing his marriage, which he calls a "Teresan ceremony" (!!!!) because, so he says, his fiancée has an aunt who's a Carmelite. I'm simply not replying.' The only fellow oblate, in fact, for whom Huysmans still retained some affection, and with whom he kept in touch for the rest of his life, was Mme Godefroy. Starved of the liturgical offices which, with the pleasures of the table, had been her principal *raison d'être*, 'Poulotte' was desperately unhappy at Ligugé. At first she thought of lodging with the Leclaires at Lourdes, but they showed no enthusiasm for this idea; then, following Huysmans' example, she applied for accommodation to the Benedictines of the Rue Monsieur. When Huysmans heard that this request had been refused, and that his friend had decided to settle at Jouarre instead, he wrote[5] to her:

If you had gone to live with the nuns of the Rue Monsieur, you would have been treated as neither fish nor fowl, and regarded with suspicion on account of a situation for which you are not responsible. Your idea of going to Jouarre is much more sensible, much more practical. And then – I'm speaking here as much for myself as for you – we two were not made to live *in* but *beside* monasteries. Within monastery walls we should be most unhappy. There is something independent in us and about us which will always result in our being held in suspicion. So we must abandon, once for all, the ideal of monastic life. This is a hard thing to tell oneself when one has dreamt for many years, as we have, of a life out of the world and in God; but we are in the same boat as the rest of humanity, who doubtless have less exalted ideals, but who suffer just as keenly from the failure to achieve them . . .

On 10 September Huysmans left Paris in the company of the Abbé Mugnier, travelling to Lille to visit Notre-Dame-de-la-Treille, and thence to Bruges for the 1902 Exhibition of Primitives. The only comment on Notre-Dame-de-la-Treille which he made in his notebook[6] was: 'A disappointment, in a city of no account.' The Bruges exhibition likewise disappointed him. 'It's full of fakes,' he told Leclaire on his return,[7] 'and what's more, it's badly installed in poorly lit rooms.' But of the city itself he wrote: 'Bruges cheered us up, in spite of the incessant rain. In a sunny interval I went back to the beguinage, which looked charming that morning, and did the tour of the canals again. The place is as exquisite as ever, and in the course of my walk I caught a glimpse of Van Eycke [*sic*] with his snow-white locks!'

Huysmans was saddened by the death, later in September, of Émile Zola, but did not attend the funeral on 5 October. This may have been partly because he took offence at the discourteous invitation he received on the 4th – 'an unstamped letter (cost, 6 sous) containing no letter, no card, no note, but simply a paper inscribed: "Funeral of Émile Zola: official pass." '[8] Another reason for his absence was that he suspected that the funeral ceremonies would develop – as, in fact, they did – into political demonstrations; and rather than be involved in anything of that nature, he 'preferred to go and pray for the poor man in a quiet corner'.[9] Writing to Leclaire on the day after the funeral, he commented: 'You will have seen how poor Zola was monopolized by the Dreyfusard mob. In those circumstances I didn't go, nor did Céard, nor did Hennique. All his old friends stayed away.' But to Céard[10] he wrote: 'All the same, these deaths stir up the ashes of the past, and when I think of it all I feel overwhelmed by an immense melancholy and by a horror of my time which grows from day to day . . .'

Throughout the autumn of 1902 Huysmans worked hard on *L'Oblat*, and on 24 November he told Leclaire that he had just written *finis* to the book.[11] The last of his autobiographical novels, this work tells the story of the two years Huysmans spent at Ligugé. It is also the story of the Abbey of Saint-Martin (thinly disguised as the Burgundian Abbey of the Val des Saints), since one of Huysmans' objects in writing *L'Oblat* was to present a vivid but accurate account of the life of a French religious community at the beginning of the century. He wished, in fact, to emulate the Flemish sculptors who, in the figurines in Dijon Museum which are described in the book, had represented 'the monastic humanity of their time, merry or melancholy, phlegmatic or fervent'. The novel is, however, much more than a sociological document. Whereas in *En Route* and *La Cathédrale* Huysmans had demonstrated how man and Nature paid homage to God, he here intended to expound the laws governing the expression of that homage. Having introduced his readers to plainchant and Christian symbolism, he now wished to reveal to them the splendours of the Liturgy.

Huysmans' friends and enemies were aware that he had other objects in view. They knew that the novelist's most cherished dream had been shattered when the monks of Ligugé went into exile; and they knew, too, that those whom he considered responsible for this catastrophe would suffer the onslaught of his invective. In Huysmans' opinion, the Catholics of France were no less guilty than Waldeck-Rousseau and Émile Combes, and in a letter to Leclaire[12] he insisted that 'this guttersnipe government hasn't sprung from a self-sown seed, but from the general cowardice and stupidity of the Catholics'. He had therefore decided that laymen, priests, and monks should all be pilloried in *L'Oblat* for having failed in their duty to God and his Church. 'By heaven, but the Catholics are going to cop it in *L'Oblat!*' he wrote to Leclaire.[13] 'They may howl as much as they like, but they, the clergy and the religious orders are all going to hear a few home truths.' At one time,[14] losing patience with the forbearing policy of Leo XIII, who in his opinion should have threatened President Loubet with excommunication, he actually extended the scope of his indictment to the Vatican, and wrote: 'Before the year is out there won't be a monastery left in this filthy country. I'm slating it, the Government, the Pope, the clergy, everything, in *L'Oblat*. The book is going to create a tremendous stink.' As the months passed, however, his anger cooled and he consequently tempered the character of his novel: while still belabouring the anticlericals and the timorous Catholic laity, he merely chided the monastic orders for their faults and failings, and his references to the Pope were, he told Leclaire,[15] 'irreproachably respectful, affectionate, and false'. And shortly before the novel was published, its author admitted[16] that, 'all things considered, and apart from one or two little slaps, it's really quite kindly . . .'

The true significance of *L'Oblat* lies, not in its polemical or liturgical content, but in its treatment of what to Huysmans was the central problem of human existence: the question of suffering. Already, in *En Route* and *Sainte Lydwine*, he had exalted the doctrine of mystical substitution. Now, in *L'Oblat*, he traced that doctrine back to its origins in the Crucifixion, and in a memorable apotheosis of pain he personified Suffering as the betrothed of Christ. After picturing her in the Garden of Gethsemane, crowning her Bridegroom with 'a sweat of rubies, a diadem of bloody pearls', he went on to show her lavishing on Christ 'the only blandishments that were hers to offer — atrocious and superhuman torments':

Mary and Magdalen, the holy women, could not follow him wherever he was taken; but she accompanied him to the judgement hall, before Herod and before Pilate; she inspected the lashes of the whips; she increased the weight of the hammers; she made certain that the thorns were spiky, that the vinegar was bitter, that the spear and the nails were sharp.

And when the supreme moment of the marriage had come, while Mary, Magdalen, and St. John stood in tears at the foot of the Cross, she, like that Poverty of whom St. Francis spoke, climbed resolutely on to the gibbet-bed; and from the union of these two outcasts of the world, the Church was born, coming forth in a torrent of blood and water from the Victim's heart. And then it was over. Christ had given up the ghost, had escaped for ever from her embrace. She had been widowed in the very moment that she had been loved, but she came down from Calvary rehabilitated by that love, redeemed by that death.

Spurned like the Messiah, she had been uplifted with him, and from the height of the Cross she too had dominated the world; her mission was now ratified and ennobled; henceforth she was comprehensible to Christians, and until the end of time she would be loved by souls who would call upon her to hasten the expiation of their sins and those of others, and would love her in remembrance and in imitation of the Passion of Christ.

In the same chapter of *L'Oblat* Huysmans showed the Virgin as being also dedicated to suffering, and described her agony of mind before the Crucifixion, thus realizing an idea[17] formulated in 1899: 'There is a Virgin in a certain spiritual condition of whom no one has spoken and whom I'm tempted to describe . . . the Waiting Virgin, she who is straining to hear whether her Son will be condemned and to what he will be condemned, the Madonna of Fear, of apprehension more terrible than certainty.' Huysmans maintained that Mary was the one human being over whom Suffering had no rights, but that in imitation of her Son she renounced this immunity, 'wishing to suffer as much as it was in her power to suffer'. Thus he united woman and suffering in a common rehabilitation, and made amends for the misogyny of his earlier novels; for in the person of the *Regina martyrum* he represented woman, no longer as Satan's catspaw, but – by virtue of her sufferings – as an instrument of salvation, the glorious mediatrix and redeemer of mankind.

Finally, fortified by the supreme example of Christ and his Mother, Huysmans accepted in *L'Oblat* the personal implications of the Dolorist philosophy, and thus infused a new meaning into the unchanging pattern of his novels. Whereas his heroes had previously abandoned their escapist dreams with reluctance and despair, Durtal now resigned himself to the will of God, declaring: 'There is much to atone for. If the divine rod is ready to chastise us, let us bare our backs for it; let us show at least a little willingness . . .'

Anxious to communicate this message to his readers, and eager to instruct them in liturgics, Huysmans gave but little thought to the form of his novel. He was content that a thin story – an account of the evacuation of Ligugé – should distinguish L'Oblat from its uneventful predecessor, and that a little comic relief should sugar the liturgical pill. 'The Liturgy is going to be rather difficult to fit in,' he told Adolphe Berthet in January 1902,[18] 'and not very exciting for the reader, I'm afraid. Still, I'm keeping his Mme Bavoil to cheer him up a little.' And to Henri d'Hennezel, who intended to write a similar work on the Liturgy in Lyons, he explained[19] how to disguise an erudite treatise in novel form:

The devices you can use – conversations, soliloquies, or personal chapters – are not very varied, but after all they serve their purpose. Obviously, as we've said before, a novel planned on those lines is a mongrel and a hybrid, but there's nothing else to be done. Otherwise your book is certain to be a flop, because no one will read a brochure on the Liturgy, the clergy least of all. And after all, you are doing useful work in masking the taste of technique with a succulent sauce.

In L'Oblat, however, Huysmans spread this sauce so thinly that his didactic purpose, and the devices indicated in his revealing letter to d'Hennezel, were only too apparent. Nor was he able to lend coherence to the miscellaneous information he had accumulated, and Léon Blum was justified in observing, in an otherwise favourable review,[20] that 'this book is incredibly disorderly. To obtain some idea of it, imagine a mixture of fragments from a treatise on ecclesiastical history, a horticultural manual, and a museum catalogue, interspersed with articles from La Croix and heterogeneous descriptions

... At no point does the composition reveal the slightest regard for artistic effect.' But if Huysmans was conscious of having produced a literary hydra scarcely less repellent than *La Cathédrale*, he showed no great concern: composition had never been his *forte*, and form was now the least of his preoccupations.

The first three weeks of December were spent revising and copying out the manuscript of *L'Oblat*, which was to be delivered to Stock on Christmas Day.[21] Writing to Leclaire on the 14th, Huysmans complained that he was continually being interrupted by visitors, among them Henriette du Fresnel.

> I'm being pestered [he wrote] by the little bird, who has flown away from her château for a few days and flutters around in the flat here for hours at a time. The worst of it is that this little *ingénue* isn't entirely lacking in cunning. As she stays with her grandmother whenever she's in Paris, and as the aforementioned grandmother is an austere lady of the noble Faubourg who would never allow her to come, she creates alibis with afternoon tea-parties, where she goes to be seen before rushing here. Finding this rather embarrassing, I went to see her confessor this morning, but I found myself faced with an inscrutable Jesuit, and after dropping a few hints I kept quiet, for fear of stirring up trouble without real cause. As for trying to remonstrate with her myself, her only reply is to make sheep's eyes at me. All the same, it's rather annoying, because it might lead to gossip and scandal-mongering, when in fact, of course, there's really nothing between us.

Another visitor in December was the young writer Myriam Harry, who in 1901 had sent Huysmans a novel of hers about life in China, *Petites Épouses*. Imagining that the author of this book was 'a male Loti, a cunning young naval officer who had disguised himself as a woman to win success', Huysmans had addressed his thanks to 'Monsieur Myriam

Harry'; and it was therefore with some apprehension that the 'impostor' called on the notorious misogynist one December afternoon. She was quickly reassured. In her memoirs,[22] and in conversations with the present author, Mme Harry has described the scene in Huysmans' study on the first afternoon of their acquaintance: herself perched on a stiff little settee, while he sat in a cane-chair by his writing-table, one slippered foot swinging as he talked, and a ray of wintry sunshine touching 'the enormous shaven skull with its bulging Memling brow, one deep-set blue eye gleaming with malice, the curled-up tip of a discoloured moustache, and the point of a silvery beard which a soft, slender hand was stroking'. From time to time Huysmans would get up and, 'soft-footed, his figure bent to one side, he padded up and down the room, brushing the bookshelves like a voluptuous cat'. His conversation with Myriam Harry ranged over the position of women writers, the stupidity of the secular clergy, succubi and larvae, and the art of the Primitives. These were all subjects which inspired interest, anger, or enthusiasm in him, but it was not until he began to speak of the Virgin that he showed of what impassioned eloquence he was capable. 'Then,' says Mme Harry, 'as he spoke, a pink flush stained the ivory of his cheeks; his delicate hands, one of which still held a forgotten cigarette, excitedly described little simple gestures; his moustache and his beard quivered; and his extraordinary eyes, his lavender-blue, amethyst-blue eyes, set beneath the proud arch of his brows, made one think of the soft blue of rose-windows lit by a sunshine of the spirit . . .'

In January, only three months after the death of Émile Zola, Paris witnessed the rebirth of Edmond de Goncourt, in the persons of his ten 'academicians'. Although the validity of Edmond's will had been established in 1900, the Academy had been obliged to apply for legal authorization under the provisions of the Law on Associations, and it was not until 19 January 1903 that Émile Combes signed the official decree recognizing its 'public utility'.[23] The members met at Léon Hennique's flat on the 12th to make arrangements for the first of their monthly dinners, which was held on 26 February at the Grand-Hôtel. The first Prix Goncourt was to be awarded at the end of the year, and in May Huysmans wrote[24] to Dom Besse: 'I'm looking for a decent piece of work to which we can give the prize of 5,000 francs. Where is that *rara avis*?' After reading through an 'appalling pile of obscene and imbecile novels',[25] he found it in *Force ennemie* by John-Antoine Nau (Eugène Torquet), a brilliant study of mental disintegration which was awarded the prize on 22 December.[26] Huysmans was delighted that the voting had gone in favour of his candidate, especially when he discovered that Nau was a poor and unknown author living in the south of France, who had got into debt through publishing his novel at his own expense, and who had not even heard of the Prix Goncourt.[27] But the choice of *Force ennemie* has not been ratified by posterity.

For some time the Leclaires had been pressing Huysmans to visit them at Lourdes, not only to gather material for a book on the town which they hoped he might write, but also to meet a young Carmelite novice who would soon be making her solemn vows and retiring from sight into the convent enclosure. To his astonishment, Huysmans learnt that this young woman, who had taken the name of Sister Thérèse de Jésus, was the daughter of his old enemy the Countess de Galoez. Leclaire sent him a photograph of Sister Thérèse in January, and in his reply[28] Huysmans wrote: 'She is indeed charming – and I can't see much of the mother in her except perhaps the mouth. Ah, but Providence has been good to her in freeing her from the clutches of that demoniac, who used to read her . . . Voltaire!'

After sending out review copies of *L'Oblat* on 2 March, Huysmans travelled to Lourdes on the 5th.[29] A week later he reported to Landry[30] that he was living 'all by myself in a villa belonging to the Carmel and not far from the Leclaires – with a view from my window of the Basilica, the Grotto blazing with light day and night, and the chain of the Pyrenees'. Though exhausted by weeks of proof-reading and illness, he was soon busy making notes on what he saw at Lourdes, and he wrote[31] to the Abbé Mugnier:

I've found a friend in a young Father of the Grotto who is giving me all the information I want and taking me everywhere. It's all very interesting. A religion peculiar to this place, a religion of apotheosis and glorification, of gold paint and electric light. But to compensate for this appalling hotchpotch there's an excellent choir, which leaves Solesmes far behind and on certain days is simply magnificent.

I'm practically living with the Carmelites and I've had some interesting conversations in their parlour, so that I shall come back splendidly documented on them. They are very worthy women whom the Leclaires have saved from ruin, and they are very grateful. What's more, they are extremely enthusiastic about *L'Oblat*, and say that it's the first time anyone has talked to them like that about the Liturgy . . .

As for the Grotto, it's delightful to be in that little fiery nook when no one else is there. Lourdes is the town of water and fire. When I'm home again I must see what symbols I can find in all this . . .

Unfortunately for Lourdes, Huysmans did not confine himself to inoffensive meditations on the symbolism of fire and water. He looked at Lourdes – at the Basilica, the Rosary, the Esplanade, and the Stations of the Cross on the slope of the Espélugues – and was roused by what he saw to a fury of invective and abuse remarkable even for such a past master in the art of vituperation. For beside the architectural and artistic atrocities which had been perpetrated in this holy place, the horrors of the Rue Saint-Sulpice paled into innocuous insignificance. To take but one example, the church of the Rosary appeared to the author of *La Cathédrale* as a cross between a hippodrome, a casino, and a railway station; as 'a gigantic crab stretching its pincers towards the old town'; as a 'dropsical circus with its rounded belly bulging beneath it'; as a 'mould for a Savoy cake, flanked by three domed boiler-covers made of zinc'. This 'plethora of vileness', this 'haemorrhage of bad taste' went so far beyond the limits of human iniquity that Huysmans could account for it only by attributing it to diabolical suggestion, the intervention of the Evil One. And after inspecting the paintings inside the Rosary, he wrote[32] in his notebook: 'It's truly frightful. These men Doze and Grellet are not even *bad* painters. Either they or the people who ordered such trash from them must have been inspired by Satan . . . The Devil has quietly intervened to make sure that nothing decent is offered to Our Lady: that is his vengeance.'

Even in the Carmel of Notre-Dame de Lourdes Huysmans was outraged by the ugliness of his surroundings, but here there were compensations. The nuns treated him with great courtesy and kindness, and on the 21st, the Feast of St. Benedict, the whole convent took communion for him as a mark of admiration and respect.[33] It was in the Carmel, too, that Huysmans met Sister Thérèse de Jésus.[34] In a letter to Georges Landry[35] he told how, one day, he was allowed to talk with her through the grille in the convent parlour. He decided that she was more like her mother than her photograph had led him to suppose, but 'angelic and young'. She sat with a work-basket on her lap and the still, veiled figure of the mistress of novices beside her, and cried softly whenever she spoke of her satanic mother. A few days later, on the 22nd, Huysmans wrote in another letter to Landry:[36] 'Sister Thérèse de Jésus will be making her profession one of these days, and I shall see her in the parlour, wearing her crown of roses, for the last time – for afterwards she will no longer be visible, even for her father.' Sister Thérèse made her final vows on the 25th, the Feast of the Annunciation,[37] and this was, in fact, the last time that Huysmans saw her. But he never forgot her, nor she him, and in one of the last letters he wrote before he died[38] he thanked her for her solicitude and her prayers.

Huysmans returned to Paris on 1 April, having decided to go to Lourdes again in September to see the great autumn pilgrimages.[39] In his flat he found a pile of books and letters which had arrived for him, including a summons to appear as a witness that very day in the Seine police court, where Henri Villars (better known as Willy) was being charged with writing and publishing an immoral novel. Remembering, perhaps, that as a young man he himself had written the first French brothel-novel and two poems of almost unprintable obscenity,[40] he hurried to the court to give evidence for his accused confrère. 'I came off with two or three words in the witness box', he told Leclaire[41] on the 4th. 'The magistrates, I must say, treated me with perfect deference, and there was a flattering murmur from the public when I appeared.' But the unfortunate Willy was found guilty, and fined 1,000 francs.

It was a busy week for Huysmans. He had to see Stock about the sales of *L'Oblat*; he had to spend a few hours with Girard, who was about to set off on another of his theatrical tours; he had to deal with the 'little bird', who was staying with her grandmother again and wanted to see him. And finally, on the morning of the 4th, he saw Jean de Caldain off on the train to Baronville, where the young man was going to train as a novice. 'Alas!' he wrote to Leclaire,[42] 'I fear no good will come of this drastic measure. He was dying of hunger, having been unable to sell any of his paintings. He's very pious, but too intelligent; he knows his monks and isn't afraid to pass judgement on them. So how will he be able to bear living with them?'

The bitterness of this comment was partly due to criticism which Dom Bourigaud had made of *L'Oblat* in the April issue of the abbey journal, the *Bulletin de Saint-Martin*. Huysmans had expected criticism of his novel – indeed, he had told Leclaire[43] that the book would 'explode like a bomb-shell' – but he had not expected it to come from the Benedictines of Ligugé. Though few of the good monks can have relished the novelist's detailed description of their facial features and personal habits, Huysmans himself was genuinely convinced that he had portrayed them in a flattering light. On the other hand, he made no secret of the malicious joy he had taken in settling old scores with the squire of Ligugé, a certain Courcy, and the parish priest, the Abbé Andrault, who were savagely caricatured in *L'Oblat* as the Baron des Atours and the Abbé Barbenton. Indeed, in a letter he had written to Mme Leclaire in December 1902,[44] he had looked ahead to the publication of his novel and expressed doubts as to 'whether the parish priestlet of Ligugé and the noble Courcy will be feeling very happy then, for I've painted portraits of them which I'm pleased to think are excellent likenesses'. It was probably in response to complaints from 'the noble Courcy' that the Abbot of Ligugé published his 'Necessary Protest' against *L'Oblat*, in which he criticized 'a fanciful setting and irrelevant episodes in which a prominent place is given to grotesque or ridiculous characters representing monks and other respectable persons'. After reading this, the novelist wrote indignantly[45] to Leclaire: 'I've made his monks grotesque indeed! – and what if I'd made them true to life and depicted Chamard and Besse as they really are? I've exalted them tremendously, and to deny this is to show appallingly bad faith.' He was tempted to make a public reply to the Abbot's article, but refrained from doing so because 'in the first place, the protest has had no effect on the Paris Press, and then . . . these are such evil times that it is good to acquire the virtues of patience and charity'.[46]

He was comforted and cheered by letters from many quarters, praising *L'Oblat* and deprecating Dom Bourigaud's 'Necessary Protest'. Dom Coëtlosquet, Abbot of Saint-Maur, Dom Pothier, Abbot of Saint-Wandrille, and Dom Logerot, now Prior of Kergonan, all made appreciative comments on the book. From Farnborough, Dom Cabrol acclaimed 'the long-awaited liturgical novel' and assured its author that it would be read in his refectory 'even in Lent'. He added: 'The poor Benedictines get a few knocks in the book, but – hear ye this – they really rather deserve them, between ourselves, very much between ourselves.'[47] But perhaps the letter which pleased Huysmans most of all was one from the Jesuit critic Henri Bremond, who wrote to him: 'Do you know that your page on Christ's betrothal to Suffering is of sovereign beauty?' Quoting this appreciation to Leclaire,[48] Huysmans remarked: 'At last, someone who has understood!'

As the weeks passed, it seemed that the storm in a teacup raised by Dom Bourigaud's reproof had completely subsided, and that Huysmans would now be left in peace. On 1 May,

Huysmans in 1903.

however, Jean Rodes published in *Le Temps* the 'Opinion of a Benedictine of Ligugé on M. Huysmans', an interview with a censorious monk (a certain Dom Paul Roche) who repeated the terms of Dom Bourigaud's protest, cast doubts on the permanence of a conversion which sprang from 'an exacerbated sensibility and an artistic dilettantism', and concluded: 'I very much fear that M. Huysmans may be another Léo Taxil, a very superior Léo Taxil no doubt, but who, like the first, will perhaps turn against us one day.' This time the provocation was too great for Huysmans to remain silent, and the next day *Le Temps* published a letter in which he accused the Benedictines of a lack of humility in 'refusing to accept any criticism, however mild'. To Leclaire he wrote: 'I've tried not to be spiteful in my letter, taking care at the same time to avoid the traps I suspect they have laid for me to make me admit that the Val des Saints is Ligugé; but if the Abbot replies, well and good, my conscience will be clear and I shall hit back hard with references to La Tremblaye and the Solesmes business.'[49] Dom Bourigaud, however, made no further comment on Huysmans' novel, and soon peaceful and friendly relations were restored between author and abbey.

In June Huysmans' teeth began troubling him once more, and he reported to Leclaire[50] that he seemed to be spending his life at the dentist's and had been put on a diet of minced-meat and eggs. The kindness and company of his friends were a great comfort to him in these trials. From the Château de la Colombière, the 'little bird' sent him baskets of flowers and new-laid eggs 'to console me for my miserable mug'. Dom Besse and Forain dined with him on the 7th and kept him amused all evening, though he continued to deplore their folly – the monk's in forever evolving bigger and bolder schemes for his monastery, and the artist's in forever buying bigger and more expensive motor-cars for himself. The Abbé Mugnier and Lucien Descaves also came to see him, and each later received his meed of affectionate praise. The priest, who would burst in on Huysmans after a long spell in the confessional, complaining that people took communion too often and begging the novelist for striking tail-pieces for his sermons, evoked the comment: 'What a dear madman!' And the writer, who had published in the *Écho de Paris* a sympathetic article on the Little Sisters of the Poor which had earned him some insults from anticlerical colleagues, was praised as 'a thoroughly decent sort: upright, outspoken, and unsectarian'.

Other visitors that summer included Mme Théophile Huc and Arij Prins. Mme Huc, the sister-in-law of the famous explorer, had been in correspondence with Huysmans since 1899, when she had been emboldened to send him the first of many consignments of southern delicacies, in an attempt to overcome his prejudices against the Midi and all its works.[51] Though he had mentioned her in *L'Oblat*, where Durtal receives 'mouth-watering sweetmeats from a friend who lives in the south and cooks them herself', he had not met her before the summer of 1903. But on 23 June he wrote to Leclaire: 'Seen Mme Huc! A charming old lady, like an older edition of little Gaëlle; the same lack of ceremony, but more calm and common sense.'

Prins arrived in Paris on 29 July and stayed at Huysmans' flat for a fortnight. 'Meanwhile,' the novelist told Leclaire,[52] 'I'm walking him gently round the museums and through the few tolerable streets left in modern Paris.' Huysmans intended to travel to Lourdes on 20 August, a week after Prins' departure, but at the last moment stomach trouble and a recurrence of the pains in his jaw prevented him from making the journey.[53]

By September he had recovered sufficiently to be present, on the 8th, at the marriage of Georges Landry to his mistress, a woman of whom Huysmans, Louise Read, and other friends strongly disapproved.[54] Memories of another wedding he had attended were evoked about this time by a letter he received from Alice Poictevin, who was now living with her husband at Menton. 'Poictevin is having more of his fits of insanity', he told Leclaire.[55] 'I suspected as much from the mad missives he's been sending me lately. The poor girl doesn't know what to do. She can be sure of one thing at least – that her marriage has been a real atonement for her illicit liaison.' There were times, however, when he dropped the scornful mask he normally wore when discussing marriage, and stood revealed as a lonely and unhappy man whose own dreams of a contented married life had been finally shattered ten years before. Such an occasion has been described by Mme Myriam Harry in her memoirs,[56] where she writes:

We had been talking about love until late in the afternoon. The maid had not come with the lamp as she usually did, and darkness and silence were invading the room. I could still see the gleam of the gold lettering on the books, and the shining reflection of the Persian plate in the mirror. The mica panes of the stove were glowing red, but on the mantelpiece the delf vases, with their bunches of box looking like dark heads of hair, were taking on a dying pallor.

'Who knows?' said Huysmans. 'Perhaps my life has been a failure. Perhaps I wasn't meant for solitude . . .'

It seemed to me that I could see tears sparkling on his waxy cheeks. I got up, feeling embarrassed and distressed. The weary head dropped on to the angel-table, and in the silent twilight I could hear Huysmans weeping . . .

A few days after Landry's wedding Huysmans left Paris on a second sightseeing tour with the Abbé Mugnier, this time in Germany as well as Belgium.[57] Their first stop was at Strasbourg, where they put up at the Hôtel des Deux Clefs, a hostelry with a 'table d'hôte for toothless folk'. From Strasbourg they travelled to Colmar, 'a town less marked by the Prussian stamp', where Huysmans spent many hours in the museum examining the paintings by Matthaeus Grünewald which he was to describe in *Trois Primitifs*. On 23 September the two friends were lodged at the Hôtel des Trois Rois in Basle; but after only a day in this 'modern and far too opulent town', this 'cosmopolitan and Calvinist city', they left for Freiburg, where they registered at the Angel Hotel. The Abbé Mugnier was travelling in his cassock and beginning to regret it, for the children of Freiburg, unaccustomed to such a sight, ran after him shouting: '*Laudetur Jesus Christus!*' and asking for his blessing. The same thing happened at Mainz, where Huysmans and the Abbé arrived on the 25th. The architecture of this town, with its 'heavy, pretentious buildings oozing luxury', displeased the novelist, while his first impression of the Cathedral, with its riot of different styles, was summed up in the words: 'Prrtt, it's a lunatic!' And finding that on one side the Cathedral was hemmed in by a row of houses, he added mischievously: 'A lunatic they've had to shut up.'

Their next stop, Frankfurt-am-Main, with its palatial hotels, imposing banks, and glittering shop-windows, impressed Huysmans above all as the capital of Jewry – and the old city, with its poor Christian population and quiet streets, as a sort of 'Catholic ghetto'. He refused to accompany the Abbé Mugnier on a pilgrimage to the birthplace of Goethe, whom he classed with Schiller as an 'inexorable bore', but went instead to see the art collection at the Staedel Institute. Here two paintings fascinated him, giving him 'sacred and profane pleasure': a picture of the Virgin by the Maître de Flémalle, and a striking portrait by an unknown artist of an unknown girl, a 'pretty and implacable androgyne', whom Huysmans later sought to identify as Giulia Farnese, the mistress of Rodrigo de Borgia.

From Frankfurt the two friends travelled to Cologne, a city which Huysmans had never liked and which again displeased him. The Cathedral in particular disappointed him once more, and he described it in his notebook as 'not very exciting, and as false as the pictures in the museum, with the exception of a few Primitives'. The 'Prussian regimentation' which had annoyed him in the German hotels, where guests were strictly disciplined by commissionaires, head-waiters, and printed instructions, manifested itself again in the Cathedral, where a notice announced, in French: 'The porters have orders to repress any riotous behaviour.' It was with a feeling of relief that the sometime Germanophile and his friend found themselves on the other side of the Belgian frontier.

In Belgium they visited only two cities: Brussels and Antwerp. In his notebook Huysmans praised a restaurant in the capital called *La Faille déchirée*, where he and the Abbé were served with Zealand oysters by a waiter who looked like an aged Forain. On the other hand, he complained that the churches were closed in the afternoon, with the exception of one dedicated to St. Anthony of Padua and equipped with an electric bell-push beside each confessional. He found Antwerp far more congenial, on account of its Hôtel Central, its quayside taverns, its museums – and its climate. Many years later the Abbé Mugnier would recall his friend pointing to the grey, melancholy sky over Antwerp, and observing in satisfied tones: 'Abbé, there's a decent sky for you!' But it was neither the climate nor the taverns nor the museums which most pleased Huysmans at Antwerp: it was an ant-eater which he saw at the zoological gardens. And with that attention to detail and that delight in the unusual and the grotesque which were so much part of his character, he entered into his notebook a lengthy description of this 'incredible animal which would have enraptured Bosch . . . a comical cross between a tapir and a wild boar'.

On his return to Paris[58] Huysmans told Mme Huc: 'We've seen some admirable Primitives and some magnificent churches, the latter somewhat spoilt by the arrogant regulations of unpleasant Teutons.' But if the German art-collections had pleased him, the German hotels and hotel-keepers had not, and in another letter[59] he wrote: 'What bliss to leave all that behind and come home.'

Even at home, however, life was far from pleasant. In October Huysmans was confined to his rooms with 'a terrible cold which makes game of potions and vesicants',[60] while in December the 'Grand Lama of dentistry' ordered him to wear 'a dear little contraption which grips my jaw and makes me feel as though I were perpetually eating green apples'.[61] Moreover, the peace he had enjoyed in his Rue de Babylone flat was a thing of the past, and in a letter to Leclaire he complained of 'the two shrews who live above me and throw furniture around from nine in the evening until eleven or even midnight. It's impossible to sleep with those madwomen in the house – and complaints have no effect at all. In their defence it must be added that the ceilings are thin, and for my consolation that they haven't a piano. But all the same, the impossibility of finding peace in this life asserts itself once more.'

Vexations of a different kind were inflicted on the novelist at this time by Henriette du Fresnel, who informed him that she had fallen in love with him and wished to marry him.[62] On 11 November he wrote to Leclaire:

I'm having a lot of trouble with my little bird. I've had some quite incredible letters from her, but fortunately when she comes here she restrains her feelings. Her mother came to see me, very annoyed by all this, but in the end she said that with an imagination like that she daren't clip her wings. So what's to be done? The little one knows very well that I shan't marry her. It's all very bothersome and ridiculous – and comical too when you consider that here Potiphar's wife is innocent and doesn't know what she wants, while Joseph isn't innocent but would dearly love to have peace. Anyway, she's making a retreat just now at the Sacré Cœur, and I hope that will calm her down . . .

This retreat apparently had the desired effect, for on the 28th Huysmans wrote to Leclaire:

The affair of the 'little bird' has taken a new turn. Ten minutes after coming out of her retreat, she came to see me, behaving very calmly and reasonably, and telling me that in the present circumstances it would be better for her to take the veil. And she added that the only problem was to decide whether to enter the Sacré Cœur or the Rue Monsieur. It's quite certain that only the cloister could save her from herself, but with an imagination like hers I doubt whether she could stay there. In any event, if she wants to become a Benedictine nun, she would do much better to go to En-Calcat, to Father Romain's monastery of Sainte-Scolastique, than to the Rue Monsieur. But will she take the veil? Her brother came to see me yesterday and didn't appear to think it a serious possibility. But what a little lunatic she is! Anyway, she's just written to tell me that henceforth she will love me only filially. That would suit me well – provided that she stayed in her château . . .

By mid-December Huysmans was convinced that he had nothing more to fear from this quarter. 'My little bird has been here,' he told Leclaire,[63] 'but with her papa – and that, as she puts it, "isn't the same thing". Still, pending Father Auriault's decision, she seems to be much calmer. It's true that she still throws me a few sad and languorous looks, but she's quietening down. If she takes the veil she can put her feelings into prayers for me, and then everything will be perfect.'

Meanwhile Huysmans continued to be tormented in his Rue de Babylone flat by disturbances which he attributed to both natural and supernatural causes. In January 1904[64] he asked Leclaire to send him some tapers from Lourdes to combat strange 'diabolical attacks' which he suffered on retiring for the night; and by lighting these tapers whenever he sensed an inimical presence he was eventually able to obtain some measure of peace.[65] But tapers could not exorcize the more commonplace annoyances to which he was subjected. One of his neighbours was learning to play the flute, and every evening practised on his instrument with great determination but little success, encouraged and abetted by his piano-playing wife.[66] In the flat above, the 'two shrews' persisted in trundling furniture about at all hours of the night, disregarding all the novelist's verbal or written pleas and protests. The only explanation of their antics which occurred to him was that one of the women was being attacked by the Devil and was using noisier weapons of defence than lighted tapers. In conversation with Mme Myriam Harry[67] he complained:

'It's the sanctimonious old woman living above me – the one you've met on the stairs, rattling her rosaries like a mare clanking its curb-chains. Ah! the old harridan! It isn't enough for her to trail larvae around in her petti-coats during the day: at night she goes completely crazy. For then she's besieged and beleaguered by Satan. She defends herself as best she can, barricading her door with furniture she drags across the room – you can imagine the din that goes on above me! And then, in spite of it all, the Devil gets in and attacks her. She throws her rosaries, her crucifix, her firedogs and her broomstick at him, retreats behind her bed, hides under the chairs. Oh, I can assure you there's hell let loose upstairs! And that goes on all night . . . Lord, what a wretched business! Shall I never find peace anywhere? Here I've barely settled down and I'm just getting accus-tomed to this hole when I have to start looking for another flat . . . All the same, Lord, you're coming it rather strong . . .'

Writing to Dom Ernest Micheau in January,[68] Huysmans said that he trembled at the thought of moving his belongings and his library of 3,000 books to yet another home. Even more appalling was the difficulty of finding a flat which offered some guarantee of peace, for Paris seemed to be occupied by an army of instrumentalists: even in the Rue Monsieur con-vent, where a friend of the novelist's called Godard had recently settled, an enthusiastic pianist spent her days creating an unholy cacophony.[69] But at last a suitable flat was found for him in his old *quartier*. It was a pleasant fifth-floor flat, commanding a view of Saint-Sulpice and Saint-Germain-des-Prés; the rent was not exorbitant; and the owner of the apartment-house was an admirer of Huysmans' works. The novelist was attracted too by the name of the street – the Rue Saint-Placide – for it was that of St. Benedict's companion, and it seemed to hold a promise of peace. On 17 February he wrote to Leclaire:

I'm moving house, beaten by the two trollops upstairs and so unstrung by the noise that it would make me ill if I stayed here any longer. The landlord finally decided that they were in the right, and there was nothing I could do but reply by giving him notice. So I'm going to No. 31 Rue Saint-Placide, where I hope to be settled in a fortnight's time. After visiting masses of flats and coming to the unhappy conclusion that I shouldn't find one to accommodate my bookcases for less than 2,000 francs, I managed to rent one in the end for 1,365 francs – a delightful flat in a smart house with carpeted stairs. It was my friend the oblate, the master at the École Centrale whom you've met here, who found it – in the house where he lives himself. He has made careful inquiries about the neighbouring tenants. There are no pianos, except at a safe distance; the street is paved with wood; in fact I have every possible guarantee. It's on the fifth floor, with a balcony, a big ante-room, a dining-room, a big study, two fine bedrooms, a bathroom, and a room for the maid. How wonderful to think that now perhaps I shall be able to get some sleep . . .

The move was made on Tuesday, 1 March 1904. The young writer Joseph Ageorges, who went with him that day to the Rue Sainte-Placide, records that he fulminated against the architect of the house for having failed to provide niches for his statues of the Madonna and wall-space for all his bookcases.[70] But on the 5th he told Leclaire: 'It's finished! Everything is in place, in a charming, sunny flat. I'm sleeping peacefully too, without any hurly-burly going on above me, and with no sound but the dull rumble of traffic on a wooden causeway.' And a week later[71] he wrote: 'This is definitely the prettiest home I've ever had . . .'

It was also his last.

8. THE MARTYR

ON the day Huysmans moved into his new home in the Rue Saint-Placide, *Le Mois Littéraire et Pittoresque* published the first of his *Trois Primitifs*, 'Les Grünewald du Musée de Colmar'; and before the month was out he had begun work on his study of the other two subjects, 'Le Maître de Flémalle et la Florentine du Musée de Francfort-sur-le-Mein'. Writing to Mme Huc early in April,[1] he declared that he was in love with 'a little monster I glimpsed in the Museum at Frankfurt, and whom I believe to be Giulia Farnese, the young fifteen-year-old mistress of old Pope Borgia! At present I'm writing something on that deliciously depraved infanta. It's going to be rather highly spiced – but then, the end of the fifteenth century in Italy was so fantastic that one can't write about it without using a little seasoning.' Yet although he was afraid that this particular study would 'make the hair stand up on Catholic heads',[2] *Trois Primitifs* was accorded a mild reception when it was published in November 1904, and the author told Mme Leclaire[3] that 'no one has taken exception to it'.

Far more controversial were two prefaces by Huysmans which were published in the same year. In December 1903 he had written to Leclaire: 'I'm busy with a work which I'm finding extremely congenial. I'm preparing an anthology of all Verlaine's religious poems – the finest collection of prayers in rhyme since the Middle Ages – and I'm prefacing them with a foreword aimed at the Catholics. They'll find in it some amusing ideas which are sure to brush them up the wrong way.'[4] Certainly he could not expect the average churchgoer to appreciate his proposition that the only noteworthy Catholic writers and artists were converts who, like Verlaine, had tasted life's pleasures and griefs to the full. Nor could he expect the clergy or the laity to understand him when he declared that the works he had written since his own conversion all stemmed from *A Rebours* – as he did in the important preface to a new edition of that novel published by the Société des Cent Bibliophiles. This edition was brought out in the spring of 1904 at the same time as Verlaine's *Poésies religieuses*, and on 29 April Huysmans wrote to Leclaire:[5]

At the moment I've got the Press nagging at me. The preface to *A Rebours*, coming on top of the preface to the Verlaine book, has had the good fortune to exasperate the Catholics and they have begun harping again on that same old string – the destruction of my earlier books. I told them to go to hell in one or two interviews, and to my astonishment this doesn't appear to have pleased them. Oh, the imbecility, the bigotry of these people! . . . The idea, too, that Verlaine was a great poet, the only Catholic poet, drives them to distraction. Again and again they come back to the point that he was a drunkard and a sodomite. They must be very pure themselves, these people, to be so fond of condemning others . . .

Huysmans was somewhat preoccupied with questions of morality at this time, for on 12 March he had announced to Leclaire:[6] 'I'm saddled with another Sol, much more dangerous than the first . . . and at present I can assure you it's all very annoying. I've avoided trouble so far, but the minx is determined to have her way.' The present author is not at liberty to disclose the identity of the woman whom Huysmans accused, in this and other letters to Leclaire, of trying to seduce him, and will therefore call her by the time-honoured and convenient name of 'Mme X'.[7] He would also point out that he has discovered no evidence to support Huysmans' allegations about 'Mme X', and would suggest that the novelist, already disturbed by Henriette du Fresnel's attentions, may perhaps have placed a mistaken interpretation on innocent demonstrations of affection. But whatever the truth of the matter, on 24 March 1904 we find Huysmans confiding to Leclaire:[8]

I feel rather happier about my amazon, in spite of her terrible remark: 'My dear, why struggle so, when you know that we must come to that in the end?' That's just what I don't want at any price – to 'come to that'. The strange thing from the psychological point of view is that the greatest help to me in this situation has come from my little bird. She writes me such sweet, affectionately chaste letters, that I've been obliged to draw a comparison between them, and have decided that if the one is very sensuous and attractive, the other, though nothing of the kind, has a charming little soul, which I hadn't noticed as long as there was no question of comparison. And since there must always be a bit of petticoat in a man's life, I prefer the little bird, who represents no danger at all and with whom it is more a question of the Blessed Virgin than of anything else. She will never know what a good service she has done me, in making me feel disgust for the other one . . .

In April Huysmans told Leclaire[9] that 'Mme X' had been to see him while he was confined to his rooms with influenza, and that he had 'persuaded her to leave me in peace and to stop asking me for *d'inutiles soubresauts accompagnés d'un peu de projection de boue blanche . . .*'

Meanwhile Henriette du Fresnel was trying to decide the question of her future; and in June, after long discussions with Father Auriault, her confessor, Dom Romain Banquet, Abbot of En-Calcat, and the Abbess, she made up her mind to enter the Abbey of Sainte-Scolastique. On the 29th Huysmans wrote to Leclaire:[10]

When the decision was taken the little bird, still feeling rather sad at heart, came to take refuge with me here for the afternoon, for the family are not taking the news very well. Oh, what melancholy days we've spent together! In spite of myself I've become very fond of her, and the thought of her leaving grieves me. A few days ago she said very sweetly to me: 'I'm not labouring under any delusions. I know that you have never loved me except supernaturally, and that you won't suffer when I leave you.' Poor kid! But it's fortunate that things are like that, because otherwise what might not happen? . . .

There will be a difficult moment when we have to say goodbye. I beg you to pray, and ask others to pray, for my little bird, that God may strengthen her sense of vocation, or give it to her if she lacks it, for it would be appalling if she came back from the cloister. I'm somewhat reassured, though, by Father Romain, who is truly a holy man; and I'm certain that he will do whatever is necessary and see clearly into her soul. My own opinion is that she's an impulsive person whom only the cloister can save from herself. But she's so independent! What an effort she will have to make to conform to monastic discipline! Still, God can arrange that. She is already greatly altered since taking her decision, and she is certainly very much in God at present. If only it will last! What a difference, all the same, between the thin, determined little creature of today and the pink-checked, merry little romp who used to bring me bunches of flowers from the park! God assuredly does well what he does. He has her in his power. This is the only possible solution to a problem of this kind.

The melancholy note sounded in this letter was echoed in others which Huysmans wrote during this summer of 1904, as he watched one Parisian convent after another closing its doors. The high altar of the Abbaye-aux-Bois had already been dismantled and sent abroad, and in July Combes ordered the closing of the Benedictine convent in the Rue Monsieur. 'Soon we shall be reduced to our parish church,' Huysmans told Dom Micheau,[11] 'until that too is closed. You can imagine that it's not without a certain sadness that I envisage this dismal prospect. No more plainchant, nothing. A few pious rigadoons on Sunday and that will be all. The bread and water of religion . . .'

Yet even the bread and water of religion in Paris was preferable, in his opinion, to the ecclesiastical confectionery of Lourdes, where the Leclaires were begging him to go once more. He had been appalled by the ugliness of the town when he had seen it during the quiet spring season, and the thought of joining the great crowds of pilgrims in the heat of summer became ever more repugnant to him. It was not as if his faith needed to be strengthened by the sight of miraculous cures, because, as he later wrote,[12] 'I know perfectly well that Our Lady can perform miracles at Lourdes and elsewhere; my faith depends neither on my reason nor on the more or less reliable perceptions of my senses; it springs from an inner feeling, a conviction based on internal proofs.' Nor did he feel any enthusiasm for the Leclaires' suggestion that he should write a book about Lourdes: though he knew that there was much in the work of Lasserre and Zola which ought to be refuted, he doubted whether the task should be undertaken by a writer who preferred the sorrowful Virgin of La Salette to the smiling Virgin of Lourdes, the medieval calm of Saint-Séverin to the noise and glitter of the Rosary. Yet at the beginning of September 1904, yielding to his friends' repeated pleas, he travelled south again to Lourdes.

The town was even noisier and more crowded than he had feared, and in a letter to the Abbé Mugnier[13] he wrote: 'I'm walking, eating and sleeping to the sound of *Ave Marias* going on day and night. Imagine a town of 8,000 inhabitants with 40,000 pilgrims sleeping, as in the Middle Ages, in the churches, for want of room, and again as in the Middle Ages, astonishing diseases, cases of elephantiasis and leprosy . . .' After spending three weeks mingling with the crowds, watching the sick being dipped in the baths, sitting in the Medical Bureau with Dr. Boissarie as he examined possible cures, and paying daily visits to the hospital of Notre-Dame-des-Sept-Douleurs, Huysmans returned to Paris on 24 September, thankful to escape from the din and bustle of Lourdes. What he had seen there had left him puzzled and perplexed, and he wrote[14] to Mme Huc: 'I don't see how I can possibly write about that strange place without laying myself open to attack by both Catholics and freethinkers.' However, he reluctantly set to work on the book, which was to occupy his attention until almost the end of his life.

During the winter of 1904 Huysmans was ill for several weeks with bronchitis and neuralgia. Alice Poictevin, whose husband had died in the spring, invited him to spend a month or two recuperating in the sunshine at Menton, but at Christmas he told Mme Huc[15] that he was 'sufficiently recovered not to go and waste my time down there'. Instead he continued to work on his book about Lourdes, as well as on 'Saint-Germain l'Auxerrois' and 'La Symbolique de Notre-Dame', two articles which were published in *Le Tour de France* early in 1905 and later included in the posthumous *Trois Églises et Trois Primitifs*. He also had to read dozens of new novels which had been entered for the second Prix Goncourt. Earlier in the year he had promised Mme Myriam Harry that he would propose and support her book *La Conquête de Jérusalem*, but in November his attention was drawn to a novel about a school in the poverty-stricken *quartier* of Ménilmontant, *La Maternelle* by Léon Frapié. Mme Harry has told in her memoirs[16] how, after reading Huysmans' copy of this work, she urged him to transfer his allegiance to Frapié, and it was *La Maternelle* which won the Prix Goncourt on 7 December.[17] But her disappointed feelings were soon assuaged and her gallantry rewarded, for in January 1905 the first Prix Vie Heureuse (later known as the Prix Femina) was awarded to *La Conquête de Jérusalem*.

According to the letters he wrote to Leclaire, the novelist's relations with Henriette du Fresnel and 'Mme X' became more complicated and troublesome than ever in these winter months. In October the 'little bird' had travelled to Stanbrook Abbey, near Worcester, for a short retreat, intending to 'elope' to Dourgne with the Abbess of Sainte-Scolastique as soon as she returned to France.[18] Her family, however, arranged that she should remain in England for three weeks until the disappointed Abbess had returned to her cloister. On 29 October Huysmans wrote to Leclaire:[19]

They are obviously prepared to do everything to prevent her from taking the veil. The worst of it all is that she doesn't seem to be as upset as one would expect. I've had a terrible letter from her saying that I knew she loved me with more than a sisterly love and that she wanted to know, once for all, whether I didn't love her in the same way – that she wished to be quite certain about this before entering the cloister! As if I hadn't told her a hundred times that marriage between the two of us was impossible! She knows this perfectly well, but she has such puerile ideas about love – kisses on the forehead, etc. I've refused all that, knowing very well – since I'm not a saint – that one evening it would end badly. So what's to be done? She refuses all the matches that are proposed to her, and it seems to me that she's not made for the cloister. If she weren't such an impulsive creature we could go on as we have for the past three years, with her coming here every month and nothing more – but she dreams of kisses! *Zut!* With her big, adoring eyes she's beginning to disturb my senses . . .

On her return from Worcester, in the evening of 6 November, Henriette took a cab from the Gare du Nord to the Rue Saint-Placide, to spend a few hours with Huysmans before catching the last train to Coulommiers.[20] As he had feared, her enthusiasm for the cloister had diminished, and she begged him 'not to send her there now'. 'She doesn't want to take the veil at all,' Huysmans lamented to Leclaire,[21] 'and declares that her cell is in the Rue Saint-Placide . . .' Worse still, to the novelist's horror and her confessor's disgust, she now set her heart on persuading Huysmans to kiss her; and to gain this end she contrived an ingenious scheme which Mother Scolastica recalled with gentle amusement thirty years later in a conversation, reported to the present author, with Christiane Aimery in 1941, and which Huysmans described in this letter[22] to Leclaire:

Her passion has now reached a point where nothing else

exists, and there are times when I have great difficulty in restraining her more dangerous outbursts of feeling. For months she has been dreaming of our kissing each other. This I've refused, knowing perfectly well where that sort of sport would lead me. But she badgered me so hard that in the end I said to her: 'Very well then, but only on condition that you obtain permission from your mother and Father Auriault.'

I thought that that would put an end to the matter – but she set to work, and by the most amazing diplomatic subterfuges extracted some sort of consent from her mother. On the other hand, Father Auriault, annoyed at her refusal to take the veil, said some extremely harsh things to her – notably that in her present emotional condition she was standing on the brink of the abyss. Whereupon I had a mad letter from her which began by saying that I must be a saint to save her, and ended by protesting that she adores me, that she doesn't quite know what Father Auriault means by the abyss, but that she's ready to fall into it with me!!!! and that she places herself entirely in my hands. The worst of it is that Father Auriault neither gave his permission for the kiss nor forbade it: he simply told her to consult her conscience. That really isn't good enough! – for her conscience will soon come to a decision, and on her next visit I shall find myself with my back to the wall.

What a terrible child she is! I can't tell you how sad and ironical it was to read the letter from little Thérèse de Jésus saying that she prays that she will take the veil and adding that 'one can rely on the Sacred Heart'. I wish I could believe that to be true, but ... there is obviously no hope now that she will ever enter the cloister. And if she did, she wouldn't stay there. I must admit, too, that my voice lacks conviction when I speak of the monasteries. They've disappointed me so much that I've no desire to send other people into them ...

In the following week events took a still more alarming

turn, and on 11 December Huysmans told Leclaire[23] that he was 'floundering in a situation which, unless there is some hope of divine intervention, is really desperate'. He went on:

Since my last letter things have come to a climax. The Devil has come on to the scene, and but for Our Lady's protection the irreparable would already have been done. The little one, staying in Paris for a few days, happened on the issue of *Femina* in which, referring to the possibility of giving the Prix Goncourt to a woman, I praised Myrrhiam [*sic*]. When the little one came to see me she began complaining about this, and was saying: '. . . I want to be the only woman you love!' when the maid announced – Myrrhiam! As she seemed really upset I was trying to persuade her at that moment that I didn't love Myrrhiam – which is true. But then she threw me such a tearful, entreating look that I said to the maid: 'Tell Mme Myrrhiam that I can't see her.' Obviously the little bird gained more in that one moment than in the past five years. Poor Myrrhiam, coming out of the kindness of her heart to ask how I was – if she only knew what a diabolical role she unwittingly played!

To cut a long story short, we ended up, as was only to be expected, in each other's arms, and in a rain of kisses.

The next day she came back and the situation became so tense that I did what I think few men would have had the courage to do (I'm not the normal type of seducer in any case) – I said: 'My little Henriette, do you know where this is leading us?' – and with deliberate brutality I explained everything to her, the ignoble mechanism of love, the shame, the disillusionment, and the consequences of it all. She was shocked and startled, of course, and said: 'Oh, but you wouldn't do that!' I replied: 'But yes, I'm no saint!' She began to sob, but in the end she said: 'You will take pity on me. You are the master, and I am only your little bird.'

I had imagined that what I said would disgust her and terrify her, and instead I myself was terrified to see her, after the first moment of revulsion, so defenceless, so unprotected! I told her: 'We mustn't play with fire any longer or kiss each other like this, and you mustn't come so often.' It was agreed – and that very evening she returned, as though driven here by an irresistible force or drawn here like the victim of a mirage . . .

After this emotional crisis, however, came a period of comparative calm, and Huysmans was able to assure Leclaire that the 'little bird' was in no danger.[24] 'To break off relations with her now', he wrote, 'would only make matters worse. That's the opinion of her mother, who knows just what she is like. Time and emotional wear and tear are the only remedies. And if she meets a young man she likes she may very well marry him – retaining only affectionate memories of one who did not take her when it lay in his power to do so . . .'

Although he spoke of marriage as a possibility, he had not entirely given up hope that Henriette might take the veil; and after telling Leclaire[25] that she was coming to Paris for the Epiphany, to hear Mass with him and later lunch at his flat, he added: 'It should be both a pleasant and a pious day – and I shall try to arrange things to be like that every time in the future. She thinks it's cutting things rather short, but she makes up for it by writing to me every day. If she comes only once a month and in these circumstances, we should be able to manage until the spring, when I still hope something may come of a retreat at Sainte-Scolastique de Dourgne.' But at the Epiphany his plans for 'a pleasant and a pious day' went completely awry, and on 15 January he complained to Leclaire:[26]

I'm living in a terrible female whirlpool, an appalling feminine vortex. I told you that I was going to take the little one to receive communion with me in the chapel of the Black Virgin. Well, she was admirably pious there, but after lunch it began all over again. I spoke to her very severely and told her we should have to make a complete break. Whereupon she went into such a fit of sobbing, following me round on her knees, that I thought she was going to lose her reason. Anyhow, she went away in the end – and in her place there appeared the terrible [Mme X] who, with her feminine intuition, sensed that I was weakening and launched a sudden attack. I got out of it safely, but I'm beginning to see myself as a kind of Port Arthur, putting up a brilliant defence but doomed to final capitulation. That minx means to profit by my chaste behaviour with the little one. All the same, it's rather a lot for one man to bear. On one side there's debauchery and on the other adultery: a third choice somewhere between the two would be more to my liking. The truth is that I'm resisting as best I can, but I'm so tired . . . so tired . . . so obsessed by now by these successive feminine effluvia, that there are moments when I feel I can hold out no longer. [Mme X] has sworn that she will bed with me. She smothers me, maddens me with kisses. I don't know how I've been able to resist her – and my resistance obviously excites her and maddens her in turn. Ah, what would become of me without my morning Mass! And every day, when I come back from it, I find a passionate letter from the little bird waiting for me. Our Lord has said that no man should be tempted more than he is able. All the same, I don't think I'm flattering myself when I say that there are few people who would have put up such a Stoesselian defence of their chastity and not surrendered long ago. Anyhow, at the moment the fortress is still holding out, and that's the main thing. It's for Our Lady to do the rest . . .

It would appear from Huysmans' letters to Leclaire that the fortress continued to hold out, and that the siege was eventually raised. After mentioning two subsequent scenes in which he claimed to have repelled the advances of 'Mme X', the novelist made no further reference to her; and although Henriette did not give up hope of making Huysmans her husband or her lover until the last few months of his life, their relations never again attained the same degree of passion. Throughout the spring and summer of 1905 he urged her to make a retreat at the Abbey of Sainte-Scolastique, and in July she spent a week at Dourgne. Informing Leclaire of the effect this retreat had had on his 'little bird', Huysmans wrote on the 28th:[27]

It has given her a little ballast, and in spite of herself she was very much taken with the monastery. The Abbess sounded her thoroughly, and one evening after Compline said very gently to her: 'I can see that you are madly in love with J.-K.' And then she talked very reasonably to her, saying: 'It can't lead to anything. Come to the cloister and eventually it will all die down. It is only here that you can turn this love of yours towards God.'

At the moment I'm waiting for Father Romain. I'm going to arrange for him to have lunch with the little one. She will probably tell him: '*He* is my vocation !' – but since that's impossible, perhaps he will win her over with his good-natured arguments. In my heart of hearts I can't help feeling very sad about the whole affair. She is really quite right in saying that there's no reciprocity – that she loves me enough to give herself to me, but that I don't love her enough to take her. Which is true.

The Abbess said to her: 'You know, J.-K. is a good man and we already loved him dearly, but we shall love him much more now that we know everything . . .'

Meanwhile, though suffering from rheumatic pains and an alarming swelling on the neck, Huysmans worked on at his book *Les Deux Faces de Lourdes*. The Leclaires were kept busy verifying innumerable details, from the highest number of communions in a month to the colour of the robes worn by the visiting Bishop of Macao; and it was they who sent Huysmans an old Lourdes ordinal which confirmed his belief that each time the Virgin spoke to St. Bernadette, there was some connexion between her words and the liturgy of the day.[28] But if he was excited by such discoveries as this, and took a savage pleasure in attacking the architects of the new Lourdes or in defending the Fathers of the Grotto against Henri Lasserre's accusations of simony, the book as a whole failed to arouse his enthusiasm. 'This youthful Virgin,' he wrote in July,[29] 'dressed in blue and white, without either Child or cross, is not the one I love best. I prefer the Mother of Sorrows of the Middle Ages.' And in September he announced[30] to Henri d'Hennezel: 'I've finished this book, which I didn't want to write, I don't quite know how . . .'

Stock hoped to publish the book in October, but the author was unable to correct his proofs: Huysmans had suddenly lost the sight of one eye. He spent the winter months in darkness, devotedly tended by Crépel, Henriette du Fresnel, and his secretary. This last was not Aubault de la Haulte-Chambre – although the 'young noble who found the comma' had helped him with his correspondence for many months[31] – but Jean Marchand, *alias* de Caldain. This young man, whom Huysmans had seen off to Baronville in the spring of 1903, had left the novitiate of the Abbey of Maredsous less than a year later, telling the novelist on his return: 'I prefer to die of hunger in Paris; I'm more likely to find salvation here than there.'[32] If there was any danger of his dying of hunger, it was averted first by Forain, who for a time found him work to do in his studio, and later by Huysmans himself, who from the autumn of 1905 employed him as his secretary and companion. As will be seen, Jean de Caldain's professional ethics were not above reproach, but there can be no doubt of his devotion to Huysmans and of the affection which the novelist felt for him.

One of the first letters which Huysmans dictated to his young secretary after his sight had begun to fail was to the Leclaires, who had recently left Lourdes to settle for the rest of their lives at Pau. It was written on 31 October and read as follows:[33]

I'm still confined to bed, with one eye which doesn't

460

open and which is the cause of terrible suffering night and day. There has been a consultation of oculists who are amazed that I haven't lost my sight entirely, while dear, devoted Crépel, who comes to change my dressings twice a day, is in despair that he can't cure me of this atrocious neuralgia. Everything is strange in this illness, and there seems to be no rhyme or reason about it. All that I can do is to leave it to Our Lady. She has given me a certain resignation and has brought me a second Abbé Ferret, a priest who preaches the Gospel to the rag-pickers of Clichy, to comfort me and bring me communion. As you can see, she hasn't abandoned me, but I think this will be a long illness . . . I should be grateful if you would inform little Sister Thérèse de Jésus of my sorry condition so that she might pray for me.

The 'second Abbé Ferret' to whom he referred was the Abbé Daniel Fontaine, parish priest of Notre-Dame-du-Rosaire in the slum district of Clichy. He had met him for the first time in November 1904, and had afterwards remarked[34] to Leclaire: 'That man has a soul: we shall see more of each other.' It is not surprising that he should have admired the Abbé Fontaine, for already, exalting the idea of a mission to the poor such as the 'apostle of the rag-pickers' conducted at Clichy, he had observed[35] to Dom Besse: 'When do the poor see a priest? When there's a baptism, a wedding or a funeral – in other words, when they have to fork out some cash at the sacristy pay-desk. Just try and convince them, after that, that religion isn't a matter of money! But if a priest were to settle in their midst, live a poor and laborious life like themselves, be kind and obliging and thus help them to appreciate religion, you would see all their prejudices disappear one after the other.' It was probably because he considered that a priest who shared the poverty of the slum-dwellers of Clichy was closer to the practices of the Early Church and the spirit of Christ than one who enjoyed the hospitality of the Faubourg Saint-Germain that Huysmans decided, towards the end of his life, to substitute the Abbé Fontaine for the Abbé Mugnier as his spiritual director. The latter was naturally hurt by the novelist's decision, but their friendship was too deeply rooted to be seriously affected, and they were completely reconciled a few weeks before Huysmans' death.[36]

As the spring of 1906 approached, Huysmans' sufferings increased. 'The lower lid of my eye is turning inwards,' he told Mme Huc in February,[37] 'and the oculists and doctors are vainly trying to restore it to its proper position. The most obvious result of their meddling has been to increase the pain I'm enduring. When the eye grows a little easier the jaw gets worse, and vice-versa. I've still got a good-sized nest-egg of suffering waiting for me . . .' A month later he told Mme Huc[38] how, on 26 February, 'I was suddenly afflicted with a throat ailment so painful that I could neither eat nor drink and yelled whenever I swallowed my saliva. That lasted until the evening of Ash Wednesday, and then disappeared. Now they are going to operate on my eyelid next week.' The operation took place on 10 March. 'It was long and painful,' reported Huysmans,[39] 'and I'm still suffering a great deal.'

On Easter Sunday, 15 April, there occurred what Huysmans acclaimed as 'a liturgical cure': his eyes were suddenly able to bear the spring sunshine.[40] 'My sight was completely restored at Easter,' he told Adolphe Berthet;[41] 'but the neuralgia is still there, and though I can now read I've decided that it would be wiser to do no writing. My flat has been turned into an electrical power-house, where gigantic appliances have been installed to suffuse my skull with blue rays. The efficacy of these instruments is uncertain as yet, but there can be no doubt whatever about their stench.' This electrical treatment failed; but in May Huysmans was back at his writing-table laboriously correcting the proofs of his book, which was now entitled *Les Foules de Lourdes*.[42]

There was naturally some speculation among his friends at this time as to his literary plans for the future, and it was generally supposed that after the publication of *Les Foules de Lourdes* he would embark on another novel. However, writing to Henri d'Hennezel at the end of May,[43] Huysmans himself discounted this idea. 'Personally,' he wrote, 'I've had enough of the novel and am abandoning the genre, which has been exhausted by hackneyed repetition.' Not only had he come to despise the novel-form itself, the old instrument of his art, but he could think of no new subject which attracted him. He had spurned the 'novel of adultery' more than twenty years before, and even when, according to his letters to Leclaire, Henriette du Fresnel and 'Mme X' attempted to seduce him, he was not tempted to write another novel of earthly passion. Nor did the world of the occult hold any fascination for him now, for after the Marseilles adventure[44] he had told Leclaire: '*Là-Bas* has been written and these harrowing spectacles are of no use to me. I know all the demoniacal ruses and these have taught me nothing . . .' There was, he knew, no turning back – but was it possible to advance farther along the lonely road he had chosen? He had already traced the history of Durtal's soul from the temptations of *En Route* to the accidie of *L'Oblat*; he had treated of Christian symbolism, mysticism, liturgy, and plainchant; he had depicted monasteries of modern times and cathedrals of the Middle Ages. Now he could find no other aspect of religious life that really appealed to his imagination; even Lourdes – as he had admitted to his friends while labouring at *Les Foules de Lourdes* – had failed to command his interest. To a man who insisted that each of his novels should break new ground, this dearth of suitable subject-matter meant an end to novel-writing. On this point Huysmans' close friend and literary executor, Lucien Descaves, was explicit:[45]

Though nothing [he wrote in 1915] can lessen the respect in which we hold his memory, we feel it necessary to state, here and now, what is our personal conviction. After *L'Oblat*, or perhaps after *Les Foules de Lourdes*, Huysmans found himself, as at the time he wrote *A Rebours*, at the end of a blind alley. Heaven, which he had considered to be an inexhaustible reservoir, had dried up for him. He had tried his hand at hagiography, notably with St. Lydwine, but had not relished the experience sufficiently to wish to repeat it. Virtue, which he regarded as an exception, inspired him no more than did heroism outside the Christian life. He disliked travelling, even in express-trains and sleeping-cars – especially in sleeping-cars . . . So what was he to do? Having reached the last stage of his life and drawn up the balance-sheet of his existence, it seemed that he would be reduced to writing trifling monographs and studies in art-criticism.

A still more cogent reason for Huysmans' abandonment of the novel-form was that, with *L'Oblat*, he and Durtal had come to the end of their spiritual odyssey: in that novel the problems of Huysmans' life – and in particular the problem of human suffering, which had dominated all his works – had finally been resolved. Like Huysmans himself, the heroes of his earlier novels had all sought to achieve some measure of happiness, but had eventually forsaken hope, abandoned illusion, and returned to the bleak realities of life – André Jayant from his search for a satisfying mistress, Folantin from his quest for a savoury meal, des Esseintes from his 'refined Thebaid', Jacques Marles from his rural retreat, Durtal from the tranquillity of Carhaix's tower and the splendours of medieval history. But if his heroes despaired, Huysmans – as *En Route* and *La Cathédrale* reveal – had clung to one last hope: the hope of attaining happiness in some claustral or semi-monastic retreat. *L'Oblat* had told how this last and dearest dream had been shattered; but it had told too of the author's final adherence to the Dolorist philosophy, to the belief that escape from life's misery is impossible and that one should accept sorrow and suffering with good grace, for the expiation of one's sins and the sins of others. Durtal had no reason to embark on yet another hopeless quest, for in the renunciation of his dreams of temporal happiness he had achieved that inner peace denied to Huysmans' former heroes. With *L'Oblat*, Huysmans had written *finis* to the memoirs of his spiritual life: it now only remained for him to put into effect the lessons of renunciation and resignation which he had learnt.

Throughout the month of June Huysmans was in the dentist's hands, as the pain in his jaw had grown worse and he was having difficulty in taking food. However, he still found the time and the patience to write long letters of encouragement and edification to two women who were considering whether they should take the veil. The first was the 'little bird', to whom the novelist wrote[46] on 20 June:

> The days pass by, and now the time has come to nestle close to the Blessed Virgin, to obtain the courage you will need in order to make the sacrifice. God truly repays a hundredfold, even in this life, and after all, what is the heroism of a few days compared with the inner joy, the certainty of being really close to him? . . . Pray well, my dear little sister – and remember that I am praying for you with all my heart in my beloved chapels, where it seems as if you are still with me in spirit . . .

His second spiritual protégée was a Mlle Marguerite de Czarniecka, of whom he wrote[47] to Leclaire:

> I'm in correspondence with one of the ladies-in-waiting at the Court of Saxony. This woman has been conscious of a vocation for the Cistercian life ever since her childhood – and has deliberately rejected it. Once, when she was seriously ill, she was suddenly cured after swearing that she would take the veil, and a saintly old priest, who offered his life to God in exchange for hers, died in her place . . . And she broke her word. She then decided to marry – and on the eve of the wedding her fiancé suddenly died. After that she lived a wearisome social life at court, until chance put a copy of *En Route* into her hands. It seared her soul like a red-hot iron. She wrote to me, hoping that I wouldn't reply. I replied. And now she is going to take the plunge and is looking for a suitable Cistercian convent . . .

Though only a few months of life were left to Huysmans, he lived long enough to see his hopes for these two women fulfilled. In March 1907, six weeks before he died, Henriette du Fresnel finally overcame the opposition of her parents and entered the Abbey of Sainte-Scolastique de Dourgne.[48] And in that same month he sent Marguerite de Czarniecka, who called herself a 'Durtal in petticoats', a sum of money to enable her to make final preparations for her entry into a convent.[49]

In June 1906 Dr. Crépel urged Huysmans to leave Paris for the summer months, and the novelist accordingly embarked on a half-hearted search for a rustic retreat not too far from the capital. After one or two fruitless expeditions with Jean de Caldain, he seems to have considered spending a few weeks with Mme Godefroy at Jouarre.[50] But one day, when out house-hunting with Caldain, he met the Abbé Broussolle, who told him that he was hoping to let his house at Issy-les-Moulineaux for a few months, in order to pay for a journey he wished to make to Italy.[51] After satisfying himself that there was a garden and that the rent was reasonable, Huysmans agreed to take this house for two months, and he moved into it on the first day of August.[52] Gustave Coquiot has left us[53] this description of the house – No. 3 Rue de l'Égalité – and of Huysmans' stay there, based on conversations with Jean de Caldain:

Contrary to his expectations, the house pleased Huysmans. It was attractive and hospitable; the rooms were comfortable and the library very well stocked with books. In the garden there were some box-trees, one or two arbours, and some plaster statues which were flaking off. Bees from a neighbouring hive busied themselves with all the flowers. There was a golden pheasant strutting up and down its cage, and there were some cooing doves perched on the roof of a little toolshed, over which a gardener in painted plaster mounted guard. Here one could imagine oneself far from Paris. There was even a hen-house harbouring some hens and also a solitary duck, which had never been near water and uttered cries of protest when an attempt was made to give it a bath. But one of Huysmans' greatest pleasures was to see the sly suburbanites in church, dressed up in their Sunday best. At High Mass the priest was not afraid to make abusive personal remarks about them, and it was a joy to study their reactions. The natives took their revenge by throwing black looks at the two strangers from the Abbé's house. Everyone wanted to know who they were, and a few of the bolder spirits invented pretexts for coming to question them. When that happened Huysmans amused himself by putting them on the wrong track, with the same verve which he showed in repulsing the advances made by the 'priestlets' from the seminary.

The 'verve' Huysmans displayed was purely imaginative and verbal, for physically he was still very weak. 'My life', he told Leclaire,[54] 'is a compound of jaw-ache and tooth-ache, and I'm obliged to use a Carrière masticator to eat meat. Add to that the usual neuralgia and stomach-trouble, and you'll see that I'm in a pretty sorry state. And then I'm not really getting back my strength. When I've taken one or two turns in the garden I've had enough, and so I'm confining myself to gulping down a little air under the trees, without tiring myself out . . .'

Les Foules de Lourdes was almost ready for publication, and on 10 September Huysmans sent the first advance copy to Mme Leclaire, who on the 16th laid it in the reliquary of the Grotto at Lourdes, in the hope that the Virgin would 'bless its pages, its readers, and its author'.[55] The book was to be put on sale at the beginning of October, and on 26 September Huysmans left Issy and returned to the Rue Saint-Placide to see to the sending out of review copies.[56] There was little serious criticism of this work when it appeared, except by the family and friends of the unfortunate Henri Lasserre. On 9 October Huysmans wrote to Leclaire:[57]

In a life made wearisome by a new treatment with the famous X-rays – after Arsonval's blue rays it's a green bulb now – and joyless sessions at the dentist's, one must have a little light relief. And it's the Lasserre mob which has provided it. Infuriated by my book they have sent me threatening letters by their pet scribe, Louis Colin. They were going to produce documents which would squash me and the Fathers of the Grotto. To which I replied: 'Go ahead! Show me a sample.' And they sent me one fit to make me split my sides with laughter – a copy of a letter from a M. Artus (?) to his daughter, a nun in Mexico, in which he declares that Lasserre is a saint. You can imagine what fun I had with Colin after that. These people haven't anything at all! If they had these famous documents with which they've been threatening all and sundry all these years, they would have published them in reply to Moniquet's book. It's all a big bluff, and I don't think the Fathers have any cause for anxiety. As for myself; being a kind-hearted soul, I invited them to bring a libel action against me, adding that I had a publisher who adored that kind of thing and would consider it an excellent advertisement for the book. They won't budge.

On 2 November Huysmans told Leclaire[58] that the book was selling extremely well. 'Seventeen thousand copies have been sold so far', he wrote. 'Apart from anything else, it's a great success for me from the artistic point of view.' But his teeth and eyes were still giving him pain, and he wrote sadly[59] to Henriette du Fresnel: 'I'm spinning days of grey wool, a little worried at the thought of a whole winter spent in these circumstances. I'm paying dearly for the success of *Lourdes*.' It seems that he had no illusions about the prospects of a complete cure, for already, on 16 September,[60] he had written to Dom Ernest Micheau: 'I am going to be taken above by a way which, for lack of courage, I would not have chosen myself.' Now, in November, he began to make preparations for the end. On Thursday the 8th – significantly enough, the day his old friend Alexis Orsat was laid to rest in the Montparnasse Cemetery[61] – he made his will, bequeathing the royalties from his works to his two half-sisters, and appointing the faithful Descaves his executor.[62]

Just as he had tried to give heart to Henriette du Fresnel and Marguerite de Czarniecka in the summer, so now, as his sufferings increased, he wrote a brave letter of encouragement to the ailing Adolphe Retté, an old enemy of his who had recently become his friend. Retté has told how,[63] after his own conversion, he had called on Huysmans to beg his forgiveness for the attacks he had made on him in earlier years, and how, 'as we embraced to seal our reconciliation, we wept like two youngsters who have clouted each other and now feel sorry for it'. In his letter to Retté Huysmans wrote:[64]

Mark well that suffering is the token of divine love. There is not a single saint whom God has not afflicted with it. Remember the reply Jesus made to St. Teresa when, overwhelmed with tribulations, she could not help complaining to him of his severity: 'Daughter, that is how I treat those I love.' So you see, he's treating us converts, us repentant rogues, as true friends! As I've said before, that's a heartening thought – but all the same, suffering is a frightful thing. I've known something about it in my time, and know more now, since I'm not precisely happy at the moment from either the spiritual or the physical point of view. But I tell myself that that is all so much less on the account to be settled in purgatory, and that's something of a consolation to me . . .

He was to have need of every possible consolation later in the month, for on 24 November he was taken to a nursing home at No. 134 Rue Blomet, suffering from a tumour on the neck. Caldain accompanied him to the Rue Blomet, and later told how the novelist, though in great pain, could not resist a sardonic quip about the 'treble clefs' or stylized flowers on the wallpaper in his bedroom. But when, glancing through an open door, he saw an operating table and a man with a blood-splashed apron, he quietly reminded his secretary where to look for his will and last instructions, 'in case of accident'.[65] He was operated on five days later by the surgeon Joseph Arrou. That same day, the 29th, his 'little bird' came to Paris to see him and was told that he had been taken away, but the maid at his flat, a girl called Marie Gaudy, could not tell her where. She spent the rest of the day looking for him in nursing homes all over Paris, and it was evening before she came to the Rue Blomet.[66] For a little while, however, she was able to sit by his bed, talking to him and comforting him.

Huysmans was told that the operation he had undergone represented only the first stage of his treatment. 'Once I'm out of this place,' he told Leclaire,[67] 'I have to have nearly all my teeth extracted. As you can see, there are more delights in store for me. Pray for me, for I no longer have the courage to pray for myself . . .'

On Thursday, 6 December, he was allowed to return to the Rue Saint-Placide, where M. René Dumesnil, then a young doctor, came twice a day to help Marie Gaudy change his dressings.[68] During the month a new swelling appeared on the right cheek, and Jacques Liouville – a young man whom Huysmans had befriended in spite of the fact that he was Waldeck-Rousseau's stepson – suggested that Professor Paul Poirier, a specialist in diseases of the mouth, should be consulted.[69] Huysmans saw Poirier on the 21st, but all that the great surgeon would say to him was: 'Ah, my poor Monsieur Huysmans! You are suffering from some *bizarre* ailments, which don't promise very well for the future.'[70] This enigmatic utterance convinced the novelist that modern medicine was powerless to cure him, and that 'what I have is beyond the scope of medical treatment'.[71] And in a last letter to Mme Myriam Harry[72] he wrote: 'I have a vague intuition that henceforth I shall be led out of the paths of literature and into the expiatory ways of suffering, until I come to die. The worst of it is that I haven't a very decided sense of vocation for that sort of life, but in the end I shall undoubtedly get into the way of it.'

At the end of the year, realizing that Huysmans had not long to live, Lucien Descaves and Gustave Geffroy called on the Minister of Public Instruction, Aristide Briand, and pointed out to him that no government had as yet recognized their friend's great literary achievements, since he owed the red ribbon on his lapel to his diligence as a *fonctionnaire*.[73] The result of this conversation was that on 13 January, to the disgust of his colleagues and of the Radical Press, Briand promoted Huysmans to the rank of Officier de la Légion d'honneur. The award of the cross did not leave the novelist unmoved, and when Mme Myriam Harry went to see him for the last time later in the month,[74] he told her: 'It isn't that I'm terribly keen on these baubles, but I'm grateful to Briand for giving it me in spite of my attacks on his nauseating government. That proves at least that there are still some men in France who put artistic probity and the desire for truth above base political intrigues.' But in a letter to Mme Huc[75] he observed with a touch of melancholy irony: 'As regards promotion in the order of crosses, I find that I've advanced very rapidly in the crucial order that is not of this world . . .'

At the end of January Huysmans' dentist, Eugène Gravollet, proceeded with the extraction of his teeth. 'The anaesthetic', he reported to Leclaire,[76] 'was badly administered, so that I came to in the middle of the operation and had to suffer the evulsion of three teeth in cold blood. And they all lost their heads and left the one tooth which it was essential to remove.' But Gravollet, to do him justice, had noticed a suspicious erosion of the tongue, which he pointed out to Huysmans' doctor. Crépel diagnosed cancer.[77]

Among the last strangers to call on Huysmans were Jérôme and Jean Tharaud, who came to thank him for voting for their novel *Dingley, l'illustre écrivain*, which had been awarded the fourth Prix Goncourt in December 1906.[78] From the end of January only his closest friends were admitted to his flat, for he was growing weaker and his doctors decided that he could not endure the strain of prolonged conversation. He now spent the greater part of every day in bed, getting up only for the pitiful meals which served as lunch and dinner, and for his dressings to be changed. Writing to Mme Hue on 27 February,[79] Jean de Caldain described this last operation as an 'agonizing martyrdom', explaining that 'I have to detach the gauze which has stuck to the abscesses, and despite all the care and dexterity of which I am capable, it takes twenty painful minutes, and that three times a day.' But Huysmans bore the pain patiently, and once when Caldain spoke sharply to Gaudy, who was helping with the dressings and had handled the gauze clumsily, he uttered the gentle reproof: 'Don't scold her like that; she's doing her best.'[80]

All who talked with him at this time testified later to his courage and resignation. He never complained to his friends of the sufferings he endured. 'Indeed,' wrote Coppée,[81] 'he welcomed them, and humbly offered them up in expiation of his past sins to his heavenly Father, to the God who died on the Cross, and also to the Virgin Mary, to whom he prayed constantly – or rather, to whom he talked familiarly and intimately, as a son talks to his mother.' When his doctors proposed to give him morphia injections to relieve his pain, he protested: 'Ah! You want to prevent me from suffering! You want me to exchange the sufferings of God for the evil pleasures of the earth! I forbid you !'[82] And with a half-smile he said to a friend: 'I hope that this time they won't still say that this is only "literature" . . .'[83]

Weakened by fever and ravaged by cancer, he no longer wished for health and life, as he told Leclaire in this letter of 11 March[84] – probably the last letter he wrote:

Only a few lines in reply, my dear friend, for writing wears me out and you are the only one for whom I don't use my secretary. May God bless little Sister Thérèse de Jésus and may Our Lady reward her for her devotion to me!

My life drags on, with influenza added to the rest. I'm not sleeping or eating, but just manufacturing abscesses to the accompaniment of never-ending toothache. Anyone who hadn't the faith and a ha'porth of courage would have blown his brains out long ago. Well, I am not unhappy. The day I said *fiat*, God gave me incredible strength of will and wonderful peace of mind. I am not unhappy. I do not wish to be cured, but to continue to be purified so that Our Lady may take me above. My dream would be for God to take me with Him like the good thief at Easter, but alas, I am unworthy of that. *Je vous embrasse.*

It seemed possible that death would, in fact, come to him on Good Friday, for in Holy Week his doctors decided that the extraction of all his remaining teeth could not be postponed any longer. On Maundy Thursday, 28 March, Caldain wrote[85] to Mme Huc: 'Five teeth had to be extracted from a mass of pus. There was some risk involved in using the anaesthetic, but still, it is over now and the teeth are out. But what a state they've left him in! My poor dear master is completely exhausted.' Even so, he lived through Good Friday, and afterwards remarked[86] to Caldain: 'It seems that God has other plans and that I'm not to die yet . . . Strange, since I was in an unhoped-for condition to appear before Him. Still, the most important thing is to obey. God's will be done . . .'

In April Caldain informed Mme Huc that the cancer was spreading and that Huysmans had asked for the sacrament of extreme unction.[87] He wrote:

Five days ago the roof of the mouth was perforated, and in a few more days all the lower part of the jaw will collapse, and then he will have to be fed through a hideous tube. Oh, dear Madame, what a terrible, slow agony in the midst of frightening lucidity! Scrap by scrap, I have to pull away pieces of putrefying flesh – and the stench is appalling!!! Our poor master has that frightful smell in his nostrils night and day! 'Don't pray for my recovery,' the master said yesterday, 'but for a prompt and resigned death!' Oh, may God have pity on his servant!

On the 21st, at half-past seven in the evening, Huysmans

suffered 'a first and rather severe haemorrhage'; and on the 23rd, his name-day, the Abbé Fontaine administered the sacrament of extreme unction.[88] The priest later recalled[89] that 'he had prepared himself for it by reading a mass of texts regarding the sacrament; and while receiving it, sitting in an arm-chair, he followed the prayers with profound attention and made the necessary responses to all the invocations. After the unctions he said to me: "I am full of confidence. Our Lady is coming to take me. I do not wish to be cured." '

He was now terribly disfigured. Twenty years later,[90] Jules Bois remembered him 'sitting up in his bed, ghostly-pale, hollow-cheeked, his throat perforated by the cancer, but still obstinately rolling a cigarette between his bloodless fingers'. And François Coppée – who, curiously enough, was to die of the same disease exactly a year after his friend – was moved to observe[91] that Huysmans 'described himself when he wrote of St. Lydwine'. Certainly he must often have meditated, in these last days, on the law of mystical substitution, of which he believed himself, like Lydwine, to be a chosen victim. 'Perhaps', he said,[92] 'I am the total of a sum. Who knows whether I am not expiating the sins of others?' In moments of great pain he would fix his eyes upon one of the various symbols of suffering and substitution which surrounded him in his bedroom: a simple crucifix, a reproduction of a Grünewald *Crucifixion*, and a photograph of Catherine Emmerich, showing her stigmatized hands and bandaged brow.[93]

Huysmans found comfort, too, in the visits of his dearest friends: Coppée, Descaves, Céard, Hennique, Forain, Landry, Geffroy, Ludovic de Francmesnil, Gabriel Thyébaut, Dom du Bourg, and the Abbé Mugnier. Nor was feminine consolation denied him, for women who had loved him in very different ways now sought to give him material or spiritual solace in his last days. Sister Thérèse de Jésus sent him her prayers, and Mme Théophile Huc some tiny pots of her own *pâté de foie gras*. From Sainte-Scolastique de Dourgne, Henriette du Fresnel wrote a letter aflame with religious fervour and joy, telling him that in another five months she would be clothed as a Benedictine novice, and that a year later, on the Feast of Our Lady of the Seven Sorrows, she would make her profession.[94] And finally Fernande of *La Botte de Paille*, the Florence of *En Route*, sent him a bag of sweets.[95] Huysmans smiled sadly when this last gift was brought to him. 'The sweets of prostitution', he said. 'We have all tasted them . . .'

As the end drew near, he carefully put his papers in order, instructing his secretary to burn many letters, notebooks, and manuscripts, including those of *La Comédie humaine* and *Notre-Dame de La Salette*.[96] 'What heart-breaking *autos-da-fé!*', Caldain wrote to Mme Huc.[97] 'But he is the master, and one must simply obey . . .' Fortunately for the biographer of Huysmans, Jean de Caldain did not acquit himself of his duties as faithfully as he led Mme Huc to believe. Aware that some of the papers which Huysmans handed him to be burnt could be sold at a high price to unscrupulous *marchands d'autographes*, he saved many valuable documents from the flames by the simple method of slipping them under the cushion of his chair when his master was not looking.[98] He thus earned the gratitude of all Huysmans scholars, and the undying contempt of the ferociously honest Lucien Descaves.

One day, among a batch of recent press-cuttings, Huysmans found a snippet which announced that he had received the sacrament of extreme unction and was in his death-agony. He made no comment, but applied himself with greater energy to his preparations for the end.[99] Another communication which made a considerable impression upon him was an invitation to the funeral of Professor Poirier, who, only a few weeks after examining Huysmans, had discovered that he himself was suffering from cancer. 'Don't you think', Huysmans asked a friend,[100] 'that he was well inspired in not charging me for his consultation? Because if I'd paid him for it we should be quits, and I shouldn't be obliged to pray for him – and just now he must be in greater need of prayers than of money.' But that same day he asked Caldain to write at his dictation the invitation to his own funeral:

Vous êtes prié d'assister
aux convoi, service et enterrement de
M. Joris-Karl Huysmans
Homme de lettres
Président de l'Académie des Goncourt
Officier de la Légion d'honneur,
décédé le   1907, muni des Sacrements de l'Église
en son domicile, rue Saint-Placide, n° 31, à l'âge de 59 ans,
Qui se feront le   à
en l'église Notre-Dame-des-Champs, sa paroisse.
De profundis.
On se réunira à la maison mortuaire.[101]

When he inspected Caldain's draft, Huysmans noticed that he had omitted the initial M of the guest's prefix.[102] He pointed this out to Caldain, adding: 'I am most anxious that the wording of the invitation should be absolutely correct. Write the letter in very clearly. There, that's perfect! Another job done . . .'

Huysmans also wrote to Dom Besse at Chevetogne in Namur, where the Ligugé community was now established, asking him to send the monastic habit in which he was to be buried. With the tunic and scapular came a last letter[103] from his old friend: 'May St. Benedict watch over your soul from above. In you God is completing his work of purification by suffering . . . You go to Him with the assurance of a son who has had experience of his infinite mercy. I send you my deepest, heartfelt affection, and say to you *au revoir* and *à Dieu*.'

The Abbé Fontaine, who gave Huysmans communion almost every day, later described how the novelist would arrange the communion-table himself, placing on the cloth a simple altar-piece, an antique crucifix, a reliquary containing a relic of Blessed Lydwine, and two multi-coloured Dutch tapers in brass candlesticks.[104]

His preparations for communion [he recorded] consisted in hearing one of the canonical hours (usually Tierce), which his secretary and I would recite aloud to him. After communion we used to recite another of the hours, and finally the *Magnificat*. He would bow his head with the deepest respect at the *Gloria Patri* of the psalms, and, when the time came to pray, would try to go down on his knees. Afterwards he used to honour me with a little Benedictine *frustulum*, generally composed of a cup of black coffee and a piece of bread. On the day before he died – the only occasion on which he agreed to receive communion in his bed – he got up to make sure that I had everything I wanted. On that occasion I had been obliged to administer a host of elliptical shape, for he could no longer swallow . . .

That same day, 11 May, Adolphe Retté called to see Huysmans for the last time.[105] He found the novelist sitting in an arm-chair, and so weak that he could only murmur, in an almost inaudible voice: 'I am going to God, my dear friend, and I am praying for you . . .'

The last letter Jean de Caldain wrote to Mme Huc concerning his master[106] prophesied a painful and long-drawn-out death-agony for Huysmans. 'The swelling', he wrote, 'is spreading towards the glottis, and that means the end may come in a choking fit with frightful deathrattles.' Fortunately, however, Huysmans was spared such final torments. He died in the evening of Sunday, 12 May, half an hour after Lucien Descaves had left him 'with a cigarette between his fingers, affectionate and weary . . .'[107] At about seven o'clock Marie Gaudy went into his room to change his dressing; unable to wake him, she ran to look for Caldain who immediately realised that death had come gently to his master.[108] The coverlet had been turned back slightly, as though the dying man had wanted to leave his bed. But the expression on his face was one of perfect peace.

Huysmans' friends were promptly informed of his death. One of the first to hear of it was probably Lucien Descaves, who was entertaining Dr. Crépel to dinner that evening at his home in the Rue de la Santé. M. Pierre Descaves has told how the family and their guest were at table when a messenger arrived with the news.[109] The boy then saw something happen which he had never seen before and was not to see again until 1921, when his elder brother died. His father, the gruff, undemonstrative ex-sergeant, broke down and wept.

On the Monday and Tuesday scores of visitors came to pay their last respects to the dead man. They found him already clothed in his black habit, a bandage tied under his chin, a rosary in his hands. It was thus that his body was placed in the coffin at eight o'clock on the Tuesday evening, in the presence of his brother-in-law, Albert Marois, Lucien Descaves, Jean de Caldain, Henry Céard, Léon Hennique, Gabriel Thyébaut, Forain, Pol Neveux, René Dumesnil, the Abbé Fontaine, and the Abbé Mugnier. Before the coffin lid was screwed down, one of those present – it is believed to have been Gabriel Thyébaut – asked the Abbé Fontaine to say a few words. The priest spoke briefly but with great emotion of the dead man. 'Lord,' he said, 'you gave him great talent, and he used it for your glory. You gave him great suffering, and he accepted it for your blessing . . .'[110]

On the morning of the 15th, in accordance with Huysmans' last wishes, the Requiem at the church of Notre-Dame-des-Champs was celebrated by the Abbé Mugnier, while the prayers of intercession were recited by the parish priest. From the church, a great crowd followed the bier through the streets to the Montparnasse Cemetery, where Huysmans was laid to rest in the family grave.[111] There can be no doubt that he would have approved of the circumstances of his burial. Nearly all his oldest and dearest friends were there; his beloved Abbé Fontaine said the last prayers, again in accordance with his wishes; there were no 'futile speeches'; and from the sad grey sky – 'a decent sky' as he would have called it – a thin drizzle was falling. It was still raining, gently and mercifully, as they began filling in the grave.

CONCLUSION

HUYSMANS' star is still in the ascendant. Indeed, it can be said that it has never declined, for Huysmans, unlike his contemporaries France and Barrès, has not known that temporary oblivion which so often follows upon a great writer's death. Each succeeding year has seen the appearance of an increasing number of theses, books, and articles devoted to Huysmans' life and work; while the informative *Bulletin de la Société J.-K. Huysmans*, which was first issued in 1928,[1] has recently resumed the pre-war practice of biannual publication. As for the Société Huysmans itself, far from being a seedy charitable association such as one often finds in France, patiently trying to fan the dying reputation of some neglected writer into flame, it is today one of the most flourishing literary societies in Europe, and numbers among its members several of France's leading scholars.

Although detailed critical examination of a writer's works is beyond the scope of a biography, some explanation of the widespread and fervent interest in Huysmans should perhaps be attempted here. This interest is not due, as some writers have suggested, to the machinations of Catholic critics or the sensational appeal of 'decadent' and 'satanist' works, since it was aroused before Huysmans' conversion and has been maintained in a period when the words 'decadent' and 'satanist' have lost their power of attraction. Nor is it due chiefly to Huysmans' criticism or hagiography, although he ranks among the greatest art-critics and hagiographers of the nineteenth century. Rather must it be attributed to his novels, and the principal merit and attraction of these lie in their autobiographical quality: they appeal to us as perhaps the most profound and candid memoirs produced by a modern writer, as an intimate record of the author's material and spiritual life.

His determination to tell the truth about himself as far as he was able, and the psychological insight, the skill, and the honesty which he showed in his efforts to achieve this ambition, continue to evoke the admiration of present-day readers accustomed to twentieth-century novels of introspection. For the analytical methods he employed were governed neither by logic nor by convention: no relevant detail was omitted for fear it should be considered inconsequential, unconvincing, or unpleasant. Thus in *L'Oblat* the anxiety which the hero feels at the ceremony of oblation about an entirely trivial matter – whether he has warned his housekeeper that he will not be lunching at home that day – is given all due prominence; in *En Route* supposedly supernatural influence is not denied, but is explicitly described in concrete terms; and the reader is spared nothing of Jacques Marles' disloyal musings, none of Durtal's obscene or blasphemous desires. The significance of dreams is also recognized in such novels as *En Rade*, with the result that Huysmans has come to be regarded by psychoanalysts as a kindred spirit and by the Surrealists as a great precursor.[2] After nearly thirty years of writing novels which together formed the most comprehensive of autobiographies, Huysmans could feel justified in stating,[3] as he lay on his deathbed: 'No one has put more of himself into his books than I . . .'

Besides their interest and importance as 'human documents', Huysmans' novels have considerable historical significance, since each of his major works epitomizes some vital phase of the aesthetic, spiritual, or intellectual life of late nineteenth-century France. Thus *A Vau-l'Eau*, the 'Missal of minor misfortunes', is permeated with the pessimistic spirit of the post-war years, and impregnated with the ideas of that period's favourite philosopher, Arthur Schopenhauer. *A Rebours*, which Symons aptly called 'the breviary of the Decadence', expresses the tastes and aspirations of an entire generation of writers and artists, and its hero, as Gustave Geffroy observed,[4] 'embodies part of the soul of the dying century'. *Là-Bas* tells of the occultist and spiritualist revival which took place in France in the eighties, and reflects the state of mind of a generation which, in its revulsion from materialism and determinism, sought comfort in spiritualism, theosophy, and even satanism, before repairing at last to the Church. And finally, *En Route*, a story of conversion written in an era of notable conversions, in the time of Dowson and Gray, Claudel and Jammes, epitomizes the Catholic revival of the last decade of the nineteenth century. Those critics who represent Huysmans as a neurotic dilettante flitting idly from pessimism to aestheticism before dabbling in satanism and Catholicism, have clearly failed to perceive that his development was not only sincere but representative – that his more important novels stand as milestones in both his own and his period's spiritual history.

Another accusation sometimes levelled at Huysmans is that his remarkable style – which Léon Bloy picturesquely described[5] as 'continually dragging Mother Image by the hair or the feet down the wormeaten staircase of terrified Syntax' – is the product of a literary charlatan. This accusation is commonly made by purists who find it difficult to believe that any French writer could or would normally express himself as Huysmans does in his books. It cannot be denied that Huysmans' style owes something to that most artificial of literary languages, the *écriture artiste* of the Goncourts; and indeed, writing to Edmond in April 1884, he declared that 'no one among the stylists of today and those of tomorrow will be able to avoid using the neologisms and turns of phrase which you have created – even when those writers have a more or less personal style of their own'. Nor can it be denied that, like any artist, he deliberately cultivated the distinctive qualities of his style, in an effort 'to render the atmosphere of our times, to describe the thousand-and-one complex nuances of modern humanity, to fix the soul of an epoch'.[6] Yet on the whole there was little difference between his literary style and the language he employed in everyday intercourse, and Remy de Gourmont has even testified[7] that 'his spoken style was exactly like his written style'. If he chose to use a tormented sentence-form, this was not, as Bloy maliciously suggested,[8] because of a perverse desire to destroy

481

the organic structure of French prose 'like a barbarian or a naughty boy who takes pleasure in destroying a beautiful thing', but because such a form was better suited to his tormented spirit than Flaubert's sonorous periods or the brief notations of the Goncourts; and, once adopted, it became a characteristic, not only of his works, but also of his correspondence. Similarly, his use of innumerable comparisons drawn from the surgery, the pharmacy, and the kitchen was not the systematic abuse of a stylistic device that it might seem; it was natural that the anaemic, neurotic, and rheumatic author should describe life in terms of the sick-room, and that the dyspeptic creator of M. Folantin should have a nightmarish gastronomical vision of the world. Yet this does not explain why, if the Goncourts' syntactical peculiarities, metaphorical eccentricities, and cult of the neologism are now regarded as obsolete and pretentious, Huysmans' reputation as a stylist should still stand high. The answer probably lies in the extreme truculence of his style, in his habit of calling an inoffensive monk 'a pious brute' and a very ordinary building 'an ignoble barrack', in his tendency to turn portraits into caricatures and grumbles into imprecations. 'You have a flair for comical exaggeration', wrote Zola,[9] 'to be found in no one else, and which, to my mind, is one of your most original traits.' But it is more than an original trait: it is a saving grace. For from an author capable of such extraordinary vehemence one expects – and accepts – tortured sentences, strange images, monstrous epithets. And Huysmans' style is seen to be no laboured essay in preciosity, but the sincere expression of a bizarre and tormented personality.

It is also, of course, the perfect medium for the story told in all Huysmans' novels, since that story is the record of a prolonged physical and spiritual calvary. Edmond and Jules de Goncourt, in their novel *Manette Salomon*,[10] have left us an excellent definition of this, Huysmans' principal achievement:

> There are certain days in the artist's life when he feels the need to spread and communicate all the bitterness and desolation in his heart. Like a man who expresses in

his screams the anguish of his limbs and his body, the artist on such days as these must express in his work the anguish of his ideas, of his revulsions, of his antipathies, of all the pain he has felt, the hurt he has suffered, and the gall he has drunk through his contact with people and things.

What the Goncourts did only occasionally, Huysmans does consistently in all his works, ranging over the entire gamut of suffering, from minor physical irritations to profound moral distress. All his senses furnished him with the painful impressions which were the precious raw material of his art: the sound of a trombone playing in the streets of Lourdes or a colleague mouthing monstrous platitudes; the throbbing agony of a decaying tooth or the prickle of hairclippings at the barber's; the smell of unwashed humanity or putrescent meat; the sight of the pious gewgaws of the Rue Saint-Sulpice or the human face at its most vacuous. He was even more sensitive to – and fascinated by – spiritual suffering. We have seen that his friends were few and his relations with the opposite sex unsatisfactory; that much in modern life and in humanity as a whole horrified and disgusted him; and that he himself suffered so many reverses, misfortunes, and disappointments that in *La Cathédrale* he could declare in all sincerity: 'To me the past seems horrible, the present grey and desolate, and the future utterly appalling.' But the cause of his spiritual suffering lay not so much in external circumstances or the spectacle of human misery as in dissatisfaction or even disgust with himself. He was too acutely aware of his moral and spiritual shortcomings ever to achieve that placid self-content for which he often yearned, but which he knew to be the prerogative of the mediocre and the obtuse. 'The genius for self-torture with which we are endowed!' he wrote in one of his diaries;[11] and his own spiritual history is indeed a record of incessant doubt, scruple, and indecision. But this mental and moral anguish was doubly fruitful, for in it he discovered both the vital principle of salvation and a supreme source of inspiration. And in another of his diaries[12] we find him writing that 'all interest lies in spiritual torment. The lack of will-power is art . . . Irresolution is the very essence of psychology, the great living subject of art.'

It may be objected that there is an element of self-pity in this exposition of suffering, and that cannot be denied. But it is offset by the very real pity which Huysmans felt for others condemned to a life of suffering: in *Marthe*, for the unhappy prostitutes; in *En Ménage* for the working man 'going home from his factory, utterly exhausted, sweating in every pore, aching in every limb, stumbling over the rubble, slipping in the cart-tracks, dragging his feet, choked by fits of coughing, bowed down under the lash of the rain and the whip of the wind'; and in *En Route* for 'old women and widow-women whom no one loves, or women who have been deserted, or women who are unhappy in their home life, praying to God that life might treat them more kindly, that their husbands might become less dissolute and their children less vicious, that the health of those they love might improve . . .' And finally, of course, the self-pity which enters into Huysmans' works is redeemed by the spirit of resignation and acceptance shown in the last novel that he wrote and the last months that he lived.

It is because Huysmans suffered sincerely and suffered well that he now commands not only the appreciation of his readers but also their affection, and that he enjoys what Frédéric Lefèvre has called,[13] in an untranslatable, unforgettable phrase, *l'immortalité selon le cœur*. It is because of that, too, that his writings are still of compelling interest to such a wide variety of readers. The twentieth-century Everyman, tormented by the petty miseries of modern life, can find in these works a reflection of his own tribulations; the twentieth-century Existentialist will discover that Huysmans was just as sensitive as he to the horror and absurdity of things; and the twentieth-century Christian can obtain from 'the admirable artist in Christian suffering'[14] the strength and comfort of his philosophy. Suffering gave meaning to Huysmans' life: to his works it gave enduring quality and significance.

BIBLIOGRAPHY

The Published Works of J.-K. Huysmans

Unless otherwise stated, the works cited below were published in Paris.

Le Drageoir à épices, Dentu, 1874.
Marthe, histoire d'une fille, Brussels, Gay, 1876.
Les Sœurs Vatard, Charpentier, 1879.
Sac au dos (in *Les Soirées de Médan*), Charpentier, 1880.
Croquis parisiens, Vaton, 1880.
En Ménage, Charpentier, 1881.
Pierrot sceptique, Rouveyre, 1881 (in collaboration with Léon Hennique).
A Vau-l'Eau, Brussels, Kistemaeckers, 1882.
L'Art moderne, Charpentier, 1883.
A Rebours, Charpentier, 1884.
En Rade, Tresse et Stock, 1887.
Un Dilemme, Tresse et Stock, 1887.
Certains, Tresse et Stock, 1889.
La Bièvre, Genonceaux, 1890.
Là-Bas, Tresse et Stock, 1891.
En Route, Tresse et Stock, 1895.
La Cathédrale, Stock, 1898.
La Bièvre et Saint-Séverin, Stock, 1898.
La Magie en Poitou: Gilles de Rais, Ligugé, 1899.
La Bièvre; Les Gobelins; Saint-Séverin, Société de Propagation des Livres d'Art, 1901.
Sainte Lydwine de Schiedam, Stock, 1901.
De Tout, Stock, 1902.
Esquisse biographique sur Don Bosco, École Typographique de Don Bosco, 1902.
L'Oblat, Stock, 1903.
Trois Primitifs, Librairie Léon Vanier, A. Messein, 1905.

Le Quartier Notre-Dame, Librairie de la Collection des Dix [1905].
Les Foules de Lourdes, Stock, 1906.

Posthumous works and collections

Trois Églises et Trois Primitifs, Plon-Nourrit, 1908.
En marge, edited by Lucien Descaves, Marcelle Lesage, 1927.
Le Retraite de Monsieur Bougran, Jean-Jacques Pauvert, 1964.
Là-Haut, edited by Pierre Cogny and with notes by Pierre Lambert, Tournai, Casterman, 1965.
Là-Haut ou Notre-Dame de Salette, edited by Michèle Barrière, Presses Universitaires de Nancy, 1988.

Works with prefaces by J.-K. Huysmans

BOIS (Jules): *Le Satanisme et la magie*, Chailley, 1895.
BROUSSOLLE (Abbé J.-C.): *La Jeunesse du Pérugin et les origines de l'École ombrienne*, Lecène-Oudin, 1901.
CAZALS (F.-A.): *Paul Verlaine, ses portraits*, Bibliothèque de l'Association, 1896.
DUTILLIET (Abbé Henri): *Petit Catéchisme liturgique*, J. Bricon, 1895.
GOURMONT (Remy de): *Le Latin mystique*, Mercure de France, 1892.
HANNON (Théodore): *Rimes de joie*, Brussels, Kistemaeckers, 1881.
VERLAINE (Paul): *Poésies religieuses*, Messein, 1904.

Principal works and articles consulted

For a comprehensive list of works by and articles on Huysmans published up to 1949, the reader is referred to tome IX of the *Bibliographie des auteurs modernes de langue française* by Hector Talvart and Joseph Place. For works published between 1949 and 1985, see René Rancœur's bibliography in *Huysmans, une esthétique de la décadence*, edited by André Guyaux and Robert Kopp, Librairie Honoré Champion, 1987, and there are also regular bibliographical updates in the *Bulletin de la Société J.-K. Huysmans*. For an up-to-date online bibliography of works by and relating to Huysmans, see the internet resource site www.huysmans.org [BK]

AGEORGES (Joseph): *Sur les chemins de Rome*, Denoël et Steele, 1936.

AIMERY (Christiane): *Huysmans*, P. Lethielleux, 1944.

AJALBERT (Jean): *Mémoires en vrac, 1880–1890*, Albin Michel, 1938.

ALMÉRAS (Henri d'): *Avant la Gloire, leurs débuts*, Lecène-Oudin, 1902.

ARMAGNAC (M.-M. d'): *Huysmans, ou les frontières du chrétien*, Maison de la Bonne Presse, 1937.

AUBAULT DE LA HAULTE-CHAMBRE (Georges): *J.-K. Huysmans, souvenirs*, Figuière, 1924.

AUBAULT DE LA HAULTE-CHAMBRE (Georges) et GERMAIN (André): 'Verlaine et Huysmans', *Revue Européenne*, 1 May 1923.

AURIANT: 'J.-K. Huysmans et Émile Hennequin', *Bulletin*, No. 14, 1936.

BACHELIN (Henri): *J.-K. Huysmans*, Perrin, 1926.

BALDICK (Robert): (i) 'Huysmans and the Goncourts', *French Studies*, April 1952.

(ii) 'Huysmans et Gabriel Mourey: correspondance inédite', *Bulletin*, No. 26, 1953.

BARBEY D'AUREVILLY (Jules): '*A Rebours*', *Le Constitutionnel*, 28 July 1884.

BAUMAL (Francis): 'Les Œuvres critiques et philosophiques', *Les Belles-Lettres*, February 1920.

BEAUMONT (Barbara): Editor and translator: *The Road from Decadence: from Brothel to Cloister. Selected Letters of J.-K. Huysmans*, Columbus, Ohio State, 1989.

BEMELMANS (Andrée): (i) 'Quelques souvenirs sur Jean de Caldain', *Bulletin*, No. 23, 1951.

(ii) 'Les derniers instants de Huysmans vus par sa servante', *Bulletin*, No. 29. 1955.

BERNAËRT (Edouard): 'Huysmans intime', *L'Univers*, 16–17 November 1908.

BERNARD (Émile): *Lettres a Émile Bernard*, Brussels, Editions de la Nouvelle Revue Belgique, 1942.

BESSE (Dom J.-M.): (i) 'Huysmans artiste de la douleur chrétienne', *Gazette de France*, 19 May 1907.

(ii) *Joris-Karl Huysmans*, Librairie de l'Art Catholique, 1917.

BIBLIOTHÈQUE NATIONALE: *J.-K. Huysmans (1848–1907): Exposition pour commémorer le centenaire de sa naissance*, Imprimerie J. Dumoulin, 1948.

BILLY (André): *J.-K. Huysmans et ses amis lyonnais*, Lyons, Lardanchet, 1942.

BLANDIN (Henri): *J.-K. Huysmans*, Maison du Livre, 1952.

BLOY (Léon): (i) *Le Désespéré*, Soirat, 1886.

(ii) *La Femme pauvre*, Mercure de France, 1897.

(iii) *Le Mendiant ingrat, journal de l'auteur (1892–5)*, Brussels, Deman, 1898.

(iv) *Les Dernières Colonnes de l'Eglise*, Mercure de France, 1903.

(v) *Sur la tombe de Huysmans*, Laquerrière, 1913.

(vi) *Lettres aux Montchal inédites (1884–94)*, F. Bernouard, 1947–8.

BOIS (Jules): (i) *Les Petites Religions de Paris*, Paris, Flammarion, 1894.

(ii) *Le Satanisme et la magie*, Chailley, 1895.

BOLLERY (Joseph): *Léon Bloy: ses debuts littéraires, 1882–92*, Albin Michel, 1949.

BONTOUX (Henri): *Les Étapes de Dehival dans les voies de l'amour*, Beauchesne, 4th ed., 1926.

BOSSIER (Herman): *Un Personnage de roman: le chanoine Docre de 'Là-Bas' de J.-K. Huysmans*, Brussels-Paris, Les Écrits, 1943.

BOUCHER (Gustave): *Une Séance de spiritisme chez J.-K. Huysmans*, Niort, Imprimerie Niortaise, 1908.

[Most of Huysmans' bibliographers cite another work by Boucher, with the promising title: *De 'Là-Bas' à 'L'Oblat', souvenirs intimes sur Huysmans*, and state that this work was published in 1910. It was advertised in advance, but it was never written.]

BRETON (André): *Anthologie de l'humour noir*, Editions du Sagittaire, 1950.

BRICAUD (Joanny): (i) *J.-K. Huysmans et le satanisme*, Bibliothèque Chacornac, 1912.

(ii) *Huysmans occultiste et magicien*, ibid., 1913.

(iii) *L'Abbé Boullan*, ibid., 1927.

BRON (Ludovic): *J.-K. Huysmans, d'après des documents inédits*, Alsatia, n.d.

BRUNNER (H.) et CONINCK (J.-L. de): *En marge d' 'A Rebours' de J.-K. Huysmans*, Dorbon aîné, 1931.

BRUNO DE J.-M. (Le P.), BRESARD (Suzanne), et VINCHON

(Dr. Jean): 'La Confession de Boullan', *Études Carmélitaines: Satan*, 1948.

CALDAIN (Jean de): (i) 'Le Satanisme est-il pratiqué aujourd'hui ?', *Le Matin*, 21 April 1908.

(ii) 'La Genèse de *Là-Bas*', *Revue des Français*, 10 April 1914.

CALDAIN (M. et J. de): 'Les Derniers Moments de J.-K. Huysmans', *Revue des Flandres*, June 1907.

CÉARD (Henry): (i) 'J.-K. Huysmans', *Grande Revue*, 25 May 1907.

(ii) Lettres inédites à Émile Zola, edited by C. A. Burns, Nizet, 1958.

CÉARD (Henry) et CALDAIN (Jean de): 'J.-K. Huysmans intime', *Revue Hebdomadaire*, 25 April, 2 and May, 14, 21, and 28 November 1908.

CHASTEL (Guy): *J.-K. Huysmans et ses amis*, Grasset, 1957.

COGNY (Pierre): (i) 'Le Pessimisme "physiologique" de J.-K. Huysmans', *Bulletin*, No. 21, 1949.

(ii) 'Baudelaire et En Rade de J.-K. Huysmans', *Mercure de France*, October 1949.

(iii) 'Aspects de la grâce chez Joris-Karl Huysmans', *Dieu Vivant*, No. 16, 1950.

(iv) 'Le Mysticisme de J.-K. Huysmans et sainte Lydwine de Schiedam', *Mélanges de Science Religieuse*, 1952.

(v) *J.-K. Huysmans à la recherche de l'Unité*, Nizet, 1953. This work is a sensitive and well-documented survey of Huysmans' psychological and spiritual evolution. It contains interesting and previously unpublished material, and is undoubtedly the best general study of Huysmans' development to date. See also the present author's review of this work in *French Studies*, July 1954.

(vi) Introduction, J.-K. Huysmans, *Lettres inédites à Émile Zola*, Geneva, Droz, 1953.

(vii) Introduction and notes, J.-K. Huysmans, *Marthe, histoire d'une fille*, Le Circle de Livre, 1955.

(viii) Introduction, J.-K. Huysmans, *Lettres inédites à Edmond de Goncourt*, Nizet, 1956.

(ix) *Le 'Huysmans intime' de Henry Céard et Jean de Caldain*, Nizet, 1957.

(x) '63 Lettres inédites de J.-K. Huysmans à Gustave Boucher', *Bulletin*, tiré à part, 1977.

(xi) Editor: J.-K. Huysmans, *Là-Bas*, GF Flammarion, 1978.

(xii) 'Un projet avorté de roman: La Faim de J.-K. Huysmans.' *Revue d'histoire littéraire de la France*, 5, 1979.

(xiii) Editor (with Christian Berg): J.-K. Huysmans, *Lettres à Théodore Hannon*, Saint-Cyr-sur-Loire, Christian Pirot, 1985.

(xiv) Editor: 'Onze lettres inédites à Julie Thibault,' *Huysmans, L'Herne*, No. 47, Éditions de l'Herne, 1985.

(xv) Editor: J.-K. Huysmans, *En Route, suivi d'un journal et de lettres inédits*, Saint-Cyr-sur-Loire, Christian Pirot, 1985.

COPPÉE (Francois): 'J.-K. Huysmans', *Le Gaulois*, 14 May 1907.

COQUIOT (Gustave): *Le Vrai J.-K. Huysmans*, Bosse, 1912.

CORSETTI (Jean-Paul): (i) 'Pour une attribution à J.-K. Huysmans de l'*Etude sur Gamiani de Musset*,' in *L'Erotisme romantique*, Carrere, 1984.

(ii) Editor: 'Lettres de J.-K. Huysmans à Jules Bois,' *Berenice* No. 25, Dec. 1988-Mar. 1989.

CRESSOT (Marcel): *La Phrase et le vocabulaire de J.-K. Huysmans*, Droz, 1946.

DAIREAUX (Max): *Villiers de l'Isle-Adam*, Desclée de Brouwer, 1936.

DAOUST (Joseph): (i) *Les Débuts bénédictins de J.-K. Huysmans*, Saint-Wandrille, Editions de Fontenelle, 1950.

(ii) 'L'Ordo 1900 de J.-K. Huysmans', *Mélanges de Science Religieuse*, 1950.

(iii) 'J.-K. Huysmans et son confesseur', *Bulletin des Facultés Catholiques de Lille*, July 1951.

(iv) 'Huysmans et l'Abbé Broussolle', *Études*, September 1951.

(v) *J.-K. Huysmans directeur de conscience*, Fécamp, Durand, 1953.

(vi) 'Huysmans et W. Kloos', *Bulletin*, No. 25, 1953.

DEFFOUX (Léon): (i) *J.-K. Huysmans sous divers aspects*, Crès, 1927.

(ii) *Chronique de l'Académie Goncourt*, Firmin-Didot, 1929.

(iii) *Les Derniers Jours de Villiers de l'Isle-Adam*, La Centaine, 1930.

(iv) *J.-K. Huysmans sous divers aspects*, Mercure de France, 1942.

DEFFOUX (Léon) et ZAVIE (Émile): *Le Groupe de Médan*, Payot, 1920.

DESCAVES (Lucien): (i) *Les Dernières Années de J.-K. Huysmans*, Albin Michel, 1941.

(ii) *Deux Amis: J.-K. Huysmans et l'Abbé Mugnier*, Plon, 1946.

(iii) *Souvenirs d'un ours*, Éditions de Paris, 1946.

DU BOURG (Dom A.): *Huysmans intime, lettres et souvenirs*, Librairie des Saints-Pères, 1908.

DUJARDIN (Édouard): 'Huysmans et la Revue Indépendante', *Le Figaro*, 14 May 1927.

DUMESNIL (René): (i) *La Publication d' 'En Route' de J.-K. Huysmans*, Malfère, 1931.

(ii) *Guy de Maupassant*, Armand Colin, 1933.

ELLIS (Havelock): *Affirmations*, London, Walter Scott, 1898.

FABRE (F.-E.): (i) 'La Vraie Source de la Bièvre', *Bulletin*, No. 23, 1951.

(ii) 'Le Centenaire d'Henry Céard', *Bulletin*, No. 24, 1952.

(iii) 'Disparition de la Bièvre', *Bulletin*, No. 26, 1953.

(iv) 'M. Folantin, type littéraire, *Bulletin*, No. 32, 1956.

FLAUBERT (Gustave): *Correspondance*, Conard, 1926–33.

FLEURY (Dr. Maurice de): 'Relations', *Nouvelles Littéraires*, 25 July, 8 August, 19 September 1931.

FRESNOIS (André du): (i) 'Quelques lettres de Huysmans', *La Vie Intellectuelle*, 15 September 1910.

(ii) 'Une Étape de la conversion de Huysmans', *Grande Revue*, 25 May 1911.

GALICHET (Pierre): 'Les Extraits de *La Cathédrale* publiés dans l'*Écho de Paris*', *Bulletin*, No. 19, 1942.

GARÇON (Maurice): (i) *Vintras hérésiarque et prophète*, Nourry, 1928.

(ii) *Huysmans inconnu*, Albin Michel, 1942.

(iii) 'Huysmans témoin en Justice de Paix', *Mercure de France*, July 1952.

(iv) 'Le Mariage manqué de Huysmans', *Revue de Paris*, December 1952.

GARNIER (Georges): 'Autour de son premier livre', *Revue Européenne*, June 1929.

GILLET (Louis): Editor: J.-K. Huysmans, *Lettres inédites à Arij Prins*, Geneva, Droz, 1977.

GONCOURT (Edmond et Jules de): *Journal. Mémoires de la vie littéraire*, 1889–96, 3 vols., edited by Robert Ricatte, Laffont, 1989.

GOURMONT (Remy de): (i) *Promenades littéraires*, 1st series, Mercure de France, 1904.

(ii) *Promenades littéraires*, 3rd series, Mercure de France, 1909.

GRAAF (Dr. Jacob de): *Le Réveil littéraire en Hollande et le naturalisme français (1880–1900)*, Amsterdam and Paris, Nizet et Bastard, 1938.

GROLLEAU (Charles) et GARNIER (Georges): *Un Logis de J.-K. Huysmans. Les Prémontrés de la Croix-Rouge*, Crés, 1928.

GUAITA (Stanislas de): *Le Temple de Satan*, Carré, 1891.

GUICHES (Gustave): *Le Banquet*, Spes, 1926.

HABREKORN (Daniel): Editor: *Correspondance à trois: Bloy, Villiers, Huysmans*, Vanves, Thot, 1980.

HARRY (Myriam): *Trois Ombres: J.-K. Huysmans, Jules Lemaître, Anatole France*, Flammarion, 1932.

HENNEQUIN (Émile): *Études de critique scientifique*, Perrin, 1888.

HUNEKER (James): *Egoists. A Book of Supermen*, New York, Charles Scribner's Sons, 1909.

HURET (Jules): *Enquête sur l'évolution littéraire*, Charpentier, 1891.

Huysmans, edited by Pierre Brunel and André Guyaux, *L'Herne*, No. 47, Éditions de L'Herne, 1985.

JACQUINOT (Jean): (i) 'Louis-Alexis Orsat', *Bulletin*, No. 23, 1951.

(ii) 'Ludovic de Vente de Francmesnil', *Bulletin*, No. 24, 1952.

(iii) 'Contesse, prototype de Carhaix', *Les Amis de Saint-François*, 1952.

(iv) 'J.-J.-Athanase Bobin', *Bulletin*, No. 25, 1953.

(v) 'Un Procès de J.-K. Huysmans: L'affaire du journal *La Comédie Humaine*', *Les Amis de Saint-François*, 1953.

(vi) 'Les Années d'enfance: la Pension Hortus', *Bulletin*, No. 29, 1955.

(vii) 'Huysmans et Octave Lacroix', *Bulletin*, No. 32, 1956.

(viii) 'Huysmans et Odilon Redon', *Bulletin*, No. 33, 1957.

JAMMES (Pierre): 'Là-Bas, Gilles de Rais et la bibliographie', *Bulletin*, No. 24, 1952.

JOUVIN (Henri): (i) 'Huysmans critique d'art', *Bulletin*, No. 20, 1947.

(ii) 'Les Lettres de Huysmans. Essai de bibliographie', *Bulletin*, Nos. 25, 23, 25, 1949, 1951, 1953.

LAMBERT (Pierre): (i) 'Un Précurseur de des Esseintes, ou l'orgue à bouche au XVIIIe siècle', *Mercure de France*, 15 December 1925.

(ii) 'J.-K. Huysmans, les bouquins et la bibliothèque de Carhaix', *Bulletin*, No. 2, 1929.

(iii) 'Une Lettre de Huysmans à Maurice Talmeyr', *Bulletin*, No. 21, 1949.

(iv) 'Des Esseintes, maître sonneur', *Bulletin*, No. 24, 1952.

(v) 'En marge de *Là-Bas*: une cérémonie au "Carmel de Jean-Baptiste", à Lyon, d'après J.-A. Boullan', *Bulletin*, No. 25, 1953.

(vi) 'Huysmans et Lautréamont', *Nouvelle Revue Française*, 1 July 1953.

(vii) Editor: J.-K. Huysmans, *Lettres inédites à Émile Zola*, Geneva, Droz, 1953. This is an important work, not only because it makes available to the public sixty letters from Huysmans to Zola written between 1877 and 1896, but because M. Lambert's notes, based on extensive research and containing previously unpublished material from the Fonds Goncourt and Zola at the Bibliothèque Nationale and from his own collection of Naturalist documents, constitute in themselves a history of Naturalism which any student of the period could consult with profit. There is an admirable introduction by Dr. Pierre Cogny. See also the present author's review of this work in *French Studies*, October 1953.

(viii) 'Les débuts de Huysmans en 1867, *Bulletin*, No. 27, 1954.

(ix) Editor: J.-K. Huysmans, *Lettres inédites à Edmond de Goncourt*, Nizet, 1956.

(x) 'Un correspondant de J.-K. Huysmans, l'occultiste Grillot de Givry', *Bulletin*, No. 31, 1956.

(xi) 'Flaubert et Huysmans au château de Barbe-Blue', Le Bayou, Houston Texas, No. 68, 1956.

(xii) 'Une Confession de J.-K. Huysmans', *La Nouvelle Revue Française*, 1 May 1957.

(xiii) 'Le Journal intime de Huysmans à la Trappe', *Le Figaro Littéraire*, 11 May 1957.

(xiv) 'Un culte hérétique à Paris, 11 rue de Sèvres', *La Tour Saint-Jacques*, May-June 1957.

(xv) Editor: J.-K. Huysmans, *Les Foules de Lourdes, suivi de carnets et letters (1903–04)*, Plon, 1958.

(xvi) 'Journal d'*En Route*', in J.-K. Huysmans, *Là-haut*, edited by Pierre Cogny, Casterman, 1965.

(xvii) 'J.-K. Huysmans, aux sources de *L'Oblat*: journal inédite de Ligugé', *Bulletin*, No. 52, 1966.

LANGE (Gabriel-Ursin): (i) *En la fête de J.-K. Huysmans*, Fécamp, Durand, 1947.

(ii) *Aubault de la Haulte Chambre*, Fécamp, Durand, 1954.

LAVER (James): *The First Decadent*, London, Faber and Faber, 1954. This is an entertaining work which presents a colourful picture of the period, but which is sometimes misleading in its account of Huysmans' life. In the interests of future students of Huysmans, some of the more serious errors it contains have been corrected in the following Notes. See also the present author's review of this work in *French Studies*, October 1954.

LE CARDONNEL (Georges): 'Comment j'ai connu Huysmans', *Le Divan*, 12 May 1927.

LEFAI (Henry): (i) 'Flaubert et Huysmans', *Bulletin*, No. 23, 1951.

(ii) 'Huysmans à Lourps', *Bulletin*, No. 26, 1953.

(iii) 'J.-K. Huysmans, ce nordique', *Bulletin*, No. 33, 1957.

LEFÈVRE (Frédéric): *Entretiens sur J.-K. Huysmans*, Éditions des Horizons de France, 1931.

LEMAÎTRE (Jules): *Les Contemporains*, 1st series, Lecène, 1886.

LEMONNIER (Camille): *Une Vie d'écrivain. Mes souvenirs*, Éditions Labor, 1945.

LETELLIER (L.): 'J.-K. Huysmans et Henri Allais', *Mercure de France*, 1 September 1951.

LEVEN (Dr. Gabriel): 'La Thèse chrétienne de la souffrance', *Revue de France*, 1 August 1923.

LÉZINIER (Dr. Michel de): *Avec Huysmans. Promenades et souvenirs*, Delpeuch, 1928.

MARTINEAU (René): *Autour de J.-K. Huysmans*, Desclée de Brouwer, 1946.

MARX (Roger): *J.-K. Huysmans*, Kleinmann, 1893.

MASSIGNON (Louis): (i) 'Notre-Dame de La Salette et la conversion de J.-K. Huysmans', in *La Salette: témoignages*, Bloud et Gay, 1946.

(ii) 'Huysmans devant la "confession" de Boullan', *Bulletin*, No. 21, 1949.

(iii) Le Témoignage de Huysmans et l'affaire Van Haecke', *La Tour Saint-Jacques*, May-June, 1957.

MICHELET (Victor-Émile): *Les Compagnons de la Hiérophanie*, Dorbon aîné, n.d. [1938].

MOELLER (Henri): 'Lettres inédites de J.-K. Huysmans à l'Abbé Henri Moeller', *Durendal*, 1908, 1909, 1910.

MONDOR (Henri): (i) 'Paul Valéry et A Rebours', *Revue de Paris*, March 1947.

(ii) *Mallarmé plus intime*, Gallimard, 1944.

(iii) *Vie de Mallarmé*, Gallimard, 1950.

(iv) Editor (with Lloyd James Austin): Stéphane Mallarmé, *Correspondance*, 10 vols, Gallimard, 1965–85.

MONTESQUIOU (Robert de): *Les Pas effacés*, Émile-Paul, 1923.

MUGNIER (Abbé Arthur): (i) *J.-K. Huysmans à la Trappe*, Le Divan, 1927.

(ii) *Journal de l'Abbé Mugnier 1879–1939*, Mercure de France, 1985.

NARFON (Julien de): (i) 'Huysmans mystique', *Le Figaro*, 16 May 1907.

(ii) 'Le Cahier de l'Abbé Mugnier', *Le Figaro*, 5 October 1907.

(iii) 'Huysmans: nouvelles lettres inédites', *Le Figaro*, 23 August 1908.

NUGUES (Émile): (i) 'Souvenirs sur Huysmans' (I), *Bulletin*, No. 29, 1955.

(ii) 'Souvenirs sur Huysmans' (II), *Bulletin*, No. 33, 1957.

PACHEU (J.): *De Dante à Verlaine*, Plon-Nourrit, 1897.

PARMÉNIE (A.) et BONNIER DE LA CHAPELLE (C.): *Histoire d'un éditeur et de ses auteurs: P.-J. Hetzel*, Albin Michel, 1953.

POINSOT (Maffeo-Charles) et LANGÉ (Gabriel-Ursin): *Les Logis de Huysmans*, La Maison Française d'Art et d'Edition, 1919.

PONTAVICE DE HEUSSEY (Robert du): 'Villiers de l'Isle-Adam intime', *Le Figaro* (supp. litt.), 13 May 1893.

PRADEL DE LAMASE (Martial de): 'Le Sous-Chef J.-K. Huysmans', *Mercure de France*, 15 October 1933.

RAFFALOVICH (Marc-André): 'Les Groupes uranistes à Paris et à Berlin', *Archives d'Anthropologie Criminelle*, 15 July 1904.

RAITT (A.W.): 'The Last Days of Villiers de l'Isle-Adam', *French Studies*, July 1954.

RANCŒUR (René): *Correspondance de J.-K. Huysmans et de Mme Cécile Bruyère, Abbesse de Sainte-Cécile de Solesmes*, Éditions du Cèdre, 1950.

REDON (Ari): Editor: *Lettres à Odilon Redon*, José Corti, 1960.

RENARD (Jules): *Journal*, Gallimard, 8th ed., 1935.

RENÉVILLE (A. Rolland de): 'L'Élaboration d'A Rebours', *Comoedia*, September 1943.

RETTÉ (Adolphe): *Quand l'Esprit souffle*, Messein, 2nd ed., 1914.

ROSNY aîné (J.-H.): (i) *Torches et lumignons. Souvenirs de la vie littéraire*, Éditions de la Force Française, 1921.

(ii) *Mémoires de la vie littéraire. L'Académie Goncourt*, Crés, 1927.

ROTHENSTEIN (William): *Men and Memories, 1872–1900*, London, Faber and Faber, 1931.

ROUZET (Georges): 'L'Amitié de Jules Destrée et de J.-K. Huysmans', *Revue Belge*, 15 July 1937.

RUDWIN (Maximilien): 'The Satanism of Huysmans', *The Open Court*, April 1920.

SEILLAN (Jean-Marie): Editor: Joris-Karl Huysmans, *Interviews*, Honoré Champion, 2002.

SEILLIÈRE (Ernest): *J.-K. Huysmans*, Grasset, 1931.

STOCK (P.-V.): *Memorandum d'un éditeur*, Delamain et Boutelleau, 1935.

SYMONS (Arthur): 'J.-K. Huysmans', *Fortnightly Review*, March 1892.

TALMEYR (Maurice): *Souvenirs d'avant le déluge*, Perrin, 1927.

THARAUD (Jérôme et Jean): 'Vieux Souvenirs d'un Prix Goncourt', *Opéra*, 19 June 1946.

THERIVE (André): (i) *J.-K. Huysmans, son œuvre*, Éditions de la Nouvelle Revue Critique, 1924.

(ii) 'Gloire de Huysmans', *Vie, Art, Cité*, July 1950.

THOROLD (Algar): *Six Masters in Disillusion*, London, Constable, 1909.

THOMAS (Marcel): (i) L'Abbé Boullan et l'Œuvre de la Réparation', *La Tour Saint-Jacques*, May-June, 1957.

(ii) 'De l'Abbé Boullan au 'Docteur Johannès', *Les Cahiers de la Tour Saint-Jacques*, VIII, Roudil, 1963.

TRUDGIAN (Helen): *L'Esthétique de J.-K. Huysmans*, Conard, 1934.

VAILLAT (Léandre): *En écoutant Forain*, Flammarion, 1931.

VALÉRY (Paul): (i) *Durtal ou les points d'une conversion*, Marcel Sénac, 1927.

(ii) *Huysmans*, A la Jeune Parque, 1927.

(iii) *Variété II*, Gallimard, 1930.

(iv) *Lettres à quelques-uns*, Gallimard, 1952.

VANWELKENHUYZEN (Gustave): (i) *J.-K. Huysmans et la Belgique*, Mercure de France, 1935.

(ii) 'Histoire d'une brouille littéraire: Léon Bloy et J.-K. Huysmans', *Bulletin*, No. 17, 1938.

(iii) *Insurgés de Lettres: Paul Verlaine, Léon Bloy, J.-K. Huysmans*, Brussels, Renaissance du Livre, 1953.

(iv) Editor: *J.-K. Huysmans, l'homme et l'œuvre, les séjours en Belgique*. Catalogue of exhibition at the Musée du Livre, Brussels, 1955.

(v) Editor: *Lettres inédites à Camille Lemonnier*, Geneva, Droz, 1957.

(vi) Editor: *Lettres inédites à Jules Destrée*, Geneva, Droz, 1967.

VERLAINE (Paul): *Correspondance*, Messein, 1929.

VEYSSET (Georges): *Huysmans et la Médecine*, Belles-Lettres, 1950.

VILLENEUVE (Roland): 'Huysmans et Gilles de Rais', *La Tour Saint-Jacques*, May-June 1957.

WALBECQ (Éric): Editor: *Correspondance Jean Lorrain – Joris-Karl Huysmans*, Tusson, Du Lérot, 2004.

WIRTH (Oswald): *L'Occultisme vécu*, Editions du Symbolisme, 1935.

ZAYED (Fernande): *Huysmans, peintre de son époque*, Nizet, 1973.

ZOLA (Émile): *Correspondance*, 10 vols, edited by B.H. Bakker, Montreal/Paris, Editions du CNRS, 1980–87.

NOTES

In these notes reference to works and articles listed in the Bibliography is made by the surname of the author and, if two or more studies by that author are listed, the appropriate roman numeral. In preparing his biography, Robert Baldick relied heavily on Pierre Lambert's extensive collection of Huysmansiana, much of which was unpublished at the time and which subsequently formed the basis of the Fonds Lambert, now held at the Bibliothèque de l'Arsenal in Paris. As much of the material from the Lambert collection cited in the 1955 edition has now been published, references in the notes have been updated wherever possible to reflect more recent and more accessible published sources. New or supplementary notes not in Baldick's original edition are marked [BK]. Although Baldick never had the opportunity to revise the English edition of his biography, he did make some revisions to the text and notes of the French edition, *La Vie de J.-K. Huysmans*, translated by Marcel Thomas (Denoël, 1958), and these have been incorporated in the present edition, as have Pierre Lambert's own list of corrections which can be found in the Bibliothèque de l'Arsenal's copy of the French edition. [BK]

The following abbreviations are used:
BN   Bibliothèque Nationale.
Bulletin   *Bulletin de la Société J.-K. Huysmans.*
JKH   Joris-Karl Huysmans.
LMC   Louis Massignon Collection.
OC   *Œuvres Complètes de J.-K. Huysmans*, Paris, Crès, 23 vols., 1928–34.
Fonds   Fonds Lambert, Bibliothèque de l'Arsenal.

PART ONE

1. *THE BOY*

1 Céard et Caldain, 25 Apr. 1908; Cogny, ix, p. 66.

2 Trudgian, pp. 15–16.

3 'J.-K. Huysmans', *En marge*, p. 52. See also H. Lefai, *Bulletin*, No. 24, 1952, pp. 234–9.

4 'J.-K. Huysmans', *En marge*, p. 56. Huysmans published a slightly tongue-in-cheek account of himself and his work in Léon Vanier's series *Les Hommes d'Aujourd'hui*, ('J.-K. Huysmans', No. 263, Vanier, n.d. [1885]). Although written by Huysmans, it was published under the pseudonym 'A. Meunier', the name of his long-term mistress. [BK]

5 *En Ménage*, chap. iii; *Croquis parisiens*, 'Ballade en prose de la chandelle des six'; *Bulletin*, No. 23, 1951, p. 135.

6 In an interview he gave on 2 May 1904 to *Gil Blas*, Huysmans remarked that his 'was not a pious childhood. I learned to stutter through a few Dutch prayers my grandmother taught me, but very badly even then.' (Seillan, p. 418). [BK]

7 *En Route*, chap. ii; Vanwelkenhuyzen, i, p. 45.

8 Céard et Caldain, 25 Apr. 1908; Cogny, ix, p. 67. The portrait is dated 1856 and not 1855, as stated by Céard.

9 'At dinner Georges was well-behaved/And ate a bit of food./ He messed around but not a lot/All in all, he's very good.' [BK]

10 Céard et Caldain, 25 Apr. 1908; Cogny, ix, p. 63.

11 Grolleau et Garnier, p. 41.

12 C. Baudouin, *Psyché*, May 1950. See also H.-M. Gallot, *L'Évolution Psychiâtrique*, No. exceptionnel, 1948.

13 G. Garnier, *Revue Européenne*, Oct. 1930.

14 These details and the following quotations are taken from *En Ménage*, chap. iii.

15 Not on 7 May 1866, as stated by Laver. See Céard et Caldain, 25 Apr. 1908; Cogny, ix, p. 71.

2. *THE STUDENT*

1 *Sac au dos*.

2 Pradel. JKH did not enter the Ministry at the age of twenty, in Apr. 1868, as stated by Laver.

3 *Sac au dos*.

4 *En Ménage*, chap. iii; *Sac au dos*.

5 If we are to believe the account of this adventure in *En Ménage*, chap. vi, which has a ring of truth about it.

6   *Marthe*, chap. iii.

7   *Marthe*, chap. i.

8   'Hoarsely the fife with whining whistle plays,/And choking sounds escape the old bassoon;/After the trombone's grunting follows soon/A screeching fiddle that's seen better days./The flageolet some feeble notes essays,/The drum's too loud, the cornet's out of tune./As for the conductor – the baboon/Who stands, pot-bellied beast, upon the dais/He'd fright a woman of the lowest kind./And yet 'tis in this polyphonic hell/That you, my dear, my love, my life, I find./Here every night some vulgar song you bleat,/Closing your lovely eyes, most gracious belle,/And smiling at the rabble from the street.'

9   In an interview with Maurice Talmeyr in 1901 (Talmeyr, p. 132; Seillan, p. 295) JKH referred to the first review for which he wrote, which he said was edited in a fifth-floor attic in the Rue de la Sourdière. All attempts to trace this review had failed when, on a visit to Paris, the present author consulted the *Bottin* for 1868 and discovered among the names of residents in the Rue de la Sourdière a 'M. Le Hir, docteur en droit, rédacteur de journaux'. Informed of this discovery, M. Pierre Lambert was able to trace Le Hir's review, *La Revue Mensuelle*, which had not been catalogued as a periodical in the Bibliothèque Nationale. M. Lambert reproduced the two articles JKH wrote for this review in an important preface to Dr. Pierre Cogny's edition of *Marthe*, published by the Cercle du Livre (1955), and in *Bulletin*, No. 27, 1954.

10 Talmeyr, p. 132. [RB] Jean-Marie Seillan calls into question the reliability of Talmeyr's book of reminiscences, which was published 30 years after the interview in *Le Matin*. In his memoirs, after describing how the wine-merchant refused to buy the bottles from Huysmans, Talmeyr quotes the author as telling him, 'J'ai dû finir par les boire!' though this was not in the original interview. See Seillan, p. 295. [BK]

11 Baumal.

12 Céard et Caldain, 25 Apr. 1908; Cogny, ix, p. 72.

13 *Les Sœurs Vatard*, chap. ix.

14 *Marthe*, chap. v.

15 *Marthe*, chap. ii; Céard et Caldain, 14 Nov. 1908; Cogny, ix, p. 117.

16 *A Vau-l'Eau*.

17 'J.-K. Huysmans', *En marge*, p. 55.

18 According to JKH's army pay-book, in a private collection.

3. THE SOLDIER

1 This chapter is based largely on *Sac au dos*, which JKH declared in his autobiography to be an accurate account of his war-time experiences.

2 Anselme is the name given to the artist in *Le Chant du départ*, an unpublished manuscript in the Fonds Lambert. In the 1876 version of *Sac au dos* he is called Pardon, and in the 1880 version Francis Émonot.

3 Céard et Caldain, 25 Apr. 1908; Cogny, ix, p. 76. In the 1876 and 1880 versions of *Sac au dos* M. Chefdeville is called respectively M. Chévillage and M. de Fréchède.

4. THE DÉBUTANT

1 Céard et Caldain, 25 Apr. 1908; Cogny, ix, p. 79.

2 Céard et Caldain, 25 Apr. 1908; Cogny, ix, p. 80. The pass used by JKH is still extant.

3 For a brief biography of Ludovic de Francmesnil; see also Jacquinot, ii.

4 Céard et Caldain, 9 May 1908; Cogny, ix, p. 94. The manuscript of *Le Chant du depart* also contains the description of a bullock's carcass later reproduced in *Le Drageoir à épices* (Fonds). [RB] In a list of corrections to the French edition, Pierre Lambert calls into question the notion that *La Comédie Humaine* was a verse-drama (Fonds). [BK]

5 Undated letter (Parménie et Bonnier, pp. 596–7; see also Cogny, ix, p. 187).

6 Goncourt, *Journal*, 23 Mar. 1886. See also L. Deffoux, *Mercure de France*, 1 May 1925. [RB] Huysmans may have been exaggerating Hetzel's criticisms for effect. Patrice Locmant, in his critical edition of *Le Drageoir aux épices* (Honoré Champion, 2003), shows that Huysmans remained on friendly terms with Hetzel and even sent him a complimentary copy of the book when it was published, together with a letter of thanks for all that Hetzel had done for him, pp. 218–219. [BK]

7 For more information on Huysmans' relations with Octave Lacroix, see Jacquinot, vii. [BK]

8 Letter from Constant Huysmans of 26 Dec. 1874 (Garnier).

9 Gabriel Thyébaut (1854–1922), whom Professor Colin Burns described as 'the literary mentor of the Naturalist generation', is a relatively little-known figure even among students of the Naturalist period. Like Huysmans, he worked at the Préfecture de la Seine and became the friend of many of those in the

Naturalist movement. Although he was not a writer in any real sense himself, his opinions and advice were respected by his literary friends; he advised Zola on matters of law for his *Rougon-Macquart* series, for example, and was a regular both at Zola's Médan retreat and Huysmans' Wednesday 'at-homes'. The sixty-eight surviving letters and notes Huysmans wrote to him have now been published in a meticulously annotated and illustrated edition. See James Sanders, *Soixante-huit lettres inédites à Gabriel Thyébaut*, Les Nouvelles Éditions à l'Ecart, 2002. [BK]

10 Céard et Caldain, 9 May 1908; Cogny, ix, pp. 99 and 108. See also Fabre, ii; and Jacquinot, iv.

11 'Émile Zola et *L'Assommoir*', *En marge*, p. 14.

12 Letter to Edmond de Goncourt of 15 Mar. 1881 (Lambert, ix, p. 67).

13 Céard et Caldain, 14 Nov. 1908; Cogny, ix, p. 115. See also L. Deffoux, *Bulletin*, No. 15, 1936. [RB] For further details surrounding the conception of *La Faim*, together with the manuscript notes of the novel, see Cogny, xii, pp. 835–46. See also Françoise Grauby's 'La Faim, la femme, l'infini. Variations sur un manuscrit inachevé', *Huysmans à côté et au-delà*, Peeters Vrin, 2001, pp. 279–97. [BK]

14 Undated letter to Céard (Céard et Caldain, 14 Nov. 1908; Cogny, ix, p. 119).

15 Pradel.

16 Laver is incorrect in stating that 'the brothers Goncourt' were engaged in writing *La Fille Élisa*. Jules died in 1870.

17 Céard et Caldain, 14 Nov. 1908; Cogny, ix, pp. 121–2; Vanwelkenhuyzen, i, pp. 10–20; see also 'Carnet d'un voyageur à Bruxelles', *Musée des Deux-Mondes*, 15 Nov. 1876 (reprinted in *Bulletin*, Nos. 29 and 30, 1955).

18 Undated letter (J. Daoust, *L'Information Littéraire*, Nov. 1951). The article mentioned is 'L'Exposition du Cercle artistique de Bruxelles', *Musée des Deux-Mondes*, 1 Sept. 1876.

19 'La Grande Place de Bruxelles', *République des Lettres*, 22 Oct. 1876.

20 Undated letter to Céard (Cogny, ix, p. 121).

21 Jean-Paul Corsetti claims to have identified the missing preface (Corsetti, i). It is now included in an edition of *Gamiani* edited by Simon Jeune and published by Editions Ramsay/Jean-Jacques Pauvert in 1992. [BK]

22 Undated letter to Céard (J. Dagron, *Nice-Matin*, 16/17 Nov. 1947).

23 Not Ludo, as stated by Laver. Nor is the hero's address given as 73 Rue du Cherche-Midi, as stated in *The First Decadent* (p. 57). These errors are presumably based on a misreading of Céard et Caldain, 2 May 1908. As a character Léo bears a certain resemblance to Ludovic de Francmesnil. See Jacquinot, ii, and Cogny, vii, p. 54.

24 Undated letter to Ernest Raynaud (Lambert, ix, p. 50).

25 Letter to Edmond de Goncourt c. 1 Oct. 1876 (Lambert, ix, p. 47).

5. THE DISCIPLE

1 Letter from Edmond de Goncourt of 27 Oct. 1876 (Lambert, ix, p. 49).

2 In the issue of 13 Apr. 1876, not that of 27 June 1876 as stated by Laver.

3 Laver (*The First Decadent*, p. 63, note) states that on pp. 7–9 of *Le Groupe de Médan* by Deffoux and Zavie, 'it is stated that Céard and Huysmans first visited Zola when he was living at No. 23 Rue de Boulogne, later Rue Ballu'. In fairness to Deffoux and Zavie, and with all respect to Laver, it should be pointed out that no such statement is made in *Le Groupe de Médan*. On the contrary, Deffoux and Zavie refer on p. 8 to 'le petit groupe d'écrivains qui s'était constitué autour de lui [Zola] alors qu'il habitait 21, rue Saint-Georges'.

4 Letter from Zola of 13 Dec. 1876 (Zola, vol. ii, p. 506).

5 *Gil Blas*, 22 Apr. 1881.

6 On 11, 18, 25 Mar. and 1 Apr. 1877 ('Emile Zola et *L'Assommoir*', *En marge*, pp. 7–39).

7 Letter to Lemonnier c. 15 February 1877 (Vanwelkenhuyzen, v, p. 15).

8 Letter from Zola of 4 Apr. 1877 (Zola, vol. ii, p. 554). This letter is commonly, but incorrectly, dated 24 Feb. 1877.

9 *La Grande Encyclopédie*, 12 Aug. 1893.

10 Dumesnil, ii, pp. 92–93. [RB] *Feuille de rose* is French slang for the practice of anilingus. [BK]

11 Letter to Lemonnier c. 15 February 1877 (Vanwelkenhuyzen, v, p. 15).

12 Deffoux, iv, pp. 44–48.

13 Letter from Zola to Céard of 16 July 1877 (Zola, vol. iii, p. 79).

14 Letter to Zola of July 1877 (Lambert, vii, p. 8; Beaumont, p. 27).

15 Letter from Zola of 3 Aug. 1877 (Zola, vol. iii, p. 84–5).

16 Letter to Hannon of 9 Aug. 1877 (Vanwelkenhuyzen, i, p. 59).

17 *Sac au dos* was published in six instalments, on 19, 26 Aug., 9, 30 Sept., 7, 21 Oct. 1877.

18 Letter to Lemonnier of Aug. 1877 (Vanwelkenhuyzen, v, p. 43).

19 Catalogue of sale at Hôtel Drouot, 21 Nov. 1934, No. 173.

20 Letter to Lemonnier of July 1878 (Vanwelkenhuyzen, v, p. 55).

21 Letter to Zola of 8 Aug. 1878 (Lambert, vii, p. 14; Beaumont, p. 31) and letter to Hannon of 13 Aug. 1878 (Cogny, xiii, p. 40).

22 Published by Gay et Doucé, with a frontispiece and three etchings by Félicien Rops.

23 This new edition was published by Henry Kistemaeckers. He wished to retain the preface, but JKH wrote to him approving Hannon's decision to omit it (Deffoux, iv, pp. 22–23).

24 'J.-K. Huysmans', *En marge*, p. 56.

25 Letters from Céard to Zola of 28 Feb. and 1 Mar. 1879 (Céard, ii, p. 66 and p. 67).

26 Flaubert, vol. viii, pp. 223–6.

27 Letter from Edmond de Goncourt of 24 Mar. 1879 (Lambert, ix, p. 53–4).

28 Letter to Edmond de Goncourt of 2 May 1879 (Lambert, ix, p. 55; Beaumont, p. 36).

6. THE JOURNALIST

1 Letter from Laffitte to Zola of 8 May 1879 (BN).

2 BN. Camille Étiévant was *Le Voltaire*'s chief sub-editor.

3 M. Talmeyr, *Le Matin*, 27 May 1901 (Seillan, pp. 291–301). See also JKH's letter to Zola of October 1879 (Lambert, vii, p. 28); and Lambert, iii. The long-suffering Alexis finally produced six articles which appeared in *Le Voltaire* from 30 Oct. to 26 Dec. 1879, under the title 'Variété littéraire: Émile Zola à l'etranger'.

4 Letter to Zola, Autumn 1879 (Lambert, vii, p. 28).

5 Letter from Céard to Zola of 15 Oct. 1879 (Céard, ii, p. 103).

6 Letter from Zola to Flaubert of 9 Aug. 1878 (Zola, vol. iii, p. 201).

7 Céard et Caldain, 24 Nov. 1908; Cogny, ix, p. 152–6; Mme E. Zola, *Les Marges*, Spring 1930.

8 No. 23 Rue de Boulogne (now Rue Ballu), to which Zola had moved from No. 21 Rue Saint-Georges (now Rue des Apennins).

9 Dumesnil, ii, pp. 146–51.

10 *Le Figaro*, 19 Apr. 1880.

11 *Gil Blas*, 21 Apr. 1880.

12 Letter to Caroline Commanville of 28 Apr. 1880 (Flaubert, vol. ix, pp. 30–31).

13 Lefai, i.

14 Articles of 15 May, 1 June, 15 June, 1 July 1880.

15 *La Patrie*, 29 July 1880.

16 Undated letter to Zola (Lambert, vii, p. 38; Beaumont, p. 38). Zola's review appeared in *Le Voltaire* on 15 June 1880.

17 Letter to Zola, May 1880 (Lambert, vii, p. 36).

18 Coquiot, pp. 123–4.

19 Letter to Zola, July 1880 (Lambert, vii, p. 40).

20 The four articles were: 'Robes et manteaux' (6 June 1880), later used in *En Menage*; 'Une Goguette' (11 June 1880), reprinted in vol. viii of *OC*; 'Tabatières et riz-pain-sel' (18 June 1880), reprinted in a much modified form as 'Le Bal de la Brasserie européenne' in the 1886 edition of *Croquis parisiens;* and 'L'Extralucide' (26 June 1880), reprinted by M. Henri Jouvin in *Bulletin*, No. 19, 1942.

21 See *Bulletin*, No. 75, 1983, p. 10. In fact, several issues of *La Chronique illustrée* were published after the first appeared on 18 Dec. 1875. Huysmans contributed three 'Chronique parisiennes' and two pieces of art criticism before the final issue of 5 Feb. 1876. [BK]

22 According to a letter from Céard to Zola of 30 Oct. 1880 (Céard, ii, pp. 153–4), a letter from JKH to Zola of 4 Nov. 1880 (Lambert, vii, pp. 52–3), and a letter from JKH to Goncourt of 26 Dec. 1880 (Lambert, ix, p. 65). The subsequent account of the history of *La Comédie Humaine* is taken largely from Deffoux, iv, pp. 28–38. [RB] In a letter to Paul Alexis written around this time soliciting a contribution, Léon Hennique announces that the journal has been founded and that the first issue is to appear on the 15th October. He also adds that they will pay five sous a line (letter in a private collection). [BK]

23 Letters to Zola of 4 and 15 Nov. 1880 (Lambert, vii, pp. 52–56).

24 Letter to Hannon of 14 Dec. 1880 (Cogny, xiii, pp. 231–2).

25 Lambert, ix, p. 65.

26 Fonds. See also Jacquinot, v.

27 Cogny, xiii, p. 238.

7. THE PESSIMIST

1 *Le Figaro*, 11 Apr. 1881.

2 'J.-K. Huysmans', *En marge*, p. 58.

3 'J.-K. Huysmans', *En marge*, pp. 56–7.

4   *L'Amateur d'Autographes*, June 1907.

5   L. Descaves, *Le Divan*, 12 May 1927.

6   *Catalogue*, No. 125, Librairie Édouard Loevy, Paris, 1952, No. 130.

7   *L'Événement*, 17 Apr. 1881.

8   Letters of 7 and 20 May 1881 (BN; see also Paul Cézanne, *Letters*, ed. John Rewald, Oxford, Bruno Cassirer, 1941, p. 153 and p. 156).

9   Entry in Goncourt *Journal*, 6 Apr. 1881.

10 Letters to Zola of 5, 6, 10, 23 June 1881 (Lambert, vii, pp. 65–76); letters from Zola of 6, 12, 24 June 1881 (Zola, vol. iv, p. 189, p. 193 and p. 199).

11 F. Lefèvre, *Nouvelles Littéraires*, 10 May 1930.

12 P. Arrou, *Les Logis de Léon Bloy*, Paris, Crés, 1931, pp. 11–19. [RB] From Huysmans' letters to Théodore Hannon it is clear that he stayed at 3 Rue des Écoles during this period. [BK]

13 Letter to Zola of 1 Feb. 1882 (Lambert, vii, p 78).

14 Like many other writers, JKH broke with the publisher as soon as he had personal experience of Kistemaeckers' sharp practice. It seems that early in 1884 Kistemaeckers published one of JKH's letters, without his permission, as an advertisement for Henri Nizet's pornographic novel *Bruxelles rigole* (Letter from Kistemaeckers to Goncourt of 5 July 1884, with copy of letter to JKH of 1 July 1884. BN).

15 Letter to Kistemaeckers of 31 Dec. 1881 (L. Deffoux, *Mercure de France*, 15 Jan. 1925).

16 Undated letter to Kistemaeckers (Vanwelkenhuyzen, iv, p. 20). In the letter, Huysmans complains to the publisher: 'I received the portrait(!!!!) this morning, alas! . . . The annoying thing is that everyone I've shown it to has burst out laughing . . .' [BK]

17 Vanwelkenhuyzen, i, p. 86; Cogny, xiii, p. 92.

18 Coquiot, p. 32.

19 Coquiot, pp. 29 and 32.

20 P. de Pressac, *Nouvelles Littéraires*, 14 May 1927.

21 Coquiot, p. 37.

22 Cogny, i. Huysmans' letters to Hannon have now been published, see Cogny, xiii. For JKH's references to impotence, see pp. 209 and 211. [BK]

23 Symons.

24 Valéry, iii, p. 239.

25 *Le Figaro*, 10 May 1924.

26 Letter to Zola of Mar. 1884 (Lambert, vii, p. 99; Beaumont, p. 53).

8. THE ART-CRITIC

1 'Du Dilettantisme', *Certains*.

2 British readers of *L'Art moderne* can gauge the accuracy of JKH's comments on this portrait of Duranty by studying the original, which is in Glasgow Art Gallery.

3 Harry, p. 46. There is no corroborative evidence for this anecdote, which may be suspect. Harry describes Degas as a 'great friend' of Huysmans, but the two men, although they knew each other, were never very close. In a letter to Odilon Redon of 2 Feb. 1886, Huysmans notes that he couldn't ask a favour of Degas as 'relations between them ended a year ago and I haven't seen him since the publication of *L'Art moderne*'. (Redon, p. 103). See also 'The Pilgrim', Note 22. [BK]

4 Letter to Abbé Broussolle of 7 Jan. 1901 (Daoust, iv).

5 Letter from Raffaëlli of 1879 (*Bulletin*, No. 14, 1936).

6 Letters published by *La Vie* on 25 May and 21 Dec. 1912; 18 Jan., 22 Mar., 26 Apr., and 24 May 1913. [RB] See also Jacquinot, viii. Forty-two of Huysmans letters to Redon are published in *Lettres à Odilon Redon*, presented by Ari Redon (José Corti, 1960), pp. 97–129. [BK]

7 Deffoux, iv, pp. 86–88.

8 Letter to Pissarro of 1883 (J. Rewald, *Cézanne et Zola*, Paris, Sedrowski, 1936, p.112).

9 Letter to Zola of 19 June 1882 (Lambert, vii, pp. 86); document entitled: *Artistes éreintés. Liste soumise à Charpentier* (Fonds); and letter to Alfred Vallette of 1890, in which JKH refers to 'a certain Charpentier, who kept a manuscript of mine for *a year and a half* without printing it' (*Mercure de France*, 1 Dec. 1946).

10 Letter to Hannon of 25 Mar. 1883 (Vanwelkenhuyzen, i, p. 85).

11 R. Marx, 'J.-K. Huysmans', *L'Artiste*, Oct. 1893.

12 Autograph dedication of 1886 (L. Descaves, Note on *L'Art moderne, OC*, vol. vi, p. 305).

13 Deffoux, iv, p. 86.

14 J. Loize, *Nouvelles Littéraires*, 7 May 1953. Gauguin's comments on *Certains* were published for the first time in this article.

15 Letter from Zola of 10 May 1883 (Zola, vol. iv, p. 388).

16 Letter from Mallarmé of 12 May 1883 (Mondor, iv, vol. ii, p. 241–2).

17 P. Guerquin, *Revue de l'Art Ancien et Moderne*, Oct. 1929.

18 Letter to Hannon of 15 Feb. 1882 (Cogny, xiii, p. 264). The title refers to the Gros-Caillou *quartier*, situated between the Seine and the École Militaire. [RB] Huysmans adapted this story for

the 1886 edition of *Croquis parisiens*, where it appears under the title 'Le Bal de la Brasserie européenne à Grenelle'. [BK]

PART TWO

1. *THE DECADENT*

1 'J.-K. Huysmans', *En marge*, p. 53.

2 Céard, i.

3 According to *Le Roi vierge*, a novel by Catulle Mendès published in 1881.

4 Not Fontenay-sous-Bois, as stated by Laver.

5 Montesquiou, vol. ii, p. 123.

6 Raffalovich. See also Deffoux, iv, pp. 96–99. [RB] Baldick may be mistaken in thinking the events referred to in Huysmans' letter stem from a period prior to 1884. The 'talented young man whose perversities are common knowledge' is most likely a reference to Jean Lorrain, and Huysmans' friendship with Lorrain didn't begin until after *A Rebours* was published. In a letter to Arij Prins of 21 Sept. 1890 which refers to a recent experience regarding the subject, Huysmans uses a similar phrase to that which he used later in his letter to Raffalovitch, which indicates that his encounter with the homosexual underworld probably took place between 1889–90 (see Gillet, pp. 204–5). [BK]

7 See Brunner et Coninck, p. 32; Trudgian, pp. 177–80; P. Dufay, *Mercure de France*, 15 Aug. 1934. There remains one important analogy which these critics appear to have overlooked: between the nightmare *finale* of chap. viii of *A Rebours*, and Baudelaire's poem *Les Métamorphoses du Vampire*.

8 For a more detailed study of Goncourt's influence on JKH, see Baldick, i.

9 Letter to Hannon of Mar. or Apr. 1883 (Cogny, xiii, p. 271; Beaumont, p. 48).

10 Brunner et Coninck, pp. 138–50; Garnier.

11 Lambert, i. [RB] Although published anonymously, the book was written by Père Polycarpe Poncelet and published in Paris in 1755. [BK]

12 Auriant (*Bulletin*, No. 14, 1936, p. 226).

13 *A Rebours*, chap. xi; B. Wirtz-Daviau, *Intermédiaire des Chercheurs*, 30 June 1936.

14 Letter to Mallarmé of 27 Sept. 1882 (Renéville; Mondor, iv, vol. ii, p. 234).

15 In his 1903 preface to *A Rebours*, JKH wrote: 'Arthur Rimbaud and Jules Laforgue would have deserved a place in des Esseintes' florilegium, but at that time they had not yet published anything . . .'

16 Letter from Mallarmé of 12 May 1883 (Mondor, iv, vol. ii, p. 242)

17 Here JKH was perhaps inspired by chap. xvii of *La Faustin*. See Baldick, i.

18 F. Enne, *Le Réveil*, 22 May 1884 (Seillan, pp. 93–97).

19 Letter to Zola c. 25 May 1884 (Lambert, vii, p. 104; Beaumont, p. 55).

20 Letter to Albert Dugripp (Mondor, i).

21 Huret, p. 137.

22 G. Moore, *Confessions of a Young Man*, London, Heinemann, 1926, pp. 177–8. For a detailed study of JKH's influence on Moore, see S. M. Steward, *Romanic Review*, July–Sept. 1934.

23 *Lippincott's Monthly Magazine*, July 1890, p. 64.

24 Whistler: Deffoux, iv, p. 51. Bourget: Fonds. Maupassant: *Nouvelles Littéraires*, 3 Aug. 1950.

25 Letter from Verlaine of 22 May 1884 (Hôtel Drouot catalogue, 29 Jan. 1927).

26 Letter from Mallarmé of 18 May 1884 (Mondor, iv, vol. ii, p. 261).

27 Letter from Zola of 20 May 1884 (Zola, vol. v, pp. 107–8). See also *Bulletin*, No. 19, 1942, pp. 255–6.

28 Letter to Zola of May 1884 (Lambert, vii, pp. 103–4; Beaumont, p. 55).

29 Bloy, iv, p. 19.

30 Bloy, iv, p. 16.

31 Barbey. Also *Le Pays*, 29 July 1884.

2. THE COUNTRYMAN

1 Bollery, p. 89.

2 Letter to Bloy of 15 June 1884 (Habrekorn, pp. 21–2; Beaumont, p. 56).

3 Letter to Bloy of 22 June 1884 (Habrekorn, pp. 23–4).

4 Letter to Mallarmé of 11 July 1884 (Renéville; Beaumont, p. 58).

5 For an admirable study of JKH's connexion with this district, see Lefai, ii. [RB] A letter from Huysmans to Bartholomé of 26 Sept. 1881 reveals that he actually discovered Jutigny the year previously in 1881 and spent a month of his annual leave there. See Zayed, p. 349. [BK]

6 Letter to Zola of 20 July 1884 (Lambert, vii, p. 109; Beaumont, p. 59).

7 *En Rade*, chap. iii.

8 Letter to Zola of 31 Mar. 1884 (Lambert, vii, p. 102).

9 Letters of 27 Sept. and 2 Oct. 1884 (Bloy, vi, pp. 21 and 23; see also Habrekorn, pp. 28 and 30).

10 Letter to Montchal of 4 Nov. 1884 (Bloy, vi, p. 28; see also Habrekorn, p. 31–2).

11 Letter to Montchal of 8 Dec. 1884 (Bloy, vi, p. 35; see also Habrekorn, p. 32).

12 Bollery, pp. 133–4, 461–3. Of the contract with the printer Florès, Bloy wrote to Montchal: 'This contract has been drawn up by Huysmans, who knows all about such things, and it is admirable in every detail.' (Letter of 2 Feb. 1885. Bloy, vi, p. 44.)

13 Bollery, p. 158.

14 Letter to Montchal of 1 July 1885 (Bloy, vi, pp. 67–68).

15 Letter to Montchal of 25 July 1885 (Bloy, vi, p. 74).

16 Jacquinot, i.

17 Letter to Landry and Bloy of 26 Aug. 1885 (Habrekorn, pp. 38–40; Beaumont, p. 69).

18 Letter to Mme L'Huillier of 5 Sept. 1885 (Bloy, vi, pp. 95–96).

19 Bollery, pp. 170–1; Bloy, vi, p. 104.

20 Letter to Zola of 12 Nov. 1885 (Lambert, vii, p. 116). Two articles entitled 'Autour des fortifications' were published by the review on 1 and 15 Jan. 1886. Others were included in the 1886 edition of *Croquis parisiens*.

21 'J.-K. Huysmans', *En marge*, pp. 51–60.

22 Martineau, pp. 33–36.

23 Letter to Montchal of 27 Dec. 1886 (Bloy, vi, pp. 272–3; see also Habrekorn, pp. 76–7).

24 Stock, pp. 297–310. Huysmans dined with Caze on the eve of the duel (See Renard, 9 Feb. 1892). [RB] For more information on Caze, see B. H. Bakker's 'Un ami de J.-K. Huysmans: Robert Caze', *Bulletin*, No. 75, 1983 and No. 77, 1985. [BK]

25 Graaf, pp. 73–87. With the exception of Dr. Cornélie Kruize, no one has yet been given access to the JKH-Prins correspondence, which is in a private collection in Holland. Dr. Kruize informs the present author, however, that this correspondence throws no new light on JKH's life or personality. [RB] The 237 letters which Huysmans wrote to the Dutch writer and businessman, Arij Prins, were finally published in 1977 (see Gillet). In the words of Dr. Christopher Lloyd, Huysmans' correspondence

with Prins is 'undoubtedly the best document we possess about his day-to-day life over a period of twenty-two years, from 1885 to his death' (*J.-K. Huysmans and the fin-de-siècle novel*, Edinburgh University Press, 1990, p. 5). It is to be regretted, therefore, that they were not utilised in the writing of the biography. Although it is true that the letters were kept in private hands until 1960, it is also true that Mme Prins was not averse to showing them to researchers who expressed an interest. Added to which, Pierre Lambert had also made a faithful copy of the letters which those in his circle presumably had access to. It would be a mistake, however, to infer from the fact that Baldick so casually dismissed such an extensive and intimate correspondence that he was either careless in his research, or, as Pierre Cogny claims in a review of the published edition of the letters, that he and Lambert deliberately played down their importance because they 'feared they would cause a scandal' due to the controversial material they contained (*Revue d'histoire littéraire de la France*, 79:5, 1979). In the first place, it should be remembered that at the time Pierre Lambert's archives were available to researchers only at the discretion of Lambert himself. When Baldick was researching his biography he was still in his twenties, and would have been dependent on, and to a large extent influenced by, the opinions of senior Huysmansians such as Lambert and Louis Massignon, both of whom had a particular image of Huysmans which they wanted to project and which, in their view, the contents of the correspondence would have undermined. If Baldick had had access to the letters at this time, then so too would Cogny, but he makes no mention of the correspondence in either of his two major works on Huysmans published during this period, *J.-K. Huysmans à la recherche de l'unité* (1952) and *Le Huysmans intime* (1959). Cogny's assertion is more justly applicable to Lambert, who though he had certainly read the letters gave no indication in his notes on Prins in his published editions of Huysmans' letters to Zola and de Goncourt either of the importance or the scope of the correspondence. [BK]

26 Letter to Zola of 16 Oct. 1886 (Lambert, vii, p. 121). Pierre Cogny has shown how much the dreams in *En Rade* owe to Baudelaire's *Paradis artificiels* (Cogny, ii). The present author has long held that they also owe something to Lautréamont's *Chants de Maldoror*, which were then practically unknown, but which JKH had read and praised in 1885 (Letter to Jules Destrée

of 27 Sept. 1885. Vanwelkenhuyzen, v, pp. 52–5). This view is shared by M. Pierre Lambert (Lambert, vi).

27 Dujardin. 'L'Ouverture de Tannhæuser' was included in the 1886 edition of *Croquis parisiens*.

28 Letters of 29 May (Bloy, vi, p. 183); and 25 Oct. 1886 (Bloy, vi, p. 251; see also Habrekorn, p. 69).

29 Letter to Montchal of 2 Jan. 1890 (Bloy, vi, p. 463; see also Habrekorn, pp. 184–6).

30 Bollery, p. 202. It should be noted that Bloy made a practice of using anecdotes his friends had told him. See Bloy, iii, 27 Oct. 1893, where he writes that Maurice de Fleury provided him with 'the most intriguing information about the Daudets, Mendès, Hervieux, Bonnetain, de Goncourt, etc., and finally *about himself*'.

31 Letter of 11 Nov. 1886 (Bollery, pp. 215–16; Vanwelkenhuyzen, vi, pp. 94–6). Jules Destrée was an accomplished author, art-critic, barrister, and politician. He opened a correspondence with JKH in 1884, and visited him in Paris in May 1886. See Rouzet, and *Bulletin*, No. 16, 1937, pp. 80–1. [RB] Huysmans' letters to Destrée were published in 1967, see Vanwelkenhuyzen, v. [BK]

32 Letter from Zola of 1 June 1887 (Zola, vol. vi, p. 148).

33 Descaves, i, pp. 74–75.

34 If Huysmans thought his name meant 'countryman' in Dutch he was mistaken. Indeed, his name seems to signify the opposite, 'huys' in Dutch meaning 'house'. [BK]

3. THE FRIEND

1 L. Descaves, *Nouvelles Littéraires*, 18 Jan. 1930; R. Martineau, *Les Marges*, 15 July 1927.

2 Descaves, ii, p. 6. See also Descaves, iii, and JKH's letter to Zola of 15 Nov. 1882 (Lambert, vii, pp. 90–1).

3 The present author has published the letters JKH sent Gabriel Mourey from 1887 to 1904, see Baldick, ii.

4 Guiches, p. 67.

5 Auriant (*Bulletin*, No. 14, 1936, p. 227). Auriant incorrectly places this meeting in 1883.

6 Aubault et Germain; Bollery, p. 280. It appears that this journey, arranged for the summer of 1887, did not take place.

7 Letter of 7 Apr. 1888 (Fonds), referring to a letter from JKH of 29 Mar. 1888 (BN).

8 Poem written at Aix-les-Bains, 27 Aug. 1889 (Verlaine, *Œuvres*

complètes, Paris, Vanier, 1899, vol. iii, p. 92). 'If his kindness isn't excessive,/It exists nevertheless, though it has to be seen,/Like a washerwoman with her washing/Slapping her laundry hard and firm./He likes it white and smelling nice,/And I think he'll have it so, whatever it takes./But this is no trifling matter/It's no job for a coward./His task is a worthy one/To take care of your linen and its distress,/Humanity, its dirt and mess,/With never a moment's idleness,/O tough kindness of J.-K.,/Slap hard and firm, old gal!' [BK]

9 Guiches, p. 89.
10 Guiches, pp. 78–86.
11 Bollery, p. 261.
12 Letter of 27 Oct. 1887 (in a private collection).
13 Letter from Louise Read to Dr. Seligmann of 18 Nov. 1887 (in a private collection).
14 Pontavice; Bollery, pp. 251–3.
15 Letter to Zola of Aug. 1887 (Lambert, vii, p. 129).
16 Letter from Zola of 21 Aug. 1887 (Zola, vol. vi, pp. 171–2). See also D. Leblond-Zola, *Émile Zola raconté par sa fille*, Paris, Fasquelle, 1931, p. 155.
17 Mondor, iii, p. 520.
18 Ajalbert, p. 189.
19 Letter from JKH to Goncourt of 22 Nov. 1887 (Lambert, ix, p. 94). Guiches incorrectly places this visit in 1889 (Guiches, p. 181).
20 L. Daudet, *Fantômes et vivants*, Paris, Nouvelle Librairie Nationale, 1914, p. 280.
21 On 26 Dec. 1887 (Bollery, pp. 267–8).
22 Bollery, p. 265.
23 Letter to Destrée of 13 Feb. 1888 (Vanwelkenhuyzen, v, pp. 138–9).
24 On 26 Apr. 1888 (G. Garnier, *Revue Européenne*, Oct. 1930).
25 Guiches, pp. 91–92.
26 Letter to de Fleury of Feb.-Mar. 1888 (Fleury, 19 Sept. 1931; Beaumont, p. 85).
27 See letters to Zola from Moore and Quilter of 17 and 18 Mar. 1888 (BN). The letters of Quilter, Edith Huybers, and JKH quoted here are now in the Fonds Lambert. Quilter's letter to JKH is in English; Edith Huybers' letters are in French.
28 The manuscript of *Le Retraite de Monsieur Bougran*, which was saved from destruction by Huysmans' secretary, Jean de Caldain, was published by Jean-Jacques Pauvert in 1964. Towards the end of his life Huysmans asked Caldain to burn a number of his

letters and unpublished manuscripts, and although Caldain ripped *Monsieur Bougran* into four in Huysmans' presence, he secreted the pieces away when Huysmans wasn't looking and reconstructed them afterwards. He later sold the manuscript to the publisher Gaillandre. On Gaillandre's death, it passed into the possession of his son-in-law, Legueltel, and after Legueltel's death, his widow sold the manuscript to M. Guerquin who finally agreed to publish it, in an edition that was edited by Maurice Garçon. In 2003, it was translated into English by Andrew Brown as *M. Bougran's Retirement* and published alongside *With the Flow* (Hesperus Press, 2003). Pierre Lambert, in a list of corrections he made to the French edition of the biography, notes that Baldick's account of the novella is slightly inaccurate. In the novella, Monsieur Bougran is forced by his superiors to retire and he is so unsettled by the loss of his routine and of all that he knows, that he gradually begins to recreate in his home the working conditions of his former job. Bougran eventually wears himself down trying to work out the solution to a fictitious legal problem he has set himself, and dies scribbling the last lines of his 'appeal' to 'Monsieur le Président'. [BK]

29 No. 5 Cottage Avenue, Winchester, Massachusetts. The present author is indebted to John L. Munro, present owner of the property, and to Mr. Price Wilson, editor of *The Winchester Star*, who in 1951 appealed on his behalf for information about Edith Reverdy. None was forthcoming. [RB] Edith Huybers (1861–1939) lived and worked as an art critic in Paris, Melbourne, United States and Brussels. She was married twice, first to the artist and wood carver Jean Reverdy, and then to the sculptor, Pierre Valerio. [BK]

30 Huysmans' replied to her request for help on 7 May 1897, see Beaumont, pp. 168–9. [BK]

31 Lambert, xii, p. 960.

32 See JKH's letter to Zola of 26 July 1888 (Lambert, vii, pp. 138–9; Beaumont, p. 87); Aubault et Germain; Bollery, pp. 280–9; Guiches, pp. 113–16. Details of a receipt for 100 francs obtained from Albert Savine, drawn up by JKH and signed by Verlaine on 26 July 1888, are to be found in *Bulletin*, No. 6, 1932. [RB] In a letter to Arij Prins of 18 June 1888, Huysmans gives a slightly different version of this anecdote (Gillet, p. 125). [BK]

4. THE MENTOR

1 Vanwelkenhuyzen, v, p. 148.

2 Letter to Hennequin of 8 July 1888 (*Bulletin*, No. 14, 1936, pp. 229–30). Hennequin died on the 13th (Auriant).

3 From a letter to Arij Prins of 1 July 1888 (Gillet, p. 127) it seems that Huysmans invited himself to Hamburg, presumably in response to the news that Prins was unable to come to Paris: 'Perhaps if you can't come to Paris, I will come and see you, in August, if you are in Hamburg then.' [BK]

4 Undated letter (catalogue of sale at the Hôtel Drouot, 21 Oct. 1934, No. 175). See also letter to Zola of 26 July 1888 (Lambert, vii, p. 138–9; Beaumont, p. 87).

5 'Le Sleeping-car', *De Tout*.

6 *La Cathédrale*, chap. xii.

7 'Lübeck', *De Tout*.

8 JKH's description of Hamburg, recorded in Goncourt, 21 Oct. 1888.

9 Letter to de Fleury of 13 Aug. 1888 (Fleury, 19 Sept. 1931).

10 The unamed correspondent was in fact Léon Bloy. In the letter, Huysmans describes how he and Arij Prins hired an acrobat and in the evenings made her take all her clothes off and perform in front of them. It was, he remarks, 'all very decent, we don't touch her'. See letter to Bloy of 16 Aug. 1888 (Habrekorn, p 131; Beaumont, p. 88). [BK]

11 Goncourt, *Journal*, 21 Oct. 1888.

12 Coquiot, pp. 103–4.

13 'L'Aquarium de Berlin', *De Tout*.

14 Descriptions of the paintings JKH admired at Berlin and Gotha are to be found in *La Cathédrale*, chap. xii.

15 *Là-Bas*, chap. i.

16 In his edition of Huysmans' letters to Destrée, Vanwelkenhuyzen dates this letter at the end of Sept. 1890 not 1888, see Vanwelkenhuyzen, v, p. 166. [BK]

17 'Huysmans is postponing his book on Hamburg' (Goncourt, *Journal*, 17 Nov. 1889). It is interesting to note that Arij Prins later embarked on a book about Hamburg, which was rejected by *De Nieuwe Gids* on account of its descriptions of an ill-famed street in that city (Graaf, p. 79).

18 Bloy, iii, p. 63 (29 June 1892). Bloy adds that he expects this statement will be used against him. He seems to imply that criticism is invalidated if anticipated. It is not.

19 Daireaux, p. 186.

20   Letter to Montchal of 23 Sept. 1887 (Habrekorn, pp. 94–6).

21   See Villiers' letter describing the interview (Bollery, p. 258).

22   Letter to Montchal of 18 Oct. 1888 (Bloy, vi, p. 437; Habrekorn, p. 135).

23   Letter of 18 Aug. 1888 (Habrekorn, p. 132).

24   Guiches, p. 99.

25   Guiches, p. 99.

26   Bollery, pp. 299–305. See also Lemonnier, pp. 208–12.

27   Letter to Destrée, Jan. 1889 (Vanwelkenhuyzen, v, pp. 153–4).

28   H. Jouvin, *Bulletin*, No. 19, 1942. [RB] For further information on the real-life model for Carhaix and the text of 'L'Accordant', see Jacquinot, iii. [BK]

29   Huysmans first complains of the rheumatism from which he was to suffer increasingly in later life three years previously, in a letter to Arij Prins of 14 Apr. 1886 (Gillet, p. 44). [BK]

30   Letter to Mallarmé of 26 Oct. 1888 (Mondor, iv, vol. iii, pp. 272–3; Habrekorn, p. 136).

31   'Eleven (are you afraid) Rue de Sevres/Refined abode where Satan/The most high; finds himself treated man-to-man/By Huysmans, whom they call J.-K.' [BK]

32   Letter to Mallarmé of 15 Mar. 1889 (Habrekorn, p. 144; Beaumont, p. 91).

33   These details are taken from notes made by JKH on 26 Apr., on his return from Barbey's funeral (*Bulletin du Bibliophile*, May 1923).

34   Guiches, p. 104.

35   Letter to Mallarmé of 1 June 1889 (Mondor, iii, p. 554).

36   Letter to Mallarmé of 5 July 1889 (Habrekorn, p. 147; Beaumont, p. 93).

37   Letter to Pontavice de Heussey of 21 Apr. 1892 (Habrekorn, pp. 219–25; Beaumont, pp. 94–8).

38   Letter to L'Huillier of 9 Sept. 1889 (Bloy, vi, p. 455; Habrekorn, pp. 170–1).

39   Bloy, ii, pp. 361–2.

40   The following details are taken from a letter from Mallarmé to JKH of 8 Aug. 1889 (Mondor, iv, vol. iii, p. 333–4). For these and other details of the marriage, the present author is indebted to his friend Alan Raitt's study of Villiers. See Raitt.

41   Letter from Mallarmé of 8 Aug. 1889 (Mondor, iv, vol. iii, pp. 333–4; Habrekorn, pp. 154–5).

42   Letter to Mallarmé of 10 Aug. 1889 (Mondor, iii, p. 557; Habrekorn, p. 156).

43 Letter of 11 Aug. 1889 (Mondor, iv, vol. iii, p. 339).

44 Mondor, iii, p. 557; Habrekorn, pp. 158–9.

45 Letter to Beurdeley of 12 Aug. 1889 (H. Mondor Collection).

46 Letter to Méry Laurent of 12 Aug. 1889 (Habrekorn, p. 160).

47 Mondor, iii, p. 557; Habrekorn, pp. 161–2.

48 The following details are taken from Deffoux, iii, pp. 13–15; and Mondor, ii, pp. 208–11.

49 Letter to Méry Laurent of 18 Aug, 1889 (Habrekorn, pp. 163–4).

50 Letter to Pontavice de Heussey of 21 Apr. 1892 (Habrekorn, pp. 219–25; Beaumont, pp. 94–8).

51 Mondor, iii, pp. 558–9.

5. *THE OCCULTIST*

1 Fresnois, i.

2 The following details are taken from Bossier; P. Dufay, *Mercure de France*, 15 Aug. 1935 and 15 June 1938; J. Saget, *Cahiers du Collège de Pataphysique*, Nos. 5–6, 1952.

3 *Portraits du prochain siècle*, Paris, Girard, 1894, pp. 17–18.

4 E. Baumann, *La Vie terrible d'Henry de Groux*, Paris, Grasset, 1936, p. 103.

5 Laver suggests that JKH's introduction to Berthe Courrière 'happened exactly as he related it in *Là-Bas*'; in fact, JKH there relates his introduction to Henriette Maillat, whose letters he quotes in his novel.

6 Gourmont, ii, p. 5.

7 See Bollery, pp. 57–58, 242–4; P. Dufay, *Bulletin*, No. 2, 1929, and *Mercure de France*, 15 June 1938. JKH copied out the letters he had received from Henriette Maillat before returning them to her; and he reproduced some of her letters, with only minor changes, in *Là-Bas*. The complete copy which he made was included in the sale of the Bibliothèque André Le Breton at the Hôtel Drouot in 1938, but was later destroyed by the Germans during the Second World War. The details given here are based on a study the present author has made of another copy, in a private collection. [RB] To compare Maillat's original letters with those reproduced in the novel, see Cogny, xi, pp. 286–98, and also *Les Péladan*, Lausanne, 1990, pp. 156–163. [BK]

8 This 'brother' was none other than Péladan himself – he and Maillat habitually referred to each other as 'Sister' and 'Brother'. The two, who had lived together since 1884 in the Rue des

Beaux-Arts, separated in 1889. See Paul Courant's article, 'J.-K. Huysmans et Péladan', *Bulletin*, No. 62, 1974. [BK]

9 Letters of 2 Jan. 1889 and Sept. 1889 (catalogue of sale of Bibl. A. Le Breton, Hôtel Drouot, 1938, Nos. 271–4). [RB] See also Huysmans' letter to Maillat of June 1892 (Beaumont, p. 120) in which he sends her a further 10 francs. [BK]

10 Dujardin.

11 Lézinier, p. 193.

12 Guiches, pp. 111–12.

13 In an interview with *Le Matin* of 27 June 1897, Huysmans states that he first met Dubus at the Ministry of Finance, where he was employed. See Seillan, p. 211. [BK]

14 Lézinier, pp. 31–43, 148–94.

15 J. Bois, *Nouvelles Littéraires*, 14 May 1927.

16 Gourmont, ii, pp. 16–17.

17 Bollery, p. 357.

18 Letter to Zola of 31 Oct. 1887 (Lambert, vii, p. 131).

19 Letter to Destrée of 30 Nov. 1887 (Vanwelkenhuyzen, v, pp. 119–20; Beaumont, p. 84).

20 Dujardin.

21 JKH met Buet at Barbey's home in the Rue Rousselet, and soon afterwards was invited for the first time to the Avenue de Breteuil (letter from Buet of 7 June 1884, Fonds). See also Bollery, pp. 409–10; Coquiot, p. 51; G. Normandy, *Jean Lorrain*, Paris, Vald. Rasmussen, 1927, p. 66; Renard, 9 Mar. 1892. [RB] See also Huysmans' letter to Landry telling him about the invitation to Buet's party (*Bulletin*, No. 91, 1998). [BK]

22 Céard, i.

23 *Être* was first published by the Librairie Illustrée in 1888; subsequent editions appeared under the title of *Les Feux du sabbat*. This may explain why it has not hitherto been mentioned by Huysmans scholars. In his admirable study *The Russian Novel in France* (Oxford, 1950, pp. 106–7), Dr. F. W. J. Hemmings suggests that JKH was inspired by an anecdote about a twelfth-century cannibal, told by Lebedev in Dostoevsky's *The Idiot*. This seems unlikely, although, as Dr. Hemmings shows, JKH was probably influenced in other respects by Dostoevsky.

24 Villeneuve.

25 Goncourt, *Journal*, 9 Oct. 1889. See also *Là-Bas*, chap. viii.

26 *La Vie*, 21 dec. 1912; Redon, pp. 119–20.

27 Letter to Verlaine of 27 Sept. 1889.

28 *Certains*. See also Barbey's dedication of a copy of *Une Vieille*

517

Maîtresse (Deffoux, i, p. 26): '*A l'ami délicat, au mystique J.-K. Huysmans, cette amoureuse et horifique* [sic] *femelle, incarnation du démon.*'

29 Letter to Joseph Boullan of 7 Feb. 1890 (Caldain, i).
30 Gourmont, ii, p. 15.
31 P. Rolland, *Étude psychopathologique sur le mysticisme de J.-K. Huysmans*, Nice, Imprimerie de l'*Éclaireur*, 1930, p. 10.
32 F. Lefèvre, *Nouvelles Littéraires*, 10 May 1930.
33 Bossier, pp. 71–72.
34 Bossier, p. 75.
35 Bois, ii; 'Le satanisme et la magie', *En Marge*, p. 91.
36 Boissier, p. 32.
37 Bois, ii; 'Le satanisme et la magie', *En Marge*, pp. 91–2.
38 Boissier, pp. 48–49.
39 This sentence was, however, removed when Huysmans republished the article in *De Tout*, Stock, 1902. [BK]
40 Lézinier, p. 207.
41 Letter to Mme Bruyère of 30 July 1899 (Rancœur, p. 22; Beaumont, pp. 191–3).
42 Letter to Abbé Moeller of 20 Feb. 1896 (Moeller, 1908, pp. 438–46).
43 Bossier, p. 73.
44 On his copy of the memorandum. See Arminius (H. Bossier), *Nouvelles Littéraires*, 14 Sept. 1935.

6. THE MAGICIAN

1 Guaita, pp. 448–88. The following account of Boullan's life is based on a study of the Boullan archives (Fonds) and of the following works: Bois, i; Bricaud, i, ii, and iii; P. Dufay, *Mercure de France*, 15 Mar. 1935; Garçon, i; Guaita; Lambert, v; Massignon, i and ii; C. Sauvestre, *Les Congrégations religieuses dévoilées*, Paris, Dentu, 4th ed., 1879; Thomas, i; Wirth.
2 Bricaud, i, pp. 74–75.
3 This interview is described in detail, but from Boullan's point of view, in chap. xiv of *Là-Bas*. See also Thomas, ii, pp. 143–4.
4 Guaita, pp. 451–4.
5 Letter to JKH (Bricaud, i, p. 35).
6 Guiches, pp. 257–8.
7 Letter to Wirth of 2 Feb. 1890 (Deffoux, iv, p. 93; Beaumont, p. 100). For Guaita's reply of 31 Jan. 1890, and Wirth's reply of 5 Feb. 1890 (incorrectly given as 3 Feb.), see also Caldain, ii.
8 Caldain, ii.

9 Ibid.

10 Letter to Boullan incorrectly dated 6 Feb. 1890 (ibid.).

11 Ibid.

12 Letter of 7 Feb. 1890 (Caldain, i).

13 Letter of 10 Feb. 1890 (ibid.).

14 Letter from Pascal Misme to Jules Bois of 9 July 1890 (Fonds).

15 Fonds.

16 Deffoux, iv, p. 94.

17 Letter of 26 June 1890, quoted in Boullan's reply of 28 June (Fonds).

18 The Fonds Lambert includes a Ministry dossier on 'a certain Comte de Lautrec who used to present churches with devotional images on which he had laid a spell, in order to bedevil the faithful' (*Là-Bas,* chap. v).

19 Bricaud, i, p. 13; Gourmont, ii, p. 15.

20 Valéry, i, pp. 18–19.

21 Bloy, *La Plume,* 1 June 1891.

22 Letter from Charles Buet of 15 Apr. 1891 (Fonds).

23 Lambert, ii.

24 Bricaud, i, p. 65.

25 Ibid., pp. 13–14.

26 For more details on Huysmans relations with Jeanne Jacquemin, see Jean-David Jumeau-Lafond's informative article 'Jeanne Jacquemin, peintre et égérie symboliste', *Revue de l'Art,* No. 141, September 2003, pp. 57–78. [BK]

27 According to an entry for 29 Mar. 1890 in the Goncourt *Journal.*

28 Aubault, p. 75.

29 R. Doyon, *Mercure de France,* 1 Feb. 1939; Gourmont, ii, p. 16; Jacquinot, iii. Another possible model for Carhaix is mentioned in Harry, pp. 55–58.

30 Lézinier, pp. 206–7.

31 A. Billy, *Bulletin,* No. 19, 1942, p. 254.

32 Lézinier, pp. 74–85.

33 According to JKH's first letter to Boucher (9 Sept. 1890) and Boucher's notes on this letter (Cogny, x, p. 3).

34 Lambert, xiv. The following description of Julie Thibault is taken from chap. ii of *La Cathédrale* and chap. i of *L'Oblat.* [RB] The version of Huysmans' first meeting with Julie Thibault given here follows that of the French edition, in which some errors of chronology were corrected. The French edition also adds new information from an article by Pierre Lambert which

describes how on the night of his meeting with Thibault, Huysmans had his first experience of being visited by a succubus, a sensation he described as being 'both exquisite and painful'. Believing that this apparition had been sent by Thibault, he felt that the time was now right to make Boullan's personal acquaintance. On the 21 September he wrote to a friend that 'the following week I am going to Lyons . . . I think I will see some strange things there, where I am sure to be received with open arms . . .' See Lambert, xiv. [BK]

35 According to undated letter from Boullan to JKH of Aug. 1890 (Fonds); entry for 26 Oct. 1890 in the Goncourt *Journal*; letter from JKH to Valentin Simond of 28 Apr. 1891 (*Écho de Paris* of that date).

36 Entry for 26 Oct. 1890 in the Goncourt *Journal*.

37 Coquiot, pp. 127–8. The first instalment actually appeared in the *Écho de Paris* of 16 Feb. 1891, as the newspaper postdated its issues. The final instalment appeared in the issue of 20 Apr. 1891.

38 Entry for 18 Feb. 1891 in the Goncourt *Journal*.

39 *L'Événement*, 21 June 1891.

40 *Le Jour*, 28 Apr. 1891.

41 *Initiation*, May 1891.

42 *L'Éclair*, 25 Apr. 1891.

43 *Écho de Paris*, 28 Apr. 1891.

44 The blackmailer's letter, of 6 Mar. 1891, and the detective's report, of 10 Mar. 1891, are now in the Fonds Lambert. See also Cogny, xi, p. 299.

45 Letter of 2 Jan. 1890 (Bloy, vi, p. 462). It should be noted that, four months after Villiers' death, Bloy admitted that no 'serious circumstance' had caused his break with JKH – an admission which suggests that his pious indignation at JKH's treatment of Villiers was deliberately worked up long after the event.

46 Letter from Bloy of 17 May 1890 (Habrekorn, pp. 190–1).

47 Vanwelkenhuyzen, ii.

48 Letter from Bloy to Montchal of 20 May 1890 (Bloy, vi, p. 499). [RB] See also Habrekorn, p. 192, where the letter is dated 21 May. [BK]

49 Letter from Bloy of 21 May 1890 (Habrekorn, p. 191).

50 Postscript to letter to Montchal of 20 May 1890 (Bloy, p. 500). [RB] See also Habrekorn, p. 192, where the postscript is dated 25 May. [BK]

51 Letter from Bloy of 23 Feb. 1891 (Habrekorn, p. 197).

52 Bloy, *La Plume*, 1 June 1891.

53 See the above article, also Bloy's open letter to Léon Deschamps, published in *La Plume* on 15 May 1891, in which he referred to 'the letters of Mme H. M. which he [Péladan] obligingly gave to M. J.-K. H'.

54 Letter to Léon Deschamps of 14 May 1891 (Habrekorn, pp. 205–6). [BK]

55 Bollery, p. 406.

56 See Aubault, pp. 27–28. M. René Dumesnil has shown the author documentary proof that in 1904 JKH sent anonymously a considerable sum of money to Bloy.

57 Letter to Abbé Moeller of June 1900 (Vanwelkenhuyzen, ii).

58 Letter of 10 Feb. 1890 (Caldain, i).

59 Huret, p. 182.

60 Entry for 15 Mar. 1891 in the Goncourt *Journal*.

61 Note by L. Descaves, *OC*, vol. xiii, p. 255.

62 Fleury, 25 July 1931.

63 Dumesnil, i, p. 41. Many years later JKH confirmed this story, in a letter to Adolphe Berthet of 1 May 1900 (Billy, p. 56).

64 Bricaud, ii, p. 27.

7. *THE CONVERT*

1 On JKH and the Bièvre, see Daoust, vi; P. Dufay, *Le Divan*, 12 May 1927; Fabre, i and iii; H. Jouvin, *Bulletin*, No. 12, 1936; G.-U. Langé, *Les Images de Paris*, 12 Sept. 1920 and *Paris-Soir*, 10 Oct. 1928; Lézinier.

2 Céard, i.

3 The editor of *De Nieuwe Gids*, Willem Kloos, was introduced to JKH by Arij Prins. For details of their relationship and three letters from JKH to Kloos, see Daoust, vi.

4 Letter from Coppée of 1 Aug. 1890 (Fonds).

5 Lézinier, p. 59. This book also contains accounts of Lézinier's walks with JKH and many photographs of the Bièvre.

6 *Le Quartier Saint-Séverin*.

7 G. Guiches, *Le Figaro*, 14 May 1927.

8 The following details are taken from *Le Quartier Saint-Séverin* and Boucher's notes on letter of 2 Jan. 1891 (Cogny, x, p. 5).

9 Letter to Boucher of 2 Jan. 1891 (Cogny, x, p. 4; see also Garçon, ii, p. 12).

10 Letter to Boucher misdated 15 Jan. 1891 by JKH (Cogny, x, p. 6; Garçon, ii, p. 13–14; Beaumont, pp. 106–7).

11 Garçon, ii, pp. 14–21.

12 JKH's diary for June 1898 (Lambert, xii, p. 960).

13 Letter of 2 Jan. 1891 (Cogny, x, p. 4–5). According to Boucher's notes on this letter, JKH was not alone when he discovered the Rue de l'Èbre chapel, as stated in *En Route*, chap. iv.

14 *En Route*, chap. iv; Gourmont, ii, p. 14.

15 Gourmont, ii, p. 9.

16 Bloy, *La Plume*, 1 June 1891.

17 Letter to Landry of 18 Jan. 1891 (Lambert, xvi, pp. 226–7).

18 In the dedication of *Là-Bas* to Abbé Mugnier (Lefèvre, p. 27).

19 *En Route*, chap. ii.

20 D. Rops, *Le Divan*, 12 May 1927.

21 F. Van den Bosch, *Impressions de littérature contemporaine*, Brussels, Vromant, 1905, p. 16.

22 Ellis, p. 199.

23 Lefèvre, p. 32.

24 Ellis; Mondor, i; Symons. Valéry's first visit to JKH was on 25 Sept. 1891. André Gide also visited JKH for the first time in 1891 (see also Mondor, i, and *Bulletin*, No. 23, 1951, pp. 129–31).

25 Coquiot, p. 48. See also Goncourt, *Journal*, 1 June 1891.

26 *L'Amateur d'Autographes*, June 1907.

27 Entry for 3 Feb. 1892 in the Goncourt *Journal*.

28 Renard, 11 Aug. 1902.

29 Letters to Jules Destrée of 29 Apr. 1891 (Vanwelkenhuyzen, v, p.178) and to Émile Edwards of 17 May 1891 (Lambert, xvi, p. 235; Beaumont, p. 110).

30 Letter to Lorrain of 4 or 5 Mar. 1891 (Walbecq, p. 48). The Huysmans-Lorrain correspondence has now been published and shows that the friendship between the two writers was more extensive than the biography implies. Baldick dated this letter 'April 1891'. [BK]

31 Boucher's notes on letter of 19 Aug. 1891 (Cogny, x, p. 11). Fernande was the 'Florence' of *En Route*.

32 *En Route*, chap. iii.

33 Fresnois, ii, p. 20.

34 Descaves, ii, p. 36.

35 Mugnier, i, pp. 7–10.

36 Ibid., pp. 10–11. On 28 May 1951, in the presence of M. Pierre de Gaulle, representing the City of Paris, and officers and members of the Société J.-K. Huysmans, H.E. Mgr Feltin, Archbishop of Paris, blessed a plaque in the sacristy of Saint-Thomas-

d'Aquin commemorating the first meeting of JKH and the Abbé Mugnier. See *Bulletin*, No. hors série, 1952.

8. *THE PENITENT*

1 Mugnier, i, p. 11.
2 Letter from Boullan of 14 June 1891 (*Bulletin*, No. 24, 1952, p. 204).
3 Fresnois, ii.
4 Massignon, i.
5 Fresnois, ii.
6 Bricaud, ii, pp. 22–23.
7 Lambert, v.
8 Billy, pp. 54–56.
9 Guiches, p. 260.
10 Ibid., p. 253.
11 Bloy, iii. entry for 11 Jan. 1893.
12 Letter to Berthe Courrière of July 1891 (Fresnois, ii, p. 24).
13 Letter to Boucher of 19 Aug. 1891 (Cogny, x, p. 10; Beaumont, pp. 113–5).
14 Letter to Boucher of 15 Sept. 1891 (Cogny, x, p. 12).
15 Letter to Berthe Courrière of 10 Oct. 1891 (Fresnois, ii, p. 46).
16 On 22 Nov. 1891. See *En Route*, chap. viii; also JKH's letter to Boucher of 21 Nov. and Boucher's notes (Cogny, x, p. 14).
17 Boucher, p. 11; Cogny, x, p. 15. The details of the séance are taken from Boucher.
18 See Bricaud, iii, pp. 8 and 20; Massignon, i; Bloy, i, p. 165, and ii, pp. 88–89. [RB] In a letter to Arij Prins, Huysmans compares the two men: 'I've found a priest [Mugnier] who can unravel most things, but he's not very potent, so I'm obliged to have recourse to Dr. Johannès of Lyons, who is in *Là-Bas*, and who is one of the most formidable theologians alive. The only thing is he's riddled with heresy, so I've got to keep an eye on him.' See Gillet, p. 239. [BK]
19 Mugnier, i, pp. 12–22.
20 Ibid., p. 23. For a detailed description of the abbey and its grounds, see Dumesnil, i. The abbey was destroyed by the Germans in 1918.
21 Narfon, ii.
22 Letter to Abbé Mugnier of 29 June 1892 (Mugnier, i, p. 25; Beaumont, p. 119).
23 JKH published this letter in *En Route*, altering only the Guest-master's name, which is given as Étienne.

24 Descaves, iii, p. 137.
25 Mugnier, i, p. 25.
26 For the text of Huysmans' letters to Rivière, see Cogny, xv, pp. 382–92. [BK]
27 Letter to Abbé Mugnier of 15 July 1892 (Mugnier, i, pp. 27–30). [RB] For the text of the 'journal intime' kept by Huysmans during his stay at La Trappe, and which he used for *En Route*, see Lambert, xiii and Cogny, xv, pp. 367–376. [BK]

PART THREE

1. THE NEOPHYTE

1 J. Huret, *Tout yeux, tout oreilles*, Paris, Fasquelle, 1901, p. 420.
2 Letter to Boucher of 4 Aug. 1892 (Cogny, x, p. 18).
3 The following details of JKH's stay in Lyons are taken from his letters to Landry of 1 Aug 1892 (Lambert, xvi, pp. 258–9) and Boucher of 4 Aug. 1892 (Cogny, x, pp. 16–19).
4 Bricaud, iii, pp. 74–75. See also JKH's letter to Adolphe Berthet of 1 May 1900 (Billy, p. 54).
5 Letter to Boucher of 4 Aug. 1892 (Cogny, x, p. 16).
6 Entry for 17 Aug. 1892 (Mugnier, ii, p. 76). [BK]
7 Since the publication of Baldick's biography, the circumstances surrounding the genesis of *En Route* have become much clearer thanks to the rediscovery of earlier drafts of the novel. In 1965, Artine Artinian came across a handwritten manuscript in a Parisian bookshop. It was an early version of the book that became *En Route*, but it lacked chapters I, III, and VI. Like the manuscript of *La Retraite de Monsieur Bougran*, it had been ripped up under Huysmans' orders, but had then been secreted away by Jean de Caldain and carefully repaired later. Artinian published this manuscript, in collaboration with Pierre Cogny and Pierre Lambert, as *Là-Haut*, the title which Huysmans preferred over his earlier working title of *La Bataille charnelle*. By coincidence, Marcel Thomas (the translator of the French edition of Baldick's biography) acquired another manuscript version of *En Route* for the Bibliothèque Nationale in the same year. This manuscript, which Huysmans had originally given to his friends the Leclaires and which was sold at auction in 1934 for 17,000 francs, actually comprised not just one but two distinct manuscripts, the first being a more complete version of the text discovered by Artinian, and the second being an almost

524

definitive version of *En Route*. In 1988, Michèle Barrière published a new critical edition of *Là-Haut*, which gathered together material from the various extant versions. In this chapter the weakness of Baldick's habit of using the novels as supplementary autobiographical material is most pronounced, as the published version of *En Route* – the only version Baldick had at hand – differed in many respects to the version Huysmans was writing and which he abandoned sometime in early 1893. In an entry in his *Journal* for 25 May 1893, for example, the Abbé Mugnier wrote that Huysmans was going to completely rework his novel on a new plan – no La Salette, only Paris and La Trappe would feature – and the new book would be 'whiter' than the original. See Mugnier, ii, p. 80. [BK]

8 Huret, p. 179.
9 Letter to Émile Edwards of 17 May 1891 (Lambert, xvi, p. 235; Beaumont, p. 110).
10 Mugnier, i, p. 33. See also Mugnier, ii, p. 72 and p. 75.
11 Letter of 7 May 1892 (Massignon, ii).
12 Bloy, iv, pp. 110–11.
13 Mugnier, i, p. 14.
14 J. Huret, *Le Figaro* (supp. litt.), 5 Jan. 1895 (Seillan, pp. 172–3). See also letter to Huret, 1 Jan. 1895 (Beaumont, pp. 142–3). [BK]
15 Letter to Brother Micheau of 25 Feb. 1895 (Daoust, i, p. 71).
16 Letter to Dom Besse of 10 Feb. 1895 (ibid., p. 68).
17 G. Docquois, *Revue Indépendante*, Mar. 1893 (Seillan, pp. 137–41).
18 Letter to Mme Bruyère of 14 Sept. 1897 (Rancœur, p. 11). See also Daoust, iii.
19 Letter to Mme Bruyère of 14 Sept. 1897 (Rancœur, p. 11).
20 See letter from Julie Thibault to JKH of 11 Sept. 1892 (Fonds) and Boucher's notes on JKH's letter of 30 Dec. 1891 (Cogny, x, p. 11); also Bricaud, iii, p. 75.
21 Bricaud, i, pp. 41–42.
22 Ibid., pp. 43–45.
23 Letter to Julie Thibault of 4 Jan. 1893 (Cogny, xiv, p. 208).
24 The interview Baldick refers to was a joint interview of Jules Bois and Huysmans by Huysmans' friend Maurice de Fleury. It was published under the pseudonym 'Horace Bianchon' (not Blanchon) in *Le Figaro*, 10 Jan. 1893. The words attributed to Huysmans were actually spoken by Bois (see Seillan, pp. 128–9). [BK]
25 Michelet, pp. 25–27.
26 Guiches, pp. 262–3.

27 Michelet, pp. 27–29.

28 Ibid., p. 30.

29 Bricaud, i, pp. 62–63.

30 Letter to Julie Thibault of 19 Aug. 1893 (Cogny, xiv, p. 208).

31 Notes on Dubus written by JKH in the Restaurant Estadier on 9 Apr. 1895 (Fonds). See also letter to C. Alberdingk Thijm of 20 June 1895 (Daoust, v, p. 23).

32 Guiches, p. 254. Anna was certified at the Infirmerie Spéciale, 12 Apr. 1893.

33 Certificate of entry to Sainte-Anne of 13 Apr. 1893, and letters from JKH to the Director of 17 Apr. and 14 May 1893 (Archives of Sainte-Anne).

34 Harry, pp. 71–72. See 'The Pilgrim', Note 22.

35 Guiches, p. 255.

36 L. Deffoux, *L'Œuvre*, 11 Nov. 1936.

37 Undated letter to Arnold Goffin (*Catalogue de la vente Andrieux-Giard*, Paris, 22–25 May 1939, No. 317 (9)).

38 Bloy, i, p. 47.

39 Bloy, vi, p. 77.

40 Bloy, ii, p. 89.

41 *Les Annales de la Sainteté au XIXe Siècle*, Apr. 1873.

42 'Autour des fortifications' (*OC, vol* i, pp. 109–131).

43 See Thérive, i.

44 Dumesnil, i, p. 113. [RB] For the full text of this letter dated 6 April 1895, see Cogny, xv, pp. 386–7. [BK]

2. THE PROSELYTE

1 *La Cathédrale*, chap. viii.

2 Letter to Landry of 26 July 1893 (Lambert, xvi, p. 277).

3 Letter to Boucher of 11 Aug. 1893 (Cogny, x, p. 21).

4 Guiches, p. 83.

5 Descaves, *Nouvelles Littéraires*, 14 May 1927.

6 Pradel.

7 *La Cathédrale*, chap. viii.

8 Not at JKH's flat, as stated by Daoust (Daoust, i, p. 7). See Boucher's notes on JKH's letter of 30 Dec. 1891 (Cogny, x, p. 11).

9 For a more detailed account of this visit, see Daoust, i, pp. 15–25.

10 Descaves, i, p. 90.

11 Daoust, i, p. 25.

12 Letter to Dom Besse of 11 July 1894 (Daoust, i, p. 54; Beaumont, p. 138).

13 Letter to Boucher of 20 Sept. 1894 (Cogny, x, pp. 25–6).

14 Letter to Thibault of 18 Sept. 1894 (Cogny, xiv, p. 210).

15 In the French edition, Baldick qualifies this statement by imply-ing that Huysmans may have visited Igny in the autumn of 1894 after all, quoting a letter to Prins of 15 Oct. 1894 as proof (Gillet, p. 267). In it, Huysmans complains of the 'bodily strain' he had had to put up with, and says that 'he preferred the Benedictines as their way of life was less harsh'. However, it is still not certain that he went to Igny, as his letter states that he has just come back from a visit to 'les cathédrales gothiques et les Trappes', and does not mention Igny by name. Pierre Lam-bert, who had read Huysmans' letters to Prins, nevertheless felt that proof of the trip to Igny had not been clearly established. [BK]

16 *La Cathédrale*, chaps. iii and xiii; also Daoust, i, pp. 28–31.

17 Besse, p. 19.

18 Letter to Abbé Moeller of 30 Apr. 1895 (Moeller, 1908, p. 43).

19 Daoust, i, p. 34.

20 Letter to Lauzet of 4 Jan. 1895 (*La Vie*, 18 Oct. 1913).

21 Letter to Boucher of 26 Dec. 1894 (Cogny, x, p. 23).

22 Letter to Dom Micheau of 30 Dec. 1894 (Bourg, pp. 14–15).

23 Descaves, iii, p. 141.

24 Register of Marriages at the Mairie of the 17th Arrondissement in Paris.

25 Antonine Meunier died in 1972. See obituary in *Bulletin*, No. 59, 1972. [BK]

26 Letter to Lauzet of 4 Jan. 1895 (*La Vie*, 18 Oct. 1913).

27 Bloy, iii, p. 348.

28 Valéry, iv, p. 53. See also Valéry, i, p. 19.

29 *Études*, 15 Apr. 1895. For extracts from most of the press reviews of *En Route*, see Dumesnil, i, pp. 92–123.

30 Bloy, iii, p. 415.

31 *Le Journal*, 7 Mar. 1895.

32 *Le Matin*, 2 Mar. 1895.

33 Coquiot, p. 171.

34 *Le Monde*, 12 Mar. 1895.

35 See the Abbé Mugnier's preface to JKH's *Pages catholiques*, Paris, Stock, 1900.

36 Descaves, ii, p. 48.

37 Letter to Dom Micheau of 25 Feb. 1895 (Daoust, i, p. 71).

38 Gourmont, ii, p. 8.

39 Bloy, iii, p. 195.

40 Letter to Dom Besse of 10 Mar. 1895 (Daoust, i, pp. 75–76).

41 Letter to Dom Micheau of 30 Apr. 1895 (Daoust, i, p. 85).

42 Descaves, ii, pp. 53–54.

43 Letter to Dom Besse of 5 June 1895 (Daoust, i, p. 89).

44 Daoust, v.

45 Letter of 5 Oct. 1895 (Daoust, v, p. 38). [RB] The friend who revealed this information to Huysmans was his Dutch correspondent, Arij Prins. See Gillet, p. 280. [BK]

46 Letter to Arij Prins of 26 Dec. 1896 (Gillet, p. 296).

47 T. Massiac, *Écho de Paris*, 28 Aug. 1896 (Seillan, p. 200).

48 G. Docquois, *Revue Indépendante*, Mar. 1893 (Seillan, pp. 137–8).

49 T. Massiac, *Écho de Paris*, 28 Aug. 1896 (Seillan, p. 201).

50 Letter to Lauzet of 5 Jan. 1896 (*La Vie*, 1 Nov. 1913; Beaumont, p. 155–6).

51 Letter to Léon Leclaire of 27 Apr. 1896 (BN).

52 O. Merlin, *Le Temps*, 14 Sept. 1933.

53 Daoust, v, pp. 34–3; and P. Lambert, *Bulletin*, No. 24, 1952, p. 248–550.

54 Letter to Abbé Ferret of 26 Dec. 1896 (Daoust, iii).

3. THE RETREATANT

1 Letter to Dom Besse of 30 Apr. 1895 (Daoust, i, p. 85).

2 Letter to Dom Besse of 5 June 1895 (ibid., pp. 90–91).

3 Letter to Dom Besse of 23 Oct. 1895 (ibid., pp. 98–99).

4 Letter to C. A. Thijm of 20 June 1895 (Daoust, v, p. 23).

5 Letter to Abbé Moeller of 29 June 1895 (Moeller, 1908, pp. 170–1).

6 Rothenstein, p. 262.

7 Letter to C. A. Thijm of 28 May 1895 (Daoust, v, p. 17).

8 Letter to Abbé Moeller of 29 May 1895 (Moeller, 1908, p. 102).

9 Letter to C. A. Thijm of 13 May 1895 (Daoust, v, p. 12).

10 Letter to Dom Besse of June 1895 (Daoust, i, p. 90).

11 Letter to Boucher of 21 May 1895 (Cogny, x, p. 30).

12 Letter to Abbé Moeller of 29 May 1895 (Moeller, 1908, p. 102).

13 Letter to C. A. Thijm of 5 June 1895 (Daoust, v, p. 19).

14 Letter to Abbé Mugnier of 8 June 1895 (Descaves, ii, p. 57; Mugnier, i, p. 39).

15 Letter to C. A. Thijm of 20 June 1895 (Daoust, v, p. 24). [RB] See also a letter to Arij Prins of 13 May 1895 in which he describes Thibault as 'an extraordinary old woman, a clairvoyant who has lived the pure religious life of the Middle Ages', and a letter to the same correspondent of 15 July in which he

admits that 'her cooking's not bad'. (Gillet, pp. 274–5, and p. 278). [BK]

16 Baldick's description of Thibault's altar is inaccurate. For a picture of the altar, see Lambert, xiv, p. 104–5. [BK]

17 Bricaud, ii, pp. 31–32. See also Lambert, xiv.

18 L. Descaves, *L'Œuvre*, 15 Jan. 1926.

19 J. Bois, *Gil Blas*, 9 Jan. 1893 (Seillan, p. 128).

20 Daoust, iii.

21 Letter to Abbé Moeller of 29 June 1895 (Moeller, 1908, p. 170).

22 Boucher's notes on JKH's letter of May 1897 (Cogny, x, pp. 41–2).

23 Letter to Dom Besse of 18 July 1895 (Daoust, i, p. 93).

24 Ibid.

25 Letter to C. A. Thijm of 5 July 1895 (Daoust, v, p. 26).

26 Letter to Abbé Moeller of 5 July 1895 (Moeller, 1908, p. 171).

27 Daoust, v, p. 24.

28 Le Cardonnel.

29 Daoust, iii.

30 Descaves, ii, p. 56.

31 Letter to Abbé Moeller of 12 Oct. 1895 (Moeller, 1908, p. 439).

32 Letter from Tours to Julie Thibault of 15 Oct. 1895 (Cogny, xiv, p. 211).

33 Letter to Dom Besse of 23 Oct. 1895 (Daoust, i, p. 99).

34 Entries for 10 Nov. and 22 Dec. 1895 in the Goncourt *Journal*.

35 Undated letter to Abbé Ferret (Daoust, iii).

36 Letter to Landry of 23 Mar. 1896 (Fonds), and Register of Marriages at the Mairie of the 8th Arrondissement in Paris.

37 Letter to Father Pacheu of 26 Dec. 1896 (Narfon, iii; Beaumont, p. 166). Laver is incorrect in stating that Verlaine was dead in 1894 and that JKH published his preface to Verlaine's *Poésies religieuses* in that year.

38 Descaves, ii, p. 10.

39 Lézinier, p. 203.

40 Notes on JKH's letters (Cogny, x, pp. 61–2).

41 Descaves, i, p. 165.

42 After Leclaire's death in 1932 this correspondence was deposited at the Bibliothèque Nationale by Lucien Descaves, with instructions that it should be kept in reserve for as long as possible. [RB] The correspondence between Huysmans and the Leclaires comprises 228 letters, and contains a wealth of material on Huysmans' thoughts and feelings, as well as a narrative of the incidents of his everyday life, between 27 April 1896

and 11 March 1907. In the first edition of his biography Baldick states that an annotated edition of the letters, prepared by himself, Pierre Lambert and Joseph Daoust, 'is shortly to be published', however this edition never saw the light of day. [BK]

43 Letter to Leclaire of 11 Dec. 1904 (BN).

44 Letter to the Leclaires of 27 Apr. 1896 (Daoust, *L'Information Littéraire*, Nov. 1951).

45 Letter to Dom Besse of 3 Apr. 1896 (Daoust, i, pp. 106–7).

46 Letter to Dom Guerry of 24 June 1896 (ibid., pp. 110–11).

47 Letter to Abbé Moeller of 2 July 1896 (Moeller, 1908, p. 445).

48 Mugnier, i, pp. 42–43.

49 Undated letter to Abbé Ferret (Daoust, iii).

50 Undated letter to Abbé Mugnier (Mugnier, i, pp. 44–45).

51 Undated letter to Abbé Ferret (Daoust, iii).

52 Letter to Abbé Moeller of 2 July 1896 (Moeller, 1908, p. 445).

53 Letter to Abbé Ferret of 10 Oct. 1896 (Daoust, iii); letter to Abbé Moeller of 22 Oct. 1896 (Moeller, 1909, p. 274).

54 Letter to Mme Bruyère of 16 Oct. 1896 (Rancœur, p. 5; Beaumont, pp. 163–4).

55 Letter to Abbé Moeller of 22 Oct. 1896 (Moeller, 1909, p. 274).

56 Letter to Jeanne Bibesco of 16 Feb. 1899 (Bulletin, No. 89, 1966, p 25; Beaumont, pp. 188–90). The complete text of this letter, together with an extensive selection of their correspondence, has now been published, see *Bulletin*, No. 89, 1996, pp. 1–45. [BK]

57 Letter to Abbé Ferret of 10 Oct. 1896 (Daoust, iii).

58 Letter to Abbé Mugnier of Sept. 1896 (Descaves, ii, p. 58).

59 Letter of 22 Oct. 1896 (Moeller, 1909, p. 274).

4. THE SYMBOLOGIST

1 Letter to Mathilde Prache of 27 Feb. 1897 (Daoust, iii).

2 Garçon, ii, p. 50. See also Albert Houtin's interesting but unreliable book, *Une Grande Mystique: Mme Cécile Bruyère*, Paris, Alcan, 1930.

3 P. P. Plan, *Le Temps*, 19 July 1901.

4 Letter to Abbé Ferret of 1 Mar. 1897 (Daoust, iii).

5 Ibid.

6 Letter to Abbé Ferret of 7 Mar. 1897 (ibid.).

7 Letter to Abbé Ferret of 1 Mar. 1897 (ibid.).

8 Letter to Abbé Ferret of 14 Mar. 1897 (ibid.).

9 Letter to Forain of Jan. 1901 (Vaillat, p. 192; Beaumont, pp. 204–5). JKH also mentions this visit in a letter to Abbé

Mugnier (Descaves, ii, pp. 39–40) in which Laver mistakenly sees a reference to Mme Bruyère.

10 Letter to Abbé Moeller of 4 Sept. 1897 (Moeller, 1909, p. 279).

11 Letter to Leclaire of 5 Apr. 1897 (BN).

12 Letter to Landry of 21 Apr. 1897 (Fonds).

13 Letter to Mme Bruyère of 8 May 1897 (Rancœur, p. 7).

14 This rough draft and Le Roy's letter are in the Fonds Lambert. Drumont's article appeared in *La Libre Parole* on 11 May 1897.

15 Letter to Leclaire of 8 May 1897 (BN).

16 Letter to Leclaire of 6 June 1897 (BN).

17 Letter to Abbé Ferret of 6 June 1897 (Daoust, iii).

18 Letter to Mme Bruyère of 11 June 1897 (Rancœur, p. 10).

19 Letter to Abbé Ferret of 26 June 1897 (Daoust, iii).

20 Letter to Dom Besse of 17 July 1897 (Daoust, i, p. 126).

21 Letter to Abbé Ferret of 17 July 1897 (Daoust, iii).

22 Mondor, iii, p. 776. Valéry met JKH on 8 July and wrote to Mallarmé on 9 July 1897.

23 Boucher's notes on letter of 11 Aug. 1893 (Cogny, x, p. 22).

24 Letter to Abbé Ferret of 22 July 1997 (Daoust, iii).

25 Letter to Leclaire of 28 July 1897 (BN) and to Abbé Ferret of 1 Aug. 1897 (Daoust, iii).

26 Letter to Abbé Ferret of 22 Aug. 1897 (Daoust, iii).

27 Letter to Mme Bruyère of 14 Sept. 1897 (Rancœur, pp. 10–11).

28 Letter to Abbé Mugnier of Sept. 1897 (Descaves, ii, p. 39).

29 Letter to Dom Besse of 14 Sept. 1897 (Daoust, i, p. 128).

30 Letter to Abbé Ferret of 22 July 1897 (Daoust, iii).

31 Letter to Dom Pothier of 13 Mar. 1898 (Daoust, i, pp. 134).

32 Cogny, iii.

33 Letter to Mme Bruyère of 30 July 1899 (Rancœur, p. 21; Beaumont, pp. 191–3).

34 Some extracts from this notebook have been published by Pierre Cogny in an interesting article on JKH and Blessed Lydwine (Cogny, iv).

35 Cogny, xiv, pp. 211–2.

36 Letter to Abbé Poelhekke of 23 Oct. 1897 (Galichet).

37 Letter to Boucher of 28 Oct. 1897 (Cogny, x, pp. 45–6).

38 Ibid. Huysmans may have implied to Boucher that he was being victimised or forced out of the civil service because of his Catholicism, but he had planned to retire in 1898 for at least five years. See Gillet, p. 253 and p. 273. [BK]

39 Letter to Dom Micheau of 23 Nov. 1897 (Daoust, i, p. 130; Beaumont, pp. 169–70).

40 Letter to Leclaire of Oct. 1897 (BN).

41 Letter to Leclaire of 30 Dec. 1897 (BN).

42 Descaves, ii, p. 114. [RB] As Jean-Marie Seillan has pointed out, Baldick, like a number of other leading Huysmansian critics of the period, was extremely reticent about Huysmans' position regarding the Dreyfus Affair, presumably embarrassed by the sporadic anti-Semitic references that litter his later work. Like many Catholics of the period, Huysmans, along with other Catholic writers such as Bloy, Barrès and Coppée, took an anti-Dreyfusard stance, believing that Jews, atheists, socialists and Freemasons were in league to destroy the ancient traditions and values of France. See Seillan, p. 86. [BK]

43 Letter to Leclaire of 27 Jan. 1898 (BN).

44 Letter to Leclaire of 31 Jan. 1898 (BN).

45 Letter to Boucher of 16 Feb. 1898 (Cogny, x, p. 48).

46 Letter to Boucher of 2 Apr. 1898 (Cogny, x, p. 53).

47 Entry for 28 Apr. 1899 (*Bulletin*, No. 9, 1933, p. 66).

48 Boucher's notes on JKH's letter of 22 Nov. 1898 (Cogny, x, pp. 72–3).

49 Letter to Leclaire of 6 Apr. 1898 (BN).

50 For example a certain Maximilien Denizet, who consulted JKH on 8 Apr. 1898 about a spell which he said had been laid upon him (Letter from Denizet to JKH of 23 Apr. 1898. Fonds).

51 Undated letter to unnamed friend (Bron, p. 64).

52 Letter to Descaves of 19 Feb. 1898 (Descaves, i, p. 18).

53 Letter of 2 June 1898 (*La Semaine Religieuse du Diocèse de Cambrai*, 1 June 1907).

54 Lambert, xii, p. 953.

55 Ibid., pp. 954–6.

56 Undated letter to Abbé Mugnier (Descaves, ii, p. 54). [RB] For other accounts of the same episode, see Huysmans' letter to Boucher (Cogny, x, p. 51), and to Prins of 24 June 1898 (Gillet, pp. 324–5). [BK]

57 Lambert, xii, pp. 957–9.

58 For more information on relations between JKH and Zdenka Braunerova (1858–1934), see John Sandiford-Pelle, 'J.-K. Huysmans, Elémir Bourges et les Sœurs Braunerova. Quatre lettres inédites de J.-K. Huysmans à Zdenka Braunerova' (*Bulletin*, No. 66, 1976). [BK]

5. THE OBLATE

1 Diary entry for 20 June 1898 (Lambert, xii, p. 958). In a letter to Arij Prins of 3 July 1898, Huysmans says that he intends to leave for Ligugé the following morning (Gillet, p. 326). [BK]

2 See letters to Mme Bruyère of 3 Sept. 1898 (Rancœur, p. 14; Beaumont, pp. 173–6) and to Leclaire of 8 July 1898 (BN).

3 Letter to Mme Bruyère of 3 Sept. 1898 (Rancœur, p. 14; Beaumont, pp. 173–6).

4 Undated letter to Abbé Mugnier (Descaves, ii, p. 55).

5 Letter to Dom Thomasson of 25 July 1898 (Descaves, i, p. 25).

6 It was probably due to Boucher that one of the rarest of Huysmans' publications, *La Magie en Poitou: Gilles de Rais*, 100 copies of which were printed in Ligugé in 1899, came into existence. This short pamphlet, which was composed of sections of *Là-bas* concerning Gilles de Rais edited to form a chronological narrative, had its origins in a lecture that Boucher had given to the Congrès d'Éthnologie et d'Art populaire in Niort in 1896. Originally, Boucher had asked permission to extract sections of *Là-bas* for use in the lecture, and Huysmans duly agreed in his letter of reply. However, Boucher then went on to publish these edited extracts of *Là-bas* under the title *La Sorcellerie en Poitou: Gilles de Rais par J.-K. Huysmans* (Librairie de la Tradition Nationale, 1897), in an edition of 100 copies, *hors commerce*. It is not clear whether Huysmans had given Boucher permission for this or not, in any event two years later he brought out his own edition, published at Ligugé, the text of which is identical to Boucher's pamphlet but which also included five photographic plates of Tiffauges. See Huysmans' letter of 9 Sept. 1896 and Boucher's notes (Cogny, x, pp. 39–40) [BK]

7 The following details of JKH's first visit to Ligugé are taken from Boucher's notes on JKH's letter of 30 July 1898 (Cogny, x, pp. 57–62) which Maurice Garçon also used for his account of the affair in *Huysmans inconnu*; and from JKH's letters to Leclaire (BN). JKH's letter to Mme Bruyère of 3 Sept. 1898 (Rancœur, pp. 13–15; Beaumont, pp. 173–6), which also describes this visit, was written to appease the Abbess of Solesmes and must be regarded with suspicion.

8 Letter to Leclaire of 8 Aug. 1898 (*Bulletin*, No. 80, 1987, p. 4).

9 Letter to Landry of 18 Aug. 1898 (*Bulletin*, No. 22, 1950, p. 71).

10 Letter to Leclaire of 17 Aug. 1898 (*Bulletin*, No. 80, 1987, p. 9).

11 Letter to Leclaire of 19 Aug. 1898 (BN).

12 The original price was 4,500 francs; JKH promised to pay 4,000

francs to Piard and 500 francs to a poor convent. The legal formalities were concluded in the office of Me Morier at Poitiers on 22 Aug. 1898 (Garçon, ii, p. 62).

13 Besse, ii, p. 22.

14 Garçon, ii, p. 69.

15 Ibid., p. 65.

16 Letter to Dom Thomasson of 2 Oct. 1898 (Descaves, i, p. 29). Descaves misdates this letter 20 Oct.

17 The dedicatory inscription, composed by Gustave Boucher, was privately reprinted for JKH and his friends. The wording is given in Garçon, ii, p. 72.

18 Letter to Boucher of 13 Apr. 1898 (Cogny, x, p. 55).

19 Coquiot, p. 208. Caldain's claim to have known JKH in 1898 may be as false as his claim to part-authorship of the *Revue Hebdomadaire* biography of JKH signed by Céard and Caldain. This work, in fact, was written by Céard, Caldain being responsible for the documentation only. The article by 'M. et J. de Caldain' in the June 1907 issue of *La Revue des Flandres* was written by M. René Dumesnil and sent to the review by Caldain, who altered the signature. Caldain died in extreme poverty in Dec. 1927, aged sixty. For an interesting and informative article on him, see Bemelmans, i. [RB] Huysmans certainly knew Caldain in 1898 as a letter to him dated 24 Dec. 1898 exists. See Cogny, x, pp. 98–9. [BK]

20 Letter to Boucher of 3 Nov. 1898 (Cogny, x, p. 70).

21 Letter to Boucher c. 25 Oct. 1898 (Cogny, x, p.68).

22 Letters to Boucher of 3 Dec. 1898 (Cogny, x, p. 74) and to Leclaire of 8 and 12 Jan. 1899 (BN).

23 A rough draft of this letter (dated 18 Nov. 1898) is in the Archives of the Abbey of Saint-Martin de Ligugé.

24 See letter to Leclaire of 11 Dec. 1898 (BN); also letter to Mme Bruyère of 2 Feb. 1899 (Rancœur, p. 20).

25 Letter to Mme Bruyère of 2 Feb. 1899 (Rancœur, p. 20). A rough draft of a similar letter to Cardinal Vannutelli, dated 12 Dec. 1898, is in the Fonds Lambert (Beaumont, pp. 187–8).

26 Letter to Leclaire of 15 Dec. 1898 (BN).

27 Letter to Boucher c. 5 Dec. 1898 (Cogny, x, p. 76).

28 Letter to Leclaire of 20 Dec. 1898 (BN).

29 Letter to Leclaire of 25 Dec. 1898 (BN).

30 Letter to Boucher c. 28 Dec. 1898 (Cogny, x, p. 84).

31 Letter to Boucher of 30 Dec. 1898 (Cogny, x, p. 84).

32 Descaves, ii, pp. 65–66.

33 Express letter of 11 Jan. 1899, signed: Sol (Fonds).

34 Letter of 7 Feb. 1899 (Bron, p. 55) Boucher afterwards claimed that it was he who had saved *La Cathédrale* from condemnation by giving a *curriculum vitae* of JKH to one Father Lhommeau, who communicated it to Cardinal Vannutelli (Notes on JKH's letter of 22 Nov. 1898. Cogny, x, pp. 72–3).

35 Letter to Boucher of 24 Jan. 1899 (Cogny, x, p. 89).

36 JKH refers to the bribing of Mme Thibault in his letter to Leclaire of 8 July 1898 (BN). The article by Jane Misme appeared in *Le Figaro* of 6 Jan. 1899. For JKH's comments on the article, see his letter to Boucher of same date (Cogny, x, p. 87) and letter to unnamed correspondent (Bron, pp. 108–9). [RB] Huysmans also complains of Thibault's venality in his letter to Boucher (Cogny, x, p. 51), and to Prins of 14 June 1898 (Gillet, p. 324). [BK]

37 Letter to Landry of 5 Oct. 1898 (Fonds).

38 Letter to Abbé Moeller of 19 May 1899 (Moeller, 1910, p. 176). JKH left for Ligugé on 20 May.

39 Billy, pp. 48–49.

40 Letter (to Alice Poictevin?) of 17 Aug. 1899 (*L'Union Séraphique*, Aug. 1909).

41 Letter to Mme Bruyère of 30 July 1899 (Rancœur, p. 22; Beaumont, pp. 191–3).

42 Letter to Landry of 17 July 1899 (Fonds; Beaumont, pp. 190–1).

43 Letter to Landry of 26 July 1899 (Fonds).

44 Letter to Abbé Mugnier c. 17 July 1899 (Descaves, ii, p. 66).

45 Letter to Landry of 17 July 1899 (Fonds; Beaumont, pp. 190–1).

46 For an account of Lézinier's visit, illustrated by the photographs which he took, and a letter JKH wrote him three months later, on 23 Oct. 1899, see Lézinier, pp. 201–18.

47 Descaves, i, p. 83. Descaves stayed at Ligugé from 25 to 28 Aug.

48 Ibid., pp. 93–94.

49 Fonds. See also the full account of the case in Garçon, iii.

50 Descaves, ii, p. 69.

51 Descaves, i, p. 90. Descaves dates this letter June 1900, but see also letter from JKH to Landry of 11 Oct. 1899 (Fonds).

52 Lefèvre, p. 58.

53 Descaves, i, p. 57.

54 Letter to Grillot de Givry of 1 Nov. 1899 (Lambert, x, p. 351).

55 Letter to Landry of 25 Dec. 1899 (Fonds).

56 Letter of 23 Nov. 1899 (Daoust, iv).

57 Descaves, ii, p. 72.

58 *Le Figaro*, 3 Feb. 1900 (Seillan, pp. 275–83).

59 Billy, p. 51.

60 See letter to Leclaire of 24 Apr. 1900 (BN); *Le Temps*, 24 Apr. 1900; *La Semaine Religieuse de Paris*, 23 June 1900.

61 Aubault, pp. 16–17. The details of this anecdote are suspect.

62 Descaves, ii, p. 71.

63 Descaves, i, pp. 141–2. In this letter JKH incorrectly calls the clothing ceremony the ceremony of oblation – probably in order to kill public interest in the second ceremony, which was to be held a year later.

64 In the French edition, Baldick adds a paragraph here to explain that, despite the implication of his letter, Huysmans was not the only candidate for oblature. As Huysmans remarked somewhat ironically to Landry, 'Boucher also donned the habit; he has even made his own, which serves as a vest and which, with its upright collar, gives him the air of a clergyman, minus the licorice pastilles – it's not in very good taste'. See letter to Landry of 22 Mar. 1900 (Chastel, p.111). [BK]

65 See Deffoux, ii, pp. 1–15.

66 Descaves, ii, p. 73.

67 JKH told Descaves of his success when he met him by chance that evening in Stock's shop. See letter to Leclaire of 7 Apr. 1900 (BN), and Descaves, ii, p. 73.

68 Rosny, ii, p. 10.

69 Letter to the Leclaires of 20 Apr. 1900 (BN). Easter Sunday was 15 Apr.

70 Descaves, i, p. 113.

71 Letter to Abbé Mugnier of 22 June 1900 (Descaves, ii, pp. 76–77).

72 Letter to Leclaire of 12 July 1900 (BN).

73 Letter to Leclaire of 19 July 1900 (BN).

74 Roche came to Ligugé for the day on 28 Jan.; Descaves stayed there from 21 to 25 Apr. and from 12 to 15 Oct.; Rivière came in June, arriving on the 8th; Girard and Landry came in August, the former leaving on the 16th; and the Abbé Broussolle arrived for a few days on 1 Nov.

75 Letter to Leclaire of 29 Oct. 1900 (BN).

76 Letter to Landry of 3 Aug. 1900 (Fonds).

77 Letter to Landry of 20 Sept. 1900 (Fonds). See also letters to Landry of 26 Sept., 6, 11, and 19 Oct. 1900 (Fonds). The Leclaires and their niece left for Vincennes on 20 Oct. Mme

Gault died in May 1902, aged twenty-three (letter to Leclaire of 23 May 1902).

78 Letter to Landry of 6 Nov. 1900 (Fonds).

79 See letters to Abbé Broussolle of 15, 23, and 24 Nov. 1900 (Daoust, iv).

80 For details of JKH's negotiations with this society, see letter to Landry of 20 June 1900 (Fonds), and letters to Leclaire of 29 Apr. and 7 July 1900 (BN).

81 Lefèvre, pp. 21–22.

82 Letter to Abbé Broussolle of 23 Nov. 1900 (Daoust, iv).

83 Letter to Abbé Broussolle of 7 Jan. 1901 (Daoust, iv). See also Descaves, i, pp. 124–5; Lefèvre, pp. 24–25; Vaillat, pp. 189–98.

84 Letter to Mme Bruyère of 30 July 1898 (Rancœur, p. 22).

85 Letter to Abbé Moeller of 25 June 1900 (Moeller, 1910, p. 494).

86 Letter to Abbé Mugnier of 22 June 1900 (Descaves, ii, pp. 77–78).

87 Letter to Leclaire of 31 Dec. 1900 (BN).

6. THE HAGIOGRAPHER

1 Letter to Abbé Moeller of 12. Feb. 1901 (Moeller, 1910, p. 499). Laver is incorrect in stating that JKH completed this work after his return to Paris in Oct. 1901.

2 Letter to Jeanne Bibesco of Dec. 1900 (*Bulletin*, No. 89, 1996, p. 37; Beaumont, pp. 202–4).

3 Letter of 13 Mar. 1900 (Bontoux, pp. 220–4).

4 Letter of 17 Aug. 1901 (Leven).

5 Letter to Jeanne Bibesco of Dec. 1900 (*Bulletin*, No. 89, 1996, p. 37).

6 Letter to Abbé Broussolle of 7 Jan. 1901 (Daoust, iv).

7 Aubault, pp. 20–23. The details of this story are suspect. [RB] As Pierre Lambert noted in his list of corrections to the French edition of the biography, the supposedly missing comma is in the Palmé edition. [BK]

8 Ageorges, p. 223; J. Guillemard, *Mercure de France*, 1 Feb. 1936; Langé, ii.

9 Letter to Abbé Moeller of 12 Feb. 1901 (Moeller, 1910, p. 499).

10 On 19 Mar. 1901. See letter to Abbé Broussolle of same date (Daoust, iv).

11 Deffoux, iv, pp. 103–6.

12 Garçon, ii, p. 88. [RB] See also letter to Landry of 22 Mar. 1900 (Chastel, p. 110). [BK]

13 Letter to Abbé Mugnier, Easter 1901 (Descaves, ii, p. 74). Descaves incorrectly dates this letter 1900.

14 Letter to Mme Bruyère of 30 July 1899 (Rancœur, p. 22; Beaumont, pp. 191–3).

15 Letter to Leclaire of 17 Apr. 1901 (BN).

16 Of Bourbon little is known except that his wife died at Ligugé and that he later took up farming in the Department of Ain. See also letter to Leclaire of 10 July 1901 (BN), and Boucher's notes on JKH's letters (Cogny, x, p. 96). Rouault left Ligugé at the same time as JKH and returned to Paris; his subsequent career is well known. Morisse opened a bookshop in Poitiers, was later on the staff of the *Mercure de France* for many years, and eventually returned to the book-trade in Zurich and Paris; he died in 1946. See Lefèvre, pp. 20–25, and *Bulletin*, No. 21, 1949.

17 On 7 May. See letter to Leclaire of 8 May 1901 (BN); also letter to Berthet (Billy, p. 65).

18 Letter to Leclaire of 30 April 1901 (BN).

19 Letter to Leclaire of 9 June 1901 (BN).

20 Descaves, ii, p. 81; letters to Leclaire of 10 and 17 June 1901 (BN); letter to Bois of 11 June 1901 (Corsetti, ii).

21 Letter to Leclaire of 25 July 1901 (BN).

22 J. Noury, *Études, 5* Aug. 1901.

23 Letter to Bois of 11 June 1901 (Corsetti, ii).

24 Letter to Abbé Moeller of 8 Aug. 1901 (Moeller, 1910, p. 500).

25 Descaves, ii, pp. 85–86.

26 Letter to Leclaire of 30 July 1901 (*Bulletin*, No. 81, 1988, p. 10).

27 Moeller, 1910, p. 500.

28 Letter to Mme Théophile Huc of 21 Aug. 1901 (Martineau, p. 71).

29 Coquiot, p. 214.

30 Letter to Landry of 7 Sept. 1901 (Fonds).

31 JKH was in Paris from 13 to 18 Sept. and from 12 to 16 Oct. (letters to Leclaire of 15 and 17 Sept. and 14 Oct. BN).

32 Lambert, xvii, p. 499.

33 Descaves, i, pp. 146–59.

34 Billy, p. 67.

35 Lambert, xvii, p. 506.

36 Ibid., p. 512.

37 Letter to Dom Besse of 2 Oct. 1901 (Daoust, i, pp. 145–7).

38 Letter to unnamed correspondent of 19 Oct. 1901 (*Catalogue de la Librairie Leroy*, Paris, Sept. 1931, No. 76).

39 Letter to Jeanne Bibesco of 29 October 1901 (*Bulletin*, No. 89, 1996, p. 40).

40 Letter to Leclaire of 26 Oct. 1901 (*Bulletin*, No. 34, 1957, p. 184).

41 Letter to Leclaire of 5 Nov. 1901 (BN); letter to Abbé Moeller of 7 Nov. 1901 (Moeller, 1910, p. 554).

42 Letter to Leclaire of 26 Oct. 1901 (BN).

43 Letter to Jeanne Bibesco of 31 January 1902 (*Bulletin*, No. 89, 1996, p. 40).

44 Letter to Leclaire of 15 Nov. 1901 (BN).

45 Descaves, ii, pp. 89–90.

46 Letter to Leclaire of 8 Nov. 1901 (*Bulletin*, No. 34, 1957, p. 185).

47 The following details are taken from Aubault, pp. 61–74.

48 Harry, p. 85. See 'The Pilgrim', Note 22.

49 Aubault, pp. 39–40.

50 Letter to Mme Bruyère of 20 Nov. 1901 (Rancœur, p. 26; Beaumont, pp. 210–1).

51 Aubault, p. 51; Descaves, i, p. 172.

52 Letter to Leclaire of 3 Dec. 1901 (*Bulletin*, No. 34, 1957, p. 186).

53 Letter to Landry, written c. 20 Dec. 1901 (Fonds).

54 Letter to Berthet of 2 Jan. 1902 (Billy, pp. 68–69).

55 Letter to Leclaire of 15 Nov. 1901 (BN).

56 Descaves, i, p. 181. [RB] Sometime in 1900 or 1901, Huysmans mapped out a plan for a novel on the liturgy that differs considerably from that of *L'Oblat*, which was first projected in 1896. Conceived as a 'novel divided into four parts', the manuscript of this plan comprises nine sheets of paper, and is entitled *Fêtes de l'Église*. It seems in part to have been inspired by Huysmans' reading of Dom Cabrol's *Le Livre de la prière antique*, which was published in 1900, as much of the plan consists of a paraphrase of Cabrol's book and includes a number of quotations from it. See *Huysmans*, L'Herne, No. 47, 1985, pp. 245–57. [BK]

57 The following details are largely taken from Deffoux, iv, pp. 107–23.

58 Letter to Leclaire of 13 Feb. 1902 (BN).

59 Letter to Leclaire of 30 Aug. 1902 (BN). [RB] Despite Huysmans' complaints, which he repeated to Abbé Mugnier (Mugnier, ii, p. 133), the published book does not appear to be missing any pages and the text of *Don Bosco* reproduced by Lucien Descaves in *En marge* (1927) is identical with that of the earlier edition. [BK]

60 Letter to Jules Bois of 9 May 1902 (Corsetti, ii).

61 Letters to Leclaire of 23 May and 30 June 1902 (BN).

62 Letter of 21 May 1902. This and other letters from M. Delmas, M. Pépin, and Mlle Duclos, as well as the rough drafts of letters from JKH to M. Delmas, Mlle Duclos, and M. Duclos, which

are quoted in this chapter, are now in the Fonds Lambert. For more detailed quotations, see Garçon, iv.

63 Letters of 7, 14, 16 June 1902.

64 Letters from Mlle Duclos of 2, 6, 8, 9 July 1902; letter from M. Pépin of 2 July 1902.

65 Letter to Abbé Moeller of 12 Aug. 1902 (Moeller, 1910, p. 558).

66 Aubault, pp. 28–33; letter to Leclaire of 18 July 1902 (BN). A more succinct version of the second account is to be found in JKH's letter to Abbé Moeller of 12 Aug. 1902 (Moeller, 1910, p. 559).

67 Letter to Leclaire of 25 July 1902 (BN).

68 Letter to Leclaire of 28 Nov. 1903 (BN); Garçon, iv. [RB] In the French edition, Baldick added the following: In trying to elucidate the origins of this strange event, Henry Lefai and Émile Nugues have discovered that both Huysmans and Naundorff had relatives who lived in Bréda. Huysmans' grandfather and uncle were professors at the Bréda Academy at the same time when Adelberth, Naundorff's son was a pupil. As a child, Huysmans had heard it said that his relatives in Bréda possessed 'royal documents, memorials and seals'. It seems likely that Rodaglia acquired some of these documents after the death of Constant Huysmans and drew entirely false conclusions from them. See Nugues, ii. [BK]

7. *THE PILGRIM*

1 Harry, p. 43. [RB] This recollection should be treated with suspicion. It is unlikely that, given his views on the subject of suffering and the will of God, Huysmans would have contemplated suicide at this period, and he gives no hint of such feelings in letters to two of his closest friends, Prins and Leclaire. He does, however, refer to the subject in a conversation which the Abbé Mugnier recorded in his *Journal* in 1892, complaining that 'demonic influences' had urged him to kill himself. Perhaps it is merely a coincidence that Harry's first public reference to Huysmans' thoughts of suicide should be published a year after René Dumesnil's *La Publication d'En Route* (1931), which contained the previously unpublished reference from Mugnier's diary (Dumesnil, i, p. 88; Mugnier, ii, p. 76). See also Note 22. [BK]

2 Letter to Leclaire of 10 Aug. 1902 (BN).

3 Letter to Leclaire of 12 Jan. 1903 (BN).

4 Letter to Leclaire of 24 Sept. 1902 (BN).

5   Letter to Mme Godefroy of Dec. 1902 (*Bulletin*, No. 57, 1971 p. 12).

6   LMC.

7   Letter to Leclaire of 24 Sept. 1902 (BN).

8   Letter to Céard of 5 Oct. 1902 (copy, Fonds; Beaumont, pp. 214–5).

9   Ibid.

10 Ibid.

11 He could not, therefore, have corrected the proofs of the book while living in the Rue Monsieur, as stated by Laver.

12 Letter to Leclaire of 8 Dec. 1902 (BN). [RB] Huysmans' frustration with what he saw as the stupidity of many Catholics was expressed in an unpublished manuscript, written sometime in 1903–04, the tenor of which can be gauged from its opening words: 'What response can one make to this insoluble question: why is it that a practising Catholic is more stupid than a non-Catholic?' See 'Les Rêveries d'un croyant grincheux,' *Bulletin*, No. 89, 1996, pp. 47–63. [BK]

13 Letter to Leclaire of 2 Nov. 1902 (BN).

14 Letter to Leclaire of 28 Aug. 1902 (BN).

15 Letter to Leclaire of 2 Jan. 1903 (BN).

16 Letter to Leclaire of 24 Feb. 1903 (BN).

17 Letter to Leclaire of 8 June 1899 (BN). This idea probably owed its origin to a letter to JKH from Dom Thomasson de Gournay, dated: '*Le jour de Ste Agnès, 1898*' (LMC). It recurs in *Trois Primitifs*.

18 Letter to Berthet of 2 Jan. 1902 (Billy, p. 69).

19 Letter to Berthet of 26 June 1903 (ibid., pp. 74–75).

20 L. Blum, *Gil Blas*, 9 Mar. 1903.

21 Letter to Mme Leclaire of 24 Dec. 1902 (BN).

22 Harry, pp. 22–34. [RB] Myriam Harry (1869–1958) can no longer be considered a reliable witness. In her account of her relations with Huysmans, published over twenty-five years after his death, she reprints a letter from the novelist supposedly written on 4 Dec. 1902 (Harry, pp. 19–20). The letter is given prominence because in it, Huysmans invites her to see him for the first time and this marks the beginning of their friendship. Harry quotes Huysmans as saying that she is welcome to visit him 'any day of the week in the Rue de Babylone', and that he has 'returned to Paris with an overcast soul' so she should 'bring a spiritual umbrella to protect her from the rain'. In fact, the letter she quotes is a composite of two different letters, the main

body of which was written two years later, on 1 Oct. 1904, when Huysmans was living at Rue Saint-Placide, and it is to this address that he invites her (letter in editor's possession). Harry's attempt to falsify the letter is also apparent from internal evidence: in late November 1902 Huysmans was already in Paris correcting the proofs of *L'Oblat* – the mention of his 'return' in the letter refers to his return on 24th September 1904 from a visit to Lourdes. It is clear from this that Harry has amended the date, address and even the content of at least one letter she reprints in her book, presumably in order to make her acquaintance with Huysmans seem of longer-standing or more intimate than it was. To a greater or lesser degree, Harry changed the content of nearly all the letters she printed purporting to come from Huysmans, so only when the originals can be checked and verified will a reliable chronology of their relationship be established. However, it is likely that she first met Huysmans either in late 1903 or early 1904: the first mention of her name in connection with Huysmans in Abbé Mugnier's diary dates from April 1904 (Mugnier, ii, p. 145), and Huysmans' letter to Leclaire of 12 Mar. 1904, in which he states that his relationship with Harry began 'a few months ago, under the guise of a visit from a fellow writer' also points to this date. Harry's memoir contains a number of dubious and unsupported claims: that Huysmans told her he had considered committing suicide in 1901, that he was going to recommend her book for the Prix Goncourt in 1904, and that he had gone to Belgium with 'La Sol'. Embellishing on the last of these, Harry recounts that during the journey 'the temptation was so great they could no longer content themselves with a platonic relationship': La Sol came to his room that night, and 'everything was spoiled'. They separated not wanting to see their 'dream dissolve into base carnal realities.' (Harry, pp. 67–8). Despite the dramatic recollection of the incident there is no evidence that Huysmans ever travelled in Belgium or Germany with La Sol, though in a letter to Cécile Bruyère of 30 July 1899 he says that La Sol went to Bruges in 1897 to solicit help from 'the demonic priest I portrayed in *Là-Bas* under the name of Canon Docre' (Rancœur, p. 22). See also 'The Martyr', Note 7 below. [BK]

23 Deffoux, ii, pp. 55–56.
24 Letter to Dom Besse of 5 May 1903 (Daoust, i, p. 161).
25 Letter to Abbé Moeller of 25 July 1903 (Moeller, 1910, p. 733).
26 Deffoux, ii, pp. 97–98.

27 Harry, pp. 61–62. See Note 22.

28 Letter to Leclaire of 29 Jan. 1903 (BN).

29 Letter to Leclaire of 27 Feb. 1903 (BN).

30 Letter to Landry of 11 Mar. 1903 (Lambert, xv, p. 255).

31 Undated letter quoted by L. Descaves in his Note on *Les Foules de Lourdes, OC,* vol. xxiii, pp. 335–6.

32 Entry for 8 Mar. 1903 (Lambert, xv, pp. 207–8).

33 Letter to Berthet of 22 Mar. 1903 (Billy, p. 71).

34 Laver states incorrectly that it was La Sol whom JKH met in the Carmel of Lourdes, explaining that 'she had undergone a spiritual evolution', an error based on a misreading of the statement that late in life '*Huysmans se trouva en presence de la fille de "la Sol", religieuse Carmélite à Lourdes*' (Rancœur, p. 22, note).

35 Letter to Landry of 11 Mar. 1903 (Lambert, xv, pp. 255–6).

36 Letter to Landry of 22 Mar. 1903 (Lambert, xv, p. 267).

37 The present author is indebted for this information to Sister Hélène-Marie de la Sainte Croix, of the Carmel of Notre-Dame de Lourdes, who wrote to him in May 1951: 'After this there is no further mention of her [Sister Thérèse de Jésus] in our chronicles. Our oldest Mothers say that she must have returned to the world soon after her profession, but I cannot give you the exact date of her return to the world.'

38 Letter to Leclaire of 11 Mar. 1907 (BN; Beaumont, pp. 234–5).

39 Letter to Abbé Broussolle of 18 Mar. 1903 (Daoust, iv).

40 *Sonnet masculin* and *Sonnet saignant* (*Parnasse satyrique du XIXe siècle,* vol. iii, Brussels [Gay], 1881; reprinted in *Poesie Érotique: quinze chefs-d'œuvre du XVIIe au XXe siècle,* La Musardine, 2000).

41 Letter to Leclaire of 4 Apr. 1903 (BN).

42 Ibid.

43 Letter to Leclaire of 17 Feb. 1903 (BN).

44 Letter to Leclaire of 24 Dec. 1902 (BN).

45 Letter to Leclaire of 4 Apr. 1903 (BN).

46 Letter to Leclaire of 20 Apr. 1903 (BN). The following 'monks and other respectable persons' have been identified: The Abbot (Dom Bourigaud), Dom d'Auberoche and Dom Émonot (Dom Jean Mayol de Lupé), Dom Felletin (Dom Besse), Dom de Fonneuve (Dom Chamard), Dom Philigone Miné (Dom Lenain), Dom Ramondoux (Dom Andoyer), Brother Souche (Dom Aimé Lambert), Dom Titourne (Dom Henri Maulbon d'Arbaumont), the Abbé Barbenton (the Abbé Andrault), the Baron des Atours (Courcy), Mlle de Garambois (Mme Godefroy), M. Lampre (M. Chaussé).

47   Letter from Dom Cabrol of 9 Mar. 1903 (Daoust, i, p. 152).

48   Letter to Leclaire of 4 Apr. 1903 (BN).

49   Letter to Leclaire of 1 May 1903 (BN). JKH had already hinted that he might have to refer to Dom Bourigaud's sympathetic treatment of La Tremblaye after the latter had taken part in the conspiracy against Dom Delatte (letter to Leclaire of 4 Apr. 1903).

50   Letter to Leclaire of 10 June 1903 (BN).

51   For further details of JKH's relations with Mme Huc, and for the text of some of his letters to her, see Martineau, pp. 50–113.

52   Letter to Leclaire of 3 Aug. 1903 (BN).

53   Letter to Leclaire of 20 Aug. 1903 (BN). Descaves is incorrect in stating that 'he left for Lourdes where he stayed until 15 September 1903' (Descaves, ii, p. 95). [RB] In a letter to Arij Prins of 29 Aug. 1903, Huysmans gave another reason for his failure to join the Leclaires at Lourdes, saying that he couldn't get a travel permit from his publishers and that 'he had no desire to spend close to 150F to get knocked around by the crowds at Lourdes'. (Gillet, pp. 374–5). [BK]

54   Letters to Leclaire of 3 Aug. and late Aug. 1903 (BN).

55   Letter to Leclaire of late Aug. 1903 (BN).

56   Harry, pp. 68–69. See Note 22.

57   The following details have been taken from Lefévre, pp. 51–54; a notebook on the German journey quoted in Descaves, ii (pp. 97–102), and in *Catalogue J.-K. Huysmans*, Paris, Librairie Dommergues, 1952, No. 48; also from a notebook on the Belgian journey in the possession of Professor Louis Massignon. The journey has been dated by the postmarks on two postcards from JKH to Mme Leclaire: of Colmar from Basle (23 Sept.) and of Freiburg from Mainz (25 Sept.). [RB] Two notebooks that Huysmans kept during the course of his trip with the Abbé Mugnier in 1903 have now been published as part of a critical edition of 'Les Grünewald du Musée Colmar', edited by Pierre Brunel, André Guyaux and Christian Heck (Hermann, 1988). Aside from the complete text of the notebooks, this immaculately produced and illustrated edition also includes the original text and published variants, and two informative essays relating to Huysmans' discovery of Grünewald and the significance of the *primitifs* in his work. See also François-René Martin's 'L'invention d'une œuvre: recherches sur la redécouverte française de Grünewald', in *Regards contemporains sur Grünewald*, Société nouvelle Adam Biro, 1995. [BK]

58 Letter to Mme Huc of 9 Oct. 1903 (Martineau, p. 77).

59 Descaves, ii, p. 102.

60 Letter to Mme Huc of 9 Oct. 1903 (Martineau, p. 76).

61 Letter to Leclaire of 15 Dec. 1903 (BN); letter to Henri d'Hennezel of 25 Dec. 1903 (Billy, pp. 78–79).

62 Letters to Leclaire of 11 and 28 Nov. 1903 (BN).

63 Letter to Leclaire of 15 Dec. 1903 (BN).

64 Letter to Leclaire of 29 Jan. 1904 (BN).

65 Letter to Leclaire of 5 Feb. 1904 (BN).

66 Descaves, i, p. 177.

67 Harry, pp. 64–65. See Note 22.

68 Letter to Dom Micheau of 4 Jan. 1904 (Daoust, i, p. 168).

69 Letter to Leclaire of 5 Feb. 1904 (BN).

70 Ageorges, p. 222.

71 Letter to Leclaire of 12 Mar. 1904 (BN).

8. THE MARTYR

1 Letter to Mme Huc of Apr. 1904 (Martineau, p. 83).

2 Letter to Leclaire of 24 Mar. 1904 (BN).

3 Letter to Mme Leclaire of 19 Nov. 1904 (BN).

4 Letter to Leclaire of 15 Dec. 1903 (BN). JKH could not have published this preface about the 'recently departed poet' in 1894, as stated by Laver, since the poet lived until 1896.

5 Letter to Leclaire of 29 April 1904 (BN)

6 Letter to Leclaire of 12 Mar. 1904 (BN)

7 The identity of the woman referred to by Baldick as 'Mme X' – and by Huysmans in his letters to the Leclaires as 'the other one' or 'La Levantine' was the writer Myriam Harry. Harry, who was still alive when the *Life* was published, had asked Baldick to suppress certain passages that would have led to her identification. In the letter of 12 Mar. 1904, for example, Huysmans explains that this second 'La Sol' is 'more dangerous than the first because she is younger and prettier and more intelligent, having in addition the exotic charm of a very real talent. Along with Rachilde, she is certainly the most talented woman of letters at the present time.' See also Mugnier's Journal entry for 25 April 1904 in which he records Huysmans' impression of Harry as 'a pagan who believes in nothing but the flesh, a real flirt' (Mugnier, ii, p. 145). Harry married the sculptor Émile Perrault on 7 May 1904, but even then she did not, as Huysmans hoped she would, 'leave him in peace', and in a letter to Leclaire of 29 June he complained that she kept going on about the

events of her honeymoon and that he would 'chuck her out if she did it again'. Huysmans' references to her are certainly unflattering and it is easy to see why Harry would have wanted them suppressed; in a letter of 24 Feb. 1905, for example, after describing how he successfully foiled one of her attempts to seduce him, he tells Leclaire that 'the bitch has spread it around everywhere that she is my mistress. I wonder what her husband makes of that!!' For more biographical information on Harry see Cécile Chombard-Gaudin's *Une Orientale à Paris*, Maisson-neuve et Larose, 2005. [BK]

8 Letter to Leclaire of 29 Mar. 1904 (BN)

9 Letter to Leclaire of 20 Apr. 1904 (BN).

10 Letter to Leclaire of 29 June 1904 (BN)

11 Letter to Dom Micheau of 31 July 1904 (Daoust, i, p. 175).

12 *Les Foules de Lourdes*, chap. ii.

13 Letter published by L. Descaves in his Note on *Les Foules de Lourdes (OC, vol.* xxiii, p. 336).

14 Letter to Mme Huc of 19 Oct. 1904 (Martineau, p. 87).

15 Letter to Mme Huc of 26 Dec. 1904 (ibid., p. 89).

16 Harry, pp. 74–77. Harry's account is not consistent with other available evidence. After the prize was awarded, for example, Huysmans was quoted in *La Petite République* on 30 Jan. 1905 as saying that although he admired Harry's book, it wasn't eligible because it was written by a woman, and to have awarded the prize to a woman would have created an 'unfortunate prece-dent' (Seillan, p. 446). In his account of the deliberations over the 1904 prize, Léon Deffoux makes no reference to Harry's book as a possible candidate (Deffoux, ii, pp. 99–101). See also 'The Pilgrim', Note 22. [BK]

17 Deffoux, ii, pp. 99–101.

18 Letters to Leclaire of 9 and 17 Oct. 1904 (BN).

19 Letter to Leclaire of 29 Oct. 1904 (BN)

20 Letter to Leclaire of 9 Nov. 1904 (BN).

21 Letter to Leclaire of 12 Nov. 1904 (BN).

22 Letter to Leclaire of 29 Nov. 1904 (BN).

23 Letter to Leclaire of 11 Dec. 1904 (BN).

24 Letter to Leclaire of 26 Dec. 1904 (BN).

25 Letter to Leclaire of 3 Jan. 1905 (BN).

26 Letter to Leclaire of 15 Jan. 1905 (BN).

27 Letter to Leclaire of 28 July 1905 (BN).

28 Letters to Leclaire of 25 Aug., 6 and 17 Sept. 1905 (BN).

29 Letter to Abbé Fontaine of 27 July 1905 (Bernaërt).

30 Letter of 19 Sept. 1905 (Billy, p. 84).

31 See Aubault, pp. 24–28.

32 Letter to Leclaire of 29 Jan. 1904 (BN).

33 Letter to Leclaire of 31 Oct. 1904 (BN).

34 Letter to Leclaire of 9 Nov. 1904 (BN).

35 Besse, ii, p. 27.

36 Descaves, ii, pp. 108–9; letter from Caldain to Mme Huc of 2 Apr. 1907 (Fonds).

37 Letter to Mme Huc of 1 Feb. 1906 (Martineau, pp. 96–97).

38 Letter Mme Huc of 3 Mar. 1906 (ibid., p. 97).

39 Letter to Mme Huc of 11 Mar. 1906 (ibid.).

40 Besse, ii, p. 35.

41 Letter to Berthet of 29 Apr. 1906 (Billy, p. 85).

42 Letters to Henri d'Hennezel of 31 May and 3 July 1906 (Billy, p. 85 and p. 87). [RB] For more documents related to the genesis and composition of *Les Foules de Lourdes* see the critical edition by Pierre Lambert, which includes two notebooks that Huysmans kept during his visits to Lourdes, a selection of his letters to various correspondents at the time, and a number of photographs and illustrations (Lambert, xv). [BK]

43 Letter to d'Hennezel of 31 May 1906 (Billy, p. 86).

44 Letter to Leclaire of 18 July 1902 (BN).

45 L. Descaves, Introduction to *Pages choisies de Huysmans*, Paris, Dentu, 1915, p. 20.

46 Letter to Henriette du Fresnel (Sister Scolastica) of 20 June 1906 (Archives of the Abbey of Sainte-Scolastique de Dourgne).

47 Letter to Leclaire of 26 July 1906 (BN).

48 Letters from Henriette du Fresnel (Sister Scolastica) to JKH of 2 and 22 Apr. 1907 (private collection).

49 Marguerite de Czarniecka first wrote to JKH from Hosterwitz on 27 June 1906. On 26 March 1907 JKH sent her a money-order for 100 francs. Seven letters she wrote to JKH are in the Fonds Lambert.

50 Letters to Mme Godefroy of 6 and 29 June and 6 July 1906 (Fonds).

51 Coquiot, pp. 224–7.

52 Letter to Leclaire of 26 July 1906 (BN).

53 Coquiot, pp. 227–8.

54 Letter to Leclaire of 11 Aug. 1906 (BN).

55 Inscription on this copy of *Les Foules de Lourdes* (*Catalogue de la vente Leclaire*, Paris, Cornuau, 17 Dec. 1934, No. 21).

56 Letter to Abbé Broussolle of 20 Sept. 1906 (Daoust, iv).

57   Letter to Leclaire of 9 Oct. 1906 (BN).

58   Letter to Leclaire of 2 Nov. 1906 (BN).

59   Letter to Henriette du Fresnel (Sister Scolastica) of 21 Oct. 1906 (Archives of the Abbey of Sainte-Scolastique).

60   Letter to Dom Micheau of 16 Sept. 1906 (Bourg, p. 19; Beaumont, p. 231).

61   Orsat died on 5 Nov. 1906 (Jacquinot, i).

62   For the full text of Huysmans' will see *Bulletin* No. 63, 1975, pp. 1–6. It was also probably at this time that Huysmans gave Descaves his 'Carnet Vert', a notebook of around 150 pages containing preliminary sketches and notes relating to his work that dated back to 1886. Pierre Lambert, into whose possession it came after Descaves' death, published extracts from it in *Le Figaro littéraire*, 2–8 July 1964 and in Lambert, xvi, and it is now in the Bibliothèque de l'Arsenal (Fonds Lambert MS 75). For more details, see 'Le Carnet Vert: 'le plus émouvant alibi de la mort,' by Sylvie Duran in *Huysmans à côté et au-delà*, Peeters Vrin, 2001, pp.245–77. [BK]

63   Retté, p. 103.

64   Letter to Retté of Nov. 1906 (Retté, pp. 108–9; Beaumont, p. 232).

65   Coquiot, pp. 231–2.

66   Letter to Myriam Harry of 5 Jan. 1907 (Harry, p. 96; Beaumont, pp. 232–3). See 'The Pilgrim', Note 22.

67   Letter to Leclaire of 29 Nov. 1906 (BN).

68   M. Dumesnil's first contact with JKH had been in 1905, when he had sent the novelist his important thesis on *Flaubert: son hérédite, son milieu, sa méthode*. JKH's comments on this work are to be found in M. Dumesnil's *Gustave Flaubert, l'homme et l'œuvre*, Desclée de Brouwer, 1933, p. 429, note. It was Lucien Descaves who introduced M. Dumesnil to JKH.

69   Coquiot, p. 230. [RB] For further clarification on the roles of Arrou and Poirier in Huysmans' case, see Dr. André Finot's 'Deux chirurgiens de Huysmans', *Bulletin*, No. 36, 1958. [BK]

70   Letter to Leclaire of 25 Dec. 1906 (BN).

71   Letter to Leclaire of 26 Jan. 1907 (BN).

72   Letter to Myriam Harry of 5 Jan. 1907 (Harry, p. 96; Beaumont, pp. 232–3). See 'The Pilgrim', Note 22.

73   L. Descaves, *Bulletin*, No. 16, 1937.

74   Harry, p. 98. See 'The Pilgrim', Note 22.

75   Letter to Mme Huc of 9 Jan. 1907 (Martineau, p. 107, where it is incorrectly dated: 9 Apr. 1907).

76 Letter to Leclaire of 2 Feb. 1907.

77 R. Dumesnil, *L'Éducation Nationale*, 11 Mar. 1948, and in conversation with the present author.

78 Tharaud. See also J. Tharaud, *Bulletin*, No. 23, 1951, pp. 136–9. Jean Tharaud was not exactly a stranger to JKH, as he had been introduced to him at Ligugé in Oct. 1899, but JKH had no clear recollection of him.

79 Martineau, p. 117.

80 Descaves, iii, p. 234. See also Bemelmans, ii.

81 Coppée.

82 Bourg, p. 31.

83 Coppée.

84 Letter to Leclaire of 11 Mar. 1907 (BN; Beaumont, pp. 234–5).

85 Martineau, p. 121.

86 Undated letter from Caldain to Mme Huc (Martineau, p. 119).

87 Martineau, p. 123.

88 Letter from Caldain to Mme Huc of 24 Apr. 1907 (Martineau, p. 122).

89 Bernaërt.

90 J. Bois, *Nouvelles Littéraires,* 14 May 1927.

91 Coppée.

92 Caldain.

93 Professor Louis Massignon in conversation with the present author.

94 Letter from Henriette du Fresnel (Sister Scolastica) of 22 Apr. 1907, in a private collection.

95 Lefèvre, p. 32.

96 Coquiot, pp. 234–5.

97 Letter from Caldain to Mme Huc of 4 May 1907 (Martineau, p. 124).

98 L. Descaves, *Le journal*, 24 July 1938.

99 Caldain.

100 Narfon, i.

101 'You are requested to attend the procession, service and interment of M. Joris-Karl Huysmans, man of letters, President of the Goncourt Academy, Officer of the Legion of Honour, who died on the 1907, after receiving the Sacraments of the Church in his home, No. 31 rue Saint-Placide, at the age of 59, which will take place on the at his parish church, Our Lady in the Fields. *De profundis*. Please assemble at the house of the departed.' [BK]

102 Coquiot, p. 233.

103 Letter from Dom Besse of 1 May 1907 (Daoust, i, p. 186).

104 Bernaërt.

105 Retté, p. 107.

106 Martineau, p. 125.

107 *OC*, vol. i, p. xxviii.

108 Coquiot, pp. 236–7. [RB] For the French edition of his biography, Baldick slightly revised his account of Huysmans' death. Although Marie Gaudy had always affirmed, in the course of her conversations with Andrée Bemelmans (Bemelmans, ii), Guy Chastel (Chastel, p201) and Baldick himself, that she found her master dead at 4 o'clock, Baldick believed she was mistaken, as her testimony is contradicted by that of Jean de Caldain, René Dumesnil, and Lucien and Pierre Descaves (see Caldain; Coquiot, pp. 236–7; *OC*, vol. i, p. xxviii; P. Descaves). Significantly for Baldick, Gaudy told Mme Bemelmans: 'Immediately after Huysmans passed away . . . Caldain was very busy; he telephoned Mme d'Etchevers and her daughter, then the doctor, and then everyone arrived.' As the death certificate (Deffoux, iv, p. 124) indicates that the time of death was 7.30, Baldick concludes that it is most likely that on going to wake Huysmans at 7 o'clock to change his dressing Gaudy found him already dead. [BK]

109 Pierre Descaves, *Mes Goncourt*, Marseilles, Laffont, 1944. p. 69.

110 Bernaërt; R. Dumesnil, *Bulletin*, No. 21, 1949; M. Dumesnil, in conversation with the present author.

111 The tombstone which Coquiot described in 1912 as 'a poor thing, turned green by the rain' (Coquiot, p. 237) was removed some twenty years later. The present stone bears the following inscription:

GODFRIED	JULES
HUYSMANS	BADIN
1815–1856	1800–1862.
JULES	V^{VE} OG
OG	NÉE BREISTROFF
1823–1867	1784–1870
V^{VE} OG	V^{VE} BADIN
NÉE BADIN	NÉE GERARD
1826–1876	1797–1876

V^{VE} ALAVOINE
NÉE BAVOIL
1800–1881

J.-K. HUYSMANS
PRÉSIDENT DE L'ACADÉMIE GONCOURT
NÉ À PARIS LE 5 FÉVRIER 1848
DÉCÉDÉ À PARIS LE 12 MAI 1907

It is interesting to note that the name of Alavoine is to be found not only on JKH's tombstone but also on his birth certificate (Deffoux, iv, p. 11), one of the witnesses who signed this document being a 49-year-old M. Louis-Emmanuel-Désiré Alavoine, domiciled at No. 5, Rue Petit-Bourbon-Saint-Sulpice.

CONCLUSION

1 The Société Huysmans did not begin issuing the *Bulletin* in 1925, as stated by the ageing and sometimes forgetful Lucien Descaves in *Deux Amis*, and subsequently by Laver in *The First Decadent*. [RB] In 1974, the *Bulletin* became an annual, rather than a biannual, publication. [BK]
2 See Breton, p. 154.
3 Letter from Caldain to Mme Huc of 4 May 1907 (Martineau, p. 124).
4 G. Geffroy, *Notes d'un journaliste*, Paris, Charpentier, 1887, p. 238.
5 Bloy, *Le Chat Noir*, 14 June 1884.
6 Letter to Mme Bruyère of 11 June 1897 (Rancœur, p. 10).
7 Gourmont, ii, p. 7.
8 Bloy, iv, p. 80.
9 Letter from Zola of 5 Jan. 1890 (Zola, vol. vi, p. 448).
10 E. et J. de Goncourt, *Manette Salomon*, Paris, Verboeckoven, 1867, vol. ii, p. 178.
11 Diary entry for 6 Oct. 1901 (Lambert, xiii, p. 511).
12 Diary entry for June 1898 (Lambert, xii, p. 955).
13 Lefèvre, p. 37.
14 Besse, i.

INDEX

★ denotes a character in one of Huysmans' works.
† denotes a character in a work by another author.

553

563

569

585